QUEEN
of SWORDS

HISTORICAL NOVELS BY JUDITH TARR

Lord of the Two Lands

Throne of Isis

The Eagle's Daughter

Pillar of Fire

King and Goddess

Queen of Swords

White Mare's Daughter

The Shepherd Kings

Lady of Horses

QUEEN

of SWORDS

J U D I T H   T A R R

A Tom Doherty Associates Book   New York

QUEEN OF SWORDS

Copyright © 1997 by Judith Tarr

This book is printed on acid-free paper.

A Forge Book
Published by Tom Doherty Associates, LLC
175 Fifth Avenue
New York, NY 10010

www.tor.com

Forge® is a registered trademark of Tom Doherty Associates, LLC.

Design by Bonni Leon

LIBRARY OF CONGRESS CATALOGING-IN-PUBLICATION DATA

Tarr, Judith.
    Queen of swords / Judith Tarr.
       p. cm.
    "A Tom Doherty Associates book."
    ISBN 0-312-85821-3 (hc)
    ISBN 0-312-86805-7 (pbk)
    1. Jerusalem—History—Latin Kingdom, 1099–1244—Fiction.   2. Melisende, Queen of Jerusalem, d. 1161—Fiction.   I. Title.
PS3570.A655Q4   1997
813'.54—dc20
                                                                                                    96-33220
                                                                                                    CIP

First Hardcover Edition: February 1997
First Trade Paperback Edition: October 2000

Printed in the United States of America

0 9 8 7 6 5 4 3 2 1

QUEEN

of SWORDS

La Forêt Sauvage

They had made an ordered place, here on the wild wood's edge: green fields and vineyards, village and farmstead, and over them the grey bulk of the castle. Its towers looked to all the world about; and all the world, it seemed, was forest. Except where the river ran, a strong slow flood running from dark into dark, wood into wood; but here it glinted in sunlight.

Old Lord Waleran's vineyards terraced the slopes on the far side, the north side, looking to the gentle south. Waleran's folly, to clear the wood across the river from the safety of his castle and plant vines that must be tended all the year through, and guarded as closely as his daughters. But God and His Mother protected them, and St. Bacchus who cherished the vine and its fruit; and the wine, Waleran's Blood as it was called, was a sweet and heady vintage, rich in its rarity.

On a fair day in early spring when the vines had barely begun to bud, the Lady Richildis oversaw the broaching of a cask. The wine flowed as always, like dark blood; as always, the steward offered her the first cupful. As always she declined. He grinned and shook his head and drank deep.

"Our wine has never traveled well," Lady Agnes observed. Neither voice nor face betrayed any expression in particular. Still Richildis fancied that she heard a hint of sharpness, saw the suggestion of a frown on the wide smooth brow. "And that was only as far as Poitiers."

"Father took a jar to Paris once," Richildis reminded her, "and it arrived in reasonable condition. Or so he said."

"Your father," said the Lady Agnes with some asperity, "could down a jar of vinegar and reckon it excellent. Whatever the number of his virtues, a palate for wine was never one of them."

Richildis shrugged. "Still: I mean to try. I'll pray to St. Bacchus, and invoke old Waleran. He'd have approved, I think, if he had known where the fruit of his vines would go."

"You always were headstrong," said Lady Agnes. She sighed, but she did not press further.

Richildis was rather surprised. Lady Agnes was never one to spare the force of a rebuke. But Lord Rogier's death had quenched her. She was the wife of his old age, no tender maid herself when she married him but a widow of lands and standing, well prepared to take in hand his scapegrace sons and his hoyden of a daughter. Everyone had expected her to outlive him. But not so soon. Not so swiftly.

Richildis' throat was tight. She had not expected it, either. There had been no warning, no omen, no clap of thunder or croaking of ravens. He had ridden out of a morning, gone to see to this or that about his lands, and simply not come back. One of the men-at-arms had found him near the forest's edge, lying where he had fallen, and his old destrier with the reins on its neck, cropping winterworn grass. The horse had not thrown him, that anyone could see. He had fallen, that was all, as if the hand of God had struck him.

The hand of God, or his own grief. The elder of his sons had died in the fading of the year, dead of a fever that struck hard and swift and left but ashes in its wake. There had been no grace in Giraut's death, and no honor. Nothing but needless misery.

Richildis stiffened her back. She had sworn on the day her father died: whatever grief beset her, she would not give way to it. Rogier had, and had died—of a broken heart, as near as made no matter. Those who were left, his daughter and his wife, had no choice but to endure.

While Richildis saw the wine decanted into jars that would, she hoped, survive the journey she was contemplating, Lady Agnes departed in silence.

Richildis found her where she most often was, these days: in the dim and stone-cold chapel. It was never a place that Richildis would have chosen, nor Agnes either while Rogier was still alive. But the chill of the old stones, that never completely left them even in the summer's heat, seemed matched to the chill in Agnes' heart.

Richildis knelt beside her on the hard cold floor, crossed herself and murmured a prayer to the Lady whose image stood beside the altar. Quickly then, before she could think better of it, she said, "Come with me. Pack your belongings and go. We'll both make the pilgrimage. We'll find my brother and bring him home again."

Agnes signed herself with the cross, slowly, as if she had not heard; but Richildis knew that she had. After a stretching while she said, "You know I can't do that."

"Why not?" Richildis demanded of her. "Thierry's a good enough seneschal. He'll hold the demesne till we come back."

"Surely," said Agnes with a hint of her old spirit, "and rob us blind while he does it. Or sell La Forêt to the highest bidder, and look all innocence when we come back, because of course he never imagined that we would mind."

"Then find another seneschal," Richildis said, "and let him take it all in hand. Father Maury, perhaps, or—"

"No," Agnes said. "I don't want to go on pilgrimage, not even to Jerusalem. I was never born here, but here I belong. Here I intend to stay."

"And when I find Bertrand," Richildis said with deliberate cruelty, "and bring him back, if he should displace us both with a wife and heirs—what then, my lady? What will you do?"

"Then," said Agnes, grimly composed, "I shall go where God and Our Lady lead me. Until then I'll stay here. I've no mind or heart to chase the wide world round, looking for a fool of a boy who cannot possibly be aware that he's the Lord of La Forêt."

"Not a boy," Richildis said, but softly, almost to herself. "Not any longer. He'll have grown. He might even—be—"

"Do not you think it," Agnes said, so fiercely that Richildis started. "Rogier and Giraut are dead, but Bertrand is alive. Never for a moment doubt that. You may go to find him, since you trust messengers no more than I trust our worthy seneschal. I shall stay here and make certain that when he comes he has a demesne to be lord of."

Richildis knelt mute, staring at her. And truly, what was there to say? People had called Richildis mad and worse, for insisting that she and no other go all the way to Outremer, to the kingdom beyond the sea, the Kingdom of Jerusalem, to fetch her brother home. But never Agnes. Agnes was as mad as she, perhaps, as persistent in her refusal to go as Richildis in her refusal to stay.

They both grieved, and both alike, although the choices that they made had been so different. Richildis could not have borne to stay, not with father and brother dead and Bertrand gone so long, doing as so many younger sons had done since Jerusalem was won from the infidel, defending the Holy Sepulcher. Richildis had raged at him when he left, hated him for going away, for abandoning her.

Now she was abandoning Agnes, leaving her all alone, and La Forêt in her hands, with no one else to share the burden.

She opened her mouth to speak, but Agnes spoke ahead of her. "No, you may not stay. You insisted on this venture; you will complete it. Your pride will allow no less."

"I am stronger than my pride," Richildis said stiffly.

Agnes raised her fine dark brows. "Are you indeed? Then let it rule you. I'll not have you growling and glooming about, begrudging every moment that's not spent in Outremer hunting down your brother."

Since that was eminently true, Richildis did not dispute it. But she said, "You'll be alone."

"I have been alone," said Agnes, "since they brought my dear lord home and laid him at my feet." She rose, graceful as she always was, and smoothed her skirts. Her face was as calm as her voice, as if the words did not matter; and in that was all the sorrow in the world. "You will go, daughter of my husband. I will stay. That is as God wills it."

And that, thought Richildis, was the end of it. She rose herself, though never as smoothly as Agnes had, and went to do as she had vowed to do. To leave La Forêt; to journey to Jerusalem. To bring her brother home again.

L A D Y *One* *and*

P R I N C E S S

(A.D. 1129-1133)

*H*elena in the markets of Acre was a force as terrible as any army of the Saracen. Armed with a purse full of silver and gold, armored in her third-best silk gown with its headdress that recalled the tribesmen of the desert, escorted by her redoubtable maid and a solid half-dozen bearded and braided Turks, she took the stalls by storm, and left the merchants in a state halfway between shock and bliss. Helena yielded to no one in the art of extracting the best price possible; but she paid well and she paid fair, and she bought goods enough to stock her own marketplace if she had troubled to establish one.

Bertrand happened across her between the street of the goldsmiths and the avenue of the spice-sellers, just as she emerged triumphant from a cloth-merchant's stall. The most villainous-looking of her guardsmen staggered under the weight of a vast bundle.

"Cotton!" she said by way of greeting, with considerable satisfaction. "Cotton of the finest, a shift for everyone and a nightrobe for me, and if you behave yourself, I might—I just might—let you have a length for yourself."

Bertrand laughed. "Only if it's crimson, and only if the dye is fast."

Her eyes slid at him—wonderful eyes, wide and dark as a doe's, painted skillfully with kohl. A smile twitched at the corner of her mouth. "You still love the color? After . . . ?"

He flushed in spite of himself. There had been a gift, one of the king's bounties, a robe of honor, and a sudden storm of rain, it being winter in Jerusalem; and he had discovered to his enormous dismay that the king had been cheated somewhat in the quality of his goods. That would have been endurable, but he had gone straight from the storm to Helena's arms. He had never known till he was naked in them, that he had been dyed as rich a crimson as ever left the vat.

It had worn off eventually, with a great deal of help from her bath-servants— and they had been discreet, he had reason to hope, though not perhaps for terror of his sword.

She had been watching him remember, following the track of his thought as she so often did. Her smile hid now in both corners of her mouth. "Ah, but the color so becomes a fair man. Even to the blush on his cheeks—"

He caught her, right there in the bazaar, and no matter who was looking, and stopped the rest of it with a kiss.

That was not quite wise. She freed herself deftly, the glitter of her eyes warning him: some things she reserved to herself, and first of them was her dignity. He did not cry her pardon, but he set a prudent distance between them, putting on the demeanor of a proper young man in the presence of a lady.

She was not so swift to forgive him, but neither did she send him away. She suffered him to follow as she continued her assault on the markets of Acre.

When she had laden another of her guardsmen with packets of spices, she inquired, "Haven't you duties to call you?"

Bertrand shrugged slightly in his fine new coat. It was silk, and of better quality than the one that had embarrassed him in Jerusalem. The king had not given it. This was the king's daughter's gift, the Princess Melisende whose eastern mother had taught her to tell gold from dross, and deep-dyed silk from middling clever counterfeit. Thinking of her, he said, "They've sighted the fleet. It should be in shortly after noon."

"And here it is, midmorning already, and you dallying in the market." Helena's brows, that needed little plucking or painting to preserve a perfect arch, drew together. "Was it but a rumor, then? You never swore yourself in knightly service to the Princess Melisende?"

"No rumor," Bertrand said, keeping the heat out of his voice. "I'll be at the quay with the rest of her train, and in good time, too."

"Then you'd best leave now," she said briskly.

"Only if you come with me."

The elegant brows rose. A curl of midnight hair had escaped her headdress. He restrained the urge to stroke it back where it belonged. "I, come with you?" Her voice was light; brittle, one might have thought. "I think not. It's hardly proper, the likes of me among the princess' attendants."

"I had thought," said Bertrand, "to find you a pleasant place to watch, where no one would crowd or trouble you."

To himself he sounded feeble, but she did not lash him with mockery—and well she might have done, if she had had a mind. "I'll find my own," she said, still lightly, still with that brittle edge. "You go. Wait on your king and his beautiful daughter."

"Why," said Bertrand with the force of revelation. "You're jealous."

"I am not," Helena said, and now her voice was cold. "Go. You'll be late."

He wanted to linger, to protest, to coax the truth out of her, but she had the right of it: he was late. He bowed over her hand, which lay still and cold in his, and left as quickly as the press of people would let him, aiming for the harbor. He could not have heard what he thought he did, nor would she have said it; yet he fancied that he heard her voice, half bitter, half wry: "Yes, go, my dear sweet fool."

The oddness of Helena's mood did not quite slip away forgotten, but Bertrand had ample to occupy him. Acre was a crowded city always; its harbor saw ships from every port in Christendom, coming and going, bringing pilgrims from the west and bearing them away again. Today however it was thronged as he had never seen it, filled to bursting. The whole High Court of the Kingdom of Jerusalem had come here, and all their servants and hangers-on, to meet the ships that sailed from France.

Bertrand struggled through the mobs, all of which seemed as intent as he on coming to the quay before the French ships reached it. He was privileged: once he had fought his way to the front, ruffled and sweating but still, he hoped, presentable, he was let through the ring of guards. The captain of this particular detachment, Richard Gaptooth, knew him; grinned and let him by into relative quiet.

It was relative only, and hardly less crowded than the streets had been. A thickening of the press marked the king: Bertrand saw him standing taller than the men nearest him, the high fair head gone lately silver, lifted easily under the weight of the crown. Baldwin of Le Bourg, once Count of Edessa, now and for the past ten years King of Jerusalem, Defender of the Holy Sepulcher, stood leaning on the shoulder of his sometime rival, often enemy, and just as often friend, Joscelin, who had taken the County of Edessa when Baldwin left it to be king in Jerusalem. Joscelin, smaller, once darker and now much greyer, was laughing at something the king had said.

Bertrand sighed faintly, hardly aware that he was doing it. They were like brothers, those two: allies and enemies, friends and devoted rivals. He had had a brother like that once, far away in Anjou.

Giraut had been a prig, as meek as a monk and much inclined in that direction; but the eldest son of a nobleman was not often permitted to indulge his religious proclivities. Bertrand, who might properly have done so, had no such calling. No, he thought, remembering the night before, and Helena's warm and scented bed: no, not in the least.

As for whether she was jealous of his princess: well, and women were strange. Melisende was a beauty as one would expect, daughter that she was of tall fair Baldwin and graceful dark Morphia of Melitene. She had inherited the best of both of them. Her eyes were great and dark, Armenian eyes, with smoke-dark lashes and strong dark brows. But her hair was like her father's, wheat-fair, and her skin was nigh as fair as his, with the suggestion of a golden sheen. The sun dyed it gold indeed, when she would let it; and that was more often than her maids would like, for she was fond of riding in the sun.

She stood in her own flock of attendants, not far from her father. They made Bertrand think of geese, milling and chattering, and among them her sisters, the little princesses, dark plump Hodierna and silver-fair Yveta. The second sister, the Lady Alys, who had married the Prince of Antioch only last year, had her own orbit and her own attendants, and kept them jealously apart, though the edges of her following blurred into those of Melisende's own.

Alys had been insufferable since she had married first, and such a splendid youth, no less than Bohemond, son and namesake of that great Norman reiver and bandit, Bohemond of Sicily. Melisende, she had been heard to observe, was marrying a mere count, and not a particularly young one, either—a middle-aged man from France, who had buried one wife already, and married off a grown son to the heiress of England, and come to marry himself to the heiress of Jerusalem.

Alys had married a prince, but the man who married Melisende would be king when Baldwin was gone. It did no one good to forget that.

Bertrand slipped in among the company of men, young and not so young, who had sworn themselves to the princess' service. Young Hugh, whose father was lord of Jaffa, shot him a glance and a grin. Bertrand grinned back. The boy was disastrously young, and reckless with it: he reminded Bertrand pointedly of himself.

Melisende stood in the ring of her attendants. Her maids were fussing about her, twitching at her robe, her mantle, her hair. She seemed oblivious to them. She had a look about her that made Bertrand frown. Alys had been at her again, he could tell, harping on how beautiful, how young, how perfectly wonderful her Bohemond was. The other half, the half that she did not trouble to say, was that Melisende's husband-to-be was none of those things. The messengers had been lavish in their praise of his intelligence, his good sense, his prowess in war; but none of them had been able to conceal the fact that he was rising forty, neither tall nor well-favored, and red as a fox.

"I hate redheaded men," Melisende had said in Bertrand's hearing. "Their eyebrows are invisible. And they burn in the sun. And peel."

Someone had remonstrated with her, rebuked her for caring so much about a man's face when the kingdom needed his strength.

"And how much of *that* does he have?" Melisende had demanded. "He's a fox, not a lion."

Since Bohemond was a great golden lion of a man, some of her attendants had concluded that she was besotted with her own sister's husband. But Bertrand did not think that that was her trouble. She had more sense than that. She was disappointed, that was all. She had hoped for something younger and more to her taste. A princess might do that, he thought, even knowing that she must marry for the kingdom and not for her own pleasure.

She was putting on a brave enough face, now that the ships had entered the harbor. They were proud to see, with their purple sails, and banners flying: white crosses and gold of Jerusalem, golden lilies of France, stalking lions of Anjou.

Bertrand strained to pick out the count from among the many faces, men crowding the decks and thronging the rails, even a few women close-veiled against the sun. They blurred together, drab brown and grey and black, pilgrim's garb or grey chainmail, and on each shoulder the blood-red cross of Crusade.

But there were flashes of brightness amid the colors of winter and the west. Prelates in their splendor, lords in what must pass for the latest fashion in Paris or in Poitiers, and—ah; at last—one man in a garment Bertrand recognized, the robe of honor that Melisende had sewn with her own hands, silk the color of blood, brocaded with dragons. It had come all the way down the Silk Road, all the way from Ch'in.

Fulk of Anjou was indeed a red man, fox-red, with the high color and freckled skin that went with it. Scarlet, Helena would have observed with delicate acidity, was not his color. And although the robe had clearly been cut and fitted to him, it was still a shade too large. He was a little wiry man, smaller than Bertrand had been led to expect: smaller than Melisende herself, who had the height and the robust breadth of her father's line.

Bertrand glanced at her. Her expression had not changed in the slightest. If her eyes had found her husband-to-be, they had wandered away again, back to contemplation of infinite space. He was reminded of nothing so much as a mare that he had seen bred to a stallion not of her choosing, hobbled and close-held, enduring what she must, because she must, unable to escape it.

"Well!" The voice was bright, penetrating, and incontestably that of the Princess Alys. "Beauty is as beauty does. Maybe," she said with the air of one seeking for the best of a bad bargain, "he can carry on a lively conversation. Or maybe he can sing."

Melisende said no word. Not one. Alys made a face, a little moue of displeasure, and turned back to the gaggle of her ladies.

TWO

*S*un struck the water and shattered it into shards of light as keenly edged as a new-made sword. Light in this place was fierce, like an enemy. Colors that in France had seemed bright, here were blinding. Even through a heavy veil Richildis blinked, eyes streaming with tears of pain, struggling to see where sight itself was struck to nothing by the sun's intensity.

And the heat . . .

She had known it well enough on the voyage, and suffered from it, and, she thought, overcome it. Until she sailed into the port of Acre, that sun-dazzled, dung-reeking, crowd-roaring westward gate of Outremer. Even from out in the harbor she smelled and heard it, as distinct as if she stood in the middle of it.

"Not long now," one of her traveling companions said with every evidence of eagerness. He had come with the embassy from Outremer, and had himself been born here, a dark slender man who looked more Saracen than Frank. He was, he insisted, as Christian as any Angevin. His name was Frankish enough, to be sure; Guibert he was called, and he came from one of the castles that ran the length of the kingdom, warding it against the infidel. He had dressed like a Frank on the voyage, but now that they had come to Acre he had put on robes and headdress like a Saracen. He looked much cooler in them than Richildis felt in her best silk gown with its sleeves lined with fur, and her woolen mantle that would have been no less than adequate in Paris at this time of year.

Hard training in court and convent allowed her to stand immobile in the sodden weight of it, though her body was dissolved in heat. Her face must be scarlet, and certainly was dripping wet; but the veil hid that, at least. She devoted much of her strength to keeping herself on her feet, standing among the few other women who had come with Fulk to Outremer, sheltered somewhat by a canopy. They were all dressed in their best, all sweltering, shocked by such heat as France seldom saw at the height of its summer—and this was only May. She did not want to think of what it would be like in full summer.

Guibert patted her hand, a familiarity that she would have rebuked if she had had the will to speak. "There now," he said. "Once we're in the city we'll see that you're dressed more suitably for this climate. Silks, my lady. Linen, cotton, fabric of Mosul—ah, lady, you'll take such joy in your splendor!"

Richildis set her lips together. Guibert was one of those men who fancy themselves irresistible to women; and he seemed to have decided that he was particularly irresistible to her. There was no space to move away from him, no help for it but to endure his chatter while the ship crawled closer to the shore and the sun beat down. The crowd's roar mounted till at last, mercifully, it drowned him out.

Blinded, deafened, and close to fainting from the heat and the tumult, Richildis kept enough of herself to be aware that they had come to land. The glitter on the quay under the banner of Jerusalem, could not but be the king and his court and, somewhere amid them, the Princess Melisende. Richildis peered through her veil, finding them a blur of faces, all much darker than faces in France, burnished by the sun.

The women, she took note, were veiled, and wore such fabrics as Guibert had babbled of, robes cut loose and full, colors vivid to the point of pain, or white as dazzling as the sun itself. So many of them, so splendid, so strange-familiar, Frankish height and bones commingled with eastern grace. Many indeed must be half easterners, as the princesses themselves were.

She swayed, but caught herself. She would stand while she must stand, then walk as she must walk, following the rest from the ship to the land. It rose up to meet her, no more solid than the sea.

"I do not faint," said Richildis. "I do . . . *not* . . . faint."

With words for a chain, she pulled herself up out of the dark. Pity: it would have been cool, and comfortable. But there was only shame in it. She struggled free of hands that caught at her, steadied herself on her feet, set herself to glare at the ever-presumptuous Guibert.

But it was not that gentleman who had kept her from falling on her face on the harborside of Acre. It was someone else altogether, a big ruddy man deep-bronzed by the sun, eyes startling in the dark face, pale grey, almost silver. They were eyes that she knew very well. She saw them in her own mirror. And the hair too, fair brown shot with gold—that gold bleached to white, the brown turned almost yellow-fair, but darker near the roots, where one could see the color that nature had made it.

She was not surprised. She supposed she should be, but God had always been incalculable. "Bertrand," she said. "What in the world are you doing here?"

His astonishment served more than well for both of them. He opened his mouth, shut it again. He looked a perfect fool.

Nonetheless he was her brother, and he had wits enough once he remembered how to use them. He peered at her, struggling to see through the veil. "Who . . . ? Richildis? You've grown up!"

"People do," she said dryly. "And here I was thinking you lost in the wilds of Outremer, or dead for all anyone knew—and all the while you were waiting on the quay for me."

"I was waiting for the Count of Anjou," Bertrand said. "What are *you* doing here?"

"Accompanying the Count of Anjou," she said. She drew a breath. The heat was no less, and she would have paid dearly for a cup of water, but Bertrand's presence was like a wall against the sun.

Ten years, and she a child when he left; but she had not forgotten how safe she always felt when he was there. All of that came back as she stood in his shadow, looking up at him, how tall he was, how broad he had grown. He was no more handsome than he had ever been, nor did a deep scar on his cheek help to make him prettier, but his was a pleasant face, a comfortable face, well lived in and apparently at ease with itself.

And how that could be when he had gone away without a word, nor sent a message, not even that he was alive, she would be pleased to know. But not quite yet. Richildis had come to herself, and Fulk of Anjou had come face to face with the Princess Melisende.

Melisende was the taller and by far the younger, and lovely as she folded back her veil: robust and sturdy and strong like the king who held her hand, reaching to lay it in Fulk's. Fulk, who had never yielded his pride to any man, seemed unperturbed to look up into the eyes of his bride. They, dark and flat and faintly sullen, looked once, hard, as if to set his face in memory, then veiled themselves in long lashes.

The princess was not greatly pleased with the bargain that had been found for her. Fulk however seemed delighted. He took her hands and raised them to his lips. "Lady," he said. That was all. No charming words, no flattery. That he was capable of them, Richildis knew well: she had been the recipient thereof, and glad of it too; for Fulk had the art as Guibert the fool did not, nor ever would. But with this princess, this Melisende, he seemed to sense that such blandishments would fail of their mark.

"My lord count," King Baldwin said. He was as tall for a man as was Melisende for a woman, big and fair-bearded, very like her and yet much warmer in face and manner. He greeted Fulk with every evidence of gladness, embraced him and shared the kiss of peace. "Welcome, my lord! Welcome to the kingdom beyond the sea."

"And very fair it is," said Fulk, whom people called the Affable. They linked arms, the count and the king, and walked together in amity no less genuine for that it was so carefully calculated.

Melisende, left to fall in behind them, seemed briefly, profoundly startled. And indeed, thought Richildis, most properly the count should have taken her on his arm and walked beside her. Instead she had to follow, seething visibly, with her ladies in a flurry about her.

"That was badly done," Bertrand observed.

Richildis raised a brow at him. "Truly? I think he knew exactly what he did. He came for the kingdom, and not for the woman."

"But the woman will be his queen," said Bertrand. "He'd do well to woo her. She's not happy to be given to an old man, and a foreigner besides."

"Old! He's barely forty. That's young enough for anything she needs."

"Sister," said Bertrand, "you've grown hard. Has it been so difficult, away at home?"

"You could say that," Richildis said, flat and rather cold. "I married, but he died. He was older at the wedding than Fulk is now, and I was younger than that child. We did well enough together."

Bertrand drew in a breath: she heard it even through the clamor of people. But he did not speak. He took her arm, much as Fulk should have done with Melisende, and guided her gently but firmly along the way that king and count and princess had taken.

She let him do it. There was little else that she could do. Her belongings were on the ship, but would be moved to the palace with everyone else's. Then, she supposed, she would be given a place to keep herself, like all the rest of Count Fulk's hangers-on; unless she asked to be taken to a convent. Some of the women had done so, and must be on their way: she could see none of them. There were only strangers about her, and her brother who had grown so different and yet was so familiar.

A convent might be wise. It would be quiet and austere and—God willing—cool. But if Bertrand was here and she had no need to seek him out, then all her plans and fears were set at nothing. She could tell him what she must tell him, find a ship that was going back to France, set them both on it and be all done with her errand before it had well begun.

That was not disappointment, no. Of course not. She had expected a lengthy search, a pilgrimage, and at the end of it perhaps another grief, another grave with a man of hers laid in it. Why else had they heard nothing, ever, not once, not even a rumor?

And here was Bertrand, alive and well and clearly prospering. Not dead at all, not lost, standing right on the shore as she sailed in, as if he had known that she would come.

She was angry suddenly, a white anger, painful as the light that struck the paving-stones beneath her feet. It stopped her short, and Bertrand perforce, caught in her grip. Behind them someone cursed. She took no notice. "Why?" she demanded of him. "Why did you never send word? Not even one short word?"

"I might ask the same of you," he said. His calm enraged her. "You could have written me a letter. I do read, you know. Or sent a message. Pilgrims come and go. One might have been pleased to find a knight among the knights of Outremer, and tell him that his kin remembered him."

"Of course we remembered! How could we forget?"

"Indeed," said Bertrand. "How could you? Easily, I should think. Considering that I was sent away in disgrace, exiled for a sin that any fool of a boy might commit, ordered never to come back, never to think of it, not though I died—"

Richildis clapped a hand over his mouth. If he had done such a thing to her, she would have bitten him, but he was a gentle creature for all his size; he always had been. He broke off his hot speech and glared at her over her fingers, standing stiff and still.

"Father was angry," she said. "He said things he never meant. You wanted him to mean them—you wanted to go away. You were wild to try your sword against the infidels."

She lowered her hand. He did not speak for a while. His eyes were pale in his dark face. "Oh, he meant what he said. He never loved me. It was always Giraut—Giraut this, Giraut that. Giraut the brilliant, Giraut the saintly, Giraut who should have been a prelate and not a simple worldly lord. I was the fool and mooncalf, the sinner who tumbled one girl too many and swelled her belly for her, and paid for it with the whole of his inheritance.

"I have a new one now," he said. "I'm a Baron of the High Court of the Kingdom of Jerusalem. I have a castle out past Banias. I have men-at-arms, and I pay knight's fee, and I give homage to the king as any lord and vassal must do. Can Giraut claim as much? Is he still moping about La Forêt, pining for the cloister?"

"Giraut is dead," said Richildis.

Bertrand, headlong on his tide of old grievances, seemed at first not to hear her. She saw him stop; she saw the words sink in. ". . . dead? Giraut is dead?"

"Dead and buried," said Richildis.

"Father must be prostrated," said Bertrand. It was light; it sounded cold. But Richildis, who knew him, heard the rip of pain beneath.

"Father is dead," Richildis said. "And not of grief, though he grieved enough. God took him for reasons of His own. I'm not one to ask what they were."

Bertrand had been standing still, and yet he stumbled. She found it in herself to pity him. She had had months to grow accustomed to the shock, first of Giraut's death, then of her father's. He had it all at once.

It said much for his fortitude that he kept his feet, that though he went pale under the sun's stain he did not topple like a felled tree. "Tell me," he said with fierce urgency. "Tell me—No." He looked about, distracted. "Not here. Come. There is a place— Just come."

ertrand led his sister—his sister whom he had thought, God help him, never to see again—by the hand through a city grown suddenly strange. Its streets in which he had walked so often since he came to Outremer, its sounds and sights and smells, blurred into namelessness. His feet carried him where he had willed to go, heedless of anything but the hand cold and thin in his, and the face in its swathing of veils, white shapeless thing, pale glitter of eyes.

Father dead. Giraut dead, by the devil's black arse. Richildis here, of all places in the world, whom he had envisioned a child still in La Forêt, with her silver-gilt eyes and her gold-bronze braids and the ant-trail of freckles across her nose. This stiff and upright lady could not be his hoyden sister, and yet he had no doubt of it.

Ages late and much too soon, they came to the place he had been seeking. It was a house like many another in this sunstruck country, bare walls unadorned, black unwelcoming slot of gate, nothing about it to betray what lay within. He waited for, and quickly heard, the intake of his sister's breath as the gate opened to his hand, the aged turbaned porter bowing and murmuring in Arabic, admitting them to a kingdom of light and coolness both, and peace: the singing of birds, the ripple of water in a fountain, the scent of blossoms on a gentle waft of air.

Servants came as they always did, by magic he used to think, taking them both in hand. Richildis clung to Bertrand, stiffer than ever but plainly terrified. "Hush," he said as if to a startled mare. "Hush, be still. They mean no harm."

She unlocked her fingers from his arm, leaving behind the throb of bruises. Her eyes rolled white within the veil as the three maidservants bore her away. He called after her, trying to reassure her. "They're only going to get you into something cooler. I'll be here when you come back. I promise!"

She was gone before she could have heard the half of it. He sighed. Marid the chief of servants, with his beautiful manners that he had learned in Baghdad, offered Bertrand all the courtesies to which he was accustomed: the bath, the silken robes, the cool and shaded room and the cup of sherbet, and dainties for his pleasure. Bertrand was glad of them all, yet with a stab of guilt, and then of anger. His father and his brother were dead. And what did he do? He brought his sister to this of all houses in Outremer, presumed on her tolerance and the householder's charity, as if he had a right to either.

In a little while one of the three maids brought Richildis to the room in which Bertrand was sitting at his ease on carpets as people did in the east. Richildis looked stiff and rather stunned. She was clean, her hair washed and curling damply about her face, her gown as modest as she might have asked for, and a veil fastened by a fillet, Frankish style and eastern fashion. Someone had chosen the colors well: soft blue, pale gold that caught the shimmer of her hair.

Bertrand mustered a smile for her. "Why, sister! You grew up beautiful."

She frowned. "Oh, I'm not that. Don't feel you have to flatter me. What is this place? Who are these people? Is this your house?"

He chose to answer the last question first. "No. My house, such as I have, is in Jerusalem. This belongs to a . . . friend."

She heard the hesitation. Of course she would. "Some other man's wife?"

Time was when he would have struck her for that. But he was grown older, and he had learned in a hard school, that one did not indulge one's every fit of temper. "As it happens," he said, "no. I've given up trespassing in other men's beds."

"That comforts me," she said. She sounded as if she meant it. She yielded at last to the maid's mute urgings, sat on the low divan that would be more to her western taste than a heap of carpets on the floor, and took the cup that she was given. She started a little: the silver would be cold, the sherbet cooled with snow.

"Drink it," Bertrand said when she hesitated. "It's good. It's made with lemons—one of the fruits of Paradise. And with sugar, which is less sweet than honey. That's snow in it, from the mountains of the Lebanon."

Richildis sipped. He saw how her eyes widened; grinned before he thought, before memory struck once more. She did not smile back, but she sipped again, and yet again.

She drained the cup and set it down on the table beside the divan. At once the servant was there to fill it. She did not reach to take it. Her hands had knotted in her lap. "You do realize," she said as if the words were part of a long and wearisome conversation, "that you are now the Lord of La Forêt."

Bertrand had not let himself understand what it meant that both his father and his brother were dead. He did not want to understand it. "I am the Lord of Beausoleil near Banias. I have a house in Jerusalem. My service is sworn to the Princess Melisende."

"You are the Lord of La Forêt," said Richildis.

Bertrand shook his head. "No. You don't understand. When I left, I left for good and all. I swore an oath on holy relics. Never, I said. Never would I come back to the place that had cast me out."

"The place never cast you out," Richildis said, merciless in her precision. "Our father, who was as much enraged by your refusal to repent your sin as by the fact that you sinned at all, spoke words that he ever after repented. When Giraut died, he told me that you would have to be sent for. It was time, he said, to end the quarrel. But he died too soon. He never sent the messenger."

"He never meant to." Bertrand turned his own cup in his hands, the sherbet growing warm, the snow melting, but he had no taste for it. He, who loved sherbet best of all the delicacies that were made in Outremer. It tasted of ashes, ashes and cold memory. "You were a fool," he said, "to come here. You're as much of his blood as I am. You should have taken the demesne, found a man to protect it for you, and ruled it for yourself."

She shook her head, as stubborn as she had ever been. "It wasn't mine. It never was. It was Father's, and then Giraut's. Now it's yours."

"I don't want it."

"Oh, please," she said. "You sound like a child. Of course you want it. It's lordship, lands, power."

"I have all those here. More than I would ever have had in Anjou. That little drafty castle, the roof that always leaked in winter, the stink of the privies in high summer—what do I want with them? You can have them. I give them to you. Take them and be glad."

"No," said Richildis.

His eyes narrowed. He looked at her, looked hard, as if he had not seen her before. "You don't want them, either."

"What I want is of no consequence. They belong to you."

But he refused to hear her. He was listening deeper, beyond the words. "A bird," he said, "in a cage, with its wings clipped. A white mare in a tight-closed stall, cut off from the open fields. You, too, little sister. You want to fly as much as I ever did."

"I do not," she said, stiff and stubborn and willfully blind to herself. "I came to fetch you home. You will come with me. You must."

"But I won't," said Bertrand. "What will you do? Seize me, bind me? Throw me in the hold of a ship and carry me away?"

"Bring you in front of Count Fulk," she said, "and bid him lay the duty on you, as your sworn and sovereign lord."

"But," said Bertrand, "he is not my lord. I never swore fealty to him. Only to King Baldwin, and after him the Princess Melisende."

"You were born to La Forêt in the County of Anjou. The Count's claim supersedes any claim that these outlanders may make."

"Fulk is count no longer—he passed the title to his heir; that was in the agreement, I saw it when it was written. He came to be king in Jerusalem."

Richildis set her lips together. Bertrand knew better than to think he had defeated her. But he had driven her into a kind of retreat.

While she mustered her forces, he nibbled on an almond-cake. He was dizzy, though not with hunger. Father dead. Giraut dead. Richildis—

"Do you remember," she asked him, as if absently, "the month of May in La Forêt? The long winter gone, and the sun returned, and the meadows all starred with flowers, and in the wood, the black wood gone green with spring, the birds singing till surely their hearts would burst?"

"I remember," said Bertrand, "that it was Martinmas when I was driven out, cold November rain, grey skies, grey walls, grey wood dripping sodden as I rode away. And all for a silly flit of a girl who found her lawful lord too fatly dull for words. He should have worn his horns with more grace—and been less public about his inability to pleasure any woman, let alone father a child."

"I rather admired him for telling the truth," Richildis said.

"He was too blind angry to lie," said Bertrand. "Idiot. Who'd have known, otherwise? He'd have had an heir, however he got it."

"You still don't repent," she said, a little sadly, a little coldly.

"Oh, I repented richly," said Bertrand. "I haven't touched a wedded woman since. But that changes nothing. He still made a fool of himself, and ended up a laughingstock. And there was no one to inherit his lands when he was dead, except the wife he lacked the will to put aside; and she would pass it to her bastard, unless she found another man to sire a legitimate heir. Did she do that, do you know? I always wondered."

"She died bearing the child," Richildis said. "It was a daughter; she's in a convent now. She'll take the veil when she's older, I suspect."

Bertrand stared at his fists. They had clenched; he had not been aware of their doing it. "Are they all dead, everyone I ever knew? Isn't anyone alive?"

"I am," said Richildis. "Lady Agnes is. She sends her love."

"Ah," said Bertrand. "Lady Agnes. I meant to say goodbye to her."

"You may tender your apologies in person," said Richildis.

"I will not," Bertrand said. "I am not going back to La Forêt."

"Are you not?" said Richildis.

He glared at her. "Don't think you can plot and scheme me into giving way. I took an oath. I mean to keep it. You go back, marry someone steady, have it all and be glad of it."

"No," said Richildis.

And there they were, at an impasse. They had fought like this as children, over this or that, blind alike and stubborn alike, and no yielding in either of them.

Bertrand was the elder. He should be the more reasonable—but not if reason meant giving up all this bright and sunlit country, and going back to France. He calmed himself by force of will, drew a long breath, said levelly, "You must be tired, and I know the heat is dragging at you. Rest here as long as you like, and ask whatever you please; the servants will be glad to oblige."

"And their mistress? Will she glad to find a strange woman here, dropped like a stray sack upon the road?"

"Helena is a wise lady," Bertrand said, "and generous. She'd rather see you here, well tended and looked after, than turned loose in the palace."

"Ah," said Richildis. "So her name is Helena. May I ask what she is to you?"

Bertrand hesitated. He felt the slow heat climb his cheeks.

She saw it, damn her. Her lips quirked very slightly—a shadow of the laughter that he remembered, as this thin severe creature barely recalled the bright-eyed child. "Ah," she said again. "No; I think it would be best if I braved the palace. Or there may be a convent that can spare a bed."

"What, are you too priss-proud to share a house with a woman of shadowed repute?"

For an instant he saw the child she had been: the flash of interest, the quick question: "Is she really?" Then the woman had returned, prim as a nun. "Please tell the servants to fetch my things. I don't think they speak the *langue d'oeil*."

"They understand it reasonably well," Bertrand said, "but I am not going to order them to do anything. You are staying here. The palace is a warren, and there's barely room to breathe. The convents will clip your wings worse than La Forêt ever did. You'll be safe here, and protected, and allowed a room to yourself."

She was tempted, he could see it. But she set her chin against him. Which only made him the more determined that she should stay. Helena would not mind. Not greatly. This was his sister, after all. Her very muleheadedness would prove it.

He turned toward the door. One of Helena's Turks stood in it, had been standing there for a while, quietly on guard; and listening, too, no doubt: they all understood Frankish, though few of them deigned to speak it. "Kutub," Bertrand said in Arabic, "in Allah's name, if it pleases you to guard this lady, I would be most grateful."

Kutub bowed gravely, though his narrow black eyes were glinting. "It would please me, lord Frank, as fair as this lady is, and so strange to all that is here. May she go where she wills?"

"She is not a prisoner," said Bertrand, "but it might not be wise for her to wander in the city. If she could remain here until your lady returns . . ."

"As you will, lord Frank; and then, of course, as my lady wills," Kutub said.

Bertrand inclined his head as easterners did, acknowledging the rights of that. When he turned back to his sister, she was glaring at them. She knew what he had said, though it was in no language that she could have understood. "This is Kutub," Bertrand said to her. "He'll look after you. I'll come back when I'm done with the duties I've been shirking."

Richildis rose as he rose, stiff with anger. "I am not staying here! I'm coming with you. Just show me to the palace; then I can—"

"No," said Bertrand. He did not bow, nor did he offer to embrace or kiss her; they had done none of that, nor would, it seemed. He simply left her.

She sprang after him, but Kutub set himself in her way. He was gentle, he was respectful, but he was immovable.

Bertrand could not resist a glance back. Richildis neither shrieked nor wept, nor did she try to batter her way past the Turk. All her rage had gathered in her eyes and focused on her brother.

He would pay, he could well see. But later. For now she was safe; and that, when it came to it, was all that mattered.

F O U R

Richildis, abandoned in a stranger's house, held prisoner by a bearded, turbaned, slit-eyed cutthroat, considered the utility of a fine and ranting fit. But there was no one to hear but her jailer. Nor would she give him the pleasure of seeing her weep.

After what he seemed to reckon a judicious interval, he bowed in elaborate eastern fashion and said, "Come, *Khatun*. Come with me."

His accent was atrocious, but she understood him well enough. She should refuse, perhaps. Who knew what he would do, infidel that he was? But she had grown weary of that room, and she was angry enough to be reckless. She followed where he led.

He conducted her through the house by ways that she had gone to be bathed and clothed, then up a stair and through an intricately latticed door. The passage behind it opened on a room less wide and high than the one below yet airy and cool, with a small black person plying a great fan, and another of the low eastern couches, and shutters that opened on a balcony. The scent of roses dizzied her. There was a garden below, in full and intoxicating bloom, red and white and gold and pink.

Even roses were more vivid here, their scent stronger. France beside Outremer was a pale and feeble country, its skies washed to grey, its colors muted, its scents dulled. She shut out the light and the fragrance of roses, and huddled on the couch. The cool dimness and the flap-flap of the fan lulled her, though she fought it. Little by little she slid into a stupor.

She must have slept. Her body was heavy. The hand that she struggled to raise was wan and pallid, like a winter morning. It was cold, yet the rest of her was feverish. Her mouth was ashen dry.

The jar beside the couch held water, cool and clean. She drank thirstily, though not without a moment's pause to wonder if there were some drug or spell laid on the cup. All that she had heard of the east were snatches and fragments, old fears, scattered tales, the scrap of a song: *Car felon sont Sarazin.*

She dragged herself up. Once she was on her feet, had reeled and then steadied, she felt a little stronger. The fan was still, its wielder gone. She was all alone.

She stumbled to the window, took a breath, opened the shutters. Fierce light stabbed her eyes. But not as fierce as it had been. Its angle was longer, its edges less blackly distinct. And was it a little, just a little, cooler?

A sound made her whirl, snatching at a weapon, any weapon; but there was none. The door was open. The Turk who had brought her here was standing in it, bowing lower than he had to her, down to the floor.

The woman who stepped lightly past him was as foreign as he, though not, Richildis could see, of his kind and nation. She was not a small woman, nor was she as tall as Richildis. Beneath swathings of silk her body was difficult to see, but it was not particularly slender. Rounded, rather, and richly so. Her skin was the color of fine ivory, her eyes great and dark, her hair blue-black and abundant, its waving exuberance held in check by tight plaits and a glitter of pins, with a drift of veil laid over it.

She was incontestably beautiful, with the great-eyed and oval-faced beauty of an eastern saint. Not that any saint would paint her face as this woman did, with what appeared to be great artifice; nor could the odor of sanctity partake of such dark richness as wafted from her: musk and sandalwood and a memory of roses.

Richildis was rather startled to hear her speak in plain Frankish with an accent so faint as to be almost imperceptible. "Lady," she said. "I'm pleased to see you awake and looking well. My name is Helena; this is my house in which you find yourself a guest."

Richildis' back stiffened. "Madam," she said in return. "I, as you must know, am Richildis de La Forêt. I must cry pardon for my brother. He compelled me—"

Helena broke in so smoothly that Richildis was hardly aware of being interrupted. "Ah; yes. My lord Bertrand sent me word that you were here. I take it that you weren't consulted?"

Richildis glared, not at Helena but at the Turk who stood in the door behind her. "I was neither consulted or given a choice."

"Aye me," sighed Helena. "How like my lord Bertrand." She turned to the Turk, spoke rapidly in what must have been Arabic: harsh and sweet at once, with strong music in it. The Turk bowed to the floor, leaped up, made himself scarce.

Helena turned back to Richildis. "Kutub has gone to set the servants in order. We'll dine in an hour. Meantime, would it please you to walk in the garden for a bit, to comfort your spirit?"

Richildis would have been deeply pleased to depart this house and never set foot in it again, but that was hardly possible. Her jailer had gone, only to be replaced by one even more vigilant and even less easily escaped. She conducted Richildis down a narrow twisting stair and into the garden.

It was not yet evening, but the sun had sunk from its zenith. It hung over the garden's wall, trapped in a net of vines.

The roses that had so dizzied Richildis' senses were but a corner of a greater garden, a sheltered court that opened on an expanse of green: a little sward, a grove of trees, a pool with fish swimming in it, bright as coins. It was all much smaller than it looked, the trees hardly higher than Richildis was tall, heavy with scented blossoms. "Lemons," Helena said, pausing to draw in the fragrance, "and oranges, and citron. Do such grow in your country?"

"Not in mine," Richildis said, determinedly polite, "but in the southlands their like is known."

"Ah," said Helena. "You come from the northern country, from Anjou, like the man who will marry the Princess Melisende."

"Like the man who left me here," said Richildis. "You do know him well, I trust. Well enough that he would feel free to drop his sister in your lap."

"We are friends," said Helena, sweetly serene. "He did believe, and I agreed, that you would be in greater comfort here than in the palace or, saints forbid, a convent."

"Perhaps it is not comfort that I crave," said Richildis.

"Perhaps," said Helena. She sat gracefully on the pool's tiled rim, took up a bowl, scattered crumbs from it upon the water. The fish flurried, swirling over and about one another in their greed for her largesse. She watched them calmly, her dark eyes quiet.

When she spoke again, it was of nothing that had come before. "I'm glad to meet you at last. Your brother has spoken often of you."

"Has he?" Richildis made no effort to keep the bitterness from her voice. "We had no word from him, not in all the years that he was gone."

"He wrote you," Helena said. "Often. Every time something happened that would make you laugh, as he said to me; or that would interest you; or that would make you proud of him."

For a moment Richildis did not know what to say. For all she knew, the woman was lying. And yet it was a thing that she could well imagine Bertrand doing— Bertrand at least as she had known him then, her tall boisterous brother who could always spare a moment for his sister. "His letters never came to us," she said at length, struggling not to sound aggrieved, and fearing that she failed.

"He never sent them," Helena said. "He was so angry at first, you see, and when his anger cooled, he grew shy. You might have learned to hate him, after all. Or simply to forget him."

"None of us ever forgot him," said Richildis. She was weary of standing, but she was not inclined to sit as Helena was doing. She wandered a little round the pool and past the most fragrant of the trees. It hummed with bees: a rich sound, and drowsy, though it little tempted her to fall asleep. She was out of her element here. It made her awkward, and worse than that, ungracious. Lady Agnes would have been appalled.

She could not bring herself to offer an apology. Easterners, she had heard, were scornful of Franks new come from the west, and reckoned them uncouth. They were slippery creatures themselves, sly and apt for treachery; Frankish directness amused when it did not offend them. Even as kind as this woman seemed, and as inclined to forgive Richildis her lapses, still she was of this country.

And Richildis had begun to suspect what kind of woman she might be. A woman who lived apparently alone, attended by villainous Turks and soft-voiced doe-eyed women; who professed intimate knowledge of a man who was not her husband . . .

She looked nothing like the painted strumpets of Paris or Poitiers. Her manners were impeccable, her bearing dignified, even queenly. Her speech was soft, its accent noble. She might have been a lady of high degree.

Perhaps she was, a widow it might be, wealthy and eccentric. Richildis was a fool and low-minded, to think her a courtesan.

The fish in the pool had eaten the last of the crumbs. Helena rose with grace that a princess should have studied, smoothed her skirts, smiled at Richildis. "I believe," she said, "that our dinner may be ready. Cook has been cherishing secrets all day long; I'll wager he's outdone himself."

Richildis opened her mouth to declare that she was not hungry; but that would have been an arrant lie. She was starving. Surely there was no sin in breaking bread with a courtesan, if courtesan this was. Had not the Lord Christ done the same?

The Lord Christ had not been a lady of good family and pristine reputation. Whose brother had left her here, as if he cared not at all for either honor or appearances.

She was angry a great deal, here in Outremer. Later she would deplore it. For the moment she needed it, to stiffen her back and her courage.

Lady or courtesan, Helena set an elegant table. It lacked the excesses of a royal feast, the parades of whole oxen, swans and peacocks roasted and clothed in their own feathered skins, elaborate subtleties depicting this extravagance or that. It was simple, but deceptively so. Fine white bread, cheeses of varied pungency, a young kid served on a heavy platter in a bed of rice and strange fruits, sweetmeats fragrant with honey and rosewater. The wine was sweet and heady, and there was sherbet too, cooled with snow.

Richildis discovered in herself a hitherto unsuspected passion for dates stuffed with almonds and dipped in honey, and for oranges eaten simply as they were, without sweetening or enhancement. Once she had determined to yield to the inevitable, she let herself enjoy flavors both strange and familiar, delicacies that she had heard of—even read of in Scripture—but never tasted. And yes, the pleasure of her companion.

Helena was not only well schooled in the manners and deportment of a lady; she was learned, could read Latin and Arabic, and Greek, too. She spoke all those languages, and both the *langue d'oc* and the *langue d'oeil* of the Franks, though not all, she professed, with equal facility.

"I've been fortunate," she said over wine and a platter of cakes of every kind and color imaginable. "My mother was a Saracen and a slave, but she belonged to a woman of a sort who is somewhat common in Islam: well born, twice widowed, wealthy and possessed of authority over a family of merchants. This woman, before she died, saw that my mother was educated—such might be wasted on our sex, she used to say, but it had served her well enough, and might serve my mother.

"When she died, my mother was left her freedom and the wherewithal to set herself up in a house of her own with a man or men of her choosing. Those whom she chose, she could choose carefully. My father was a Frank, a sergeant in service to one of the great lords. He could never marry my mother, of course, since she was an infidel, but he looked after her as he could, and after me when I was born. Between them they saw that I had teaching well above my station in the world. Mother had won herself a sergeant; she meant me to win a prince."

"My brother is hardly that," Richildis said. The wine was in her; it made her warm and rather silly, but not so silly as to forget who she was.

"Your brother is a baron, which is rather better than a sergeant," said Helena.

"He'll never marry me, of course. It's much better for his position if he finds a woman of suitable rank and property, and makes her the mother of his sons."

"If he does that, she might make him give you up."

Helena favored her with a long dark stare. "Is that how it's done in France? Does a man give up his mistress once he's taken a wife?"

Richildis should have blushed, but the wine had a will of its own. It made her say, "That depends on the wife."

"He would find a sensible one," said Helena. "Men are few here and women many, at least among the Franks. Sons die young or in battle. Daughters fill the noble houses and overflow. Only look at the king: four daughters and never a son, so that he must send for a man from France to be king after he dies. The woman in this country who finds herself a noble husband knows better than to interfere in his more private pleasures."

"Such pleasures are a sin," Richildis said.

"How severe you are!" said Helena. "Was life so bitter for you, away in Anjou?"

Richildis blinked. "Bitter? What's bitter about proper Christian virtue?"

"Why, everything," said Helena.

"Are you not a Christian then? Are you an infidel?"

"I have never professed the Faith," Helena said, "and I was baptized at my father's insistence, in the Latin Church and not the Greek. I was never sufficiently devout. I think I may be a kind of pagan."

Richildis shivered. Everyone who was not Christian was infidel; that, she had been raised to believe. And anyone who, once baptized in the Church, thereafter repudiated it, was worse than any infidel, who after all had the excuse of ignorance. "Do you mean to say," she said, breathless with the shock of it, "that you are apostate?"

"Of course not," said Helena, no more angered by this than by anything else that Richildis had said. Her equanimity was remarkable. Or perhaps she was a marvel of deception. "I'm not passionate enough to be either heretic or apostate. There's so much in the world, you see, that isn't endless fretting over the number of angels in the eye of a needle."

"Head of a pin," said Richildis. "It's the camel that—" She stopped herself. Folly, all of this; pure folly. Sitting in this place, drinking too much wine, conversing with this woman who was nothing that Lady Agnes would ever have approved of.

For a surety, she had had more wine than she needed. When she tried to rise, the world reeled. A hand steadied her, attached to that same rogue of a Turk whom Bertrand had set on guard over her. He was infidel. His very touch sullied her.

The thought was impossibly ridiculous. Once she had begun to giggle at it, she could not stop. Even when he carried her away in ignominy, gave her into the hands of silent expressionless women, and went wherever servants went when their duties were done.

And where *did* they go? She had never stopped to wonder before. Servants served. What they did, where they went, when they were not performing their service, a lady did not ask.

Perhaps a lady should. With that markedly heretical thought, Richildis came to a conclusion. She was not going to try to escape from this peculiar prison. She would stay, and study it, and let it entertain her. Then, when her brother came to release her, if he came . . .

Of course he would come. He was honorable, in his way. That could not have changed since he was young.

So much wine, rivers, oceans of it, and she could still think. She was pleased with herself. Oh yes: very greatly pleased.

ichildis was not so pleased to wake to a stabbing agony of light, and a voice like drums beaten in her skull, and her brother's face staring down at her, looking as if he struggled not to laugh. She shut eyes tight against the light and that irresistibly grinning face, clapped hands over her ears, burrowed into bedclothes too richly scented with herbs. Her stomach heaved, but that she mastered.

"Sister," Bertrand said above her, echoing in her brainpan, "your most humble pardon, but you've been granted a great gift: the Princess Melisende will see you this very day."

Richildis crawled out of hiding, ruffled and scowling. "Gift? Why is that a gift? I never asked to intrude upon her presence."

"No," he said; "but I did. She's been in need of a lady to wait on her, someone sensible and intelligent, who can converse with her on subjects other than this new fashion and that new beauty from France."

"I'm sure every princess needs such a companion," Richildis said, "but I am not in need of a lady to wait on. As soon as we can find passage, we are returning to Anjou. La Forêt has need of its lord."

"I am not going back to Anjou," Bertrand said. "And since you are hardly likely to leave until I do, I've found you a place and a purpose."

"You have to go back," said Richildis. "You can't stay here."

"Can't I?" He said it without anger, nor with any particular emphasis, but she sensed the iron beneath, the will set firm and immovable.

Wise of him, to know that she would not go until she had succeeded in prying him loose. Wiser still to find her something to do; though if he thought to bind her with friendship to that lovely, sullen princess, he was not as wise as he fancied himself.

He retreated as she rose from the bed, withdrawing in favor of the maids who had waited on her the day before. She had a clouded memory of their bathing her—twice in a day; how decadent—and putting her to bed. And here they came to bathe her again, dress her in another gown that must have been cut hastily to her measure, and weave her damp hair into an intricacy of plaits.

She had never been so conscientiously clean before. It felt sinful. To feel her skin so smooth and scented; her hair clean, freed of its burden of small visitors;

her garments fresh that very morning, scented with sweet herbs—surely the priests would condemn her for a harlot. But ah sweet saints it was wonderful. She said a prayer against vanity, and another against pride; and when that was said, she followed one of the servants to the room in which she had dined, where Bertrand was, and Helena looking as fresh as if she had never drunk the night away.

Richildis wished that she could look as well. She rather suspected not: there was an art of paint and kohl that she did not have, nor had she suffered the maids to practice it upon her. Her bleared eyes and her pallid cheeks were as God had made them. The gown at least was becoming, sewn of a marvelous fabric that, the maid had told her in hesitant Frankish, was raw silk. Its color was somewhere between amber and gold, its sleeves embroidered with gold, and the shift beneath of cotton as whitely pure as the robe of a virgin martyr. The gown caught the lights in her hair, the maid had observed, and suited her well. It would not shame her in front of the Princess-Heir of Jerusalem.

It seemed she had decided to play the game as Bertrand wished to play it—if decision it could be called, to abandon open resistance. She had not failed to take note that if she served the Princess Melisende, she must of necessity live in the palace and not in this house, with this courtesan whom she should not, she truly should not, like as well as she did.

Helena's smile warmed her as she entered. There was a place laid at the table for her, on her brother's right hand as Helena sat on his left. In France one broke one's fast as one could, a sop of bread in wine perhaps, or a bit of cheese. Here one ate in greater dignity, from an array of breads and cakes, cheeses and fruits, and more of the perpetual sherbet.

Richildis' stomach heaved, and yet oddly she was hungry. She ventured to nibble on a flat round of bread that was, Helena told her, the common bread of the east. It was surprisingly good to be so unassuming. And there were oranges; she had discovered in herself a passion for oranges. She ate two and restrained herself from a third.

Somewhere between the bread and the oranges, Richildis had lost the greater part of her wine-sickness. Her brain was dull still, and her head ached dimly but persistently; but she felt like a living creature and not the walking dead.

The others helped by not insisting that she make conversation. They spoke little themselves, but not as strangers; as friends so comfortable and so long accustomed to one another's company that they had no need to fill the silences with words. They did not act like lovers, that Richildis could see: though that might be played for her benefit. They acted like friends and long companions.

She had never seen a man and a woman act so before. Man and man, yes; or woman and woman. These two seemed not to regard the differences of sex and station. There was no deference in Helena's manner, and no condescension in Bertrand's. Nor did they touch one another as lovers did, to lay claim to the body.

It was strange. Almost disturbing. Richildis was glad to finish breaking her fast, to bid farewell to Helena with ample and suitable gratitude; to let Bertrand carry her away to the place that he had found for her.

• • •

She had in some fashion expected the royal residence in Acre to be such as she had seen in France: crowded, drafty, reeking of smoke and humanity. Of course it was crowded, but the rest was profoundly different. It was a castle, yes, a strong fortress, but its halls were open and airy, its courts clean and swept, and its gardens rich and strange. The people therein were Franks, well enough, but dressed in eastern fashion, moving with eastern grace, greeting one another with eastern effusion. The newcomers from the west seemed greatly uncouth, ill-washed and ill-kempt and sweating in garments much too heavy for this place.

She could not avoid a moment's relief, and a moment's shame too, because she had been made into an easterner. Not in heart, God knew, but in the body certainly. The flow of her garments washed her in coolness as she walked; the whisper of silk followed her, compelling a more supple stride. Her feet in silken slippers stepped delicately on the pavements. The crown of plaits gave her no choice but to hold her head high, as if she were royally haughty and not simply afraid that the whole edifice would collapse and slither down her back.

Bertrand was well known here. He was admitted not only through the outer gate as any man might be, but through the inner as well, past companies of idlers and unoccupied persons, petitioners to the king or seekers of his favor. When one of those tried to slip in in Bertrand's wake, the door-guards warned him back with lowered spears.

Some of the idlers had even called to him, addressing him as a personage. "My lord! Lord Bertrand! If you would, if the king could spare a moment—"

"My lord, if you have a moment—"

"Lord Bertrand, do remember, we were together at—"

He strode through them without rudeness but without slackening of pace, smiling at this one, nodding at that, and neatly evading speech with any of them. Richildis had seen the King of France do less well in this princely art than her brother was doing. She found it as disconcerting as everything else he had done and said in Outremer. He was her brother still, her Bertrand whom she had loved, but he had changed—more than she would ever have believed, away in La Forêt, when she spoke so lightly of bringing him home again.

The inner courts of the king's residence were full of elegant personages, silk-clad and musk-scented gallants trailing clouds of hangers-on. Among them like lions among deer strode men in mail, armored as if for battle, with the cross of Crusade on the shoulder. Their faces were deeply seared by the sun, and often scarred; their eyes were hooded under heavy brows. They bade Richildis remember that this was no soft and effeminate country, however great its comforts. It was a nation born in war, sustained in battle, the eastern bastion of Christendom against the hordes of the infidel.

Warrior and elegant alike greeted Bertrand with respect. Here he could not move so quickly. He had to stop, if only for a moment, to speak to this man or that. Names blurred in Richildis' memory. Faces she remembered more clearly: alert, keenly aware of her as a stranger. The men of war were mostly warrior monks, Templars and Hospitallers. The men in silks were lords of the High Court or their heirs; but some of those, she saw when she was closer, wore mail under their handsome robes.

One or two she did remember. Joscelin, who was lord in Edessa: she had heard of him even in La Forêt, for his name was sung among the great ones of the first Crusade. He was aging now, his shock of hair tonsured by time, the remnants of it gone iron grey; and his face was grey, too, under the sun's bronze, as if he had been ill. But he greeted her with courtly grace, kissed her hand and said, "You're most welcome in Outremer, my lady. And how do you find it, now that you've seen a little of it?"

"It's . . . strange," Richildis said, feeling like a fool and wondering where all her wits had gone. People were staring. Too many people, too many strangers.

She had never been shy; she had been raised to be stared at, as all noble ladies were. But there had always been familiar faces, people whom she had known since she was small, who had seen her grow from child into woman. These, except for Bertrand, were all unknown to her.

Lord Joscelin seemed not to mind the inanity of her response. "Oh, indeed," he said. "It's uncommonly strange when one first comes here. But in time it grows familiar. I've nigh forgotten what France is like—the sun's burned it all away, and left me with memory of nothing but this most holy country. You will be visiting the sacred places, yes? If you have need of escort, only ask, and I would be more than pleased to oblige."

Richildis murmured something, she hardly knew what. Lord Joscelin excused himself to greet a man in armor, a Templar by his habit. Bertrand touched her hand, drawing her away.

"That was well done," he said when they had gone a little distance, through that particular hall and up a stair and a passage and past another pair of guards. "Milord Joscelin is a great power in this country, and a strong friend. If he's taken a fancy to you, most of the greater lords will follow."

"What is it about me that he fancies?" she asked with some asperity. "Is he in want of a wife?"

"Not at the moment," said Bertrand, refusing to be baited. "Don't tell me you never learned to cultivate friends in high places. Or were you in the convent so long, they all but made a nun of you?"

"I left Ste-Mathilde when I was twelve years old," Richildis said, "to marry Thierry de Beaumanoir."

"You married *Thierry?*" Bertrand sounded honestly appalled. "God's bones! What was our father thinking?"

"Our father was thinking that it was time I made a suitable marriage, and Beaumanoir would match well with La Forêt."

"But Thierry was a lout," said Bertrand. "An idiot. A miserable excuse for a knight, and not much of a man, either."

Richildis stopped in the passage, which happened to be empty. She rounded on her brother. "Father made for me the best marriage that he could find. If you had been there, no doubt he would have heard your objections. But you were not, and he did as he judged wise. I was not unhappy. I only regret that I gave him no son. One of his bastards is lord in Beaumanoir now: I gave it up when he died, to go back to La Forêt."

"Gave it up? Or fled?"

"I left," said Richildis with all the serenity she could command. "I never learned to love Beaumanoir. My heart called me back to La Forêt; and Father said nothing, nor cast me out. My dowry came back with me, and a consideration from my husband: as it happens, enough to pay my passage here. I did well enough, though not as well as Father had hoped."

Bertrand, alack, was no fool, and he knew her better than he had a right to. "He beat you. His bastard tried to. Did he rape you, too?"

"Which? William Bastard?" Richildis could not prevent her lip from curling. "Of course not. He called me a cold and milkfaced excuse for a saint, but he lacked the force of will to keep me prisoner. I took what I pleased and left when it suited me."

"As you left La Forêt to come to Outremer?"

"You know why I came here."

"So I do," Bertrand said. "I wonder: do you?"

She could hardly turn on her heel and stalk away from him. She did not know the way ahead, and the way behind was full of strangers. She settled for walking swiftly forward. He followed as she had hoped he would, then in a long stride set himself ahead, guiding her onward.

The ladies of Jerusalem had their bower in a high turret, looking out over the city and the blue brilliance of the sea. Their assembly was like a garden of flowers: bright gowns, bright jewels, bright glitter of eyes at the stranger who had been brought among them. But for the guards at the door and the singer with a lute, there were no men in their company. Richildis was a little surprised at that. She had expected that Melisende's knights would flock about her, but there was none here, except Bertrand.

He bowed with grace that he could only have learned in this country. The princess, seated in the center of her ladies, seemed less sullen a creature than she had been on the quay of Acre. Her smile at sight of Bertrand was vivid; Richildis saw no affectation in it. She held out her hand. He took it and kissed it. "Highness," he said, "I have the gift I promised."

Melisende's glance left his face to settle on Richildis. Vivid indeed, Richildis thought. Alive, alert, and much too intelligent for its own good. She was a woman grown by any reckoning, well past her first courses, old enough that a sister who had been born after her was a full year a wife; and yet she struck Richildis as a brilliant and thoroughly spoiled child.

She spoke charmingly enough, with an accent that spoke to Richildis half of the north of France and half of the east. Her mother had been Armenian: Richildis saw it in her dark eyes and in the faint golden cast of her skin, though the rest of her was as straightforwardly Frankish as King Baldwin himself. "A handsome gift," she said, "and one well given. Milady . . . Richildis, yes?"

Richildis inclined her head.

"Richildis," said Melisende. "Come, sit by me. Do you sing?"

"Not with any great facility, highness," Richildis said.

"Your brother told me otherwise," said Melisende.

"My brother remembers the child I was," Richildis said, "and not the woman I am now."

"Brothers will do that," said Melisende, "or so I am told." She beckoned, graceful and imperious. "Come! Sit. Will you take wine? Or have you acquired a taste for sherbet?"

"Wine will do," Richildis said, "highness." She sat where she was commanded, taking note of the ladies who shifted to make room. Their mouths smiled but their eyes were dark and flat, as if they weighed her and found her wanting. They all seemed to be of eastern blood, in part or in whole. Of them all, only Richildis seemed to be pure Frank.

She could not feel excessively tall or pale: Melisende was tall and fair. But she felt as much an outlander as she had yet felt in this country.

She veiled her discomfort well, or no one cared to notice. Melisende dismissed Bertrand with another of her blazing-bright smiles. "Go, greet the sky, defend the Holy Sepulcher. I'll guard your sister well, you have my word on it."

Bertrand bowed low. As easily as he had abandoned his sister to Helena, he left her with the Princess of Jerusalem. And there was not a word she could say against him. That was the lot of women in this world: to be disposed of as men saw fit, however little they themselves might wish it.

elena was better company, but Melisende was infinitely more respectable. Stranger she might be, surrounded by strangers, in a strange country, but she was still a Frankish lady. Her manners had the silken softness of the east, but her speech and her expressions were of the west, learned as it must be from her father.

As idle as she seemed to be, in fact she was doing a great deal, in the inimitable fashion of princesses. While the singer sang his songs, some of Provence and some wailing oddities of the east, Richildis saw how Melisende had set each lady to a task: sewing on bits that would become a robe of state, or making lists that must pertain to the court's moving to Jerusalem for the wedding, or running on errands. She herself, seated in comfort, listening to sweet music, kept pace with all of them. The woman next to her, who was reading from a book, read not tales of old knights or lives of the saints, but the accounts of a great demesne.

Indeed, thought Richildis. Melisende would be chatelaine of her father's holdings, since her mother was dead. Strange to see with how much pleasure she seemed to regard her duties, and yet she so clearly was not pleased with the husband who had been chosen for her.

Gossip was the same here as everywhere. The names were strange but the scandals were the same. And there were many of those, if these ladies' chatter was any guide; but none of them named Fulk, or told tales of him.

Richildis could well remember when she prepared for her wedding, how the talk had never failed to come round to the man whom she would marry. There had been a certain delicacy in it, in that no one had dwelt too long on his sins of the flesh and the spirit, but still they had had much to say of him, of his bastards, of the wives he had had before her. She had come to know him very well, as she fancied, by the time her hand was laid in his before the church door, and she spoke the words that made her his wife.

Here, no one spoke of Count Fulk. That seemed rather a pity: by every account that Richildis knew, he was a better man by far than Thierry de Beaumanoir. Instead they chattered of everyone else, names that she had heard in legends of Crusade, still other names that were strange to her, and not a few words of her brother.

She was not, it seemed, expected to mind their speculations as to his prowess in the bedchamber, still less their lighthearted wagers as to when, and if, he would

take a bride. She sat beside the princess, alone of them all in having nothing to
do, and nothing to say, either, since she was a stranger.

It might have been an hour that she sat there, saved from boredom by the singer's
excellence and her own growing fascination with the Princess Melisende. The
spoiled and sulky child of the quay was little in evidence here. This was a lady who
performed her duties well and skillfully. She was managing the wedding herself, or
nearly; the errand-runners went several times to the king's seneschal and more than
once to the king himself, but the word they brought back was always *It is well; do
as you see fit.* Melisende did not seem disconcerted; indeed, from her conduct, she
had expected to be given a free hand.

It seemed that this odd mingling of pleasure and duty would go on all day. But
when an hour had passed, as close as Richildis could tell, Melisende rose abruptly.
What moved her, Richildis could not see. No bell had rung, no messenger come to
summon her. Perhaps she had merely grown tired of sitting in one place.

Richildis, who had thought herself forgotten, now felt the full force of the princess' eyes on her. "Come with me," said Melisende. As others of the ladies stirred
and some rose, Melisende lifted her hand. "No; stay. That robe must be done by
morning. Anna, take Marie and Cecilia and investigate the cellars. I'm in some
doubt as to whether there's wine enough in Jerusalem for the wedding feast. We'll
take what's here, if it's of sufficient quality. Martine, there's an oddity here in the
accounts for the month of March. See if you can discover why the sugar-mill pro-
duced so much for the first half, and then nothing for the second. Brother Robert
should know; that's his writing in the ledger."

The various ladies returned to their places, or bowed and went to do as they
were bidden. Richildis found herself swept in Melisende's wake, out of that room
and down the stair and out of the tower. The abruptness of it made her dizzy, and
put her in mind, oddly, of battles. Armies did such things, she thought. Waited for
days—months, sometimes. Then leaped into action.

The place to which Melisende took her was hardly deserted. There were women
there as well, but only a handful: older ladies than had gathered in the tower, sitting
in a circle, sewing on a splendor of gold and jewels and silk that must be the princess'
wedding robes. They looked up as the princess entered, bowed their heads and
smiled, but did not either rise or offer greater reverence.

This Melisende must have expected. There was an alcove in the chamber, a
rounded niche with a window too high to look out of, and a bench built into the
wall, curving round it from edge to edge. It made Richildis think of the chapter
house in Ste-Mathilde where she had spent her childhood. It had the same air of
stony quiet.

From the niche she could see the waiting-women laboring over the princess'
gown, and no doubt they could hear if she spoke; yet she felt set apart, alone with
this stranger, this Princess of Jerusalem.

Melisende must have brought her here for a purpose, and one urgent enough to
sweep her abruptly out of the tower, but she seemed in no haste to come to the
point. She sat under the window, arranging her skirts and her veil. "Sit," she said.

Richildis obeyed as she had before, sitting near the edge of the niche. Melisende's
eyes glinted. "France is a warrior country, too, I see," she said.

"Is there any that is not?" Richildis asked her. It might have been courteous to address her by one of her titles, but this place somehow did not encourage it. Therefore she left the question bare, as if they were equals.

The princess did not rebuke her for it, nor seem to notice the lack. "I had heard that Provence is a soft and pleasant country," she said, "where even the barons live in peace with one another, and no one does battle unless he must. They are all poets there, I'm told, and singers of songs."

"Provence is rather less full of ravening beasts than most places in the world," Richildis conceded, "but even it has its wars and its quarrels."

"None as great as here, surely," said Melisende. "We live eternally on the edge of death. Which, the priests will tell you, is the lot of mankind; but it's most perceptible in the Kingdom of Jerusalem, where every house is a fortress, and none is safe from the maraudings of the infidel. France is free of that at least."

"There are the Norsemen," Richildis said, "and Saracens, sometimes, in the south. But the heart of France has nothing to fear but its own contentious nobility."

"They say that in Byzantium there are whole cities that have not known war in generations, and men who have never raised a weapon in battle. Can you believe that?"

"I admit I find it difficult to credit," said Richildis. And added, at last, "Highness."

"Lady," said Melisende, "we'll not stand on ceremony. Nor did I bring you here to contemplate the universality of war. I had wanted to ask you . . ." She paused. Richildis did not believe that she was shy. She hunted for the words, that was all, so as to give the least offense. "I wished to ask you if your brother told me true. You came to fetch him back to France."

Richildis nodded. "Yes. Yes, I did. He's heir to a barony in Anjou."

"He is the Lord of Beausoleil, that my father gave him for his feats against the Saracen. It's a small holding, but rich enough, with an olive press and a sugar-mill, and two knights in fee to the king. Is your Angevin barony as well endowed as that?"

"I have to admit," said Richildis, "that it is not. It has only one knight in fee. But it has a vineyard, and its wine is well thought of, though it's said to travel ill. I brought a cask of it to Outremer. I'll make you a gift of it, once I know what's become of my belongings."

"They are here," Melisende said. "You'll be housed among my ladies in the chamber just outside of my own. I'll have you taken there when we're done here, if you've a mind to see for yourself."

"I believe you," Richildis said. "You want to keep him here, then."

"Of course I do," said Melisende. "We have women enough and more than enough, but strong fighting men are much too rare for comfort. Did you think we'd give up even one, even to take a barony with a vineyard, away in Anjou?"

"One might consider honor," murmured Richildis, "and obligation." But before Melisende could respond to that, she went on, "Yes, I do understand. He has honor and duty here, and both are of great moment to him. He refuses to go home to Anjou."

"His home is here," Melisende said. "He's made it so, by his own merits and the strength of his arm."

"So I can see," said Richildis. She paused. Melisende made no effort to fill the silence. "And so you have taken me in hand, to keep me from vexing my brother."

"Hardly that," Melisende said. "He asked me to honor his sister with a place among my ladies. I was glad to oblige him. It's a coup of sorts, to have a proper Angevin in my train, and she a lady of both presence and probity."

"You may find me stiff and ill-suited to the lighter amusements," Richildis said. "I have little patience for frivolity, even of the most royal sort."

Melisende laughed, startling her. "Oh, he told me true! He said you had a tongue as blunt as any in France, and no reluctance to wield it. Do you think me frivolous, then?"

"I think," said Richildis, "that you are not quite what a stranger might expect. How many people, seeing you with your ladies and your luteplayer, have reckoned you no more than an ornament?"

"Fewer than you might think," said Melisende. Had she been a cat, the tip of her tail would have been twitching. "When I was small I begged to wear armor and carry a sword. I raged when my nurses informed me that such were not for women. Women are weak, they said, and much too light of mind for the rigors of war."

"I am certainly less strong than my brother," Richildis said, "and I would be hard put to lift his sword, still less to wield it against an enemy."

Melisende raised her hand to the window's light and turned it, flexing the fingers. It was a long hand, large for a woman's and strong. "I wonder," she said as if to herself. "Sometimes I wonder . . . what would have happened if I had had my way. I was indulged in much, but in that my father would not be moved. I was not to learn the arts of war, not even the bow as some of the Turkish women do. Horses only he would let me have, and for a while I was a figure of terror, reckless to insanity.

"But I grew older," she said, "and I grew wise. Not all or even most of ruling has to do with war—no, not even here, where war is every man's pursuit. Someone has to feed and equip the armies, and house them when they're home from the field, and maintain the kingdom at their backs. Men fancy that that too is theirs to do; but women know better. *I* know better. I may be compelled to accept a man who can wage war in proper fashion, and call him lord and king; but while he rides about defending the kingdom, I remain at home, ruling it as I see fit."

Richildis regarded her for a long while in silence. She was not greatly alarmed by the words that Melisende had said. Most women thought them, though few spoke them aloud. Those who were firstborn as Melisende was, who had perforce to see their inheritance taken by a brother who might be still a child or less than competent, were hard put to maintain their equanimity. And yet . . .

"It does appear to be God's law," Richildis said, "that man rules and woman serves, in silence if she can."

"And if she has wit enough and patience, in the end she rules, though it might be in a man's name." Melisende shook herself a little. "I'm glad I don't shock you too unduly. It's a friend I'm needing here, more than a servant; and your brother is very dear to me. I had hoped that his sister would find it in herself to suffer her exile in my presence, since she has vowed not to return to Anjou without her brother."

"Am I given a choice?" Richildis asked.

"Do you want one?"

Richildis thought about it. "No," she said after a while. "No, I see the sense in it. Though I'll not forgive him soon, for disposing of me so summarily, without thought for what I might wish."

"Even he is a man," Melisende said, "after all."

Richildis met the level dark stare. There was laughter in it, and sympathy, and— yes—calculation, too. A princess had need of every friend she could find. As what woman did not?

How strange, thought Richildis. She had so disliked this woman at first meeting; and so misjudged her.

Or, no—not misjudged. She had failed to see all that there was of her. As with Helena, she was much more than she seemed, and much less simple to dismiss.

The same indeed might be said of all this country. Richildis began to think that she might find living in it bearable, for however long she must, until her brother's resistance was worn away, and he agreed at last to return to La Forêt.

he wine had traveled neither well nor ill. It was not the satin-smooth vintage that it would have been if they had drunk it in the hall at La Forêt, but neither had it turned to vinegar or worse. Melisende pronounced it very pleasant. Her father the king, to whom she sent a jar, was pleased enough with it that he asked to see the giver of the gift.

Richildis by then had found her belongings in the ladies' chamber, and a bed which she must share with two of them: a privilege, that; the rest had to spread pallets on the floor. She had spent the rest of that day learning the extent of her new duties, and when the princess went to the daymeal in the great hall, she went as one of the princess' waiting-women.

It was there that Melisende presented her father with the tribute from La Forêt. He was said to be less skilled in the colder arts of kingship than that Baldwin who had been king before him—no kin, and no likeness save in the name—but his good humor was well known even in France. He received the cup with a smile that reminded Richildis vividly of his daughter's, drank deep from it, and bowed low not to Melisende but to Richildis herself. "A fine gift," he said to her, "and sweet, like the memory of your fair country. It's long years since last I walked in it. Would it please your grace to remember it to us?"

Richildis stared at him. She was no jongleur, to spin sweet words for a royal feast. Nor could she bring any stories to mind. Her wits had all fled.

God be thanked, one man at least saw how she floundered. Count Fulk spoke smoothly in her silence, with a smile that calmed her as it was meant to, and a turn of the head that drew all eyes to him. "Indeed, majesty, shall we remember our fair France? Her forests, dark and deep yet dappled with sunlight; her rivers, the Seine and the Loire, the Rhone, the Rhine that flows away into Germany; her fields and vineyards, her orchards in bloom, her little hills all gold with the harvest. Ah, we remember her, here in this land of iron and of sanctity. And yet, majesty, would you truly wish to go back there? Would you give up your kingship to be a baron in France?"

"Sometimes," said Baldwin, "I would give my heart's blood to be there again. But my crown and my kingdom . . ." He shook his head. "No. No, I would not."

"Nor, I think, would I," Fulk said. He raised his hands. "It's as they say, is it not? This is the land that was made for us. This is the earth that God has blessed above all others. God wills that we dwell here, my lord of Jerusalem. God wills it."

"*Deus lo volt*," someone echoed him, down among the knights of the kingdom. Someone else took it up, and another with him, and yet another, till they had made a chant of it, the cry of the Crusade. "*Deus lo volt. Deus lo volt!*"

Fulk of Anjou had no memory for names or faces. His famous affability, it was said, was assumed for safety's sake: he must of necessity be pleasant to all he met, since he could never remember which of them he had met before.

This could be a difficulty, or it could be a notable advantage. Richildis did not expect to be remembered as one of the handful of ladies who had come on pilgrimage under Fulk's protection, nor was she. When Melisende began to use her as a messenger between the two of them, bearing word of this matter or that with regard to the wedding, Fulk did not vex her with inquiries as to her comfort here or the success of her journey. He saw her simply as she appeared, as one of the princess' ladies.

She pondered approaching him and demanding his aid in compelling her brother to return to France, but Bertrand had argued too well. Fulk would hardly wish to offend his bride by depriving her of one of her knights. He was pressed as it was to repair the miscalculation of that first day, when he had ignored Melisende to keep company with the king.

He had a name in certain quarters for charming manners with the ladies; but with this princess he seemed condemned to ineptitude. At the feast in which he had conducted so handsome a rescue of Richildis' wits, he had presented Melisende with a gift: three rings of gold, one for her finger, one for her arm, and one for her brow. The speech he made was pretty, forgotten as soon as it was uttered. He made it from the far side of the king, so that he could not gracefully present the rings himself. One of his knights perforce did that.

Better, thought Richildis, if Fulk had come down off the dais and knelt in front of the princess and played the lover, no matter the cost to his dignity. As it was, he seemed unwilling to approach her or touch her, nor would he speak face to face without her father between.

Melisende accepted the rings with cool grace and murmured thanks. She did not look at the giver, nor offer him any greater intimacy than he had offered her.

She kept the full force of her outrage for her ladies, in her bedchamber after she had left the hall. They struggled to undress her and take down her hair and ready her for bed, while she stalked the room, fists clenched, face white and furious.

When she had with difficulty been undressed down to her camise, and her hair freed to ripple down her back, she halted at last. "He shames me," she said clearly, though her teeth were gritted shut. "He insults me. If I were a man—oh, God, if only I were a man! I'd have his head for what he does to me. How much clearer could he be, that he wants nothing of me but the crown I can give him?"

None of her women ventured to speak, but Richildis was less wary or less cowed by so magnificent a display of temper. "It may be," she said, "that he thinks to win you over gently, and not to force himself on you as a man might on a woman of lesser rank. After all, you are a princess. Princesses are notoriously delicate in their sensibilities—and who more so than the Princess of Jerusalem, whose mother was the flower of Melitene?"

"Do I look delicate?" Melisende demanded. "Do I look as if I need to be held at arm's length? Marriage most certainly is a transaction for the good of the kingdom, but may a woman not ask that her husband treat her as flesh and blood and not as a prop for a crown?"

Richildis set her lips together. The marriage of Baldwin and Morphia had been a favorite of the singers: a love match, they had said, that rarity of rarities, half a sin and all a wonder. They had esteemed one another, the songs said, and cherished each other, body and spirit, and conceived their daughters in evident joy.

If Melisende hoped for another such marvel, then she could not but fail. Richildis, looking at her, did not think that she wanted to hear of Richildis' marriage to a man whom she neither loved nor liked, with whom she had managed some degree of contentment. Contentment was not what young creatures dreamed of.

After a while, since Melisende seemed to be waiting, Richildis said, "You could do the courting of him."

Melisende laughed in incredulity. "What? A woman court a man?"

"Why not?" said Richildis. "It doesn't have to be blatant. You can send him gifts—you have some for him, no? And send him messages. And after a day or two, ask to meet, and be your gentlest and most enchanting self. Let him see that you're worth wooing."

She held her breath. Melisende's brows drew together. She would resist. Even she, rebellious in her womanhood, would not wish to take the man's place in the delicate art of courtship.

Suddenly she laughed again—pure mirth this time, and no mockery. "Yes! Yes, I'll do it. But," she said after a pause, as the laughter shrank and vanished, "I don't think I'll ever like him. He's too old. And I hate redheaded men."

"Age can be made to matter little," Richildis said. "As for the rest: a man is only as handsome as his deeds. Fulk's are very handsome indeed. You needn't ever like him, if only you admire and respect him, and give him the son you need."

Melisende tensed as if for another surge of temper, but subsided, sinking slowly and wearily to her bed. "Marriage is a cold thing, isn't it? There's nothing in it that the blood can warm to."

"It serves honor and propriety," Richildis said, "and assures the prosperity of the kingdom. If through it one gains respect, and perhaps a friend . . . well then, one is blessed. And if not, then, God willing, there are children. It's not all grim duty and forced smiles."

"I do hope not," Melisende said.

Therefore Richildis found herself entrusted with the task of bearing messages from Melisende to Fulk, then back again. She made a poor go-between as the songs would reckon it. She offered no embellishments, nor undertook to seduce Fulk with the charms of his bride. Melisende must do that for herself.

Melisende's gifts to her bridegroom were small things, consciously so: a little casket containing nothing but a pearl, a chaplet of flowers from the garden, her singer with an hour's worth of songs. Fulk, engrossed in making himself known to the high ones of the kingdom, seemed bemused by the gifts, but accepted them gracefully enough. In between, Richildis bore word of this preparation or that— impressing on him that his bride, for all the delicacy of her gifts, was a practical woman, a princess born, bred to rule a kingdom.

Richildis could not tell whether he understood the things that he was being shown and told. When on the fifth day after he had come to Outremer she took to him the message for which all the rest had been prelude, inviting him to attend the princess in her bower, she waited for him to put off the invitation.

But he did not. That, she thought, was the first sensible thing he had done to Melisende since he left his ship. She came within a breath's expanse of warning him to conduct himself with greatest care; but it was never her place to do such a thing, even if he had remembered who she was.

She returned to Melisende with his reply. Then for the first time she did indeed embellish it. "I'll come," he had said, no more than that. Richildis framed it with greater grace: "I'll do all indeed as my lady wishes."

Guilt stabbed her even as the words escaped. Melisende's sudden smile did little to assuage it, nor the lift in the princess' spirits as she waited for him to appear. It was a small lift to be sure, and could hardly be likened to eagerness, still less to joy, but it was with serene face and no evidence of sullenness that she received word of his arrival at her door.

"Remember," Richildis said in her ear, "woo him, even if he seems distant or cold. I doubt he's honestly either. He's never wed a princess before; I'll wager he's shy, and even a little afraid."

She could only hope that she spoke the truth; that she had not heaped lie on lie. She shaped a small prayer for forgiveness, and sent it where it best might go.

Fulk came to his bride as she sat not in the bower in which Richildis had first seen her, but in another that lay outside of the tower. It was a very eastern place, a colonnaded gallery that might be as old as Rome or as young as Islam, with high louvered windows and intricate patternings of tiles, and at the far end a fountain in the shape of a leaping seahorse. The soft fall of its water struck counterpoint to the notes of the lute on which one of her ladies played.

Richildis did not entirely approve of her lady's choice. Better the tower room, which Fulk would find familiar as any lady's bower in the west. This in its lines and colors and its elaborate tiling was alien.

Melisende at least had agreed to put on a gown in the western fashion, though made of eastern stuffs, silk over the fine light fabric of Mosul. Her ladies mirrored her, even those whose blood and faces were more of the east than of any western country. They were a pretty picture, plying their needlework and listening to the luteplayer, eyes lowered demurely and hands carefully busy as Fulk made his entrance.

He had come accompanied as one might expect, by a handful of his knights. These must be the most presentable, the least inclined to cling to western habits: they were clean, well shaven, and quiet in their manners. Having seen what some new pilgrims seemed driven to do, and heard of worse, Richildis was glad of Fulk's tact and pleased with his wisdom.

He approached Melisende without visible hesitation, bowed over her hand, and said, "My lady. How fair you look!"

Melisende inclined her head. "Will my lord sit?" she asked.

There was a chair for him, and a bench or two on which his knights might settle themselves if they wished. He took the chair. The knights sat, some of them; the rest stayed on their feet, sliding glances round at the ladies, the fountain, the tiles not only on the floor but on pillars and walls and ceiling.

Fulk, wisely, kept his eyes on Melisende. "My lady is well?" he inquired.

"I am well," she answered, stiffly formal as a court dance. "And my lord? Has our climate been kind to you?"

"It is," he admitted, "somewhat warmer than it tends to be in Anjou. But I was here before; I grew accustomed to it then, and expect I shall again."

"I remember," Melisende said. "You came to court, and my father showed you how to wear the Arabs' headdress."

Fulk smiled. Richildis looked for discomfiture, but found none. No doubt he was accustomed to his failures of memory, and resigned to them. Certainly he could remember plans of battle and the disposition of a demesne. It was only people whom he could not remember. "Ah, so you were there then? There was a bit of a scandal among certain of my compatriots, that I should wish to look like an infidel."

"And you replied that the infidels at least were cool in the heat." Melisende managed a smile of her own, not overly warm, but not cold, either. "It's well thought of here, for a westerner to follow the ways of good sense—and such are many of the ways of the infidel."

"Including their prayers to Allah?"

That was wicked. Melisende bridled a little at it, but then suddenly she laughed. "Oh, but Allah is our God, they'll tell you, and they are people of His Book, just as are we. But their faith is newer than ours, and therefore, they believe, more current."

Richildis found that shocking. So, she noted, did several of Fulk's knights. But he grinned, looking more like a fox than ever. "So what is new is to be preferred to the old and true? How foreign."

"I did say that many of their ways are sensible," said Melisende, "but not all of them. They do believe as fiercely in the errors of their religion as do we in the truths of ours. That's the heart of our war here. Without that passion of theirs, there'd never have been need for Crusade."

"Indeed," said Fulk. He studied Melisende as Richildis had seen him study a young squire whom he had in mind to raise to knighthood. He had roused, Richildis thought, to the same awareness that she had. This was not a spoiled child or a pretty toy. There was substance in her, and strength of will and mind that would grow as she grew, till perhaps she was too strong for any man's mastery.

Small wonder then that Baldwin's embassy had asked the King of France to choose them a man of years and seasoning. A raw boy, however pleasant to look at, could not have kept this princess in hand.

Richildis watched as Fulk's eyes narrowed, as he seemed to come to the same conclusion. If indeed he had done that, he betrayed none of it in speech. He said,

"Some I've heard here—and more than any in the west would credit—are contending that we should understand the infidel in order to defeat him. But surely that way is perilous. One might slip, you see, from wearing his clothes and eating his bread to believing in his god."

"True faith is never so easily shaken," Melisende said. "And for a fact, if donning a turban and drinking sherbet makes a man a Muslim, then he was never much of a Frank to begin with."

Servants chose that moment to appear with platters of sweets and dainties, and pitchers of sherbet. It could not but be coincidence; but Melisende was Melisende. She might have bidden the servants enter precisely now, as she said precisely this.

Fulk's grin flashed again. It did not flatter his face or his teeth, which were not of the best. But he was remarkably free of the sin of vanity. He accepted a cup of sherbet with a good will, and when she also had been given one, raised his own and saluted her. "To true faith," he said, "and to the Crusade."

here was not going to be love between Fulk and Melisende, nor great passion of the body, but Richildis had reason to hope that they might come to something less sinful and more lasting. Respect for one another's intelligence. Concern for the kingdom. Willingness to meet as husband and wife should meet, to breed the sons that this country so badly needed.

"How cold," said Helena. "How practical."

Richildis had not thought, once she left Helena's house to enter the princess' service, to return there. Yet here she was, and here she sat, at dinner with Helena and Bertrand as she had when first she came to Outremer. The court would move to Jerusalem on the morrow, and on the day after they had arrived in the Holy City, Count Fulk would wed the Princess Melisende. The court feasted with even more than its usual exuberance, but Melisende as the virgin bride was permitted an attack of the vapors. She had been put to bed with a posset.

Vapors, Richildis would not call what beset her headstrong lady. Melisende was thoroughly out of patience with the court's fussing, as she put it. The fussing of her ladies annoyed her even further. She had sent them all away, all but the one quiet older lady who would stand guard over this, their last night in Acre and one of the last of her maidenhood.

Richildis would have taken the opportunity to rest and to read from the book that she had brought with her all the way from France, but a messenger had found her in the ladies' sleeping-chamber. He was a most exotic creature, as black as an infidel's heart, dressed in a scarlet coat and a spotless white turban. He had bowed to the floor as infidels did, and said in lisping but clear and barely accented Frankish, "My lady Helena wishes you to know that, if your princess is indisposed and your time is your own, you would be most welcome to dine with her in her house in the city."

Richildis opened her mouth to refuse out of hand. But the messenger was so very young and his eyes so very hopeful that she found herself asking instead, "Will my lord Bertrand be attending as well?"

"Lady," said the messenger, "since he also serves the princess, and the princess is indisposed, his time is also his own."

Which meant, Richildis supposed, that Bertrand would be permitting his lover to entertain him. And did he know that Helena had summoned his sister as well?

"Very well," she said in something close to wickedness, "I'll come."

• • •

Bertrand, as it happened, had incited the invitation. "You haven't set foot outside the women's tower since you went in there," he said when Richildis appeared, escorted by the messenger and by that one of Helena's Turks whom she had begun to think of as her own, the scarred and discreet Kutub. "Aren't you going wild with boredom?"

"Ladies, like nuns, learn to find interest in very small space," Richildis said.

"Or they die of creeping accidia." Helena beckoned Richildis to the seat that she had had before. As she settled there, servants began to bring in the first course of what was to be a surprisingly elaborate dinner.

"And what is this in honor of?" Richildis inquired. "Not, surely, the princess' wedding?"

"That," said Helena, "and your presence as my guest." She caught Richildis' glance as it lowered. "Yes, I know what you've been thinking of me. I'm flattered that you came here, even as little reason as you have to either love or admire what I am."

"Love is a long thing, and must be earned," said Richildis. "Admiration has little to do with simple courtesy. Might I not have been glad to escape, as you put it, accidia?"

"The sin of ennui," Helena said. "Yes. Not that I believe you've suffered it in the princess' service. Not with her wedding to prepare for. Still, one may wish to vary the walls that close one in."

"That's a gift seldom given to women who've taken the veil," said Richildis.

"Is that why you didn't do it?"

Richildis stiffened a little. But she was ready for Helena now; she had had days of Melisende's moods and sudden brilliance, to teach her that outspokenness was surprisingly common among these eastern women. They did, it was true, restrain their tongues in public, but in the privacy of their bowers they were often shockingly blunt.

Richildis responded with aplomb therefore, and rather more calm than she felt. "I was summoned home before I was to take vows, to marry as my father dictated."

"And if he had not summoned you home, would you have taken those vows?"

"I thought so," Richildis said. "Now . . . I wonder. I had no vocation, not as some of the others did: passions, ecstasies, clear calls to God. Mine was a duller thing. I was there; the veil was waiting. I would take it, since it was a great and honorable calling."

"But your heart was never in it."

Richildis shook her head. Imagine, she thought: examination of a vocation that she had long since laid aside, if she had ever had one, by a courtesan in Outremer. Grim old Mother Adele would have been horrified.

Somehow, from that unlikely beginning, the conversation had wound through the courses to the wedding of count and princess, Anjou and Jerusalem. "Cold practicality," Richildis told Helena, "is the best state in which to enter a marriage. The heat of passion blinds good sense. When it dies, naught's left but ashes."

"Have you ever loved a man?" Helena asked her.

Truly, Richildis thought, this was a most indecorous woman, for all her appearance of elegance. And there was Bertrand, who had been remarkably silent, watching and listening, apparently enthralled. And that indeed was as remarkable as Helena's lack of proper discretion.

"If I had sinned so badly," said Richildis, "do you think I would confess it?"

"To your confessor, I should hope so," Helena said. "What have you loved, then? Not God, it seems. Your demesne in France? Your mother? A favorite lapdog?"

"Are you mocking me?" Richildis demanded.

Helena seemed surprised that she was angry. "Of course I'm not. I had wondered, that was all, how people think of such things in France. It seems that Count Fulk has no need or desire to play the charming lover. Are you all as practical as he?"

"I now see," said Richildis, "why my lady is so full of fancies. That must be an eastern thing, to transform holy wedlock into a sin of the flesh."

"But do you love nothing? Nothing at all?"

Vexed out of all patience, Richildis burst out with the first thing that came into her head. "I love La Forêt! I loved my father, though he could be a stern and unlovable man. I loved my brother once, too, until he left us. I am not the chill stick of a woman that you must be thinking me. I am . . . practical, that's all. And virtuous, as a godly person should be."

"I think that you could be much more," Helena said in her low sweet voice, as if she had mused long on it, and not simply come out with it to provoke Richildis into a fury.

Richildis refused to be baited further. She rose with scrupulous care. "I thank you for your hospitality," she said.

Helena raised a brow, but made no effort to stop her. She departed in great dignity, without, she hoped, betraying how close she was to tears—or how little she understood why she wanted to weep.

"That wasn't kind," Bertrand said to Helena.

She sighed, shrugged. One might think her callous, but Bertrand knew her better than that. "And haven't you ever told a young page the truth, the hard and unpolished facts of his existence? Such truth is pain, but pain that heals. Yon's a wounded creature, my love, and scarred to the heart."

Bertrand shook his head. "No, it's not—she's not. She grew up with nuns, that's all. And then, married off to Thierry of all people—no wonder she turned into a stick. He was never one for the lighter moments, was Thierry."

"You may have known your sister once," Helena said, "but I think I know her better now. I've seen her like before—too often. Such women become nuns not for love of God but for escape from the world that gave them so little pleasure."

"Richildis won't take the veil," said Bertrand. "Not if she hasn't already."

"Her like," Helena said, "may deny that it has a vocation, and may flee the cloister for long and long—but in the end, there it finds itself, locked in walls that grow ever narrower, going slowly mad with the boredom that destroys the soul."

God's feet, Bertrand thought. It was not only Richildis who was hearing hard truths tonight. He still refused to believe that she was so badly wounded as Helena had said. Not Richildis. Women were never as soft or as weak as the priests liked to think them, but his sister was stronger than most, strong as a steelblade.

He said so to Helena. "That's what you're seeing," he said. "Not the stiffness of the green stick but the strength of tempered steel."

"Even steel may crack," Helena said immovably, "and the best blade will break if struck too hard. I'm glad she came to Outremer, though she may not be thinking so, just now. She'll find her heart here, and—who knows? Perhaps even her heart's love. If he's anywhere in the world, here he'll come, seeking till he finds her."

"By Saint Venus," Bertrand said, half in anger, half in admiration, "what a dreamer you are! And here I'd been thinking you as practical a creature as any Frenchwoman."

"My practicality is tempered with sense," Helena said. She filled her cup that was empty—with sherbet, he noticed, and not with wine—and sipped reflectively, watching him over the rim of the cup. Her eyes were as dark as a doe's, but never as gentle. "She'll keep coming back. She won't be able to help herself. Her higher faculties are convinced that I'm the Evil One's own sister, but her heart knows better. Wait; you'll see. Next she'll try to convert me to the ways of righteousness."

"She may surprise you," Bertrand said.

"I hope she does," said Helena. She set down her cup and held out her arms. "Now, sir. Come here."

Bertrand was not as obedient as she might have been hoping. He held back, frowning at her. "Maybe she does see clear. Maybe you are a devil."

"Surely I would know," Helena said calmly. She lowered her arms, and rose as Richildis had. "Goodnight, my lord. Rahman will see you out."

Ah: Bertrand had done it at last. He had succeeded in vexing Helena. He should have been triumphant. Alack for his victory; it rang all hollow.

He refused to beg for her pardon. No more would he let himself be dismissed as if he had been a stranger, and one who paid ill besides. "I think I'll stay," he said.

She barely paused. "Very well," she said, as calm as ever. She raised her voice slightly. "Rahman! Prepare the blue guestroom. Lord Bertrand has need of it."

Bertrand's teeth clicked together. So that was how the land lay? Well and well, he thought. His temper was up. God help him if he let a woman get the better of him, even such a woman as Helena.

He suffered himself to be conducted to a room at the end of a long corridor, as far as possible from Helena's chamber. He let himself be offered a bath, a light robe, a last cup of watered wine. But when the house was all quiet, when Rahman had departed to his guardroom and the only light that Bertrand could see was in the lamp hanging over the bed, he lit a smaller lamp from that, and went where he well knew to go.

Helena's door was guarded, but it was only the boy Karim. He did not try to stop Bertrand, though he wavered visibly in thinking of it. Bertrand slipped the latch and walked in.

As far as he could tell in the dim glow of the nightlamp, Helena was honestly and deeply asleep. He stood a moment nonplussed. He had fully expected her to be waiting, knowing that he would not be dismissed as easily as that.

She lay on her side with her cheek resting on her hand. Her hair was plaited for the night, but some of it had worked loose already and framed her face in curls. She looked hardly more than a child.

He bent over her, braced to wake her; then sighed. He who had no mercy on an enemy in battle, could not bring himself to wake a single sleeping woman.

It was not, he reflected, that she had not warned him. Long ago, when first he sought out the famously beautiful Helena, the courtesan who chose her own lovers, she had told him outright: "You came to me because I'm a novelty; because I don't take every man who can pay. Remember that I choose who shares my bed and who does not. I choose you now, because I find you interesting; but if you ever grow dull—and dullest of all is the man who wants me for himself alone—then I shall revoke the choice. That is the freedom I keep for myself."

He liked to think that she loved him. She never quite said she did; but since she chose him, she had taken few others, and of late, that he knew, there was none. Had she not come to Acre to be near him?

Much though it stung his pride, he admitted what might be the truth. She had come to Acre as everyone else had, to see the princess marry the Count of Anjou.

"She does love me," he said fiercely, but softly, lest he wake her. "I know she does. I annoyed her tonight, that was all. She'll want me back when her temper's cooled; she always has before."

But this time, said a small niggling voice in the back of his eyes, might be the time when she did not. He could not know until she woke; and if he woke her now, he would betray himself.

He left as quietly as he knew how, returned to the guest chamber only to gather his belongings, and slipped out into the black dark of night in Acre. No servant followed him. He took a torch from the wall by the gate, lit it at the lamp that burned there, and when it had flared to life, let it light his way to the palace.

God, or God's Adversary, defended him. No robber or footpad came upon him. The city was deep in sleep, even to the young bloods of the court, who gathered strength for the journey to Jerusalem and the wedding thereafter.

A wedding without love; love with altogether too much contention. What a world this was. He would have laughed, if the silence had allowed it. But it was deep silence, silence weighed down with stars. He slipped voiceless through it, clutching his little bit of light.

he transfer of the High Court to the city
of Jerusalem was an undertaking as great as any war. It gathered like an army, and
like an army surrounded itself with armed and armored men. The lumbering wagons
of the baggage train and the ladies' brightly curtained carts and horse-litters traveled
in the center, well guarded—for in Outremer, even under a strong king, the roads
could be perilous.

Melisende however did not conceal herself among the great mass of ladies but
rode a-horseback in the van with the king and the great lords and her husband to
be. Most of her ladies preferred the wagons, but a handful accompanied her for
propriety's sake—and, thought Richildis, because they could not endure the stifling
confines of a horse-litter.

Richildis had not had to ask to be counted among the princess' guard of women.
Melisende had asked her rather, a day or two ago, "Do you ride?"

Richildis had nodded.

"Do you ride well?"

Richildis raised a brow. "I could shoot a bow from horseback once, though that
was long ago."

Melisende nodded as if satisfied. "Good. Then you'll ride with me. This is to be
a royal progress, and I'm not intending to shut myself up in a wagon. You'll need
clothes to ride in. Ask Dame Agatha to see to it."

Therefore Richildis rode in the van of what could well be a Crusading army, clad
in something very like Saracen riding-dress, with loose trousers under a flow of robe,
and a headdress that could be raised to shield her face against sun and staring eyes.
The horse under her was one of the king's, bred from Saracen stock. It was lighter
and smaller than horses in France, but very strong as she had been assured, and
fiery enough to keep her occupied for a good distance outside of Acre.

She managed still to look back at least once, to bid farewell to the city. She had
not come to love it greatly, but it had become familiar. She raised a hand to its
walls and towers, and to the blue glitter of the sea.

What lay ahead—her heart thudded. Jerusalem. The Holy City. Heart and soul
of Christendom. The Lord Christ had not walked in Acre that anyone reliably knew,

but in Jerusalem he had walked and taught and—she bowed her head and crossed herself—died.

In France, May was a gentle month, clear sun and soft rains, and seldom the cruelty of biting cold or bitter heat. Here in Outremer, the sun grew stronger with each day that passed. Richildis had heard that it rained, even snowed sometimes in the winter, but not now; not in this sunstruck season. The roads were thick with dust; in short order therefore so was she.

And she was fortunate. She rode near the front, without need to breathe the dust of a whole shambling army. It moved slowly, the pace of the foot-travelers and the oxen that drew the wagons, crawling across a land that seemed, to her eyes, unbearably barren.

And yet two men near her were marveling at the lushness of the greenery this year, the gift of strong winter rains. It was all dust and sere leaves, stones and sharp edges.

One must learn to see richness in a few straggling bushes, and the promise of water in a clump of thorns. Richildis' eyes felt dried by the dust, dazzled and burning. She drew her veil up over them, checked her mare before she skittered into the rump of the stallion directly ahead, and hoped that, when at last they paused to rest the horses, there would be shade.

There was not, in the event, a surfeit of shade, nor did it grow more common as they crawled southward. They were five days on the road from Acre, pausing it seemed at every village and town, so that the people could come crowding out to gape at the king and his daughter and the man who, if God willed it, would be king when Baldwin was dead. Richildis grew excessively familiar with her saddle and with the mare who wore it, cross-grained fretful creature who nonetheless possessed a certain fascination, if only for that she never seemed to tire.

Richildis would happily have ridden decorously behind her lady, but the mare's crotchets compelled her to ride up and down the column at frequent intervals. She was not such a fool as to slip past the line of armed men who guarded it, but unless the road narrowed greatly to slip through a cleft in a hill or descended with breathtaking suddenness to a scent of water and greenery where a little river burst out of the rock, she had ample room to wander.

Even as slowly as they rode, they were not vexed by bandits. They were too large a company, and too well-armed; and the Saracen was raiding far from the road to Jerusalem. They rode with an air of warlike holiday, a strange mingling that to Richildis seemed the essence of Outremer. Those who could sing sang often, and those who could not were often minded to try. As she rode up and down the line, she heard jests both coarse and witty, snatches of conversation, commentary on this or that, all let loose as it were to wander on the wind.

She was, she realized on the fifth day, surprisingly happy. They had risen before dawn and left the castle in which they had paused for the night, ridden out with its lord and half the countryside, into a morning like the first morning of the world. The sun rose in a shower of gold, and all the hills were gold, even the dust that rose to veil their passing.

On this day she would see Jerusalem. She could hardly take it in, the nearness of it, the sheer overwhelming imminence of the Holy City. Her mare was fresh but, oddly, less fractious than usual. The road wound away under her feet.

• • •

And there at last in the burning noon she saw it. Jerusalem on its high hill among the barren hills of Judea. Tall dun walls and loom of towers, and in the east of it, like a second sun, the golden flame that was the Dome of the Rock.

Many of those who had come in new from France flung themselves from their horses or mules and dropped to their knees in the road. Some even cried out, opening their arms to the sight that lay before them.

Richildis neither left the saddle nor made a sound. Fools. The rest of the line had to halt, knotting and tangling, lest they trample these idiots who could not keep their piety to themselves.

She supposed that Helena was right. She was hopelessly practical. She looked at that city, so like and yet so unlike every other city in the world, and her heart was full. But not so full that it would slow her progress toward the gate, still less put herself at risk of being ridden down.

The king and his barons, she took note, and those who had lived in Outremer all or most of their lives, were calm enough, nor had anyone lost his temper with the newcomers' extravagances. It must be common, then.

She saw how one nodded, another lifted a brow, a third moved off to lift a prostrate pilgrim onto his horse. Others farther back did the same. The column sorted itself out. The newcomers got themselves in hand, or were got in hand by those nearest them. In remarkably short order, they had resumed their march to the city.

Richildis found herself accompanied. She glanced once at her brother, and then away. She had not spoken to him since the dinner in Helena's house, nor had he approached her. She had rather hoped that he would continue to avoid her.

"I see you aren't unduly moved," he said.

His voice held neither mockery nor curiosity. She determined to be as calm. "I am as moved as I have any need to be. Would it profit me at all to throw myself down and get in the way?"

"That depends," he said, "on whether you see advantage in advertising your piety."

She shot him another glance. He was giving her nothing, no expression, though his mail-coif was down and his great helm entrusted to a squire's care. "Do you believe," she asked them, "that yon display was false?"

"Much of it, no," he said.

She did not reply to that. She hoped that her silence would drive him away, but he seemed content in it. He rode like a wall between herself and the eastward hills, as if to guard her from the threat of the infidel. She could not quite despise herself for feeling safe. He was a big man, armored from chin to toe, his mail covered in the fashion of this country with the loose white garment, sleeveless and cut for ease on horseback, that people here called the surcoat. A cross was sewn on its shoulder, blood-red on white.

She wore no cross on her shoulder. She came as a pilgrim but not as a warrior for God.

"I could be more ostentatious," she said after a while. "If I knew what good it would do."

"Why, none," said Bertrand. "You look as if you were born here. You dress sensibly, you ride a horse bred for the country, you preserve a remarkable calm at sight of the holiest city in the world. You're much admired, you know. People are impressed. It's not often that someone new from the west manages to settle in so quickly."

"Did you?"

His teeth flashed white in his sunburned face. "God and His Mother, no! I was as raw as they come. Did you know that if you insist on wearing wool in summer here, and don't clean or change it often enough, you get boils? I could have given a holy hermit advice on mortification of the flesh."

"I'm sure he would have thanked you for it."

He laughed long and free. "Oh, sister! I've missed you."

"I'm glad I can amuse you," she said tightly.

She thought he was refusing to see the sparking of her temper, till he reached down from his tall warhorse and patted her shoulder. "There, there," he said. "Chin up. You're doing splendidly; I'm proud of you. You'll be the delight of the High Court, just wait and see."

"I would rather be the delight of La Forêt."

"Would you?" He turned away still grinning, devils take him, and spurred his big bay horse, sending it into a lumbering canter.

Her mare fretted and thought seriously on bucking in protest that she could not follow. Richildis set her mind to getting the beast in hand. And when that was done, to thinking not about her infuriating brother, but about the city that drew ever and ever closer.

A little while—though long enough to be exasperating—and she was all caught up in it.

They rode in through David's Gate under the frown of its tower. The city had come out to greet them, streaming along the road, shouting, singing, waving palms and scraps of banners. Almost Richildis fancied that she heard the ancient holy song, *Hosanna! Hosanna to the son of David!*

But that was fancy, and dangerous. They were calling the king's name, the name of his daughter, and that of the Count of Anjou; calling down blessings on them, health and joy and long life. A choir stood by the gate, their voices sweet and remarkably strong over the shouting of the crowd, chanting one of the Psalms of David that he wrote in this very tower that rose so high above them.

The king shall joy in thy strength, O Lord; and in thy salvation how greatly shall he rejoice!

And indeed the king was rejoicing, and at his side the Count of Anjou.

The princess . . .

Richildis blinked a little, dazzled as so often by the light in this country. Melisende was not happy, she did not have that look. But resigned, yes. Accepting, because she must. And even, as they passed under the arch of that great gate, in no small measure exalted.

TEN

Fulk, Count of Anjou, took Melisende of Jerusalem to wife on a blazingly hot day in May, in the city of Jerusalem, in the kingdom across the sea. He wore mail as befit a lord of a warrior kingdom, and over it the wedding surcoat that she and her ladies had made for him of cloth of gold. She was resplendent likewise in cloth of gold, and the silk of her gown was the green of young leaves. It reminded Richildis rather poignantly of spring in France.

Melisende had risen before dawn like a young knight preparing for battle: head high and back stiff, with a hint of unsteadiness that clearly she fought to hide. She had to endure the wedding bath with its ancient humiliations: long-wedded ladies waiting on her with ribald pleasure, and one who must investigate and swear to her husband that she was as God had made her, with no man's hand laid upon her—or, as the old harridan said, any other part of his body, either.

If she had had illusions as to what a man did with a woman on the wedding night, by the time she was glistening clean from head to foot, she could have had none left. Richildis hoped that she was wiser than Richildis had been, and less gullible. The old jests about stallions had alarmed her terribly, left her in stark and shuddering fear, imagining like an idiot that a man put on something more than his natural member in order to deflower his virgin bride. As little as her body had yearned toward aging, scrofulous Thierry, she had been greatly relieved to discover that he took her with nothing more than nature had given him; and that was by no means as mighty a weapon as the one that Wat the stableboy had wielded against the goosegirl behind the stables, one day when Richildis happened to be visiting her pony.

She had concluded later that there was a saint in command of nervous brides, because she had not burst out with that observation while Thierry sweated manfully to perform his duty. She had thought too of trying the goosegirl's tricks, the wriggling and moaning and the concluding shriek, but she had been too embarrassed. Thierry had dropped like a stone when he was done, snoring before he struck the bed; and in the morning he had slapped her meager rump and declared that she would do, she would definitely do. He liked his casual women lusty, she learned, but he preferred his lady wife to be quiet. She had never had great difficulty in giving him what he wanted.

Odd sad thoughts to be thinking as she prepared a princess for her wedding. She would have liked to silence the nattering women; but she had no such authority.

Perhaps Melisende was too preoccupied to listen. Her face had a white, set look. She allowed them to dress her as if she had been a lifeless thing, an image carved in wood and painted in gold and white and red.

Stiff she might be, betraying none of the quick intelligence that was so much a part of her, but there was no contesting that she was beautiful. The woman who with clever fingers applied the paint to her face and lips and eyes, had the sense to do so lightly; to let the living flesh shine through. Her hair had been bathed in herbs and eastern unguents till its gold shone as clear as the living metal. It was a pity to conceal it beneath a veil; but the veil was the merest drift of a thing, no less golden than the hair beneath.

She was all gold and fragile green, a May princess in this fiery country, where the leaves turned grey or white with dust before they were well unfurled, or blackened with the sun. "Ah," said one of the most ribald of the women as she stood in front of them, and there was nothing of ribaldry in her voice or her face. "Ah, lady, you are as beautiful as any bride I've ever seen."

"Beautiful as the morning," came the chorus, inevitably.

Melisende with her wits about her might have snapped them all into silence. But wherever her mind had gone, it was nowhere near this gaggle of women.

They half led, half herded her out of the ladies' solar in the palace of the kings of Jerusalem, mindful of drifting veil and sweep of train, gathering maids and attendants as they went. No men this morning. This was a women's procession. All the men were waiting on Count Fulk, away in the city, where he had been housed near the Temple of Solomon. Even Melisende's knights were not hers today; they were dismissed to serve the man who would be her husband.

The rest of the procession waited in the court of the great gate. The choir had begun its chanting already, sweet voices of nuns and white-robed children. Melisende's sisters were here, Alys leading them in her capacity as second eldest and only married woman. So too were the ladies of the High Court and the women of the king's household and a great crowd of hangers-on, not all of them either savory or female.

A litter waited for the princess, but she ignored it. There was a scramble, a check in the choir's chanting; then all was in order again, and Melisende on the back of a milk-white mare. A mailed guardsman led it, which could not have been to Melisende's liking, but she seemed content to have won as much as she had. Servants in white and gold raised a golden canopy above her. So arrayed and in royal splendor, she rode out of the palace and into the city.

The streets were lined with people, the way kept open by men with spears and swords. Down the Street of David that led from the gate, past the Pool of the Patriarchs, then up the Patriarchs' Way to the Street of Palms and the Church of the Holy Sepulcher. It was not the Way of the Cross—that way led from the far side of the city—and yet it was holy, and every stone was blessed.

Richildis, walking behind the princess, guided in the press by the dip and sway of the canopy, felt all about her the deep throb of sanctity. Some who came to Jerusalem, she had heard, went mad. So much holiness overwhelmed them. They began to hear voices and see visions. Some dreamed that they were great saints and martyrs, even the Lord Christ himself, riding through the Holy City on the colt of an ass, bowing his head to the hosannas of his people.

She was too much of earth. She noticed that the stones were worn and old and not remarkably clean. The people were as people everywhere: noisy, flatulent, reeking of dung and garlic. The brightness of banners celebrated the royal wedding just as they might have done in Paris or in Poitiers. There were no beggars to be seen, but people in plenty scrambling for the coins that the youngest maids flung from baskets into the throng: copper mostly, and silver worn to nothing by time and judicious paring. The lepers were all kept away, driven to the middens beyond the walls, lest the sight of them bring ill fortune to the count and his bride.

The road was strewn with palm-branches and with the petals of flowers. Their sweet bruised scent struggled against the stronger redolence of humanity.

Richildis stumbled. A miracle of sorts rested by her foot: a whole and nigh unblemished rose, a bud just opened, red as new blood. Without thinking she took it up, careful of the thorns, and slipped the stem beneath the roundel of her shoulder-brooch.

The procession turned into the broader street before the great church, and thence into the arched colonnade. In the court beyond waited the procession of men, king and lords and Count of Anjou. They were clad in mail as defenders of the Holy Sepulcher, but in the splendor of silk above it, and no weapon to stain the peace of God's holy place.

They were a fine and warlike sight, even disarmed. So many tall sun-burnished men; so bright a sheen of mail.

The king and the count, Richildis took note, wore plain grey steel. Baldwin's surcoat was of scarlet silk, Fulk's of cloth of gold. The king was crowned, the count bareheaded as if in humility. They stood side by side in front of the colonnade, the tall fair man and the slight fox-red one, an image of amity to warm a troubled heart.

Baldwin came forward as his daughter approached, and with his own hands lifted her from the saddle. Perhaps they spoke. If so, Richildis was too far away to hear. Melisende stood straight and tall beside her father. He took her hand in his and led her toward the door of the church.

There waited the Patriarch of Jerusalem in the full splendor of his rank. There were tales of him, rumors of ill feeling and contention with the king. But on this day such things were put aside. At the door of the Church of the Holy Sepulcher, Baldwin laid his daughter's hand in that of Count Fulk, and the Patriarch laid his own over it and spoke the words that bound them in the eyes of God and man.

When truly they were bound—Melisende without visible tremor, erect as ever, standing a good half-head taller than her husband—they were led within to the singing of the Mass before the tomb of Christ. It was a white Mass, a Mass of great joy, casting light and splendor in that dim and holy place.

The words washed over Richildis, familiar almost beyond understanding, though she was learned in Latin and could comprehend them if she tried. The church, half Byzantine, half half-built Frankish, breathed holiness about her. She had made no effort to come closer to the Sepulcher than she was already, caught in the knot of women just below the high altar. Later she would be a pilgrim. Now she was simply here, as they were who had lived here their lives long: standing in that space, hearing a mass, not oblivious to the Tomb behind them, but not openly aware of it, either.

Just in back of her was the center of the world. She might not have known it, but someone in the palace had told her. When the new choir was all built, that one had said, it would be marked in the pavement for pilgrims to marvel at. Now it was as simply there as she was.

Here was the heart of Christendom. Here was its soul, the empty tomb, the place so holy that it had needed might of arms to protect it from the infidel. Here: an empty tomb, an absence in which resided every article of faith, a three days' resting place for the Son of God made man.

It was too much to bear. Either she must go happily mad, or she must turn her mind to the mass that was sung before and about her. The choir of eunuchs and children had followed them in, and the choir of monks and canons joined it, clear high voices lifted up to heaven, deep voices solid as stone underfoot.

And what, Richildis wondered, was Melisende thinking as she knelt with her new husband before the altar? Her back told Richildis nothing, not even in its rigidity. Her voice in the responses was inaudible. She had slipped her hand from Fulk's where her father had placed it, and claimed it for herself. The ring that Fulk had given her gleamed softly in the dimness. It looked strange on her finger, as if it had yet to find comfort there, or to be settled in its place.

One learned to live with strangeness. This mass Richildis knew, these words in which it was sung, even the secret mutter of the Canon that made flesh and blood of earthly bread and sweet eastern wine. Here where the heart of Christendom beat close and terribly strong, it was still the same; still the old rite, the rite that she had loved since she was a child. She clung to it. She let it enfold her, and suffered it to comfort her. It softened the blow of sanctity a little. It lightened the weight of the world.

nce Melisende was safely married to the Count of Anjou, the kingdom settled to wait in a kind of joyful anxiety. And to be sure, by the middle of what would have been autumn in France, Melisende was incontestably with child.

She announced it with neither the joy nor the trembling of the usual young bride. Her marriage did not sit ill on her, but neither had she bloomed in it. Fulk had done his duty as often as the needs of war and kingdom permitted, and, it was evident, as capably as a man of his years and experience might be expected to do. She had not appeared to suffer from his attentions, had not come from the bridal chamber bruised and quenched as some few virgin brides did. Nor did she look as if she yearned to be there. Outside of the marriage bed she was much as she had always been. When he had gone away with her father for the summer's round of skirmishes with the infidel, she did not appear to pine for him. She greeted him warmly enough on his return, but no more warmly than she greeted such of her knights as were her friends.

Pregnancy did not suit her at all. Long before the kingdom knew that the princess carried an heir, her women could not mistake it. Greensickness that began in the morning and lasted much of the day; storms of tears or rage alternating with an oxlike placidity; a sudden and flat refusal to entertain her husband in the evenings—the older women nodded wisely. The younger ones bit their tongues lest they say something indiscreet.

The men were happily oblivious. All but Fulk. He was not a remarkably perceptive man when it came to women's foibles, but, as he said to Melisende the third time she made to slam the door on his face, "Lady, I was married before, and long enough to learn a little sense. How long till the baby's born?"

She would have slammed the door regardless of his presence in it, if he had not somehow managed to set himself on the inside of it. The few maids whom she suffered of late in her presence, Richildis among them, had perforce to see and hear it all, since it was the ladies' solar he had entered, and the only escape was inward, toward the bedchamber.

Melisende stood just out of his reach. She did not press hands to her belly as women did to protect their unborn children. Clearly, precisely, and without expression she said, "He will be born in the spring."

"He?" Fulk asked. "You think you know?"

"It is a son," Melisende said. "Just as my father and the kingdom wanted. Once he is born, and if God wills that he lives, Jerusalem has its heir. And I have my freedom."

Fulk's brows went up. "Freedom, my lady? From what? One son alone is hardly enough to build a dynasty."

"He will have to be," she said. "I won't go through this more than once unless I must. And no, I'm not going to demand that you put me aside. You can be king when the time comes. You'll be good at it. But no more of this childmaking."

Truly, thought Richildis, Fulk looked astonished. She was mildly surprised herself. She had not known Melisende felt so strongly about it. It was good Christian asceticism, of course, but Melisende had said nothing of that—no word of piety.

Fulk, it seemed, thought much the same. "Would you make yourself a nun?" he asked her.

Melisende shook her head sharply. "This is not religion. This is what I wish. One son, my lord. That should be enough. If he dies I'll give you another."

"As easy as that?"

"You seemed to have no great difficulty in getting this thing that roils my stomach and slows my wits."

"Lady," said Fulk, drawing out the word, as if he needed the time to think. "Lady, do you hate me so much?"

"I don't hate you at all," said Melisende. "I resent this state I find myself in. When it's done, I don't want to do it over again."

Fulk seemed at a loss—which in him was a rarity. Clearly he thought of saying something further; equally clearly he thought better of it. He bowed. "Lady," he said. "As you will."

After he was gone, Melisende said composedly to the air where he had been, "I would sleep now."

Her ladies mustered wits to rise, to assist her. She did not speak to them. She allowed herself to be undressed, her hair combed and plaited for the night, her bed turned down and herself settled in it.

Richildis was the last to bow and retreat. Melisende held out a hand. "No," she said. "Stay."

Richildis turned back toward Melisende, folded her hands in front of her and waited.

"You look like a nun in chapter," Melisende said. She had no great air of distress, now that she was alone. She was preoccupied, that was all. "Do you severely disapprove?" she asked Richildis.

Richildis did not see that her opinion was of any great moment. But Melisende, for whatever reason, seemed to value it. She answered honestly, "No. I can't say I approve, either. The duties of a wife and a princess—"

"I am doing them," Melisende said. "Or as much as I can, with this to make me stupid. That's what I hate, you see. Not being able to think. And when I try, it's all milky sweetness. It's disgusting."

"I don't think," said Richildis after a moment, "that I've ever heard a woman object on quite those grounds before."

"Most women don't care if they can't think. They're happy enough to let their men think for them."

"Isn't that the way of the world?"

"If it is," demanded Melisende, "then why did God give me the capacity to think at all? Cows don't think. Sheep don't think. Why should a woman? And why should she care, if she wasn't meant to in the first place?"

"You never ask the easy questions," Richildis said, half to herself.

Melisende sat up in her great white-canopied bed, with her face flushed and her hair slipping out of its plait. She looked like a child. "Fulk is going to fight this, you know," she said. "He'd like to keep me pregnant and ox-witted so that he can rule without interference. He's not pleased that Father lets me sit in court and in council—*lets*, he says, as if there were any question of my right to sit there. I am the eldest and the heir, though I lack certain vital parts that would make it possible for me to be king. Parts that, mind you, my son will have."

"Fulk's son, too," Richildis said mildly.

"My son," said Melisende. "Men may claim them, but women have the bearing and the raising of them. And the shaping, too, if they're wise. As I plan to be."

"Then," said Richildis, "you had best not say such things to Fulk as you've said to me."

"Not a word," said Melisende. "Not one. God's witness to it."

It seemed to Richildis that Melisende had already said more than enough to alarm Fulk. Or perhaps not. Melisende was young, she was beautiful. As strong-willed as she was, she was still a woman. Fulk might well convince himself that her pronouncements were but the vaporings of new pregnancy. It was a frightening thing, after all, to bear a child. Each child that was born took its mother to the gates of death. A young and innocent woman might well transform that fear into resistance—resistance that would be easy enough to break, he might think, once the child was born.

For the moment he allowed his lady her fancies. He was gentle with her. He brought her dainties. He sent her a player on the harp whom he had captured on campaign, who could sing even more sweetly than her luteplayer. When she wished to be left alone, he obliged her; but when she was in need of company he was there, or if he was occupied, he sent someone charming to entertain her. It was usually one of her own knights, sometimes one of his.

More than once it was Bertrand. Richildis had found it easy enough to maintain a chilly distance through the summer while he rode on campaign with the count and the king. But in this season that began in dusty heat and ended in the startling chill of winter, men tired of war. They returned to their own domains, but for high feasts and saints' days they came to High Court in Jerusalem.

Bertrand seemed to divide his days equally between his castle and a house in the Holy City. She had not seen his demesne, nor had she been invited to see it. When she went with the crowd of pilgrims round the holy places and down to Jordan, she thought of going on till she found her brother. But she could nurse a grudge most excellent well—and he had given no indication that she was welcome there.

He was affable enough when he came to entertain his princess. He might have forgotten their quarrel; except that he never asked to see Richildis outside of her lady's presence.

Richildis brooded on this, one day in winter. It was the sort of day she had dreamed of while she sweltered in the heat of summer: grey, dim, and chill, with rain in the air. It had snowed in the night on Mount Hebron, someone said, and the mountains of the Lebanon were white, the great cedars weighed down with snow. The feast of the Lord Christ's birth was nearly upon them. The king would celebrate it in Bethlehem, as every pilgrim then in Outremer strove to do. Melisende wanted to go, but her pregnancy was not going as well as it might. If her father and her husband had their way, she would stay safe in Jerusalem, sheltered and warm, while they braved the rains and snows and the throngs of pilgrims on the road.

She was in a great temper over it. Richildis had escaped into the bazaar, using as pretext the need for an oddment or two. She had not begun alone, but the maids who went with her had strayed in the crowd.

Richildis was not unduly perturbed. She had come to know the city well, had walked in it often on errands for her lady or herself, or simply because she was free to go where she would. Women of the infidels did not have that freedom, she had heard; nor indeed did the unmarried daughters of the Franks. But she was a widow and her own woman, and she could choose to walk abroad.

Today she did not mean to go far. A thin rain had begun to fall, little enough in the covered arcades of the city, but it brought with it a penetrating cold. Summer's sellers of sherbet had given way to sellers of wine warmed over braziers and enriched with spices.

She paused to buy a cup of it, strong and sweetly pungent. As she drew in the scent, someone else slipped past her into the wineseller's booth. She drew back, to be courteous, but the crowd in the street swelled suddenly, jostling them into one another.

Richildis looked into a face she knew, even veiled in silk. Helena's smile was swift, artless, and transparently glad. Richildis could not match it.

She could at least be civil. "Madam," she said.

"Lady!" said Helena. "It's been ages since I saw you. Have you a moment? My house is near here—it's warm and out of the rain, and cook has been baking. Won't you come?"

Richildis opened her mouth to refuse, but she had already been swept up in a cloud of silk and perfume, borne away she knew not how, and taken out of the chill and the rain into a warm and fragrant house.

The house in Acre had been borrowed only. This was Helena's own. Richildis knew enough now of the city to recognize that it was as old as Rome but made new under the Saracen. Its grace was infidel grace, its warmth a Roman thing, a memory so old that one would have thought it long forgotten.

"Yes, there is a hypocaust," Helena said. "They're gone, most of them, but I was fortunate: this house has been well kept up since Rome went away. There is one old man whose family has served the people here for all that time, who knows how to keep the furnaces running and the channels clear."

It was a marvel. Richildis had been coaxed out of her rain-dampened clothes and into soft warm robes and slippers that let the warmth from the floor seep into her feet. She was tempted to drop down from the chair in which she was sitting, to lay her hands flat on the floor, to feel the worn tiles of its mosaic and the heat that resided in them.

But this was not a friend's house, not a floor on which she could lie like a child or a basking cat. She sat rather stiffly and drank warm spiced wine and tasted cakes that seemed made of every spice and sweetness that was known in the east of the world.

It was difficult. She had not seen Helena since the spring—not since Acre. And they had not parted in amity. Helena had said things that were not easily forgiven. Things that not even kin had a right to say.

Helena seemed to have forgotten them, or to have willed them away. Perhaps it was a courtesan's skill; perhaps an easterner's. She made a virtue of Richildis' silence. She broke it not to chatter aimlessly but to speak of things that might be of interest: the spices that flavored the cakes, the summer's wars, the princess' pregnancy. Richildis answered in nods or in monosyllables.

After a while Helena fell as silent as Richildis, but with greater comfort in it. She nibbled cakes, drank wine. A servant came in once, bowing, apologetic, with somewhat that must be decided quickly. She dealt with it where she sat, and sent the servant away.

Then she sat watching Richildis, though Richildis was doing nothing but sit with her hands folded tightly in her lap. "You could have left," Helena said. "And yet you stay."

"I can think of no polite way to leave," Richildis said. It felt as if she blurted it out, but she sounded quiet enough to herself.

"You can excuse yourself and go," said Helena.

"Do you want me to?"

"I don't think *you* want to," Helena said. "It distresses you, doesn't it? That you find me interesting."

"To a saint no doubt any sin is interesting," said Richildis. "I'm no saint, mind you. But—"

"But I must be an egregious sinner." Helena sighed and shook her head. "Oh, I am probably as vile as you imagine. I'm steeped in sins of the flesh."

"With . . . many men," Richildis said, not wanting to, but it slipped out of her.

"Actually," Helena said, "there have been six. Your brother is the sixth. And, in the past year and more, the only one whom I haven't sent away."

"Then how do you—"

"How do I live?" Helena seemed neither amused nor offended. "I was left well provided for. And my . . . patrons have been generous."

"Including my brother?"

"I take nothing from your brother," Helena said, "but love."

"And love-gifts?"

Helena flushed and then paled. Richildis was surprised. She had always been so serene; so impossible to move.

Richildis resolved not to ask. But something—some sign in the way she sat, in the way she looked, even the sheen of her hair in the light of the lamps—sharpened Richildis' eyes. And after all she had been looking at Melisende day after day, all through the summer and the autumn.

Just as Fulk had asked of Melisende, Richildis asked of Helena: "When?"

And just as Melisende had, Helena answered, "In the spring. At Easter, or near enough." She laughed, breathless, too painful for mirth. "I was always so careful. Always so meticulous, to make sure—that—" She broke off. "Now you know me for a mortal sinner."

Richildis bit her tongue before she pointed out that she knew it already. She was not cruel, not if she could help it.

Helena's serenity had well and truly cracked. She twisted a fold of her robe between her fingers, over and over. "There isn't anyone I can tell. The servants know, of course. Servants always know. But everyone else—"

"Not my brother?"

"He last of all."

"I doubt he'll be angry," Richildis said. "He might be glad."

"Lady," said Helena with an air of tight-strung patience, "a man does not come to a courtesan to find himself father of a bastard. I know why he left France."

"He left France because the girl was married to someone else, and that one was not pleased to admit that he needed another man to swell his wife's belly for him. I heard how my brother wept, how he mourned that he would never see the child."

"No," said Helena. "Men never care. And as for those on whom they get the bastards—"

"I think you misjudge him," Richildis said.

Helena shook her head. She had lowered it, looking for once as young as she must actually be: not greatly older than Richildis. She was no slender delicate creature, but just then she looked fragile and hollow-boned like a bird.

Richildis did not think that Helena fared as ill in pregnancy as Melisende did. But her skin had a certain transparency, and her mood was brittle, like the smile she directed at Richildis. "And now I've betrayed myself. You'll tell him, I suppose, and let him dispose of me."

"No," Richildis said. She kept anger out of it.

Helena was surprised: her eyes had gone wide.

"It is never my place," Richildis said, "to tell another woman's secrets. I do believe that he should know, and soonest is best; if he discovers it too late, he'll be far more angry that you kept it from him than that it's happened at all. But if you refuse—"

"I can't tell him," said Helena. "Not . . . till I have no other choice."

"What will you do, then? Let him think you've turned cool to him? Invent a new lover? Go away on pilgrimage?"

"I don't know," Helena said. She sounded ready to weep, though more from exhaustion than self-pity. "I've held it in so long. I haven't thought—I haven't been able to think—"

"That happens," Richildis said a little dryly.

Melisende would have rounded on her in anger. Helena smiled a crooked smile. "My Turks are set to sweep me away into the wilds of Asia, where, I suppose, I can live on mares' milk and the flesh of camels, and raise my child among the horses."

Richildis tried to imagine Helena as a wild tribesman. She nearly laughed. Helena in her fine gowns, with her perfumes and her eyepaints, was perfectly a creature of eastern cities. Richildis could not even see her in a Frankish castle, let alone in a tent among the tribes.

Helena sighed. "I honestly don't know what to do. I suppose I'll hide it from him for as long as I can, then find an excuse to go traveling for a while. I have kin in Damascus—distant, I fear, and not overly kindly disposed toward me, but willing enough to take me in if I have need. The Prophet, after all, enjoins charity upon every true believer."

"You have kin among the infidels?"

"That surprises you? I'd think you'd be sure of it—it's of a piece with the rest of me."

Richildis shook her head. She did not know what she was thinking—what to think. Except that she liked this woman very much; and more, every time they met. It was not proper at all. It might not be particularly Christian. Although the Lord Christ had kept company with harlots, a woman of good family should be more circumspect.

Suddenly she was very tired of circumspection, of propriety, of the sheer niggling weight of being a respectable woman in a country much too holy and much too ancient to be respectable itself. She shook herself hard, faced Helena squarely, and said, "You must do what you judge best to do. Whatever it is, I'll help you as I can. But I think—I really do think—you should tell my brother now."

"No," said Helena. "No, I can't."

Richildis bit her tongue. When it had stopped stinging she said, "Very well. Do you have any friends? Is there a woman who can come in and assist you, who can guide you when it's time, either to a convent or, if you insist, to Damascus?"

"I have my Turks," Helena said. "No women, no. Only you. Women of decent family," she said with the faintest hint of bitterness, "do not befriend a courtesan. Women of . . . indecent family have their own trades to ply, and seldom suffer a rival."

Of course. Richildis should have known that. She swallowed a sigh. "You do need someone you can trust, to help you—who won't be urging you to turn yourself into a Turkish tribeswoman."

"A *khatun*," Helena said. "They would make me a princess of the tribes. I'd ride and shoot like a man, and travel in a wagon when I was tired, which of course I'd never be. And when my baby was born, I'd wash it in mares' milk and set it on the back of a new-broken colt and turn it into a perfect little Turk."

"All that Frankish blood," Richildis said, "would betray the poor creature. It would wither and fade—and so would you, away from cities."

"It's Damascus for me, then," said Helena, "and soon. My cousins will need fair warning."

"No," said Richildis. "No, stop it. We'll think of something else. Or you'll tell Bertrand. He'll cherish you."

Helena shook her head. She was unreasonable as women in her condition could be. She would not hear of telling Bertrand.

Foolish. If she kept that of all secrets, she would do herself far more harm than good.

But she was not to be moved just now, and Richildis knew it. She would have to be subtle—a Frank outdoing an easterner in subtlety; now there was irony.

"We'll think of something," she said again. "Somehow. If God is with us."

"God," said Helena, "has been known to be kind to a courtesan."

"Let us hope He'll remember," Richildis said.

elena would not relent. She would not tell Bertrand. He could not escape the fact that his lover and his sister had become friends—it was a mild scandal in certain quarters of the court. Not however with Melisende, who was too deeply absorbed in her own troubles to care what Richildis did, nor with Bertrand himself. He could have disapproved; after all a man could have a mistress without encouraging his lady sister to befriend her. But he was not ashamed of the woman whom he so dearly loved, nor did he fear that she would corrupt his sister.

Richildis began to understand the dilemma of the priest who must keep the silence of the confessional. She had promised Helena that she would say nothing to Bertrand. No matter how great a folly she might reckon it, she had given her word. She would not break it.

And they said that women had no honor. Richildis wished it had been so. She would have been happier, and less constrained with guilt.

The quarrel with her brother, the distance that had risen in Acre, served them rather too well now. That she could be Helena's friend but not return to amity with Bertrand . . . he could only reckon it incomprehensible, a vagary of the female mind. And that too served them well.

She confessed the whole sin of deceit. Her confessor, the same elderly priest who performed the office for Melisende, set her a penance that made her wonder if he had even listened: a handful of prayers and a day of bread and water. She did as he bade her, but she did not feel absolved. The deception went on, nor could she see any end to it. Not at least until the baby was born.

Between the two women, princess and courtesan, she was beset with bearing and birthing. There was no escape but from one to the other. And the winter wore on, colder than she would have imagined possible, and after it a startling, brief, and breathtakingly beautiful spring.

Then as Lent trod slowly toward Easter and the sun grew warm again, Helena left Jerusalem with Richildis' knowledge if not her full consent. They had between them found a place for her to go, a house of holy women near Bethlehem. Helena would not be expected to cloister herself, nor would they compel her to live as they lived. They were content to accept her as guest and sometime penitent, to house her and the servants whom she brought with her—even to the Turks who would have appalled any house of holy women in France. But this was Outremer. Turks tamed and clearly loyal to a Christian lady were, if not ordinary, then certainly not incomprehensible.

Richildis could not visit her often. Melisende had more need of those she trusted, the closer she came to bearing her own child. At best Richildis could send and receive a messenger, the Turk Kutub more often than not. He seemed able to come and go as he pleased, slipping in in morning or evening, slipping out as softly as he came. He brought the same word always, that his mistress was well; that she oc-cupied herself in reading and in contemplation; that she would, if Richildis were kind, be pleased to have word of Bertrand.

Richildis sent back such word as she could. She tried not to rebuke Helena for enforcing silence. Bertrand only knew that Helena had taken it into her head to retreat for a time.

"It's because of me, isn't it?" he said to Richildis.

The inevitable had happened. He had stalked her to the ladies' chapel and found her there alone. She gone to pray, and not least for Helena, who must be near her time.

When Bertrand spoke behind her, she barely jumped. She had been expecting such a thing for so long that it came as no surprise at all.

She finished the prayer that she had begun, though she could feel him seething at her back, like hot iron held close to the skin. She crossed herself, rose, turned.

"You know where she is," Bertrand said. "And why. She's gone to be away from me."

Since that was manifestly true, Richildis could not deny it. She said, "She loves you very much. She needs peace, that's all, and a little holy quiet."

He was not listening. "I've hardly seen her all winter, hardly spoken to her, let alone—" He broke off. He was pale enough still from winter to show the flush that rose to his cheeks. "I know how these things go. A woman finds another man, a courtesan another patron. I suppose I'm being let off gently. But who—God's bones! Who else can there be?"

"No one," Richildis said.

"Of course there's someone! There always is. Couldn't she have told me first? Couldn't she have let me know that I'm no longer pleasing to her?"

Richildis shook her head. She did not know what to say. Had she been anything but Helena's friend, she would have been glad that Bertrand misunderstood so badly; that he would so simply if never easily break off his long round of sinning with a woman whom he could never marry.

But she was Helena's friend and unwilling ally. She could not betray a secret. She set her lips together and locked her fingers till they ached, and let him snarl himself into silence.

He took a long time about it. It was as monotonous as a monk at prayer. He cursed Helena, blessed her, castigated himself and her and the rest of the world. He never once bethought himself of the truth.

At length he seemed to remember that Richildis was there. He rounded on her.

"*You* must know who he is. Women talk to one another. Gossip's the whole world to them. Tell me who has taken Helena away from me!"

"No one," Richildis said again, for what good it would do.

"It can't be possible you don't know," Bertrand said. He was pacing as he said it, from wall to wall in front of the altar, halting, spinning on his heel, stalking back. He halted in front of her. "You're lying for her."

Richildis bit her tongue, tasted blood.

But he was blind to her. "Or she didn't tell you. No, she wouldn't, would she? She knows you'd tell me. A sister can't keep secrets from a brother. I'll have to ask—who would know—"

"*No one*," Richildis said with all the force that she could summon, "has taken Helena from you. She has gone to a convent to contemplate her sins and to cultivate a little peace. That is all she has done. You insult her by the very thought that she would abandon you for any other man."

"She is a courtesan," said Bertrand. "That is what courtesans do."

Richildis' expression must have been terrible: he actually flinched. "You," she said in white cold anger, "do not deserve any woman of either sense or probity— and Helena is both. Whatever she is, in whatever state of body and soul she may have been when she came to you, she has given herself to none but you since she accepted you into her bed. She has taken no other lover, admitted no other patron. Only you."

"Then," he said with the air of a man who snatches at any advantage, "how has she lived? I've never made her rich."

"Her patron who was before you," Richildis said out of her still and freezing center, "happened to die before she met you. He left her well provided. She's a wealthy woman, Bertrand. Don't tell me you never knew."

He blushed, he truly blushed. But he was a man. He was too proud for decent sense. "She lives well because her patrons pay her well."

Richildis brought her fists down on his shoulders. He wore mail under his tunic: he was as hard as chain-woven steel. "Oh, you purblind fool! First you go half mad because she must have taken another lover, then you tell me she's been living all along on the spoils of her lovers."

"No!" he half-shouted back. "*You* are the fool. She's always had lovers, a courtesan does. But she never turned me away. Never—till this winter and spring. Someone else stands closer to her heart, or to the cashbox where her heart should be."

"Have you ever," Richildis demanded of him, "paid her one copper penny for the use of her body?"

"She is not a whore!"

"Then you've given her nothing, paid her nothing, and still she never refused you her door."

"I gave her gifts," he said thickly. "She must have—"

Richildis spun away from him in perfect disgust. "Oh, go. Go! I'm ashamed to be your kin."

She thought that he might linger, might try to defend himself, but he did not. He left her headlong, blind and hopelessly deceived.

"Helena," Richildis said to the air. "Oh, Helena. We'll all pay high for this."

ertrand was cursed. He had been driven out of France for his folly with a woman, sundered from his father and his kin, compelled by the heat of a quarrel to seek the heat and dust and holiness of Outremer. Now, when he had thought it all done and gone, the curse struck again. He had quarreled with his sister, and for a woman whom he had thought he loved.

He left Richildis in anger, speechless with it. What he did for the rest of that day and somewhat of the next, he barely remembered. He must have sat through a session of the High Court, for that was why he had come to Jerusalem. He engaged in an hour's vigorous sword-practice with some of the other young men of the court, and had bruises to show for it. When he came to himself he was in the king's stables, readying to ride with a handful of knights and squires who had taken it into their heads to go hunting gazelle in the hills beyond Olivet.

A hunt would do him good. A fast ride, the wind in his face, the hot sweet scent of blood. Short of a good bruising fight, there was nothing better for such a mood as his.

But as the groom brought out his best hunting mount, the strong swift grey that he had bred of a Frankish dam and an Arab sire, something caught his eye. Amid all the coming and going of the stable at the height of Easter Court, still one movement struck him with both its strangeness and its familiarity. Out in the hills near Beausoleil, that skulk, that flick of robe, would mark the passing of an infidel. Here it was strikingly out of place.

He thought he recognized the shape of the skulk. Leaving the groom to look after grey Malik for yet a while longer, Bertrand slipped through the crowd of men and horses. Almost he was too late—but the skulker had been hindered by a quarrel among hunting hounds and was just eluding them as Bertrand came in sight of him.

Bertrand opened his mouth to call out the man's name. Kutub—Helena's man, the Turk Kutub.

But he held his tongue. Inspiration struck, strong as the hand of God. He slipped back toward the groom and the horse, moving as swift as he knew how; snatched rein, flung thanks over his shoulder, sprang into the saddle without pausing to set foot in stirrup.

Malik had been in a stall for a hand of days. He was eager to be out and running.

Bertrand let him go at his own speed, darting through the court, ignoring the hunting companions who called his name. He had other quarry now, and better sport.

It was a great folly to imagine that a Frank could outstalk a Turk from the steppes of Asia. But this Turk did not appear to be looking for pursuit. He rode openly once he had left the palace, sitting his ugly-headed little Turkish pony, passing through David's Gate to the southward road.

Fortune and the season favored Bertrand's hunt. The roads were heavily traveled, thronged with pilgrims. He had no little fear of losing a single man in the press, but there were few enough in turbans, and none with the point of a helmet thrusting through the snow-white wrappings.

Kutub rode at ease in his high sheepskin-cushioned saddle. Pilgrims crossed themselves as he passed, or muttered imprecations against his infidel presence. He took no notice. A Muslim who had lived his life among Christians, learned not to hear what Christians said of him.

Some distance outside of Jerusalem, when the city had shrunk to a shape of walls and towers and one blinding golden dome, the Turk seemed to wake as if from a drowse. Bertrand, who had been nearly asleep himself, kept awake only by the need to keep that turbaned helmet in sight, nearly lost him then; but God was looking after his wayward knight. Bertrand saw the turban shift, the rider slant across the line of travelers on foot and on muleback and in carts. The road's verge was kept clear by and for the swift passage of men on horseback: messengers, errand-riders of this lord or that.

As soon as Kutub's pony reached the road's edge, the Turk set heels to rough-coated sides. The pony sprang willingly into a gallop.

Bertrand cursed and wrestled his own horse through clots of pilgrims. They were too intent on piety to give way, even before a Frankish knight on a tall horse. Some might have ridden them down. Bertrand, alack, was soft when it came to such things. He pushed through as best he could, stopped short in the midst of a huddle of black-robed monks, crossed himself rather furiously and escaped, God be thanked, into nearly empty space. Malik snorted and lashed his tail and, even before Bertrand could bring spurs to bear, leaped in pursuit of the Turk on his pony.

No sane horseman, alone and ungifted with remounts, kept his horse at a gallop for long. Bertrand knew some long moments' fear that he had erred; that Kutub had indeed supplied himself with a change of horses, and would not slow till he reached posthouse or caravanserai. But after that first, heart-stopping gallop, he settled to the pace of the horseman who must travel swift but spare his horse: gallop to walk to canter to walk and back again. The tough little steppe pony did not need rest and water and forage as some might, but Kutub pampered him: stopped at intervals to let him breathe, graze if there was forage to be had, drink from well or cistern.

Bertrand followed his lead. The press of pilgrims eased as the road stretched toward Bethlehem, but they were still numerous enough to provide a sort of cover. Better yet, the road's verge was not entirely deserted. Twice couriers overtook him, swift riders wearing the badge of the king. More than once he passed riders who had set a slower pace than his own, though still swifter than the trudge-and-pray of the pilgrims.

If Kutub recognized the one who followed him, he betrayed no sign of it, nor made any move to elude pursuit. Bertrand considered overtaking and capturing him; but if the man was indeed bearing messages from Helena to Richildis and back again, then he might be bound to refuse aid to Bertrand. Else why had he not come to Bertrand himself, and brought word from Helena?

Or perhaps, Bertrand thought blackly, the message had not been for Richildis. Maybe it had been for another man, some lord or knight who had captured Helena's fancy. Or Richildis herself was using Helena's man for some intrigue of her own. Or—

He was thinking like a fool. There was no escaping the fact that Helena was not in Jerusalem—Bertrand had gone to her house, had found it shut up, empty but for the porter, who would not tell him where the lady had gone. Kutub must be on his way to her, wherever she had gone. There were castles in plenty along this road, demesnes of this baron or that, towns and villages in which a man could entertain a woman away from the prying eyes and wagging tongues of the city.

As the pursuit lengthened, he began to wonder if he had been mad to begin it. Food he had, provisions for a day, thanks to the diligence of his servants. There was even a bag of barley for Malik, and a waterskin that Bertrand filled at the pilgrims' wells while Malik drank his fill. There were hostels, monasteries, caravanserais, all dedicated to the succor of pilgrims. He could go on, if he must, all the way to Elin on the Red Sea, though that would tax his resources to the utmost.

Then if it had been a trick, or if Kutub did not lead him to Helena—what then? No one knew where he was. He had said no word to anyone. The last that was known of him, he had ridden away like a man possessed, blind to everything but his sudden quarry.

If that was God's will, then God willed it.

There was a dizzy freedom in it, a headlong recklessness that he had not known since he fled La Forêt with his father's curses on his head. He had taken more with him then, had gathered his belongings, his warhorse and his palfrey and his armor and such of his inheritance as he reckoned was due him, even a scared yet eager servant who had died of fever after they took ship for Outremer.

That had been a greater anger, a wilder escape. This was temper purely, and outraged pride, and—God help him—love that had been wounded to the heart. His squire, wicked little *pullani* that he was, would find another knight if Bertrand failed to come back. That was Messire Gabriel's great charm: like a cat, he always landed on his feet. As for Richildis . . .

Richildis could look after herself. Bertrand hardened heart and mind against her.

He was, perhaps, a little out of his head. He should be in Jerusalem being a Baron of the High Court, joining in the festivities for Easter, waiting about for Princess Melisende to produce the child that, she was convinced, was the prince-heir of the kingdom. Not riding out headlong after a courtesan's infidel servant, in hope and fear that the man would lead him to her hiding place.

If she hid—if she cared as much as that.

The road wound away under Malik's hoofs. The sun reached its summit and began to fall. Just before they came to Bethlehem, Kutub left the pilgrims' road and turned toward the hills.

Bertrand's heart thudded. The Turk had seen him—would elude him.

And if he had not been seen, how could he avoid it, now that there were no throngs of pilgrims to hide in?

A hunter knew the ways of that. Bertrand had intended a hunt today, though never so far from the city. There were not, unfortunately, any servants to tend his horse while he forayed on afoot, but neither did Kutub abandon his pony.

The way that he took, while twisting and patently deserted, seemed well enough traveled: it was wider than a foot-track, grooved with the wheels of carts. Bertrand, keeping out of sight if not of earshot, saw the prints of hoofs: small narrow donkey-hoofs, and the larger marks of a mule, and several that belonged to ponies or small horses. Turkish ponies, perhaps, like the one that Kutub rode.

Surely, thought Bertrand: surely Helena was somewhere near, if her Turks were hereabout. But where . . . ?

He should not have let himself think. He should have kept his eyes on the track and his ears on the man ahead of him. Well after he should have noticed that the sound of hoofs had stopped, he came round a steep and narrow corner into a little bowl of a valley. On the other side of it, perched on a hilltop, stood a shape of walls and one low dome crowned with a cross—church or monastery, and no doubt of it.

And there in front of him on the path, with cliff-wall on one side and sheer drop on the other, bow strung and bent and arrow aimed straight between his eyes, stood Kutub. His pony had gone on down the track: Bertrand saw it with the clarity of one who looks death in the face, grazing amid a startling patch of green.

"Lord Frank," Kutub said in the Frankish that he occasionally admitted to speaking. Bertrand bridled. That was an insult. He spoke Arabic better than Kutub spoke Frankish, and Kutub knew that very well.

Still, he thought. If the Turk was minded to talk, he might not be minded quite yet to shoot. In Frankish himself, Bertrand said, "Messire Turk."

"You followed me," Kutub said.

Since that was glaringly obvious, Bertrand forbore to respond.

Kutub looked him over without visible evidence of anger. "I am ashamed," he said. "Bitterly, bitterly ashamed. We were a full league out of Jerusalem before I knew that I had a companion on the road."

"Yet," said Bertrand, "you led me onward."

Kutub shrugged expressively. The arrow never wavered from its target. Bertrand knew how much effort it took to bend the Turkish horseman's bow. He would not show it, but he was impressed. For so little and wiry a man, Kutub was remarkably strong. "I was undecided," Kutub said, and now he spoke in Arabic. "I could lose you, I could lead you astray, I could kill you. Or I could pretend that I had never seen you. It is difficult, sometimes, to know what one must do and remain loyal."

"So she is hiding something," Bertrand said, but not in Arabic; let the other wonder if he understood the meaning of the shift.

A thought struck him, perfect in its horror. "That's a convent yonder—my sister said—it's not—" He paused to breathe. "She's not ill. She hasn't succumbed to—"

Kutub's teeth flashed. They were as whitely sharp as a wolf's, and as long in the fangs. "No, she's not become a leper. From that at least, God has preserved her."

"Thank God." Bertrand crossed himself with heartfelt relief. "Then why is she hiding? She wouldn't take the veil, not Helena. Take me to her!"

"She said," said Kutub, "that you above all were not to be admitted into her presence."

Bertrand flung up his head, heedless of the arrow that hovered so close. With all the arrogance of his birth and race and breeding, he commanded, "Take me to your mistress."

The arrow hung unwavering a moment longer. Then it dropped. The bow unbent. Kutub slipped arrow back into quiver, unstrung and slung the bow, never taking his eyes from Bertrand's face. Bertrand could not read the thoughts that flickered there.

Kutub held out both hands, startling him almost into drawing sword. "You should take me prisoner," he said. "Bind me. Beat me a little. Overpower me."

"She'll never believe it," Bertrand said at once, and no need to think about it, either.

"What, and I a little bowlegged bandit of a Turk, and you a great tall broad-shouldered knight?" Kutub laughed as his kind did, almost without sound: as a hunter would, or a tribesman on a raid. He crossed his wrists and held them under Bertrand's nose. "Where's your arrogance, sir Frank? Take me captive. Make me lead you to my lady."

By God, Bertrand thought. The Turk was on his side. Astonishing.

Unless of course it was a trap.

No Frank ever did himself any good gnawing and fretting at if-it-weres. Bertrand plucked a spare strap from his saddlebag and bound Kutub with it, not so tight as to endanger the flesh nor so loose as to threaten the deception. The Turk grinned at him over the bound hands, looking for once like his accustomed self: lighthearted and a bit wicked, with a fine eye for absurdity.

It was perfectly absurd to mount Malik and capture the grazing pony and herd it and its master along the track to what was, indeed, a convent of nuns. From the look of the place they were Greek rite and not Latin, but in this circumstance it mattered little. Bertrand in his mail and weapons and on his big half-Frankish horse was little enough to frighten the doughty woman who peered from the shutter in the gate, but his captive widened her eyes.

"I would speak," said Bertrand in Greek, "with the Lady Helena."

The nun did not try to deny that such a person resided here. Nor did she admit it, or him. "Wait here," she said, and went away. He heard the slide and boom of a bar.

Kutub, who was a man of sense, sat on his haunches in the shade of Bertrand's horse, rested bound hands on knees and to all appearances went to sleep. Bertrand would have liked to follow suit, but he had not the gift. He left horse and pony nibbling together at a bit of dry grass near the gate, and wore a circle in the dust, pacing and peering up at the blank unwelcoming walls. There was not even a banner hung from a turret, only the windowless stone and the dome of what must have been the chapel. The cross on the summit was dark and dull. If it had ever been gilded, wind and dust and sun had long since worn the gilding away.

How odd to feel gilded himself in sensible leather over mail, with his horse-trappings that were as plain as a knight could properly allow. They were all very fine for their plainness, handsome and nearly new. In such a place as this, that was luxury, and no doubt faintly sinful.

A house of holy women that admitted Helena and her outlandish servants might not be as troubled as some by worldly vanity.

While he consoled himself with such thoughts, the wait stretched long, and the shadows with them. He would have to spend the night in or near this place. In it, he hoped, if there was a guesthouse hidden away somewhere.

When at last the shutter opened again, Bertrand was caught by surprise. He had wandered down the path, kicking stones to make them fall in companies. He had to scramble ungracefully back to the gate, too well aware of the amusement in the round black eyes. "She will see you," the nun said. The voice through the shutter betrayed no expression. "You cannot come in here. Go round the hill to the gate there. Someone will let you in."

Bertrand's heart leaped as it had when he saw Kutub in a court of the king's palace. The same wildness possessed him, the same headlong impulse. He would have taken no thought for horses or captive, if Kutub had not thrust out a foot to trip him.

He fell hard and rolled. As he fetched up winded against a rock, Kutub's booted foot came down lightly on his throat. A firm thrust could have crushed it; but he looked up without fear and in a great deal of temper.

Kutub grinned at him. "Shame," he said, "to be so unwary. Come, sir Frank. Get up. Drag me cruelly to my lady and fling me at her feet."

A bark of laughter escaped before Bertrand could stop it. He caught the boot that rested on his throat, thrust up and back. Kutub toppled. Bertrand surged up after him, grasped the end of the strap that bound his wrists, pulled him up and shoved him forward. It was by no means all feigned. He was no more delighted than any other man, to be made a fool of.

he track on which Bertrand had been set was narrower than the one that led to the gate, little more than a footpath against the wall. For a man leading a captive and two horses it was adventurous, particularly where the hill fell away and dropped sheer into the valley.

Fortunately horse and pony were surefooted and Kutub offered no further ambushes. They came unscathed to the postern gate, for so it must be: small, narrow, looking down on emptiness. It opened as Bertrand approached. Another nun stood in it, a little round dumpling of a woman in a faded black habit, veiled to the eyes. She said nothing, only held the gate as Bertrand led horses and prisoner in, then shut and barred it firmly and led him across what in France would have been called a cloister garth: a tiny garden tucked into a fold of wall, with trees trained flat against the stone like images of the crucified Christ.

There was indeed a cloister past that, a shaded colonnade, dim this late in the day and remarkably cool. Yet another small round nun relieved Bertrand of the horses there but left him his captive, with a glance that seemed to approve the infidel's condition. Kutub showed her his teeth, and not amiably, either.

The colonnade opened on a court and what must be a guesthouse: a stone building set apart, built into the outer wall. Bertrand, observing it with an eye accustomed to measuring fields for battle, took note that it opened on another way, one that surely must lead to the greater gate. But that way was the dome of the chapel, and no doubt the good sisters of the convent, who must not be tainted by the sight of a man within their walls. The portresses and the nun who had taken charge of the horses must have a dispensation; must be required to confess each time they suffered the world to touch them.

However that might have been, he had seen no random passerby, nor did he think that he would. His guide led him to the guesthouse and through yet another small and unobtrusive door.

The house was small and very plain. The room into which he was led had no more furnishings than a bench and a table, no carpets or ornaments, nothing that would comfort the eye or the heart. There was an icon on the wall, some great-eyed dark-faced eastern saint. A curtain covered a doorway. There would be another room beyond, and perhaps a stair.

In that bare and comfortless place, Bertrand was left alone with Kutub. He could hear nothing but the stifling silence of the cloister. No bells for this was between the hours, no clear voices singing, not even the call of a bird. Wherever the Turks were, whatever had been done with their horses, no sound came as far as this room.

He opened his mouth to demand an explanation of Kutub, but, thinking better of it, forbore. Kutub squatted on the floor at Bertrand's feet, in apparent comfort. The glances he shot Bertrand were full of wicked mirth.

The light died while Bertrand sat there. No one came to light the clay lamp that rested in a niche below the icon. While he could still see, he took out flint and steel from his purse and performed the office for himself. The lamp was filled with oil, faintly and sweetly scented. Its light traveled not much farther than the icon's painted face; but it was better than sitting in the dark.

Before the last of the light was gone, the bell rang in the chapel. A little later Bertrand heard voices, the faint sweet chanting that he had been listening and straining for, all unaware, since he passed the outer gate. It sounded soft, almost too soft to hear, and unreachably remote.

He began to think that he had been left here to cool his heels till morning. No food, no water had been offered him. Nothing but this place to sit and wait and, no doubt, pray. But he had no prayer in him. What was he supposed to ask for? That Helena should not have taken the veil? The longer he waited, the more it seemed he was too late.

Still, said the reason that was left to him: would she have kept her Turks if she had vowed herself to God? The God who cherished these nuns would hardly be pleased to entertain a pack of infidels.

The chanting dimmed and faded and died. The bell rang again. With full dark the lamp seemed to gain power and presence. It illumined the room surprisingly well. Bertrand could see the icon's face clearly, the lines of it limned in gold. Its eyes seemed to come alive, to fix on him in supernal disapproval.

He had, like a fool, left his saddlebags on his saddle, with their stock of provisions. The purse at his belt held a few dried dates wrapped in a withered leaf. He offered half of them to Kutub. The Turk declined politely. Bertrand wrapped them frugally and laid them away again.

Patience stretched thin and snapped. Just as he rose to explore the rest of the house, to venture forth if need be and demand water, food, an explanation, he heard the sound of a door opening, and booted feet on the bare stone floor. The curtain swayed; a brown hand lifted it.

Another of Helena's Turks stared down the length of Bertrand's sword. His narrow black eyes were as fearless as Kutub's. "Come," he said as if a sharp steel point did not menace his windpipe.

Bertrand hauled Kutub roughly to his feet—to no visible response from Kutub's countryman—and followed yet another damnably silent guide.

Perhaps this was not a guesthouse after all. Perhaps it was a place of detention for unwelcome visitors. It looked out on a stone-paved court and another house like it but larger, and with the light of life in it.

There were Helena's Turks, the whole lot of them, regarding Kutub with lifted brows and glances that understood too well. They had settled well and comfortably into the lower portion of this second house, with all their gear scattered about, and carpets on the floor, and sleeping-mats spread and mostly occupied. Three of the six were playing at knucklebones under a hanging lamp. The one who was not either captive or guide, lounged indolently by the wall, propped up on a saddle, mending a bit of bridle.

Ayyub the guide led Bertrand through them. They greeted him in their fashion, bowing where they sat or lay, evincing no surprise, nor any dismay at Kutub's captivity. A stair led out of their guardroom into a darker, dimmer space, rooms divided by walls and a passage and lit by another of the clay lamps. The rooms were empty, all but the one at the end, which was a little larger and rather brighter. A pair of lamps burned in it, casting a yellow light on a bed as narrow and no doubt as hard as a nun's, a low stool on which sat a woman in a black habit, the inevitable icon.

Bertrand saw all of that in a soldier's glance, recording and setting it aside. The center of it, the thing that focused the whole of him, sat in a tall stiff chair beside the bed, wrapped in a dark mantle. She cradled something small, that began suddenly and powerfully to howl.

Truth had a force like a lance in the vitals. Helena, rocking the swaddled and crimson-faced baby, crooning to it, cajoling it to be silent, did not trouble to be oblivious to Bertrand's presence. She raised her eyes to his face.

They were as dark and calm as ever, no hint of either fear or defiance. Yet she must have known both. Else why hide this from him—this of all secrets that she could have kept?

"Is it not mine?" Bertrand demanded abruptly. "Is that why?"

"It is yours," she said: her sweet voice, lovely as always, unshakably serene.

"How do you know?"

She did not flinch from the blow, nor lower her eyes. "I know," she said.

"Then why?"

She did not answer that. She folded back the swaddlings from the face and the small flailing arms. The baby, having rested sufficiently, began again to howl. Helena's voice carried through it, pitched low and very calm. "This is your son," she said. "I named him Olivier, for the Mount of Olives. He is very beautiful, they tell me. I'd not know; I'm no connoisseur of babies. I think that he is very strong, and will grow up as big as his father."

All the while she spoke, she rocked him. His wailing went on unabated. The nun, whom Bertrand had all but forgotten, rose suddenly and took him from his mother's arms. At once and completely he fell silent. She took him back to her stool and sat cradling him, never raising her eyes to Bertrand's face, never even admitting to his existence.

"I have too little milk for him," Helena said. "There is a woman coming in the morning, a villager from nearby here, who is said to have milk enough for three— and she lost her own just yesterday. Sister, you are sure that he'll be well until she comes?"

The nun nodded. She would look into Helena's face, showing a pair of large and very beautiful eyes in the shrouding veil. Perhaps her body was lovely, too: more slender than the others he had seen, graceful even in rest, with white long-fingered hands.

He called himself to order. Now was no time in the world to distract himself with the guesswork of finding a woman inside a nun's habit.

And yet he could not help it. He was angry. So angry that he did not trust himself; not unless he found refuge in something other than the truth of what Helena had done.

She had borne him a son. She had hidden it from him. She had lied to him while she was in Jerusalem. When she could not have lied any longer, she had gone away—had run from him as if from an enemy.

How a man could love a woman so much and be so blindly, relentlessly angry, he could not imagine. He wanted to crush her to him and never let her go. He wanted to cast her away and never look on her face again. Both at once. Both with all his heart.

She sat mute, with those great eyes resting still on his face, as blank as the icon's, as empty of human feeling. If they had looked away, if she had spoken, he might not have said what he said then. But she did neither, and his tongue was its own master.

"If you had been as truthful with me," it said, "as I always was with you; if you had told me when first you knew, I would have raised and cherished that child as tenderly as father ever did. Because you lied, because you ran from me, I cannot do that. Not now. Not ever. That is no child of mine. I will not acknowledge him. I will not give him my name or my countenance or any of my worldly substance. You conceived and bore him without a father. Let him live without one: bastard, fatherless, without name or honor or nation."

Still he could not move her, could not shift the calm in those eyes. It might be a mask, such as courtesans learned. Yet if it was not . . .

"Why did you do it?" he asked her again, though it weakened the power of his curse.

Again she did not answer.

He turned from her as he had from his sister, in rage that was like a sickness. He had to escape from this place—even in the dark, even with his horse taken away he knew not where, even with the road as treacherous as he knew it to be.

There would be a moon tonight. Enough to see by, with anger to sharpen his eyes.

Already in spirit he was on that road, even while he stood in front of Helena. She must have seen it: for the first time her calm cracked; her eyes lost their look of endless distances. He heard the intake of her breath, swallowed in the sharper one that marked another of the baby's wails. Hunger, temper, blank insensate rage— oh, yes. He knew them all.

"You have sown," he said to Helena. "Now reap."

He left her to think on that, if she deigned to. Who knew what she thought? She was a woman, and worse: a courtesan.

Some dark angel must have protected him. He found his horse in a stable not a dozen paces from the guesthouse door, found saddle and bridle and gear all tidy beside the stall, and the stallion picking at stray bits of fodder on the bottom of his manger. He had eaten well from the look of it. Good: he would travel the better for that.

Gates that were barred from without were easy of access from within. Bertrand could do nothing to secure them behind him, but no one came to stop or assist

him. He said a prayer for the convent's safety, and could only hope that that would
suffice till the nuns rose for the Night Office.

The moon was up indeed, waxing to the full. It lit his way well enough, and
Malik was both sharp-eyed and surefooted. He never slipped nor stumbled, nor
misstepped though the road was steep. And when they had come down off the hill
and out through the valley and back to the pilgrims' road, empty and open in the
moonlight, Bertrand had no need of spurs. Malik was glad to stretch his stride, to
make haste toward Jerusalem.

ertrand was in Jerusalem only
long enough to gather his belongings and his servants and to return to Beausoleil.
Richildis knew that he had vanished out of the stable court just before he was to
have ridden on a hunt, but not that he had come back and gone away yet again—
not till somewhat after the fact. Melisende had been brought to bed at too long
last in her own estimation, and set about producing a prince-heir to the Kingdom
of Jerusalem.

It was not a terrible labor, as labor went. It was women's battle as combat at
arms was men's. Melisende fought it as well as her father had ever fought on the
battlefield, fought and won and emerged alive, with a fine strong son bellowing his
objections to the cruelties of the world.

He took after his mother, fortunately: big and fair, but his midwives judged that
his eyes would not be dark as hers were; they would be blue, or grey perhaps. The
more doting of the women called him handsome. Melisende, and Richildis in the
privacy of her thoughts, reckoned that he was much as any other newborn manchild,
red and wrinkled and rather hideous.

"He'll grow," said one of the elder ladies.

"And thank God for it," said Melisende, cradling him competently enough but
without particular affection. That she left to the nurse who had delivered herself of
a mere and weakling daughter a few days before, and who had more than milk
enough for both.

While the plump and placid woman cooed over the baby, Melisende refused to
rest until she had spoken to her husband and her father. "They are Jerusalem," she
said, "or would be. Let them see together what they most longed for."

No one dared to protest that it was deep night, midway between the monks'
Night Office and the dawn. Melisende in triumph was as irresistible as any horde
of Saracens.

Neither man had been sleeping. They had, the messenger told Richildis later,
been getting very drunk together in a corner of the great hall. The scent of wine
came in with them, but they were clear-eyed enough. Baldwin entered first, of Fulk's
courtesy, but Fulk was hard on his heels.

They were as eager as boys, crowding the great bed on which Melisende lay. The
nurse had consented reluctantly to return the child to his mother's arms. They were

a pretty picture in the clean and sweet-scented bedclothes, Melisende in a fresh new shift with her hair in a plait, the baby swaddled in her arms.

Baldwin bent to kiss his daughter on the brow. Fulk lifted the child from his wrappings, cradling the newborn body with the ease of a man who has done so more than once before. There was no mistaking that here was a son, or that he had a strong pair of lungs. He bellowed lustily as his father raised him.

Fulk laughed, a low sound of pure pleasure. "Yes," he said. "Yes, this is an heir for Jerusalem, if God wills that he live."

"He will live," Melisende said from the bed. Her voice betrayed none of the exhaustion that must be dragging at her. "Does he please you, my lords?"

"He pleases us immensely," Baldwin said. "And you, daughter? Are you well?"

"Very well indeed," she said, "now that it's over."

She did not add that she had no intention of entering that battle again. Richildis wondered if Fulk thought she had forgotten. If so he was a fool. Melisende closed her eyes: honest weariness, but there was calculation in it, too.

The nurse took the baby from Fulk's hands, cradling him again, giving him the plump brown breast. His bellowing muted to gurgles and then to the sounds of vigorous sucking.

"My lady," Fulk said to his wife, "I do believe you—that he will live and grow strong."

But Melisende was asleep, or feigning it. For all that she would admit to knowing, her husband had barely acknowledged her existence, still less her part in the birthing of his son.

That was, of course, if she wished to quarrel. Richildis did not know that she did. She had labored for a night and a day to produce this child, this prince whom his father, with a hand on his soft downy head, named Baldwin.

He had not asked her what she would name her son. Still it was well chosen. It was a good name, a royal name, a name of honor and precedence in this kingdom. This prince would wear it well, as his grandfather had before him.

Fulk kissed his wife as her father had, on the brow. She must truly be asleep: she never stirred. He smiled and brushed her cheek with a finger, the first tenderness that he had shown her where anyone could see. It struck at Richildis strangely, with a poignancy that she had not expected.

She was still a little raw with it, come morning, when the city woke to the ringing of bells and the crying of the word from the old minarets: A prince! A prince for Jerusalem! While the city burst forth in jubilation, Richildis found herself possessed of an odd and restless mood, and no joy to be found in it, even on Melisende's behalf.

It was then that she learned of Bertrand's brief return and swift departure. No one knew why he had done it.

But she remembered that Kutub had come with a message, the second since Helena's son was born; and that he had left her not long before Bertrand was said to have ridden headlong out of the stable court. It might be folly, it might be nonsense, but if Bertrand had caught sight of Helena's Turk—and if he had done that, and had followed the man, and discovered what Helena would not have him know . . .

Richildis might be seeing consequence where was only coincidence. But God did not, in her experience, rule the world so.

On impulse that she found herself regretting even as she acted on it, she asked and received leave to depart from her lady's service for a few days' span. Melisende had a surfeit of attendants just then, though most of them hovered about the infant prince. "Go," she said to Richildis. "Take as long as you like. Only be sure to come back."

Richildis bowed lower than she was wont to do, which raised Melisende's brows; but the princess did not say anything.

If she had, Richildis might have reconsidered. But she had been given leave, and with it, she could presume, some degree of authority—enough to secure a horse, provisions, and escort with a company of Hospitallers on its way to one of the castles in the north.

They had another lady with them, a widow on pilgrimage, traveling with a gaggle of maids, a veritable caravan of baggage, and servants enough to look after a small army. Her name was Lady Elfleda. She came, she said, from England, where her family had held lands since long before the Normans came in with their great trampling feet.

"Of course," she said, "we made sure we had a Norman to speak for us, and married into the family, too, though it wouldn't have done for one to have inherited the lot—oh, no. It wouldn't have done at all."

"And the Normans let it happen?" Richildis asked.

Lady Elfleda smiled. She was a fat, fair, comfortable woman, yet her smile had somewhat of the curve of an axeblade. "Why, of course," she said. "How not, when the loveliest of the earl's daughters had set her heart on the overlord's favorite son? So determined was she to have him, that she had her brothers invite him to hunt the red deer with them, and when the hunt was done and they feasted on the spoils, she filled his cup of mead with her own white hand.

"Imagine his expression," said Lady Elfleda, "come morning when he woke naked beside her, and her maiden blood on the sheet, and she crying to all who would hear, that he had taken her by force. Her brothers were in a fair taking, and would have taken the offending parts of him, had she not invoked their mercy—and beseeched the one of them who was a priest to bless her with the name of wife."

"And so a Norman married into your family," Richildis said. "How very clever."

"How fortunate," said Lady Elfleda, "that after he had finished snarling at them all for base traitors, he found in himself a great and insatiable passion for the lady who had tricked him. He wasn't a bad man, for a Norman—and not bad-looking, either, as I remember him when I was young: and he was getting on a bit then. They say he was quite the pretty boy when Aunt Frideswide plied him with the good white mead."

"And would he have known the good from the bad?" Richildis wanted to know. And added, lest her companion be puzzled, "We're in the way of vintners ourselves, away in Anjou. Mead's not a thing any Frank knows a great deal of."

"Of course not," Lady Elfleda said. "And maybe it wasn't the best that was in the casks, but it served the purpose well enough. He never could abide mead after that, could milord Jehan."

"And yet he could abide your aunt of the difficult name?"

"How odd," Lady Elfleda said. "He said the same of her, and insisted on calling her Willa. Oh yes, he endured her very well, and esteemed her too, once he'd been brought to see the sense in her stratagem. It kept our holdings safe, let his father claim to be their overlord, but let us go on much as we always had, though we had to speak a different tongue in court thereafter."

"That was more than threescore years ago," Richildis said. "Surely, you yourself couldn't be—"

Lady Elfleda laughed. "Oh, no! But everyone remembers. Because it's the family, you know."

Richildis did know that. She reflected on it as they rode among the Hospitallers in their grey mail and their white habits, the warrior monks taciturn in the presence of women, but not ungracious. Nights they spent in Hospitaller holdings, honored guests, set apart and protected. Days they passed in the saddle, Elfleda on her soft-paced white mule, Richildis on her crossgrained Saracen mare.

Part of one day and a night they spent in Nablus, that ancient city in its girdle of gardens and orchards—like, said Lady Elfleda who knew all of these places, a little Damascus. Its beauty was the more blessed after the bleakness of the lands about, the bare and dusty hills and waterless plains. And yet Richildis was not soothed into peace.

It had been nigh on a year since she came to Outremer. So long, and passed to so little purpose. Bertrand was not one step closer to removing himself from this country than he had been on the day Richildis found him in Acre.

She had written of this to Lady Agnes, and more than once. As slow as letters were, still she had had answers, written in slightly stilted Latin in the hand taught by the nuns at Ste-Mathilde. *Be patient*, Lady Agnes said. *Endure. Be at ease for La Forêt. All is well here; everyone prospers; no one is sick or has died. The demesne waits in comfort for the return of its lord.*

Richildis did not wish to be either patient or comfortable, but there was little else that she could do—not, at least, till now.

Bertrand had retreated to Beausoleil north of Nablus. From Helena there had been no word—no messenger, nothing. If Richildis had erred—

Well: and if she had erred, then her brother would be delighted to see her, and she would be a guest at last in his castle.

Richildis left Nablus with few regrets, even for its cool springs and its green orchards. She was almost glad to be on the road again, to be choking on the dust and battling the stinging flies. She was doing something. That was all, at the moment, that she cared for.

The road outside of the city grew swiftly wilder. Passers were few and heavily armed. They bore rumor of robbers, of reivers farther on. The Hospitallers, hearing this, put on their armor and hung their helms from their saddlebows, and kept bow and sword and lance to hand.

They traveled so for all that day and into the next, in vigilance that did not abate, the farther they traveled. Past noon of their second day out of Nablus, one of the Hospitallers' scouts came in at the gallop. He pounded to a halt, already calling out to the knights in the van. One of those set horn to lips and blew. At the signal, all of the knights and the sergeants hastened to the van, gathering into council, leaving only the men-at-arms and a sergeant or two to guard the rear and the ladies.

The caravan slowed to a halt. Lady Elfleda's maids were most of them reasonable women, but the silly one, whose name was even more difficult than that of Elfleda's aunt, began to shriek and carry on. "Raiders! Murderers! Infidels!"

One of the other maids, with remarkable presence of mind, clapped a hand over the idiot's mouth before she had quite managed to rouse the dead. In the blessed almost-quiet, one of the Hospitallers halted his horse beside Lady Elfleda's litter. "Raiders?" she asked him with the calm of one who has traveled far and seen much.

He nodded. "Alas, lady, yes. They're but Bedouin; they'll give us little trouble. But they are a nuisance."

"And we should be quiet and not interfere," Elfleda said. "We understand, Brother."

The Hospitaller bowed in the saddle, wheeled his horse and returned to the front of the line.

The lady's caravan, it was evident, had dealt with such nuisances before. The servants drove mules and baggage to the center and set themselves on guard about it, producing a gratifying array of weaponry: knives, bows, spears, even a sword or two. The women were set—trapped, in Richildis' mind—within the circle of the baggage.

They were not to wait to be attacked. They would continue, it was clear, if more slowly than before, and in stricter order. The Hospitaller knights had mounted the destriers that were kept fresh and only for fighting, put on their great helms, stepped their lances that had been borne on sumpter mules, made themselves into moving towers of flesh and steel. They were held in great terror, Richildis had heard, among the Saracens.

Yet this was a rich prize, and raiders could not help but know it: Lady Elfleda was not one to travel even on pilgrimage without proper ostentation. The knights were not numerous and were thinly spread round the limits of the caravan. The rest were lighter armed on lighter horses, squires and sergeants who must defend where the knights could not be.

Richildis found that she was not afraid. She was exhilarated. Was this what young knights felt when they waited for a battle? The only one who had ever been honest with her was Bertrand, and he had told her that he was stiff with terror. "Everything is fear," he had said. "Every thought, every breath, every move that anyone makes. And when the enemy strikes, the fear grows so great that it's beyond comprehending. That's when you can move. When there's nothing for it but to fight, and fight well, because if you fail, the fear will be your death."

Maybe Bertrand was a coward. And if so, then so was every knight and hero, because even in his youth Bertrand had been known for his reckless courage.

Richildis had the recklessness, it seemed, but not the leavening of fear. It was a startling thing to discover when one had been crediting oneself with a fair excess of good sense. She resented the necessity that compelled her to cower among the women and the baggage, that prevented her from gaining a clear view of the fight. She did the best that she could do, which was to establish herself near the edge of the innermost ring of baggage, mounted on her unwontedly still and watchful mare.

From that vantage she saw how the road passed between a pair of hills, how sweetly shaped the place was for an ambush; and how the first raiders appeared as if from the earth.

They were a little disappointing. These were not the emirs and princes of nobler battles, clad in silks and mounted on fine horses. They were tribesmen from the desert, ragged and filthy, clinging singly and in pairs to the backs of scraggy ponies or motheaten camels. Their weapons were as unprepossessing as themselves: worn and tarnished knives and swords, battered spears, bows that had seen better days.

And yet their poverty and the pilgrims' evident riches made them desperate; and desperate, they were dangerous. They were many and they were determined, and they descended from every side, shrieking, yowling, calling to one another like wolves, or like jackals of the desert.

Word came down from the front, shouted from man to man of the Hospitallers: "Press on! Get out of the valley!"

The women and the baggage were driven like cattle, and lowing like them, too. Richildis, by design or by accident, found herself slipping away from them, her mare pressing ahead as if she had understood the command. The Hospitallers' own baggage, much less in quantity than Lady Elfleda's, was possibly richer: they were conveying chests of Frankish gold and silver to one of their castles in the north, for aid in fighting against the infidel.

Near those chests and the mules that carried them, Richildis persuaded her mare to slow a little. She had no weapon, nothing to fight with but the little dagger she carried at her belt, that was barely sharp enough for cutting meat at dinner. A bow might have served her well, if she could remember the way of it: such a bow as she had seen the Turks wield.

All that ran swift through her head while she held her mare to a dancing, crabbing walk, and raiders fell on the caravan like crows on carrion. Darting, yelling, striking, whirling away—evading the heavy armored knights and their ponderous horses, seeking gaps and weaknesses, thrusting as deep as they dared before the line closed against them. They struck to wound, not it seemed to kill; to drive the defenders from their treasure, to seize and carry away the prize.

A knot of raiders plunged straight at Richildis; at her and at the mules beyond her, weighed down with their burden of gold and silver. Of its own accord her hand dropped to her belt and drew her little dagger. Her mare snorted and lashed her tail and pawed impatiently.

Shrieking voices, no more human than the yipping of jackals. Dark faces, black pits of mouths, yellow gleam of teeth. Glitter of whirling steel. The song of it hummed in her bones.

She saw, or some saint guided her to see, in the hand of the foremost a strung bow. In the other an arrow, but not yet nocked to string. Without thinking about it at all, she clapped heels to the mare's sides. The mare leaped as if on wings.

As easy, as light, as calm as if she plucked a blossom from a passing bough, Richildis won bow and—O marvelous—the arrow that had been meant, no doubt, for her heart. And she was past the raiders, wheeling behind them, and there was steel near and about her, Hospitaller steel, but none was close enough to stop her.

Memory was set in the bone. Nock arrow, lift bow, draw, find it not quite too much for her strength; and loose—careful, careful of the horse's movement, the swing and sway and sudden veer. In a hunt one aimed. In a battle one had no time. One simply loosed and prayed.

She had only the one arrow. But God's grace showed her a quiver hung from a raider's saddlebow—for laziness, convenience, stupidity, she never knew. A swoop, a wheel, and it was hers.

Oh, it was easy, this thing called battle. If one had a swift horse and a keen eye—if one were a woman and therefore, in every man's mind, helpless—one could have one's way with such raiders as these. Poor baffled underfed infidels, taken from behind by a woman with a bow, and shot with their own arrows, too.

When one of them fell with an arrow in the eye—pure luck and a waft of wind, and even in her fit of exultation she could not call it more—they retreated as they had come, headlong and yelling, seeking simpler prey.

And there she was, all alone, with her arms aching from the unaccustomed effort of bending a bow, a still-full quiver slung behind her. The raiders, she saw with numb surprise, had withdrawn from the whole of the caravan. They would not come back, she did not think.

As unthinkingly as she had done everything else since that battle began, she unstrung the bow and coiled the string and, for lack of a better thought, slipped it into the purse at her belt. The bow she held in her hand, till she could find a place to put it.

The caravan did not stop, barely paused to gather the wounded and to dispatch a mule that had been gutted by a raider's knife. Luckily it had carried nothing of consequence: a tent and its poles, that went simply enough atop other mules' burdens.

Richildis wondered if she should go back to Lady Elfleda. The Hospitallers who had come back from fighting along the caravan's edges, seemed certainly to think so. "And where were you," she demanded of them, "when the Saracens came to steal your Grand Master's gold?"

Being men, they had an answer for that, and it was pure bluster. She ignored it. They could hardly get rid of her without removing her bodily. If any thought of that, he did not act on it. She was suffered to stay where she was, as alone as ever, even with Hospitallers all about her.

Of course they would not admire her for protecting their treasure. She was a woman. Her competence was an insult.

Time was when she might have been troubled to think such a thing. Now, with the heat of battle gone and a chill clarity in its place, she was, if anything, amused. Imagine: all her life long she had thought herself a right and proper woman, gentle and rather weak. And the first time anyone brought a killing fight to her, the first raid that by a peculiarity of fortune she had ever been a part of, she had discovered that she thrived on it.

It was dreadful, of course. Horrible. Against nature. But that was the way of it.

God's irony, she thought. And men's considerable distress. They would never understand why she smiled; would only edge away, keeping a careful distance, as if she carried some contagion.

ady Elfleda was much less dismayed by Richildis' accomplishment than the Hospitallers were. Yet even she could not entirely approve of it. She was glad, Richildis thought, to bid farewell to her oddity of a traveling companion. She remained with the caravan as Richildis turned aside from it to ride through the village at the foot of a steep hill that like the castle above it was given the name of Beausoleil.

It had been called something else before the Franks came to Outremer, Richildis was sure. The people were natives of this land, slight dark people, the men bearded and in turbans, the women swathed and veiled in black. They were not Christian, that she could discern: there were no crosses in evidence. The structure that might have been a church, with a cracked and weathered dome, was crowned with the thin spire of a minaret.

The castle itself had a look both new and old. The walls were well made, and recently repaired from the signs. The gate was new, bound with black iron. The tower above it was worn somewhat with weather, and there were marks on it that might have been dealt by the hurled stones of a catapult; but it had neither crumbled nor fallen.

It was a larger castle than she had expected, larger than most in France. Within its curtain wall was a broad and spacious court and a handsome keep.

Her escort left her at the gate, the Hospitaller sergeant and his handful of men, bowing and handing her over in silence to the men who stood guard. There were two at the outer gate, two at the inner. Each pair was half Frank—or German, or perhaps Flemish: the big white-fair man at the inner gate spoke a guttural patois that resembled only faintly the *langue d'oeil*. They were well equipped and clean, and kept good discipline.

So too the people she saw in the courtyard. They were all men. She had seen women enough in the village, but here there seemed to be none. The person who took charge of her horse was pretty enough to have been a girl, but his voice was well and distinctly broken, and as he bowed she saw the sheen of the first beard on his cheek.

The stableboy was an easterner, like most of the others she saw. Except for the burly Frank at the outer gate and the German at the inner, she saw no other western face until she was brought into the great hall.

There as elsewhere was a kind of elegance that would have been unusual in the house of a great prince in France, but seemed ordinary enough to mark a simple baron's castle in Outremer. The floor was covered in carpets rather than rushes, and the walls were rich with hangings. The march of columns, the delicacy of pointed arches, marked an eastern builder; even in their strongholds, it seemed, the infidels had cultivated a certain grace.

There in a shaft of light from a high pierced window, two men sat over a chess-board.

One was a big fair man, a Frankish knight. The other was a—Saracen? A dark and bearded man in a silken robe, frowning and stroking the rich curls of that beard as he pondered the array of pieces on the board.

No, he was not a Saracen. A golden cross glinted on his breast beneath the beard. Nor was his face of quite the same quality as Saracen faces that she had seen. It was handsome enough, but blunter, with a long straight nose and large, very dark eyes.

By the eyes she knew him. She had seen just such eyes in the icons of eastern churches. When he spoke she was sure of it. His Frankish was excellent, but his accent was pure Byzantine Greek—and noble, too, as she had heard it in the court of Jerusalem.

"Your king is mine," he said to the Frank, who was of course her brother.

Bertrand did not look well. Someone was looking after him: he was clean, shaved, well dressed. But his cheeks were hollow, his eyes dark-circled. He glowered at the board, nor would he look up, even at the stir of Richildis' presence. "There is a way out of this," he muttered. "There must be."

He did not seem to be speaking entirely of the game. There was too much intensity in it.

His companion had turned to see what had the hangers-on in the hall staring and murmuring among themselves. His eyes were even more vivid, seen direct, than when they had been bent on the board. For all their resemblance to the black mute stare of an icon, they were alive and lively, with an air of wicked humor. She found herself smiling as she met them, bold as a well-brought-up woman should never be—but what was well brought up about a woman in dusty traveling clothes, with a bow and quiver slung behind her?

She must have looked frightful; should have let herself be taken away to a bath, food and drink, proper clothes. But she had been too eager to see her brother.

Now that she saw him, she knew that he must know. He did not see her at all. And this stranger, this Greek with his extraordinary beard and his even more extraordinary eyes, made her want to grin like a fool.

Probably she was a little off her head. Outremer could do that to a pilgrim, what with sun and heat and holiness. And she had killed an infidel yesterday, shot him dead. It was a just battle and therefore it was not murder, but her confessor would hear of it when she came again to Jerusalem.

The Greek rose as if he had just then remembered courtesy, and bowed in the fashion of his people. "Lady," he said. "On behalf of its lord, I welcome you to Beausoleil."

Beausoleil's lord started, and woke as from sleep. He blinked at Richildis. For a moment she doubted that he knew her.

Then he said, "You knew. *You* knew."

Richildis could pretend incomprehension, but she had never played that game well. "Yes, I knew about Helena. She made me swear to keep silent."

"She made you swear." Bertrand said the words dully. "Damn her. Damn you."

"You sound," she said, "precisely like a lover in a story."

He glared at her, his eyes red-rimmed, with the look of a man who has not slept in far too long. "What do you know of love and lovers?"

"Why, little," said Richildis. She gripped his shoulders and pulled at the heavy resistant weight of him. "Get up. Here, get up. Sir!" she called to the Greek. "Help me."

He seemed pleased to oblige. He was a big man for a Greek, though not as big as Bertrand; he was strong, and easy in his strength, heaving Bertrand to his feet. "There, my friend," he said. "Indulge a lady."

Bertrand swayed but held himself erect, with both of the others braced to stop him if he sank down again. "And how do you think I came to this?" he demanded. "For indulging a lady."

"For indulging yourself." Richildis tugged him forward. "First you eat. Then you sleep. Sir," she said to the Greek, "do you know his servants? If, of your courtesy . . ."

He grinned through his black beard and bowed with an edge of extravagance that he had not had before. "To so fair a lady," he said, "I can deny nothing."

Richildis laughed, not to mock him, but because he managed somehow, by the look in his eye and the turn of his head, to delight her. And he a Byzantine, too: one of that endlessly devious people. Who would have thought it?

He went to fetch Bertrand's servants. Richildis stayed with her brother, who once compelled to stand seemed disinclined to sit again. He might be ill, she thought, with a kind of fever born of too much brooding and too little sleep.

Anger could do it, too: the anger that is a deadly sin. Bertrand had always had a temper. It rose swift and endured long. Had it not brought him into Outremer, and kept him even from sending a message to his sister that he lived?

Now, it seemed, he had turned it against Helena.

"And that," she said, "is a great pity."

He turned his reddened eyes on her.

"So you followed Kutub," she said. "And you found Helena. And you're too furious to think."

"She lied to me," he said.

"She kept a secret from you," said Richildis. "That was not wisely done, but it's hardly worth this grand passion."

"You know nothing of it," Bertrand said, thick in his throat.

"I know that children sulk so when their toys are taken from them. What do you think it must have done to Helena for you to depart from her in anger? She's just had a baby. Your baby. Your son."

"I have no son," Bertrand said.

"Kutub says he bears a considerable resemblance to you," said Richildis. "Particularly when he howls for his dinner."

Bertrand was not to be distracted by absurdity. "She wanted me to know nothing. When was she going to tell me? When he was grown to manhood, when she could send him to demand a share of his inheritance? I'm surprised she didn't drown him like an unwanted puppy. Isn't that what harlots do?"

"No," said Richildis, tight and cold. "They rid themselves of such inconveniences long before they can be born." While he gaped at her, astonished that she should know such a thing, she said, "She wanted this child. She loves him as she loves you."

"Then why," Bertrand demanded, "did she refuse to tell me that he existed?"

Richildis drew a breath. There was a question that Helena had never answered, not to anyone's satisfaction. But Richildis tried as best she could. "She was afraid. She loves you, trusts you—but she was raised to put no trust in men. Men, she was told, love women only as long as nothing interferes with that love. And the worst interference of all is the natural consequence of what they do together. Never let it happen, her masters taught her. If it must happen, be rid of it soon. And if you cannot bear to do that—conceal it, bear it in secret, raise it away from the eyes of its father. No man loves a bastard, they said, over and over until she was like to weep. No man wants to be the father of one."

With each word she spoke, Bertrand stood a little straighter. His face hardened. His eyes began to burn. When she had done, he raised clenched fists and slashed them down, so sudden and so fierce that she flinched. "They *lied* to her!"

"And did you not prove it to her," said Richildis, "beyond any hope of doubt? You fled from her. You swore that this would be no child of yours."

"Not because she bore him! Because she hid him from me."

Richildis shook her head. "It makes no difference to her. Abandoned is abandoned; and she has a child without a father."

"How can I accept him now? After what I did and said?"

"Easily enough," Richildis shot back. "Swallow your pride, if you can. Go back to her. Beg her pardon. Take up your son and acknowledge him."

"No," said Bertrand.

Richildis sighed. "So," she said. "They didn't lie to her. They told her the exact truth."

Bertrand opened his mouth, but he did not speak. Servants had come with platters and bowls and jars, bearing a minor feast. The Byzantine followed them. He saw to it that they set a table on its trestles and spread it with a cloth, and laid upon it places and victuals for all three.

Richildis should not have been hungry, not in the middle of a quarrel, but it was long hours since she broke fast with Lady Elfleda. She was glad of fine white bread and good cheese, the haunch of a gazelle, fruits sweetened with honey, sweetmeats in the eastern fashion—more varied than she had often had in the palace in Jerusalem, and of better quality, too.

"My lord has an excellent cook," the Greek said as they sat to eat—Richildis hungrily, Bertrand with reluctance, the Greek with relish. "He came in fact with an excellent recommendation: he had been in the service of the Lady Helena."

Bertrand snarled at the name. "Eat," Richildis commanded him with iron will.

He bared his teeth, but he obeyed her.

She raised a brow at the Greek. "And you?" she inquired. "Are you also excellently recommended?"

He shrugged: wry, amused, a little embarrassed. "My name is Michael Bryennius," he said, "of the one and most excellent City, the heart of the Roman Empire, Constantinopolis. You, lady, I know by the name that your brother called you."

"Richildis," she said, nodding, "of La Forêt Sauvage in the County of Anjou."

They bowed to each other over the plates and bowls, with Bertrand between them glowering impartially at them both.

"You came here alone," her brother said to her, "without even a servant to attend you. Have you taken leave of your senses?"

"Rather less than you have," she said tartly. "I rode with a caravan from Jerusalem. Hospitallers guarded it. An English lady kept me company. It was all quite proper."

"Even that?" He jabbed his chin at the bow and quiver that she had laid on a bench by the wall.

She flushed slightly, but she kept her head up. "There was a raid. Circumstances compelled—"

"That you become an Amazon?" His lip curled. "Oh, I'm sure. What do I know of women, after all? What do I know of anything?"

"Oh, do stop that," Richildis said in impatience that she regretted as soon as it was done. But she could not undo it. He was wallowing as he had been wont to do when he was younger, indulging in great fits of thwarted temper.

And since he had eaten all that she thought he was going to, she beckoned to the servants who hovered just beyond the table's edge. "Now, sleep. I'll send someone with wine in a little while, with something in it that should help you forget your troubles."

"Nothing can do that," he said, as inevitable as summer's heat in Outremer.

"It can try," she said grimly. "Are you going? Or should I pursue you and strip you and trip you into bed?"

"I will go," he said. He did not say it kindly, but he said it.

When he was gone, escorted by servants, the hall seemed suddenly and vastly quiet.

There were people in it, curious faces, folk of the castle coming and going with evident if sometimes transparent purpose. But in the corner in which the table had been set, there were only the two of them, Richildis and Michael Bryennius. The Greek was still eating, partaking calmly of a bowl of something white and milkily sweet. He held it out to her. "Will you take a little? It's quite pleasant."

She moved to decline, shrugged, accepted a spoonful. It was indeed lovely, delicately flavored with almonds and honey and a hint of rosewater.

Over the spoon she met the bright dark eyes. "Is it a custom of your country," she asked, quite without thinking, "to stare at a woman who is a stranger?"

His eyes lowered with gratifying abruptness. Did he flush? It was difficult to tell. His cheeks were dark and his beard grew high on them.

She had never liked a heavily bearded man. She wondered always what it was he needed to hide: weak chin, ill-shaped mouth, bad teeth. Somehow with this man she did not think such things. Those lines of his face that she could see were well and cleanly drawn. His lips she had seen, and they were not ill shaped; his teeth were excellent. She could discern a firm chin under the black curls. He was a handsome man, but he did not carry himself as handsome men too often did, with too keen an awareness of their own beauty.

She liked him altogether too well for a stranger and a foreigner, a man whom she had never seen before this hour. She was not given to swift judgments or to sudden likings. It was almost alarming. As if, she thought, he had cast a spell on her.

Only fools contended that all Byzantines were sorcerers. If this man worked any magic on her, it was the simple one of fine dark eyes and charming manners. And, beyond that, something else. Something she could not put a name to, a sense of ease with him, comfort that had nothing to do with reason.

She did not believe in such things. No more could she escape it, or hope to deny it.

There was nowhere now that she could go. Her brother was sent to his bed by her own command, with the Byzantine's assistance. She did not know this castle or any of the people in it. As far as she had seen, it was entirely a house of men, as rigid in it as a monastery.

And that was strange, from all that she had heard of Outremer: how few the men were, how many the women. To be sure, most of those she saw seemed to be native to this country, but there were Franks enough, sergeants and men-at-arms, and one tall gaunt knight of middle years who appeared as she was wondering what to do, bowed and said, "My lady, a place will be prepared for you if you wish it."

She inclined her head in return. "I do wish it," she said, "and I thank you. Sir . . . ?"

"Amaury, my lady," he said. "I come from near Cluny in France."

"I know Cluny," Richildis said. "The monks there are wonderfully severe."

The gaunt knight betrayed the faintest sword-edge of a smile. "So they are, my lady."

And perhaps, she thought, he had reason to know it. She did not ask. One did not, in Outremer.

Another knight came in behind him. Younger, this one, and plainly born in this country: his fine olive features and his dark eyes would not have looked ill beneath the turban of a Saracen emir. He bowed lower than Messire Amaury had, with a notable store of grace. "Ah, lady! They spoke truth who said you were fair. May I wait on you? May I worship at your feet?"

Messire Amaury drew breath to remonstrate. "Daniel—" he began.

"Amaury," said the younger knight, but his mockery was gentle. "Yes, yes, I know. I'm too forward. My lord will be ashamed of me. But so fair a lady—how can I help myself?"

"Easily," said Amaury, "if you had any strength of will."

"But how can I?" Messire Daniel asked, "if I was never raised in Cluny?"

Richildis intervened before they could begin to quarrel. "Messires! Messires, if you will, I'm weary and I've traveled far. A bath would be welcome, and a bed, and time to rest."

That diverted them handily. Daniel was all limpid apologies, Amaury nigh rigid with embarrassment. "At once, lady," Amaury said; and Daniel cried in his sweet eastern-accented voice, "Lady! No sooner need you speak than it is done."

And all the while they vied to serve her, she was aware, subtly, in her bones, of Michael Bryennius' manifest amusement.

here were women in Beausoleil after all. The two who waited on her in the bath appeared to be Saracens, someone's sisters perhaps, or his wives: plump young creatures with doves' voices and intensely curious eyes. They spoke little Frankish. She spoke only a word or two of Arabic.

Somehow they managed. Their names were Leila and Yasmin. They waited on her very well, with the deft hands and keen perceptions of well-trained servants. She had not been so well looked after, for a fact, since she left her maids behind in La Forêt.

The place in which they bathed her must have been built before the Franks became lords of Outremer. It was like one of the old baths in Jerusalem, an eastern *hammam*, luxury above luxury in a stronghold two days' journey by caravan from Nablus. It was tiled in blue and green, water-colors, and it had a cistern that was kept filled, and a hearth and a cauldron for the heating of water, with an ingenious arrangement of pipes that directed water both hot and cool to the little tiled pool in which the bather could sit or lie. There was only the one room, to be sure, and not the several of a *hammam*, but even one was a wonder in such a place as this; and the water could be as hot or as cold as one liked.

Richildis had long since been seduced by the allure of the eastern bath. She basked in it for so long that she nearly fell asleep. Then Yasmin and Leila lifted her gently out and laid her on a soft couch and worked sweet oils into her skin.

Under their hands she did indeed slip into sleep. If she dreamed she did not remember. When she woke, the room that met her eyes was strange.

She was not disconcerted. Memory had followed her into sleep. She knew that she was in Beausoleil. She lay in a high carved bed fit for a princess in France, swathed in delicate netting as was the custom here, to keep out the stinging flies. The coverlets were silk, and the cushions mounded about her. The sheets were fine white fabric of Mosul.

She struggled out of them. The room in which the bed was set was not excessively large but very bright and airy for a room in a castle. It had a window which bore out her guess: that she was in a tower. She looked down from on high to the clustered houses of the village and the patchwork green of fields and orchards, and thence across bare brown hills to the flicker of brightness that must mark the banners of another castle.

So it was in Outremer: castles strung like jewels in a necklace, each in sight of the other, all the length and breadth of that beleaguered kingdom. In Jerusalem one was not so much aware of it: the city itself was so great, so very much the center of things, that one forgot that there was anything else in the kingdom.

Out here one could hardly avoid the truth. This was a land at war, shaped by war.

She was not dismayed. She was exhilarated. As she had been in the raid on the caravan, she felt intensely, keenly alive. She was like a lady's lapcat, kept in the bower, petted and fed and shut out from the world: one day she had slipped past some unwary pair of feet and escaped, and discovered that she was a wild creature, a hunter, a conqueror of the great world.

"Silliness," she said as she leaned on the windowframe, with a soft warm wind brushing her cheeks. It was not much past sunrise, when it was still almost cool. The light on the hills was mellow gold.

There must be a chapel in this castle. She should find it, discover if a priest said morning mass in it. But she was too lazy to leave the window, even when, by the magical art of servants, the two maids appeared to wait on her.

They had brought breakfast: a sop of bread in wine in the Frankish fashion, but sugared almonds too, and an orange. It was a delightful welcome to the morning. And when she had eaten every bit, there were clothes for her, not her own that had been so sadly soiled, but robes in the eastern fashion, and slippers, and a silken veil.

She thought briefly that these must have been castoffs of Helena's; but they were made for Frankish height and breadth. Perhaps they had been a man's: there was little enough distinction in eastern dress between a man and a woman, the same loose trousers and long shirt and silken overrobe. These were white, all but the robe, which was a quite beautiful shade of crimson.

So dressed, Richildis ventured with Leila and Yasmin for guides, out of the tower and into the hall of the castle.

Bertrand was not there, nor was either of his knights. There was a squire mending a shield, a curly-headed, wicked-eyed eastern-looking boy who ducked his head and applied himself conspicuously to his work. And there was the Byzantine, Michael Bryennius.

Morning light suited him well, even falling high and faint through the louvers of the hall. He had been breaking his fast, from the evidence in front of him. He read from a book as he sipped from a silver cup, murmuring too softly for her to understand. His brows were drawn together in concentration. He seemed oblivious even to the sudden rampant excitement as a pack of hounds burst baying through the hall.

They had escaped, it seemed, from the kennel and come in search of their master. It took a handful of servants and the squire and a pair of harried dog-boys to capture them and wrestle them all out again.

Richildis had seen one brindled bitch escape and bolt up the stair at the back of the hall. But if no one else had noticed, she did not see that she should draw attention to it. Her sympathies were rather more with the dog than with the men who bayed after her kennelmates. If the dog found Bertrand . . . well then. Bertrand had always been excessively lazy of a morning.

It was wonderfully quiet after the dogs' removal. Richildis advanced boldly to sit across the table from Michael Bryennius.

He greeted her with a smile, held out the winejar, lifted a brow in inquiry. She declined with a tilt of the head. She was listening intently, but no sound came from the realms above. No barking; no roar of human outrage. She was disappointed.

"She'll have climbed into bed with him and gone to sleep," Michael Bryennius said. He sighed a little himself. "Pity. It would have been wonderful to hear how he would like to be licked awake by a loving hound."

"You have no sense of propriety," she said.

"No more do you," said Michael Bryennius.

If anyone else had said such a thing—even, especially Bertrand—she would have bridled. But this man seemed able to say anything that he pleased, and she could only laugh.

"I've never met anyone like you before," she said—and that too she would not have said to anyone else.

He raised his brows. "Oh? You've never met a man of the City?"

"Several," she said. "None of them was like you. They were all . . ." She paused. She should not say it; but she could not stop herself. "They . . . slithered."

"Ah," he said without perceptible offense. "The subtle serpents of Byzantium."

She flushed. "They do earn their reputation."

"And I don't?"

"Are you insulted?"

He seemed to ponder that. "I think I should be. But from a Frank, such would hardly be flattery."

"You are probably as subtle as any other of your people," she said. "It is only . . ."

"Only?" he asked when she did not go on.

She raised both fists and struck them on the table. "Oh! You are mocking me."

"I could," he said after a careful moment, "understand that. If I tried desperately hard. If I were given the wisdom that God gives a woman."

She laughed. It hurt. She was hot and cold at once, blushing and going stark pale. "It is only that my whole heart persists in trusting you, and none of your race, in every tale that's ever told of them, is to be trusted."

Having said that, she waited for him to go all cold and serpent-soft, or else to burst out in sudden rage.

He did neither. He said slowly and rather wryly, "How odd. Because it's said of your race that you speak your mind invariably—but what that mind is, is as variable as the moon, and rather less predictable. If it serves the moment's purpose, your whole heart and soul is in it, and every grain of your belief. But a moment later it's all changed, and all your will is turned about. You swear great oaths, it's said, and break them with terrible ease. You have no faith; no heart-deep honor."

"I am not like that," she said, soft and still.

"No," he said. "You are not like that. You would keep your word, I think. Even to a courtesan; even against your own kin."

"It is true," said Richildis, "that to some an oath sworn to an infidel or to a sinner has no force to bind the soul. Unfortunately for me, I am not one of them."

"That is difficult," he said.

"As difficult as being an unsubtle Byzantine?"

He flinched a little, perhaps. Perhaps not. "I did," he said, "say somewhat that I should not. Once. More than once. Often enough to be invited to amuse myself in another country."

"And I," said Richildis, "swore that if my brother was alive, I would bring him back to his lands in Anjou, nor return except with him beside me."

"And he of course is not about to go back."

"You can hope for a change of emperor," Richildis said. "I have to hope for a change of heart—and that is not likely to happen soon."

"Oh," said Michael Bryennius, "it wasn't the emperor I offended. It was someone worse. It was one of the chamberlains. One placed very high. In a position from which only death will dislodge him—and he is neither old nor feeble. He'll not be poisoned; he's too clever. It's likely he'll outlive me."

"That is terrible," Richildis said.

"Isn't it?" Michael Bryennius said, lightly, as if it did not matter. "I can't even curse him to the thousandth generation. He's a eunuch: he'll have none."

"Then I should think him sufficiently cursed," Richildis said. "And maybe he'll die soon, or forget what you said to him."

"I don't think so," Michael Bryennius said. "That's what I said to him, you know. About his offspring. After I had called him a king of fools and upbraided him right royally for some bit of nonsense. I wish it had been something noble, something with grandeur in it: a battle lost, an embassy destroyed. It was nothing more earth-shaking than the order of seating for a court banquet. He would have set the ambassador from the courts of Baghdad beside a certain very eminent scholar of the Jews, as if everyone at court had not heard how cordially they detested one another. And then—and then, my lady, he proceeded to order that they be served a course of wild boar roasted in thyme and Hymettus honey."

Richildis could see that she was expected to be appalled. She could not precisely see why.

He saw. He was perceptive, that one. "Muslims," he said, "do not eat the flesh of the pig. No more do Jews. It was a perfect insult, calculated to offend them both, and to anger them both alike."

"It could have been intentional," Richildis said.

"I'm sure it was," said Michael Bryennius. "It was also monumentally stupid."

That, she could see. "And you were exiled for it? For having sense?"

"Sense is not greatly prized in an imperial court."

"Evidently not," Richildis said. "It can be in short supply even in the High Court of Jerusalem."

"Truly?" He seemed slightly taken aback; or perhaps that was mockery, again. "And here I had been thinking that I might be safe there."

"You're probably safer here," said Richildis. "My brother is only an idiot at occasional, if regular, intervals. He's not usually inclined to exile people for speaking the truth."

"Rather the opposite, in fact," Michael Bryennius observed, "from what I can tell."

"How long have you been here?"

He barely blinked at the shift. "I arrived in the winter. I'd been traveling through in a caravan; it paused here, and I found it congenial. Your brother invited me to linger."

"You've been here so long? And you never went to Jerusalem?"

Michael Bryennius shrugged. "It's a very old city. It can wait to see my face."

Her eyes narrowed. "You're afraid of it."

"I am not," he said. "I am . . . wary. I hear things of it. How it conquers the heart. How he who has seen Jerusalem is never the same thereafter."

"That's fear," Richildis said. "And it's Byzantine, isn't it? To avoid it. To stay away, not to face it and conquer it."

"Franks are great folk for headlong charges," he said. "We prefer to wait; to consider the field. To act in our own time and for our own purposes."

"To skulk and hide and slip away, and never fight unless you have no other choice."

"And isn't that plain good sense?"

"It's cowardly," she said.

"It's practical."

The word startled laughter out of her. Helena's word, condemning her to eternal dullness. And here was one who was duller yet; who was practical beyond the worst that Richildis could have conceived of.

She tried to explain, but it would not come out as it was meant to. It was as alien to him as the cause of his exile was to her. So small a thing, so insignificant to have begotten so much grief.

He stopped her before she could tangle herself beyond redemption. "We are different," he said, "and yet very much alike. Imagine. A lady of the Franks and a Byzantine courtier. Marvelous is the mind of God."

"I think," said Richildis, "that this may not be remarkably proper."

"It's amusing, certainly," he said. "I can't remember when I've been so entertained."

"What, not even in the imperial court?"

"The imperial court is dreadfully dull. Imagine," he said, "the longest, most stupefying rite you ever stood through in a basilica, forms so rigid in a language so old that even the priests barely understand it. Then imagine that it goes on from first dawn till long after the sun has set, relentlessly, round and round, without change or shift or easing of its severity. That is the order and the protocol of the emperor's court. He himself is powerless to change it. He's caught like a spider in a vast and ancient web, closed in, forbidden to move except as rite and custom decree."

"That is horrible," Richildis said. "Our kings complain of the rigors of courts, but none is as merciless as that."

"That is why it's Byzantium," said Michael Bryennius. "It's Rome, new Rome, Constantine's empire and his city in the east of the world. It's old and strong and knows no way but its own."

"I do not think," said Richildis, "that I want to understand it."

"I understood it too well," he said. "Once. Till I grew sick to death of it. I wanted to be out, free, away."

"And now you are."

"Now I am," he said, "if exile is freedom. Though, to be sure, it's not called exile. It's called a pilgrimage of indefinite duration. I may go back without penalty—but not yet. Not for a long while yet. Not, if my adversary has his way, ever."

He did not sound terribly cast down. Gloom, Richildis thought, was not his natural condition. A cheerful Byzantine—that was as unexpected as one who told the truth, and who practiced no deception.

He might of course be deceiving her so perfectly that she could detect no sign of it. But she did not think she was quite as innocent as that. She would know.

"Someday you'll go home again," she said.

"I do hope so," said Michael Bryennius.

ertrand came down late and
surly and escorted by the scapegrace dog. For all his scowl and his tardiness, he was
moving like the man she knew, not half creeping, half staggering as if he did not
care where his feet fell.

This morning he walked like a man and a knight, and he carried himself erect.
It might be outrage rather than pride, but it was to be preferred to the stoop of a
broken man.

He strode direct to Richildis where she sat with Michael Bryennius, stood over
her and demanded without greeting, "What brings you here?"

"You," she said.

He tossed his head slightly, as if at a stab of pain. "Oh, do tell! You wanted to
know if I knew about Helena. I do. Now you can go."

"What if I don't want to?"

"You have duties," he said, "and service. Or have you been dismissed?"

She drew herself up. "I asked to be let go for a while. Until," she said, "I hammered some sense into your head. Will you come to Jerusalem with me?"

"What? Not La Forêt?"

"Jerusalem first," she said. "Then La Forêt."

"No," said Bertrand.

She had expected nothing else. Nor was she minded to argue. Not just yet. She
sighed and shook her head. "You were always obstinate," she said. "I'm not going
to stay here until you give in and follow me. I'm not even going to insist that you
go back to Helena."

"Then what will you do? There's no caravan passing through. I can't spare my
knights just now; there are raiders on the roads."

"I know," she said. "I fought them. The Hospitallers have a message for you. If
you're minded to join forces, they say, they'll be well pleased."

He rubbed his jaw where the razor had nicked it, frowning, but not, for once,
with temper. "Yes, that would do. That would do very well."

"You are not," she said sternly, "to get yourself killed."

His eye flashed on her. His lip curled. "Why, do you think I'm as poor a fighter
as that?"

"I think you're at least as great a fool as that."

"I am not," he said with a nasty edge. "And you are not coming with me. Bow or no bow."

"Did I ask?"

"I anticipated you."

"Good, then," said Richildis. "I'll stay here in comfort, unless I hear you've been an idiot. Then I'll ride after you with fire and sword."

"You do that," Bertrand said.

Once Bertrand had made up his mind to do a thing, he did it. Within the hour he was gone, taking with him the younger of the knights and his squire and a company of men-at-arms mounted on the swift light horses of this country. He looked, as he rode out, properly alive again.

When he was gone, the castle seemed a darker and smaller place. Until Richildis turned in the gate and saw Michael Bryennius standing in the sun of the courtyard.

Odd how a dark man could so brighten a place. And he looking a little rueful, too. "I suppose I should have gone with them," he said.

"Did you want to?" she asked.

He shrugged. "I can fight. It's not something I choose to do as often as some. By which I suppose you reckon me a coward."

"Were you asked to go?"

"No," he said.

"Well then," said Richildis.

She doubted if he understood, but he did not speak of it. He stepped back gracefully to let her pass, and followed her into the castle.

For a few days that stretched into weeks and then into a month, Richildis lived in Beausoleil, as free as she had not been even when she was a child. The castle was run to its own satisfaction; she had no need and no desire to take command of it. There was no one who expected her service, nowhere to go that was not of her choosing. Bertrand stayed away, pursuing Bedouin raiders far from his lands and easing his troubles thereby.

She could do as she pleased. The village was Muslim as she had suspected, and had its own mosque and its own rites, but there was a chapel in the castle and a priest to serve it. Father Garamond was elderly and rather deaf but learned and pious. He had a library of books that should have been a wonder in this part of the world, books that he had copied himself or that he had traded for in a lifetime of traveling.

He was delighted to find in her a person who could read Latin and a few words of Greek, and who was minded to learn more of the latter. "Not that I can teach it as well as Messire Michael can," he said.

"But he has no books, Father," Richildis said, "and you, he says, have many."

"I do have a few," he conceded. Then with transparent eagerness he said, "Would you learn, then? So few have the will or the heart for it."

"I would learn, Father," Richildis said.

Therefore every morning after mass she came to Father Garamond's workroom and read Greek. More often than not Michael Bryennius was there, reading from books too lengthy or difficult for her fledgling knowledge. He would not intrude on Father Garamond's teaching, but he seemed more than pleased to answer when asked; and he was asked often.

When the lesson was done, when the priest had gone to other duties, Richildis could go where she pleased. She could take a book away to an eyrie in one of the towers, or have her mare saddled and ride in the fields about the castle with a man-at-arms for guard and escort, or sit at the chessboard with Messire Amaury. Or she could go down to the village, where she was greeted at first with suspicion but thereafter with welcome.

She did there as she had done at home: visited the women in their houses, brought salve for a child's sore eyes, nursed an old man who was ill of an ague. These people would not take bread from infidels, but oranges from the trees in the castle garden they were glad of; and she made a sacrifice of her gluttony for them.

It seemed that, whatever she did, Michael Bryennius was somewhere in evidence. It was not so small a castle as to fling together the people in it—for whole days at a time she never saw Messire Amaury who was steward in her brother's absence. But Michael Bryennius never seemed to be far from her.

She could not say that he haunted her. He always had a reason to be there, as when he read Greek in Father Garamond's workroom. Nor did she begrudge his presence. He was excellent company.

"He's courting you," Yasmin said. She and her sister had a little Frankish, and they were teaching Richildis a little Arabic. Their conversation would have sounded odd to unaccustomed ears, composed as it was of a mingling of both languages, but it made sense enough to Richildis.

"He likes you," said Leila as she combed Richildis' hair out of its nightly plaits and bound it up for the day. "You can see it in his eyes when he watches you, when he thinks that you can't see. He's in love with you."

Richildis flushed hotly, and why she should do that, God knew. "That is nonsense," she said. "He's bored here, and he doesn't know it. He finds me less tedious than the others. There's no more to it than that."

"Bored?" Yasmin could barely speak for giggling. "Why, lady! He's never known the meaning of the word."

"Certainly not," Leila said. "He dreams of you, I'm sure. He can't stop yearning after you."

"Foolishness," said Richildis, sharp with temper. "Here, stop chattering. I'm late for mass."

In fact she was early. Michael Bryennius did not come to mass in the mornings. The rite was Latin and he was Greek. He could not, as he had professed, accept the Credo as it was sung in the manner of Rome.

But when mass was over and she had gone to her lesson, he was there with his book, reading by the window. He was in fine looks this morning, hair and beard new-washed and still a little damp, falling in glossy curls. He was wearing the coat of his that she liked best, the one that was the precise color of the sky at evening. It was an exile's coat, starkly plain, and yet it suited him.

She had become much aware of how he looked; how he moved; how his hands turned the pages of his book, long fingers, finely made and yet strong. For all that he professed to shun battle, he had calluses that she recognized from a lifetime among men of war. Sword-calluses, calluses from the bow, set indelibly in the flesh as they could only be if he had been archer and swordsman from his childhood.

He could hunt, she knew. They had hunted gazelle in the hills more than once in company with men of the castle. He rode well, and he was a skillful archer. On one such hunt he brought down a fine big buck; and they had dined on it that night. She could still remember the flavor of the meat, pungent with herbs and garlic.

And yet here he sat as if he had never been more than a soft-bodied scholar, working his way through a volume of Aristotle. The sun found blue lights in his hair. He frowned a little as he read, reading in silence as people could do who learned in monasteries.

She shook herself hard. Her maids were idiots, full of foolish fancies. He was a handsome man; Richildis was the only woman of rank in the region. Of course they imagined a grand passion. Infidels were given to that. Bodily love was not for them the sin that it was for a Christian. A Muslim woman, she had heard, was required by her faith to marry and to give her husband children. There was no place in that world for the virgin martyr, no blessing in their religion for the man or woman who shunned the allure of the flesh.

She had been shocked when she first heard that. A faith that made no virtue of virginity, except as a gift that a bride brought to her husband—how dreadfully strange.

Michael Bryennius was a Christian, though he would not admit that the Holy Spirit proceeded from both the Father and the Son. He would not indulge a craving of the body, no more than Richildis herself would.

Not, she admitted to herself, that that was easy, if he saw her as she saw him now, bathed in sunlight, so engrossed in his book that he did not know how she stared. She dragged her eyes away, found her own book on the chest where she had left it, sat to wait for Father Garamond to finish in the sacristy. He was unwontedly slow this morning: his joints were paining him, she had seen it while he said the mass. Later, when she was done here, she would brew him a cup of willowbark tea.

The silence should have been comfortable, and for the most part it was. But her eyes kept sliding away from her simple exercises, the bit of Homer that had been an aid to the learning of Greek since long before the Lord Christ was born, and finding their way back to his face. Sullen Achilles had been a redheaded man—like Count Fulk, not like this dark Byzantine. So: who was he then? Wily Odysseus? Clever Diomedes? The beautiful and unfortunate Paris who loved another man's wife, stole her and ran away with her and destroyed his whole nation in war?

Richildis' husband was well and safely dead. Richildis had come to this country of her own will, abducted by no man, and with every intention of departing as soon as she had carried out her errand.

A widow, if she had no father or brothers to compel her, was free to make her own choices. Bertrand had presumed to make none for her. Though if she asked him to give her to this Byzantine—how outraged would he be?

Preposterous. She was alone in this place with no other woman of rank. Her mind was sliding toward the sins of the flesh—inevitably, as any good mother abbess could have told her.

She should leave, now, take her belongings and her mare and such escort as was willing, and go back to Jerusalem. She had service there, a princess to wait on, noblewomen to surround her and protect her from her own follies.

And yet she could not muster the will to rise, still less to do as she properly should.

Just so did one fall into sin, through this idleness of the spirit, this inability to move when one should move. Still, such a sweet sin. So harmless. Watching a man read beside a narrow sunlit window. He would never be closer to her than this, never threaten her bodily virtue. How could he? There was no way that a Byzantine exile could unite himself with a Frankish lady.

Oh, but there was a way. A very simple way. Two people together, alone in a room, with the sun to warm them. A kiss here, a touch of the hand there, and in a little while . . .

Her breath came thin and fast. She was going to faint. She rose abruptly, thrust her book aside, fled.

Richildis did the proper thing, the correct thing. She left Beausoleil and returned to the safety of Jerusalem. Messire Amaury sent her with a company of men-at-arms led by a middle-aged, deeply scarred, and thoroughly sensible sergeant. He also sent, for propriety's sake, the maids Leila and Yasmin. "Keep them, lady," he said. "Your brother would wish it, and their father is delighted. He has a houseful of daughters and insufficient men of means to marry them to."

"There will be no Muslim men of means in Jerusalem," Richildis pointed out.

Messire Amaury shrugged. "If there is a way, those ladies will find it. Go, take them. They'll serve you well. If when you come to the city you have no further need of them, send them back with Giraut and his company."

Richildis could hardly in courtesy refuse. She bowed to his will, which was also and patently the will of the two women.

They were delighted beyond belief, if never beyond words, to be given into her service; and better yet, to be sent to Jerusalem. They were adventurous spirits, though they had been born in the bodies of women of Islam.

"The imams would be shocked," Yasmin said, "but I'm glad we were born under the heel of the Frank. That way we get to look after you. You go places. You do things. You have adventures. No one has adventures in the harem, unless she has one with one of the master's friends—and he can be killed for it, and she can have her nose cut off."

"Or her head," Leila said with a shudder. "You who walk the world without a veil—you can't imagine how deadly dull it is within those walls."

"I grew up in a convent," Richildis said. "I can imagine."

All the way to Jerusalem, she wavered between taking the veil and turning her horse's head and galloping back and flinging herself into Michael Bryennius' arms.

Of course she did neither. In company with armed and mounted men, and with her brother and his allies hunting Bedouin far away from the road on which she traveled, she met no raiders. The road was quiet except for the stream of pilgrims and the occasional caravan. She traveled in safety, undelayed and unmolested, until she passed again within the walls of Jerusalem, bowed before her lady and returned to the life that had been made for her.

There in the city of peace she found what peace a woman could find who had believed herself free of the temptations of the body. Was she not a widow? Had she not welcomed the day that freed her from her wifely duties?

And yet in the nights, while she slept in her third of the bed with Dame Agnes snoring next to her, she remembered the glint of sun on blue-black hair, and the line of a hand as it turned the pages of a volume of Aristotle. But it was only memory. She prayed till it went away. However long that took. However difficult it might be.

hile Richildis dallied in Beausoleil, grief had come to the palace in Jerusalem.

It had begun in the winter while Melisende waited in growing impatience for her son to be born. Her sister Alys, who had never been kind to Melisende for that she was wedded to a man past his youth and ungifted with beauty, had become a widow all untimely. Her princely husband was as ambitious as he was beautiful—and he had taken it into his head to take back all the lands that his great Crusading father had ever won. Richildis had heard him vaunting at Melisende's wedding—and had heard older men, Fulk among them, observe with palpable irony that youth would, will they or nill they, have its say.

That winter Bohemond had decided to act on his ambitions. One of the Cilician princes was dead, and his heir with him, leaving a realm that had been conquered by the first Bohemond. This second Bohemond set out to seize the principality. Young as he was and full of himself, he took with him no great army; he thought to conquer by sheer force of princely presence.

But the old prince's brother had taken the throne, and though a Christian had made alliance with the infidels. These allies, Turks of one of the great tribes, fell on Bohemond's little army and destroyed it utterly. His head they took to their lord; and he in his turn sent it to the Caliph as a gift of honor.

The kingdom had mourned the young Prince of Antioch—even Melisende, who had no reason to love the thought of him. After all, as she said, he was male and he was good to look at, and he had not made too ill a prince. There had been rumblings of revenge, young hotheads set to gallop off and destroy the Turkish armies singlehanded.

But the king was too practical a man to indulge himself in fancies. As winter wore into spring, he kept the more passionate of his knights at bay, held them off with a promise of battle when battle was wisest—which, he let them think, would be soon.

Soon after Melisende delivered herself of her son, while Richildis rode to Beausoleil, news came that caused the king to call the council of his trusted advisors and to closet himself with them for the greater part of a day.

There was no grown heir to Antioch. Princess Alys had presented her husband with a single child, a daughter, whose name was Constance. When word of her husband's death came to her, Alys had taken the regency without troubling to consult the king.

Melisende, on hearing of it, had shaken her head. "Father won't like that," she said.

But the king had chosen to bide his time. He had no vassal great enough or strong enough to hold Antioch, let alone to master the princess who held the throne and the city. Fulk would have done admirably; but Fulk was hardly likely to give up the prospect of kingship in order to become a mere prince—even if the Church would have allowed him to put aside his wife in favor of her sister.

While Baldwin delayed and temporized and kept his knights in hand, Alys strengthened her rule in Antioch. She meant, it was said, to seize throne and coronet for herself; to shut her daughter in a convent or wed her to a man too lowly or too craven to claim the title that accompanied his bride. If that was true, then in her way she was as ambitious as her late and lamented husband.

The king, hearing this, set out at last for Antioch. When Richildis came to Jerusalem she heard the worst of it. Alys in her ambition, or in her folly as many reckoned it, had done a thing that no Frank, no child of Crusade, should ever have done. She had sent a rich gift to the Turk who ruled in Aleppo, to the greatest of the infidels that she or anyone knew of, and begged him to make her strong against the armies of her own father.

"That blazing idiot," Melisende was saying even as Richildis returned to her old place by the princess' side. Melisende was in her solar as usual with her women, returned to her old strong self again, and holding the reins of city and kingdom while her father contended with the most wayward of his daughters. She had risen as the messenger delivered his message, and sat down again with an effort that Richildis could easily see.

"That fool," she said with banked heat. "What in the world does she imagine the Turk will do, once he's been invited into Antioch? He'll seize it and her, and set at naught everything her so-beloved husband fought for."

"And, not incidentally, deprive this kingdom of one of its greatest demesnes." Richildis had not meant to speak, but she had got into the habit in Beausoleil of speaking her mind when and as she chose.

Melisende did not bid her be silent, though some of the other women lowered their brows and looked disapproving. "Clearly my dear sister never thought of that," Melisende said. "She never did think before she did whatever came into her head. She and her late husband were well matched."

Richildis could not disagree. And in time word came back to the city. Alys had shut the gates of Antioch against her father. He, having captured and hanged her envoy to the Turk, was in no very forgiving mood. Nor, it seemed, were some of her own servants. They opened their city's gates to Baldwin's commanders—to Fulk and to Joscelin of Edessa. Alys locked herself in a tower, in fear of her life. Only the promise that she would live, and her father's solemn oath thereon, persuaded her to come out.

He forgave her. What else could he do? She was his daughter, the child of his body. And, as Melisende observed, she was a pretty creature, with a talent for melting a man's heart. She could not have the princedom; she had lost all chance of that when she turned to the Turk against her king and father. But she had her life, and exile to her dower lands. Her daughter she gave up to the care of Count Joscelin, who would rule as regent until a husband could be found for her. Since the little princess was all of two years old, no one was in great haste to see to it.

Shame as much as grief accompanied every word that came down from Antioch. And when the king came back, he was—not a broken man, no. But not the hale and robust man that he had been. He who had always been so strong, who had seemed firmly established in the prime of his life, was suddenly grown old.

He had been no child when Pope Urban preached the first Crusade, and that was five-and-thirty years ago. Now all his youth was gone, both the truth and the semblance of it.

The three of his daughters who were untainted with exile gave him what solace they could. Melisende was never one for tender displays, but she could and did bear him company more often as summer faded into the hot and dusty autumn and thence into a grey winter. Baldwin, as greyly wintry as the sky that dripped cold rain without ceasing, fell ill of an ague such as beset many in court and city that winter. They recovered fully. He never entirely did.

It was as if a life of war and struggle and kingship had fallen on his head all at once, bowed and bent him till he was nigh to breaking. He was weary, perhaps weary unto death.

It was a long winter and a grey spring in the High Court of Jerusalem. Bertrand, having returned direct to Beausoleil after the settling of Antioch, appeared at last for Christmas Court, but went away again without visiting either Helena or his son.

Richildis made no move to compel him. Helena had left the convent in the summer and returned to her house, which after all was her own. She was living there quietly, her gates shut to the men who came courting—for rumor ran as rife as it ever did, and had her long and truly parted from her knightly lover. Of her son people were saying remarkably little. She would not suffer it; and Helena, when sufficiently determined, could stem even the tide of gossip in the court.

One rumor she could not suppress, or perhaps did not trouble to: that Bertrand had rejected the child because it was not his own. That, to anyone who had seen him, was patent nonsense. He was growing up big and fair, and his eyes as he grew out of infancy were the grey of winter rain. He spoke his first word early, with the same stubborn set of jaw as Richildis had seen often in Bertrand himself: "No," he said. He said it, for a while, in response to everything.

He did not say it to Richildis as often he did to everyone else. She was no lover of children, had never doted on babies as other women did. But this one she looked on with a fierce tenderness that surprised her, even frightened her a little. He was hers—her kin, her blood. No matter his bastardy; no matter that his father would not even look at him.

The name that his mother had given him was Olivier, but the Turks called him Arslan, Lion—a favorite name of theirs, Richildis gathered, for a strong manchild. Saints knew, enough of their chieftains bore some form of it.

This lion-cub answered to it more easily than to his given name. Arslan he was, then, and a strong young lion he was growing into.

• • •

On a fine afternoon in the octave of Easter, not long after Arslan had entered his second year, Richildis sat with Helena in the garden of Helena's house. The almond tree was in bloom, and the lemon tree was dizzy with fragrance. Arslan played with a pair of Helena's Turks. One was his mount, a fierce war-pony. The other was his ferociously snarling prey. They were hunting lions, it seemed, with much noise and exuberance.

"They grow so fast," Helena said. "I used to hear the women saying so, gossiping in the market, and I thought them impossibly foolish. But they told the truth. Babies become children become men in an eyeblink."

"So I had noticed," said Richildis. She had not meant to broach the subject so soon, but her heart bade her say then, "He'll be a child for yet a while—a long while, one would think. And yet, as swift as time flies . . . have you given any thought to what will become of him?"

Helena did not glance at Richildis, but kept her eyes on her son as he completed the triumphant slaying of yet another turbaned and villainous-looking lion. "I think of it constantly," she said. "He'll never make a Turk, though they insist that he would cut a splendid figure among the tribes: he's too big and fair. Yet what kind of Frank can he be? He has no father to speak for him."

"He has," said Richildis, "an aunt." And as Helena's eyes flicked toward her: "Mere female I may be, but I flatter myself that I have some little influence in the court of Jerusalem. Would you consider sending him into fosterage?"

Helena's breath hissed. Her face had gone still, a mask that betrayed itself by the fact of her putting it on. "I do consider it. My heart flinches. Give up my baby? Surrender him into the hands of strangers? And yet," she said, "he's not a daughter, to raise as I was raised, perhaps in that generation to snare a prince. A son becomes a boy and then a man. And this one will want what Frankish men have: war and feats of arms, and a knighthood if he can get it."

"Or an emirate."

Helena raised her brows. "What, send him to my cousins who are infidels? You would allow that?"

"No," said Richildis, "but you might."

"No," Helena said. "If he were less his father's child—if he had more of the eastern look and spirit . . . I might. But not this one. Though he answers to a Turkish name, he's as fine a young Frank as ever came swaggering out of Anjou."

"So he is," said Richildis. She looked at him and sighed a little. "I have been thinking," she said, "that there is a prince of the same age and much the same heart and breeding, who has neither milkbrother nor close companion. Would you be willing to let him go for an hour or two every day, to keep Prince Baldwin company?"

Helena's eyes widened. Richildis knew better than to think that she had not pondered just such a thing—but still, to have it offered to her who was a courtesan, whose child had no father who would accept the name . . . that affected her to a visible degree.

Richildis held her tongue. Helena was not one to be compelled to anything, even the furthering of her son's fortunes.

After a while Helena mused, "His father will see him. Will perhaps forbid—"

"Not likely," said Richildis, "until it's far too late. The knights never come to the nursery, nor are welcome there; nor care what goes on within. When the two of them come out together from among the women, when both are much older than they are now, no knight, though he be a baron of the High Court, will have either the power or the influence to divide the royal heir from his friend."

"You plot as cleverly as a Byzantine," Helena said.

Richildis did not know why she blushed. "I have a care for my kin," she said, "whether acknowledged or no."

"Your brother may not forgive you for this."

"He has so much to forgive me for," Richildis said with lightness that was not entirely feigned. "What's one thing more?"

Helena smiled herself, if somewhat faintly. "You can do this?"

Richildis nodded without speaking. She should, she thought, have spoken with Melisende first. If the princess did not agree . . .

The princess was not, that week, in the best of moods. Her husband had been vexing her again as she put it, pressing her to begin another child—this despite the fact that young Baldwin had yet to be ill for so much as a day, or to complain of anything but the pangs of teething. He was in all ways a robust child, sunny of disposition, with his mother's looks and his father's affability. He was growing up well and strong, but Fulk was a prudent man. The succession, in his mind, was best assured with more than a single heir.

Melisende had been simmering for some time. As had been her custom since well before Richildis knew her, she did the greater part of it in solitude, praying in her chapel or in one of the churches in the city. When prayer failed her however she turned to other consolations.

Richildis had become one of them. On days when duties and pleasures allowed, she would find her lady in this church or that, and walk with her back to the palace, often by circuitous routes. There were always guards. Sometimes they were mounted, sometimes afoot.

That day Richildis came back from Helena's in company with Kutub the Turk, whose presence deterred anyone from interfering with a woman of apparent means and rank walking alone. She had known that Melisende would be praying in the Church of the Holy Sepulcher today—proof enough of how far her husband had taxed her patience, that she stormed heaven from the very navel of the world.

Melisende was coming out as Richildis came in, with small escort and in little state. At sight of Richildis she dismissed her maids and all but a pair of guards. They did not approve, but neither did they dare to protest.

As they departed slowly down the Street of the Sepulcher, Melisende turned in another direction, toward the east of the city. The two guards and the Turk, who knew each other from other such expeditions, exchanged warily respectful nods and fell in, Kutub ahead, the Franks behind.

So protected, they walked where Melisende willed, which seemed to be nowhere in particular. The streets closed in about them, ancient and twisting, some covered over against the sun of summer, others open to the sky. Pilgrims and people of the city did not know their princess in a dark mantle and with small attendance, striding out as much as one could in crowds, walking with clear purpose, though that was simply to walk as far and as fast as she could.

By the Dome of the Rock she paused. Its gates were open, Templar knights on guard. She passed between them into the vast court and garden, wide as a city in France, with its golden dome to the east and the silver dome of the lesser mosque, the Father Mosque, to the west. There were people within, but surprisingly few: Templars most of them, and none minded to interfere with a pair of women and their guardsmen coming quietly to look on the holy place.

They passed into the shrine of the Rock, the raw undressed stone from which, the infidels believed, their Prophet had been taken up to heaven. All about that rough stone was wide and shimmering space under a dome like a dream of heaven. If one looked up too suddenly, one reeled, dizzy with splendor.

Richildis, who had learned that lesson the first time she came here, kept her eyes carefully on the pavement till she had followed Melisende into the high hall. It had been a mosque before the Crusade won it, built atop the ruins of Solomon's Temple. The Templars had taken it and made it their stronghold, set a cross atop the dome, stabled horses in its sacred spaces. They had made it a proper Christian and Frankish place, and yet she could not help a moment's regret, perhaps even a flush of anger, for the people who had made it so vast and so beautiful and so deeply holy.

That holiness lingered, though trampled under Templar feet. Pilgrims came here in hordes as to every other place in the city, had stolen slivers of the Rock till it must be barricaded against them, but on this day, by some whim of the world, there were no gawkers at the shrine.

Melisende genuflected to the altar that had been set atop the Rock. Richildis followed suit. The princess, having paid due tribute, began to walk slowly round the circle of the holy place. She could walk so for hours if need be, her restlessness concentrated in this soaring, singing space.

Richildis could wait, endure the long and circular pilgrimage, follow her lady back to the palace at last and wait the proper moment. Or she could say as they strode out together past walls of figured marble, pillars crowned with gold, arches marching in an endless round, holding up the golden vault: "I visited my nephew today."

Melisende shot her a glance. Richildis had not made a secret to her of Arslan's existence. It had seemed from the first like a thing that the princess should know.

"And how was he?" Melisende inquired.

"Very well," answered Richildis. "Growing. He looks like the prince."

"Most babies look alike," Melisende said rather indifferently. She did not dote on her child, no more now that he was walking than she had when he was an infant at the breast. When he learned to speak intelligently, she often said, she would begin to find him interesting. Until then she left him to his nurses.

"I had thought," Richildis said, "that since he and the prince are so close to the same age—"

Melisende shot her a glance that was not indifferent at all. "Do you expect me to foster your brother's bastard?"

Richildis paused, drew a breath to steady herself, remembered perhaps too late that her lady was far from the slowest-witted of women. With strangers and in court she kept her impatience at bay, let the rest of the world stumble its slow way to conclusions that she had reached at the first fall of a glance. But with Richildis she did not trouble with pretense.

"Lady," Richildis said, "he is my nephew and my blood kin. I had no thought of fosterage. I had considered that perhaps, for an hour every day, your son might welcome a playmate."

"Playmates become treasured friends," Melisende said. "Treasured friends become indispensable. How long were you going to wait before you spoke of fosterage? Till he was five years old? Six?"

"Seven, I had thought," Richildis said. "But until then, why should they not be allowed to play together?"

"Why?" Melisende curled her lip a little. "It might be pointed out that a courtesan's offspring is hardly proper company for the heir to the Kingdom of Jerusalem."

"It might also be pointed out," Richildis said swiftly, "that a courtesan's son will learn to be unimpeachably loyal to the prince whose indulgence gave him honor and standing in the world. He has no inheritance to protect, no family to contend for his allegiance—"

"And yet," said Melisende, "he is your nephew."

"Do you doubt my loyalty?"

Melisende paused, turned to face her. "No. But you are a woman. He will be a man. And what of his father?"

"His father is your faithful servant—so faithful that he's bound me here these three long years, and will not go back to Anjou to take the lands that are rightfully his. Would you not bind the son as you bound the father?"

"The father will not acknowledge the son."

"My brother is stubborn," Richildis said. "So am I. I think they would do well together, those two children."

"The bastard's presence will be a taunt to his father. How will my baron's loyalty endure that?"

"Rather well, I think," said Richildis. "And by the time the boy is old enough to be a page, my brother's mind may well have changed."

"Miracles do happen," Melisende conceded. She turned, began to walk again. "Bring the boy to me tomorrow. Let me see what he is—and his mother, too. Her I've never met. I want to know if she is as rumor makes her."

"She is a lady," Richildis said, "my lady. Whatever fools may say of her."

"Let me see," said Melisende. "Let me judge for myself."

*H*elena preserved her composure, even faced with a summons to the palace and the princess. She would not let Richildis come to fetch her; she came herself at the time appointed, with her Turks for escort and her son in the arms of one—for he had refused to be carried by any personage as lowly as his nurse. Richildis was suffered to meet her at the gate and lead her inward, guards and all.

They would have made a fine stir if they had gone through the public courts. But Melisende had commanded and Richildis agreed that it would be best to be circumspect. They went by quieter ways, round corners and down passages that were not so well frequented as most.

Melisende received her guests in one of the private chambers, one that abutted on her bedchamber. It had the virtue of quiet, and of being apart from the ladies' solar. It was dark and somewhat close, but the servants' ingenuity had brightened it with a bowl of roses, red and white, that had been set to catch the light from the one narrow window. Those and a bank of lamps that burned sweet oil made the room seem brighter and airier than it was.

She sat there with only one attendant, one of her sensible older ladies, who happened to be both discreet and rather deaf. Such care might not be necessary, but Richildis appreciated the taking of it. These matters could be delicate, this being a court, and courts being what they were.

Helena made obeisance with both grace and correctness, and the Turks behind her, the turbaned heads lowered, the proud knees bent. Only Arslan kept his head up. His eyes were wide, staring at the splendid stranger.

Melisende regarded him with interest. "He does look like Baldwin," she said to Richildis.

Richildis nodded. Helena, who had not been invited to rise or to sit, sat comfortably enough on her heels, with her Turks again mirroring her. Their calm was an eastern thing, the calm of people who expected nothing more of their rulers, and nothing less.

It might be that Melisende understood. Her lips quirked slightly. She beckoned to Helena. "Come, there is a chair. Sit."

Helena inclined her head and did as she was bidden. She had the manners of a great lady, but with more graciousness than many a noblewoman could claim.

Richildis watched Melisende study her, swift sweeping scrutiny that judged and decided all at once, without a word spoken.

"You are not what I expected," Melisende said.

"And what did you expect, your highness?" Helena asked her.

"Less than you are," Melisende answered.

"Younger? Prettier? More common?"

Melisende sat back in her chair. The sudden smile bloomed, startling Helena into widened eyes and a flash of expression: astonishment, pleasure, dawning amusement. "I do see," said Melisende, "what my lord Bertrand saw in you." She sobered suddenly, and that too was startling, like a cloud over the sun. "Do you honestly think that your child is worthy to be fostered with my son?"

"I think that it would serve him well, highness," Helena said.

"So it would. But how would it serve me?"

"I believe," said Helena, "that you have already had this argument with his lady aunt."

"So I have," said Melisende. "She tells me that I can expect a loyal friend for my son, one whose ambition will never exceed his grasp. Can the same be said of his mother?"

"This was not my doing," Helena said.

"Yet you allowed it."

"My lady Richildis is persuasive."

Melisende glanced at Richildis, a touch like the passing of a steel blade. "Convince me that I should believe you."

Richildis drew breath to protest, but Helena spoke before her. "I will do whatever I must for my son. If not here, then in Islam; if not in Islam, then in Byzantium. Somewhere in the world is a place for him."

"There is no better place than here," Richildis said with more heat than perhaps was strictly prudent. She rounded on Melisende. "Lady, do you mean to insult us? Look at the child! Does he look unworthy?"

"He looks like a child," Melisende said. "Too young to speak for himself, too small to contest whatever we choose for him. Suppose that I told you to give him up, to surrender him into my care and that of my son's nurses. Would you do it?"

"Not yet, highness," Helena said levelly. "Not till he's older."

Melisende paused. Was that approval in her glance? "The answer is no?"

"The answer is yes," said Helena. "Later. When he is older. When he is ready to leave my care."

"Then so be it," Melisende said. "Up, now. Come with me."

Swiftness of decision was a commander's virtue—or a king's. Melisende had chosen to exercise it now. She took Helena to the nursery, and Helena's son with her.

Young Baldwin had been driving his nurses to distraction with demands for this or that—some in words, some in wails that waxed in strength, the slower they were to gratify him. One such was just rising to a crescendo as the strangers entered his domain.

He stopped as abruptly as a child can who has been well and wisely distracted. Arslan in the arms of Ayyub the Turk captivated him wholly. Richildis wondered if he had ever seen a Turk before.

The nursery was scattered with toys and diversions such as would delight a child of Baldwin's age. Arslan caught sight of something—an army of wooden Saracens, Richildis saw, with wooden swords, mounted on painted horses. He yearned out of Ayyub's grip, slithered to the floor, made for the wooden army at a purposeful trot.

Baldwin, not yet so adept on his feet, squawked once, escaped his nurse's clutches, crawled rapidly after the interloper. When Baldwin reached him he had dropped to his rump and won for himself a fiercely mustachioed Saracen with a silver-painted sword, astride a dapple-grey horse of remarkable fire and ferocity.

Baldwin snatched the prize from Arslan's hands. Arslan, nothing deterred, snatched it back. Baldwin regarded him in flat incredulity. Never in his life had anyone contested his will.

They all braced for war. Only Arslan seemed unperturbed. He looked at the wooden Saracen, then at Baldwin. His eye shifted toward the rest of the army. There was one golden-turbaned emir on a foaming and head-tossing black stallion. He surrendered the soldier on the grey with as much grace as his mother had shown the princess, and took for himself the emir on the black.

Baldwin was perhaps not deceived by apparent generosity. And yet he accepted it, settling contentedly enough to play at soldiers with this stranger-child. He had won in short order most of the Saracen army, all but the emir, who remained in Arslan's possession.

"There," said Melisende of her son, "is a king."

"And there," said Helena of hers, "is a man who will serve a king well—and keep a portion for himself."

"But no more perhaps than he is due." Melisende turned away from the children. What they were now was of little interest to her, or what they did once they had proved that they could endure one another's company.

Richildis indulged herself in a moment's satisfaction. Now let Bertrand do what he would. Fatherless or no, Arslan would prosper.

King Baldwin was not so fortunate. As the warmth of spring passed into the heat of summer, Richildis' third in this country and, it seemed, far from her last, the king began perceptibly to fade. A day came when he could not leave his bed to go to his throne; when he lay breathing lightly in a flurry of vassals and servants, making no move to rise or to walk.

But he had voice left still, and strength of will to command that he be carried to the house of the Patriarch beside the Holy Sepulcher that he had fought for and won, and had defended for so long. No one presumed to contest him. They took him up as he bade them and carried him in procession from the palace.

It passed slowly, like a funeral cortege, in a wailing of eastern grief. Those whom the king's guard caught were silenced, but they could not silence a whole city, still less a kingdom that knew the truth beyond a doubt: that their king, their lord and commander, the Defender of the Holy Sepulcher, was dying.

Fulk had gone alone that summer on such campaigns as there were: small battles, defenses of the borders, shows of strength lest the infidel think the kingdom weak in the absence of its king. But when Baldwin was laid in the Patriarch's own bed under a golden canopy, banked and raised in cushions so that he could look out upon the dome of Holy Sepulcher, Fulk came back in haste to Jerusalem.

Melisende attended her father as often and as long as she could. Tenderness was not her way, no more now than ever, but he seemed to take comfort from her brisk manner and her refusal to permit an excess of weeping and mourning in his presence.

Still someone must attend the matters of the kingdom, and she as the heir was best fit to do it. On the day that Fulk returned to Jerusalem, she was holding audience in the king's stead. Her chair was set beside and below the throne, on which rested the crown and the scepter of the kingdom. Richildis had not seen her glance at them, nor marked that she was aware of them. And yet she must be. Her husband would take them up once Baldwin was dead, and hold them until their son, their Baldwin the younger, was grown to manhood.

Fulk came to her there, straight from the road by the look of him, though he must have paused to wash off the stains of travel: his armor was clean, his surcoat unblemished. He who had never been precipitous, put an end summarily to the rambling petition of a *rais* from a village in the hinterlands of Nablus, and dismissed the court.

Melisende had not moved since he burst into the hall. The day was searing hot without, but here it was cool, with a scent of stone and lamp-oil and the heavy, mingled perfumes of courtiers. He stood in front of her in a tang of blood and iron. She, sweet-scented with roses, met his glance with the ring of steel on steel. "My lord," she said, soft, almost gentle, "you are not yet king."

Fulk took no heed of the warning. "He's still alive, then?"

"Do you wish he were not?"

He shook his head, sharp as if with impatience. "We had a messenger on the road. Come quickly, he said. Come before the day is out. The king will take the vows of a monk and lay down the life of this world."

Melisende retained her composure, though Richildis, standing with the maids behind her, saw how her shoulders tightened. "Word has not come here," she said, "that his condition has changed. Go, sir; take off your armor. Make yourself fit to visit a king on his deathbed."

"We'll go together," Fulk said. "And the boy, too. That was the summons I was given."

"As you wish," said Melisende, but it was not capitulation. Richildis wondered if Fulk even understood what she was doing. By the laws of God and man, a woman must be obedient to her husband. But Melisende was royal born and far above this man who had been born a mere count. She would yield because it was expedient; never because she intended to make a habit of it.

They went in processional to the Patriarch's palace, count and princess together, and their son between them. The city watched them go. No one could fail to know what it meant that Count Fulk had returned to Jerusalem, or that he came with his wife and son to the king.

The sun was fierce even so close to its setting, the heat like a hammer on Richildis' skull. It seemed somehow in keeping with this solemn passage. They went in silence, without music or singing, and for once no one chattered among the ranks of attendants. As brilliant as the light was, still there was a darkness on them. Almost she could fancy that the Angel of Death walked with them, mute and strangely companionable.

In the Patriarch's residence was a hush beyond the stillness of a holy place. People moved softly, spoke seldom. The Patriarch himself sat by the king's bed in the high chamber with its curtains of silk and its bed of gold.

Baldwin did not lie in the high bed, at ease on its soft cushions. He had had a pallet spread beneath the window, no more than a mat on the floor. On that he lay in the plain black habit of a monk. His gaunt face, his wasted hands, were white against the dark rough wool. He had the air of one who has been shriven for the last time, an air of exhausted peace.

There was little left in him of the man that Richildis had first seen by the harbor of Acre, the robust knight, the proud king of a warrior kingdom. Only the spirit was left, a white heat of devotion, shining out of him as he lay dying.

He would die, if not tonight, then very soon. Not much of him was left to linger in the world. What there was of him started awake as his daughter and her husband entered, even raised him slightly, stretching out his hand.

Melisende took it in both of her own, kneeling in a billow of skirts, taking no heed for them. She did not weep or wail; that was not her way. When her two youngest sisters were brought in—not Alys, never Alys whose folly had broken him; that one was kept well away in her place of exile—they burst into tears. Melisende hissed at them. Hodierna subsided into audible sniffles. Yveta, less circumspect, required firm hushing from her nurse.

Baldwin sighed, a rattle in his chest. Melisende focused on him, sudden and complete. He beckoned. Fulk drew closer, took his hand that was still free. To Fulk's shoulder clung his son, young Baldwin staring, perhaps not recognizing this gaunt and hollow-eyed stranger-monk as his kingly grandfather.

"God," said Baldwin in a shadow of his old voice. "May God bless you all. My love upon you; my blessing. Be king, son-in-law. Be queen, my daughter. Rule well; and when your time comes, grandson, be such a king as the world will pause to marvel at."

They bowed before him. He slipped his hands free of theirs and rested each upon a lowered head, for a little while, before his strength failed him. "God keep you," he sighed. "God protect you. And his kingdom—his Jerusalem. Guard it well. Cherish it. For God—for Holy Sepulcher. God wills it.

"*Deus*," he said: "*Deus lo volt.*"

aldwin of Le Bourg, knight of the Cross, Count of Edessa, King of Jerusalem, Defender of the Holy Sepulcher, died gently in his sleep before dawn of the day after he had given his heirs his blessing. Fulk woke from what by all accounts was a troubled sleep, to find himself king.

Melisende had not slept. She had remained with her father throughout that long night. He died as she knelt beside him, with the Patriarch and half the priests of the city praying over him, and barons of the High Court standing guard about him. His soul slipped free as softly, as quietly, as the light of dawn that crept into the room.

He who had fought so hard his life long, died as a saint dies, in supernal peace. He was fortunate, Richildis thought. All his battles, his grief, the betrayal that had broken him—none of them mattered in the end, to him whose eyes were turned to a light beyond the simple light of sun or moon. He died in the city of peace, within sight of the Holy Sepulcher, as near to Calvary as he could come.

With news of his death came news of another. Joscelin of Edessa too was dead, wounded in battle against the infidel. There was no great lord left who had come in the first Crusade, no prince or nobleman who could claim that he had seen the taking of Jerusalem. All who remained were younger men—lesser, some muttered, but others begged to differ.

A world had passed, as it were. A new world rose in its place. Fulk's world; and Melisende's. As always with the passing of kings, grief and joy were inextricably mingled. It was embodied in the people's chant.

The king is dead. Long live the king!

They buried King Baldwin in the Church of the Holy Sepulcher, near the empty tomb which he had defended for so long. Then when the time of mourning was over, a score of days and one, three weeks altogether, Fulk and Melisende were crowned at the altar before which Baldwin had lain in state. There in front of the Holy Sepulcher they promised solemnly to defend it, to protect it from the infidel, to guard any and all Christian pilgrims who should come to the holy place.

There was no kingship like it in the world, and no joy greater than Fulk's as he stood side by side with his tall golden queen, head raised high under the weight of the crown. For this he had come to the far side of the world. For this he had taken to wife a sullen and often difficult child, a princess who had protested far more than once that she must accept a woman's lot, weakness and servitude and submission to a man.

She seemed submissive enough to his will in the coronation and in the festival that came after. She was stunned, Richildis knew. Grieving for her father, struggling to comprehend a world without him in it. For Fulk it was sorrow enough, for he had been Baldwin's friend. But for Melisende it was the loss of both father and king. And—yes, friend too, perhaps. They had been much alike, they two. Had she been born a man, there would have been no question that she was fit to be king.

While the kingdom accustomed itself to the ways of a new king, and Melisende kept her counsel, bided her time, said and did nothing to contest her husband's rule, Bertrand returned at last to Jerusalem. He could not in courtesy have refused to attend the coronation—to do so would have been too much like an objection to the name and presence of the new king.

And, he told himself, he was being a fool. There was more to the city than a single woman who had in her way betrayed him. He knew that she was there: he could hardly avoid it. Of her son he had heard nothing, except that he was alive and undisposed of.

Her son. His son. It had all roiled together in such confusion that he could not think of it without a twisting of sickness in his belly. Fighting did little to ease it. Hunting and killing infidels, laying siege to a city with a renegade princess in it, riding here and there on the track of another battle—in the end it left him impossibly weary.

Times were when he wondered what would happen if he let go. If he surrendered as the elder Baldwin had, gave in to the weariness, let it carry him off.

But he was too young. His body was too strong, too little inclined to succumb to a few hard rides and a wound or two. The wounds would not even oblige him by festering. They healed swift and they healed clean. He was up from the last one well before the coronation, with the summons waiting and no useful way to escape it.

Therefore he came to Jerusalem. He sat through the festivities. So much joy, so many bright banners—and only a month ago the whole city had been draped in black and in sorrow, awaiting the death of its king. One would think that everyone had forgotten.

He could try to forget one woman among so many. A courtesan, yet: a woman who lived by her body, who took her sustenance from the men she preyed upon. He was not lacking for women, even if he persisted in shunning both maidens and married ladies. That left women who could be bought and paid for, both courtesans and their lowlier sisters; and servants; and ladies whose widowhood set them free from the usual constraints. Ladies quite unlike his sister, whose virtue was notorious.

It seemed that they flocked to him, as if they knew that he was hunting. So must birds know when it is time to mate, or bees when the season comes for swarming.

Thus it happened that he lingered in Jerusalem past the festival and the first

High Court in which Fulk sat as king, dallying in his house, dangling about the court with others of like persuasion. They made excuse that the king would need such aid he could find, if certain rumblings became open conflict. Princess Alys, it was said, was not displeased that her father was dead; was stirring in Antioch with an eye toward forcing Fulk's hand as she had failed to force King Baldwin's.

Bertrand lingered, and idled with a lady or two, but never to much purpose. He was dallying so one afternoon in the palace garden among the fading roses. The lady who had lured him there—with him well aware of the ruse but too lazy to resist it—had slipped the veil from her crimped yellow curls and was letting her bodice slip from the swell of milk-white breasts. She hoped, it was clear, for a comparison between white roses and red, and white breasts with their nipples redder than nature alone could have managed.

He was bored enough, and yet aroused enough, to contemplate lifting her skirt and having his way with her; but as he set hand to the rumpled silk, he looked into a face that he barely knew, a little round kitten-face with sullen mouth and greedy eyes, and such revulsion rose in him that he dropped her unceremoniously in the path. He heard her gasp of startlement and then of outrage, but by the time it mounted to a screech, he was long gone.

He came up short against a wall—God's teeth; had he come as far as the spice-market, and with no memory of leaving the palace? He was all alone, no squire, no servant, no attendants. He had his sword at least, which he vaguely remembered keeping on because she said that it excited her. Everything excited that one—she was like a cat in heat.

Not like Helena. Not like Helena at all. Helena had come joyfully into his arms, but only when she chose, and never with the panting desperation of a woman who cannot get enough of it. It was a pleasure to her, but not an obsession. Sometimes he had thought that she was happier simply being with him, talking to him, sharing a cup of wine or a bit of gossip, than she had ever been in his embrace.

It came to him with the force of inevitability, that he was only a street or two away from her house. His feet had taken him this far but then faltered. And well they might. He did not want to go crawling back to her, to beg her forgiveness for the thing that she had done to him.

Yet as he gathered himself to turn away, to go back to the palace, he found himself walking onward.

Her house was the same as it had always been. And how long had it been? Two years? That long?

Surely not. Surely it had only been a few months.

And yet when he walked away from her in anger, Baldwin had been king, strong as if he would go on forever. Now Baldwin was dead and Fulk was king. The world had gone on as the world always did, while he seemed to stand still, fixed in his fit of temper.

Richildis would have pointed out that he had done just the same when he left La Forêt: sustained his folly for years out of count. As if she herself had not done precisely the same, staying in Outremer like a living reproach, persisting years past any reasonable expectation. "Lady Agnes is content," she said when he taxed her with it. "She has no objection to continuing as chatelaine until you deign to return."

Which he would never do—that was an oath, taken when he took ship across the sea. He had taken no such oath before Helena.

He halted in front of her gate, breathing harder than so brief a walk could warrant, with his heart hammering with something very like terror. Perhaps, he thought half in hope and half in dread—perhaps she did not live here any longer. Perhaps a stranger would greet him when he set hand to the gate, and not her ancient yet endlessly hale porter.

Vain hope; vain terror. Marid had altered not at all, not even so much as to regard Bertrand with surprise. Nor did he shut the gate in Bertrand's face. He bowed and let him in as always, as if it had not been years since last Bertrand stood in this place.

Marid had not changed, nor the house; but the way of Bertrand's welcome had. He could not walk in with ease, go questing for the mistress of the house. The servant who met him was a stranger, a woman of years and dignity, who greeted him courteously as she might any noble visitor, and left him in an anteroom until, as she put it, "My lady is disposed to see you."

Milady, it seemed, was not either quickly or eagerly disposed. He sat for as long as he could bear it; stood to go, paced instead, circling the room, finding nothing in it to engage his mind. It was an eastern room, ornate of carpet and hanging, rather bare of furnishings, with nothing in it but a chair or two, a table empty of either wine or sweets, and a bank of lamps, only a few of which were lit. He could remember when Helena had kept unwanted visitors waiting there with nothing to do until she took pity on them and had them summoned.

Such visitors, too. Tradesmen. Petitioners for alms or charity. Would-be guards or servants. Men young and old who fancied that she might wish to accept them as lovers—some bearing rich gifts, or offering payment well above the ordinary for a courtesan in this city.

He had no gift for her. Nothing but his inadequate self. She had other lovers now, of course she did. A courtesan must; or how was she to live?

Richildis said that Helena was rich and had no need of patrons. What did Richildis know? She was a woman of iron virtue, gently reared. She knew nothing of the ways of courtesans—even though she claimed one, rather preposterously, for a friend.

He stopped pacing, dropped to one of the chairs. It groaned under his weight. He thrust himself to his feet again. Saints and angels; what was he doing? He was not welcome here. This room, this neglect, made that abundantly clear.

"Out," he said aloud. "Away. Away from here."

And yet he could not make his feet carry him out. He was still standing so, flatfooted like the idiot he was, when a step sounded in the passage without. He turned toward the door, breath drawn to address whichever servant had come, to bid her conduct him to the gate.

It was no servant who opened the door and stood in it.

She had not changed. That was his first thought, a dull thought, uninspired, but true enough. A year could make a great difference in a woman of her age, no longer in the first bloom of youth though some distance yet from the fading of middle age. She had never told him how old she was, but he could guess at it, from things that she had said. Older than Richildis; younger than he. Five-and-twenty, let it be: perhaps a little more, perhaps a little less.

She did not look like a girlchild—not like the one he had left in the garden, who must have been all of one-and-twenty, but who contrived to look like a child of seventeen. This was a woman, wearing her years lightly but not invisibly. She was no more beautiful than she had ever been, and no less. Her face was carefully and skillfully painted, her gown well chosen to suit her figure. Now as always, she was the image of elegance.

He braced himself to be met as a stranger, to be dismissed with cold words and hard truth: that she had put him behind her.

He was not at all prepared for what she did do. She came to him and took his hands and looked up into his face—how far up, he had forgotten: she loomed rather larger in the spirit than in the flesh. She said simply, and as honestly as a child, "I'm glad you came back."

A whole spate of words surged up in him: hard words, cruel words. "I didn't come back. I don't want you. I only wanted to know—" What? Whether he had been supplanted?

He said none of it, and wisely enough, too. Still he could not keep from asking, "Is there anything to come back to?"

She shrugged slightly, a faint lifting of shoulders in her heavy silken gown. "I am here. There's no one else. I never wanted anyone who was not you."

"Even before you first saw me?"

Her eyes crinkled in the corners. "I knew that there was someone whom I wanted. Just not anyone that I knew then."

He could feel himself slipping into the warmth of her smile, melting as he always had, heart's slave to her as he had been from that first meeting. He pulled away sharply, suddenly. "No. This isn't reasonable. After the things I said, did—"

"Certainly not," she said with composure that he remembered too well. "I never pretended to be reasonable. I'm not going to be reasonable now. I'm going to give you leave to court me again. To win me back."

"But I'm already—" he began, and stopped.

She nodded as if in approval of his belated restraint. "I said I don't want anyone else. I may not want you, either. You have my permission to convince me otherwise."

"And if I don't want to?"

"Then you don't want to." He could not tell what she felt: regret, amusement, anger—he could not read her at all.

"And—the cause of contention?"

That had been difficult to say. She appeared to have no such difficulty in her reply. "You do not have the right, yet, to ask me that."

His throat was tight enough to hurt. He could still speak, though his voice was thin and strained. "I hear he's alive."

She inclined her head. He waited, but she did not say anything else.

That was her revenge, then. To refuse him the son whom he had refused. There was a bitter fairness in it.

And a truth even more bitter. She was not going to force the child on him. She was not even going to admit him to the boy's presence. If he would court her, he would court her alone, without encumbrance.

Was that not what he had wanted? Then why was he so troubled by it? He had refused to acknowledge a bastard. The bastard's mother should be exerting her every fraction of strength to force his hand. And she would not even tell him whether the boy thrived.

It was a deception. Of course it was.

Except that Helena did not do such things. Helena had not even told him that she was with child. She wanted nothing of him for the boy, not one thing.

Anger stirred, but it was feeble. It had lost itself somewhere, perhaps in the light of Helena's eyes. A courtesan who took no lovers but one, a mother who asked nothing of her child's father—how like her; how unlike any other woman that he knew.

He bowed to her, as deep as to a queen. When he straightened he had his voice in hand. "Lady," he said with admirable steadiness, "may I have your leave to court you?"

She paused so long that he came near to anger again, anger at late refusal. But then she said, "My lord, you may."

Any other pair of lovers—past or yet to be—would have fallen into each other's arms. But Helena did not move, and neither therefore did Bertrand. He ventured to take her hand and kiss it. That she allowed. But no more that day; no more than a few moments' conversation and a cup of watered wine, and after that he was in the street again, staring at the gate.

Passersby must have thought him mad: for as he stared, he began to smile, and then to grin, and then to laugh. Maybe he was mad. But what else could he do? That was Helena—that was Helena to the bone.

"God's feet," he said to the gate. "You drive me straight to distraction. But ah God—ah, lady, how I do love you."

While Bertrand courted Helena, a dance both delicate and prolonged, two very different dances played themselves out in the High Court of Jerusalem. The first was expected, a dance of war and treachery. The second was perhaps inevitable, but no one had looked for it.

The second followed upon the first, though it was not precisely born of it. In the first dance, after a winter of rising discontent, the Princess Alys rose up again in Antioch. This time she had the sense not to look to the infidels for allies. She turned instead toward good Frankish malcontents.

Joscelin of Edessa, who had died not long after King Baldwin, had been made regent of Antioch in the name of Alys' daughter Constance. The child, who was by all accounts as headstrong and haughty as her mother, was still so young as to be a simple counter in the game of princes. Alys insisted that a mother was best entitled to serve as regent for a minor heir. For ally she called on, of all people, Joscelin's son, named likewise Joscelin.

The father had been greatly feared in Edessa, if never greatly loved. The son was neither loved nor feared. He had risen to claim the principate, in full expectation of getting it; but the barons had refused. He was not fit, they declared, to be prince of a warrior state. For as his father lay dying of a terrible wound taken in battle against the infidel, word had come of yet another infidel attack. The elder Joscelin had bidden his son to go to the aid of the beleaguered fortress; and the son had refused. Edessa's army, he had said, was too small to be of use. Therefore the elder Joscelin had had himself set in a litter and borne in haste to the siege; and he had raised it, and won the battle, and died in the winning of it.

The younger Joscelin had an ill name in any event as an idler, a layabout, and a lover of luxury. His father had been no perfect saint; but whatever anyone said of Joscelin the elder, no one had doubted that he could both rule a realm and do battle to defend it. In the considered opinion of the barons of Edessa, the younger Joscelin was fit for neither.

He of course took issue with them. Edessa was his, he maintained, by right of blood and law. He looked to Alys, likewise deprived of her rightful place and title, and she to him; and when the winter was out, Fulk had a rather pretty war on his hands. It was much the same war that had broken Baldwin, but without the distress of an infidel alliance.

Fulk was a younger man by far than Baldwin had been, and he had not fought over half his life in the brutal land and climate of Outremer. He could have wished for time to strengthen his position in the kingdom; but such a gift was seldom given a new-crowned king. He gathered his forces and marched out of Jerusalem, riding north toward Antioch.

Melisende remained behind as she had always done when father or husband went away to war. Always before however she had been left with court and kingdom to manage. This time Fulk took with him what he could and left the rest to chancellors and seneschals. There was nothing for the queen to do, even to be chatelaine of the palace—that office was given to a seneschal.

Fulk's meaning was abundantly clear. Melisende's meek looks and quiet manners had not deceived him. He told her in this that she would continue to be as she pretended; that she was not to claim or to seek power. Her purpose was one and simple: to produce heirs to throne and kingdom.

And she had been refusing him her bed. Locked doors, doubled guards, and early retirement after banquet or festival had drawn the lines of battle. Fulk, rather than lay siege to her bedchamber, had withdrawn—only to leave her with nothing whatever to do, once he was gone, but sit in her bower and ply her needle and read such books as she found available to her. Most of those, as she discovered, were tractates on the wife's proper place in Christian marriage.

Thus began the second dance. Not all of the knights and nobles of the High Court had gone to Antioch with the king. The kingdom must be defended from enemies without as well as within. And there were some who, having left their demesnes in trustworthy hands, saw fit to visit the holy city and, perhaps incidentally, to relieve the queen of her boredom.

Chief among these was Hugh, Count of Jaffa. Hugh was an old friend of the queen, a companion from her childhood. They had grown up together, played together. Some whispered that their games had not all been innocent—though Richildis doubted that that was more than spite.

Now Hugh was a man grown, as Melisende was a woman. He had married a great heiress and widow whose sons were nigh as old as he; she doted on him by all accounts, but her sons loathed their stepfather. He was the kind of man whom women loved on sight but men too easily despised: handsome almost to prettiness, with his fair curls and his ready smile, tall and straight and slender, graceful as he bowed over a lady's hand.

With him as with Melisende, there was more than met the eye. His smile and his easy chatter concealed a shrewd enough mind, if little inclined to exert itself. Why should it? He had only to look charming, to be given whatever he wanted. He was rather dreadfully spoiled, and rather appealingly aware of it.

Hugh was in Jerusalem that summer while Melisende cooled her heels and Fulk waged war in Antioch. His countess had matters well in hand in Jaffa. He could linger, dally, keep the queen occupied. She unburdened herself to him—more than she ought, perhaps, but she had known him so long; she did not see that there was any need for propriety, no more than between brother and sister.

They looked well together, two tall fair handsome people, with the gleam on them that comes only with youth and wealth and pleasure in each other's company. Her anger at Fulk transmuted there, became something both gentler and more dangerous.

Richildis was no great master of intrigue, nor had she ever had much to do with the sins of princes. Yet even she could see what was happening. It was evident in a glance, in the touch of a hand. Perhaps they had not thought of such a thing before. Melisende had been a maiden when she married, with a maiden's innocence; and then she had been with child. Now she was neither.

As little as her husband pleased her, still he had shown her what it was that a man did with a woman. He had roused the flesh; and it was calling to this other, this youth who also had been mated with wise and practical age.

A brother could hold a sister's hand while they conversed, and it was simple courtesy that they should kiss at meeting or at parting. But for touch or kiss to linger . . . that was not brotherly, nor sisterly either. And there was much lingering that summer; many silences that might conceivably be guilt.

Melisende would not hear anyone who begged her to be more circumspect. "This is my friend," she said. "I will not cast him off for a mere and pernicious rumor."

No one quite dared to ask the question that was in every mind. Was it a rumor? Or was it truth?

Richildis did not know which it was. Some days she thought it must be false. Others, when she had seen the two of them riding side by side or sitting together in the solar, hand clasped in hand, fair head beside fair head, deep in intimate converse—she wondered not whether but how they managed it. He could hardly creep in at night; Richildis slept outside the queen's bedchamber, and she would have known. But during the days—who knew? They were not always in sight of every one of their attendants. On hunts in particular, they could escape in the confusion, meet and do as they pleased, and return with no one the wiser.

She rebuked herself for thinking such things of a Christian queen. Melisende was devout indeed—but she was a queen, and she was in too many ways as free of her thoughts as a man. Richildis had heard her declare with a strong sense of injury: "Yes, and a man can sire bastards as he pleases, and Mother Church forgives him. Let a woman look once at a man not her husband, and the whole world calls her a harlot. Is that just, I ask you? Is that fair at all?"

A man sired bastards. A woman conceived and bore them. Richildis saw nothing fair in that, and yet it was the way of the world. God had willed it so.

But Melisende would not listen to any such wisdom. She was headstrong always, but that summer she seemed possessed by a demon of perversity. Like a child whose father is overstrict, or a woman whose husband leaves her nothing to do in his absence but feed on her impatience, she devoted herself to defying him. What greater defiance could there be than cuckolding him, if only in rumor?

As the days crawled on and the heat mounted, they grew ever less discreet. A kiss on the cheek became a kiss on the lips. Simple companionship, riding side by side or sitting together at table, darkened and deepened into the queen riding pillion behind her knight, as she called him; or leaning against him as they sat together; or even sitting in his lap.

In fairness to Count Hugh, he was shyer than she, and less inclined to flaunt the passion that clearly possessed him. She was not besotted, Richildis did not think; simply angry at her husband, sulky and rebellious, and minded to punish him for his treatment of her. But Hugh was desperately, hopelessly, irretrievably in love.

It betrayed itself in everything he did. When they were apart he yearned for her.

When they were together he could not hold himself aloof. His eyes never left her; he even seemed to breathe as she breathed, each breath drawn together and drawn alike.

Richildis pitied him. But what could she do? Melisende's mind and ears were locked shut. Hugh was no more amenable to reason. When certain of the bolder courtiers ventured, gently, to remonstrate, he either laughed them off or bade them be silent. One he even threatened with his sword.

And there she was, one day when the sky was hammered brass, dawdling in front of the house that he kept in the city, trying to tell herself that he would listen to her—a mere woman, and one of the queen's women at that. Still she could not refuse to do it. Word had come that matters in Antioch were settled, more or less. Alys was returned to her exile. Her allies were quelled or at least persuaded to withdraw. Fulk was calling it a victory.

And he was coming home. Melisende, on hearing that, had dismissed her women and retreated to what some might perceive as a monstrous fit of the sulks. Richildis was more inclined to think that the queen was brooding on her wrongs and plotting revenge.

In any event she had shut out even the most trusted of her ladies, had locked herself alone in her chambers and refused to come out. Richildis had judged it useful then to come this far, to consider whether she might persuade Hugh to return to Jaffa before the king arrived in Jerusalem. Rumor was running at fever pitch. Not an hour ago she had heard a pair of courtiers giggling over an assignation that she knew had never happened: she had been with her lady at the time, safely and respectably established in the palace chapel, listening to the chaplain discourse with painful dullness on the doctrine of transubstantiation.

Why she thought she could or even should prevail on the noble Count of Jaffa when he barely knew her face, let alone her name, she did not precisely know. But she was in her way as desperate as Melisende, and—yes, nigh as bored. Her dreams of late were full of dark eyes and a white smile, and a soft rich voice with a Byzantine accent.

Richildis gathered her courage and approached the gate. The porter was an affable fellow, rather disconcertingly incurious as to why a woman should come to call on his lord with a lone veiled maid and a single borrowed guardsman, and he a Turk at that, none other than Helena's Kutub. She could not help but wonder how many women had done the same—and how virtuous any of them could have been.

In any event she was let in without a murmur, shown to a chamber and left there. There was wine on a table, and a bowl of sweets. She ignored both. No one had said anything to her of fetching the count—but neither had anyone declared that he was absent. She began to wonder if they had been expecting someone else, some other woman on a less hallowed errand. If that one did come, would they turn her away?

From what she had seen of it in courtyard and passage and chamber, this was a gracious house, well appointed, but rather carelessly kept up. The wine was decent, the sweets flyblown. The carpets were fine but thick with dust, and there were cobwebs in the corners. The pick of the servants, she suspected, were in Jaffa with Hugh's lady wife. Those whom he had here were easier in their manners, unconcerned with a little dust and a spider or two.

It occurred to her as she sat watching flies devour the sweets, that Bertrand's near-monastic retreat in Beausoleil could have been as frowsty as this. And yet like a monastery it had been scrupulously clean, meticulously ordered, looked after with both care and devotion. In this house no one seemed to care.

Yasmin the maid was sitting by the door, giggling over something with Kutub. Both of Richildis' infidels got on very well with Helena's Turks—too well, she sometimes thought. She suspected that one or both of them was doing more than giggle in doorways with one or more of the Turks; but when she had called her maids to account, they had assured her solemnly, "Oh, lady, we would never sell our virginity so cheap. Those are *slaves*. We're saving ourselves for an emir at least."

Possessed of an impulse that she lacked will to resist, she slipped past the maid and the guardsman into the passage that led to this room. It did not end here: it went on into a pallid light that might be the light of sun in a courtyard or an open space, shining obliquely through a window.

Investigation yielded a window indeed, heavily latticed, and a meeting of passages. One, from the angle of light, led somewhere that was under the sky. The other ascended a stair. Although the window illumined it well enough, lamps burned in niches all the way up. They must have been lit some time ago: they burned low and smoky, and one flickered, close to going out.

She followed the line of the lamps, not thinking of what she was doing, simply doing it. The lamps led her to another story, a corridor of closed doors, another stair. That one ended in a door that hung slightly ajar, with light streaming through. She opened it a little more, slipped round it, stood dazzled and streaming-eyed in full sunlight.

Slowly the painful brightness eased. She blinked away tears. She stood, as she had suspected, on the roof of the house. A high parapet rimmed it, and a garden grew in a corner of it, trees in pots, flowers, a bank of crimson roses. The neglect that vexed the rest of the house did not make itself known here. Someone loved this garden and tended it, trained the roses over the parapet and up into a sort of bower, trimmed away the dead blooms and cherished the living ones, and made them beautiful in this unexpected place.

Under the bower of roses, on a soft green bed that was, perhaps, a cloak, two bodies lay twined. There was no mistaking that fall of wheat-fair hair, all loosed as it was, streaming over white shoulders.

Neither of them was naked, or particularly immodest. He was fully clothed. Her gown had slipped low, and her shift with it, baring her shoulders, but the rest of her was covered well enough. Their embrace, so passionate at first glance, on closer scrutiny seemed almost chaste.

Melisende lay with her head back, eyes closed, face perfectly and utterly blank. She might have been asleep or in a trance, or somewhere very far away.

Richildis made herself a shadow, a breath, a whisper of wind. They seemed oblivious—but one never knew.

After a while Hugh raised his head from where it had lain on Melisende's breast. "Oh, lady," he said. "Lady, I love you with all my heart."

Melisende's eyes did not open. No part of her moved, except her lips as she responded. "Yes," she said. Only that. And no more expression in it than in her face.

He rose over her, looking down on her. "It's not the same for you, is it? Men love you. You love none of them."

"I am fond of you," she said. "I like you much better than the king."

"Why? Because I'm prettier?"

She slid from beneath him. He lay on his side and stared at her. Next, thought Richildis, he would beg her to forget what he had said. But she spoke first, without perceptible anger. "You are prettier. And you talk to me as if I were something more than a child."

"He is," said Hugh, "a very good lover. They say."

Nothing else that he had said had sparked her temper. This did. She bridled. "Who says? Who would know such a thing?"

Perhaps he flushed. It was difficult to tell. "People. Courtiers. He knows how to please a woman. He can please her very greatly."

"What is pleasing about getting children?"

He was not astonished to hear that. Richildis, who was—not that Melisende had said it but that she had said it to this man who by all appearances was her lover—began to understand a little.

"Lady," he said, "you will never let me show you. These kisses—these . . . other things—they are only prelude. If you would only let—"

"I do not want another child," she said with iron will. "None of you men can comprehend that. *You* are not forced to endure both the inconvenience and the pain."

"Do you say this to torment me?" he demanded.

"I say this because it is true. I like you very much. I reckon you my friend. You warm me as he never could."

"And yet he loves you, too," said Hugh, "and you love neither of us."

"I like you," she said. "I don't like him. I never shall."

"Liking is not enough," Hugh said, "to be worth what everyone is saying of us."

She looked levelly into his face. "Are you ashamed? Afraid? Then go. Take yourself off to your doting countess. I'll be no worse off than I was before."

"You would be bored to insanity," he said.

"I will find somewhat to do."

"What? Foment a rebellion? Seize the throne?"

"Don't tempt me," she said.

"You shouldn't," said Hugh. And when she did not reply: "You wouldn't."

"Sometimes," she said, "I dream of it. It wasn't a husband my father wanted for me, you know. It was a keeper. A man to chain and kennel me, to prevent me from declaring the truth: that I am as fit to rule as any man."

"Your sister has done just that," Hugh said—dangerously, Richildis thought.

Nor was she far off the mark. Melisende sat up. Her back was rigid. "My sister is an idiot. She needed simply to come to Jerusalem, speak sweetly to my father, convince him to give her the regency. And when he died, she should have done the same with my husband. She should also," said Melisende, "have taught her people to love her. She never thought of that, either."

"The people love you," Hugh said, as if pondering it.

Melisende smiled. "They do," she said. "Indeed they do."

Richildis remembered herself with a start. She backed farther into the shelter of the stair. What she had seen and heard cast little shame on her lady; but it would not serve her well to be found here. She retreated as softly as she could, gathered her servants, withdrew to the palace. And prayed God and His Mother that the rumormongers would tire of this sport before Fulk came back—for there was nothing that she could do, not with either of them, or God would have seen fit to bring her to Hugh's house while its master was safely alone.

Which was cowardice, and she knew it. But she could not work herself up again to the proper pitch of righteousness. Not after what she had seen and heard.

ulk returned to Jerusalem in no wondrous good mood. He had won a victory, or so it was proclaimed, but it was a feeble thing. He had done no better than King Baldwin had, and perhaps worse. It had gained him little, and lost him a summer's campaigning against the infidel.

And as he came back to the Holy City, he found it and every town and city near it simmering with rumors of his queen and the Count of Jaffa. The mildest of them had them cuckolding him in the queen's own chambers. The more outrageous were enough to drive a husband mad, if only with laughter.

From one rebellious sister he had come home to another. She greeted him with her own defiance: a sweet face and a queenly graciousness, riding out to him on the road beyond the city's walls, and bowing before him, and welcoming him to Jerusalem. As if, he was heard to mutter, it were her city and not his; as if she were queen and he a pilgrim stranger.

She did not abate her insolence when they had come to the palace. At the feast of welcome she conducted herself as host, as if he were guest and not lord returned to his domain. He was given the place of honor, accorded every reverence—but again, as if he were a newcomer.

Kings learned to master their expressions. Fulk, but lately come to kingship, was not yet entirely master of his face. The anger mounted on it, the more sweetly his wife spoke to him, the more elaborately she made him welcome. She would have done better to have neglected him and bidden him make his own way home.

His temper did not escape him that night—or if it did, it did so where no one saw or heard. He was not made welcome in his wife's chamber, nor did he seek it. He went to his own rather earlier than usual, locked himself within, shut out all but his squire and a loyal bodyservant, neither of whom was given to gossip.

The storm broke on the third day after he came back to Jerusalem. Nothing in particular had happened. Hugh was not much in evidence, but neither was he shunning the court.

The festival of the king's return was not yet entirely past. That day the court had indulged in another feast, and thereafter in dancing. The hall was vivid with silks and brocades and fine fabrics of Mosul, gleaming in the light of lamps and candles, hundreds of them as it seemed, and pale shafts of sun through high windows. Musicians strove mightily against a tide of voices and laughter.

The court had its feuds and factions. No court was ever without one—even, it sometimes seemed to Bertrand, the court of heaven. Else why had Lucifer fallen, and there been war among the angels?

Dangerous thoughts. He kept them scrupulously to himself, though he might venture a hint of them to Helena later, when he went to call on her.

That too was dangerous to think of. It made him impatient. Dancing had always struck him as a waste of good muscle; why trouble with it when one could be out on a horse, wielding a lance or a sword? The games of courts bored him silly.

They bored Melisende, too, he thought. When she was given a share in ruling the kingdom, she was in her element. Those factions, those feuds and alliances, were life and breath to her. Many of them were born and fed here, but she was given no part in them, nor asked to do anything but sit on a gilded throne and wear a crown that was a lesser image of the king's.

Melisende had occupied that throne and worn that smaller crown for nigh on a year. Bertrand could see how thin her patience had grown, how sullenly she sat, drumming her fingers on the arms of her throne. He was not surprised when she rose, twitched her skirts into order, stepped down into the swirl and sway of the court.

The latest round of factions had centered itself around Hugh of Jaffa. His allies bore him close company or else gathered in knots here and there, eyeing with distinct disfavor both those who were his enemies and those who were simply not his friends. It was a difficult thing to walk the edges of all the camps, particularly since Melisende's friends had of necessity aligned themselves with Hugh's. And that, Bertrand could not help but notice, set them against the king's party.

Melisende joining in the dance, swirling from circle to circle, laughing and tossing her head till the crown nigh flew from its binding of plaits, spun tension close to open warfare. Inevitably she made her way to the place where Hugh stood with the closest of his friends. That was as far from the king as the hall would allow, lit by a circle of lamps. Hugh's hair gleamed hardly less gold than the circlet that bound it.

He was a handsome man, even pretty, but people seldom called him beautiful. Hand in hand with Melisende, pacing the measures of a stately dance, he seemed more beautiful than real. They were splendid together, tall and fair, she in white and gold, he in deep and luminous blue.

Bertrand, caught in an eddy that fetched him up at the far end of the hall, came nearly face to face with Fulk. The king had been conversing, affably it seemed, with a number of the older barons and a Templar or two. But his eyes were not on them. They watched the queen. As her head bent toward Hugh's, the king's expression turned stony.

One of the Templars said something—Bertrand heard a snatch of it, something about affairs in Damascus. Fulk nodded. He had been nodding for some time, evidently without hearing a word that anyone said. Certainly he could not be agreeing that the infidels should be amassing an army in Damascus to march against Jerusalem.

Melisende must know that her husband was watching: her gaiety grew ever more pronounced. She began again what had first given rise to rumor: she clung close.

She twined her fingers in Hugh's. She whispered in his ear, and laughed as he laughed, and in all ways conducted herself with unqueenly shamelessness.

Fulk at last could bear it no longer. He left his barons discoursing gravely of high matters, simply and abruptly strode away from them.

Fulk at his best was no more than a small man, but in anger he bulked as large as any great bull of a Norman. He clove the press as if it had not been there, leaving the startled and the indignant in his wake. He swept down on Hugh of Jaffa, sundered him from the woman who pressed so close, flung him aside as if he had been a man of straw and seized the queen in a grip that won a gasp from her. In silence that by now was absolute, he said in a still cold voice, "Madam, you will come with me."

Any other woman, or man either, would have been taken aback. But Melisende was extraordinarily strong of will. She set her heels and made herself a stone. He could shift her, but not with either ease or grace. Equally softly, equally coldly, she said, "Surely, my lord, there is nothing to say that cannot be said here."

"Do you think so?" he asked her. "Do you truly think so?"

Her eyes glittered. She was exhilarated, Bertrand realized. What was it with these women, that they were most alive when they were most contrary?

She smiled a smile that was meant to drive Fulk mad: white, wild, and no shame in it at all. "I do think," she said, "that you may be jealous. Are you, my lord? Are you jealous of simple friendship?"

"Simple!" And there Fulk lost the battle: his temper escaped its bounds. "Friendship! Aye, madam: in Provence, so they call it. But in Anjou we have another name for it. We call it rutting. Like the bull and the cow, madam. Like the stallion and his mare."

"And unlike the king and his queen?" Melisende lifted her chin. "Yes, you are jealous. And with no reason. If you are not admitted to my bed, who could beget legitimate heirs, then I assure you, neither is any other man."

"That thing need not only be done in a bed."

"Why? Can you enlighten me? Is it true what I've heard, that you did it with a camp-follower once on the back of a destrier, and won a wager by it? What was it you won? A fine Damascus dagger, wasn't it?"

Fulk's face was crimson. It clashed remarkably with his hair. "My deeds or misdeeds are not at issue here."

"Oh, are they not? And why may a man tup a whore on horseback, but a woman may not even kiss her friend on the cheek?"

"It was not his cheek I saw you kiss."

"No: it was his hand. Men kiss my hand with tedious regularity. May not I, just once, return the favor?"

The court by now had gathered round as if at a duel. The weapons were keen-edged words, the combatants fierce, giving no quarter. Fulk clearly no longer cared who heard this quarrel. Melisende clearly had never cared at all.

Their factions had divided as they had, gathering to one side or to the other. No one spoke or laughed. Even the musicians had given up their playing and drifted toward the edges. There would be tales told of this, songs sung. Bertrand could only hope that they would not be dirges.

"Remember," Melisende said, "what right you have to rule in this place. Without me there is none. I have given you the heir that we both require. If I may not enjoy my friendships, if I must keep myself like a nun in a cloister—if I must have nothing to do with myself but stare at these walls—I swear to you, my lord; I swear to you by the Virgin's white breasts: I shall go mad."

"So that is it," Fulk said. "You are angry with me. You defy me with this puppy, because you think that you should be king."

"I think that I should be queen!"

"As your sister is princess in Antioch?"

Melisende drew herself to her full height. She was sufficiently taller than he that, when she made the effort, she towered over him. "Perhaps," she said, "she has the right of it. Maybe it is wisest to take and not to ask—particularly if one is a woman."

"Not," he said, "while I am king."

"So," said Melisende with curl of the lip. "I take my amusements where I can find them."

"You will find them amply supplied in your own chambers," he said, "guarded by women of my choosing. Or would you prefer a convent?"

"I would prefer," she said, "to be what I was born to be."

"You were born a woman. You will be whatever your lord ordains that you shall be."

"I was crowned queen," she said. "I shall not forget it. Nor will my people. Be wise, my lord, and be warned. If I am not given somewhat useful to do, then I will do whatever I please."

Fulk stood as stiff as she, but he could never stand as tall. He seemed to have become aware, all at once, of where he was and what he did there. "Madam," he said, "you will make yourself useful. Apart from yonder puppy."

"I will choose my friends as it suits me."

"Your friends," he said. "Not your sweet friends."

"Of the latter I have none," she said, soft and tight.

"We shall see," he said, "madam."

Fulk had capitulated. That was not perhaps what he had meant; it was clear to eyes that could see, that he meant to withdraw and rejoin the battle later on less public ground. But the court judged him by what it knew of itself. Fulk had retreated before his wife. She was the victor of the field.

He left it. She remained, defiant in her gaiety, calling the musicians to play an estampie, whirling off into it with a peal of sudden laughter.

If that had been all that that gathering came to, it would have been talked of for days after. But as it came about, it was talked of for years, might indeed not be forgotten.

The king's quarrel with his queen had unleashed tempers in more quarters than one. Enemy confronted enemy, and not a few wives, emboldened by Melisende's example, declared war against their husbands.

In the midst of them, loud and raw, a voice lifted itself out of the hum and babble. "Hugh! Hugh de Le Puiset!"

Hugh of Jaffa was just about to succumb to Melisende's persuasion and join in a dance with her. He turned at the sound of his birthname, no little irritated.

It was not the king who challenged him. Walter Garnier, his own stepson, thrust through the press to plant a solid body in front of him.

Walter was little younger than his stepfather, and notoriously displeased with that fact. He also, the gossips opined, was jealous of Hugh's beauty. He was a thickset, dark-faced young man, so heavily bearded that his chin was never smooth of stubble. Women found him attractive; he was strong and he was famously virile, and his dark looks were not by any means unpleasant.

But tall fair Hugh with his open face and his ready humor was calculated by his existence to eat at the liver of a man like Walter Garnier. They had been at odds since Hugh married Walter's mother. Now it seemed Walter had seen in Hugh a fair target.

"Hugh!" he bellowed as if across a battlefield, although they were face to face. "Tell the truth here before the king and all his nobles. Tell them what you were really doing when you were thought to be kissing in corners with her majesty the queen. Tell them! It was the king's life you coveted—not his wife. You were plotting to kill the king."

Hugh laughed, a light and incongruous sound. "Oh, come! Walter, don't be a fool. Why in the world would I want to do that?"

"Because," said Walter Garnier, "if he were dead, you would have his wife. And with his wife comes the kingdom."

"That is nonsense," Hugh said. His lightness had shrunk and faded. No one was smiling at the absurdity. Too many faces were scowling, and not at Walter Garnier.

Hugh looked about. He must have seen no friendship anywhere near. Melisende had gone when the estampie was ended, departed with her victory and with the flock of her ladies. His own allies had drawn away from him. Whether they did it in revulsion or to avoid being suspected of the same collusion, it was difficult to tell. Perhaps both.

Walter's wild words had not roused Hugh's anger, but this silence, these stares, the desertion of those he had thought his friends—those struck fire in him. Then he did not seem so pretty, or so much the ornament of courts. "You, sir, are an arrant liar."

Walter Garnier ripped the glove from his hand and flung it at Hugh's feet. "Prove it. Prove it to me, king-killer. Meet me in the lists, the two of us alone, and show the world the truth."

Hugh snatched up the glove, slapped it against his palm, seemed inclined to fling it in Walter's face; but he flung it down at the other man's feet. "Let the world know that I am no traitor. Let us meet in the field of battle."

"So be it," said Walter Garnier in evident satisfaction.

ews of the duel between Walter
Garnier and Hugh of Jaffa ran from end to end of the kingdom. Stepson did not
often challenge stepfather to combat, still less in the king's name.

Melisende was remarkably quiet, remarkably subdued—if one did not know her.
Hugh had left Jerusalem for Jaffa the morning after the challenge, to prepare himself
for the fight. Walter had done the same, withdrawing to his domain of Caesarea.

One or two people wondered why there could not be a less bloody trial than
mortal combat, with proper inquiries and searches into the truth of the accusation.
But they were reckoned eccentric if not actually craven. Men were fallible, but God
was the one and only just judge. He would prove guilt or innocence where knights
were best served, in the lists before the assembled nobility of Outremer.

Any that had not come for Fulk's return, came now for this. Duels were not
uncommon, but a duel over a plot to slay the king—that was a novelty.

The king himself could not fail to be pleased by what had happened. He was no
friend of Hugh, nor were his friends Hugh's friends. Their factions, that had been
clear enough before he returned from Antioch, were now drawn full and distinct.

And best of all perhaps, his quarrel with Melisende had been eclipsed altogether
by the quarrel of the two lords. Any shame that he had had was faded or forgotten.
No one ventured to suggest that the queen had joined with Hugh in the supposed
conspiracy.

"There is no conspiracy!"

Melisende should have been content, like a cat in cream. She had appeared that
morning in the court of justice, and had not been either dismissed or ignored. She
had taken the seat that was her own from when her father was alive, and spoken
as she had then, as one with a right to speak; and no one had silenced her. It was
a test, a venture of the rights and powers that Fulk would allow her, and it had
proved her victory. She was to be allowed a place in the ruling of the kingdom.

She had tested again thereafter in receiving a company of noble pilgrims from
Germany and Hungary. Again she was not forbidden to sit beside the king, nor
advised to hold her tongue when she spoke with authority.

Yes: she should have been content. Yet here she was, having eaten and drunk little of the daymeal, pacing restlessly in her bower. She had sent her ladies away, all but Richildis and Lady Agatha. "There is no conspiracy to kill the king," Melisende said. "If there had been, don't you think I would have known? Hugh couldn't tell a convincing lie if it would save his soul, or keep a secret for God's own mercy. He's charming, intelligent, and completely without guile. Walter Garnier, however . . ." She paused, scowling; reached the wall; spun on her heel in a swirl of skirts and stalked back down the room. "You know, I do wonder. If he had conspired himself, and cast the blame on Hugh . . ."

"They say he's a strong fighter," Richildis said. "If he has something to hide, he may think to conceal it completely in Hugh's grave."

Melisende rounded on her. "There will be no killing!"

Her vehemence took Richildis aback. Lady Agatha, less evidently startled, said placidly, "I suppose you think you can stop them."

"I can try," Melisende said. "Agatha, fetch my writing things. I have a message to send."

Melisende's box of pens and inks and parchment lay near to Agatha's hand. She set it on the table where Melisende could come to it.

Melisende could write well and quickly, in a good if not elegant hand. She murmured the words as she wrote them, perhaps for the others' benefit.

" 'To Hugh de Le Puiset, Count of Jaffa, knight of the queen,' " she wrote, " 'from his queen, greetings. My lord, this fight is folly. What can you gain from it? How can you prove either guilt or innocence, when it is known that your adversary travels hither and yon in search of battles to fight and duels to win, whereas you only fight if necessity commands it? If there is a conspiracy, it is that of your stepson and his allies against you. They whisper in the king's ear. They teach him to hate you for no reason but that you are my friend. They convince him that you were better dead or maimed than alive to mock their follies.' "

She paused, flexed cramped fingers, considered what she had written. Her frown deepened. After a moment she bent again to the page. " 'My lord, that man will kill you if he can. He is known for his hard hand and his disregard of the rules of combat. If you insist on facing him, face him at least with all your defenses raised, and pray to God that He will protect you from that murderous hate.' "

She laid down her pen and sighed. "They always hated him, the twins, Eustace and Walter. Now Eustace is dead—I wonder, does Walter blame Hugh for his brother's succumbing ignobly to a fever? Is that why he accuses Hugh so furiously, to punish him for an imagined crime? Or simply for marrying their mother, and for being so much beloved?"

"What if there is a conspiracy?" Richildis inquired.

"How can there be?" Melisende demanded. "What profit would he take from it? What that fool said—that he would seize me and make himself king—nonsense! Hugh is charming, intelligent, and quite without ambition. He wants what he has, and no more."

"I think he wants you," Richildis said.

"I know he wants me. Me, not my crown or my lineage. He'll never have me. He knows that, too." Melisende flung up her hands in disgust. "God! Men are such fools."

She bent to write again. " 'My lord, be wise. Shun this foolish battle. Armor yourself in your innocence, but let it protect you far away from Walter Garnier. He means you nothing but ill. He will kill you—right and justice be damned.' "

She stopped. Her fist clenched. She rent the parchment in two. "No! He's a man. He'll never listen. It has to be face to face. But how can I—" Her face lit. "Yes. Yes, I will do that."

That, as Richildis saw, was to begin another letter, this to Countess Emma of Jaffa: widow of Eustace Garnier, mother of Walter and the younger Eustace, Hugh's lady wife who by all accounts doted on her beautiful young husband. It said a great deal for either Melisende's arrogance or her innocence, Richildis thought, that Melisende could write to this woman whom rumor made a rival. Her letter was brisk, frank, and civil, and said much of what her discarded letter to Hugh had said. " 'My lady,' " she wrote, " 'guard your husband. Prevent him from this folly. You know what your son is, and what my lord Hugh is. Hugh cannot defeat Walter in combat. If he loses this fight, he is maimed or he dies. My lady, if your wisdom can see a way—keep him from the fight. Together by God's grace the two of us will salvage his honor. A sudden sickness, perhaps—a fall on the hunt—my lady, whatever will help him, for your husband's sake, do it.' "

She signed the letter with her titles, sealed it with the ring that she wore, that had been her mother's; summoned a messenger and sent it on its way to Jaffa—all so swiftly that no one could have remonstrated.

But once the messenger was gone, Melisende sagged as if the iron had gone out of her. "Pray God I did the right thing," she said. "Pray with all your hearts."

Richildis was already doing so. She added a prayer for Hugh. Poor pretty creature—if he had plotted anything, she doubted that it was of his conceiving. Melisende had the right of it. He did not covet power; not beyond what was his already. He wanted Melisende; but that was a wanting of the body, not of the mind.

She could find it in herself to pity him. So simple a creature should have been left alone, and not vexed with venomous stepsons or fancied conspiracies.

The day of the duel dawned clear and warm. By noon the heat would be powerfully fierce—unusual so late in the summer, so close to the gate of winter. The lists were ready, the field laid out on sacred ground, within the walls of the Temple of Solomon. People crowded there, as many as could pass the gates, the poor and the pilgrims as well as the great ones of the High Court. For the king and his high lords a dais had been set up, and for the barons ranks of benches. The rest must stand or sit as they could, and see what they might.

Banners hung limp in the still air of the morning. Their devices were hidden, but by their colors one could tell: white and gold for the Kingdom of Jerusalem, white and scarlet for the Templars, white and black for the knights of the Hospital. On either end of the field a tent had been set up, a pavilion in the eastern style, white and gold for Jaffa, blood-scarlet for Caesarea.

Already before the dawn people had gathered at the field. By full light only the king and his highest lords, the queen and her ladies, had yet to arrive.

Bertrand had elected to stand well down the field among the common people. The view was better there than from a bench among his fellow barons, and he could move about as it pleased him. His squire Gabriel was wandering now, gossiping as he so loved to do. The boy wore Frankish dress and spoke the *langue d'oeil* without accent, but in heart as in face he was utterly an easterner.

In time he wandered back, slid into Bertrand's shadow, made himself as much at ease there as a favorite hound. "Walter's here," he said, "sitting down yonder in the tent that's as red as his wrath, sharpening his sword and breakfasting on iron nails. The other tent is empty. Hugh's not there. Nor, they say, is he even in Jerusalem."

Bertrand's brows went up. "What, he's not in the palace, with the queen to hold his helm, and the queen's ladies to serve as his squires?"

"Not at all," said Gabriel, "they say. They say he never left Jaffa. He may be ill, it's said. Maybe a fever. Maybe an attack of the galloping terrors."

"That doesn't sound like Hugh," Bertrand said. "I'll wager he's here, he just hasn't troubled to announce his presence."

Gabriel shook his head. "No, the people who are talking know people who know the guards on the city gates. Nobody with Hugh's face has come from Jaffa. He's not in the city."

"I don't believe it," Bertrand said. "Hugh has more looks than sense, but he's never been a coward."

"Maybe not Hugh," Gabriel said, "but you know women. The queen adores him, everybody knows that. So does his lady wife. What would you wager that one or both of them leashed and muzzled him and kept him from coming to be cut in collops by Black Walter?"

That, unfortunately, Bertrand could almost credit. But Hugh must be here. A man did not accept a challenge to his life and honor, not such a challenge as this, and then fail to appear. Not simply because he had his honor to think of—because any man of wit or sense would know that if he ran away, he proved not only that he was a coward but that he was indeed guilty of the charge against him. Treason—conspiracy to murder the king.

Hugh was a bit of an idiot, but not as much as this. Surely not.

And yet as the sun rose higher, no one came to the white-and-gold pavilion. The king did not appear, nor the queen. Did they know something? Had they had word that had not yet found its way into the common talk of the city?

The crowd began to grow restive. Walter Garnier came out of the scarlet tent in his mail and surcoat, with a squire behind him carrying the cumbersome weight of the helm. His warhorse waited, big stolid black creature, hipshot and evidently asleep. No such horse stood by the other pavilion, no squire or attendant. It stood all alone and empty.

Even from half the distance of the field, Bertrand could see how red Walter's face had grown. It was nigh as scarlet as the tent.

By now the whole field was buzzing with the rumor that Bertrand had heard. Hugh was not here. Hugh was still in Jaffa. Hugh was coward, traitor, false to his oath and his king.

The mood was growing ugly. Walter flung himself onto his horse's back, woke it with a raking of spurs, drove it lumbering down the field.

What he would do, whether simply to gallop about or even to mount an attack of pure frustrated fury on some baron whose expression did not please him, no one was about to discover. For as he reached the middle of the field, trumpets rang. A man on a light Arab horse rode swiftly in. He wore the garb of a king's herald, and his voice was both stronger and clearer than the trumpets. "My lords, my ladies, people of Jerusalem, and my lord of Caesarea! The king bids you disperse. There is no battle. Hugh, Count of Jaffa, has failed to come as he agreed. By his absence he confesses his guilt. God gives you justice, my lord of Caesarea. The victory is yours."

Walter Garnier hauled his mount to a halt. Bertrand could see no joy in that dark face—none at all. Indignation, yes. Thwarted rage. Bloodlust that must now be unfulfilled.

It would not matter to such a man that he had won. He wanted blood. He wanted his enemy dead, and at his own hand; not alive and dishonored in his mother's arms, and no doubt at her instigation.

Some sons, Bertrand reflected rather distantly, were less than sane about their mothers. Add jealousy of golden beauty, and one had pure poison.

Walter spoke not a word, not to the herald, not to anyone on or near that field. He gathered his squire and his attendants, swept up everything that was his, and left the city in a storm of wrath.

He did not even wait for the king's council to declare Hugh guilty by default—as it must. Even Hugh's allies could not defend him in his absence. If there had ever been a plot, it was broken. If there had not, then Hugh was a fool and his countess was worse, to think that they could escape the consequences of what could only be read as cowardice.

If Hugh had had any respect in the kingdom, he lost it through that, and through what he did thereafter. When word of the declaration of guilt came to him in Jaffa, he fled in what must have been a madness of fear—fled to Ascalon that was held by infidels from Egypt. He cast himself on their mercy.

And they brought him back to Jaffa, a lord of the Crusade riding as an ally of the infidels. He kept his head up, said those who had seen him, and rode as if he had no shame, side by side with turbaned Saracens. Yet that must have been bravado, or purest idiocy. Certainly he was not in command of his new friends. They deposited him in the city with a kind of casual contempt, and rode out to harry the plain of Sharon.

It had to be idiocy. Melisende insisted on it. She had demanded to ride with the king to take back Jaffa, but Fulk, who had been denying her nothing, stood firm against her. He gave her instead the rule of the city and the kingdom.

She could not fail to understand the meaning of that. He would allow her to prove herself trustworthy. He would not punish her for the folly of her friend.

"It was idiocy," she said more than once. "His own, his wife's—what matter? Why in the world could they not have contrived a simple bout of fever, or a plain accident and a broken bone? Why did they sit like fools at a synod, helpless to act—and then leap to Ascalon? Ascalon, of all places! Why not Antioch? Why not Constantinople? Why not, for God's sweet sake, somewhere safely Christian?"

"Ascalon was closer," Richildis said, but Melisende was in no mood to hear the obvious. She could never abide fools, and Hugh had been fool and worse than fool. To evade the fight—that was common sense. But to run from it to the infidel made no sense at all. It only proved to those who sought such proof, that he was indeed a traitor.

The infidels to whom he had fled were infidels from Egypt, and that was an ill thing; but the infidels of Damascus, seeing the kingdom in disarray, had begun to move themselves, casting an eye on the Frankish castles along the borders of their own lands. Fulk must settle this trouble swiftly, or see his kingdom beset from within and without.

It was as if all the fears and resentments of a kingdom perpetually at war, the shock of a king's death and the accession of a king from across the sea, the rebellion in Antioch and the endless shifting sands of alliances among the infidels, had foregathered to vex the beginning of this second year of Fulk's kingship. Hugh's folly, and Melisende's folly born of Fulk's ill judgment, heaped blunder on blunder until the whole of it tottered and bade fair to fall.

But Fulk could learn through suffering, and had. He was no more at ease with his queen than he had ever been. The shadow of their quarrel lay over them, never entirely banished. Yet there was no open war, and no skirmishes in the dark; simply a deepening of the constraint that was always between them.

She ruled while he led his army to Jaffa. She contemplated following him in defiance of his command, but she had too much sense. She remained in Jerusalem, and waited with tight-reined impatience for every messenger, and did what she did best, which was to hold in her hands the keys of the kingdom.

Jaffa fell without bloodshed—for which the people sang thanksgiving in every church of the Holy City. The infidels were gone as quickly as they had come. They had seen no profit in their alliance, had simply taken their horses and their booty and ridden back to Ascalon. Hugh had no choice but to bow before the king.

Fulk startled him—startled everyone. Fulk showed him mercy. "I see," he was heard to say, "that we are condemned to the same fate: to love a woman whose heart will never be given to any man."

What Hugh said, no one reported. Nothing, perhaps. He submitted. That was reckoned to be enough.

His sentence was light. Three years of exile, after which he might return to his domains. Too little, many reckoned—Walter Garnier not the least of them. But the king's will was firm. Hugh alive was little enough threat to the royal life; and from exile he would be hard put to set the kingdom in greater jeopardy than he already had. Hugh dead made far too convenient a martyr. His friends would remember him then, and remember their dislike of the king.

It was much too practical a sentence for the wilder youths of the king's court. Their complaints met deaf ears. "It is done," the king said. "So let it be ended."

or one last time before he sailed away to Italy, Hugh was permitted to come to Jerusalem. A pilgrim could not be denied the Holy City, nor a penitent its consolations.

But his pilgrimage was not to the Holy Sepulcher, nor did he make his confession to a priest of that great shrine. On a day of wind and rain, just at the middle mark between Christmas and Twelfth Night, he presented himself at the palace and asked humbly for audience with the queen.

She could have refused him. She should have, most felt; but he had been her friend. She valued friendship, who dealt it out so rarely. She suffered him to come to her.

She received him in the hall of audience. It was late in the day, most of the petitioners gone in search of warmth. The roof here was solid enough, and no rain seeped in; but the high walls and lofty arches that were so cool in summer's heat, were clammily cold now.

The queen had a brazier nearby her throne, and a stone warmed in a fire and wrapped in wool to warm her hands. Her mantle was lined with fur, soft grey vair that shimmered against the gold of her hair. Her beauty would never be ethereal—she was too robust, her face too strong in its bones—but the mingling of rainlight and lamplight laid a shimmer on her that seemed to dazzle the man who entered and bowed at her feet.

Hugh of Jaffa had not prospered in his adventurings. He was thinner, his cheeks pale as if with sickness or captivity. He had been kept close in Jaffa, Richildis had heard, by both his infidel allies and the king's justice. His prettiness was faded, his beauty grown wan.

Melisende, secure in her strength, might have pitied him. It was difficult to tell. "Sir," she said. She did not invite him to rise, did not offer him her hand to kiss.

He lifted his head. "Lady? Is that all the greeting you have for me?"

"Sir," said Melisende again, "you were bold to come here."

"I wanted," he said, "I needed—I had to say goodbye."

"Goodbye? So easy a word, for all that you have done and have still to do?"

He flushed. "I did ill. I atone for it."

"And why did you do it?"

He of all people was accustomed to her directness. He must have expected it: he flinched slightly but held his ground. "I was afraid."

"Because what was said was true? Did you conspire to slay the king?"

"No!" His vehemence might be pretense, but Richildis thought not. "I was ill —a griping in my belly. And when I went to demand my horse and armor, all doors were locked and the servants deaf. I was trapped. And then my lady—my wife—" His face twisted. "May God damn her. My lady wife informed me that I was to go nowhere unless it were back to bed to recover from an illness that, unless I am altogether a fool, she had the making of."

Melisende sat back. It might have been relief; it might have been annoyance. "You were ill? Then why did you let the world think you hung back from cowardice?"

"I was bound to the privy for a day and a night. By the time I came out, it was all decided. Any protests I uttered, any truth I told, would be mocked as lies."

He was angry, but not so angry that he could not speak clearly. Melisende either did not see it or did not care. "You are weak."

"My stomach is weak—and my wife's potions were strong."

"Do you think that she should have been exiled in your place?"

He met her hard dark stare. "She did not lose her wits and run to Ascalon."

"So calmly you speak of it," said Melisende.

"Some devil was in me," he said. "It drove me in a madness of anger and fear. I had been betrayed—I was reckoned a traitor—then let it be true; let them have cause to judge me as it seemed to please them. I would be what their judgment made me."

"You did not judge well," Melisende said.

"That is what the king said," said Hugh. "He chose to be merciful."

"The king does as he chooses."

Hugh looked her in the face. "I ask no mercy from you, not even your blessing. Only let me know that you keep me in your memory."

"I remember," Melisende said slowly, "that we were friends once."

"Then go on remembering it. I will get my honor back—I will remember my courage. And when I come back, I'll offer it at your feet."

"I want no offerings," she said.

"In three years' time, the heart can change much," he said. "Will you, my lady? Will you agree to remember me?"

"I can hardly forget you," said Melisende.

Bertrand had heard that Hugh of Jaffa was in the city. It was the talk of certain quarters, that a man accused of cowardice and worse should come openly there of all places. Bertrand had evaded most of the gossip, taking refuge in Helena's house. She only gossiped when it suited her, and tonight she was in no such mood. Her house was a haven of warmth, the dinner she served him as excellent as ever. Of the child he saw nothing, no more than he ever did—it was fostered out, he supposed, or disposed of. He never asked. Helena never mentioned it.

And yet for all the comfort of house and heart's love, he left them both to venture the city at night. He had wooed her into bed quite some time before, but tonight she was not inclined toward him. She had begun her courses, which for her were always painful. She would have kept him there in spite of them, housed him in the room she reserved for guests, spared him the trouble of traveling back to his own house in the dark. But the rain that had been falling when he came was gone away, a keen wind blown the clouds from the sky, laying bare the frosty stars. In company with his squire and his torchbearer and, at her insistence, three of her Turks, he was well escorted.

It was bitterly cold, but he was warm with spiced wine and Helena's parting kiss, and his cloak was heavy, of thickly woven wool lined with fur. He rambled a bit, going home. It was still rather early, hours from midnight. People had come out to breathe the clean air after the long grim rain. On the Street of the Furriers he saw a huddle of men in a doorway, dicing as people liked to do here, with torches to light them and a jar of wine for warmth.

Just as Bertrand was approaching, one of them moved. The light caught fair hair, made distinct a turn of the head.

Bertrand paused. Oh, surely not. That could not be Hugh of Jaffa, dicing in a doorway as if he had not a care in the world—he who should be shut up behind thick walls and guarded against the crowd of his enemies.

The man in the doorway looked up, laughing at a jest. Yes, it was Hugh. Bertrand hung on his heel, torn between the cowardice of ducking his head and slipping away or the courage of offering a greeting to the king's convicted enemy.

As he hesitated, a shadow stirred behind Hugh, sliding into the darkness of the doorway. Instincts honed by years of fighting brought Bertrand to the alert.

He could not move fast enough. A knife flashed in the torchlight, stabbing viciously down. Blood sprang scarlet. The knife flashed again and yet again before the Count's companions could think to move.

Bertrand, far enough away to be slow in coming but also to have had a better view of the attack, lunged through staring, witless bodies—God's nose; what a stink of wine!—and fell on the shadow with the knife. It was a man, substantial enough, and well wined too from the smell of him. He did not struggle. His voice rasped in Bertrand's ear. "The king! I did it for the king!"

Hugh of Jaffa lay in the Hospital of St. John, tended by the holy brothers, wavering between life and death. He had bled terribly from head and body. Not even the chief physician of the Hospitallers could tell whether he would live or die.

"Then he needs a physician who knows his craft!" cried Melisende, and sent one of her choosing: a bearded and turbaned yet avowedly Christian gentleman who had studied in the schools of Cordoba and of Baghdad. He did not endear himself to the Frankish physicians—the gentlest word he had for them was *butchers of swine*—but with the queen's authority and a handful of her most formidable knights, he set to work on the wounded man.

Melisende was in a white rage. Hugh's cowardice and his flight had angered her, but his wounding roused her to a royal wrath.

The whole mighty weight of it fell on her husband the king. The knight who had assaulted Hugh, a Breton born, enjoyed no great rank or distinction, but he had ambition. "I did it for you, majesty," he insisted when he was brought before the king. "That traitor walked free in your own city, mocking your mercy with his presence. I disposed of him for the honor of your name."

"And thereby besmirched it nigh beyond redemption," Fulk said, no little angered himself. He gestured to the guards who had brought the man in, to whom Bertrand had surrendered him at the palace gate. "Take him to the prisons. He will be tried by the High Court—tried and, if God wills and the Court is wise, put to death."

The knight wailed like a woman. "*Majesty!* I did it for you!"

"You did it for yourself," said Fulk. His voice was iron. "Take him away."

Melisende heard of that, even professed to approve it. But her rage was no less. While Hugh lay neither alive nor dead, she would not see Fulk. When her physician sent word that the Count of Jaffa would live, though much weakened and scarred, she went in her own person to the hospital. Hugh was deep in a drugged sleep, bandages concealing the worst of his wounds. His beauty would not be the same thereafter, but she looked on him without revulsion. She looked long. Then she turned on her heel and went back to the palace.

Fulk had been in his workroom, going over accounts with his Constable and an officer or two of the chancery. He had dismissed them and sat at the table to eat a bit of bread and cheese with ale, all the meal he would take on such days as this, when he was too preoccupied with kingship to care what he ate or drank.

Melisende in her fury burst like a storm-wind into that small and windowless room. She was almost too large for it. Those ladies who had kept pace with her were caught without, but they could see and hear well enough: Melisende had not slammed the door behind her. Fulk blinked, as stunned by the force of her as any lesser man.

Her voice when she spoke was soft enough to be startling. "Tell me," she said. "Tell me true. Did you put that murderer up to it?"

"Do you take me for that much of a fool?" he asked her with remarkable presence of mind.

"All men are fools," she said with grand contempt. "Tell me. Did you?"

"I did not."

"Swear in God's name. Swear by Holy Sepulcher."

"I do swear," he said without hesitation.

Even yet he had not appeased her. She shook her head, tossing it. "It doesn't matter. Whether you ordered it or simply let it be known that you wanted it—a man, crying your name, stabbed the Count of Jaffa in the back. Exile or no, coward or traitor or simple idiot, he never merited so vile a thing."

"I did not do it," Fulk said. "I did not order it or will it. I did not wish harm to him. If I had, don't you think I would have had him put to death when first I took Jaffa? The whole kingdom would have abetted me then."

"Not all of it," Melisende said with grim precision.

"Lady," said Fulk. "Nothing in the world that I do is sufficient to please you.

Now even knights who claim to be mine—whose oath I certainly never took—
conspire to feed your hatred. I grant you right and queenship. I give to you all that
your father gave, of ruling and commanding in this kingdom. What more do you
want of me?"

"I want that murderer's life," Melisende said, "and his limbs one by one. And I
want the Count of Jaffa kept safe until he recovers, then sent guarded to Italy. Let
no one so much as look at him with disrespect."

"I had intended that," Fulk said.

"Then do it." She whirled on her heel.

But he was on his feet, swooping across the table, seizing her hand. She snapped
to a halt. "Lady," he said. "It was not my fault."

She would not turn to face him, though his grip must have twisted her arm
cruelly. "Prove it," she said. "Prove it so that no one alive can doubt it."

Fulk did what he could. The High Court judged the miscreant, but every lord and
baron there knew the king's will. They condemned the man to death—to his great
horror; but he had stopped shrieking that he had done it for the king. Rumor had
it that certain of his jailers had promised him an unusually slow and painful exe-
cution if he said any such thing.

The sentence laid down on him was quite terrible enough. He would be destroyed
limb by limb, one by one, and only last and after he had again confessed, would he
be granted the mercy of beheading.

That was Melisende's wrath, though it wore Fulk's face and authority. Any who
ventured to think that Hugh himself deserved a similar sentence for his betrayals,
did not dare to speak aloud. Neither the king nor the queen was to be reasoned
with, and the High Court was in no remarkably obliging mood, either.

Count Hugh's would-be murderer was put to death before all the people. His
screams echoed for days in many a dream, and his blood ran, as each arm, each leg,
and last and only when he had confessed that the king had had no part in his
crime, his head, was sundered from his body.

Hugh himself was taken away while still so weak as to need a litter, set gently
on a ship and dispatched to Italy. The queen did not bid him farewell. There were
many who said that she had no need. Her anger was tribute enough. The chiefs of
Hugh's enemies walked in terror of their lives, dreading a knife in the back. The
king himself, it was whispered, slept with no very easy spirit, and kept a knife ever
near to hand.

It was, in the end, a victory for Melisende. She found no sweetness in it, or none
that she would admit to. She had lost a friend, perhaps her only one, for a bit of
vaunting folly. He had promised to come back; but he was sorely hurt. He could
die of that on the voyage, or die in Italy of that country's famous fevers.

And she remained in Jerusalem, queen in fact as in name, ruling beside her
husband as was right and proper. Alys, the rebel who lacked an essential grain of
sense, remained in exile in her dower lands about Lattakia. The two younger sisters,
no longer quite so very young, had the wits to be quiet.

Hodierna was almost old enough for a husband; one would be found for her soon.

Sweet-faced Yveta professed to want no husband but Christ. She had been odd since she lived for a year as hostage to the infidels. She had gone away a lively and often frivolous child, but come back silent and withdrawn and conspicuously devoted to the forms of Christian prayer. It would be the convent for her when she was older, and a life of prayerful quiet now, attended by nurses of suitably pious nature.

So it was settled, at least in Jerusalem. There was still the matter of a prince for Antioch, but Fulk had found new strength to contend with that. The likelihood that while he was away his wife's temper would cool, proved a marvelous stiffener of the will.

She had already come to a kind of thunderous stillness. Her farewell to him as he rode yet again to Antioch, was almost gentle. Perhaps she had grown resigned to this marriage that had been made for her, now that she had power as well as title. Perhaps at last she had understood that, where men were concerned, she had no heart. She was as alien to the thing called love of the body as a virgin saint.

Richildis could wish that she shared such a blessing. The month she had spent in Beausoleil should have faded long ago in her memory. Yet she still dreamed of it, of dark eyes and black beard and long fingers turning the pages of a book.

The Byzantine had never come to Jerusalem, never written to her, never sent her word or message. That she had never done any of those things, either, managed not to matter in the scale of her indignation.

And then, early in the spring after Hugh left for Italy, a letter came to her by the hand of her brother's squire. Gabriel professed not to know its contents, but its sender he knew very well. "Michael Bryennius sends greetings," he says, "and hopes that you remember him."

It was all Richildis could do to thank the boy civilly—too much aware of the wicked glint in his eye, the too-knowing slant of his brows as he bowed and suffered himself to be dismissed. She realized when it was too late that she should have offered him something of value as well, a coin or a trinket.

Later. She would make sure of it. Now . . .

She needed to be alone. Melisende's ladies were variously ignoring her in favor of their own concerns, or regarding her with idle curiosity. For the benefit of the latter she tucked the letter into her girdle and went back to the sleeve that she had been embroidering.

She barely saw the stitches. Most would probably need to be ripped out on the morrow. But they passed a slow and necessary hour, until she was free to go for a while where she would.

She went to a place that she had come to favor, the chapel of the palace. It was quiet outside of the hours of mass and office, not often frequented by anyone except, once in a while, the young Princess Yveta; and she was never inclined toward conversation, except with God.

There was no one in the chapel today. Someone had been there a little while ago: there were candles lit on the altar, living prayers for this cause or that. Richildis knelt and crossed herself and murmured a fragment of a prayer.

Then at last, by the light of the candles, she took out the letter. It was sealed with a device that she had seen before, carved in the ring he liked to wear: a very old stone, old as Rome, a wolf nursing twins under a branching tree.

She broke the seal abruptly, before she could waver further. And why her hands should shake and her heart beat hard, she did not know. It was only a letter from a man she had known for a little while, two years and more ago.

It began simply enough. "Michael Bryennius of the City Constantinopolis to the Lady Richildis of La Forêt in Anjou, greetings and good health. I hope this finds you well and your lady content.

"I had meant to write you before now. I remember how you taxed your brother with his silence, so that you never knew even if he lived. But one grows shy in absence, and you were in the heart of things, and might have forgotten a stranger with whom you shared a book or two.

"Still," he said, and she could hear it as clear as if he spoke in front of her, "I hope that you will remember, and of your charity, permit a stranger to call on you. I am leaving this country. My enemy is dead; my kin have summoned me back. It seems I'm heir to more than I knew. Of course I have to go; I have no weight of refusal to keep me here.

"Yet there is one farewell I would make, and that is to Jerusalem. And, I confess, to you. Will you allow that liberty?"

There was more, but it mattered little: phrases of closing and parting, polite inconsequentialities that weighed nothing beside the truth of what he had said. That he was going away. That he wanted to see her.

That he was going away.

She had not seen him in a pair of years. Why should it matter if she did the not-seeing with him in Beausoleil or with him in Byzantium?

Yet it did. Beausoleil she could visit if she would. The City of the Byzantines . . .

If she would, if her will and her resources were strong enough—she could.

If.

lady in the service of the queen might properly receive a visitor in the ladies' solar. But Richildis did not find pleasant the prospect of meeting Michael Bryennius again in front of the whole flock of the queen's ladies. Even those with whom she shared alliance or even friendship, might be too intensely interested in her words and her manner when she spoke to her guest. They had little enough else to occupy them; they were always looking for a new love-affair or a particularly delicious scandal.

Richildis' virtue had been troubling them for quite some time now. With so many women and so few men, it was no devastating disgrace for a woman to remain unclaimed—even a widow of property, and that property in France, which made it all the more enticing. But Richildis had had no lack of would-be claimants. Young knights mostly, second or third or fourth sons with no hope of inheritance unless they married it, but a baron or two as well, lords of rank and substance in search of a beautiful young wife who would bear sons to fight for the kingdom.

She had turned them all away, gently if she could, firmly if she must. She did not want to marry again. Someday she supposed she must. But not here—not in Outremer. A pleasant gentleman in Anjou, a man of substance perhaps, who had sired heirs enough and who desired a lady to look after his estates, to bear him company, to be his friend and confidante in the ruling of his domain . . . that, she might welcome, if it were the right man and the right demesne.

Michael Bryennius was none of that. He was a foreigner, a man of evident property but never in any Frankish country.

And why was she imagining such things? He had never said a word to encourage it. She could look at a man reckoned handsome by the women of this court, a golden vision or a dark eastern beauty; concede the delight to the eyes, grant the pleasure to the senses, but remain unmoved by any quiver of the heart. She was cold, people said. She was ice and iron, untroubled by the living flesh.

They did not know how she trembled now, how she fretted over what she would wear, how she would loop her veil, whether her hair should be braided beneath it or free, which jewels she should choose to adorn the whole. In the end she tossed them all aside with a hiss of frustration, flung down the drift of silk that veiled her plaits, called her maids to do it all again. Yasmin and Leila were far from annoyed;

they thought it a grand lark. She would have slapped them if she had been a better mistress.

In a plain gown the color of mist over a northern sea, with a veil a little nearer in color to silver laid over her free hair, and a silver fillet binding it—that and a simple silver brooch that held her mantle at her shoulder, the only ornaments that she wore—and escorted by her two conspicuously unfrivolous maids, Richildis made her way through the city to Helena's house.

Helena was away from it, visiting her house in Acre as she liked to do at this time of year, conquering the markets and tending to the more mercantile of her holdings. She had made Richildis free of her house in Jerusalem, and left Kutub and Ayyub there at Richildis' disposal: generous, and very like her. Richildis slept there some nights, where it was quiet, and she need not contend with a bedmate who snored.

The servants had been warned to expect more guests than Richildis. They were at their duties as Richildis came in, preparing dinner, tending the garden, standing guard at the gate. Michael Bryennius had not arrived. It was early—of course he was not there.

She had time to establish herself in the reception room, to see that the wine and the cakes were present and satisfactory, to send her maids to the kitchen to report on the progress toward dinner. To which she had not invited him. To which he very likely would not stay. She had ordered a suitable repast nonetheless, one of the eastern delicacies, a whole lamb roasted and served on a bed of rice with spiced fruits and flat unleavened bread and an array of dainties. Because he had expressed a liking for the Arabs' bitter yet oddly appealing kaffé, she had ordered that, too, and sugar to sweeten it, and confections of half a dozen kinds.

The servants would feast tonight, if Michael Bryennius did not.

She did not torment herself with fears of his failing to come at all. He had asked for this audience. He would hardly wish to forgo it.

Just at the ringing of the bells for the hour of Nones, when in the palace they would be sitting down to the day's feast, she heard his voice in the passage, and the sound of his step. The certainty with which she knew them was astonishing—disturbing.

But of course she had been expecting him. And his accent was distinct. He was exchanging banter with Kutub, the Turk's voice lighter, harsher, with a different accent altogether.

Kutub admitted him to Richildis' presence with becoming gravity—and a wicked glint in his eye. Michael Bryennius was smiling himself, bowing low as one did in the court of the emperor, an extravagance that she found dreadfully appealing.

He was much as she remembered: black eyes, beautiful black beard, elegant hands. And yet he was different. He had a new coat, she could not help but notice, of gold-embroidered crimson silk. It was the coat of a wealthy man, a nobleman, a courtier. She had never seen him in colors before, only in black or in twilight blue. She did not know if she liked it.

Of course he was different, she told herself sharply. He was no longer an exile. His rank and station had been returned to him, and all his properties, which evidently were extensive. She had not known how much so—though she should have guessed. Men of limited means did not claim both kinship and familiarity with the emperor of the Byzantines.

As he straightened from his bow, he took her hands with such ease and such lack of affectation that she could not think clearly enough to pull away. Then she was trapped, held in a grip both light and strong, as a young and skittish mare is held by the horseman's hand on her rein.

Michael Bryennius smiled at her. She felt the heat rise from her toes to her crown, a swift fiery ascent. Oh, there was nothing holy in this, nothing chaste or safely spiritual. This was pure white-hot lust of the body.

And yet . . . and yet. It was not only that he was a man, and that she yearned for his touch. It was the light in his eyes, too; the way he smiled, a little crookedly, with his teeth shining white in his beard. And his voice, his lovely deep warm voice, saying in that elegant accent, "My lady. You are more beautiful than ever."

He hated it when she denied that she was beautiful. She caught herself biting her tongue on the denial; heard herself say, "My lord, I thank you. And you are beautiful as always."

His cheeks flushed scarlet, as hers must surely be doing. "Do you like my new coat?" he asked her.

"It's very vivid," she said.

He raised his brows. "Too vivid? Gaudy? Ridiculous? They told me it was all the rage in the City."

"I'm sure it is," she said. "It's quite beautiful, really. It just looks a bit odd. You used to be so somber."

"I was somber," he said. "I was an exile."

He was still holding her hands. They were still standing near the door—and how had she come so far from the room's center? She backed slowly, and he followed, letting her lead him to a chair while she took another at a prim and prudent distance.

It was almost a physical shock, the parting of their hands. She sat quickly, hastily for a fact, and knotted her fingers in a vain attempt to keep them from trembling. He seemed little less disconcerted: he was staring at her, eyes wide, faintly shocked.

He recovered first, or perhaps his tongue was simply smoother than hers. "Lady, after I've done the things that a pilgrim does, I'll return to the City."

And why should her heart thud at that, and her throat tighten as if with tears?

She mastered her voice and made it say, "I'm glad for you. Exile is never joyous, even among friends."

"Yes, I have friends here," he said. "I'll not stay away forever. Only long enough to remind the City of my existence, and to make order of my affairs."

"That could consume a lifetime," she said: "affairs in your City being what they are."

He laughed, but with a catch in it, as if of pain. "I hope for a decade at most. I've been thinking, you know. Of what it would be like to live as I please. To travel, to look on stranger things than I've yet seen . . ." He paused. "Isn't it odd? Three years I was an exile. Three years I clung to your brother's castle, nor set foot beyond his lands, even to visit the holy places. Now that my exile is ended, now I'm free to go home, I want only to visit, to set matters in order, to go away again—far away."

"That's it," Richildis said. "You're free. While you were not, you rebelled; you refused to move. Now you can go where you choose, and no part of the world is forbidden you."

He blinked as he considered that. "Mary Mother," he said, half amused, half dismayed. "What a contrary creature I am!"

"I think you are perfectly sensible," she said. "My brother, now—he's not only free, he's lord of a demesne, and he refuses to set foot in it."

"That's why," Michael Bryennius said. "Lands and lordship bind a man tighter than any shackles."

"He has both here," she said, "and he never flees them."

"But they're here," said Michael Bryennius. "Not in Anjou. Not in the place from which he was driven."

"And who has come to fetch you," she asked, "and will not go home until you do? Have you a sister? A cousin? A bride-to-be?"

"None of those," he said, "lady. Not one. Simply a messenger from my mother's household, who waits on my convenience—but that should not be delayed too long. My mother is hungry to see my face."

"No bride waits for you?" Richildis inquired. "Ah: but your mother will have seen to that. No good mother could forbear."

"Mine has," he said. "I made a bargain with her long ago. I would choose my own wife. In return she would rule the family as she saw fit, and never fear that a bride of mine would displace her."

"She'll want you to choose soon. Every house needs heirs."

"Mine has them in plenty. Two of my brothers married well and profitably, and proceeded to sire armies of offspring. Sons in profusion—I can have my pick of them."

"How reassuring," Richildis said.

He grinned at her. "Disgusting, isn't it? I'll be beset when I go back—there are half a dozen perfectly reasonable candidates for the position, and only room in it for one."

"Set a task," she said. "Offer a contest. The one who composes the best verse in Homeric Greek, or the one whose bow shoots the farthest, or the one who shows the most sense in a matter of consequence—let that one be your heir."

"I was thinking," he said, "to ask for the one least willing to defer to me simply because I can make him head of the family."

"But a well-brought-up child must have respect," Richildis said severely.

The lift of his brow mocked her primness. "Respect," he conceded, "but not obsequiousness. I'll not be lied to by some fool who will trample my body when I'm dead. Better the truth, and honest insolence. *That* I can reason with."

"Is all your family as odd as you?"

He mimed elaborate startlement. "Odd? Why, no. It's the rest of the world that's strange. You'd like my mother, I think. She's very severe, very virtuous—and wonderfully wicked when she pleases to be."

"I am not wicked," said Richildis. "I have poor control over my sense of propriety."

"That's not wicked?"

"That's distressing." She glared at him. "I hope your mother thrashed you often when you were younger."

"She never needed to," he said. "Her tongue was enough to flay me to the bone."

"Mine has never dealt the smallest wound."

"No?" He shook his head. "Lady, you have no perception."

"My flaws are myriad," she agreed.

"Myriad and enchanting," he said.

"So much so that you endured them for a single month, abandoned them for a pair of years, and now you go away again."

"You could come with me," he said.

His voice was light, as if he made nothing of it. She should have responded in kind. But she could not make herself utter a word.

Go with him? Go to Constantinople? With Michael Bryennius?

With him she would go to the ends of the world.

But.

Her brother. Her purpose, already years unfulfilled. La Forêt, and the lady waiting there, growing no younger, professing no impatience as the lord and his sister tarried in Outremer.

Her heart yearned to run away, to vanish with this stranger whom she knew, somehow, as well as she knew her own kin. Her heart, that should be perfectly cold, perfectly chaste, was burning to be near him.

The heart was flesh, raw throbbing blood-swelling thing. The spirit was above it, was air and ice. Or tried to be. She forced it to speak through her. "You know I can't go," she said. And the heart crept in while her guard was down, only for a moment, only long enough to add, "Someday, maybe . . ."

"Someday," he said, regretfully—but not as if his heart would break.

It was only friendship he wanted. After all.

"Dine with me," she said abruptly. "Make it a farewell feast, if you like."

She held her breath. He would refuse. Of course. Why should he accept?

He accepted. And was charming, witty, no more or less warm to her than any friend. It was a delightful dinner, well prepared, well served by her two maids and the Turks. He spoke of everything but one, the fact of his departing. He did not try to compel her to change her mind. If he had truly wanted—if he had meant—

And in too brief a moment it was over. The delicacies were all consumed, the wine was gone. He was rising, casting an eye toward the windows, that had gone dark since he sat to dine.

She yearned to snatch at his hand, to pull him back. Coldly, sternly, she cast down that yearning. A little of that coldness lingered in her voice. "Kutub and Ayyub will escort you to your lodging."

He bowed slightly. "I thank you," he said.

There was a silence, stiff and uncomfortable—the first such discomfort since they met again. Richildis could not make herself break it. Not to drive him out. Not to beg him to stay.

It was he who spoke, and not as she would have wished. "I must go," he said. "It was a great pleasure. If you should come to the City—"

"If I should come to the City," she said, faint and a little cold, "I will remember your name."

"Yes," he said, "lady. Do remember. Unless I come to Jerusalem before then."

Her heart should not leap—by all the saints, it should not. "I shall pray that you come back," she said; unwisely perhaps.

"Then I shall do my best to answer your prayer," said Michael Bryennius.

"You could," she said, "not go at all."

This silence was not merely uncomfortable. It rang like a gong. As before, it was he who broke it. "Lady, you of all people know that I must."

Her head bowed. Unwillingly she said, "I do know."

"We are both much too dutiful," he said. He took her hands. Again, as when he first came, she felt the world sway underfoot. Ridiculous; she was a woman of both virtue and strong will. Yet his touch was almost more than she could bear.

Either he sensed it, or he was shaken himself. He let go—too quickly, and yet never quickly enough. "God keep you," he said, "until we meet again."

"If . . ." she began, but she could not finish. "God keep you," she said.

And with that, so swift and yet so slow, he was gone. Almost—almost—she called out after him, ran in pursuit, did any number of utterly foolish things. But she was too wise, too deadly practical. She remained where she was. In Jerusalem, from which it seemed she would never depart—never, for Bertrand would not return to La Forêt.

She had admitted as much to herself, for long and long. But never so clearly. Never with such devastating finality. Michael Bryennius had returned to Constantinople, to the world and the kin and the obligations that had called him. Bertrand would not follow his example. This was Bertrand's country now, this his world and his heart's home. This, and not La Forêt.

And she knew it, and she would not leave. She had her vow; she had her stubbornness. Maybe Bertrand would alter his will. Maybe he would surrender. Someday. Not soon, perhaps not while youth remained to him—but someday he well might.

Until he did, this was her world, too, and if not her heart's home, then the resting place of her spirit. Was it not the holiest city in the world? Was it not Jerusalem?

"God wills it," she said, aloud in the silence. There was no one to hear, no one to wonder at her. The servants were all gone about their business. She was alone. She said it again, for the truth of it, and to make it true beyond doubting. "God wills it. And I . . . maybe I, too. Maybe."

Two

QUEEN

REGENT

(A.D. 1143-1149)

he autumn after Prince Baldwin passed his thirteenth year, the High Court traveled as it often did in this season, to take the sea air and to populate the markets of Acre. Baldwin had been desperate for a diversion, or so he professed. Jerusalem had grown deadly dull—meaning that there had been no good wars of late, and his father was not minded to start any.

Baldwin had been remarkably bloody-minded this year. Arslan thought it was because after a promising start he was small for his age, and his voice was still unbroken. Baldwin did not believe his mother when she said that he would grow, and soon. Of course his mother would say that. Mothers were supposed to say such things.

Arslan, who had had the poor taste to shoot up nearly to man-height over the summer, and to break out in a voice like—Baldwin said—a sick frog's, had to labor mightily to preserve a friendship so old it went beyond memory. Sometimes it made him very tired. But now, for once, Baldwin held up his end of the bargain.

They had escaped the palace not long after dawn, armed each with a purse full of copper, determined to take the market by storm. The price for their escape was one they bore with some semblance of fortitude: Baldwin's brother Amaury. Amaury was just old enough to be a page, a tall thin fair child who never had much to say for himself. Baldwin barely tolerated him. Arslan rather liked him. He could keep quiet, and he hero-worshipped his elders, as was only fitting.

Baldwin had wanted to lose him in the crowds that would be heavy even so early. Arslan had always been less ruthless. "Oh, let him stay with us," he said as they passed the guards at the citadel's gate.

Baldwin rolled his eyes. "He's a nuisance."

"That's what Lady Richildis said we were," said Arslan. There were people staring, watching them come out of the citadel. He put on a bit of a swagger for them.

Baldwin was not paying attention. He was saying to Amaury, "You know why you were born, don't you? Because I got sick, sick enough that people thought I might die, and Father finally convinced Mother that one of us was not enough. Now they say two of us are two too many."

"Father had to woo Mother for years," Amaury said serenely, "before she would let him make me. For you he only wooed her for a season."

Baldwin would have fallen on his brother, right there in front of the gate, if

Arslan had not pulled them apart. "Stop that!" Arslan commanded them in his new deep voice, which betrayed him halfway through by breaking into a squeak.

The squeak saved him. Baldwin, instead of leaping on him, fell down laughing. Even Amaury smiled. Arslan swept them with him, one on each arm, away toward the city and the market.

"I never should have given in," Melisende said. She had roused for mass long before the boys were sent out in the name of an hour's peace. Now mass was sung and her soul well purified; it was a little while before she must hold the morning's audience. She had paused to be dressed for it, to have her hair plaited, the better to wear the crown.

That was done, all but the placing of the crown. Most of her ladies had gone to array themselves for court. Richildis, who had dressed already, paused in taking the crown from its chest. "A husband should do his duty by his wife. Occasionally. Once every seven years."

"So he said," said Melisende sourly. "I told him no. Two are enough. One should have been—but he had to master me. He had to demand his rights—and win them by sheer force of persistence."

"Persistence," Richildis said, remembering, "and a cask of wine from France."

"It had traveled badly, too," said Melisende. "I had the most hideous headache after."

"And another son coming, and a husband who was most pleased with himself and his wife."

Melisende made a sound of disgust. "Drunkenness is a sin in the face of the Lord. I paid high for it, and have done penance."

"But do think," Richildis said. "Two living sons, and none lost or died aborning—God blesses you."

"So he does," said Melisende. "I'll not vex him a third time. No matter how my lord may press me."

Richildis shrugged slightly. She had never seen the profit in that old war. Christian marriage and Christian chastity warred unreasonably, and when a husband desired his wife, it was expected that she oblige him. Melisende was extraordinary in her resistance, that had failed only once in twice seven years—and then, Richildis sometimes suspected, she had allowed it, whether for weariness or because she did indeed see the sense in getting more than the one son. Baldwin had had a spate of fevers that year, enough to warn any mother that her child was not immortal.

Now Baldwin was approaching man's years, and Amaury was old enough to be a page in his father's household. Fulk would be thinking that a third son might be well considered, or even, it might be, a daughter. Fathers did want daughters, once they had had a son or two.

Melisende had had no greater interest in the younger son than in the elder, nor did she express any desire to bear a daughter. Children were not a thing she had much care for. Beyond bearing them and handing them to nurses and waiting till they were, as she put it, old enough for decent conversation, she took as little notice of them as she might. And since to her decent conversation meant something close to the art of dialectic, even Baldwin was barely of age yet, and Amaury, studious as he was, was still too much a child.

Richildis sighed faintly. Twice seven years in Melisende's service had taught her much of the manners and mores of queens. They were not as other women, not even as other noblewomen. Power was meat and drink to them. Richildis had heard the same of empresses of the Byzantines, and she had read of the queens of the old time, of Rome and Greece and Egypt. They were all the same. It was as if, to be a queen, a woman needed to be something other than woman; to be not a little like a man.

Such wisdom, she thought as she took Melisende's crown from its coffer and laid it on the woven crown of braids. There was no thread of grey therein, no suggestion of advancing age. Melisende was still a great beauty, richer and fuller of body than she had been when she awaited her affianced husband by the harbor of Acre, but lovely as ever, with her ivory skin and her dark eyes and her hair like a wheatfield in the sun.

Richildis herself felt no older than she had been when she first came to Outremer. And yet she must be. Had she not been here for fourteen years? Bertrand was still lord of Beausoleil, still intransigent in his refusal to return to Anjou; and still married to no lady of this kingdom or any other, although the common rumor made Helena his wife. Certainly he had no other woman that was known of, nor was Helena called a courtesan now except by force of habit. She had long since ceased to take any client but Bertrand; and from him she took nothing but his love and such gifts as he was pleased to bestow.

Time ran swift, here in the country beyond the sea. Richildis herself, unwedded, unbedded, still sought after but still unminded to take any husband, had grown thinner perhaps, more severe of face, but no older in her heart than the young woman who had sailed with Fulk. It was strange to think that she might stay here her life long, bound by her vow and by her own obstinacy, while La Forêt slipped farther and farther away down the stream of years.

She shook herself hard, willed herself to rouse. Melisende was ready. The court was waiting, as it had waited every morning for time out of mind. She was watching Richildis, brow lifted slightly, as if she had followed the track of Richildis' thoughts.

"Do you know," Melisende said, "we haven't done anything interesting, short of traveling from Jerusalem to Acre, since I don't remember when."

"There was the great dance and festival," Richildis said, "and the tournament at Pentecost."

"Ah," said Melisende with a flick of the hand. "Pentecost. That was whole seasons ago. And nothing to do, really, till the Christmas feast. Not even a war to send the men off to, to keep them occupied. They'll be fomenting conspiracies next, or challenging one another to duels."

Richildis held her tongue. Melisende refused to maintain silence on a subject that to any other woman would have been painful. Hugh of Jaffa was ten years dead. He had come living to Italy, but died there of his wounds and, perhaps, a broken heart. Melisende had mourned him fiercely but briefly, then put him resolutely out of mind.

It was true enough that knights and barons, when suitably bored, were given to duels and conspiracies. Richildis raised a brow. "And have you a cure for knightly ennui?"

"I might," said Melisende. "Tomorrow if the weather's fair, I'll conceive a yearning to ride out. Those who wish can hunt; those who love idleness can dine in the field. We'll shake the dust and gloom out of our spirits, and let the men out for a run."

"Boys, too," Richildis said, thinking of Baldwin and his brothers—both the foster-brother and the brother of the blood. "They're always the better for fresh air and the opportunity to kill something."

Melisende clapped her hands. "Yes! And I'll award a prize for the finest gazelle. And if someone kills a boar or a lion, I'll make him the king of the feast."

"That would do," Richildis agreed. "That would do very well."

"Go," Melisende said with eagerness that recalled the quick-tempered young woman she had been. "See to the beginning of it. I'll come when I'm done with audience; we'll muster such a hunt as they'll be talking of till Yuletide."

Richildis dipped in a curtsey, not at all dismayed to be granted reprieve from the tedium of the court. She was already ordering in her head the servants who would be needed, the masters of hunt and hounds, the falconers, the beaters, the cooks to prepare the feast in the field. Melisende was gone before she noticed; then she was on her way herself, going about her lady's business.

No matter how fast Baldwin and Arslan ran or how twisty they made their path, Amaury managed doggedly to keep up. He was as tenacious as a Bedu bandit after a caravan, and so they pretended he was. After the second time they ambushed him, he vanished.

Baldwin first heaved a sigh of relief, then went white. "Mary Mother! She'll kill me if we lose him."

She was Queen Melisende, as always. There was only one *she* in their world, only one woman worthy of honest terror—though Lady Richildis had her moments. The queen was a figure of perpetual awe, a tall and terrible shape on the borders of childhood dreams, a woman crowned and mantled in gold, to whom one bowed low and offered one's deepest respects. Children were beneath her. Boys who were almost men were almost worthy of her notice. It was Arslan's tenderest ambition to be worthy not only of notice but of a smile.

She had smiled at him once. He did not delude himself that she had noticed who he was, or cared; but he had done her service, brought her hot spiced wine on a day of winter when the hall of audience was achingly cold, and she had smiled and murmured thanks as she curled blue-tinged fingers around the cup.

He suppressed a sigh. Of course he was in love with the queen. All the pages were. So was the king—though he had to be stern about it or be thought a weakling. It was difficult for Baldwin: one should not be in love with one's mother, but awe alone was never enough. He had to settle for alternately worshipping and defying her.

And now he had lost Amaury. They had gone all the way to the Royal Market, and the press of people was so tight that they could barely breathe. There would be no finding one small boy in a crowd so innumerable. The game that they had been playing on the quieter side street was folly here; but a child would not know what was foolish and what was not.

Arslan could see nothing for it but to keep going in the direction they had been going in. Turning back would only confuse Amaury if he had laid an ambush ahead. He tried to tell Baldwin as much, but Baldwin was too distraught to listen. Arslan only avoided losing him by getting a grip on his belt and bracing his own superior weight, and refusing to budge until Baldwin stopped trying to run in circles. Then he pulled the prince after him, pushing through the crowd. He was already as tall as a man, and though nowhere near as broad as he was going to be, he was broad enough. He could cut a respectable swath when he put his mind to it.

They had been going to look at daggers. Amaury would know it. He had been coveting one for days now, a damascened blade that was, even Baldwin admitted, rather exceptionally fine. Of course a child just old enough to be a page could not muster the price of such a thing, nor could he ask and be granted the wherewithal; not so young.

He was not there, yearning after the dagger. Arslan was not worried, not yet, but he would be in a little while. He kept Baldwin busy admiring a strange broad-bladed sword with a hilt that was, the merchant said, the actual horn of a unicorn—and truly it was strange, twisting and spiral-grained, but the sword was a dull thing without sheen or temper. Foolish to set so much value on a hilt when it was the blade that made a sword a sword.

Still it was a marvelous thing, and Baldwin could not stop tracing the twisting shape of the hilt. While he was so engrossed, Arslan searched with eyes and ears for sign of a lone small boy in a blue tunic. No such creature appeared, nor hid under a table, nor leaped from a shadow like a bandit from his lair.

God, Arslan thought, would not allow the king's second son to be snatched away by slavers, not from the heart of the king's own market in the king's own city while the king was resident therein. And yet, for all his milk-and-water manners, Amaury was an attractive child—and with his white-fair hair and his clear grey eyes, more than attractive to the black-haired, black-eyed people of the east.

Arslan should not panic. Amaury could take care of himself. So for that matter could Baldwin; and Baldwin in a panic was likely to do something drastic. Best to be calm. To keep eyes and ears keen. To pray as he could, if any saint or angel was listening, that at the very worst Amaury had gone back to the palace in distress because his brother did not welcome his company.

Eventually even the unicorn-sword failed to hold Baldwin's interest. He had wherewithal to buy a knife for cutting meat, and did, choosing a plain one but sharp and well willing to hold an edge; he bargained well, too, almost as well as Arslan's mother, and that was saying something. But when he had done that, he looked about, and Arslan knew what he would say before he said it. "I don't see him. Where is he?"

Arslan opened his mouth to say something, though exactly what, he was not sure. Before he could manage a word, a tall man appeared as if from air, looming above the knife-seller's display. A much shorter figure hung back a little, as if seeking safety in his shadow.

All words fled from Arslan's head. Arslan was tall—as tall as many men. This was a tall man indeed, though he was not reckoned a giant: big and fair and somewhat battered by weather and fighting, as a good knight and baron of the Franks should be. No one had ever called him a beauty, but women liked him and men respected him, and they all said that he was easy enough to look at.

Arslan found it difficult to keep his eyes on that face. He knew it, of course. Everybody did. There was no one who did not know Lord Bertrand.

Least of all Arslan's mother.

Lady Richildis told him he was too young to be bitter; but he could not stop his heart from going tight and small whenever he saw that one of all the men in the world. The one who was, or so his mother said, his father.

Bastardy was not such a stigma that men could die of it. There were bastards enough in the court: by-blows of this lord or that, sons born out of wedlock to noblemen in the west, offspring of unions that for one reason or another were not sanctioned by holy Church. A bastard could not be a priest, but he could be a knight and even a lord, and by his merits and the force of his arm become a great man in the world. Had not William Bastard of Normandy become King of England?

That was nothing to make Arslan bitter. Legitimacy was a little enough thing, he liked to reflect, in the eyes of God if not of the Church. But other bastards had something that he had not. They had fathers.

Fathers who acknowledged them. Fathers who admitted to the sin of begetting them, and showed no shame of it. Fathers who would look their sons in the face and speak to them as kin to kin, and not coldly, brusquely, as to any stranger not of their blood.

Not that Lord Bertrand was particularly brusque or cold. He was affable mostly, but distant, as a man is with a stranger. Arslan did not believe that he did not know who Prince Baldwin's foster-brother was.

True, few people did. It was even said that he might be a late by-blow of old King Baldwin himself. But that Bertrand should not know—how could he fail to? Arslan was his own son.

And here he was, bringing Amaury back to his brother, and not troubling to rebuke either of them for losing him. He barely acknowledged Arslan, which was probably proper but which hurt nonetheless. He spoke to Baldwin, and jostled the prince right out of his sulks and into laughter that, to be honest, much better became him. It was not even anything in particular that he said: only the way he said it.

He and Baldwin bent over the merchant's display. "Now that is a fine blade," Bertrand said, indicating one that was rather well made, though the one next to it, Arslan thought, was better. Baldwin did not say so, if he knew to. He was still yearning over the unicorn's horn.

Arslan's eye caught Amaury just as the boy showed signs of slipping away again. His hand shot out, snared an arm before its owner could escape. "Where did he find you?" Arslan demanded. "We could have been in miserable trouble if you'd been taken away by slavers."

Amaury snorted. "Slavers! That's silly. I was laying an ambush for you by the sweetseller's stall, the one with all the cakes with cinnamon in them. You were supposed to go there first."

"We always come here first," Arslan said. "You know that."

Amaury thrust out his lower lip. "You always buy cakes with cinnamon in. So I had three. I was going to have another, but *he* came and said I'd get sick. I never get sick to my stomach. So I had a honey sweet instead, and then he said I should go look for you, so we did. I don't know why people think you're my uncle really. You look just like him. Sound like him, too, when you get all growly."

Arslan discovered that his mouth was open. Amaury was given to flights of the tongue, but this was remarkable even for him. Arslan retrieved his jawbone and clapped it back where it belonged. "I do not look like him! I hate him."

"You don't either," said Amaury. "Hate him, I mean. You *do* look like him. Nurse says that's because—"

Arslan clapped a hand over his mouth. "Don't say it. Don't you . . . dare . . . say it."

It was not the hand that stopped Amaury—such things had never troubled him overmuch. But Arslan's expression must have been horrifying: the grey eyes went wide over Arslan's hand, and when Arslan took it away, he was suitably and appropriately mute.

Bertrand had heard not a word of it, nor Baldwin. They were debating the merits of a pair of daggers. One was prettier, one more fit for use but not as well suited to Baldwin's hand. As Arslan watched, Bertrand proposed a third, which the prince at first declined, then considered with greater attention.

They looked a little alike: both fair-haired and light-eyed. It was no surprise that people thought Arslan kin to the prince, if he was as like Bertrand as Baldwin was. But Arslan could never have bent his head to Bertrand's as Baldwin was doing, never have been so much at ease with him, never have claimed the friendship that Baldwin claimed as his simple right.

It had never hurt so much before. There was no reason that it should. But the heart never had reasons: that was a maxim of his mother's.

His heart was coming to a decision. But it wanted to take its time; and it could do nothing in front of the princes and the knife-seller and the pack of squires that came roistering in, looking, the loudest of them professed, for a sword "as long as Jeannot's yard."

He would wait. But not too long. Then he would say what he must say—and let God grant that it was wise.

he morning of the queen's hunt dawned clear and golden-splendid: not always a certainty in this season. Most of the court that was in Acre had chosen to accept the invitation; as Melisende had hoped, the young men were delighted by the diversion, and the women pleased with the choice: to hunt with the men or to take their ease among the women and the elderly. It was a grand processional, riding out of Acre in the morning. Horses and hawks and hunting hounds, bows and lances and the heavy spears that alone would suffice for boar or lion. Ladies rode if they were bold, reclined in horse-litters if they were proper, attended by their maids and their servants. Not all wore hunting gear; some went out in silk and cloth of gold, bright as peacocks in the royal garden.

They rode through the fields and the orchards, the rich country about the city, striking toward the wilder land beyond. The young men whooped and shouted, racing one another as they went, swirling dust about the more sedate line of courtiers.

Bright sun and early morning and unwonted freedom made them all a little dizzy. Arslan would have loved to join the races, but he was still only a page, and was required to ride close in the queen's train. Next year, when he was a squire, he would enjoy much greater liberty.

His mount was as restive as he was: a foal of Lady Richildis' cantankerous mare, gifted with its Frankish father's common sense but its mother's endurance and blinding speed. He thought more than once of letting slip the firm rein he was keeping, but he was too proud of his horsemanship. Better if far duller to stay where he was, close behind the queen and her ladies, with the bay colt fretting and tossing foam from the bit. He could let Barak dance a little for the ladies who rode by, and did, pretending not to notice when they stared and giggled.

Girls were terribly silly things, but of late they had become suddenly fascinating. Embarrassing, too, when he had other things on his mind: the queen's service, the imminence of the hunt, and the thing that had kept him awake all night dreading and yearning for the morning.

The object of that yearning rode ahead, one of the barons who was privileged to ride close by the king. He was still the queen's knight, strictly speaking, but she never thought ill of him for that he enjoyed the king's favor. He had greeted her when they came out of the palace, kissed her hand and told her she was beautiful, which had made her blush like one of the girls. Arslan did not quite understand that. People were always telling the queen how lovely she was. She should be used to it.

Now Lord Bertrand was among the men where a lord and knight belonged, not the tallest but by no means the shortest either, riding easily on the young dapple grey that he had ridden since old Malik was retired to stud. He was a fine horseman, as fine as Arslan wanted to be, better than most Franks who sat like wooden men on the backs of their big heavy horses—so few like the Turks and the Saracens, who rode as if they and their horses were one creature.

There, at last: the field beyond the farthest tilled field, a hollow in a circle of hills, kept green by a spring that flowed out of a rock. A grove grew there, so ancient that it could remember the old gods, the gods who had been here even before the God of Israel. It was a beautiful place, sheltered from the wind, cool with shade in summer, warm in winter; in this season, neither summer nor yet winter, pleasant in its greenery, sweet with warmth and the scent of wet cool earth.

There the ladies would settle to wait for the hunt to finish, and there they would all gather later to take their dinner. Already there were tents pitched, bright pavilions with the sides rolled up to let in the morning air. Cooks and servants had set up their kitchens, dug a pit to roast an ox whole. Bread was baking, and cakes fragrant with spices and sweetness.

It was all very pretty and very tempting; but Arslan wanted to be where the men were, gathering on the hillside for the hunt. To his great relief and no little delight, the queen showed no sign of stopping as everyone had expected. For a fact they should have understood what it meant that she wore clothes fit to ride and not to hold court in, simple gown and divided skirt, plain mantle and her hair in tight plaits under a veil wound like a turban. One of the servants brought her bow and filled quiver.

And there was Lady Richildis with her bow that she had, people whispered, won from a Saracen in a fight, and one or two other ladies of bold heart and restless nature, all ready to ride a-hunting with the king. Arslan swallowed a whoop. Prince Baldwin had already galloped off to join his father—taking as his right that he could do it. Prince Amaury on his pony was not even asking if he could come: he was keeping quiet and trusting that no one would notice him, to stop him.

They were all moving now, riding toward the king and his barons. Arslan let Barak have his head, not long, just long enough to pull in front, to mingle with the king's party. He heard Melisende call out and Fulk answer: more amicable than they usually were, a little wild maybe with sun and wind and the prospect of the hunt.

"My lord!" Melisende cried. "I'll wager you a pearl that I bring down quarry before you."

"And I'll wager you a falcon that you do not!" he called back. He was seldom so exuberant—old man that he was, more grey than red, he sounded as light as a boy. He laughed and clapped heels to his horse's sides. "*Avant!*"

They rode headlong over the rough and stony hills, driving toward the line of beaters that had gone out long before them. Well out of sight of the green place they met the first wave of animals running before the shouts and cries and the smiting of earth and covert. Gazelle in a herd, tossing horns and leaping bodies; a knot of wild asses braying protest; a startlement of birds, too many and too swift to count.

A shrill yell, a gazelle-leap collapsed into gracelessness: someone had made the first kill. The king of course, or someone very near the king. Arslan had a little Turkish bow, and he had strung it, but had not moved yet to shoot. He was watching Lady Richildis instead. There she was in front of him with arrow to string, riding like a Turkish archer, so effortless that one forgot how very difficult that was. Arslan had never noticed that she could ride this way—never stopped to think that she might be able to.

While he hung suspended in amazement, Barak carried him past her, past the queen, into the king's escort. It had stretched thin as the lesser horses flagged and fell back. The king's own mount, Arab-bred, could gallop most of the day if it pleased, and the king was not holding it back.

Roughness of ground and sudden darts and dodgings of quarry divided the hunt into twos and threes and fours. Arslan lost the king in a sudden copse and a near-collision with a heap of stones that might have been a ruined tower. Barak veered, bucked as the ground fell away, surged up a slight but steep rise.

The hunt had vanished, all but one or two riders struggling likewise with the obstacle. And one behind them, slowing prudently or with foresight, pausing to judge the ground before he rode his horse over it.

Arslan's heart, already in his throat from the suddenness of the check, throbbed painfully and then seemed to stop. Lord Bertrand, here, as if God had sent him; and the others had ridden away already, cursing their ill fortune on losing both king and quarry.

Arslan rode toward him almost without volition. Barak had whickered, glad to see another horse when all the rest had gone away. Bertrand's stallion pawed and snorted, impatient to be going.

Arslan could think of nothing better to do than call out, "Sir!"

Bertrand fixed on him the same look as always, recognizing him but not as anyone who mattered. "I saw the prince with his father," he said, assuming no doubt that Arslan would want to know that first.

"So did I," Arslan said, and blushed at his own ungraciousness. "I know where he went. I was ahead of you." And that was worse.

Lord Bertrand must be inured to blushing and barely coherent pages. He offered no rebuke, simply said, "We'd best go after them. They'd have gone east, I think."

"East and possibly north," Arslan said, hoping devoutly that he sounded sane and ordinary. "The king had his eye on a boar up there. Or so I heard."

"You heard rightly," Bertrand said.

They fell into silence as their horses went on side by side, Bertrand's at a sensible walk, Arslan's at a walk interspersed with eruptions of prancing and head-tossing. Bertrand seemed in no haste in spite of his words; or else, like an old soldier, he knew when to let the land compel a more restful pace.

Past the copse and the scattered stones, he kept to a walk. The land was more open here; Arslan saw a rush of movement that must be more of the hunt, hot in pursuit of something low and dark. Boar? No, too fast. Gazelle? Jackal, even, startled from its lair?

Nothing ran past them. A bird flew overhead. Arslan made no move to shoot it, nor did Bertrand seem inclined to string the bow that rode in its case on his saddle.

"Sir," said Arslan in silence that suddenly was too much to bear, "do you like to hunt?"

Stupid, stupid question, but Bertrand did not sneer at it. "I like it well enough," he said.

"I would like it better," said Arslan, "if I could do it the way the desert people do it: one by one and with skill, and no beaters."

"The sheikhs and the emirs use beaters and all the rest of it," Bertrand said.

"But I'm neither," said Arslan. "I could hunt alone, to live; not in great crowds and armies, for little more than the sport."

"Most young things would like to run away and be free," Bertrand said. He could have sounded insulting, but somehow he did not.

Arslan remembered that Lady Richildis had told him of how and why Bertrand had come to Outremer. He bit his tongue before he asked another foolish question, said instead, "I am glad to be out of the city. Sometimes I think I should run away with the Turks, be a tribesman on the steppe, and forget that I was ever a creature of cities."

Lord Bertrand was staring at him. He could not imagine why. He had said nothing too shocking, though enough to be rebuked for silliness. This was a look of striking intensity, piercing him deep.

Then it went away. Arslan nearly lost his grip on the reins, so strongly had those eyes held him and so suddenly did they stop. "Are you not," Bertrand asked, "after all, a Frank? You look like one."

The hot blood rushed to Arslan's face—staining it, he knew from times before, a rather ugly crimson. "No, I am not King Baldwin's bastard, though you are far from the first to wonder. And yes, I know who my father is."

He kept his eyes on Bertrand, but saw no flinching in that face, no shock in the eyes. How that could be—God, was the man blind? Or had he willed not to care, and done it so long ago that he could not change it even if he wished to?

"At least," said Arslan with no little bitterness, "I know who my mother says he is. And I do look like him."

Bertrand flinched a little at that. Maybe. Minutely. Barely to be seen.

Then he said, "I . . . had a son. His mother assured me of that, and took him away, and never begged me to acknowledge him. He's where you want to be now, I suppose. Running wild among the Turks, or studying to be an emir in Damascus."

For a moment Arslan's head was empty of words. When they came, they were weak to his own ears, and faintly petulant. "You don't know?"

"I could never ask," Bertrand said. "It . . . isn't something she allows."

Arslan, who knew his mother, could well believe it.

What he could not believe was that he was riding here, picking his way down a steep and rather stony slope, being told such things by Lord Bertrand as he did not think anyone—still less a page attached to the prince—had ever been told before. No, not even Lady Richildis, and certainly not Helena. Was it the blood that did it, calling even through ignorance? Or was it a game Lord Bertrand played, a cruel sport with his never-acknowledged son?

It did not sound like a game. He was talking as if to himself, or perhaps to his horse's ears. "He would be—Lord God, would he be as old as you are now? Where do the years go? And I saw him once, but I never looked at him. I was too preoccupied with berating his mother for the secret that she kept, the fact that she was pregnant at all. In reply she kept the secret deeper still, took him away, never told me where he had gone or what she had done with him. Sometimes I dreamed that she had had him killed, or smothered him in his cradle—but not she. Not milady Helena. She can be coldhearted, but she's no murderer of children."

How strange, Arslan was thinking as he listened. How utterly peculiar. Helena had hidden her son in plain sight—and this idiot of a man had never guessed. Surely he had only to look at Arslan's face and then find a mirror, and see how like they were.

But King Baldwin had been a fair-haired, strong-boned Frank, too, and there were a dozen more in the High Court of similar shape and likeness. Prince Baldwin himself could have been Arslan's brother, give or take a hand or two of height. Arslan was nothing remarkable at all in this land of Outremer.

Lady Richildis would have said, acidly, that a man saw what he wanted to see. She had said it more than once, and often of her brother. Where better to conceal an unwanted bastard than under his father's very nose, attached like a shadow to the prince?

Arslan had known it all his life. Had borne it, lived with it, suffered in silence. But he had had enough. Lady Richildis and his mother would have called him mad. Maybe he was; yet he had to say it. "She never murdered me. She never even sent me away."

For a long while he did not think that Bertrand had heard. There was no response, not even the flicker of a glance. He did not stiffen and set his horse to dancing. He made no move at all.

Until he said, "Say it again."

Arslan did, word by word, clear and distinct. "My mother never murdered me. She never sent me away."

"You are a fortunate child," Bertrand said. He could not be thinking when he said it. Or else he was so deep in oblivion that he had not understood; no, not at all.

"Do you even know what my name is?" Arslan demanded in some temper.

"Actually," Bertrand said, "no. Should I? He calls you something, doesn't he? Lion? Eagle?"

"Arslan," said Arslan. "I've been called that since I was small. Ayyub gave me the name, because I roared so fiercely when I was hungry. My given name is Olivier."

No response still. Had Helena ever told her lover what his own son's name was? "Olivier," Bertrand said. "Olivier-Arslan. How like this country."

"My mother's name," said Arslan, and he could not keep the anger out of it, "is Helena. My father's name is Bertrand. Bertrand de La Forêt, Lord of Beausoleil near Nablus."

"Is that what she told you?" Bertrand asked.

Oh, he was a madman, or an idiot. Arslan wanted to hit him. But a page did not hit a belted knight, not if he wanted to come home without a broken head.

Bertrand's horse halted. It might have done so of its own accord: they had climbed a hill and found a patch of thorny scrub, on which it began to graze. Bertrand did not move to prevent it. Arslan's own Barak was less hungry than eager to go on, but he snapped grudgingly at dusty branches. He understood, maybe, that if he indulged in temper now, Arslan would have no patience with it.

Bertrand had turned his face to the sky, to the sun that rode halfway to noon, with a cloud meandering across it, and a winged thing circling—vulture, from the shape and soar of it. Arslan heard the sigh as he drew it. "How logical," he said in a light, calm voice. "How typical of her. Right in front of my nose. I don't suppose she laughs at me?"

"Not often," Arslan said.

"Why?" Bertrand turned suddenly, so suddenly that Arslan's horse shied. "Why now?"

"Because I couldn't stand it any longer."

"She didn't put you up to it?"

Arslan wanted to shriek—with laughter, rage, he did not know nor much care which. This was not at all the way he had imagined it would go. Bertrand would either cast him off in outrage or clasp him to a sobbing breast; not this preposterous calm that was almost acceptance.

"My mother," said Arslan, "would be furious if she knew. So would my aunt. They are of the opinion that if you have no desire to ask what became of your own son, then you won't be troubled with an answer. They think that it's enough for me to be where I am and what I am. And mostly it is. Except that you come and go, and I know and you don't, and that I can't bear it one moment longer. You can beat me now and drive me out. I don't care. Just as long as you know who it is you're doing it to."

"Why in the world," Bertrand asked as if he expected an answer, "would I want to beat you?"

"For being alive," Arslan said.

"That's hardly your fault," said Bertrand.

"Don't beat my mother! It's not her fault, either."

"Oh, isn't it?" Bertrand shook his head before Arslan could burst out with another indiscretion. "No, don't. It's mine, too. Both of us. And maybe God's."

Arslan had thought the same thing, and reckoned himself a terrible sinner for it. To hear it from this man—to know that they thought so much alike—was more disturbing than he might have expected. Other people were not supposed to think like that. It was blasphemous.

"So then," said Bertrand, cutting through Arslan's musings with a briskly practical air. "What are you asking of me?"

Arslan could not answer. Not for lack of one—for an excess of them.

"Surely there's something," Bertrand said after the silence had stretched. "Acknowledgement, I suppose. Fosterage you have. An inheritance? A settlement?"

"No," said Arslan. "Just . . . to know that you know."

Bertrand stared at him. He stared back. "You do mean it," Bertrand said.

Arslan nodded.

"And what am I to do with the knowledge?"

"Whatever you like," Arslan said.

"You are a strange child," Bertrand said. "More like your mother than I would have guessed."

Arslan did not know what to say to that. He did not look anything like Helena. If he thought like her, he did not know it. She was herself. He was someone else. Who he was, he did not know yet.

He should have been more satisfied that he sat here on Barak's back, with the sun climbing higher and his father looking at him with recognition at last—knowing who and what he was. It was not an ill feeling, but not a greatly joyous one, either. It made things very complicated.

"I have to think," Bertrand said. "Do you understand that?"

Arslan nodded.

Bertrand looked hard at him, as if to search out the truth. Since the truth was all he had, he could offer nothing more than silence.

Bertrand gathered the reins abruptly. "Come," he said. "Come back to the hunt with me."

Arslan's heart swelled till surely it would burst. Such simple words—but they meant so much.

He kept his face as calm as he could, loosed rein on Barak, let him follow Bertrand's grey. Following his father. Riding with him to rejoin the hunt.

*T*he hunt was in full cry when Arslan and Bertrand returned to it. They had come to a broad open valley—one that was, Arslan saw with some surprise, not far at all from the place where the ladies had camped. They had ridden in a great circle.

As neatly as partners in a dance, hunters who had wandered afield now came back. There was much laughter and jesting, much brandishing of quarry. The king and the queen were the center of it, she boasting a pair of fine gazelle, he a string of wild geese that he had shot one by one out of the sky. "And who wins the wager?" someone shouted.

"Why," said the queen, "all of us!"

The king laughed and bowed in her direction. "Now there is grace," he said, "and victory for everyone."

"And a falcon for me and a pearl for you," she said, "and for the rest—a feast!"

They all cheered. The young and the bold spurred to a gallop. The sedate kept their mounts to a canter. Melisende grinned a rare and wild grin, and clapped heels to her mare's sides.

It was the sun that made her so, and the cool air, and the exuberance of the hunt. Fulk, catching fire from her youth, loosed rein on his stallion. The beast leaped as it were into flight.

Arslan was close behind, Bertrand beside him. He saw Lady Richildis beyond, keeping pace with the queen; and Baldwin riding ahead, reckless in his speed, laughing over his shoulder. That was perilous, Arslan would remember thinking. He should not—

It was blurringly swift and yet very slow, as some men said battle could be. The king at the full gallop. The queen a horselength ahead. A flash of brown on the brown earth, long ears, white tail—a hare started from cover, leaping full into the headlong hoofs of the king's stallion. The horse staggered. Its legs tangled. Slowly, slowly, yet swift as thought, it careened end over end.

The king fell free. Arslan, still caught in that slow crawl of time, saw him roll, saw him flail the earth, wide-eyed, battling shock, as the great wheeling weight of the horse crashed down on him. Arslan saw the high saddle, how it fell with monstrous inevitability, merciless as an executioner's axe.

The stillness was entirely of the mind. People were reeling, shouting, screaming.

Horses were hurtling hither and yon. People were hauling at the king's horse, the horse was struggling, flailing with hoofs, and the king—Arslan could not see the king at all.

The horse rolled away, scrambling to its feet, staggering lame. Its leg was broken. No one seemed to see. Arslan got down off Barak, not even noticing whether his own horse stood still or reared in terror. The king's stallion stood trembling, its poor leg dangling. Arslan had no weapon swift to hand, only the knife at his belt. It would do: he knew where to strike. Straight in the great vein of the neck, steady and deep, and the horse barely protesting, staring at him with its big dark eye, afraid and in pain yet trusting him—a man, a lord of creation—to take away the fear and the pain.

The horse sank down in a gush of bright red blood. Arslan stepped back out of reach of it, turned, let mind and eye know again what it had refused.

The king was not still, not mercifully dead. He jerked and convulsed over and over against the arms that restrained him. His skull—dear God, his skull was crushed and yet he lived, and his face—

Arslan swallowed bile. It was the queen who held the king down, the queen whose wailing seemed to fill the world: Melisende the cold, the perpetually calm, the queen to her fingers' ends, keening for the husband whom she had not, by any reckoning, loved as dearly as he loved her.

For three days Fulk lingered, racked with convulsions, dying yet refusing to die. They had carried him back to Acre with deathmarch slowness, laid him in his bed in the citadel, surrounded him with priests and physicians. And not one of them— not a single one—could do more than pray for his soul.

Melisende who had been so calm when her father died, who had borne her mother's death, it was said, with Christian fortitude, whose strength was so commonplace a thing that no one remarked on it—Melisende had broken when her husband fell. She had not loved him. She had barely esteemed him. Perhaps it was regret, and perhaps it was love waking late—no one knew.

After the first extravagance of grief she had gone quiet. She stayed by Fulk's side, would leave it for nothing, not to eat, not to sleep. She held his hand. It was slack, all bones and blue-white skin, a dead man's hand. It gave back nothing. The life lingered in him: he breathed, he shuddered at intervals, he shaped words with his broken mouth. They all strained to hear, but he said nothing that mattered, nothing that they could make sense of.

Baldwin's calm was deeper than his mother's, his shock if anything more profound. He had to eat and sleep and go about duties and lessons—his mother insisted, and he lacked will or desire to defy her. He sat with his father when he could. When he went to his bed, he lay as if asleep, but Arslan next to him felt the stiffness in his body, the stillness that was too deep for sleep.

He would not talk about it. Arslan, never given to pressing for words where words were too much or not enough, let him be.

When he was ready, he said what had been festering in him for nigh three days— since he turned in his headlong gallop and saw his father fallen, his head all broken by the saddle, and his mother keening like an eastern woman. He was lying in bed.

Outside it was deep night, the hour between matins and prime. A cold rain had crept in, rattling against the shutters, sending drafts of chill dampness through the room.

Beside Arslan, Baldwin stirred slightly. "He's going to die."

Arslan nodded. Baldwin's eyes were dark in the nightlamp's glimmer. They did not see Arslan's face, though they might seem to be resting on it. Arslan doubted that they saw anything at all.

"He's going to die," Baldwin said again, "and I will be king."

Arslan stayed silent. He had not had a father till three days ago, not one who knew who he was, and he had never had an inheritance to think of. Nor therefore had he had to think of what it meant to be a lord or a king—of the truth that some people thought too little of, and some too much. That in order to be king, a prince must lose his father. The king must die, that the king might live.

"I'm not supposed to be king this soon," Baldwin said. "I'm supposed to be much older. Much closer to a man."

"Then there will be a regency," Arslan said, since that much he did know.

"Like Aunt Alys and Cousin Constance in Antioch?"

Irony was not a frequent thing in Baldwin, but it was not unheard of, either. Arslan gave it the raise of brows that it deserved. "I don't think so," he said. "Your mother wouldn't sell you to the highest bidder, to rule instead of you."

"Wouldn't she?" Baldwin lay on his stomach, propped on his elbows, frowning at the wall. "They say her mother—my grandmother—was a warm and loving woman. She loved her husband. She took an interest in her daughters. But they grew up different."

"They grew up to rule," Arslan said. "Princess Yveta is like her mother, mostly— or like her mother as people tell of her. I like Princess Yveta."

"Aunt Yveta should have children," Baldwin said. "So of course she'll never marry. She'll be a holy abbess and spoil the novices instead."

"I don't think," said Arslan, "that your mother will do anything too terrible to you. You're too old, for one thing. For another, you're much more sensible than Princess Constance."

"Cousin Constance is a horrible child," said Baldwin, who was in fact a year younger than the lady in question. "No wonder Aunt Alys despises her, if she was like that as a baby. Can you imagine? She must have screamed for everything she wanted, and kept on screaming till she got it."

"Just like her mother," Arslan said, not charitably; but he did not like either Princess Alys or her daughter. Princess Alys was a haughty creature, given to sneering at anyone less lofty than herself. Princess Constance . . .

He schooled himself not to growl. Children were never kind, least of all to a bastard, but in the court he had fought his way to a position of respect. None of the pages could take him in a fight, nor could a good number of the squires. Nobody called him Olivier the Bastard to his face, or behind his back either—except Princess Constance when she visited her kin.

Lady Richildis said she liked him. That was why she curled her lip at him, found frequent occasion to slight him, called him ill names and galloped headlong over any defense that he could utter. He had stopped defending himself long ago, since that only fed her malice. If such was liking, then he did well to shun it.

"You are *nothing* like your aunt and her daughter," he said with vehemence that made Baldwin start. "Nor is your mother."

"She'll want a regency," Baldwin said after a pause. "She'll take it, too. I'm not ready to be king. Oh, God. I wish . . ."

Arslan waited, but he never actually said what he wished. Instead he shifted abruptly as he could do, shook himself, said, "I have to see my father."

By the time they had dressed and made themselves presentable—though who would care, Arslan could not imagine—it was nearly dawn. The king's chamber was guarded as always, the guards stiff and somber. Within, nothing was different. Still the same priests, the same physicians, the same stink of blood and sickness and something ripe and rotten-sweet that made Arslan think of death. They had been burning incense to cover it, and to invoke God, too; and there had been something noisome burned not long before, some nostrum of the ancients, most likely.

Queen Melisende sat by her husband's bed as she had sat for the past nights and days. Her face in the lamplight seemed a lifeless thing, a carving in pale stone. She glanced up as the two pages came in: swift, blinding, like lightning in the dark. This was not a woman gone mindless with grief—not any longer. She was thinking. Planning. Letting the long dark hours, the ruined face, the people coming and going, all the confusion of this sudden and yet drawn-out dying become for her a place of quiet.

Quiet like a storm before it breaks. Baldwin bowed to her, homage that she barely acknowledged, and knelt beside his father. There was nothing alive there, nothing aware, only the rattle of breath, the twitching of a body that had lost volition long since. The soul had gone out of it.

Baldwin did not weep. He simply knelt, head bent, eyes closed—praying, perhaps. Arslan started a little guiltily at that, thought that he should pray, too. A few words at least, begging the Blessed Virgin to be kind to this poor broken thing—to let it die soon, and not linger any longer.

She answered him—and that he had not expected. It was a long while before he understood the meaning of the silence.

There were sounds still: the rustle of cloth in a priest's robe, a cough, a soughing that might be wind. But something was missing. Everyone who breathed, breathed softly. No rattle and catch of tortured breath. No bubbling of blood in the broken throat.

The king was dead.

Baldwin's head came up as if he too had heard what was no longer there to hear. His face was stark white. "Father?" he said. "Father!"

Arslan caught at him before he could rise, before he could violate the dead with shaking. He fought, but Arslan was braced for it. Arslan held him and withstood him and waited till he went quiet again. Then, when it seemed safe, he let go.

Baldwin stood straight. He could not have cried himself out—but he had remembered what he was; what this moment made him.

So had Melisende. Arslan, lifting his eyes over Baldwin's tousled fair head, looked full into her face.

He hoped that he would never see such a face again. It was even whiter than

Baldwin's, and even starker. Its eyes were burning. Grief, yes, and pain, and guilt—whatever that was for. And a kind of white, fierce triumph. As if she had won something. As if . . .

"The king is dead," she said. "The king is a child. Baldwin!"

He snapped about, sharp as if her voice had been a lash.

"Baldwin," she said more gently but with no less intensity, "you do understand? What I must do?"

"If I didn't," he said, "would it make any difference?"

"It might have been easier," she said. She sounded almost regretful. "When your time comes, you will be king—you will be fit to be king. Until then, you will accept my right to command you."

He did not bow his head, though perhaps he should have. He said steadily, "I understand you."

"Good," said Melisende. "We'll do well, then. You will," she said, "be a good king. When your time comes."

"If it comes," Baldwin said: but too low perhaps for her to hear.

elisende had studied the example of Antioch. She had been careful to win the people to her side, to be charming to the lowly as well as to their princes, to be a queen whom they loved and whom they judged worthy of respect. They were ready to hear that she would be regent in her son's minority.

One more thing she had learned from her sister. She did not attempt to set aside the child who should rightfully rule. When she stood in front of the council of the kingdom, two days after the king's death when all who could come to Acre had done so, she stood with Baldwin at her side. The likeness between them was inescapable, and she had fostered it by ordering him dressed as she was in white and gold, the colors of the kingdom.

She laid her arm about his shoulders, there in the great hall of the palace of Acre, and said to the assembled lords and barons, "Here is your king. Because he is young, he requests that I rule with him. I who was born the heir to the Kingdom of Jerusalem, who was raised to be queen and to rule at a king's side—I have accepted the trust that he places in me. Do you also accept it? Will you permit not regency only, but queen regnant beside youthful king?"

She was not asking, not really. Arslan could tell that much. The barons could, too, most of them. He was watching his father: Lord Bertrand less shocked than some of them were to be here, approving a new reign, where but a week before had been a king of unblemished vitality. But he had been there at the hunt. He had seen the king fall. He had known what it meant, nor denied it as so many did.

People did not grieve for Fulk as they had for the old King Baldwin. They had not loved him so much. They were already rising out of grief, looking to the queen and her son, seeing what they were given to see. They were happy—a kind of delirious happiness in some of them, the laughter that comes after powerful shock. They rose, right there in the hall, rose and lifted a shout, ragged at first but then more nearly together. "Baldwin! Melisende! Melisende! Baldwin! Melisende! Melisende! Melisende!"

Melisende's grief for Fulk was real. There were many who doubted it, but Richildis who knew her—Richildis saw the truth of it. Much of it was regret, and guilt too:

that she had not known what he was to her until he was lost beyond recalling. "I never told him," she said in the night after Fulk was buried in Jerusalem near the Holy Sepulcher, not far from Melisende's own father. "He never knew that—after all—"

Richildis had no words of comfort to offer. The easy, the gentle, the not quite false but not quite perfectly true things that most women could utter as easily as they breathed, had never come to her when she needed them. She could only say, "It's said the dead know all."

Melisende laughed, no mirth in it, only pain. "Then he knows everything—every slip and folly, every moment that I resented him, every time I looked at him and wished that he had been anyone else—almost anyone at all."

"And the end, too," Richildis said, "when you repented of it."

"But did I?" Melisende had been sitting while Richildis brushed out her hair. She rose and began to prowl. "I never loved him. Even now I don't love him. He did love me—I think he did. He said he did. He told people—" She broke off. "Ah, God. It's my fault. If I hadn't taken it into my head to go hunting—if we hadn't—"

"Stop that," Richildis said briskly.

Melisende's eyes glittered, but she stopped ripping at herself with words. "I don't love him. What I feel—I could have esteemed him more. He was a good man, an affable man, and not too ill a king. Not a great one, no. He never had the gift. But he did well enough."

That was tribute, in its fashion. It was as much as Melisende would give him.

And when he was laid in his tomb, when mourning had turned as it inevitably must, to the joy of a new reign, Melisende at last was in her element. Melisende the princess had waited in taut-strung patience to be queen; then when she was queen she had fought to rule beside her husband. Now that husband, that man who had been required by law and precedence to give her the rank and title to which she was born, was dead.

She had still to rest her right on the head of a male, a boy who must wear the crown and sit as king beside her. But a boy, a child both young and small for his age, would not constrain her to accept his will or his precedence. She could rule now in truth, rule as queen.

Their coronation was a splendid thing. Ill prepared the kingdom might have been to crown a new king, but with Melisende to drive it, it wrought miracles of magnificence. Every great lord and prince and prelate who could be in Jerusalem for the Christmas feast, who could come there from countries as far as Italy and Byzantium—they all came to celebrate the birth of Lord Christ and to see Baldwin crowned beside his mother Melisende, young king and queen regent.

The streets were hung with silk and cloth of gold, banners that had been made for Fulk's crowning brought out and cleaned and others made new. A feast was spread in the city every day within the octave of Christmas, laid out in the square before the Patriarch's palace: fine wheaten bread and oxen roasted whole and sweets over which holy pilgrims squabbled like children. For the great ones there was a high feast in the Tower of David, day after day of it, and the queen sitting above it like an image of joy.

So quickly one forgot the dead, when the dead was king and a king was crowned thereafter. Baldwin remembered his father—probably one of the few who did, by the time he came to his crowning—but even he was caught up in the glory of it. Fear had died or was buried deep. He stood up when it was his time, lifted his head as the choir sang the antiphon, remembered only as the crown descended that he should bow beneath it.

It was his father's crown. It had needed no alteration but a rim of padding, to fit his head. The weight startled him: Arslan, standing as his squire, saw how his eyes widened. But when he stood up, lifted by the roar of the people, it seemed as light as living air.

Arslan had his own wings of exultation to carry him aloft. He who had thought to endure another year as a page, who had expected no preference for that he was Baldwin's foster-brother, had been roused before dawn on this day of coronation, sent to bathe, and dressed in clothes that he had never seen before. Then the king's servants—Baldwin's now, as the king's old chambers would be his when this day was over—told him that he would take the squire's place, carry the sword of state. "And by God," the king's bodyservant said, "if you love him or your own new rank, have a care that you don't drop it."

Arslan bit his tongue rather than gratify the man with a declaration that he could hold a sword, by God's bones—was he an infant, to be so weak? It was as well he restrained himself. The sword when he was given it was enormous, a heavy weight for a man grown. He carried it, and with pride, too: all the way in procession from the Tower of David, through the city with excruciatingly dignified slowness, into the Church of the Holy Sepulcher and up to the altar, there to stand through the splendid tedium of a high mass and a coronation after.

At least he could set the sword between his feet and rest his hands on the hilt for the mass—and fight the shaking that ran through his arms and shoulders from holding the thing upright for so ghastly long. Come the coronation he must grit his teeth and lift it again, so that it gleamed behind the king, sign and symbol of the power that God had given him.

Pride sustained Arslan—pride and a kind of desperation. He must not fail Baldwin. He was the king's squire, the bearer of his sword. In battle he would carry the royal arms. In the palace, he supposed, he would look after them and do what needed doing with them, and lock away this ruddy great sword that would be no earthly use in a fight.

The new Constable of the Kingdom, Manasses, a man new to Arslan but not to the queen—he had married her father's sister—was carrying a sword nearly as large, with much less apparent effort. He was a big man, as big as Arslan expected to be, with a kind of leonine grace that Arslan envied. Arslan was fast on his feet, but not particularly dignified. Mostly he scrambled, except when he stopped thinking about it; then he was deft enough.

The two of them stood side by side, swords held upright, as king and queen were crowned. Queen first—which was not the wonted order. But she had commanded it. She could not rule alone—that was the law and custom of the kingdom. But she could and would insist that she be first in each of the rites; that her son follow her as befit a child whose mother had ruled in this kingdom since before he was born.

If he resented it, he was not showing it. He was king—king under regency, but king nonetheless. He was full of it, singing with it. He wore the crown as one born to it. He had been studying his mother, and his father, too: he was gracious, royal but not haughty, with a bright edge that made people smile.

They loved him. They were delighted with their new young king, and with the queen who had won their hearts long since. If anyone muttered against them, he did not do it where Arslan could hear. Everyone was glad. The whole kingdom sang, celebrating the new king and the new year.

Richildis was too tired to sing. She had been laboring without rest since the morning after King Fulk died, to set all this in train, to hand it to those who would carry it on, to serve her lady as she best might. The dances, the feasting, the trappings of festival, all slipped past her in a blur of crowding duties.

She was aware amid the rest that there were embassies to be accommodated. The Saracens had sent ambassadors, so that both Damascus and Egypt saw the king crowned with his mother the queen; and Baghdad had sent a grave turbaned scholar and a caravan of gifts, including a brace of hunting cheetahs that enthralled the king. There were emissaries from the princes of Armenia, from the cities of the coast, from Italy and France and even distant England whose queen was wife to Baldwin's brother, Fulk's son by that earlier marriage from which, widowed, he had come to Melisende.

Baldwin's much elder and suitably noble brother, whose name was Geoffrey, had taken his father's place as Count of Anjou. He could not of course have known that their father was dead; not so soon. His embassy had come out of goodwill, that was all, bearing greeting to his father and his kin across the sea. But his envoy's presence spoke well for him, and gave him a voice in the affairs of the new king's court.

Byzantium had sent an embassy of suitable pomp and splendor, led by one of the emperor's own cousins. She noted them only insofar as the ambassador insisted that he be accommodated more nobly than the ambassadors from Cairo and Damascus—which, since he had come later than they, was not simple to accomplish. She had cursed, she had maneuvered, she had housed them all in a house precisely like those in which the others were lodged, but slightly closer to the Tower of David. That had appeared to satisfy them; there had been no further complaints.

The day after the coronation, between feast and feast, she paused a moment perforce. She had been running an errand in the city, a triviality that was of mighty importance to the baroness for whom she ran it, and had sent that lady's page back to her with the packet of spices that she must, simply must have for her husband's nightly hippocras. And what Richildis, a lady of rank and standing, was doing running at the beck of an imperious but not excessively lofty lady, she could not have said. Running away, perhaps. Indulging herself in something simple, in preference to the complexities that waited for her in the queen's workroom.

In fairness to Lady Emily, she had not expected Richildis to run the errand; she had asked her to find a maid who knew the markets, who could do it quickly. People did not presume with Richildis, unless she chose to let them.

She took her time walking back to the palace. Her perpetual shadow, the Turk Kutub—not Helena's Turk any longer, really, since he had attached himself to Richildis—was comfortably quiet and comfortingly there. He guided her gently past throngs of drunken revelers, round the square in which the public feast was spread, through quieter ways that, if crowded, were crowded with the reasonably sane and sober. She was content to be so guided, to let her mind rest for a little while.

Since Fulk died, Richildis had felt oddly old. She who had been as good as ageless for so long, with the passing of that man who had meant surprisingly little in the end to her or to her lady, now felt the sudden weight of years. It was like an autumn of the spirit. One moment bright summer, sun and warmth and burgeoning youth. The next, grey chill rain and fallen leaves, sere grass and the breath of winter.

She shaped the image in her head, to write down later. Often she wrote such things in letters: to Lady Agnes away in Anjou, yes, but to another more often than that, a memory of presence nigh a dozen years gone. Michael Bryennius had never come back to Jerusalem, nor indicated that he would. He wrote on occasion, letters brief but as warm as his smile. Small bits of gossip, wishes for her health and the health of her kin, a line or two that had to do with him: busy always, keeping a large and obstreperous family in order, managing its affairs, seeing to this estate or that, selling one amid mighty uproar till he reaped the profit; then he was the delight of all his kin.

In reply she wrote volumes, and sent them too—shyly at first, half determined to burn them instead, but after a while, though his replies were short, they seemed clear enough in their desire to hear more of her. So she wrote whatever came to her head, daily doings, this escapade or that of the prince and his headstrong foster-brother, snippets of court gossip; but mostly inner things, things that she told no one else, not even Helena who was her heart's friend. She knew that people thought her cold, and even Helena reckoned her reserved, not easily persuaded to open her heart; but in ink on parchment she was peculiarly free.

She had told him of her suitors, how they still kept coming though she was no longer particularly young; how none of them appealed to her sufficiently to merit the marriage vows. She told him of Arslan, in no great fear of breaking confidence— Michael Bryennius of all people would never betray her. She would tell him now of this odd new light on the world, this sense of years running away, when before they had seemed to stand still.

I wonder, she would write, *how much of it is the fact of a king's death, and how much of it is my own encroaching mortality. I'm hardly an old woman—I've half my natural span still to live—but the fact that half is gone . . . it matters. It didn't matter when I was twenty years old and a new widow to an old and rather unpleasant man; but that was fifteen years ago.*

I look at the men who approach me—three yesterday, can you believe it? Three bold brawny knights of God, three noblemen in search of a fine dowry—for surely the queen would endow me richly—and a handsome wife. I am handsome, aren't I? After all. I always denied it, but age brings clarity of eye, too, and a greater willingness to admit the truth.

So I look at them, dear friend, and I can only wonder what they want with such a juiceless stick as I am. Saints know there's no lack of buxom maids in this woman-

*heavy kingdom, and most with dowries, too. What makes them come to me? Do
they fancy that a widow of as much longevity as I, must be excessively eager to
renew the pleasures of the marriage bed? Or do they imagine just the opposite, that
I'm so desiccated as to be undismayed by a husband who seeks his comforts elsewhere?*

Dark thoughts, those, and rather silly—maybe she would not write them after
all. He would want to know of the coronation, surely, and all the festivals attendant
on it. If at the end she noted that she was feeling rather older than she had before,
she would not make a great issue of it. Why vex him? He was older than she, and
feeling it too, no doubt, with the family that he had.

But no wife. More than one letter had remarked wryly on his mother's efforts to
unite him with this lady or that. There was never one who quite suited him, never
one with whom he would go to the trouble of a wedding. When his mother lamented his perfidy, he reminded her of his brothers and their wives and their numerous progeny, any dozen of whom would have done perfectly well to supply that
branch of the family with an heir.

Richildis was not so richly endowed with kin, but there was Arslan; and she had
not given up hope that Bertrand would find himself a suitable lady and sire a legitimate heir or three. Foolish hope to be sure, as long as Helena lived, but Richildis
had not stopped hoping, either, that in the end he would go back to La Forêt.

"All things are possible," she said aloud, pausing as a procession of notables filled
up the narrow street. She recognized the Byzantine delegation by the silks and the
long beards and the air of self-importance; took note that the house she had chosen
for them was nearby, that in fact she was about to pass it. They must be going to
the Patriarch's palace for an entertainment in honor of the young king and his
queenly mother.

Richildis should be there herself, if she was strictly dutiful. But she was not
dressed for it. By the time she could come to the Tower of David, put on a gown
of suitable state, and summon a litter to take her to the fête, it would likely be
over.

She indulged a moment's guilt by way of tribute, and flattened herself in the
niche of a gateway while the procession strutted and jostled past. They were all in
grand panoply, robes and tall hats and a sweep of fur-lined mantles, perfumed so
strongly that her eyes watered. One of them had a monkey on a chain, riding his
silken shoulder; the little wizened creature was dressed in silk, too, proud in its
finery.

Most of them were mounted. The few who walked afoot must be servants. Several
were beardless but too old to be boys: eunuchs of the court. Richildis shivered a
little. Eunuchs made her uneasy.

Near the end of the line, one sat a fine bay horse, riding with more ease than
most, and more apparent pleasure. Richildis' eye caught on him and lingered. He
was a handsome man, not young but not old, either, dressed in crimson silk with a
mantle of rich dark fur—marten, she thought; beautiful and sleek, as he himself
was.

Her heart knew him before her wits did. He could not be here, of course. He
was hopelessly tangled in a broil of affairs that had taken him all the way to Nicaea

and kept him there through the summer. She had had a letter from him just the other day—or was it last month, before the king died? He could not be in Jerusalem, riding in the train of the emperor's ambassador, turning his horse from the track of the procession and halting in front of her, and smiling, the smile exactly as she remembered, as warm as a hearthfire in the chill chamber of her heart.

"My lady," he said, the same deep voice, the same accented Frankish, charming and familiarly foreign.

She looked up at him and considered anger. It was foolish, of course. A letter might have gone astray, or still be on the road and he had traveled ahead of it.

He slipped his foot from the stirrup and held out his hand. Anger could easily have become outrage—what, make a spectacle of herself in the public street? She forbore to indulge herself, clasped his hand and set foot in stirrup and let him draw her up behind him. His horse was amenable: a solid, broad-beamed creature, spirited but sensible, and not at all dismayed to carry two.

She could easily enough have held to the saddle's high cantle, but his waist was more comfortable, and more secure. She did not know why it felt familiar: she had never ridden behind him before. It was as if she had dreamed it, and the dream had been as real as life.

The procession of his countrymen had gone on its way while they lingered here—staring and muttering, no doubt, and wondering what brazen female that was who had captivated Michael Bryennius. He looked over his shoulder, a slant of bright dark eye, and said, "We could ride in state to the Patriarch's entertainment, or we could be dreadfully undutiful and run away like children."

"You wouldn't," said Richildis.

"Wouldn't I?" His smile gleamed like a sword, then flashed away. The bay's haunches bunched under her. She clung to Michael Bryennius' waist as the beast cantered down the nearly empty street.

THIRTY ONE

*I*t was absurd, outrageous, ungodly to run away like this.

It was wonderful.

She could not do it. Kutub—she strained, twisting against the horse's movement, looking in vain for sight of his lovely villainous face. There was no sign of it.

"Kutub," she said to the fine woolen mantle in front of her face. "Where—"

She felt the laughter through her hands, though there was nothing for the ears to hear. "Ah, Kutub. That pearl of Turks, that bright banner of Islam. I trust he's taking a well-earned holiday."

She went stiff as it all came clear. "That wasn't an accident. You bribed him to bring me to that particular place at that particular time."

"There now," said Michael Bryennius with no evidence of contrition, "I'd hardly say I *bribed* him. Consulted with him, rather. Agreed that we should meet again, you and I."

"You could," she said acidly, "have submitted yourself to the palace and applied for admission to my presence. It would have been granted."

"Surely," he said. "And I would have found you at your most prim and proper, being the perfect servant to the queen." His tone softened. "Isn't this better? Won't you admit it? There's no constraint on either of us, and no eyes to watch and pry and spread rumors of our impropriety."

"No," she said. "Only the whole city of Jerusalem that sees me carried on the crupper behind a man not of my kin or household or even of my nation, riding away who knows where, for who knows what purpose. You will," she said, "let me down. Now."

For answer he quickened his horse's pace a fraction, just enough to make it unwise to leap free. She would have done it regardless, except that her arms would not unlock from about his middle. It could not be fear, surely. It was prudence. Not—of course not—a deep unwillingness to let him go. She could not be wanting to go wherever he took her, wherever in the world he chose.

Whither thou goest . . . The words had never meant much to her: old words and holy, woven into the substance of her faith, but of no greater weight than many another. Now all at once they meant the world.

She should leap from this horse's back, run as fast as she could, as far as she might—away from this temptation.

Ah, and temptation to what? Bold as he might seem, Michael Bryennius was no man to ravish a lady unless she asked to be ravished. Wherever he was taking her, surely it was somewhere harmless—not back to the Tower of David, they were going in the wrong direction for that, nor to the Patriarch's palace where everyone else was, but somewhere in the east and north of the city.

It was a clear brisk day, with a strong wind blowing, snapping and straining the banners that ornamented every roof and balcony. Fusty old Jerusalem smelled almost young, almost clean. She was, she realized with a shock, giddily happy.

Just as she decided to ask him again where they were going, and this time compel an answer, he drew his horse to a halt. They were on a street that she did not know, except that it was off—well off—the street called Jehoshaphat. It was a quieter street than some, lined with blank walls and locked gates, like any street in any eastern city. The degree of its cleanliness and the absence of beggars and pilgrims spoke of a greater prosperity than some. From the roofs of its houses, no doubt, one could see the golden dome of the Temple gleaming against heaven.

From the street below there were only walls, and gates both shut and barred. Michael Bryennius had halted in front of one. Nothing distinguished it from any other. They all had worn stone carvings above their gates, marks of old wealthy houses, she supposed—Jews, in this quarter; though all the Jews were gone, driven out in the first Crusade. The one above her head depicted a Hebrew letter or word, she did not know which: she could recognize but not read the language of the Lord Christ's betrayers.

"It says *Life*," Michael Bryennius said, as if he had known that she would want to ask. "Just the one word: *Life*."

"How strange," said Richildis.

He swung his leg over the high pommel of his saddle, slid down, turned and caught her just as she slid to join him. She stumbled against him for an instant— too great a pleasure in the touch; she backed away. She was unreasonably annoyed that he let her.

He let go one of her hands, but kept a grip on the other. It was not so tight that she could not escape if she chose, but she did not so choose. "Come," he said.

The gate was not locked after all. It gave to his touch, opening on darkness. She heard his mutter of annoyance, a rattling and scrabbling and the harsh sliding of a bolt.

She blinked, dazzled. He had opened an inner door, revealing the place in which she stood to be a porter's niche. On the other side of the door was bright sunlight and the murmur of water, pool and fountain such as were beloved of people in this country. They filled the center of a courtyard with a colonnade, and walls rising above that, pierced with latticed windows.

It was all well kept, the pool and fountain clean, the vines that wound the columns cut close against the chill of winter. Yet no one came to greet them, no porter nor servant, nothing living but a cat that sat beside the fountain, upright and still as an image cast in copper. It was a red cat with a white breast, its eyes the clear gold of coins, regarding the interlopers with calm interest.

Michael Bryennius drew Richildis forward, into the sun. "Come," he said. "Come and see."

But this time she dug in her heels. "Whose house is this?" she demanded.

"Why," he said, "mine."

That did not surprise her. "Really? I hadn't known you had a house in Jerusalem."

"I didn't," he said, "until yesterday. It was to be ready when I took possession. Come with me and see if Messire Moishe has done as he promised."

"Messire Moishe?" She seized on that rather than the rest, as simple to unravel. "Not a Jew, surely."

"A Jew," he said, "surely, of a great and noble house that claims descent from a daughter of David. This was his father's house before the Franks in their ignorance drove out the Jews. I've taken it until the Franks in their turn are driven out, on the understanding that if the next rulers of this city are less horrified by Jews than those who hold it now, it will revert to him or to his family. For a suitable compensation, of course."

"How Byzantine," Richildis said. "I'm amazed that he was able to sell it to you. All properties were confiscated under Godfrey—that much I know."

"Not all," said Michael Bryennius, "not in perpetuity. Jews are wise in the ways of persecution. They seek out agents, calculate contingencies, do whatever they can to preserve what their labor has earned. Think of me as Messire Moishe's agent in this season of the world. Or if that makes you uncomfortable, simply think of me as owner of this house. It's quite beautiful. Will you see it with me?"

Richildis could hardly object to walking through a house that had belonged to a Jew. This whole city had been a house of Jewry, long ago. The Lord Christ himself . . .

She drew herself up as if for a battle. "Show me," she said.

Michael Bryennius did not say anything, but she saw how his body eased, a tension that she had not been aware of till it was gone. And why should it matter to him that she would walk through a cold and empty house? Despite the name that it was given, house of Life, it had not even servants to bring it alive. Only the empty rooms, clean and swept, and a few furnishings, and carpets that looked as if they had been rolled for long and long and only recently spread again.

"It will be a few days yet," Michael Bryennius said, "before it's fit to live in. But do you like it?"

"It's very handsome," she said. And when that did not seem to be enough: "Beautiful. The way the rooms flow into one another; the tiles on the floor; the garden, though it's wild yet—it will be lovely in spring."

He nodded. "Lovely, yes. I've hired a master gardener. He'll be here tomorrow or the day after. The servants, too. I brought some of my best from the City; they're looking into finding others here. By Candlemas, they've promised me, this will be a household both ample and complete."

Richildis turned slowly in place. They had come through the house to a room that must be meant for entertaining guests: larger than the rest, with a vaulted ceiling and a small fountain that, unlike that in the court, was dry and dead. It would come alive, she supposed, when the servants were in residence. Maybe it was meant to run with wine—though this seemed hardly a house for such ostentation.

For all its beauty and its spaciousness, it was not a pretentious place. It was simply what it was, lovely and quiet.

She liked it very much. As for what it meant, and what he had said—"You're going to live in Jerusalem?"

She must have sounded more incredulous than she meant. "Yes," he said with a touch of sharpness. "I am."

"But," she said, "your heart is in the City—in Byzantium. What possessed you to shift yourself here? Have you offended another chamberlain?"

"No," he said, still sharp, sharper than she might have expected. "May I not live where I please?"

"Ah," she said. "Your mother pressed you too hard to find a wife."

"She pressed me till I yielded," he said.

Richildis' mind ran on past him; stopped abruptly; went still. "And . . . you bring her to Jerusalem? Is she a native of this city?"

"No," he said, "and no."

She was all confused. It must have shown in her face: he took her hand once more and led her to empty fountain, and urged her gently down on its rim. She looked up at him, at his expression that she could not read. "Your mother must be furious," she said, "that you defy her so: agree to take a wife, but buy a house for her in Jerusalem."

"She doesn't know it yet," he said without evidence of guilt. "My brothers are managing the family's affairs as well as can be expected. None of them knows that I may be . . . delayed in coming back."

"Surely your bride-to-be knows," Richildis said. "You would have paid her that courtesy. Yes?"

He looked down. Was he blushing? The light in here was less bright than under the sky; she could not tell.

He took his time in answering. When he did, it was less boldly than heretofore. "It could be," he said, "that I bought this house as a favor to Messire Moishe, and because it gives my family a foothold in the Holy City. Need I have intended it for my putative intended?"

"You did say—" she began, but stopped. He had not. Not really.

He had never been so difficult to understand when he was in Outremer before. But he had been younger then, trammeled by his exile, with no certainty that he could return to his City or his kin. Far fewer years than this could change a man utterly.

No, she thought. He had not changed. Her heart told her he was the same. It was a foolish thing, but it would not let her be; it would not yield to the cold light of reason.

"I did," he said, "tell my mother that I would take a wife, if she would have me. I never told her where I would go or what I would do when I came there, or how long it might take. In this I sinned, and will do repentance. But this . . ." His hand took in the room and the house in which it lay. "This is my choice, my exile if you will. I gave the City and my kin the years that I felt I owed them. Now that those years are given, I take a handful for my own."

"How very free," she said.

"By which you mean libertine," said Michael Bryennius with a flash of teeth in the black beard. "Yes, I am, aren't I? I was careful that all the family's affairs should be well and fully seen to. I left nothing that could not be left in others' hands. No one suffers for my absence. No one loses by it."

"But why?" she asked. "You never loved this place so much before you left it."

"Then I was exiled by another's will," he answered. "Now I exile myself."

"*Why?*"

He met her eyes. "I am going to marry you," he said.

Richildis blinked. She said the first thing that came into her head. "Whatever for?"

"Because," he said, "I will have no one else."

"That's foolish," she said. "Wouldn't it have been simpler to insist on a monastery?"

"I have no calling to the monastic life," he said.

"Nor I," she said before she thought. She caught herself, but too late: it was tumbling out in spite of her. "This is impossible. We come from different worlds. You could never live in Anjou—you would loathe it. I could never live in Byzantium: I'd tangle myself in knots."

"Hence," he said, "this house in Jerusalem, where we can both be happy." He paused. Gathering courage, perhaps; if he had any need of such a thing. "I don't ask you to answer now, or even soon. Simply to consider it."

"Consider . . ." Her eyes were fixed on his face. She could not look away. She never had been able to, not without great effort. It was a handsome face, there was no denying it, but there were others as pleasant to the eyes, and some even pleasanter. That was not what fascinated her. The light that shone out of him, the spirit, whatever it was—he could have been the ugliest of men, and it would not matter. He was always and unmistakably himself.

Consider, she thought. What was there to consider? She did not want to marry again. She did not need to marry again. This man knew it—better than any, after the letters she had written.

Or had he never read them?

He had read them.

"I—" she said. Her voice died. She should refuse him now. To linger was cruel.

She could not say the words. What came at length was nothing that she had meant to say. "I should not," she said. "I should never even think of it. What we are—what our nations make us—it doesn't matter, does it? After all."

She could not tell if he held his breath, if he cherished hope. His eyes were dark. His face was still. Fortunate man, with such a beard to hide behind. No grey in it, either, though he must be past forty.

Her mind wandered. Almost she let it escape; but she lacked the will for any such thing.

"I . . . think I want to marry you," she said. "Does that make me as mad as you are?"

"Madder, most like," he said.

"Then I'll do it," she said. She was dizzy with daring. She had never done such a thing in her life. God in heaven, she should be excoriating him for going away for ten years and more, and coming back, and demanding almost the moment he saw her, that she bind herself to him. He had even bought this house to keep her in. The gall, the sheer and brazen gall—

It was glorious.

Which of them moved first, she never knew. He was as tall as she, solid and warm, sleek in fur and silk. She in her plain go-to-market gown had no such splendor, except in her heart.

Dull brown autumn, had she been? She was as gaudy as the Kalends of May. She had not felt so youthful when she was young—oh, not she, who had gone from the convent to Lord Thibaut's bed. This would not be the same, at all, at all.

He was staring at her, arched back a little within the circle of their embrace, so startled that she laughed. "I never knew you could sing," he said.

"I can't," she said. "That's my heart you hear, warbling like a lark as it rises."

"Beautiful," he said. "Wonderful."

"Preposterous," said Richildis.

mpossible," Bertrand said.

Richildis could not say that she was taken aback. She rather agreed. She faced him in Helena's receiving room, with Helena silent and—she thought—somewhat amused, and Arslan trying to make himself small beside his mother. Michael Bryennius had not yet arrived for the dinner that was being prepared in a waft of savory scents, nor would he appear for yet a while.

Which was exactly as Richildis had intended. She had presented the facts baldly, with few preliminaries—struck him with it, she admitted, nigh as soon as he came in the door. "I'm going to marry Michael Bryennius," she said.

And of course he said, "Impossible."

"No, it's quite possible," she said. "He's in Jerusalem with the delegation from his emperor. The Patriarch may not agree to marry us—there is the little matter of schism—but I may become a devotee of the Armenian rite, and so avoid the conflict."

Bertrand looked ready to spit. "I know he's in the city! I went tavern-crawling with him the night before last. That devious, low-minded, damned impudent son of a—"

"I beg your pardon," Richildis said stiffly, which stopped him; but not for long.

It was Helena who brought him to a halt. "Don't tell me you let yourself be entertained by ladies of tarnished reputation."

Bertrand flushed bright scarlet: glorious to see. Poor fool, he had never considered the reflection on himself. "We did not!" he cried. "We most certainly did not. I am a man of faithful heart, and he—"

"He is going to marry me." Richildis met his glare with calm that she knew would drive him wild. "My dear and beloved brother," she said, "you may be my eldest and only legitimate male kin, but I am a widow of many years' standing, with rank and position of my own. I never swore fealty to you as my liege lord, since you refused to take the demesne to which you are heir. You have no authority over me, nor right to forbid me."

"I have every right," he said. "I *am* your male kin."

"Then I shall disown you," she said.

"A woman can't disown her own brother."

"May she not?" Richildis asked with lifted brow.

"She may not," he said firmly. "Nor will the queen be of any use to you. She can't pass a law that would allow a woman to refuse such authority. It would look too much as if she wanted it for herself."

"That is manifestly true," Richildis said, unshaken. "But the queen is my liege lady—and yours. It requires no alteration in the law. She may simply, upon petition, overrule any objection. I will petition her, Bertrand. Don't doubt it for a moment."

His jaw had set hard, but he was not altogether a fool. "He should," he said, "have asked my leave."

"So he will," said Richildis. "He's coming to do just that."

"And if I deny him?"

"I go to the queen."

Bertrand struck the winetable with his fist. The jar rocked. Cups wobbled. Helena caught one before it fell, staining her sky-blue gown with crimson. He looked only faintly guilty. "I can't let you marry that—"

"That old and much-loved friend of yours, with whom you went tavern-crawling just the other night?"

"That Byzantine!"

"Oh," Helena mildly, sweet as birdsong amid the roaring of a storm. "Of course one must have nothing to do with a foreigner, a person of blood far removed from good Frankish stock."

Bertrand reared back. Helena smiled.

"My love," she said, "you're being absurd. Your objections are all very proper—if you were a proper Angevin lordling with a proper wife and a castleful of proper heirs. If you had gone to Anjou when your sister first came to fetch you, you would be all of that. And she would never have met so unsuitable a suitor."

"But—" said Bertrand.

"Father, don't you like him?" Arslan looked startled at himself, as if he had not meant to say anything but could not help it. "You always seemed fond of him. When I heard you talking of him—when Mother told me—"

He gave up in confusion. Bertrand had shied a little at the title of father, but had rallied admirably. He spoke to Arslan with gentleness that he had not shown the women—though not so gentle that it was an insult. "Yes, messire, I am fond of him. As a friend. As a drinking companion. As a brother-in-law—how can I be? That's my sister he's daring to touch, as if he had a right to her."

Richildis burst out laughing. She should not have, and she knew that, but there was no help for it. He was simply too ridiculous.

As he rounded on her, furious, she swallowed the last of her laughter and said, "Oh, Bertrand, listen to yourself! You're being a perfect monster of rectitude. When did you grow up so straitly? When did you become our father?"

Bertrand went white. She had gone too far—perhaps.

She would not back down. Let him think, or let him be too blind with rage to think. She hardly cared which.

When he spoke, his voice was barely to be heard. "You give no quarter."

"I never did," she said. "I want this man, Bertrand. I've wanted him since I saw him in your castle, destroying your armies in a chessboard. I never knew, nor knew that he wanted me. When he went away I thought myself cured of him. But he came back—and he came for me. He's wanted no woman as I've wanted no man. For each of us there is only the other."

"I would never have dreamed," he said, "that you could think such things."

"Nor I," she said in a kind of wonder, "until I said them. Mind you, I won't die if I can't have him. But I will die to the world. I'll take the veil."

"You never wanted that," he said.

"Nor do I want it now," said Richildis. "But without this man I want the world even less. I could do very well. A scholarly order, a life of contemplation, no interruptions but the round of the holy offices: there's much worse in the world in that."

Bertrand shook his head. He seemed more awed than angry now, and more wry than either. "I can't win against you, can I? You've prepared all your battles, even the ones I would never have thought of."

She nodded, unsmiling. She was not here to revel in victory, or to be glad that she had prevailed over her brother. "If you won't bless us, the queen will."

"I'll bless you!" He made it sound like a threat. "I am your kin. I have the right."

"And I," she said, "won't petition the queen to overrule it."

Bertrand was blessedly polite to Michael Bryennius. Polite—not cordial. He was in fact a little stiff.

Michael Bryennius was amused. When they had eaten one of Helena's cook's simple yet marvelous dinners, when Helena had ordered up a jar of the best wine from the cellar, he sat back in his chair, turning the silver cup in his hands. "My dear friend," he said to Bertrand, "out with it. How dare I presume to ask for your sister?"

"And how dare she accept?" Bertrand sighed heavily. The tension in him eased—not altogether, but enough to notice. "She's informed me that whether I will or no, she will marry you. I might resist her, but she invokes the queen, who surely will take her part. I can hardly challenge her majesty."

"A very sensible conclusion," Michael Bryennius said.

"You don't have to sound so damned smug," Bertrand said.

Michael Bryennius grinned. "I am, aren't I? She's the glory of the Franks, my friend. Small wonder you're reluctant to give her up to a foreigner."

"Don't be silly," snapped Bertrand. "She's attractive but she's not sublime. There are half a dozen prettier—"

"Not to me," Michael Bryennius said, soft as a purr.

Bertrand blinked. A brother could forget, Richildis thought, what a lover would want to hear. No man's sister should be beautiful to him.

He turned to look at her. She fought the urge to say something cutting. Apparently he saw something in her face that he had not seen before: his eyes widened; he blinked again, not in surprise, not exactly. More as if a sudden light had dazzled him.

Well. She was not a great beauty, but neither was she ugly. That might startle a brother whose perception of her face had blurred into familiarity when she was a gaptoothed child.

Bertrand shook his head slowly. "Now I'm amazed that no one's asked for you before."

"The queen could tell you otherwise," Richildis said. "When I first came, there was one every month. Now it's one or two each season. Some men prefer a widow of a certain age but young enough still to bear a child or two."

"Why didn't I know this? Those must be men I know. If one them has insulted you, or refused you, or—"

"The queen dealt with each according to his deserts," Richildis said.

He ran his hand over his face as if it hurt him. "Do you women have any genuine need of men at all?"

"Not," she said, "as a general rule. No."

"You see," Michael Bryennius said, "how she honors me by pretending that she needs a husband."

"Need has nothing to do with it," Richildis said tartly. "Now if you speak of wanting . . ."

He smiled at her, sweet enough to weaken her knees. Love was a disease, the ancients said. She knew it for truth. Such a disease as made one want more of it and not less, till one expired in a haze of bliss.

Not that bliss was her common lot in this man's vicinity. Annoyance rather, and startlement at whatever he took it into his head to say next, and a marvelous deep warmth whenever he looked at her. She had not tried to imagine what it would be like to be his wife. She would do it, that was all. God would help her if He would; if not, not.

Her poor brother was completely baffled. Well; and he should not be. He had chosen the lady of his heart long ago, though he had never married her.

This would be a grand jest in Provence, or in Aquitaine where such a thing was called *fin amor* and much prized and sung. But then people in the south of France were all famously hot-blooded, or so they professed themselves to be. Northerners made less noise about it.

She schooled herself to serenity, drank the rest of her wine though she barely tasted it, and did her best not to stare too often at Michael Bryennius. He was wearing what must be his courtier's face, amiable and rather empty, and not turning his eyes toward her at all. What, shy? Or merely and belatedly circumspect?

Bertrand put an end to the discomfort abruptly, rising and saying to Arslan, "Come, sir. It's time we went home."

Since home to Arslan was the palace, and home to Bertrand was his house in the city, Arslan looked rather understandably startled. He did not, Richildis noted, utter a protest. Wise child. He was taking very well to the late advent of a father— better perhaps than the father was taking to the late discovery that his son had been living under his nose for all these years. Arslan had enough of his mother in him to be undismayed by shocks that would flatten a lesser spirit.

Michael Bryennius waited till they were both on their feet and turned toward the door, with a servant coming with their cloaks, before he said, "I gather we don't have your blessing, then."

"You have it," Bertrand said, biting off the words. "What, do you want a kiss on both cheeks, too, and a brother's welcome?"

"Such would be pleasant," Michael Bryennius said. "Eventually. I'll give you time to accustom yourself to the prospect."

Bertrand growled wordlessly. "God's teeth! You two deserve each other."

Michael Bryennius smiled and bowed where he sat, as if he had been paid a compliment. Richildis laughed. Bertrand snarled again, but with a catch in it—he was trying not to laugh, she could tell. He did not want to laugh. And there was Arslan, hopelessly confused. She hoped that Bertrand could explain to him later just why, after all the growling and snapping, everyone was suddenly helpless with mirth.

The young would never understand. For that one needed years and scars and no little recent pain. Laughter was born of these; and if it ended in tears, those tears washed the heart clean.

"You," Bertrand said when he could speak again, "will do what you damned well please. Rather than look like an idiot, I'll play the game with you. But don't expect any brotherly love until I'm good and ready."

"Oh, we would never expect that," Michael Bryennius said gravely. "Never at all. No."

Bertrand coughed: laughter again, with perhaps a roar of rage buried in it. But he said nothing. He bowed to them all, kissed Helena on both cheeks—making a point of it, surely—and left, taking his son with him.

After he had gone, it was as if a storm had passed, leaving them all a little weak. Helena sent the winejar round again. Richildis was minded to refuse, but Helena had filled the cup before she could object. The wine was sweet and strong, barely watered. She drank deep, deeper than she was used to, till she was dizzy.

Michael Bryennius spoke for them all. "Victory," he said, "but at a price. Who would believe so affable a man could be so terrible in battle?"

"The lion is a lazy beast," Helena observed, "except when he's pricked to anger."

"That's not lion-anger," Richildis said irritably. "That's a boy's tantrum. How dare his sister do a thing without begging his leave? And if he were my liege lord, maybe I would have."

"Did you ask the queen's leave?" Michael Bryennius asked.

She glared at him. "Of course I didn't. I will when she's done with all this festival."

"And if she says no?"

Richildis rebuked her heart for stopping. "Then we'll try the Emperor of the Byzantines. And if he refuses . . . well then. We'll find someone who won't. The lord of the spice countries, maybe. The man who rules the silk country. Even a Caliph or two, or the King of France. His queen is young, they say, and a little wild. Maybe she'd find us amusing enough to indulge us."

"A vast plan," Michael Bryennius said, "and ingenious. I salute you."

She bared her teeth at his mockery. "I am not going to surrender to the rest of the world, now that I've surrendered to you."

"But it was I," he said, "who surrendered to you. What is it the knights say in the lists? Yield! I yield! And all power to the Queen of Beauty."

"They don't say that," Richildis said.

"Then they should," said Michael Bryennius.

elisende had much less to say of Richildis' folly than Bertrand had, and rather more to the point. "You will do this?" she asked.

"Will you forbid me?" Richildis asked in return.

She watched the queen consider it. For all her bold words to her brother, she was not greatly enamored of wandering the world around in search of a ruler who would bless her union with a Byzantine.

But if she must do it, then she must.

Melisende sighed at last, bowing her head under Richildis' hands that ran the ivory comb through her hair. "No, I won't forbid you. The man is a schismatic and a Greek, yes?"

"He reckons himself a Roman."

"That might be worse." Melisende shook her head. "No, no. Marry him. The Patriarch will see to a dispensation, if one is needed."

"As easy as that?"

Richildis had not known she spoke aloud until Melisende said, "Which? The Patriarch, or your marrying the man at all?"

"All of it," Richildis said. "You don't even know him."

"On the contrary," said Melisende. "He applied to me for audience the day after I was crowned. I granted it finally yesterday. He's an interesting man."

"Yes," said Richildis.

Melisende looked over her shoulder. "When you go flat like that, I know you're thinking rage at me."

"No," Richildis said—flat; she could not help it. "Lady, neither of you said a word to me."

"We judged it best," thought Melisende, "to spare you any vexation. As it happens, I like him very much. He's less slippery than most of his kind. Where ever did you find him?"

Richildis did not know that she was prepared for a comfortable gossip with the Queen of Jerusalem; but Melisende was in an amiable mood. Richildis struggled to meet her at least without sharpness. "My brother found him. He was in Beausoleil for three whole years and more, and would never come to Jerusalem."

"His exile, yes," said Melisende. "He told me of that. He would be an unfortunate courtier, particularly in that court. What does he expect to do in this kingdom?"

"He didn't tell you?"

Melisende's eyes flickered. Richildis had presumed; but she refused to flinch.

"He told me," said Melisende, "that he expects to live quietly, to administer such of his family's affairs as can be done at this distance, and to make you deliriously happy."

Richildis blushed furiously. "He did not say that!"

"Those are his very words." Melisende let a smile escape, one far less fitting a queen than a hoyden princess. "I told you that I liked him. He's wealthy, I gather, but his family may not be so pleased when he fails to return from his embassy. There's a charter waiting for you, title to an estate that's in my bestowal. It's small but profitable, with an olive press and a sugar-mill and the beginning of a vineyard—and what may suit you well, it's within a day's ride of Jerusalem."

That was more than generous. It was a gesture of friendship. Richildis felt her throat go tight. "I . . . thank you," she said.

"You may not when you see what needs to be done at Mount Ghazal."

"Mount Ghazal? Is that what it's called?"

"Indeed," said Melisende. "It's a village of devout Muslims, a few Frankish pilgrims scraping a living beside them, and a castle that was barely finished before its lord was killed in a Bedu raid. He had no wife and no heir. There will be servants, a steward, a knight I think, unless he transferred his service elsewhere. You will owe one knight in fee; or provide twenty men-at-arms to the levy of the kingdom."

Richildis bent her head. This was labor on labor—worse perhaps than what she had done to help prepare the coronation. And she was glad. High, bright, singing glad. To serve a queen, that was honor, and by now most familiar. But to be lady of a holding, a barony with even—God help her—a vineyard: that she could do from her youth.

She reined herself in. "My . . . husband"—her tongue stumbled; so did her heart—"might be otherwise inclined. He does insist that his wealth is enough for us both."

"He did," said Melisende. "He eventually agreed that you would be happier with somewhat to do, and a place of your own in which to do it. A fortress in the chain of castles, a house in Jerusalem: that's very proper for a baroness in this kingdom over the sea."

"And how did he take to the thought that he would be a baron of the High Court of the Kingdom of Jerusalem?"

"Why, not at all," Melisende said. "He'll be no baron. He continues to be a nobleman of Byzantium, kinsman of the emperor. You are a baroness of the High Court."

"You can't do that," Richildis said.

"The queen may dispose as she pleases of the lands in her bestowal," said Melisende. She took great pleasure in saying it: her eyes were as bright as they had been when she was crowned. "Do you offer further objection?"

"I don't object," Richildis said. "I'm . . . taken by surprise."

"You shouldn't be," said Melisende.

Richildis bowed to that.

• • •

Richildis was married to Michael Bryennius on the feast of Epiphany, before the chapel door of the Tower of David, by the queen's own chaplain. The Patriarch would not do it, though he had given dispensation. Father Walter was more willing, perhaps in hope of converting a schismatic to the true faith.

Except for a slight flaring of the nostrils in the mass that came after their vows, when they had been admitted to the chapel, Michael Bryennius preserved his peace. He had not let Richildis' hand go since it was placed in his during the taking of vows. Their fingers were twined as if they would never be divided.

He was warm beside her in winter's chill, with the faint sweet scent of spices that he favored over the heavy perfumes of his countrymen. His coat was new, brocaded silk the color of ripe Damascus plums, so deep a blue it was almost black. It made her remember the clothes he had worn in Beausoleil, somber and always elegant.

She had somewhat unwittingly matched him, choosing a gown appropriate to a widow who married again, a blue nigh as deep and nigh as rich as his. Pearls were sewn upon it like stars in a midnight sky. Her camise was fine linen the color of ivory, her veil deep blue over ivory, her hair plaited beneath it and bound with a fillet of silver. The fillet pressed on her brows, not quite heavy enough to ache. She was ridiculously happy.

It was a small wedding, no more than kin; no press of the court, no crowd of hangers-on. Bad enough that people were whispering, telling tales of a Frankish lady who would not choose from among her own kind but must go seeking among the treacherous Byzantines. So they had been married in quiet, in an hour of the day when most sat to their daymeal. The queen was there with those of her ladies who were most well disposed toward Richildis, having eluded the feast in the court; Baldwin the young king and Arslan his friend and Amaury the young prince in his page's livery, Bertrand and Helena and, outside the door where infidels must stay, Helena's Turks with their turbans and their wonderful wicked faces.

The wedding banquet was laid in Helena's house, that being closest and Helena being most strong-willed about the excellence of her cook. Richildis rode to it in a litter, the others as suited them best, laughing and singing and brandishing torches in the grey sleet-lashed evening. It could have been high spring and bright day for all they recked of the weather.

Helena's cook had outdone himself. He refused to roast an ox whole—vulgar ostentation without finesse, he called that. Instead he had prepared a round of dishes: lamb in dates and spices, gazelle rubbed with herbs and roasted on a spit, geese stuffed with apples, pies and pasties and sweets in delirious profusion. Richildis could have her fill of oranges if she wanted them, and wine from Italy, wine from France, wine from La Forêt itself.

She could eat none of it, could drink only a little. She made herself nibble, or seem to. Everyone else, even Michael Bryennius, seemed happily ravenous. She could only feign interest in the feast, beautiful as it was.

She had been much less dismayed at her first wedding—and much less willing, too. Then food and wine had dulled the edge of her dislike for the man whom her father had chosen. She had calculated that if she drank enough, ate enough, nothing that happened after would matter.

It had been unpleasant, but not as unpleasant as she had feared. Thierry could be gentle enough when he wished.

What it would be tonight . . .

She shivered a little, though the room was warm with braziers and lamps and the heat of human bodies. The thing that made a marriage a marriage was the one thing she had forborne to think of. They had not even kissed, the two of them. They had touched hands. That was all.

Maybe he would be content to live as brother and sister, to share a household in Christian chastity.

Ah: but would he? And would she?

She was almost sorry when the last of the wine had gone round, when the plates and platters and bowls were carried away. As little as she had partaken of them, as silent as she had been while the revelry went on around her, it was a shield of sorts. When it was gone, there would be nothing left but the two of them. And then . . .

And then. They were delivered to Michael Bryennius' house—their house—with rather too much shouting and laughter, wine and torches and ribald singing. She did not recall that there had been so many at her first wedding, or that so many had been young men, knights and squires armed with torches. Someone had mustered an army. She would lay the blame on Bertrand, but he seemed as taken aback as she. She had to glimpse Baldwin's face in a flare of torchlight, to see the expression of wicked glee—and Arslan looking as if he had been the master of the plot.

She would kill them. Later.

They sang and roistered and drained wine from skins outside in the sleet, while the more proper guests saw bride and groom put to bed. Melisende and Helena oversaw Richildis' bath in a brazier-heated room, clothed her in a shift of fine white linen and a gown of sea-blue wool lined with soft grey vair, combed out her hair and scented her with oil of roses. She had trembled herself into stillness.

The chamber was golden with lamplight, the bed freshly made and strewn with herbs and rose-petals. Richildis could only think, looking at them, of bare skin and rough dried leaves and the discomforts of luxury.

She dared not burst into giggles: if she did, she would not be able to stop. She let them, her queenly servants, arrange her in the bed, spread her hair about her shoulders, draw the coverlet up just so far and no farther. All of it would come off, of course, but he would expect to find her so. Every new husband did. Did he not?

Who knew what a Byzantine would expect?

They bowed and smiled—even the queen, enjoying herself immensely, Richildis could see—and withdrew. Leaving her alone with her overscented bed and her overwarmed chamber and her overarching edifice of fears. She had not been so afraid last night; no, not even in the wedding, when she spoke the vows that bound her to this stranger.

Stranger, foreigner, man whom she had known for a month and then not seen for ten years and more. And when he had come back, he had demanded that she marry him. And she, like a fool, had agreed.

Her heart had done all the choosing. Her head ruled now, when her heart should be strongest. Fool of a creature, to be so contradictory.

The outer door opened slowly. The charivari outside the window drowned out any footstep, yet Richildis felt his coming. She could not move. She lay like a scared child, a maiden bride arrayed for her beast of a husband.

Michael Bryennius' voice sounded without, calm but very firm. "No, I do not require an escort. No, you will not put me to bed. Now go."

Then the door was shut and barred and he was inside of it, looking much less calm than he had sounded. He was as damply clean as she, his cheeks flushed, his eyes a little too bright. The door bulged behind him as some ox of a knight flung shoulder at it. But the bolt held. It was a sturdy thing, new-forged from the look of it, and with this night in mind, Richildis had no doubt.

He took a step away from the door, then two, then three. And stopped. "You look," he said, "like—"

"Like a frightened fool." Richildis flung back coverlets and mantle, rose on legs that wobbled but held, and approached him as if he were a Saracen and she had a mind to conquer him. He did not recoil, which spoke well for his courage.

She did not know precisely what one did. Thierry had expected her to be lying in bed, as flat as she could manage, and had grunted and heaved on top of her till he was satisfied. That was not the way she had heard people speak of it elsewhere. They began, it was said, with a kiss.

Her arms fit well about his neck. His scent was of musk and spices, light and clean yet somehow strong enough to dizzy her. One kissed . . . so. He was not the innocent that she was. He knew the art that she had only heard of. She was clumsy, but he was a willing teacher, patient and not too conspicuously amused.

His patience would have won her heart if nothing else had. It won her head, too, which was more to be marveled at. Fear lingered, that he would seize her after all and throw her down, but he never did.

It was she who grew impatient at last, who wearied of touching lip to lip and tongue to tongue, with the rest of the body burning, and not so slowly, either. If this was a sin, then sin could be sacred.

Blasphemy.

She did not care. This was like battle, like riding wild in the hunt: a white exhilaration. To let go, to free oneself of fear and doubt and shame of the body— to make a sacrament of the flesh as the Church had made them of the spirit . . .

"No wonder they won't allow folk to marry inside the church door," Richildis said in a pause, "if it leads to this."

He did not answer, not in words. He lifted her in his arms and swept her up, only to lay her down again rather quickly. She was spare enough, but her bones were solid. She laughed breathlessly, sinking down and down in the featherbed, and the deeper she sank, the more beautifully startled he looked.

Before she vanished utterly, she reached up and caught hold of him and pulled him in with her. She felt him try not to fall on top of her. That only made her laugh the harder. In a tangle of legs and arms, elbows and knees and garments that needed undue amounts of time to be rid of, they found at last the meeting of body and body.

She gasped. He tried to pull away, but she held him till he yielded. "I hurt you," he said. He sounded as if he would weep.

"No," she said. "No, no, no. You would never hurt me. Not you, not ever."

"But—"

"Be quiet," she said. "Love me."

It was she who had vowed to obey him. But he was a wise husband. He chose to obey her.

ount Ghazal was not as dreadful
as the queen had led Richildis to expect. It was in some disrepair, to be sure. Its
knight was long gone, and she would have to find another, or equal him with twenty
men-at-arms. Its steward was old and not well, nor had he a wife to rule in his
name. There was however a young clerk in his workroom, a weedy boy with the
squint of the nearsighted, who appeared to know where everything was, if not always
what to do with or about it.

Richildis appointed him steward, to his manifest dismay, and set him to work.
For the men-at-arms—knight, she could not find quickly, nor truly wanted to—she
turned to Kutub. She had only to raise a brow. "I saw," he said, "some strapping
young men in the village. I can make fighters of them, I think."

"You think?"

"They aren't Turks," he said. "If they were . . ."

"Can you find any?"

His brows went up. "You would take a whole score of wild tribesmen? If I could
find them?"

"I'll take what I can get," she said.

"Then if you'll trust me," he said, "I'll see that you're well served."

She inclined her head. He bowed and went away. Truly away—out of Mount
Ghazal. God—or Allah—knew where.

She had little enough time to fret over him. There was the castle to set in order,
the *rais* of the village to receive in proper dignity, the affairs of the holding to see
to, each in its turn.

And Michael Bryennius coming up from Jerusalem on the morrow, after he had
settled affairs of his own. She would like to see the castle clean at least, and a
chamber readied for him, and food to feed him that was not cold roast mutton and
days-old bread.

She kilted up her skirts and mustered her forces and set herself to work.

Michael Bryennius found a clean hall and a horde of busy servants and, ankle-deep
in the mud of the stableyard, his wife. She was looking over a fine colt while a
dark-eyed boy held the halter of its dam. "He was bred here?" she was asking in
quite decent Arabic. "His sire?"

"Lady," said the boy who held the mare, "he didn't exactly have a sire. We tethered her out, you see, where the Banu Yusuf like to water their flocks. They have a good stallion. If it happened that he covered her . . . well . . ."

"And if it happened that some knight on a hulk of a destrier had ridden past first?"

The boy lowered the lids over his big beautiful eyes. "Oh, lady," he said demurely, "there were no knights in the region that day; no, not one."

"I hope you didn't lure one over a cliff," Richildis said, "or into a lion's den."

"Oh, no, lady!" the boy said fervently. "Of course not. We're horsebreeders, not murderers. One did come, but my cousin Suraya was filling a jar at the spring. Suraya is very pretty."

"Worse and worse," sighed Richildis. "Did he—take advantage of her?"

"Of course not, lady," said the boy. "He thought of it, of course, but Suraya's nine brothers happened to come by on a boar-hunt, with their spears and their bows and all. They persuaded him to take his hulk of a destrier and find his pleasure elsewhere. He was remarkably willing to oblige," the boy said, remembering with evident fondness. "He was standing in the saddle, and moaning every time his horse took a rough stride."

"They flayed him?" Richildis asked in morbid fascination.

"No, lady," the boy said. "Suraya has a dangerous knee. Most dangerous, lady. My cousins have some doubt that the knight will sire children after this—even weakling daughters."

"Is that so?" Richildis said. "I should like to meet those cousins—and their sister Suraya."

"And do you like the colt?" the boy asked with an air of innocent persistence.

"The colt is splendid," Richildis said. "I do wonder what the destrier was doing while Suraya was disposing of his master."

"Covering the mare, I would guess," Michael Bryennius said.

Richildis whirled. The light in her face was enough to stop a man's heart. It was always there when he came to her, reflection of that in his own face—nor did time seem likely to lessen it.

She restrained herself from embracing him in front of strangers, greeted him demurely as a wife should greet her husband. "You do think the colt is a halfbred?"

"I think the destrier must have been a very fine horse indeed," Michael Bryennius said. "You don't see such bone or such size in the desert stock—even the best of it."

The colt, which had been standing quietly on the lead, decided just then to rebel. As it went up, Richildis brought it firmly down again. She rebuked it as if it had been a wayward child, and in God's truth it lowered its head and looked ashamed.

"Even infant stallions give way to you," Michael Bryennius said to her much later in the chamber with its fresh rushes and still faintly damp bed-linens. Everything looked as new as this morning, except the carven monstrosity of the bed, which some long-gone lord must have hauled with him all the way from Germany. Richildis had thought of having it taken away and burned, but it was too useful. Perhaps its ghastliness would grow less as she grew accustomed to it.

She was letting her mind wander. Her husband let her do it, smiling at her in the lamplight, doting shamelessly.

"I think I'd like to stake the mare out again in the spring," she said, "and see who else rides by on his destrier."

He grinned like a boy. "I have a better plan. Invite a guest or two—and choose each for the quality of his horses."

"I don't know," she said, "that I want to submit a guest to the knee of the lovely Suraya—or the gentle ministrations of her nine brothers."

"Them, you would do well to take on as men-at-arms," he said.

"Even the sister?"

"Her above all," he said, flinging himself backwards onto the bed, spreading his arms for her to fall into.

When they had sorted themselves out with the laughter that had become an inextricable part of what they did together, Richildis rested her head on his shoulder and let him cradle her with the whole of him. "I don't suppose you'll like it much here," she said. "It can't be like anything you'd choose to do."

His voice was a rumble in his chest, thrumming against her ear. "What makes you think that?"

She held him a little more tightly, as if to stave off anger. "You come from your City, yes? This is an outland castle in poor repair, and a holding in sore need of good management. So much of it must seem unnecessary to you. Unnecessary and excessively countrified."

"Are you regretting marrying me?"

She lifted her head from his shoulder, raised herself against his grip. It tightened, then dropped away. She stared into his face. It was very white, his eyes very dark. "I could never regret marrying you," she said.

"Then why," he demanded, "are you perpetrating such utter nonsense? Yes, I was born in Constantine's City. Yes, I've spent much of my life there. But not all my family's holdings are in cities. There is an estate in Illyria, a lone tamed island in a black sea of mountain and forest, where the hunting is astonishing. Someday I hope you'll see it. Then tell me in all truth that I would find this place impossibly rustic."

Richildis bit her lip. "I . . . didn't mean to make you angry."

No? And had she not?

She silenced the mocking voice in her mind and said, "We know each other so well, and yet so little. A month, nigh a dozen years ago. Letters at intervals since. A few days in Jerusalem, and now here."

"That's more than most new-wed folk are given," he said. "Some never meet till the day they're married."

"They don't marry for our reasons, either," Richildis said. "They are practical."

"And we are not?"

"If we were," she said, "I would have married a Frankish baron years ago, and you would be mated to a suitable young woman of your City."

"And we would both be miserably unhappy," said Michael Bryennius. "I don't think I believe in being practical."

"You may have to learn, if you're to find any kind of contentment here."

"I'll surprise you," he said. "Watch and see."

She much preferred to kiss him long and deep; and then, because it was late and the day began early, to curl up in his arms and go to sleep.

Michael Bryennius made a very capable consort to the baroness of a holding in the hills of Jerusalem. He could keep accounts, which spared the young seneschal for efforts elsewhere. He knew horsebreeding and, also excellently to the point, the breeding and keeping of goats and sheep. He could fight when it pleased him, and train men to fight, which resulted in the appearance in the courtyard every morning of a dozen stalwart young men from the village with blunted spears and wooden swords, and the setting up of butts for archery in the field beyond the castle's wall.

A loud splash one morning, and a yelp immediately thereafter, told Richildis that one of the would-be men-at-arms had lost the usual wager: victory in this contest or that, or an involuntary swim in the cistern. Michael Bryennius insisted that such silliness kept them keen. The cistern had been built in some ancient time for who knew what purpose; Richildis meant to have it drained and cleaned and over time refilled, to bolster the newer well in the castle's heart. Meanwhile it was a reasonably vile example of its kind, green and scummy, with things swimming below the surface that no one liked to think too much on. Richildis hoped that none of the daily vanquished took sick from the foul water.

So far none had, and they took noisy delight in the game. Their clamor interrupted her going over of lists with Charles the steward, but rather more pleasantly than not. It was a good sound, like the clucking of fowl in their coops by the kitchen, the sound of hammering and hewing as workmen repaired a crumbling corner of the east tower, the squeal of a mare in the stable. They were all living sounds, lively sounds, sounds of a castle setting itself in order.

She was sitting there smiling, alarming poor Charles, who had stammered into silence. "Go on," she said to him. "I'm listening."

He stammered as he obeyed, but steadied as he went on. She had hopes of him. His shyness was crippling, but he had a good mind and a fine eye for detail. He needed someone to assist him, she thought: someone to speak for him when his stammer overwhelmed his wits. She would find a suitable person, a clerk from Jerusalem, or someone more local perhaps, someone from the village, if any there could read and write Latin and the dialects of Frankish as well as Arabic. One of the Frankish settlers, perhaps. She set the task in her memory, to do when there was time.

She had no proper page yet—another task: to find a noble family with a son to spare, for her to foster—but there were always young things about the castle, offspring of servants or workmen or, perhaps more often than that, people in the town who were curious about their new lady. One of these appeared breathless at her side, and said in Arabic too rapid almost for her to follow, "Lady-there's-a-riding-coming!"

She deciphered that with little enough difficulty. "People? Franks?"

"Franks!" said the child. "With banners." It sighed as if in rapture. She would think it male, but dressed as it was in a grubby white shirt and a blue bead on a string, it could as easily be female. "Many many Franks, lady. Four, five handfuls."

Richildis could not allow herself to become alarmed. This was the lot of any who held a castle in a world of war: any noble traveler could come as he pleased, with all his retinue, and expect guest-right for however long he wished to stay. She had dared to hope that no one would come until the castle was ready.

But it seemed that God had other intentions. She suppressed a sigh and rose, and went to make herself ready for guests.

They were as she had expected, nobles of the High Court going home from court and coronation. Their curiosity was palpable. She had made no secret of her marriage, but neither had she made a great public outcry.

That might not have been wise after all. In the absence of truth, rumor will fly— and she had not only married a man from the Byzantine embassy, she had vanished from Jerusalem fairly promptly thereafter. These were the outriders of an army, perhaps, come to see for themselves what she had done.

She had no shame to offer them. Such order as she could manage, she kept, and she received them into it with all the grace that blood and training had given her. When Michael Bryennius came in from wherever he had been—inspecting the sugar-mill, he told her much later—the hall was full of strangers.

He took it in in a glance, and her with it, seated on the dais with the two barons of lesser holdings and the heiress of one as great as the others put together. In a lull in their high and pointless chatter she rose, stretching out her hands. "My lord!"

"Lady," he said, advancing with the same impulse that had come over her, taking her hands, kissing them one by one. His eyes laughed up at her. She bit her lips to keep from grinning back. When she had mastered herself, she turned with her hand in his and said, "My lords, my lady: my husband."

They were forced to be courteous, not an easy thing when their eyes were so wide and their minds spinning so furiously. She wondered what monstrous bride-groom rumor had given her, that they should actually seem disappointed by her elegant Byzantine. Had they been telling one another that she had married an infidel? Her notorious Turkish guard, perhaps?

And she had married a Christian, if a schismatic, and one who spoke Frankish besides. Rumor would never love that as it had loved the wilder speculations.

She enjoyed herself rather more than she had expected to, sitting next to her husband in her own hall, playing host to the first guests that she had received as lady of Mount Ghazal. And only a month ago, she had had no thought at all of gaining such a thing, still less through marriage to a man whom she had not seen in so long.

"Strange are the ways of God," she said to herself, unheard amid the murmur of conversation. Not even her husband heard her. He was engaging in lively debate with the lords and their squires, over the best way to dress a deer in the field.

She should make conversation with Lady Gisela, and not suffer her mind to wander even farther afield than the men's poor slaughtered deer. The lady had been chattering on for quite some time, as far as Richildis could tell. It was mindless chatter, court chatter, comfortably simple to fit oneself into. One had only to nod, smile, murmur a word at suitable intervals.

Such was the lot of a lady in hall. She found that it suited her, even as tedious as it could sometimes be. Yes; it suited her very well indeed.

utub had gone out not long after Epiphany to find men-at-arms for Mount Ghazal. On the threshold of summer, around the feast of the Ascension, he came back with an armed company. They were all Turks, and all young, and all nearly as villainous to look at as he was himself. There seemed to be several dozen, but the count of them, on the rare occasions when they could be persuaded to stand still, was ten.

"These are my cousins," Kutub said, marking the half-dozen who stood together. "And these," he said of the other four, "are my nephews. There would have been more, but the city-sultans have been paying well this year, and the rest of my kin had promised themselves already to this one or that."

"That's well enough," said Richildis. "We have a dozen here, learning to fight in the Byzantine style since we lacked an armsmaster of the Turks."

"Well," said Kutub, "and now you have him. Show me these dozen of yours."

It was hardly appropriate for a servant to command his baroness; but this was Kutub. Richildis acceded to his wishes, nor sent someone either, but went herself, out to the field where Michael Bryennius had mustered his soldiery. They all had bows, each in his fashion, and were shooting at targets.

Michael Bryennius did not believe in interrupting such proceedings unless there was great need. In that it seemed he was like Kutub. The Turk went to stand beside him, greeting him with an inclination of the head. He followed the example that Kutub set, indulging in no effusions of welcome, watching in silence as the young men from the village nocked arrows, aimed, and shot, over and over.

"You waste their time," Kutub said at length, in a tone of careful consideration. Michael Bryennius raised a brow.

"The shooting in a fight," Kutub said, "is most often from the back of a horse."

"These won't be horse-archers," Michael Bryennius said. "The Franks don't use them as the Turks do."

"Perhaps they should."

"Undoubtedly," Michael Bryennius said. "But the fee we owe the queen is a fee in men-at-arms in the Frankish fashion. We can but oblige."

"My kin will never fight like Franks."

Michael Bryennius looked past him to the uneasy huddle of his young relations. They were wild creatures, the dust of the steppe still in their long plaited hair, and hardly enough beard on the lot of them to befur the face of a single Byzantine. He grinned at them. They glowered back. "My dear young things," he said in Arabic, "you will cut a remarkable swath among the soldiers of Jerusalem."

"They will fight for the lady," Kutub said, "and for the queen she serves. No one else."

"That will do for the purpose," said Michael Bryennius.

Richildis could only be relieved that there would be no war. Kutub would hardly contemplate harm to his lady's husband, but his kin might have no such compunctions about their rivals from the village. Villager and wild tribesman had been at war since the world was born—but while the men who commanded them were at amity, they could not break the truce.

Or so she could hope. Infidel honor was an odd and fragile thing. It resided in a man's right arm and the weapons it bore, in the bodies of his women, in the name and prowess of his tribe. If he decided that loyalty to his commander stained his honor, then he would go where his honor bade him.

She would have to hope that both Kutub and Michael were deft enough to keep the balance. Perhaps she should find a Frankish sergeant to command the lot of them, setting Kutub free to be captain of guards, and Michael Bryennius to be her consort.

Another thing to set in the annals of her memory. She had made a whole edifice of them, a house of rooms that grew more numerous each day. The exercise, that she had had from a nun of great learning, suited her well; she felt the honing of her mind upon it, the keenness that she had thought lost when she was taken out of the convent. Solitary study had not been enough; nor had she found anyone with whom to talk of what she read, except in her letters to Michael Bryennius.

She would have to learn to talk to him as she had written, without constraint. She was still too new to this, her days too full, the nights more often spent in deep and exhausted sleep than in either lovemaking or conversation. There was always someone listening, someone standing by, someone needing something that must be seen to just then.

Perhaps she should have done what he had hoped she would do: linger in Jerusalem, be a new bride, let her barony wait till she was ready to devote herself to it. But she had been too restless for that; too determined to do what she judged to be her duty. And, she admitted in the quiet of the nights, she had to force this choice of hers on her husband, to see what he would do—to lose him if she must, and quickly, before her heart bound itself any more tightly to him.

It had been too late for that, she thought, before he left Beausoleil, years ago. And he seemed at ease here at Mount Ghazal, as he had been in Jerusalem, as he had been at Beausoleil. Surely he was at ease in Byzantium, too, and wherever else God and his fate had led him.

An enviable gift, that. Perhaps she could persuade him to teach her the way of it.

· · ·

Her house of memory grew, and rooms were opened and closed, altered and divided, as time and necessity demanded. Outside of it, in the world of the body, winter passed into spring, and spring into summer. She returned to Jerusalem for the great feasts, for High Court, for attendance on the queen who was still her liege lady.

The first time she came back from Mount Ghazal, for Easter Court, Melisende allowed her to perform proper obeisance as a baroness to the queen, but lifted her after and looked long into her face. Rather than lower her eyes or admit to embarrassment, Richildis returned the scrutiny. There was nothing new to see. No encroachments of age. No marks of strain or sorrow. Queenship suited Melisende. She prospered in it.

"You," said Melisende, "look . . . young. Is that the fountain of the ancients in your courtyard, then? Have you found your youth again?"

"Not my youth," said Richildis, "which I rather misspent. Joy. That's what I've found. Joy."

And so she had. In the summer she knew what she had suspected when she returned from Easter Court. It so startled her that she could not speak of it even to her husband. With Thierry there had been nothing—and he had sired bastards enough. She had reckoned herself barren.

Now, with increasing clarity, she saw that she was not. She knew what misfortune had followed Helena's refusal to tell her beloved that he would be a father. Yet she could not say the words. Could not stand in front of her husband and say, "I'm going to have a baby."

He said it for her, one night in the fullest heat of summer. The well in the castle flowed with cool water, a blessing indeed in a country and in a season in which water was precious rare. They had granted themselves a vast indulgence: a bath together. They were still damp, still scented with the herbs that had made the water sweet.

She was slender still—spare as she had always been, without much meat on her bones. But her breasts were fuller, she had noticed that.

So, it appeared, had he. He kissed the tip of one. She shivered in pleasure. "Beloved," he said, soft as a cat's purr. "When will the baby be born? Somewhere about Epiphany, yes?"

Richildis' mind went briefly dark: a moment's swoon of pure relief.

But if he was angry—

He did not seem to be. He was smiling, looking into her eyes.

"Epiphany," she said, "or a little after."

"It will spare the most ribald of the jests," he observed.

He must be angry. He had shown no joy, none of the deep delight that she had expected. She reached for him, not knowing what she would say, not certain that she could cry his pardon.

When the words came, they came of themselves. "I'm sorry. I didn't think—I knew I was barren."

"God knew better," he said.

Her hands found him, locked behind him. She buried her face in his breast. "I'm afraid," she said.

"All women fear the curse of Eve," he said.

She struck his back with her clenched fists. He gasped: she had not tried to be gentle. "Don't be obtuse," she said. "I'm afraid of the pain of childbearing—who wouldn't be? But that's not what terrifies me. It's . . . that this child may not live. That I may not be able to—"

"Hush," he said. "God will do as God wills. Pray that He wills that the birth be easy, the child strong, well fit to grow into man or woman."

"Man *or* woman? You don't care which?"

"Either or both," he said.

"You are not the usual run of man," said Richildis.

"I should hope not," he said with some indignation. "How dull that would be. How painful: for then you would never have looked at me."

"You're easy to look at."

"But if I weren't myself, would I look like myself?"

"You make my head ache," she said, but not to complain of it. She did something small and very wicked, that made him yelp and nigh cast her out of bed.

As she lay grinning with her hair spilling on the floor, he mustered his breath and his dignity. "You are treacherous," he said.

"You begged for it," said Richildis.

"I did not."

"You did," she said. And stopped; and gasped. Her hand flew to her middle.

He leaped, all foolishness forgotten. The sheer white terror in his face made her want to laugh, but she dared not. "No," she said, fending him off. "No, please. Stop panicking. It was only—it moved." She paused as the words made themselves real in her awareness. "It's alive, my love. It moved!"

She was laughing, crying, she hardly knew which. And so early yet. So fragile a thing, that flutter within; so long a road to travel before it could live and breathe in the world outside the womb.

It would not flutter again for its father—contrary child; she would speak to it sternly if it persisted. He professed not to care. "You felt it," he said. "You know. Your word is all I need."

"Such trust," she said. "Your family will disown you."

"My family may try," he said. "It won't get far. I'm master of its affairs, after all—even here."

Her eyes narrowed. She searched his face as it hung over her. "You said," she said, "that you had left them in others' care. That—"

"Others look after them," he said. "I remain master of them. I haven't given them up, my lady. Not even to gratify the indignation of my mother."

"You'll go back someday. Won't you?"

"I and you and the whole flock of our children," he said, "in a grand caravan. Yes, we will go back—to visit, to see the glories of the empire, to make the acquaintance of my kin who are now yours. Did you think I'd exiled myself here forever?"

"That's what it is to you, isn't it? Exile."

He shook his head sharply. "No. No, damn it. You're all raw edges tonight, looking for hurt where there is none. Do you forget so easily the vows we took? Whither thou goest, I will go. I live here of my free choice and because you choose to live here. When we're older, when our children are grown enough to travel, why shouldn't we think of traveling to the City? Is there some oath that binds you here?"

Richildis opened her mouth to reply that yes, there was; but the words would not come when she called them. She was bound not to go back to La Forêt while Bertrand refused to take the lordship of it—old oath grown worn with use, but no less strong for that. But where she went else, that mattered little. She could see the wonders of East Rome, the splendors of Byzantium, perhaps even the fabled palace of the emperors. Was not her husband one of the royal kin?

"You see," he said as if she had answered his question. "You're not sworn to stay in or near Jerusalem till life forsakes you. Someday we'll sail to Byzantium, you and I and our children."

"One child," Richildis said, "and the life of that one is in God's hands."

He bowed his head and crossed himself as the Greeks did, backward. Something in the gesture melted her heart. Perhaps he never fully understood why she sprang on him just then, overset him, nigh overwhelmed him with the ferocity of her embrace.

hile Richildis made Mount Gha-
zal a place fit for a child to be born in, the world had gone its round as relentlessly
as ever. In the autumn the peace that had for the most part prevailed in the kingdom
since King Fulk died, shattered suddenly and with terrible force.

The balance of kings and emperors in this part of the world had always been
delicate. Now there was a new king on the throne of Jerusalem, an emperor hardly
less new on the throne of Byzantium, the father of each dead the year before. In
Damascus the infidels were watching, always watching, alert to capture what they
could from weak or unready princes.

Not only in Damascus, either, or among Saracens. Both Antioch and Edessa had
grown restive under Fulk's rule. Under what they reckoned to be the feebler rule of
a woman and a half-grown boy, Joscelin of Edessa and Raymond of Antioch broke
out in open rivalry.

Raymond of Poitiers had been chosen for Constance, heiress of Antioch, as Fulk
had been chosen for Melisende—and in much the same fashion, for he was in
England when the messengers found him, as Fulk had been seven years before that.
Fulk had been seeing his son married to the heiress of England. Raymond was in
attendance on the heiress' father. He had been amply willing to forsake that liege
lord in favor of a young and beautiful princess. That she was also headstrong, arrogant, and notably free of her tongue, did not appear to dismay him. Nor was he
perturbed that she was, at the time of their marriage, all of nine years old. "She
will grow," he was heard to observe, "and she has beauty in her bones."

The princess' mother Alys had been led to believe that this handsome man of
seven-and-thirty had come to take her as his bride. Only so could he come to
Antioch unmurdered, and only so could he claim it as the king's vassal, too quick
and too subtle for her to prevent him.

Something broke in Alys when the truth was laid before her. Where Melisende
would only have grown stronger, more determined to win back what was hers, Alys
proved herself of lesser mettle. She retired to her dower lands, nor would she come
out for any summoning, even that of her sister the queen. She was said to spend
her days in alternation between the chapel and the winejar.

All the steel that had been in Alys seemed to have passed on to her daughter.
Constance grew up as beautiful as Raymond had professed to expect, the image of

her father Bohemond, white-fair hair and sea-blue eyes and a face like that of a marble saint. For all that anyone knew, she doted on her tall handsome husband, heeding him as she heeded no one else.

That would have been better, in everyone's estimation, if Raymond had been a wiser man, or less ambitious. His wings had been severely and properly clipped by the last emperor of Byzantium, who had actually taken Antioch in its prince's absence. Raymond had been compelled to pay homage to the emperor as to an overlord: an act that had galled him in the doing and forever after.

But now that emperor was dead. Antioch was safe from his claim of suzerainty—though the new emperor would no doubt make his own claim. But not yet. Raymond breathed free at last, looked about him, and set to the delightful task of expanding his territories and claiming back those that the Byzantines had taken from him. He was also, and with relish, quarreling with Joscelin of Edessa over numerous insults and injuries, not least of them Joscelin's distaste at having been forced to accept the Prince of Antioch as his liege lord.

It was all very tangled, very complicated, and very ill for the strength of the Franks against the infidel. When Franks quarreled, people said, infidels rejoiced—and infidel joy was expressed most keenly in war.

In the autumn of that year, the year after Baldwin was crowned king beside Melisende his mother, the knots and tangles of alliances in the north began rapidly to unravel. Antioch and Edessa were at odds if not yet at war. Edessa had failed to keep its half of a bargain with Antioch, that would have added greatly to the lands of both. Joscelin had chosen instead to swear truce with infidel Aleppo, in hopes of bettering his fortunes in that direction rather than in servitude to a haughty overlord—those being the words of his that came in rumor even to Mount Ghazal. His overlord the Prince of Antioch was greatly displeased, perhaps to the point of sending an army against Edessa.

While the Franks quarreled, the infidels struck. Zengi the Turk, who wielded power in Mosul, was not content to rule a single city. He would be lord of all Syria if he could, of all the world if Allah favored him. He mounted an attack against one of the infidel allies of Joscelin. Joscelin, bound by oath to aid his ally, marched out of Edessa—and Zengi, who had laid the trap with such cunning skill, marched in behind him and laid siege to the city.

Joscelin was intermittently and sometimes belatedly prudent. There were many indeed who called him a coward. He did not turn back in furious haste to break the siege and win back his city. He retreated to Turbessel with an army that, to be sure, was not remarkably large or strong, and was probably no match for Zengi's horde of Turks and Kurds and Turcomans.

The queen, with the High Court in hastily summoned council, gathered an army and set her Constable in command of it, and sent it to the aid of Edessa. It was a great army, splendid as it marched out of Jerusalem. But not great enough. It needed Antioch.

And Antioch would not stir. Joscelin had betrayed his vassalage, had made alliances with infidels, had paid for his perfidy in the loss of his city. "Let him learn his lesson," Raymond said before he stopped receiving messengers from the queen or her commanders. "He never had much sense when it came to people, or fighting, either. Now he pays for it—and far be it from me to ride to his rescue, unless he begs me himself, on bended knee."

But Joscelin would not do that, would not grovel as he said that Raymond had done before the late emperor of the Byzantines. And so the quarrel went on: silly, petty, and dangerous.

The price of warring pride was Edessa. Zengi took it after a month of siege. On the very eve of Christmas his tribesmen broke down the wall and ran wild in the city. Every Frankish male was put to death, and every Frankish woman and child sold as a slave. The Latin churches were broken down and their sacred things taken or trampled in the dust. Everything that had been built or wrought or begun under the Franks was shattered. Edessa was again, as it had been before the Crusade, a city of infidels and of eastern Christians.

Edessa was fallen. The infidel crouched at the northern gate of Outremer. The queen's armies had failed to withstand him. Antioch had refused, and still refused, for its prince's blind ambition. Nor had Joscelin grown wiser in adversity. First he had failed to do what he could, while he could, to weaken Zengi's siege of Edessa; he had chosen instead to wait for the queen's army, loitering in Turbessel while his city fought alone. Now from Turbessel he defied the authority of Antioch, repudiated his oath of fealty, and declared that he would stand alone until the whole of his realm was restored to him.

"Idiots!" Melisende, unlike Joscelin, thrived on adversity; but it was as much as she could do to wait patiently in Jerusalem while men made such a shambles of both war and alliance. "If even one of them could see past his own nose, it would be a sacred miracle."

"Shall we pray for it?"

Richildis had come to Jerusalem in the new year, after she judged herself recovered from the delivery of a miracle of her own: twins, Gisela the firstborn and Alexios her brother. She had wondered, late in her pregnancy, if there were two to make her so vast and unwieldy, but she had never believed it till Gisela was born and the pains went on, and her brother sprang yelling into the world. Two at once, as if to make up for all the barren years.

She had come this morning to pay her respects to the queen, and Melisende had asked that she stay. The twins went home with their father and their nurses. Richildis returned, if briefly, to the familiar round of the queen's service. She stood with the other ladies through the rest of the morning audience, then adjourned with them to the solar, where a new and talented singer was matching his voice to the wailing of a flute. He was young enough to be beardless, but Richildis wondered if he was one of the Greek eunuchs. No one else had a voice of such power and purity.

There a messenger had brought word of yet another calamity in the fall of Edessa: another refusal on the part of either Raymond or Joscelin to be even faintly reasonable.

"There will have to be a Crusade," Melisende said. "I see no other hope for us. With Antioch stalking the edge of treason, Edessa fallen, Edessa's lord intent on his feud with the lord of Antioch, and the infidel laughing as he takes the spoils . . . we need more than we have, to win back what's been lost. We need the knights of the West."

"But will the pope preach a Crusade?" one of the ladies asked. "There has been none willing in fifty years, since Urban preached our fathers and grandfathers into taking Jerusalem."

"Then it's time one was willing, yes?" said Melisende. "I'll offer Antioch one chance to redeem itself: I'll consult with its council on the sending of an embassy to Rome. Raymond is a bloody fool, but his vassals may have better sense."

As it happened, they did; and an embassy set sail for the west, but not in as much haste as might have been expected. That was a strange year, this second year of Melisende's reign with Baldwin, beset with urgency yet vexed with delays. No one seemed able to act, except Raymond of Antioch, who ran to the emperor of Byzantium to beg for aid. Raymond gained nothing, not even, at first, an audience with the emperor. His humiliation was the talk of Jerusalem. People did love to see a proud man fall on his face.

Arslan was not greatly sorry, either. His dislike for Princess Constance had not abated in the least as he grew older. Her husband was as insufferable as she was: the same overbearing manner, the same haughty disregard for anyone he regarded as beneath him. And that, Arslan certainly was. Even if his father had formally acknowledged him, which Bertrand had never quite taken time to do, he was still a bastard.

It did not hurt as much as it used to. Over the spring and summer, Baldwin got his growth at last, and his voice changed, too; suddenly he was a great growling lion-cub of a creature, neither boy nor man. After he knocked down the sergeant who had been teaching him swordplay since he was small, wrested the sword from him and beat him with the flat of it, the queen determined that her son was getting out of hand. She gave him a new tutor, one who would not, she opined, be as easy to overmatch as Reynaud had been.

"There isn't anybody," Baldwin said that night before he went to sleep. "I'm better than all the sergeants."

"She'll put a knight in charge of you," Arslan said. "You'll see."

Baldwin lifted a shoulder in a shrug. He was going to be big, like his grandfather before him; his fears of ending as small as his father were long since proved groundless. Arslan would always be bigger, but not by so very much.

At the moment they were much of a size, but Baldwin was all elbows and knees. Arslan was a little more grown into himself.

"The younger knights are all weaklings," Baldwin said. "None of them has the least idea what to do with us."

"*I* have always tried to be an obedient student," Arslan said with an air of injury. "So did you before you shot up like a weed. Now you're as tall as a man, do you think you're as strong as one? You're just a clumsy pup. You've years of growing in you."

Baldwin surged across the bed. "I am not a clumsy pup! You take that back!"

Arslan was ready for him—and stronger, too. It was more of a struggle than it would have been two seasons ago, but he won as always, wrestled Baldwin down and sat on him. "Do think," he said from that vantage. "Your mother had her grim face on, the one that means she's going to do something nobody else will like but she will enjoy immensely. With your luck, she'll hand you over to your Uncle Manasses, and make him make a man of you."

"Uncle Manasses would be too soft on me," Baldwin said—all the admission Arslan would get that Arslan had been right. "He's too lofty, too. Unless she means to foster me out—but she can't do that. I'm the king. I have to stay in the court."

King indeed, Arslan thought, letting himself fall backwards onto the bed. "We'll know in the morning," he said, "who's to break you to bit and saddle."

Baldwin made a horrible face at him, but was too lazy or too prudent to try another attack.

In the morning they knew indeed. They were roused as always by the king's body-servant, but at an hour so unwontedly early that Baldwin yowled a protest. "Her majesty commands," Radulf said with a hint—a merest hint—of satisfaction.

Dressed, combed, and lightly fed, they went out to face the fate that Queen Melisende had ordained for them.

A knight. Indeed. A baron of the High Court, no less, and big enough to give even Baldwin pause. Lord Bertrand inspected his charges with an eye that found little to approve of—though it did glint a little, perhaps, on Arslan.

Arslan could have excused himself. He was under no obligation to be taught as Baldwin was. No one had commanded him. He had no orders from the queen, nor had the king said a word.

The king did not need to. His eyes said everything that needed saying. If Arslan loved his friend and liege lord, he would stay. They would suffer together as they always had.

Arslan swallowed a sigh. No hope that his father would spare him for kinship's sake. Quite the opposite, if he knew Bertrand. He would lead as always, break ground for his lord the king, and take the blows meant for the king, too, if he must.

"You will take your own blows," Bertrand was saying as if he had been listening to Arslan's thoughts, "and pay your own prices for them. No hiding behind friends or servants. The king enjoys great privilege, but it comes at a great price. Whatever he does, for harm or good, he bears the burden of it."

"There are always people who will bear it for me," Baldwin said with a lift of the chin that told Arslan much: that he was afraid, that he was angry at himself, that he would strike however he could, and wound as deep as he might.

Bertrand was oblivious, or perhaps impervious. "While I am your tutor, no one but you will do penance for your sins."

"So you say," Baldwin said, still in that tone of studied insolence.

Arslan did not see exactly what Bertrand did. It was too fast to catch the whole of. One moment he was standing at ease, listening to Baldwin. The next, Baldwin was flat in the dust of the practice-yard and Bertrand was standing over him, holding out a hand to help him up.

Baldwin grasped the hand, made as if to rise, tugged with sudden ferocity.

Bertrand braced his feet. "Not bad," he said. "Not bad at all. Now, up. There's work to do."

ork indeed. Earlier tutors had
driven them hard, or so they thought. But none of those was Bertrand. He drove
them from before dawn till long after dusk—and not only with weapons, either.
They were to read and write in Latin and Frankish and as much Greek as they had
wit for, and they would speak Arabic well enough to be sure that their interpreters
were honest. And when they were not doing all of that, they were learning the arts
of courtiers: everything from dancing and the lute to the intricacies of state councils.

Once in a great while they were permitted to stop for a moment and breathe.
Such moments were never given them when they expected any. Bertrand would
fail to appear on the practice field, perhaps, or a page would be standing in the
schoolroom, ready to rattle off a message: "Lord Bertrand says go away, do something
frivolous, don't come back till evening." There was never any pattern in it, whether
they behaved well or ill before the gift was granted them. It had nothing to do with
feastdays or saints' days, when they worked harder if anything, since, as Bertrand
informed them, a king's duties never paused, not even when he slept.

When autumn had slipped into winter again, the year Edessa fell, the page came
on them just as they readied to go to the field, with the same message as always, in
the same maddening treble. This was not the usual page however: it was Prince
Amaury, and he must have studied that shrill tone to have it down so perfectly,
since his ordinary manner of speaking was no more unpleasant than anybody else's.
As soon as the message was out, he added in his own voice, "I'm coming with you."

"You are not," Baldwin said at once. "You're waiting on Lord Bertrand today."

"Lord Bertrand has gone to visit his sister in Mount Ghazal," Amaury said. "He's
not coming back for a hand of days at least."

Arslan's throat hurt suddenly. "He never told us," he said.

"He didn't want you to think you could get away with anything," Amaury said.
"Tomorrow someone's going to take his place till he comes back, but today you
have for yourself. He said to enjoy it, it won't come again soon. And I'm going
with you."

"Not," said Baldwin, "if I have to tie you up and stuff you down the garderobe.
Go find someone else to pester."

Amaury folded his arms and set his jaw and looked immovably stubborn. Baldwin
picked him up, tipped him through a doorway, and bolted.

• • •

When they were out of David's Tower and well lost among the throngs of Jerusalem, Baldwin stopped to get his breath. Arslan was glad of the opportunity. "You," he said between gulps of air, "dumped that poor child into—"

"I said I'd stuff him down the garderobe," Baldwin said. "I'm a man of my word."

"We'll get a flogging when milord finds out."

"But not until then," Baldwin said. He looked about keenly, with a clear purpose in mind. "And it will be worth it. Are you with me?"

"That depends on what I'm getting into," Arslan said.

"Come and see," said Baldwin.

Arslan was a fool, maybe. He held his tongue and followed.

They went to a part of the city that they had not often been in before. Baldwin seemed to know where he was going, though Arslan thought he heard him counting turnings under his breath.

The streets were narrow and seemed as crowded as ever. Most of the people who thronged here were shabby in one way or another: pilgrims much worn with travel, ragged squires and threadbare knights, men-at-arms in worn leather, passersby of less determinate provenance and purpose. Sellers of sausages and pasties did a desultory business—and no wonder, from the pie Arslan unwisely bought: it was mostly onion, and the meat in it was probably dog, unless it was rat. He grimaced and gave the remains of it to a beggar.

Baldwin had not wanted a pasty, had barely paused to let Arslan buy or begin to eat it. Arslan had to thrust through a knot of pilgrims to catch his friend—Mary Mother, if people knew that the King of Jerusalem ran loose and ill escorted in the back alleys of his own city, there would be an outcry to rival anything Arslan had ever heard.

That was not a thought he usually let trouble him. But this was not their usual run, either. Mostly they went to the bazaars with a crowd of squires, or went hunting, or found something to do in or about the Tower of David.

Baldwin halted so abruptly that Arslan ran into him, and turned equally abruptly. The door he turned to had nothing to distinguish it, not even a mark cut into it. It was simply a door.

But what was behind it . . .

Arslan had heard about houses of pleasure. All the squires talked about them. Some had even been in them, though for how long and to what effect, he sometimes doubted they told truly. The priests said that even thinking about them was a mortal sin. Going to one, and doing what people did in it, must be direct damnation.

This was a house of pleasure. There was nothing else it could be, unless by some freak of luck they had stumbled into an infidel's harem. It reeked of perfume and of flowers and of other, earthier things. Its walls were hung with gauzes that fluttered in the breeze of people's passing. There were rooms, stairs, crannies full of whisperings and laughter. The light was dim, deliberately so, and tinged as if with blood.

Arslan wanted *out*. But Baldwin had a grip on his wrist, and it was too strong to break.

They stood in what must be one of the anterooms, unmet and unattended, but there were eyes in the walls. Arslan could feel them, could almost see them glinting, laughing at a pair of boys huddled together as if in terror.

Arslan was not afraid. He was furious. He twisted his free hand in the neck of Baldwin's mantle and pulled him in close. "Whose brilliant idea was this? Who told you how to get here?"

"Galeran," Baldwin said.

Arslan growled under his breath. "Galeran! That witless fop. What does *he* know of whores and whoring?"

"A lot," Baldwin said, "from all he says. He knows about this place, doesn't he?"

"Aye, and how? Because he was born here?"

"You know who his mother is," Baldwin said impatiently. "She's as noble as you—as I am."

"As I'm not," Arslan said. "You were going to say that next, weren't you? And say how odd it is that I'm being such a saintly sister, considering where I come from and what my mother is."

"I was not," Baldwin said fiercely. "You can't help it if Lady Helena won't marry your father. Everybody knows she's no whore, and hasn't been a courtesan since before you were born."

"Everybody isn't quite that kind about it," Arslan muttered. "So why else did you bring me here, except that you thought I wouldn't mind?"

"Don't you ever think about women?" Baldwin demanded of him.

He felt his face go hot. "Not *this* kind of women."

"What other kind is there? Women are women."

"Then let's go back to the Tower," Arslan said. "Let's see if one of the kitchenmaids would like a tumble. They're all panting to have a go at you, I'll wager."

Baldwin was blushing, too, and not becomingly: blotched with white and crimson, with a look that would have been murderous if it had not been so absurd. "They don't want *me*."

"So you think you have to buy it?"

"Buying's better. They . . . know more. And they don't—they don't—",

"Laugh?"

"Laugh," said Baldwin a little thickly.

"You did it, then," said Arslan. "You asked Fleur."

Fleur was one of the maids. She had a face remarkably like a rabbit's, hair the color and texture of saffron wool, and the round lashless eyes of a fish. She also had breasts as big a man's head, and a reputation among the squires that was, as far as Arslan could determine, richly deserved.

"I asked Fleur," Baldwin said, too low almost to hear.

"She laughed?"

Baldwin's eyes burned under his brows. "She didn't laugh. She said, 'King or no king, and I like you very well, mind, I don't take tumbles with boys. Come back when your beard's in.' "

"So you think *this* will get your beard going?" Arslan's hand took in the room they were in, the shielded lamps, the wavering draperies, the reek of unguents. "Believe me, if that were what did it, Jeannot would have a beard to his knees."

Since Jeannot was so fair as to be colorless, could grow exactly six pallid hairs on his fine white chin, and had by his own account tupped more women than a ram had ewes, Baldwin did understand the reference. He hissed at it. "Don't be silly! She meant, stay away till I've made a man of myself. Doesn't this make a man?"

"Years make a man," Arslan said.

"I have enough," Baldwin said. "What I lack . . . it's here. Galeran said so. He said ring the bell and ask for the Rose of Sharon."

"Or the Lily of the Valley?" Arslan ducked a half-hearted blow. "Why not ask for Mary Magdalen, and see what comes to meet you?"

"You are blasphemous," Baldwin said.

"What else should I be, in this place?"

Baldwin bared teeth at him. The bell was hanging by the wall, with a heavy curtain next to it. Baldwin leaped as if he feared that Arslan would stop him, seized the cord, tugged hard enough almost to pull it down. It jangled unmusically, a sound that could carry, surely, no farther than the curtain beside it.

Yet it seemed that someone heard, or was waiting for the signal. The curtain stirred. Arslan's breath caught in his throat.

The vision that appeared was nothing that he would call lovely. It was a woman, he supposed, or possibly a eunuch: a vast edifice of flesh, clad in garments that billowed like the hangings. A turban concealed its hair, if hair it had. Its voice was astonishing: pure as snow from the mountains of the Lebanon, sweet as honey from the comb.

And that was poetry, and Arslan was maundering. "Yes, young gentleman?" the apparition inquired. "How may we serve you?"

"The—I need to—I'm supposed to—" Baldwin stammered.

Ah well, Arslan thought. No one would ever expect the king to manifest himself as a stumbletongued gawk of a boy. Arslan said it for him, since he was so clearly set on it: "If you would—we seek the Rose of Sharon."

"Do you indeed?" said the apparition. Arslan had nearly concluded that it was a eunuch. "And who may I say is inquiring?"

"Two seekers after the truth that she imparts," Arslan said, winning a glance of pure incredulity from Baldwin. He met it as blandly as he could. If this was a game, then he would play it and be damned. If it was not—then God help him.

The eunuch seemed unperturbed by Arslan's floridity. Perhaps he was accustomed to it. He paused as if to consider, then said, "She is not wont to give audience to every man who asks. But it might be . . . she may be persuaded."

Arslan was no stranger to the ways of the east. He searched in his purse till he found a bit of silver.

The eunuch did not inspect it vulgarly, bite it to determine its purity, do as a vendor would in the bazaar; he simply slipped it into the recesses of his robes. His eye was keen and his expression sardonic as he bowed and said, "I shall do what I may to persuade her."

"I hope you paid him enough," Baldwin muttered when the eunuch was gone. "That is a he, isn't it?"

"I think so," Arslan said. "You owe me for this. I'd saved that bit of silver for a bridle I had an eye on."

"I'll give you a bridle chased with gold," Baldwin said, "if you help me get through this."

"Do I have any choice?" Arslan asked, more of the air than of his idiot king.

They waited long enough to be almost certain that they had been abandoned. While they waited, they heard sounds that might be others coming in, the soft laughter of women, whispers and sighs and a rhythmic grunting that made the slow heat crawl up Arslan's cheeks. Oddly enough considering that the sight of a girl's ankle could set his banner flying, he was as limp and juiceless as yonder eunuch. This place excited him not in the least. He only wanted to be out of it.

But Baldwin refused to go. "Kings do such things," he said, "to keep petitioners humble. Be patient."

Arslan rolled his eyes and sighed vastly and assumed the attitude he favored when he was on guard: relaxed, alert, but resting as he could. Baldwin, whose training had been as thorough as his, sat as a king sits, erect and still.

They must have been a strange vision for the messenger who came to them: not the eunuch now but a reed-thin girlchild in a drift of lurid draperies. She regarded them in something like terror, but managed to beckon and say, "Come."

Baldwin shrank into a scared boy again. Arslan levered himself up.

The child led them down a dim and whispering passage and up a stair and down another passage, this one lined with doorways. Near the end she stopped, lifted one of the curtains, dipped in a bow.

Neither Baldwin nor Arslan allowed himself to hesitate. Arslan went first as a guard should, hand to the hilt of his meat-knife, which was all the weapon he was allowed to carry outside of arms-practice. He felt Baldwin behind him, pressing close, peering over his shoulder.

No enemies leaped from behind the arras. No army waited to fall upon them. There was only a room so small it was no more than a cubicle, with a bed in it, not remarkably clean, and a chest for clothing, and a heap of rugs and carpets, and enough of the gaudy gauze to drape a hall for a feast. A tree of lamps lit it, stingy of oil: the wicks were smoky, the flames low.

On the bed, cross-legged like a storyteller in the bazaar, sat a woman. She was clothed in the eastern fashion, silken trousers and loose tunic. Her face was veiled.

Arslan stopped just within the door. He had expected the room's tawdriness; had been braced for any kind of naked debauchery. But this quiet, composed person took him aback.

Her veil was thin enough to see through. She was not particularly beautiful, though she had fine eyes, large and dark. Her profile was pleasing, if somewhat sharp. Her figure, as far as he could see, was much the same.

She did not look or act as one might expect of a whore. Her gaze was direct, assessing them as they assessed her. He could not tell what she thought. Their youth amused her, perhaps, but did not arouse her outright contempt.

"Come in," she said as the silence stretched. Her voice was rather ordinary, low and pleasant. When they hesitated, her brow rose. "You asked to see me, yes?"

"We asked," said Arslan, "to see the Rose of Sharon."

"And so you see her," she said, bowing where she sat, with a flicker of a glance at both of them.

"We heard," Baldwin said behind Arslan, "that you are . . . unusual. That you choose your clients. That not everyone who comes to you is admitted to your presence."

"You heard part of the truth," she said. "I do enjoy a certain degree of freedom. But I must also eat, and pay the keeper his fee."

Arslan thought he understood. He reached for Baldwin's purse. Baldwin let him take it, rifle it, come out with enough assorted silver to, perhaps, begin to appease her.

She did not even look at it. "Please. Keep your silver. If any of it is needed later, I'll tell you."

Arslan, astonished, dropped the coins back into the purse and let it fall jingling to Baldwin's side. "Does this mean you won't—"

"I don't know yet what I will do," she said. "Sit down."

They gaped at her. Baldwin mastered his wits first, looked about, discovered nothing better to sit on than the floor; unless he sat on the bed beside the woman. He seemed no more inclined than Arslan to take that liberty.

The floor was comfortable enough with all its carpets. They sat side by side. Arslan made himself look directly at the woman on the bed. "What is your name?" he asked her. "Really?"

"What is yours?" she shot back.

"Arslan," he answered before he thought.

Her eyes widened slightly. "Such a name, to go with such a face. Are you a Turk in disguise?"

"Turks had somewhat to do with raising me," Arslan said. "They gave me the name I answer to."

She nodded as if that made sense, which to most people it would not. "And you?" she asked Baldwin. "Do you have a name, too?"

"Yes," Baldwin said. And no more.

She waited till it was clear that he would not answer. Then she laughed. "O remarkable! I have names enough, with all that men choose to call me. I do like best, however, to be called Nahar."

"Nahar," Arslan said.

She inclined her head, gracious as a queen. "May I suppose that you came for the usual purpose?"

Arslan did not blush. He was astonished. "I—" he began.

Baldwin overrode him. "I was given to understand that you can provide such tutelage as few of your kind are capable of."

"Ah," said Nahar, "you are eloquent. And educated. Are you a clerk, then? I'm not fond of breaking clerks' vows for them."

"I am under no such vows," Baldwin said.

"I'll trust you to be truthful," said Nahar. She reached up to let fall her veil. She was no more beautiful than Arslan had thought. In fact she was rather plain, with her strong features and her forthright expression. "Tell me who told you of me," she said.

Baldwin frowned. "Does it matter?"

"I think," Arslan said, "it does." He looked Nahar in the face. "It's a joke, isn't it? A callow fool told my—friend to look for the Rose of Sharon. Leading him to expect the usual run of woman in such a place as this, but knowing that he would find something quite different."

"It is possible," Nahar said without sign of offense, "that this fool of yours had heard of me from another, but lacked the courage to discover what I might be. I am not to the taste of every man, or boy either."

"You remind me of my mother," Arslan said without thinking. But when he did think, he decided to let it be. "She tells the truth, too. And she's not in the common run of women."

"Your mother is a great lady," Baldwin said with rather more heat than the occasion warranted.

"My mother was a courtesan when she was young," Arslan said levelly. "She only ever wanted one man at a time, and then one man at all. That would have served her worse if God had not given her my father."

Nahar listened in apparent fascination. "I'm very unlike her, then," she said. "One man alone would never be enough for me."

"Have you ever tried it?" Arslan asked in honest curiosity.

"Several times," she said. "There was never enough of him, and always too much of me. The man is rare to vanishing, who will share a woman as women are forced to share a man. After the last one, who tried to beat me but I showed him how well I can wield a dagger, I gave it up. I came here. Here men know better than to be jealous—and if they are, Little Maimoun gets rid of them for me."

"Little Maimoun? Is that the person who met us down below?"

"Oh, no," said Nahar. "That was Constantius. Little Maimoun you would remember if you had seen him. He's a whole ell taller than the tallest man you knew before him."

"I hope we won't need to be got rid of," Arslan said.

"I hope we get what we came for," Baldwin said crossly.

"What did you come for?" asked Nahar.

Baldwin went scarlet.

She took no pity on him. "You should have known to ask for one of our preceptresses. They have great skill and practice in the art of transforming boys into men."

"May he ask for one now?" Arslan wanted to know.

Her brow went up again, very like Arslan's mother. "He? Not you?"

"I didn't ask to come here," Arslan said.

"Well then," said Nahar. She clapped her hands. The girlchild appeared as if from the air. Nahar said to her, "This young gentleman would like to visit Petronilla or Lys, whichever of them has the night to spare."

"Lys," said the child. "She's bored tonight."

"Then by all means, we must relieve her," Nahar said. She gestured to Baldwin. "Go with Ceci."

Baldwin looked ready to turn tail and run, but he was too proud for that. He followed the child with wobbling step, but steady enough to send him where he wanted to go.

Arslan, left alone with the Rose of Sharon, said rather wryly, "You must think me a remarkably juiceless young thing."

"Not at all," she said. She sounded as if she meant it. "I think you're sensible, and not inclined to run away with your passions. That's remarkable in a boy of— fifteen?"

"Almost," Arslan said.

"You do look older," she said as if she felt the need to reassure him. "Your friend betrays you—and, I confess, a certain air about you."

Arslan shrugged. "It doesn't matter. Really. *He* cares, but I never could. I'm odd, I know. My mother's a very self-contained person, too. We make people want to scream at us, just to see if we'll crack."

"And do you ever?"

"Sometimes," he admitted. "Some things do put us out of patience."

"Yes," said Nahar. She stretched out on her side, to be comfortable: meaning no seduction by it, he did not think. Nor was he seduced. She was too much like someone who could be his friend.

The thought was hardly unthinkable, considering what he was and where he came from. Still he wondered at it. Of all places to find a person who thought like him, with whom he could converse in comfort and without pretense, a brothel was one of the most unlikely.

He shrugged inside himself. Why not, after all? And such a tale he could tell when he went back to the Tower of David, if he chose to tell it: how he spent the greater part of a day with the Rose of Sharon, and gave and received great pleasure, and was invited to come back again.

"But not too soon," she said. "I have a living to make, after all. And no, I won't take your silver, or your friend's either. Some things are worth more than silver."

He did persuade her to take a little, to pay her reckoning to the brothelkeeper. "As a gift," he said, "in friendship."

"In friendship," she said, sounding as bemused as he was, and amused, too. It was a grand joke after all, though Galeran the callow would never in all his life understand it.

aldwin had done extraordinarily well with the enchanting Lys. He was so full of it and of himself that he never seemed to notice how quiet Arslan was, nor asked Arslan how he had fared with the Rose of Sharon.

That was as well. Arslan was in no mood for explanations. He did venture a question. "Will you go back?"

"I don't think so," Baldwin said without either hesitation or regret. "I have what I needed. Fleur will look at me now—or if not Fleur, then someone else."

Arslan hoped that Baldwin was right.

"And you?" Baldwin asked him. "Will *you* go back?"

Not so full of himself after all, and not so oblivious as to forget that he had gone with a companion. Arslan managed not to answer, assisted by their arrival at the Tower of David. A page was waiting there with something that the king must do, and do quickly. When that was dealt with, Arslan could hope, Baldwin would have forgotten that he had ever asked Arslan a question, or that Arslan had failed to answer it.

Arslan went as often as Nahar would let him, which was not often. She would never meet him elsewhere than in that cell of a room, nor seek him out. She knew who he was, of course, by the second time he saw her, and guessed who Baldwin was. She did not speak of it, not directly. She only said, in passing, a word or two that told him that she knew.

He was a fool, perhaps, but he trusted her not to make it the talk of the taverns. She had her honor, did Nahar. She could not love one man alone, nor had the birth or wealth to indulge herself as she pleased. She did as well as she could in the world that God had made for her.

One afternoon as they conversed of something aimless and yet interesting, she stopped all at once and said, "It's time, I think."

Arslan blinked at her, baffled. "What? For me to leave? Surely it's not that late— I just came here."

"No," she said. They had been sitting on the bed, decorous enough, one at each end. She swooped across the space between. Before he could move or speak, she had captured him. Her arms were strong, her lips insistent.

He did not know at all what to do. Girls giggled at him, blushed when he looked at them, but never seized him and kissed him, least of all like this. It was like being swallowed whole.

When he dreamed of this, he had not dared dream so far: strong brown limbs, heavy ropes of black hair, eyes that a boy—or a man—could drown in. She was not particularly fair-skinned nor large-breasted nor rich of body—she was not what the squires talked of when they yearned after women. When he looked at her he thought less of roses than of thorns, of fierce dry hills and desert places.

But even in the desert there are havens, oases of green, with water and rest. Nahar led him there and guided him through all their delights. He had never known there were so many.

Maybe for most men there were not. This was a master of the art, no doubt of it; even he could tell. She seemed to take pleasure in it. She not feigning that, he thought, or hoped. She smiled at him through curtains of her hair, showing him yet another thing that he could do, that perhaps would pleasure her as much as it pleasured him.

We are sinning, he thought somewhere in the midst of it. *I'll have to do penance.*

It did not matter. Not then, not after, when they lay in a tangle and he felt the onslaught of sleep, but there was enough of him awake to hear her murmur, "Sweet child."

He roused at that, with a prick of temper. "Is that all I am to you?"

"You are what you are," she said. She kissed him, not dizzyingly as she had before, but softly, lips and cheeks and brow. "Sleep a little. I'll wake you before too long."

He was not strong enough to resist her, or foolish enough to doubt her word. She drew him back out of the warm dark, urged him up and helped him dress and ushered him out, all before he could bring his wits to bear. He was in the street and the sun going down before the essential thing came to him. He had not paid her. He had to pay her.

The door was shut to him, and would not open for any of his calling. He went away in despair, reeking of sin, too much the sinner to go in search of his confessor.

This was the end, of course. Nahar had had what she wanted of every man; as with every man, she would not want to trouble herself with him again, not in friendship. If he went to her, it would be to buy pleasure as any man did.

He was too proud to do that, and too ashamed. He would not go begging to her, nor do penance for having failed to resist her.

And there was no one he could talk to. No one who would understand. Baldwin who was his friend, perhaps the only friend he had, would never see why Arslan had to do what he had to do. Baldwin was a king, accustomed to taking what he wanted. He had never known what it was to want but not to have.

Not that Arslan knew what he wanted. Nahar as a friend? She was older than he, an infidel, a whore who had told him outright that she would never belong to any single man. He had no wealth to give her, no house and lands and properties as that long-ago patron had done for his mother, to make her a woman of means and to give her choices. He had not even paid Nahar for the afternoon's pleasure she had given him—and had been locked out, he was sure, because of it.

He went back in the end because of that: to pay her, and for no other reason. Or so he told himself.

Rather to his surprise, he was let in. He allowed himself to be set in the anteroom where he had been before. But as soon as the doorkeeper left, he slipped out. He knew the ways well by now, the passage and the stair and the one door of many. He met no one. It was quiet today, only one or two stirs or murmurings behind the curtains. The noisy one as he liked to think of her, the woman whom he had never seen but had often heard whooping and sobbing like some demented beast, was silent.

He hesitated at Nahar's door-curtain. There was no sound within. It struck him belatedly and with a shock of shame, that she did not spend all her life in that one cell of a room. She must be out, in the house perhaps, in the city, who knew? She was not there. He would leave his bit of silver on her bed, nor care if she knew who had brought it.

He raised his hand, but stopped. Someone was inside. The sounds were soft, but he had heard them often enough in that place and, for that matter, in corners of the stable.

Why his belly should clench so, he did not know. He knew what she was. She had a living to earn.

He wanted to leave the silver in front of the curtain, turn, bolt. But he could not do it. He moved away, set his back against a wall, slid down it. He should go back to the anteroom and wait to be called. He could not do that, either.

After a moment or an hour, the curtain stirred. Arslan did not know the man who came out. He was a man, that was all, a Frank, neither well nor badly dressed. He could have been a tradesman, a pilgrim, a man-at-arms, even a poor knight. Arslan could not hate him. There was nothing there, really, to hate.

The man left as men did here, a little furtive, a little proud of himself. Some crept and clung to shadows. Some walked as if they had won the world. This one did neither. He might have been coming from a business engagement, one in which he had done reasonably well.

Arslan stayed where he was. The curtain lifted again. Nahar stood holding it up, looking straight at him. The man had not seen him, huddled against the wall in a pool of shadow, but she saw. She said, "Come here."

He did not want to, but he did as she bade. He had his purse in his hand. "I came to pay you," he said.

"You owe me nothing," she said.

His step faltered. Her eyes held him. They drew him in with her, past the curtain into the familiar room. It seemed smaller than he remembered, small and mean.

She made him sit on the bed where he had sat so often before. She sat in her own place, at a careful distance, with her feet tucked up. Then for a while she let the silence stretch, till he was ready to burst out in words, any words, simply to break it.

"You owe me nothing," she repeated. "If you come to me and ask, yes, you pay. But what we did . . . I wanted it. That was for me."

"And not for me?"

"Should it have been?"

"I don't understand you," Arslan said.

"I am very understandable," said Nahar. "If I were a man, I would be perfectly simple."

"But you aren't a man."

"No," said Nahar.

Arslan shook his head to clear it. "You're too confusing. You make me dizzy."

"But you came back," she said. "You sit here. You don't say what must be in your mind, that after all I am a base and blatant harlot."

"I don't think words like that," he said. "I don't know what to think. I was shut out, you see. The last time. When I tried to come back and pay."

"Because there was no payment owing," she said. "If you insist, you may buy me something that I would like."

"But I don't know what you would like," Arslan said.

"Surprise me," said Nahar.

They had not touched or kissed, they had said nothing tender at all, but when Arslan went away again, his heart persisted in singing. He had no idea in the world what he would buy for her, except that it would be something extraordinary. Something different. Fripperies were not to her taste, gauds or ribbons or bits of silk. A dagger she might like. Or . . .

Illumination was wonderful. Alarming, too. Worrisome. It was different indeed. But it seemed, the more he thought about it, to be exactly right.

It was several days before Arslan could go back to Nahar. There were duties, obligations, a festival in the court—a conspiracy as it seemed to keep Arslan from doing what he intended to do. But at last he was set free for an afternoon. He retrieved his gift and shut it in its basket, not without relief, and all but ran into the city.

This time he did not go up till he was summoned. He was not asked to wait long, which pleased him.

Nahar must have been out in the city: she was dressed as he had never yet seen her, in a Frankish gown of modest color and cut, with a veil and a fillet. She looked odd and rather out of place.

She seemed glad to see him, greeted him with a smile and another new thing: the offer of a cup of wine. He took it but did not sip it at once. His basket weighed heavy beside him. She was determinedly uncurious, drinking her wine and chattering of he knew not what.

While Arslan hesitated, waiting for his moment, the basket made its own decision. With only the slightest of warning scrabblings, the lid erupted, and with it his gift.

Nahar sat on the bed in her modest grey gown, face to face with a ruffled and tail-twitching kitten. Its eyes were perfectly round and still infant blue, fixed on her in an expression of pure indignation.

She committed an unpardonable sin in the world of cats. She laughed.

The kitten, affronted, launched itself straight up and forward. She gasped as its claws found purchase in her shoulder. With great care she pried them loose, but did not fling the kitten away. It clung less painfully, worked its way up and inward, burrowed into her hair and began to purr.

Arslan was holding his breath. A lover of true finesse would have given his lady a hawk or a hound or a fine palfrey. But he lacked the wherewithal for those, nor did he think that Nahar would have any use for them. A cat, however, could bear her company, hunt the mice and rats that scrabbled in the walls, and keep her warm on nights when she had no man to do it for her.

Not that he would say such a thing. He knew better than to insult her.

Maybe he should have given her a gaud after all, a ring or a bit of silk.

Then she smiled. It was a smile such as he had never seen in her, broad and delighted. "I've always wanted a cat," she said. "But none ever came to me, and no one ever gave me one."

"You do like it?" Arslan asked, almost choking on it. He was trying too hard to be calm. "Would you rather have had a necklace? A pair of gloves?"

She stroked the kitten's grey-striped head. Her expression was almost fierce. "No! Any fool can give me gloves or a necklace. Nobody ever thought to give me a cat."

Arslan drew a breath. "So I did the right thing?"

She bent toward him, kitten and all, and set a kiss on his forehead. "You did exactly right. Aren't I clever, for knowing you would?"

Arslan smiled a bit uncertainly. This matter of men and women, he was coming to see, was both simple and endlessly complicated. He did not know if he would ever master it.

But today he had done well. She was pleased with his gift. So pleased that she took him to bed again, and pleased yet again by his surprise that she should do such a thing. "You are a marvel and a rarity," she said to him, so that he blushed furiously and lost his stride and had to fumble till he found it again. She waited till they were done before she went on. "Don't change, not even a little. No other man is like you, and certainly no boy. There's only one of you in the world."

"If you ask my mother," muttered Arslan, "one of me is more than enough."

"Your mother adores you," Nahar said. "Come here, stop chattering, let me show you something else that a man can do if he is both wise and agile."

"And young?" Arslan asked, panting with the effort.

She laughed much longer and more freely than his feeble wit might be judged to warrant—laughter that was like a release, shaking the bed, sweeping him up with it till they lay giggling helplessly in one another's arms. The cat, its patience exhausted, uttered a sound of pure disgust. It stalked across them to the bed's edge and thence to the floor, and went hunting either mice or quiet in the darkness under the bed.

he twins were ill. They had been ill
before, had recovered with prayer and tending, but they had not thrived thereafter.

Richildis knew as every mother did in this age of the world, that children were
fragile. They died. She had lost one in the autumn, hardly after she had known she
carried it—too young even to know whether it was son or daughter.

She was not well herself, from that. And as the twins grew thinner and paler,
she lost will and strength. She was not aware that she was fading; rather that the
world was fading about her. It did not trouble her greatly. She would have said, if
anyone had asked, that for all her troubles she was still happy. She had a husband
whom she loved, a demesne that she had made prosperous, a house in Jerusalem, a
place in the High Court, friends and kin, a whole world in which she belonged.
God would preserve her children. Would He not?

Except that He would not. She saw it before anyone else would admit to it. Her
husband could not see, or would not. He was oblivious as men could be, visiting
his children, finding them much as ever, going on about his business in castle or
city, wherever they were.

They were in Jerusalem that winter and spring, before word came from the West
that Crusade had been preached and would come when it came. That could be
within the year, or it could be years, while the infidel settled deeper into Edessa,
and the Court persisted in doing nothing to dislodge him.

Richildis had always drawn strength from the Holy City, but this year she had
none to draw. On Good Friday her children slipped away, so softly and so quietly
that one might barely have noticed. They had been ill of a rheum that week, no
worse than anything that had taken them before, till it flared up in fever and
consumed them.

Gisela died in her arms, one gasp among many, and then nothing. Alexios lived
not an hour longer. She sat in their nursery, cradling them both. They did not grow
cold as she had expected. It was an early summer, the heat already fierce. Even
within the walls of the house the air was warm.

Michael Bryennius had been out somewhere—in the market, she supposed, or
visiting the Byzantine embassy. He came in like a storm breaking, burst through the
door, stopped at sight of her. His face in the black beard was white. Not as white,

she noticed, as the faces in her arms. There was life in his features, and strength even in their absence of color.

She could not say anything. What was there to say? When he broke down weeping, raw choking sobs, she could not move. Her arms were full, her heart all empty. Nothing in the world could fill it. Not even the sight of him at her feet, prostrate with grief.

The stillness went on and on. People came and took the children away. Other people came and coaxed their father to retreat. They would have done the same to her, but she made herself a rock, a stone, immovable. She would not move though the world shifted beneath her.

Her tormentors muttered to one another. "Mad," they said. "Grief has driven her mad."

That was not true at all, but she lacked inclination to say so. She simply did not wish to speak, nor to stir, nor to do anything at all but sit in this darkened room with its smell of death.

She must have been there for a long while. Days, perhaps. There was water in the jar, which she drank. Sometimes there was food. She ate a little bread, a bit of cheese. It was not death she wanted, not to slay herself with hunger and thirst. She simply wanted quiet.

The quiet shattered in a blast of light and sound. The room was full of people, great loud-voiced men in dusty armor.

It was only Bertrand, and Arslan behind him, and the whole half-dozen of Helena's Turks. They looked as if they had come riding headlong to battle.

Richildis regarded them with neither fear nor surprise. They all stared back. She was mildly startled to see that the Turks were not boys any longer, nor particularly young men. There was grey in Ayyub's beard, now that he had finally grown one. Some of them had married, she had heard, one even to a Frankish woman who had buried a husband and gone looking for another.

How swiftly time flew.

Then she was flying herself: swept up in Bertrand's arms and carried out into the hurtful, hateful light. She flinched away from it; felt him flinch in return, and heard the mutter of his curse. It seemed the house was in disorder and its master gone from it. She had not known that Michael Bryennius was away. Perhaps he had gone back to Byzantium to escape his sorrows.

Bertrand carried her to the baths and set her in the hands of the servants. They were looking flustered, as well they might. They might have been weeping.

With hot water and vigorous scrubbing, some of her wits began to come back. She fought that. She did not want to feel again, to care what happened to her. Better to be not-there, to be buried in quiet. Then was no pain, no sorrow. Only emptiness.

But her kin were not so merciful. Bertrand had come, it seemed, straight from some campaign or other, and Arslan with him; and they had fetched Helena, and she was putting the house in order. Richildis was not at all astonished to find the king himself in the hall in which she entertained guests, helping Arslan and a handful of the servants to prepare the hall for dinner. Of the dead she saw no sign, nor of her husband.

She went looking for them, came on Helena instead, imposing a reign of gentle terror on the kitchen servants. Helena broke off her dressing down of the sullen and scowling cook, to turn to Richildis with such an expression that Richildis wanted to recoil. Instead she said, "I can't find my husband. Is he dead?"

"We don't think so," Helena said, direct as always, though she looked as if she wanted to weep. "He saw the children buried, but no one since has seen him. Or, for that matter, you. We thought he might be here."

"No," Richildis said. "He went home, maybe. I don't know. I know so little now."

"I don't doubt it," said Helena. "Here, come with me. You've been too much in the dark. You need the light in your face."

"I don't want light," Richildis said.

"Nonetheless," said Helena, "you shall have it."

Nor would she rest till Richildis was settled in the garden, in sunlight a little muted by a canopy of leaves, with a bowl of oranges—for the brightness, Helena said, and for the taste—and a cup of the strong sweet hot stuff that the infidels called kaffé. Helena called it medicine and made her drink it. It was notably less vile than many another potion she had had forced on her, and it did what Helena wanted: it began to rouse her.

Helena sipped at a cup herself. Her hands trembled a little but her gaze was steady. "How long have you been ill?" she asked.

Richildis blinked. "Ill? I haven't been ill."

Helena shook her head. "Don't lie to yourself. You haven't been well in spirit since you lost the baby in the winter. And now this. Do you know where your husband might be?"

"No," said Richildis. "Unless he went back to Byzantium."

"I don't think so," Helena said. "Nor is he in Mount Ghazal. He must still be in Jerusalem."

"I don't see why," said Richildis. "There's nothing to keep him here."

Helena reached out and grasped her shoulders and shook her once, hard. "Stop that! He has you—he loves you. What did you do to him? How did you drive him away?"

"I did nothing," Richildis said. "I said nothing."

Helena hissed in exasperation. "Nothing is a great deal. It's a sin, you know. The sin of despair."

"I don't know," said Richildis, "why I should succumb to such a thing. People die. Children in particular. The world goes on. No one cares, except for a moment."

"So you would kill the love your husband has for you, and the children who would be born of that love, because God chose to take those you had and reclaim them for Himself?"

Richildis curled her lip, "Oh, please! That is not God. Or if it is, then God is no better than the Evil One."

Helena did not shrink from what was, after all, blasphemy. If anything she looked glad of it. "Yes," she said. "Be angry. Feel something."

Richildis shivered. "I don't want to," she said. But it had begun. Only embers yet, but they were color in a grey world, heat in the empty cold. When they flared into fire she would be alive again—and she wanted that not at all.

"There are times," Helena said as if to herself, "when the spirit ebbs. When the soul has had enough. There may be no cause, or none that makes itself apparent, until the world is grey and nothing seems to matter. If the soul gives in, it dies. If it's to live, it has to find the light again."

Richildis laughed painfully. "Light? Where? Have you ever been as alone as I am now?"

"By my own choice," Helena said, "once, yes."

Richildis shut her mouth with a snap.

"I think you should find your husband," said Helena.

Damn her for wisdom. Damn her for laying open the empty places and lancing the wounds beneath them. It was as rough a surgery as any on a battlefield, and well might kill Richildis, too.

Richildis went hunting. She did not know precisely where she was going. She dressed for the city, veiled for modesty, with Kutub her shadow as he had always been. It was no lonelier than sitting in the dark, no more futile than waiting for the stillness to swallow her. He was on his way to Byzantium, most likely; she was a fool to seek him here. But seek him she did, because if she stayed one moment longer in that house she would lose her soul altogether. She might welcome that, but Bertrand and Helena would never allow it.

To escape them she went hunting a man who could be anywhere. But there were places where he had been known to go. The house of the Byzantine ambassador. The street of the jewelers and the street of the silk merchants, where he conducted certain transactions in his family's name. A place where men of means gathered, too elegant to be called a tavern. Even one of the churches, one in which the Greek rite was sung, the priest of which was some distant connection of his family, and in the cloister of which he sometimes sat and disputed philosophy with a scholar or two.

He was in none of those places. Nor was he in Holy Sepulcher amid the flocking pilgrims, nor gaping at the Dome of the Rock, nor wailing at the Jews' Wall where even under the Crusade a few veiled and mantled men rocked and lamented the fall of their temple. They should not be there, but when the guards were lenient they crept in, disguised sometimes as pilgrims and often as merchants, to say their prayers and weep their tears.

There were no tears in Richildis. She was weary of walking, of fighting currents in the city, of finding nothing wherever she went. Yet instead of turning her steps homeward where grief and darkness were, she let the road lead her out of the city, through the gate that led to the Mount of Olives, up the hill and into the grove that was more ancient and holy even than the city that rose beyond it.

Whatever guided her, God or His angel or something darker altogether, there she found him. He was not among the pilgrims kneeling and praying and being exalted in the Garden of Gethsemane. He had set himself alone under the ancient trees, seated on a stump that must have sprouted when Joshua was an infant. So many pilgrims of so many nations, and not a few of his own, and yet she knew him, that strong yet elegant man in black with his rich black beard.

No miracle healed her then. No light blinded her with revelation. She went to

him, that was all, and sat on the ground beside him, and waited till he became
aware of her. That seemed a very long time. The stillness into which she sank was
different from the one that had possessed her till now. It was a stronger thing
somehow, a presence rather than an absence.

After a while a thought came to her. She reached out a hand and found his, and
clasped it. His fingers were cold. She warmed them with her breath. He did not
move, did not return her grip. Nor did she slacken it.

When he spoke, she had stopped expecting it. "I thought you would die," he
said.

"Everyone dies," said Richildis.

"I meant," he said, "now." He paused. "I had them buried in St. Alexios."

And she had been there, and she neither known nor looked. She tightened her
grip a little. Tears were still alien to her. Her grief was too shallow, or far too deep.

"I thought that I would bury you, too," he said.

She shook her head. "I'm not that close to death."

For the first time he looked at her, dark eyes, white face, burning intensity. "You
were."

Maybe she had been. "Not now," she said.

"What woke you?"

"The horde of my kin."

He snorted. It was laughter: unwilling, unlooked for, but laughter nonetheless.
"Let me imagine. Bertrand, then Olivier-Arslan, and when they had swept through
with fire and sword, the Lady Helena with her devastating good sense."

"How well you know them," Richildis said. "They've made order of chaos, and
sent me out to hunt you down."

"Of course," Michael Bryennius said. "Anyone else would have kept you close
and under guard lest you do harm to yourself. They sent you out all but alone, on
a hunt that might take you clear to the City."

"They said you were in Jerusalem," Richildis said. "Why didn't you leave?"

"You were here," he said.

As simple as that, and yet not simple at all. "You left the house," she said. "You
left me alone."

His brow went up. "Are we quarreling?"

"No," said Richildis.

"Good," he said.

"Will you leave Jerusalem now?"

"Only if you come with me."

"No," she said again.

"Then I stay," he said.

Richildis drew a breath. Her throat hurt. It had been too tight for too long. "You
needn't stay for me."

"Need I not?"

"I don't want to bind you," she said.

"I remember," he said, "what the priest said on the day we were wed. 'What
God hath joined together, let no man put asunder.' "

"But if—" She stopped. "I don't want to go home," she said. "Where else can
we go?"

"Mount Ghazal," he said.

"No," said Richildis. "Not even there."

"Then," he said, "if you can go anywhere in the world, where will you go? Anjou, perhaps?"

She shook her head. "Not there."

"Ah," he said. "Old vows. Old chains. And yet you said to me when we married, that you were free of the world, all but Anjou. Would you run away with me? Would you travel into my own country, even to my City?"

Her heart quivered. It was waking, perhaps to fear, perhaps to something else. "May we go on a caravan? May we go to such places as I've never seen?"

"All the way to the silk countries, if it pleases you."

"I don't think," said Richildis, "that we need to go so far. But to go away . . . yes. Yes, it pleases me."

"Then we shall go," said Michael Bryennius. "Today, tomorrow, whenever you like."

Practicality possessed her, sudden and not unwelcome. "In a week. That's brief enough—the servants will have fits. If we can find a caravan—"

"There is one," he said, "traveling to Nicaea nine days from now, if we are minded to be part of it."

"Let us be," said Richildis.

"Then we shall be," he said.

FORTY

Lady Richildis and her husband had gone away. It was not running away, Arslan's mother said, though to him it sounded very like it. They had taken a caravan to Nicaea, and beyond that they did not know— perhaps to Constantinople, perhaps into Asia. It was a strange thing to do, but people did it; except that mostly they called it pilgrimage and came to Jerusalem, or went to Rome or Compostela.

Someday Arslan would see Rome. Paris, too, and Anjou where his father was born. He was too young yet, and too busy learning to be a squire and then a knight. When he had learned it all, when he had fought in the Crusade that everyone said was coming, and grown into a man, then he would go. He had made a vow to himself. Not even Baldwin knew of it. It was too strong a thing to tell anyone but God.

Now Lady Richildis was gone away, and Michael Bryennius too; and there was an empty place where they had been. Arslan tried to fill it with duties and pleasures, hours with Nahar and hours in the hunt or on the practice-field. And in the summer and autumn there were campaigns, little wars in which the knights of the kingdom honed their skills. Sometimes the king was permitted to join in them; and when he did, Arslan went with him. When he did not, Arslan expected to stay in Jerusalem or Acre; but that summer, when a company of lords and barons went to put down a rising of bandits near Banias, Bertrand took Arslan with him.

This was the proving ground. These little wars, these marches and encampments, these rough skirmishes with Turks or desert tribesmen, had little enough of the pageantry that the king brought to his greater battles. Here one learned thirst and privation, heat, dust, flies on the bloodied faces of the dead. Here one became a man, or one died. There was no room for children or for cowards.

Arslan took a wound in one of the small battles. They had been scouring raiders near the eastern border, out past Lake Tiberias. Things were stirring among the infidels. Zengi was dead, murdered near Damascus; Islam was in uproar, princes quarreling like dogs over the unburied carcass. The tribes ran wild as they always did when they had the scent of death, and some ran into the Frankish country.

It was a bloody, yelling skirmish like any other, in among the rocks and scree of that bleak country. Arslan, spurring in his father's wake, took a bolt in the side, straight through his mail: one of the raiders had got hold of a Genoese crossbow and learned how to use it, damn his devilish wits. Luckily for the next unwitting target, he was far slower to wind and reload than he was to shoot. Bertrand wheeled his horse in time to see Arslan fall, and clove the bowman in two with one great furious sweep of his sword.

He carried Arslan out himself, and cut the bolt from the flesh, and tended it with rough mercy. Rough to rouse pain, and merciful because pain grew till it cast Arslan into the dark.

When he woke the fight was over. The pain was not much worse than he had taken in buffets on the practice field, but it clawed deeper, and he was much weaker. "You lost blood," Bertrand said when he tried to struggle up. It was night, there was a fire, there were stars, and somewhere someone was weeping.

"Who—" Arslan tried to ask.

The weeping stopped. Bertrand's face betrayed nothing. "Rogier got it in the belly. He wouldn't take the mercy-stroke."

"Nor would I, it seems," Arslan said. He had managed to sit up, though he nearly gagged with the pain of it.

"You weren't gut-shot," Bertrand said, "or you wouldn't be thrashing around like that. You're not bad hurt, unless it festers. It's more a graze than anything else."

Arslan did not want to think about wounds that festered. He was alive—his body screamed the truth of that. "I'm thirsty," he said.

One of the squires brought him a cup with water in it, tasting of leather and a ghost of wine. It could have come from the pure springs of heaven, as welcome as it was. Arslan drank it down, and had a little bread after, though the bit of roast gazelle was more than his stomach could bear.

All the while he drank and tried to eat, Bertrand sat by him, asleep perhaps, or near to it. The firelight caught the scar on his cheek, the one that ran from temple to jaw—knife-slash, Arslan had heard. Someone had stitched and tended it well: it was barely visible in most lights.

It must have hurt like fury when it was new.

One grew accustomed to bruises and buffets. Maybe one could grow accustomed to wounds, too. Arslan was in no comfort, nor could he sleep now that he was awake. In the morning he must ride, or be carried in the wagon with the provisions and the few others of the wounded.

He would ride. Whatever it cost him, he would sit up on his horse like a man.

It was not so easy to cling to his pride in the black dawn. His whole body had stiffened while he lay in an uneasy doze. He creaked like an old man, getting up. When he stood erect his stomach revolted.

There was little in it, which was a blessing; and no blood, which was a relief. When it was empty he could walk, though the stabbing in his side made him dizzy if he moved too quickly.

His horse was waiting for him, saddled, and Bertrand's too though Arslan as his squire should have seen to that himself. He pulled himself into the saddle, paused for breath. Through the dark that crowded the world, he did not think he could see anyone staring. They were all preoccupied with breaking camp and riding out.

He rode because he must, and because he was too stubborn to stop. When he could think, which was seldom, he wondered why he was doing this—what possible good was in it. If he died of a wound taken in a skirmish that proved nothing, that drove back a tribe of bandits who would only raid again in another season, what would he gain, or anyone else either?

He was feverish. He clung to the saddle, letting his body ride while his mind drifted. Pain anchored it, tugging whenever he floated too far, pulling him back to remembrance.

Saints fasted and prayed and tormented themselves in search of revelation. Arslan found it in a wound that was not even particularly serious; in pain and its endurance, and in the beating of the sun upon his head. Until now he had been a child, though a great and hulking one to be sure. He had thought little on what he did or why, nor sworn oaths that were his own, out of his heart. They were always someone else's: Baldwin's mostly, since Baldwin was king and Arslan was the king's squire.

On that ride from pain to pain, Arslan made no vows to himself. But something deeper than a vow—that, he came to. He was bound by birth to the Crusade. When he had given it whatever he had to give, he would find a world for himself. It might be this world and this country. It might be another altogether. But he would find it.

Baldwin was jealous of Arslan. "You took a wound in battle," he said, "while I sat here wrapped in wool, with servants leaping if I so much as stumbled over a crack in the floor."

"You're the king," Arslan said. "You have to stay alive and well."

"Why?" Baldwin asked with bitterness that had grown more frequent of late. "I don't *do* anything. If it's not the Constable or the barons, it's my mother doing it all."

"That will change," Arslan said.

"Not fast enough," Baldwin muttered. "Maybe not at all. They like the feel of the reins in their hands. They'll not let them go, least of all to me."

"All the more reason for you to watch yourself," Arslan said. "You'll have to be ready when your time comes—ready and strong."

"If that time ever comes," said Baldwin.

To the queen Baldwin said nothing. He would never admit to fear of her, but respect he most certainly had; and she never asked his leave to rule as she saw fit.

She ruled like a man, with a man's sure hand. Except, Arslan reflected, that she did not lead armies to war. She left that to the men under her command—and to Baldwin, who for all his complaining was never forced to sit at home when there was a war to be fought. Skirmishes and raids, no; but wars he led, as befit the king.

There was a strong war brewing now among the infidels. Raymond of Antioch and Joscelin of fallen Edessa were at odds again. Joscelin had in mind to take Edessa back. Raymond called him a ramping fool with a pitiful nothing of an army, and left him to it. He, who might conceivably have been persuaded to wait until he had more men and better strategy, was pricked to move regardless.

To everyone's astonishment, including perhaps his own, he won the city; but not the citadel, which was the city's strong heart. Without the citadel he had won nothing. The garrison there would easily, once the infidels came with their armies, crush him between them. He could not help but know this, but he did nothing of any use, sat confused in the city where he had once been lord, and waited for someone to show him what to do.

Inevitably the infidel came, in the form of the lord Nur al-Din from Aleppo with his hordes of Turks and Saracens. Then Joscelin remembered his wits, or what passed therefor. Though trapped between army and citadel, he slipped away by night with his men and with Christians of the city, striking for the river.

There in the morning the infidels caught them. The messenger who came to Jerusalem was wounded, but not badly. He told his tale as all such tales are told, with stark precision. Joscelin defeated, wounded but alive. Joscelin's ally, the lord of Marash and Kaisun, dead in the fight. "We were standing fast," the messenger said, "till Lord Joscelin took it into his head to break out and fall on the infidel. Not that I'd presume to judge a nobleman, your majesties, my lords and ladies," he said to the assembly of the court, "but he could have been wiser."

Joscelin had escaped to Samosata. The Christians of that country who had followed him, abandoned in his flight, were slain to the last man. Their children, their women were taken slaves. Edessa was emptied, that ancient Christian city; emptied and laid waste.

And still no Crusade came to the kingdom's aid. It was begun: the pope had preached it in France, and kings had taken the cross; but it would be months before they wended their way eastward. Wars so great were never either easy or swift of accomplishment—least of all among the Franks, who did not stand perpetually in battle order as did the men of Outremer.

In the wake of Edessa's second and final fall, God's goodwill seemed to take leave of the kingdom, and with it a great deal of its common sense. The devil of the infidels seemed to have claimed mastery over the Kingdom of Jerusalem.

It began simply enough, if anything to do with the infidel was simple. Jerusalem was then allied with Damascus in one of the complex weavings of the east, in which enemy might share cause with enemy against a common adversary. In the spring of the third year after Edessa's first fall and the year after its second, one of the lords who served the lord of Damascus appeared in Jerusalem. His name was Altuntash, and he governed Bosra and Salkhad.

He rode in in state, a man of lordly height and girth on one of the slender little horses of this country, with an escort of Turks and Saracens under the banners of Islam. Arslan could read some of what they said: verses from the Koran, warlike and holy.

Altuntash was an apostate, an Armenian who had forsaken the Lord Christ for the infidels' Allah, but because he came as an ally he was welcomed with studied courtesy. He stood up in front of the High Court, in the hall of their assembly, and addressed them through an interpreter though Arslan had heard him speak perfectly intelligible Frankish.

"Majesties," he said, bowing with florid grace to the queen and the king. "My lords. My ladies. Knights and barons of the Kingdom of Jerusalem. I bring you alliance, if you will have it."

"We are already your allies," said Manasses the Constable from his place at the queen's right hand. "Are you not a vassal of the lord of Damascus?"

"My lord," said Altuntash with another, less florid bow, "I was. I am no longer. I have divided myself from that allegiance. I come to lay it in your king's hands, if he will take it. I bring Bosra and Salkhad under your rule."

"And what," inquired Manasses, "would you ask in return?"

"Only, my lord," Altuntash said, "that you make me lord of the Hauran in which Bosra and Salkhad are."

The Court stirred at that, not with surprise unless they were utter fools, but in interest and the beginning of debate. The Hauran was a Christian country, if not of the Latin rite. It might therefore be a proper conquest for the Crusade.

"From there," someone said among the ranks of the barons, "we have Damascus within our reach."

"Damascus is our ally," someone else reminded him.

"Today it is," said the first man. "Tomorrow . . . who knows?"

The debate ran back and forth. On the one hand the old alliance, the oaths sworn to stand on the side of Damascus in the infidels' wars; or at the least, not to interfere between Damascus and its enemies. In return Jerusalem gained Damascus' assurance that the might of Syria would not fall on the kingdom, and Syria's protection against the rest of Islam. This new alliance, on the other hand, would shatter the bond with Damascus but gain lands and power that Jerusalem had not held before. It would be a thorn in the infidels' side—a Christian realm in the heart of Islam. That thought endeared itself greatly to the younger and hotter-headed of the barons.

The older and the more sensible walked warily round promises of princedoms. "How do we know he can give it to us? What will it cost us to hold it? Damascus' alliance costs us nothing and gains us a measure of safety."

"Until a new sultan supplants the old, and all alliances are made void."

"But they might not be. This man Altuntash—what do we know of him? Unur in Damascus we do know, all his loyalties and his treacheries."

And on it went, through the day and into the night, with the queen sitting silent while the Court ran on. The king, rather to the barons' surprise, did not like Altuntash at all, and would not speak for him.

When it was very late, when the barons growled like dogs with hunger and exhaustion, the queen spoke at last. "I believe that we should do this."

Those who had spoken against it broke out in a roar of protest. Her son led them, his voice higher than some, clearer to hear. "We can't do that! We'll break faith with Damascus."

"We break faith," she said, "to wrest a Christian country from the hands of the infidel." She rose, set down the scepter that she had held in her lap through all this long day and evening. "In the morning, my lord Manasses, you will summon the levies."

He bowed. If he would have spoken, she gave him no time. She had swept out, and a tide of people after her, seeking food and rest.

• • •

Baldwin wanted to pursue her and no doubt shout at her, but Bertrand stood in his way. "Not now," he said.

"Then when?" Baldwin demanded hotly.

"In the morning," said Bertrand, cool to the king's heat. "Come now. You should eat, sleep."

Baldwin set his jaw as if he would resist, but after a moment he surrendered.

When he was asleep in his own bed, or feigning it, Arslan went out of the king's bedchamber into the anteroom where the squires were most of them asleep already, and past that to the outermost room, the one in which he preferred to sleep. It was cold in winter but it was quiet, and no one else seemed inclined to spread his pallet there.

Bertrand was sitting in it now, eyes closed, hands folded over his middle, to all appearances asleep.

Appearances could deceive. "My lord," Arslan said, not loudly but not softly either.

Bertrand opened an eye. "That was quick enough," he said. "He's asleep?"

Arslan shrugged. "He seems to be."

"Good enough," Bertrand said. He closed the eye, sighed, opened them both. No sleep clouded them. "In the morning I want you to keep him busy. Keep him away from the queen."

"You don't want him to dissuade her?"

"I don't want him to convince her that she should do this mad thing."

"You think he'll do that if he tries to talk her out of it."

"I know he will," Bertrand said. "He's just of the age to object to his mother's rule. And she's not giving it up."

"She should," said Arslan. "She should have done it when he turned fifteen. But she never said a word. Nor did anyone else."

"Not even Baldwin." Bertrand stretched more comfortably in the big carved chair, crossing his ankles and studying the toes of his fine crimson shoes. He was still in his court dress, odd to one who had grown familiar with him in dusty armor and wayworn riding-gear. "No, no one said anything. She's a strong woman, is Melisende, and she knows—she believes she knows—precisely how to rule this kingdom. If she were a man, with the blood and right she carries, would anyone even be suggesting that she should abdicate in favor of an untried boy?"

"She's not a man," Arslan said.

"Alas for her high heart," Bertrand agreed, "she is not. But do you see? If Baldwin starts shouting at her, she'll be all the more determined to do as she pleases and not as he would like her to do."

"Is that," Arslan asked slowly, "why she chose Altuntash to begin with? Because Baldwin wanted to stay with Damascus?"

Bertrand shook his head, but slowly. "No, I don't think so. I think she sees greater advantage in possessing the Hauran than in appeasing Damascus."

"Do you?"

"I'm not the queen," Bertrand said.

Arslan nodded. "I don't either. It's too much risk for too little certain reward."

"And there is the matter of broken faith."

"That never comes to much unless we want it to," Arslan said, which won him a slightly startled glance. He bared his teeth at it. "I'm not a child. I know how kingdoms are ruled and how wars are fought. Loyalty is a thing to be set aside for expedience's sake, and oaths and promises are valid only as long as they're convenient. With Damascus . . . Altuntash holds out a tempting prize, but something in me dislikes the feel of it."

"It's not the prize," Bertrand said. "It's what we might have to do to hold it. We're weak against the full force of Islam—at least till the Crusade finds its rambling way here. We can't risk a defeat now on the heels of Edessa's twofold fall. The next city to fall might well be Jerusalem."

"The queen will argue that a strong Damascus could turn from ally into enemy in an eyeblink: if someone other than Unur takes power there, he might refuse to honor Unur's pacts. Why not take the lands were offered, and use them to strike at Damascus before Damascus strikes at us?"

"And yet if we do that, Damascus might strike before we can be ready; and that will be very ill indeed."

"Round and round it goes," Arslan said, swallowing a yawn. "We heard it all today, and we'll hear it tomorrow, I'm sure, and for days thereafter. Is there something else I can do for you, my lord?"

Bertrand looked ready to fall asleep himself, but roused with the hint of a start. "No. No, I'm dallying, I should be home long since. Keep Baldwin quiet and keep him apart from the queen, if you can at all. Now's not the time for him to challenge her. He has friends, but not enough. She's stronger than he is, and she will win, no matter how hard he may fight."

"Are you," Arslan asked carefully, "taking the king's side in this?"

"No," said Bertrand. "I'm doing my duty as his tutor."

That could well be true. Arslan stood for a while after Bertrand had gone, thinking about it, wondering why he was so set against the queen's decision. It made as much sense as the other, when he stopped to think—and yet his heart insisted that it was wrong.

It was probably as simple as a sharp dislike of Altuntash. A man who had forsaken the Lord Christ to turn to Muhammad, who had then forsaken his sworn lord in Damascus to turn to Jerusalem, must be a slippery ally at best, and perhaps not a great judge of causes.

Arslan sighed. He was tired to the bone, but he had no desire to sleep. After he had spread his bed and undressed and lain down, he lay a long while awake. The world was turning, he could feel it. Dame Fortune's wheel was poised with Jerusalem at the top of it, ready to stand or to fall.

Whichever way the wheel turned, he rode with it. His faith was not so very strong, perhaps, but he was loyal; and he was his king's man.

FORTY ONE

Baldwin did not want the course that his mother had decided on, but when it came time to march to the war that she had forced upon him, it was he and not she who led the armies of Jerusalem. Led them indeed more truly than heretofore: not only riding at their head with his crowned helm under the glittering splendor of the True Cross, but speaking in the councils of war, and what was more, being heard.

The queen stayed at home in Jerusalem, holding the reins of the kingdom while he and the barons rode to enlarge it, or perhaps to defend it if Damascus proved too great a gobbet to swallow. She bade farewell to her son with no evidence of apprehension, no apparent fear that he would be captured or killed. "Fight well," she said. "Bring honor to the kingdom."

He bowed, looking bold and manly in the new armor that had been made for his broadened shoulders and his newly noble height. Arslan supposed he felt, inside, as small as he had ever been, and too excited to be afraid—as Arslan did himself.

There was a new edge to Arslan's excitement, a sharpness like a memory of a bolt piercing his side. The wound was healed, with a scar that pulled if he moved too suddenly, and in odd moments a ghost of pain. He did not talk about that, nor complain when his armor, less new than Baldwin's and beginning to strain at the shoulders, began to catch and rub. He padded it after the first day, and it subsided to a nuisance.

Royal war moved much more slowly than raids across the border. The army wound its stately way out of Jerusalem through hills going brown with summer's coming. At the Jordan they slowed amid the hordes of pilgrims, crossing in battle array while men and women in the rags of sanctity bathed and wept and prayed on the banks and in the turgid water. Many of the pilgrims called out to them, begging for a blessing; or in their eagerness to touch and kiss the cross of Crusade that marked each man's shoulder, got in the way of the footsoldiers. One even sprang onto the crupper of a destrier, clawing at the knight who rode it, setting that fine blooded warhorse to bucking and squealing.

The horse shed its unwanted passenger and nearly its rider as well, turned on the fallen man and trampled him as it had been trained to do. His screaming followed the army for a while after, and no one else was mad enough to try what he had tried.

They forded the river and turned north through Galilee. At Lake Tiberias they camped by the walled city and the beautiful waters, the last that they would see under the sky until they came to Damascus. If they came to Damascus.

And when they had left there, with many looks back; when they had passed the chain of fortresses that guarded the Franks' lands against the infidel; then indeed they were gone out of Christendom and into the House of Islam.

Here was the proving ground of prophets, the desert in which God spoke clear to those with ears to hear: the fasting, the thirst-wracked, the mad. Allah was born in desert as deadly as this, in the dry land without respite of green.

There was no water here. No living thing. Locusts had come in their hordes, a plague out of old Egypt, but no Moses was here to soften the blow for God's chosen. They ate what they brought with them, drank what their mules and laden oxen could carry. They advanced no faster than the beasts could, slowed immeasurably as the infidels began to gather.

They came like vultures to the feast. They circled and struck, flocked and squabbled, gave the army not one hour's peace, not by day, not by night. The farther the army went, the thicker the enemy grew, as if every raider and reiver and soldier of the Faith had gathered to this one place against this army of Jerusalem.

At last they could barely move for the massing of the enemy. Each step was fought for, every inch of that bitter ground.

Baldwin had never known such terror before, never suffered such privation. The last war that he had led had been a triumph, not a man lost, as if the blessing of God had been upon him.

Now God's hand seemed taken away. Yet Baldwin was not crushed down. The darker the way, the brighter he seemed to burn. His people had always loved him; he was like his mother, a golden creature, with a gift for winning hearts. On this march that was like nothing that even the older knights had known, that broke down stronger men than he had seemed to be and left them weeping and imploring God's mercy, he rode straight and tall in front of them.

"This is the forge," Bertrand said to Arslan as they rode side by side in a rare lull in the storm of infidels. Masses of them blackened the horizon, but none rode just now against the army. Franks were making what progress they could, moving as quickly as wounds and thirst would let them.

"This is the forge," Bertrand said again, "that tempers the steel in the core of a man."

"I think he must be solid steel," Arslan said of Baldwin, not with envy, not really. A king had to be stronger than an ordinary man. He had to hold the kingdom on his shoulders, its loyalty and its strength of will. Arslan was glad that Baldwin was proving himself so well. One never knew till the steel was hammered and heated, whether it would emerge the stronger, or crack and fail.

Just then Baldwin paused, so that father and son found themselves riding up on either side of him. "Give the order to camp," Baldwin said. "Tell the army to pretend that there's not an enemy to be seen. Trust in God to defend us, and in our own courage. We'll not be shattered by these hordes of Allah."

His voice was pitched to carry. The men who were nearest sent up a ragged cheer. It ran down the line, and the king's words just ahead of it, while he sat his big white horse in his bright armor, head up, unbowed, as a king should be.

No one ventured to gainsay him. It was getting on for evening, the sun sinking over the barren hills. Water there was none. What they carried, they reserved for the horses. Some, Arslan among them, had been sparing of their waterskins; had gone thirsty when others drank deep, and reaped the reward now, in a sip of warm and leather-reeking water before they set to work pitching camp in the waste.

They did it as Baldwin had commanded, in careful order: tents pitched, horselines set up, men set to work digging pits for the privies. It was all as if they were in friendly country, unbeset by infidels. Those who would have flung themselves down where they halted, were beaten or shamed into obedience. "Show those devils a bold face," Arslan heard a sergeant snarl. "Front to or backside up, I don't care. You heard his majesty. *Do it!*" And they did, for the king and for the preservation of their own sun-parched hides.

The sun sank. Night brought little relief from the heat. The stars were dim, veiled in dust.

One by one and in pairs and small companies, the lords gathered to the king's tent. Baldwin had not summoned them, had had no need. He sat under the canopy with the sides rolled up to admit what breeze there was, with his armor off—raging folly, some muttered, but most were rather comforted by the sight of their king in a tunic that was almost clean, with the dust wiped from his face, and his fair hair combed and glistening in the light of a lamp. He had had his servants broach a cask of wine, the next to last, and share it out. It was heady with no water to weaken it, but it was wet; bliss enough, though there seemed too precious little of it.

Even as they gathered they were arguing. Whether to go on or to turn back; whether to stand and fight or to retreat in such order as the enemy allowed. "It can only be worse ahead," someone said in Arslan's hearing. "This is madness, this whole misery of a war."

Arslan did not think that Baldwin would beg to differ. But he was in the middle of it, where his mother had set him, and he showed no sign of shrinking from it.

Quite the contrary. Altuntash the apostate had ridden with them, worse than useless as a guide, nor loved at all for this country that he had brought them to. Baldwin was courteous to him, a gritted-teeth courtesy. "Sir," the king said now. "Tell us truth. Is there water in this country? Can we go on?"

"Better to ask," someone muttered, "if we can survive till morning."

He was ignored. Altuntash bowed as he always had, a little too low, a little too elaborate. "Majesty," he said in Frankish though the interpreter hovered, "there is water in deep wells. My guides know how and where to find it."

"Indeed?" asked Manasses the Constable with a lift of brows. "Then we go thirsty now for nothing?"

"No," said Altuntash, "sir. This is the barren country. We come soon into Trachonitis, which we call the country of the caves. It seems bleak, bleaker even than this, yet men live in it, burrowing deep in the earth. Wells sustain them, and gardens in the rock."

"And will they share their water with us?" Manasses inquired.

"Sir," Altuntash said, "we will take it, whether they give it or no."

" 'We,' sirrah?"

Baldwin spoke before Altuntash could reply, quelling his kinsman with a word. "Then you believe that we can go on."

"Majesty," Altuntash said, "I believe that we must."

"And I, that we must not!" cried one of the barons. "Sire! Will you listen to this man? Traitor, twice and thrice traitor—he'll betray us into the enemy's hands."

"That is possible," Baldwin said while Altuntash stood unmoving. His face, wiped clean of its obsequiousness, was harsh for all its full floridity, tight-lipped, cold-eyed. It was the face, perhaps, of a traitor.

"But," said Baldwin, "if we retreat now, we fall into dishonor. And we disobey the queen."

"Who is the queen?" someone shouted from the back of the gathering. "Is she here? Why isn't she leading us into this debacle?"

A growl went round at that. "Yes, she sits in her perfumed comfort, with water whenever she wants it, and fountains pouring out wine. Whereas we—"

"Sirs," Baldwin said, not raising his voice, yet it carried far and firm. "We are not here to question the rights or wrongs of a royal decision. It is made. We must accept the consequences. It is my will that we go on, if and as we can."

The king's will carried the council. The lords and barons went away still muttering among themselves, but none made move to defy him.

Manasses was the last to go, except for Baldwin's squires and his servants. The Constable did not smile; this was not a night for smiling. But he nodded. "You'll do," he said.

"From him," said Baldwin, "that's high praise."

It was not quiet in the tent with the sides rolled down, but there was an illusion at least of being set apart from the clamor of the camp. The infidels were drawing in, whooping and shouting. Some of the Franks were baying back. Somewhere, a pair of stallions were fighting.

But within these thin walls, there were only a pair of servants, and Arslan to do squire-service. The others were gone about this errand or that.

Baldwin let himself be readied for sleep. Many in the camp would sleep in armor tonight, but Baldwin settled for his sword as a bedmate and his armor nearby. Arslan would sleep next to it, ready to leap up and get him into it if the enemy attacked in force.

"Not that I think they will," said Baldwin, sitting on the bed, too restless to sleep. In council he had looked a man, if a young one, tall and firm and strong. In the tent, in lamplight, and stripped for sleep, he showed himself for the boy that he was, too tall for his bones, awkward and gangling. But the voice was still the king's, the mind running on, galloping on paths of its own.

Arslan had not seen it quite so clear before. This war had grown Baldwin up. The sulky boy who had left Jerusalem was a man now, a commander of armies. It could not have happened all at once—it had to have come on slowly as they fought their way through the Hauran—but Arslan was just now coming to see it.

He was not entirely sure he liked it. The Baldwin he had known, the bright-eyed and rather ordinary boy, had transmuted into something that he was not sure he recognized. That something, maybe, was a king.

It was still Baldwin sitting on the bed, frowning at the air. "We can try to hold our ground here, or we can make a break for it. God will have to help us—He knows we can't do it ourselves. May He damn that Altuntash to perpetual torment! He did nothing to prepare us for this country, or for the hordes of infidels who infest it."

"We could have expected the latter," Arslan said dryly, "and found guides to tell us the former."

"We were told," Baldwin said sharply. "We just weren't *told*. It's one thing to say, 'Oh, yes, sire, it's deep desert, dreadful country, the Devil's own,' and quite another to be in it."

"Yet we are in it," Arslan said, "and there's no end to it, they say, till we come to Bosra."

"Do you think we should turn back?"

Arslan looked hard at Baldwin. It seemed an honest question, and from the Baldwin he knew it would have been; but this Baldwin, this king, he did not know.

After a while Arslan decided to answer it honestly, whether it were honest or no. "I think it would probably be prudent, but prudence has little to do with the winning of wars."

"I think that, too," said Baldwin. "Do you look at it, Arslan, and see not just a mess of blood and dust and struggle, but a kind of overarching whole? Can you feel where this wing should go, and where that one should be, and how it should come together?"

Arslan had never thought about it. "I suppose so," he said. "Is it like looking down from a height and knowing where everything is?"

"Just like that," Baldwin said.

"Then yes," said Arslan. "But I see the blood and the sweat, too, and hear the wounded crying."

"So do I," said Baldwin, "but when I'm in the high place, it matters less. I have to be king then, you see. I have to do what a king should do."

"I'm glad I'm not a king," Arslan said.

"I think I'm glad I am," said Baldwin. "Even here. Or is that arrogant?"

Arslan shrugged. "God set you where He wanted you to be. He could have made you a woman, after all. Or a commoner."

"Yes," Baldwin said. He paused. Arslan thought he might let himself fall over then and try to sleep, but he remained fiercely awake. "I'm glad she's not here," he said.

There was no need to ask whom he meant. "So that you can be a man?" Arslan asked.

"So that I can be a king." Baldwin did lie down then, flung himself flat, arm over his eyes. "She got us into this. If we get out of it, I'll have to go back and be a child again, do as she tells me, submit to her regency."

"Do you hate her?"

Baldwin stiffened a little, but spoke calmly enough. "No. I don't hate her. I wish she would be a natural mother, and give me what is mine."

"Why don't you ask for it?"

Baldwin laughed, a sound like a grunt of pain. "Are you fool enough to believe I could? Or she would grant it?"

"How can you know for certain till you try?"

"I know," Baldwin said. "And so should you."

Arslan did, rather, but he was feeling contrary tonight. He was hot, he was thirsty, he itched. There were untold thousands of infidels swarming without. He was somewhat past fear. It made him say, "You're afraid of her."

"And shouldn't I be?" Baldwin asked without evidence of anger.

"Not if you're the man you want to be."

"Then I'm not a man yet," said Baldwin. "Only a king." He sighed heavily. "In the morning we break out of this trap. And trust in God that He brings us safe to Bosra."

FORTY · TWO

*I*t was madness, what Baldwin wanted to do—purer folly than his mother had committed in forcing this war upon them all. Not to retreat but to force their way forward. Step by step, every inch bought in blood, they hacked their way through the hordes of infidels, striving grimly toward Bosra.

Arslan fought at the king's side, clinging to it through every wave and surge of battle that sought to sweep him away. Baldwin was defended, warded in ring upon ring of knights and men-at-arms, but even they were not enough to hold back the shrilling demons who vied with one another for the glory of killing the king of the Franks.

For Arslan it was a nightmare of shouting, shrieking, the clash of metal on metal, the hot sweet stink of blood, the gagging reek of cloven entrails and bowels loosed in death. And heat, heat like the forge of God, sharpening thirst to burning pain, searing through heavy leather and padded gambeson as if they had not been there, as if the sunstruck mail were laid directly on his skin.

But of all the pains and terrors that beset him, one small thing vexed him out of measure: the gall of the saddle through mail and leather and padded cotton against his sweat-raw privates. He had heard that saints could turn such pain into virtue, make of it a sacrifice to God. He could only dream of cool baths and soft silks and a houri or two to soothe his hurts.

It was a lovely dream, too lovely for this hell of a battle. His body fought without him: stand and charge, stand and charge. His lance was long lost. His sword was notched—it had caught on the spike of a helmet. When it broke he would resort to a mace, but that weapon he disliked; it was heavy and lacked subtlety.

As if there were anything subtle about mortal combat. Kill or be killed, that was the only law. Defend one's king, gain what ground one could, keep oneself and one's horse alive. For God, for Holy Sepulcher. For raw burning thirstridden life, and for a queen who sat in her cool bower and played armies like pawns on a chessboard.

They won through. Staggering, bloodied, dying for lack of water, but alive and moving. Their dead they carried with them, by Baldwin's order. The field was full of bodies, but they were all infidels, the living enemy drawn back in awe of Frankish hardihood.

Or perhaps they had seen the country into which the march would take the

Franks, and had determined to let it do their killing for them. It was a black country, fields of ash like the pits of hell. If the lands they had passed through before were barren, this was desert among deserts.

And yet people lived here. They dwelt in caves beneath the earth, burrowed like beasts in the ground.

Where there were people, there was water. There was heat like fire, there was dust, there was nothing green on the blasted earth—but water there was, their guides assured them of it.

And when they found the deep wells, sent down their waterskins on the long ropes that they had knotted together of every rope and line and cord that they could muster, knives far below cleft the ropes or slit the skins. They brought up nothing, no water, no relief from the heat and the thirst.

Arslan had still one flask of wine. All the water that he or anyone had was doled out in pitiful sips to the horses. The wine he drank in drops, barely enough to moisten the center of his tongue. Even that little was enough to dizzy him.

He had lost count of time, caught in an eternity of thirst and exhaustion, but those who could still keep count reckoned four days in that black and burning desert. Four days; and then at last they came in sight of heaven.

It was only Bosra. Crowded dusty infidel city—but there were green things growing in it. And outside it a miracle: pure water from the rock. Springs bubbling from the ground, miraculous in this hideous country.

The army fell on them in a delirium of joy. Lords and sergeants fought as hard as they had in all their battles, to keep order among the troops, to keep the springs clear and un-muddied and the horses watered without gorging. The wise knew to fill their waterskins and sip slowly. Yet the temptation to wallow, to drink till the stomach revolted, and drink and drink again, was nigh irresistible; for some, impossible.

The king would not drink till his men were satisfied. It was a sacrifice, and noble. When he had had his share however, and his council had gathered in something like comfort, he contemplated the frown of the walls and the barred gates, and said, "God will give us this city."

"Will He?" That weary voice was the Archbishop of Nazareth. His faith was strong enough by all accounts, but he was as weary as the rest of them. Wearier perhaps, for his was the greatest charge: to carry the jeweled splendor of the True Cross, and to uphold it as a banner in battle.

"He must," Baldwin answered him. "Have we not suffered terrible trials to come here? What were they for, if not to earn us this victory?"

"Perhaps to warn us that there can be no victory." The Archbishop lowered his face into his hands. "No, don't listen to me. I shake your faith—such faith as we all need now, or we die."

"God defends us," Baldwin said. "We have to hope in Him. What else is there to hope for?"

No one had an answer to that.

The council disbanded to find what rest they might, for in the morning they would begin the attack on the city. Baldwin slept, or feigned to. Arslan sat on his own pallet across the flap of the tent, knees drawn up, exhausted beyond sleep. He had drunk his fill, enough to send him twice to the privies. As he thought again of venturing into the dark and the hordes of stinging flies, a flurry without brought him to his feet.

He had no premonition, no stab of fear. Nothing but a kind of exhausted curiosity and a dim thought: that if this was a messenger, he should wake the king.

The king was awake, sitting up, no sleep in his eyes. The messenger was let in by the grim-faced guard: a man in eastern dress, much stained and soiled, as if he had fought his way with difficulty from a heavily guarded place.

The word he brought was ill, as ill as it was possible to be. "Betrayal," he said. "The wife of Altuntash has surrendered the city to Unur of Damascus. All its Christians are driven out. The towers, the citadel—they teem with Turks. All the armies that beset you in the black desert are as nothing beside what waits for you within yonder walls. The House of Islam is raised up against you. Nur al-Din himself, the terrible lion of Islam, has come to destroy you. There is no hope for you, King of the Franks, or for the army that you have brought here."

Baldwin heard him in white-faced silence. When he had finished, when he had bowed to the carpets, the king said in a soft, still voice, "See that he is fed and given water as he pleases. And call my council."

They came straggling through the night. Some were in bits and oddments of clothes, some in full armor, others somewhere between. Not many had been sleeping, from the look of them.

The messenger, fed and somewhat refreshed, conveyed his message to them as he had to the king. Then he was suffered to go, to rest as he might; but they were given no such gift.

They would be at it till dawn, Arslan thought. Shouting one another down. Crying out in protest. Yelling for attack, retreat, both, neither, all at once and all in a clamor of shock and betrayal.

The loudest voices, those which held forth the longest, cried a counsel of greatest folly. "We are lost," they said. "Only let the king take the swiftest horse that can be had, and the True Cross in his hand, and ride away. God will keep him safe till he comes to Jerusalem."

"And the rest of you?" Baldwin demanded. "What will you do?"

"Die," they said.

Baldwin reared up, eyes glittering. "If you are fortunate—yes, you will die. If not, then you live as slaves."

"God wills it," they said.

"God does not will it!" Baldwin cried. "This whole war is a monster of folly. I fought it because I was compelled. God has proved what my heart knew: that we should never have begun.

"But I will not lose you. I will not cast aside the whole army of Jerusalem to run like a coward back to my lady mother. We will go back together, or we will die. I will not leave you."

"What is the kingdom without its king?" they asked him.

"My mother rules as queen in Jerusalem," he said. "My brother sits at her side, as biddable in his youth as I ever was. Our kingdom has no lack of royalty to rule it."

"Sire," said one of those who had urged him to flee, "royalty we may have in plenty, but of you there is only the one."

Baldwin paused. Perhaps he had not known before how they loved him, or not understood what it meant. Or perhaps he was simply tired, and needed to grope for the words. "I will not leave you," he said. "We live together or we die together. I will not ride away and abandon you to the infidel."

"Maybe God will give us a miracle," Arslan said out of nowhere that he could discern; and well out of place, too, a squire in a council of lords and princes. He was rather mercifully ignored.

Those who spoke in favor of storming the city were shouted down, though they were loud enough and numerous enough to make it a battle royal. To attack would be certain death, if the messenger told the truth—and there were those who doubted him, too. But the king chose the counsel of retreat, a slower death and a less certain one, and honorable enough in the circumstances. Arslan saw what it cost him to make that choice, how his lips drew thin and his face went tight, and he looked wan and strangely old. He had done what his mother commanded; through no fault of his own he had failed.

In the grey light of dawn they broke camp. Already the enemy were gathering, streaming out of the city, boiling up from the earth. The air itself seemed turned against them: hot already, searing as the sun climbed over the horizon. None dared count the leagues to Jerusalem. Step by step, pace by hard-fought pace, they would win their way home, or die in the trying.

No one spoke unless he must. No one sang, not even the priests who might have raised up a hymn to hearten them. They marched in grim silence broken by the shrilling of infidels and the clashing of swords.

By sundown they were out of sight of Bosra, even as slowly as they had advanced. The enemy granted them a respite in the hour of prayer; they pressed on through it, and camped as it ended, ringed with guards and surrounded by Saracens. Those who could sleep did. Most lay awake, clad in their armor. The dead slept in the wagons—Baldwin had forbidden that they be left behind. "We leave nothing," he had said, "for any infidel."

He walked among them far into the night, perhaps to reassure himself; but in the doing he lightened their hearts, sitting by this campfire or that, sharing a bit of hard bread, a sip of water, a tale or two of other and happier marches. Arslan followed as his guard and shadow, no more able to sleep than he.

Dawn came suddenly, caught them by surprise. Baldwin was almost preternaturally awake. He bade the priests sing mass. "Make a joyful sound," he said, "unto the Lord. Let the enemy make of it what he will."

It was a doleful enough sound in the event, crying out to God for help, beseeching Him to look with compassion on His children. And when the mass was all said, those shriven who wished to be, and all consecrated to God, they set themselves again on the long road back to Jerusalem.

hen Arslan died, he was not going to mind if he was sent to hell. He had lived in it—for eternity it seemed, though it could hardly be a month since he had ridden out of Jerusalem. He had not slept in longer than he could recall. Nights were a hell of fighting and standing still, days a hell of fighting and pressing onward. He sank into a kind of trance as he went on, a dream in which he never let go his sword, never took off his armor.

The king was commanding that even the wounded and the broken carry drawn blades, to make their numbers seem greater. If the dead could have obeyed, no doubt he would have commanded them, too. They at least could feel no hunger nor thirst, no heat, no weight of mail bearing them down.

Each day the heat grew worse. Men went mad with it. Arslan kept finding them in the line of the march, fallen or dismounted from their slat-ribbed and staggering horses, struggling to get out of their armor. "It burns," they cried. "It burns!"

Arslan helped to bind one of them to his saddle, lashing him with his own spare saddlestraps, while he fought to get down again, to escape from the stifling prison of leather and steel, to run away God knew where. He was beyond reason. They all were—those who persisted in going on quite as much as those who fell down raving.

As he walked beside Messire Roger's horse, leading his own, a clamor of shouting at last came clear. "Fire! *Fire!*"

This plain was waste, but waste that in another season had been green: thickets of thistles and brambles, dry thorny things that caught in horses' tails, crept through the rings of mail, pierced leather as if it were fine silk. The enemy had set it all afire.

Had he thought it hell before? That had been mere purgatory. This was the Devil's own kingdom. Sun beating down, fire roaring up, smoke parching the throat and catching in the lungs till men died of it—died coughing blood and black bile.

"God has no mercy." The voice was a croak, the face a blackened devil's, the eyes clear grey in it, too clear for sanity. Arslan stared blankly at his father. Bertrand stared as blankly back. Behind him rose a wall of flame, the fire of which the smoke had been the outrider, rearing up as if to crash down on the army beneath it.

"God," said Bertrand, louder. "What happened to God?"

One of the smoke-dimmed, soot-stained creatures marching near them was an archbishop. Arslan knew that not because he was any different from any other armored man, but because he clung to the bridle of a mule that in happier times had been white, whose pack showed still a glimmer of gilding. The Archbishop of Nazareth was given in charge the great treasure of the kingdom, the True Cross itself. Even here he would not forsake it.

He raised his head at the sound of Bertrand's voice. His eyes were as mad as anyone else's, but they had lit with a clarity of purpose. Still stumbling beside the stumbling mule, he began to tug at the wrappings of its burden.

No one tried to stop him. No one helped him, either, nor could Arslan turn aside from where he walked, half leaning on, half dragging his horse.

The Archbishop freed the True Cross from its swathings. It shone unbearably bright in the smoky air, gold and jewels brilliant, untarnished, like a vision of heaven from the depths of the Pit.

He raised it up, and his voice with it, preternaturally clear: chanting in Latin a hymn to the Cross.

And in the moment, the very moment, that it rose erect, just as he began the verse of the *Vexilla Regis*, the wind shifted. It turned, veered, blew back the way it had come—swept the smoke away from the Franks and into the faces of the infidels.

A cry went up, a long deep roar of wonder and awe. "A miracle! God loves us. A miracle!"

"See?" Baldwin said to Bertrand. "God is here. He is with us."

Bertrand said nothing. Nor did the Archbishop pause in his chanting. That too was a miracle: that clear voice unroughened by smoke or thirst, rising up to heaven.

All that day he bore the Cross before them, and no infidel came near him, though they had barely paused in harrying the army. God had not seen fit to drive the enemy away, only the fire that the enemy had set. The war was theirs, He seemed to say. Let them go on fighting it.

Arslan would never understand God.

They fought on, pace by pace, league by league, back as best they could to the Sea of Galilee. One miracle had sustained them for a while, but it had not deterred the enemy to any great degree. At night and in the mornings when they prayed together, they sang a litany that had been born in the dark years before Charlemagne raised the Frankish kingdom to an empire: *From the terror of the infidel, O Lord, deliver us.*

When they had half of the way to go, when it seemed that the whole distance and that much again must lie before them, and only death between, they made camp as they could while the enemy paused to pray. The evening prayer of Islam had been their salvation before, and would be again, God willing.

It ended too quickly as always, with the full fall of dark. Many no longer pitched tents, lacked the strength to begin, but Baldwin's tent went up as always, because the king must be the strongest of them all. They set the Cross before it though it might be a beacon to the enemy, to hearten the army.

Smoke had not stained it, dust barely dimmed it. It gleamed in the last of the sunset, and glimmered in torchlight thereafter. Men prayed near it, briefly most of them, as if they had wandered past and seen it and yielded to the urge.

Arslan had no prayers to say. The farther they traveled, the grimmer the fight, the more devout most of the army became. They had had one miracle in the wind that blew the fire away. They stormed heaven incessantly for another, till surely God wearied of the sight and sound of them. Baldwin himself was with the priests at every halt, except when he was walking through the army, comforting the wounded or the weary, spending himself without heed for the cost.

Where he went, Arslan went, armed and watchful—as he had since they were children together, and as he would do until God sent him another purpose. When Baldwin consented at last to rest, Arslan lay near him, tumbling into a sleep nigh as deep as death.

He swam out of it, gasping as if he had been drowning. A shape of darkness loomed over him. He surged without thought, battling air and unyielding iron.

It caught his hands, held him till he stopped struggling. He looked into a face that he knew too well for recognition, that he had not seen in longer than his dimmed brain could remember. "Kutub!"

"Hush," said the Turk who, the last Arslan knew, had been safe in Mount Ghazal, looking after it with Lady Richildis' steward while she wandered through the east. He was wrapped in a dark cloak, a hood over the turban that would have betrayed him as an infidel.

Arslan lowered his voice, at least somewhat. "What are you doing here?"

"Hush," Kutub said again. "Come."

Arslan might have argued, but he had been trained from infancy to that singular tone and expression, to shut his mouth and quell his curiosity and follow.

Kutub led him straight out of the camp, past guards oblivious to two shadows passing in shadow-quiet, to a hollow that opened suddenly and nearly pitched Arslan into it. There were people in it, Turks younger than Kutub but all like enough to him to be kin, and a handful of strapping young men who must be the levy of Mount Ghazal. The last he saw of those, they had been safe in the army, or as safe as anything Frankish could be in this outland of hell.

They all greeted him with inclinations of the head, wary eyes and a frown here and there but no open protest. Kutub wasted no time: once Arslan was in the midst of them he said, "You levies are here on sufferance—because my cousins refused to do anything without you. You, my young lord, are here because we need your voice in front of the king. Some of those out there are my people, my own tribe and kin, but they will not spare this army because of it, nor will I betray my lady's people to them or to any other. You should know this, because your death is waiting on this plain. The armies of Islam are sworn to destroy every man of you."

"Aren't they always?" Arslan asked.

"Not," said Kutub, "as a rule, with such determination. They're herding you, you know. Driving you away from water. Slowing your march till you die of thirst."

"We've found water," Arslan said. "Sometimes."

"You should be finding it at every camp," Kutub said swiftly. "I see none here—yet I know of a spring not a league distant. Have you guides? For if you do, I'll wager they've betrayed you."

Arslan could hardly doubt it. "Is that what you came to do, then? Guide us?"

"Not I," said Kutub. "This isn't my country. I never hunted it in my youth or wandered through it in the madness of my young manhood. But this one may be of use." He pointed with his chin.

It was one of the Turks, taller than the rest and fairer of skin, but otherwise as like Kutub as a brother. He grinned at Arslan, baring very good teeth, and said in his own dialect, "Ho, young lion. You look like an imp from the Pit."

Arslan had no doubt that he did, what with dust and soot and grim exhaustion. He bared his teeth in return. "Then we are brothers, you and I," he said.

The young Turk laughed. "My name is Mursalah," he said, "and a Frank had somewhat to do with the making of me."

Arslan peered at him. "That's not terribly easy to see."

"Oh," he said, setting hand to breast, "but my heart knows it. Will you hear what yonder so-wise man has in mind?"

"I doubt I'll be given a choice," Arslan said rather dryly. He paused. "Mursalah . . . Are you an angel or an emissary, then?"

"Now that," said Mursalah, "is why I bid you listen to my cousin Kutub. He has a plan, you see. He thinks that he can bring your army home."

Arslan would not let hope leap too high in him—not yet, not after so long in hell. Hell, after all, was both absence of God and absence of hope—and any hope offered would inevitably be snatched away.

"Listen to me," said Kutub, "and forbear to laugh until I'm done."

Arslan listened. In the event he did not laugh, except in wonder, and somewhat in admiration. "Yes," he said. "Yes, it's mad, but it would work."

"You think so?" Kutub honestly seemed to care that Arslan approved: remarkable in that most insouciant of Turks.

"I think," said Arslan, "that we Franks are ripe for a miracle. If miracle you can offer, then let us have it. We're dead else."

"Go, then," said Kutub, "and let these mooncalves from Mount Ghazal go back too and keep their tongues between their teeth until it's time to cry the miracle. Then let them be as loud as they please."

They all nodded eagerly, as apt for this blessed wickedness as the Turks were. Arslan knew a pang: he was sinning, he could feel it. But if it brought the army back safe to Jerusalem, what matter a stain or two on a soul already black?

He would have sung if he could, if it would not have betrayed him to the guards. Not for joy, not exactly. For hope; for relief. For the pain, too, of being alive again, of seeing the world clear, of feeling the dry kiss of the wind in his face. It had the faintest whisper of coolness, a wan hint of dawn.

He looked back once as he left the hollow. It was empty already, or seemed to be, all its shadows gone, no sign of any presence, man or horse. He might have wondered if he dreamed it, if he had not held in his hand the pledge that Kutub had sent: a little Turkish dagger with a verse of the Koran carved on the blade. It was far too dark to read, but he knew the verse from long ago.

By the winds, the messengers, sent each in its turn,
By the winds of wrath,
By those which bring back life to the earth and its fruits,
By the Winnowers,
By the Reminders—
Surely what thou hast been promised shall be brought to pass.

Surely, he thought as he made himself a shadow to slip through the guarded edges of the camp. Surely man would make a miracle, if God would not.

*I*n the morning as the army broke camp, they looked upon an unwonted thing: a plain empty of enemies. They did not credit it, not even as a miracle. They set themselves in battle order and marched out as they had each morning, armed and ready, even the wounded with their swords beside them.

As they marched away from the sun with their shadows long before them, in heat as merciless as it had been since they abandoned Bosra, a shadow seemed to grow out of their shadows. The riders in the van saw it first, Templar knights who rode always ahead, to be the first in battle, the first to fight and the first to die.

Hands leaped to swordhilts. A lance or two lowered. But it was only one man. They could see far enough beyond him, and no one followed. No one lurked in ambush. He rode alone. As he came closer, riding easily, they saw that he wore mail washed with bright silver, and a surcoat of white unmarred. He carried a banner the color of blood, and on it no device.

He must be a Frank: his armor was Frankish. His horse was as white as foam on the sea, tall as Frankish horses were, but with a look about him of the eastern breed. He shone almost too bright to bear, a dazzle of pure brightness.

Just before he entered the line of the Templars, he halted. He had no face to see, only the blank and silvered steel of the helm. Yet it seemed that he scanned them all, took in the whole of them. He raised his banner. It swept up, forward.

They followed him. Any who might have doubted him was silenced by his own silence. He spoke no word. He rode before them, never beside them. He approached no one of them, not even the king.

For all most of them knew, he could have been leading them to destruction. But the light on him, the gleam of his armor, his horse's white coat, seemed too splendid to be mortal.

He led them on ways that they had not gone before, ways that might perhaps be easier; that were, if not empty of enemies, then less desperate than they had been heretofore. That, O miracle, led from water to water, from oasis to oasis; and the Turks who followed seemed powerless to prevent them from drinking their fill.

In the evening he brought them to a place that was well made for a camp: set up above the plain yet with a well that brought up clear water and plentiful. They could defend this camp from the enemy that circled below, rest high under the stars and be as much at peace as they had been on all this grim retreat.

When they looked for the guide, to see where he pitched his tent, or what tent he had, they found no sign of him. He had vanished with the evening light.

Arslan waited on the king as always, brought him water—enough even to wash his face and hands, luxury unbounded in this hell of dust and stone. Baldwin had taken a little while to be by himself in quiet, before he went among the army. He accepted the water, drank and bathed himself, sighed and closed his eyes.

When he opened them, Arslan had set the basin carefully aside for himself and the rest of the servants. Baldwin noticed: a brow went up briefly. He said, "That's the one you told me of. Yes?"

"I think so," Arslan said.

"You think? You don't know?"

Arslan shrugged, uncomfortable. "It must be Mursalah. But—"

"But?" Baldwin asked when he did not go on.

He did not like to say it, did not particularly want to, but there was no simple way to avoid it. "We didn't need to do anything. The people we had ready to cry a miracle, to urge the army on—none of them had to say a word. Everyone followed him. What if—I find myself thinking . . . what if it's somebody else? Somebody from . . ."

"An angel of God?"

"That's what his name means, you know. Mursalah: Emissary. What if it's not a blessed lie? What if God made it the truth?"

"God can do that," Baldwin said calmly. "Does it matter? He led us here. We're safe for the night. Come morning, we'll do whatever we have to do, to leave this place alive."

That was wisdom. Arslan wanted to ignore it, to worry away at the skin of his doubt, but Baldwin had risen and donned his mantle and gone to walk among his troops. Arslan had to scramble to follow.

In the morning when they broke camp, as the sun hovered on the horizon, the glittering figure rode out of it. Again he led them; again he chose ways both easy and short, found water for them, and at evening brought them to a place that again they might defend from the hordes of their enemies.

His powers seemed somewhat limited. He could not keep off the enemy or protect them from storms of dust or the terrible heat. Those they must fight for themselves. Yet they reckoned him an angel of God, nor looked for him to lead them astray.

On the second night Arslan left Baldwin to make his rounds of the camp with another of the squires, and sought the campfire round which sat the men from Mount Ghazal. They greeted him gladly enough, passed him a round of bread fresh from the coals. He took it with thanks. He had had a little to eat at the king's fire, but this bread was fresher.

While he ate he searched the faces in firelight. They were all eastern faces, but no Turks; no fierce scarred cheeks, no threefold plaits. "So where are they?" he asked at last.

No one asked him whom he meant. One of the young men answered with a tilt of the chin. "Out there. Distracting the tribesmen, or so we can hope."

"Treachery?" Arslan asked.

"Not against us," the easterner said. He shrugged. "It's all the tribe, the clan, the kin. One fights for God—for Allah. But if the jihad, the holy war, comes between self and kin . . . one decides as one best may. That may be to give up a pursuit that after all is useless, and go back home to one's own kin and one's women."

"It's not all or even most of the ones who come after us," said Arslan.

"Well," said the easterner. "It's some of them. Isn't that better than none?"

And there was Mursalah, who guided them through this country, shortened their path and made it less brutally difficult. Arslan granted that it was considerably better than nothing.

Mursalah led them home: out of the desert and to the Sea of Galilee. Before Tiberias he left them, slipping away into the glare of the setting sun. None saw him vanish. One moment he was there, and the city beyond him, and the gleam of the lake; the next, city and lake remained, but of him there was no sign.

All who were alive gave thanks to God in the city of Tiberias. Of their queen's war they had nothing, only the ranks of the dead, the wounded, the broken and battered. Altuntash was gone. Word came that he had gone to Damascus, and there fallen afoul of the law, not for treachery but for an old perfidy to a brother. He had blinded his own kin; and that kin demanded recompense. So his eyes were put out, but he was let alive, nor condemned as a traitor.

Strange were the ways of the east. Bertrand, though he had lived here so long, still was a Frank at heart. He would go in time to Beausoleil; but first he paused in Jerusalem. He went with his son to visit Helena, the two of them coming not as victors but as weary travelers.

Her house was a place of rest as it had always been, cool and quiet. They had indulged in an orgy of water and coolness in Tiberias, but here was comfort of the spirit as well.

She was the same as ever, sufficient in herself. She had a new thing, a carpet from Tabriz, like a weaving of jewels. She had hung it in the dining-room, where it glowed behind her as they ate.

In the way of young things, Arslan slipped direct from bright, almost fierce wakefulness to nodding where he sat. His mother had him taken away to a bed in the house, against which he protested, but feebly.

When he was gone, the two who remained sat in sudden quiet, sipping the last of the wine. Neither was minded at once to speak. At length Helena asked, "Was it as terrible as they say?"

"Worse," Bertrand said. He left his chair to sit on the carpet at her feet, rested his head on her knee and sighed as she tangled her fingers in his hair.

"You are thin," she said, "as if the sun has eaten you. And limping—what was it? Arrow? Sword?"

"Not a thing," he said, "but old Time and too many days a-horseback. I'm not the boy I was—or that he is."

Arslan, he meant; and she understood. He heard the smile in her voice. "Isn't he splendid? He looks just as you were when first I saw you. A golden youth, beautiful and shy."

"I wouldn't call Olivier-Arslan shy."

"Wouldn't you? But there; you're not a woman."

"Nor to him are you, who are his mother."

She laughed and tugged on his hair, not quite hard enough for pain. "I see well enough, O my lord. All men are shy in front of women."

"I yield to your wisdom," he said. He drew in the scent of her. Sleep was close, but not yet upon him. He said, "The queen chose ill in her alliances. Now Damascus is against us, and the truce is broken."

"And the king?"

"The king, who is wise in his youth, says nothing."

"And the people see, and hear of what he did in that failure of a war, and love him for that silence."

"Exactly," Bertrand said.

"Clever, clever boy," said Helena.

Bertrand raised his head. She was only half smiling.

"That will come to a crux, you know," she said. "He's a man now, old enough to rule a kingdom. His mother will have to let go; let him wield as well as wear his crown."

"He's young still," Bertrand said, not comfortably. Even to Helena he was not pleased to voice the thoughts that had been vexing him for years now, since Baldwin came of age and his mother failed to acknowledge the fact. "She'll wait, I think, till he's old enough to be knighted—then she'll have to set aside the regency."

"Except," said Helena, "that it's not a regency. She's queen to his king, ruler beside ruler. But in everything she takes precedence. I understand her, I think. So often a woman is far more capable than any man, yet the world compels her to hide behind a man's name. Her majesty would have done well to raise that child differently, made him weaker, more dependent on her; less his own man and far more his mother's."

"She wouldn't do that," Bertrand said sharply. "That's not in her. She despises the weak. She's proud of her strong son."

"Yet she refuses to grant him the reward of his strength: to let him be king without her."

"Ah well," Bertrand said, half growling it. "When they're both ready, we'll know."

"Pray the lesson isn't taught in war," said Helena.

"What, such a lesson as we just learned, in rampant ill-luck and folly?"

"Just so," she said. She bent to kiss him on the forehead and then on the lips, lingering over it. Her mouth tasted of herbs, cool and sweet.

He could never cling to temper when she kissed him so. He sighed and let himself ease against her. "I dreamed of you," he said. "You brought me cool water to drink.

You touched me, and weariness went away; I forgot pain and fear, and remembered only you."

"I dreamed," she said, "that I brought cool water, and that you drank your fill, and were healed of a wound."

"I wasn't hurt," he said, "except in the soul."

"And do you blame the queen who sent you?"

He snapped taut. "No!"

Yet as she sat silent, offering no apology, repenting nothing that she had said, something made him say, "I don't blame her. But I do think that she chose ill, and cost lives and blood and the honor of the kingdom. Worse for her: people will remember that the king obeyed her against his will and to his great pain and suffering, while she sat at ease in Jerusalem. That will be reckoned against her."

Helena nodded. "A woman can only fail, you know. Either she is weak and proves that weakness, or she is too strong and is excoriated for it. There's no mercy given a woman who errs—not if that error brings grief to a kingdom."

"Men err, too," Bertrand said, "and are punished for it."

"But not as a woman is—perpetually." She slipped from her chair into his lap, a rare unbending, and one that took him slightly aback. But he was glad of her in his arms, folding them about her, losing himself in the scent of her hair. She said nothing more for a long while, nor on reflection did he. It was safest so.

From the roof of a house high up over the Golden Horn, Richildis looked down on the teem and seethe of the City and the harbor. There below her, near enough almost to touch, were ships from every nation in the world, and markets full of strange and wonderful things, and streets crowded with people such as she had never dreamed could be. Great tall black men from Africa, sleek golden people from the silk countries, Indians with their great eyes and their slender grace, huge ice-fair bearded men from the Rus—Turks, too, and Saracens, and Franks looking both rough and familiar, and always, in multitudes, the Byzantines themselves.

There was a houseful of them below her, most of this branch of the Bryennioi, with the matriarch ruling them all with a terrible gentleness. The Lady Irene had called a council of her sons, to which the sons' wives were not invited. They had responded in their various ways: some with equanimity, some in flight to friends or market, and Richildis to the roof from which she could perceive the world like one of the old gods, high and remote and yet irresistibly present.

She stroked the amber silk of her gown, loving the feel of it. It was not Byzantine silk, though of that she had a quantity, but the rarer, costlier weaving of the farthest east. She had found it in a bazaar in Tashkent, at the easternmost stretch of her journey. The caravan had gone on, all the way to Ch'in, but she had turned back with Michael Bryennius, summoned to this council in which none not of the blood was welcome.

She forbore to resent the exclusion. Lady Irene was feeling her mortality, had taken it into her head to surround herself with her sons for, as she maintained, one last time before they scattered again to the ends of the earth. One of them had come farther even than Michael: Constantine had come in late the night before, burned almost black by the sun of Africa, with gifts of ivory and gold and amber for all the ladies. He had been to places that, he swore, had never seen a man of his nation or complexion, nor imagined that he could exist.

They were an adventurous lot, these Bryennioi: nothing like the run of Byzantines, and yet one of their cousins had been an emperor. Michael in exile in Outremer had been a poor shadow of Constantine in Africa, Nikos in the Rus, Demetrios on the silk roads with a caravan of cutthroats and merchant princes.

None stained himself with trade, yet trade fed the lands that gave the Bryennioi their nobility. It was a subtle dance, as Byzantine as one could imagine.

Richildis folded her arms on the parapet that rimmed the roof, laid chin on them, watched a fleet sail in from somewhere far and strange. Its sails were purple, faded with salt and sun to the color of watered wine.

She sighed, and felt herself smiling. She had smiled a great deal in the past year or two, on caravan with Michael Bryennius. There had been quarrels—how not? But laughter most often, even when the road was hard, or bandits beset them, or a way taken proved less short or less easy than guides had promised. Snow in the mountain passes, sun in the desert—his hand reaching to clasp hers, and his smile as their eyes met, as if they were not wife and husband at all, but friend and sweet friend out of Provence or Aquitaine.

A step sounded behind her. She glanced over her shoulder. It was not Michael Bryennius as she had expected, but his brother Constantine.

All the brothers were much alike: tallish dark-eyed bearded men with warm deep voices. Constantine was the tallest and, at the moment, the thinnest, though from the depth of his chest and the width of his shoulders, Richildis suspected that he could be a big and burly man. The sun that had deep-dyed his skin had faded his hair to bronze. His face was clean-carved, his brows level above eyes that had seen stranger things than she could perhaps imagine.

He was a handsome man, handsomer than his brother; and she looked at him and felt never a quiver. Warmth, yes, for the smile that he shared with his brother, and for the likeness, and because, from the moment that she met him, she had liked him.

She returned smile with smile. "I never grow tired of this," she said, sweeping city and harbor with a hand, pausing at the clustered domes of Hagia Sophia. "Or do time and custom make it all seem ordinary?"

"I think," said Constantine, "that one would have to be a connoisseur of boredom to be bored by our City."

"Is that why you travel so far? To keep it fresh?"

His eyes widened. He laughed—incredulous, perhaps. Or delighted. "Do you know, no one's ever understood that before."

"I understand your brother," she said. "You're very like him."

"Branches of the same tree," Constantine said. "Our father was a dull stick, but one wise thing he did in his life. He married our mother. She was reckoned beneath him, a tradesman's daughter from Ephesus—but she brought a handsome dowry and a certain beauty of her own, and a way about her that fed the family's fortunes till they grew richly fat."

"And she bred sons who were nothing like the run of their kind." Richildis half-turned from him to look on the city again, but her mind was on him still. "Sons who could, when they pleased, take thoroughly unsuitable wives."

"Ah," said Constantine, "but Frankish wives are all the rage. The emperor himself has fallen to the fashion, wed himself one of those big fair German princesses about whom one always wonders . . . can she lift a whole ox?"

Richildis laughed. "I'm a feeble thing, then. I can barely lift a lamb."

"I hear that you can bend a Turkish horseman's bow."

"And where did you hear that?"

"Round about," he said. "I half expected to see you in armor, with a dagger plaited in your hair."

"Do I disappoint you?"

"A little," he said. He was grinning, as wicked as ever his brother could be. "You're not a savage at all. You look reasonably civilized."

"I cry your pardon," said Richildis.

"Do forgive her," Michael Bryennius said behind her. "Whatever she did, I'm sure she did it with perfect intent."

She turned to greet him. Constantine, stranger though he was, was a comfortable companion; but Michael Bryennius was like a part of herself come home to rest. He took her hand and kissed it and sat beside her.

In a little while they were all there, all the brothers, a little wild in their gaiety, like pupils escaped from a stern master. Richildis' presence constrained them remarkably little.

"Free at last," Nikos said. He was the youngest and usually the most sober, but for once he was showing his relative youth. He sat on the parapet with a fine disregard for either propriety or safety, and turned his face to the sky. It was clear today, vivid and hurting blue, but never as blue as the sky of Outremer. "Am I the only one," he asked, "who believes that our mother grows more formidable with age?"

"You'll never hear me doubt it," Michael Bryennius said. "She's as frail as a flower of steel—and will outlive us all."

"Amen," the others said.

"So," said Constantine when they had paid due tribute of silence. "Is it true what I've heard? Franks are coming, and bringing a Crusade?"

"Franks are here," Nikos said. "The emperor's kinsman, the German king, emperor, whatever he calls himself—he's pillaging everything he can get at, around Philopatium. It's driving our emperor to distraction. And there's an army of West Franks behind the Germans, and English too for all any of us knows. The emperor wants them gone as quickly as they came. They're a frightful lot, no manners at all."

Richildis caught Constantine's eye and bit back laughter. Nikos, oblivious, swung a leg over the edge of the parapet and said, "I hear the French queen is a remarkable creature."

Richildis found that they were all staring at her. She spread her hands. "Sirs, sirs! I left Anjou nigh twenty years ago. She would have been a child then, barely out of leading-strings."

"Pity," said Demetrios. He was the coldest of them, and she thought perhaps the most intelligent. "It's said she loves luxury. She might make certain persons very rich, if they were both clever and resourceful."

"Are you suggesting that we bilk the Queen of the Franks?" Nikos whooped and nigh fell off the parapet; saw the dropped jaws and sudden pallor, and only laughed the harder. "What shall we instruct our mercantile gentlemen to sell her? Silks? Pearls? Swine?"

"Stories," Richildis said.

It had slipped out of her, without her thinking. And they were staring at her, waiting for her to go on. "She comes from Aquitaine," Richildis said. "In that country, the nobles are most fanciful. They sing—her grandfather was a troubadour. They tell stories. They live for their lovely lies."

"They sound like courtiers," Constantine said.

"But do think," said Michael Bryennius. "A nation that trades in stories. What could we tell them, all of us? Have we any dreams to sell?"

"That's base trade," Demetrios said.

"And we only do that through our mercantile gentlemen," said Nikos with little evidence of dismay. "Pity we couldn't pack them off on a caravan for a thousand nights and a night—the emperor would love us perpetually."

"They'll be off to Outremer soon enough," said Michael Bryennius. "Then they'll be a plague on that country instead of ours."

"We hold title to a portion of Outremer," Richildis reminded him.

Her voice sounded small and cold in her own ears. It seemed that it did in his as well; he glanced at her in surprise. "Yes," he said. "So we do. It's safe, surely. Those we left to look after it—"

"Have you seen what the Germans have done at Philopatium?" Richildis demanded of him.

She was no less startled by her vehemence than he was. It had come flooding, no warning at all: memory of Mount Ghazal and the hard labor that she had done there to make of it a place both prosperous and pleasant. Grief touched her still at the thought of it, but lightly. The hard blow that had struck her down, that had sent her in flight half across Asia, was faded and all but gone.

Michael was watching her steadily. His brothers chattered of something else, out of tact perhaps, or lack of interest or understanding. "Do you want to go back?" he asked her.

"Yes," she said. Simply, and without hesitation.

"This very moment?"

"No," said Richildis. And that too she was sure of. "We needn't leap on a ship within the hour. We needn't even look for the next one that sails, or a caravan or a riding of pilgrims."

"Or a Crusade?"

She shuddered a little. "I don't want to travel with the Germans."

"Nor I," he said with evident relief. "Maybe when the French come? They'll be here inside of a month—sooner, if they're as close as people say."

"I'll think about it," Richildis said.

And she would. Instinct tore her in two, between yearning to see her own countrymen again, to hear the *langue d'oc* and the *langue d'oeil* spoken by tongues that had been bred in Provence and in Anjou; and wanting to run away even farther than she had run before, clear into the east of Ch'in. Outremer was home, more so than any caravan, yet she dreaded the thought of it. Kin, friends, memories of pain as well as joy . . .

She drew herself up. She was strong again, had been for a long while. She could endure the homecoming. To be home: that was a dream she had had for a while, and not of La Forêt either, but of her castle in the hills outside Jerusalem.

She was healed, maybe, or nearly so. Outremer would complete the healing or undo it utterly. She could not know which until she went there, until she knew again the heat of that sun, breathed in the scents of dust and dung, felt in her bones the thrum of holiness that underlay every living and unliving thing in that of all lands in the world. Nowhere else, not even Rome, dwelt so strong in the heart, or called so clearly once one had let oneself hear.

mperor Manuel had set the Germans well on their way and scoured the palace at Philopatium inside and out before the French were let in. Their advance guard had been notoriously revolted by the savage Germans, had shunned them and professed great relief when they were sent away into Asia. It was distressing for the French, Richildis had heard, to be forever in the wake of such pillage and plunder, to be guarded like prisoners lest they do the same, and forced to pay vast prices for provisions because the Germans had taken most of what was to be had.

"And to think," Richildis said to her husband, "that three hundred years ago they were all one empire, East Franks and West Franks—but the East Franks gave way to the wild Saxons, and there's all the trouble in a word."

"And you are a West Frank?" he asked from amid the cushions of the bed. He was nigh buried in them, in an orgy of comfort.

She sat crosslegged in a corner, too wide awake to sink down into the warmth of him. "I am an Angevin," she said, "and that is a Frank, yes. There's no Saxon in me. I'm a barbarian of an older blood."

"A charming barbarian," he said, "and distractingly beautiful. Your French are almost civilized, then—and not at all happy to be reckoned together with the bloody Germans."

"Would you be? If you were a Frank?"

"Not in the least," he said. "They wrought dreadful havoc by all accounts, no better in their manners than wild beasts, and no more grateful to be netted and hauled away. And to think: the empress is one of them. She's mortified, I hear, and has let her kinsman the German king know it."

"I could almost wish I had been there to hear her."

He peered from amid the cushions, bright dark eyes and lifted brow. "Do I hear a suggestion of wistfulness? Are you wanting to be presented at court?"

"Could I be?"

"You haven't asked."

"So I could," she said. She was a little angry, though for no good or proper reason. She had not even been in the City for a fortnight, and she had shunned courts and kings through all her wanderings through the east. He could hardly be faulted for expecting that she would be the same here. Indeed she should. But . . .

"One hears such things," she said. "The birds that sing, and the lions roaring, and the throne that rises and falls as the emperor ordains."

"Well then," he said, struggling out of his cushions. "You shall have your moment in the court. It will take a while to arrange. If you would rather go home . . ."

"I'll stay," she said a little sharply. "But wait, let all the French come here, the king and his queen, and not only the Lorrainers and the vanguard. I'd like to see their faces when they stand in front of the emperor."

"You never ask for the easy things," he said, but he did not sound unduly cast down. "I'll do it if I can. If not—will you accept a more ordinary day in court?"

"If you can't give me the stars and the planets," she said with sudden lightness, "I'll accept the moon instead."

"Generous lady," said Michael Bryennius. "Practical, too. I'm glad I married you. Another man might not have appreciated you properly. Such virtues as you have . . . they're not in the common way."

"No; they're often reckoned vices."

He grinned. "Come here," he said.

She did not always obey him, vows or no vows; but at the moment she was inclined to be indulgent. She let herself fall into his arms, laughing as cushions billowed around them. Laughter was his gift to her as always, and love that followed fast upon it, in a cloud of feathers from a burst cushion.

The French king and the queen and their great lords marched in from the west on a splendid day of autumn. They were not admitted at once to the city, not after the Germans' depredations; rather they were diverted and stopped at Philopatium, where amid the cleared rubble of their predecessors' camp they set up their own tents. The high ones of course had the palace, a roof over their heads and elegant pavements for their feet, with servants to wait on them as they desired.

If the vanguard had been closely guarded, the army itself was nigh held prisoner, and not to its liking, either. Byzantium did not trust any Westerner in arms. But the king and his lords were let into the city, conducted to the palace and presented to the emperor.

The emperor had decided that it was neither safe nor particularly politic to receive the King of France in his golden hall of audience with its magical and mechanical splendors. Instead he received them in a great open court under the vault of heaven.

Richildis was there: Michael Bryennius had kept his promise as best he could. She was choosing not to mourn the birds that sang, or the golden lions. She had a place among the ladies who were permitted to attend, in a court robe that had seen a dozen reigns at least and was grimly determined to see a dozen more. She could see very well, since she was taller than the women in front of her. The emperor came late and last, but while she waited there was ample to see. All of the court who had been invited were there, processionals of princes coming each to his place with his retinue, lords and ladies protecting their fragile skin under silken canopies, chamberlains massing and fluttering and herding flocks of courtiers this way and that.

She had seen gold in plenty—had she not seen the Dome of the Rock, and

Hagia Sophia with its great dome and its lesser domes and its mosaics like none other in the world? But gold here was as plentiful as sand, as if it might be strewn underfoot and trampled on, and no one would notice. Every robe was silk, every neck and ear and brow seemed adorned with pearls, lucent in the sunlight. She in her antique court robe from the chests of House Bryennius, the pearl drops in her ears and the pendant about her neck and the coronet atop her crown of braids, was distinct from the rest in her height and fairness, but there were a few other tall fair ladies and lords, Macedonians perhaps, or even French or Germans. She did not think she was stared at for that, but because she was a stranger, in robes that the ladies about her must recognize.

It seemed that here one did not converse as one did in court in France or in Outremer. One maintained a hieratic silence, in boredom that over time might become monstrous, or be transformed into a sacrament.

She saw her husband across the broad space, standing among the lords as she stood among the ladies. He looked as bland as the others, one dark bearded face among many. He did not glance at her. One did not do that, either, she supposed.

To her vast relief, just before she was ready to erupt in a fit like a small and thwarted child, a ripple ran through the assembly. The court was filled as far as she could see with silken-gowned and coroneted nobility. At the far end the gate had begun to open, the great gate that, she had been told, admitted noble embassies and petitioners to the emperor. So high was it and so wide that for a moment she did not see the people dwarfed within it.

Then she saw the chamberlains in their silks, with their beardless eunuch faces. She saw the French in their finery, such as it was to eyes accustomed to eastern splendors: little silk, much wool and fur and cloth of gold. She remembered vividly the discomfort of such garb in this hotter, fiercer part of the world. She could not tell if they were as miserable as she had been when she arrived in Acre: from this distance she saw little but a blur of sunburnt faces. Even the queen had fallen victim to the sun, an unlovely scarlet that clashed with the crimson of her robe. Her hair however was a ripple of gold, flowing down her back and nigh to her heels.

That of course Richildis could not see at first; it came clear as the procession advanced. They were not required to perform the nine prostrations that were expected in the hall of the throne—reason enough for Manuel to have chosen this greeting instead, without its burden of ritual. They could approach in dignity, upright and without groveling, as would well suit them in the pride of their position.

As they advanced, the emperor came out at last. He walked on his own feet in the crimson boots of his rank. Guards surrounded him: great tall Varangians with their famous axes. They were taller than he, but he was no small man, and no dark one either: fair hair beneath the crown with its pendant pearls, fair beard grown as full as it might be, which to be sure was not very. The Frankish custom of shaving the beard might have served him well. He managed nonetheless to look both regal and handsome, not at all as Richildis had imagined an emperor of the Byzantines.

France's anointed king, having completed his procession through the court, stood in front of the Emperor of the Romans. Louis was another of the fair Franks, almost white-fair, with eyes so blue that even from amid the court Richildis had caught the brightness of them. He was tall, slender, fair of face—everything, one might think, that a king should be.

And yet there was something lacking in him. He was a little too fair, a little too pale—a milk-and-water creature, graceful without honest strength. His voice in speech was light, musical, without particular depth. He spoke words through the interpreter, bland and politic words that meant little and offended no one.

He was very pious, Richildis had heard, and certainly he showed it; alone among the princes of France, he wore no finery, no handsome robe nor golden adornments, but the plain worn robe of a pilgrim. He looked all the more unprepossessing beside the golden splendor of his queen. Her face under the crown was lively rather than beautiful, long and rather narrow, with wide eyes of a color interminate at Richildis' distance: grey perhaps, or green. Where the sun had not burned her unbecomingly she had a very fair skin, whiter than the king's. Her figure was tall, graceful, strong as a steelblade: a strength that the king so signally lacked.

The king and the emperor were guided by chamberlains to two tall chairs under a canopy of purple and gold. There they sat with the interpreters and, as far as Richildis knew, continued their blankly amiable converse.

The queen meanwhile had been brought face to face with the empress. Irene, she called herself now; but in Germany in her childhood she had been named Bertha. For all the elegance of her dress and manners, she was still a big, florid, broad-beamed German woman—bigger and broader than the slender Eleanor, with strength but no grace. They did not, Richildis thought, like each other on sight. Rather the opposite in fact.

But queens were queens, and where they must be politic, so they would be. Empress Irene bore Queen Eleanor to her own palace within the walls of this great palace of the Boukoleon, to a colonnaded hall in sight of the sea, where she had laid a feast for the French queen and all their respective ladies.

Richildis was one of them by her husband's contriving, through the right of House Bryennius to set a wife—even a Frankish wife married in distant Jerusalem and brought here on a whim—in the empress' august presence. She hoped that her manners were adequate to the task. She did not expect that she would be noticed particularly, or given any greater favor than that she be present and share in the banquet.

She was startled therefore as she made to seat herself near the foot of the table, to be approached by a soft-voiced eunuch and bidden in very decent Frankish to follow him. He led her to the table's head, to a place within reach of queen and empress. She hoped that she did not look as foolishly disconcerted as she felt. For the empress smiled at her and said as if they ever had been introduced at all, "Ah! Lady Richildis." And to the Queen of France: "Lady Richildis is the wife of one of our nobles, a lady of Anjou in your own country, and a Baroness of the High Court of the Kingdom of Jerusalem. Yes, if you will believe it: baroness in her own right and by grant of the Queen of Jerusalem, without recourse to her husband or to any man."

In the full light of Queen Eleanor's attention, one forgot the long face, the long nose, the severe lines of the mouth. One saw only the eyes, wide, grey-green, and perfectly focused. They made her beautiful.

"How wonderful," she said to Richildis. "That you should rule as you please—and your husband never objects?"

"My husband finds it rather amusing," Richildis said, "majesty." She took the chair that was offered, with a faint sigh and an inner shrug. It was not as if she was a stranger to royalty.

These were queens as Melisende was, secure in their strength. But in Eleanor there was an edge, an almost frenetic gaiety, as if something in her was stretched too tight. She seized on Richildis like a child on a new toy. And such a toy: a baroness of Jerusalem, a bulwark of the Crusade, a warrior against the Saracen.

She said it just so in her musical accent, so that Richildis remembered that her father's father had been a troubadour. It was in the blood.

"In truth," Richildis told her, "we live much as we would in France. We have our castles, our holdings, our duties to king and court."

"And yet," said Eleanor, "you live, it's said, in luxury that we can hardly dream of, eating off golden plates, clothing yourselves in silk. The wealth of the East is yours, and you make joyously free of it."

"You do dream well, majesty," Richildis said.

"One becomes accustomed," Eleanor said. "France would seem squalid to you now."

"France would be beautiful," Richildis said as composedly as she could. She did not want Eleanor's words to be the truth, though she had heard them before; though she had seen how her eyes had changed, how the noble pilgrims from France seemed drab and ill-washed. Even these in their Byzantine finery: she saw how they scratched, if discreetly, and marked a certain sharpness under the perfumes of the East.

She could not be so lost to her own country as that. She had not changed so much.

Queen Eleanor had gone on as if oblivious to the quality of Richildis' silence. "You must come with us, of course. We have guides, and of course the emperor is generous"—this with a glance at the empress—"but a lady of our own nation, wedded to a Byzantine, in service to the Queen of Jerusalem: how perfect that is! We can hardly let you go."

"I had," Richildis said, "intended to go home in a little while."

"Then you shall go with us," Eleanor said. She clapped her hands. "Oh, that will be splendid! You can teach us the songs of Outremer, and speak to us in Arabic. You do speak Arabic?"

"A little," said Richildis.

"There, you see?" said Eleanor, turning to the empress with an air of great delight. "She is wonderful—just as you said. Is her husband as great a marvel, too?"

"All the Bryennioi of that branch are . . . unusual," the empress said. It was difficult to tell whether she approved or disapproved. She approved, Richildis rather thought, but it would be less than imperial to betray it.

Her stolidity stood in great contrast to the French queen's liveliness. It was not the hieratic stillness that Byzantine royalty were said to cultivate in their cradles, but a stony German immobility. It served well enough; it presided over this banquet with monumental graciousness. It even preserved Richildis from an excess of Queen Eleanor's attention, diverting the French queen to this lady or that, or calling on her to pass judgment on yet another delicacy from the imperial kitchens.

Richildis was glad to be left to herself. The gossip that ebbed and flowed about her was little that concerned her, either of France or of this court and palace. She missed her husband, his warm presence, the amusement that she did not doubt would touch him at the posturings of the various ladies. But women did not dine with men in this empire. In old Rome they had done it, but in the newer Rome they followed an ancient custom of the Greeks. Richildis much preferred the lesser feasts of the Franks, in which she might sit beside her sweet friend, touch hands beneath the table, laugh together over a particularly delicious scandal.

And maybe he was missing her, or maybe he was not. This was his own country, his own custom. He would find nothing strange in it. It must have been far stranger for him to share a table with ladies as well as lords, and his lady at his side in what, in Byzantium, would be great impropriety.

She was almost glad to be reft out of her thoughts just then by the French queen with another question, another eager seeking after legends—for such was her vision of Outremer. She did not want to hear of ordinary things. She wanted the exotic, the strange: lepers on the dungheaps as well as princes in their palaces. Richildis sighed and gave her something of what she asked. And why not, after all? Soon enough she would see the truth of it.

ueen Eleanor and her ladies had a conceit, a grand fancy. It had carried them through the wilds of Europe and to the edge of Asia. They meant to carry it even into Outremer.

"Amazons!" cried Eleanor as Richildis presented herself at the palace of Philopatium. It had taken some doing to find the queen: she was not in any of the places in which one might expect to come on a royal lady. But in the field behind the palace, beyond the ranks of tents in which resided the armies of the French, a company rode in armor bright-burnished in the sun.

They were all women. They bore helms at saddlebows but rode here bareheaded but for silver fillets, hair plaited down their backs or streaming free. They all carried bows and wore swords forged to woman's measure. They were a very pretty company; and Richildis saw at last how Eleanor had come by the scarlet that dyed her cheeks.

"We revive the Amazons of old," the queen said after she had brought her white mare to a rearing halt in front of Richildis and dismounted in a flurry of skirts. She was armored to the waist, clad in woman's fashion below, but Richildis had caught a glimpse of braies and very sensible boots; and the skirts were divided for riding. It would be very comfortable, if more than mildly scandalous.

That thought made her say before she thought about it, "What, no bared breasts?"

Eleanor laughed. She had a laugh as hearty as a man's, yet with a lilt in it that was unmistakably a woman's. "Can you imagine what my husband would say to that? Poor milk-and-water boy, he'd die of the shock."

"Yes, and isn't he the one to come to bed in a robe like a monk's. He crosses himself as he begins, and says a Paternoster for each thrust. And when he's done— and that's not long at all, please God—he runs to his confessor to confess the sin." The lady who had spoken seemed no more brazen than the others, nor did the queen frown at her, even when she tossed back her head and laughed.

"Poor boy," said Eleanor. "The priests got at him early. By now there's no hope for him."

"Indeed," said another of her ladies, "if you can't cure him, who in the world can?"

"Ah well," Eleanor said. "What's to do? He's the monks' child, and there's no curing him of it. But they left him enough sense to spare me the worst of his piety."

"Aye: and he knows better than to forbid this pagan pastime." The Amazon who had spoken whooped and spun her mount about and galloped off down the field, with the others in hot pursuit.

But Eleanor remained with Richildis, with a guard or two for company, and a lady of quieter mien than the rest. "I'll have you fitted for armor," the queen said. "You will ride with us, yes? I'm told you know how to bend a bow."

"I learned it when I was a child," Richildis said somewhat reluctantly, "but I never learned to wear armor."

"Why, no more than we," said Eleanor. "It's not so hard. It galls abominably at first, of course, but after a while you grow used to it."

"I don't think—" Richildis began.

"I do think," said Eleanor. "Come, we'll talk to the armorer. There's a coat or two already made, that might fit you."

As always with queens, one did well to do as one was told; to let oneself be swept up and carried off to whatever fate her majesty decreed.

Richildis could hardly fault herself. She had wanted to return to Jerusalem, and had thought to attach herself to the French. But not quite so firmly, nor ever so close to the counsels of its princes. Folly, of course: how could she not be singled out, with such names and titles as she brought with her?

So she paid for her own failure to be ordinary. Armor, yet, and a flight of fancy, as if a company of ladies from France could claim to be descended from the Amazons. They all rode well. Some could even shoot a bow and find the vicinity of the target. What earthly use they would be in a battle, she could not imagine.

Michael Bryennius heard her tale with ill-bridled amusement. "And to think: I was bored half to tears, listening to his pious majesty rehearse a whole spate of sermons. You had the more interesting part by far."

"Too interesting for my blood," Richildis said darkly. "What is that story you told me, of Alexander and the Amazons?"

"Which, the true or the false?"

"The true," she snapped, "and well you know it."

"There," he said, though he knew better than to stroke her. "There now. You *are* in a taking. What, do you mean the young ladies whom Alexander met on one of his marches, who rode out in grand array, even to the bared breast, and delighted his soldiers immeasurably? But they were only young maidens of that country, no better with weapons than young maidens are wont to be, got up in pretty armor and with gilded bows, to pique the conqueror's fancy."

"Exactly," said Richildis, only a little mollified. "And what did he do with them? You can wager he didn't take them on as soldiers of his army."

"No, it's said he gave them pretty presents and sent them home again, and was gracious to their kinsmen who had conceived the game."

"I don't think," Richildis said, "that the Saracen will be as charitable. So many fair-haired ladies would fetch a grand price in the slave-market of Damascus."

"I suspect they're not such fools as that," her husband said. "From what I hear, Eleanor is far more intelligent than his majesty the king. She sees some advantage in this revel of hers, or I'll wager she'd not do it."

"Of course she sees an advantage. She sees how shocked everyone is. She loves to be shocking. I think it's in the blood. All that line are given to excess."

"You sound as sour as King Louis," Michael Bryennius said, which was not wise at all. She pitched him out of bed and swept up the bedclothes and stalked off to the couch in the antechamber.

She was sure that he would follow her. Yet he did not. It was cold in the outer room, and lonely, and the couch was hard. She tossed on it, cursing her own temper and his refusal to see what idiots these Frenchwomen were. Playing at war, as if war were a game and not grim bloodstained truth.

Pride would not let her crawl back into bed with him, though she tossed and cursed the night away. He must have laughed himself to sleep. None of her moods and frets had ever shaken him in the least.

"Damn him," she muttered in the dark.

He was awake when she came back, his arms warm, welcoming her with all her prickly temper. "I don't deserve you," she said.

"No one deserves such a fate," he agreed.

She kicked his shins.

He yelped. "*Ai!* Your feet are cold."

"And whose fault is that?"

"Yours," he said. He kissed her from brow to chin, warm and warming kisses.

But she was not ready to be kissed into submission. "I do not want to wear armor," she said. "I'll feel a perfect idiot."

"You'll look a perfect delight," he said. "And consider: it's practical. It will protect you well on the march, and ward you from arrows."

"That can't be what she's thinking of," Richildis said.

"Why not? She's more sensible than she looks, I think. She loves the grand gesture—but she makes certain that it serves her purpose. Why do you think she insists on good Frankish mail and not the rather less . . . complete warding of the old Amazons?"

"I don't think they wore much of anything," muttered Richildis. She considered kicking him again, but her feet were warm now, nigh as warm as the rest of her. "Why do you have to be so damnably sensible?"

"One of us should be," he said. "Usually it's you. It's rather pleasant, for once, that it's not."

"If you tell me I'm beautiful when I'm angry, it won't be your shin I kick."

"I wouldn't dream of it," he said in all apparent sincerity.

Richildis suffered the armor because it was practical. Certainly it was not comfortable, and getting into and out of it was an exercise in sweaty frustration. She did not think that she looked grand in it, though some of the ladies preened themselves as if they had worn the finest silks. They ornamented their mail with ribbons, fastened plumes to their helmets, wound garlands about their horses' necks.

One thing Richildis did that set a fashion. She had made a surcoat such as knights wore in Outremer, marked on the shoulder with the red cross of Crusade. The white silk was thin yet strong, and kept off the worst of the sun. It looked well enough, too, and discouraged excesses of ornament.

While the ladies fretted over fashion, the emperor was preoccupied with ridding himself both swiftly and cleanly of his guests. The Germans had been a monstrous inconvenience. The French, hard on their heels, were better behaved but in the end no more welcome. They were armed, they were many, they were ready for war. Byzantium had no desire to loose that war on itself.

Manuel himself escorted the French king and his queen and all their following across the Golden Horn and into Chalcedon, and thence on the road into Asia. His well-wishings seemed honest enough. He was a great lover of the West, was the Emperor Manuel. But not so close; not in his own city, pillaging his people.

Richildis rode with the queen, and her husband with the king. They had bidden farewell to House Bryennius, but it was the adieu of the Franks and not the forever farewell of the Romans. They would return. It was expected. Nor was Richildis altogether dismayed by the expectation.

Most of the family had remained in the house as they rode away, but Constantine had followed them to the harbor and the ferry. The French were on the other side, had crossed the head of the Golden Horn the day before and camped for the night in Asia. Richildis and her husband would meet them on the road past Galata.

They had a little while before the ferry was ready to cross. They spent it in speaking of small things, the doings of this cousin or that, and whether Michael had remembered to pack the court robe that his mother had insisted on. He would not go before kings, she had said, in his usual drab old rags.

"And no," he said before Constantine could ask, "I did not pack the parade armor, too. That would need a whole pack-mule to itself. The plain mail will have to do, and Father's drab old sword."

Since Father's drab old sword had been forged in India and was as fine a blade as anyone knew of, they grinned at that. Michael slapped the hilt, which was plain enough, to be sure. Just then the ferryman bellowed the call to board. He left unsaid whatever new sally had occurred to him; pulled his brother into an embrace instead, and his brother drew Richildis with them in a threefold farewell.

"God go with you," Constantine said to her, "and protect you from harm."

"God keep you," she said, "until we meet again."

"Let that be soon," he said.

"Come to Mount Ghazal," said Richildis, "when the Crusade is over. We'll hold a festival in your name."

"If God wills," he said, "I'll come to you."

Michael Bryennius touched her arm. The ferry was slipping from the quay. All their baggage was on it, their horses, their sumpter mules. She gasped and ran, with a last glance back at her husband's brother. As she would expect of him, he was laughing.

That was a fine thing to take away with her: the mirth of a Bryennius. And another Bryennius at her side, breathless with running, holding her up as she held him, as the boat made its ponderous way across the Golden Horn.

anuel had hoped that once the French were across the Horn, they would go swiftly on their way. But Louis could be indolent at inconvenient moments, as Eleanor herself attested. The camp that he had made at Chalcedon showed signs of remaining indefinitely.

That was not at all to the emperor's liking—nor Richildis' either, and certainly not Michael Bryennius'. There was little that a pair of mere nobles could do. An emperor however could wield the power of his position. A pilgrim from Flanders provided him with a pretext: in rage over some slight difference in price between the bread that he had bought and the bread that his friend had found in another baker's stall, he gathered a mob and nigh tore the camp apart.

The king hanged him out of hand, but the emperor had closed down the markets, stopped the ships and the caravans that supplied the army, and made clear through his messengers that he had no intention of indulging these barbarians further.

An army could not march on an empty stomach. In that much Manuel perhaps had outsmarted himself; but he played a greater game than the simple one of dislodging unwelcome guests. King Louis called a council before it could call itself. The emperor's messenger attended; and another in worn and dusty traveling clothes, who carried himself with care, as one who is in pain.

They were no more or less unruly than any other council Richildis could remember. In a rare unity of opinion, they condemned the fool who by inciting a riot had attracted the emperor's attention.

"And we are most sorry for it," the king said, not seeming to reflect that apology was hardly a kingly thing. "Such amends as we can make—"

"Yes," the Byzantine envoy said, "there will be amends. His most serene majesty will consent to feed your army in return for a small concession."

"And that is?" the king inquired, again not as wisely as he might have done.

"That you and your lords agree to restore certain lands that were taken from us, and to pay homage to the Emperor of the Romans for such of those lands as you intend to dwell in."

A snarl rose from among the barons. It was as wild a sound as the howl of a wolf, and purely dangerous.

And the king said, "If we do that, he will feed us again?"

"If you will also agree to depart within the week, and make your way toward Nicaea."

"We did mean to do that," said the king.

The snarl had gone on while they spoke. In the moment of silence before the envoy's reply, if reply there was to be, it burst into a roar.

Louis could no more stop it than if it had been a wave of the sea. Never at all would the lords and barons of France grovel before the emperor of the Byzantines— no, not though they starved.

When the worst of it had run its course, a clear cold voice cut through it. "Do please think, my lords—if you can."

Eleanor had neither risen nor raised her voice, and yet they both saw and heard her. The exuberance of the Queen of the Amazons was gone. Here was royalty bare, too lofty for contempt.

"My lords," she said. "We may starve, and proudly, but we are sworn to Crusade. Jerusalem awaits us. Must we perish here for our folly and for the Greek emperor's pride?"

"He humiliates us!" they cried.

"One may pay homage," she said, "without giving one's soul."

"But—" they said: milder now, baffled, beginning to think like men and not like beasts.

"You are sworn to the King of France," she said, "and to the Crusade that was preached by the Pope of Rome and by the great Bernard. Such oaths would supersede any that you swear here. I think you should swear them, asking God's forgiveness; for without them there is no Crusade."

"There is a German Crusade," someone said.

"Possibly not," said Eleanor. She inclined her head to the man who hitherto had sat silent, slumped in weariness or in the weakness of a wound. He drew himself up with a visible effort of will.

"My lords," he said. His accent was that of Lorraine, with a hint of German heaviness. "Majesties. I come from Dorylaeum, where once was a great victory for another Crusade. But for this one . . ." He sighed. He seemed too exhausted for tears, or even for despair. "Disaster, messires. Defeat. The whole army of the Turks came on us there as we were nigh to dead from the rigors of the march. They slaughtered us, my lords. Our army is gone. The remnants were to make their way as they could, back to Nicaea. I was sent as they began, to bring word to you. For all that I know of them since, the Turks destroyed them all."

The silence that followed on his words was profound. Not even a breath marred it.

When Eleanor spoke, some of them started as if she had struck a blow. "Half of God's army is gone, if this man's tale be true. Will we, who are all that remains, grant the infidel the victory? Let us bow to the Byzantine, if he wishes it. He asks for nothing that we have now, only for what we may win—and we may choose to win nothing that Byzantium can rightfully claim."

That made them think, even through the shock of the word from Dorylaeum. It was too much for most, perhaps, all at once; but that too she must have calculated. She would grant them no mercy until they had chosen as she wished them to choose. Nor did she seem to care that the emperor's messenger had heard every word of it. The emperor must know how they would resign themselves to accepting his terms. Perhaps he even knew of the German defeat. There was little that would escape the imperial eye.

Games within games; expedience upon expedience. They won their provisions, at cost to both pride and honor. And—which could only delight the Emperor Manuel—they had no choice now but to depart from Chalcedon, to make haste for Nicaea in hopes of finding what remained of the Germans' army.

"We are the poor relations of the world," Eleanor said the day before they came to Nicaea. It was an ill day for traveling, grey and cold, with a thin rain falling. The Amazons had veiled their plumage, the knights and the men-at-arms and the hordes of hangers-on wrapped all in the same drab mantles dark with rain.

They had made early camp, pitched tents closer together than their wont, lit such fires as they could with damp fuel. The queen's tent was warm because of a gift from the Empress of the Romans, a brazier that glowed with blessed heat. They took turns standing close by it, all the ladies and a fair portion of the king's suite as well, wandering in at the rumor of warmth.

Eleanor held court amid them all. She had sent wine round, and sweets from a store that had also been the empress' gift. She nibbled on a honeyed date, held up the remnant of it, grimaced. "Poor relations. Fed, clothed, indulged for a brief while, then sent away to trouble another of the family. What is Crusade to old Rome, that it should trouble itself unduly?"

"Do you want Byzantium in your Crusade?" Richildis asked. "It would use you, you know, to do the fighting and dying; then march in over your bodies and claim the lands you won."

"It means to do exactly that," Eleanor said, "if we let it."

She stretched, luxuriating like a cat. Some of the knights looked away.

The king never even saw. He was playing chess near the brazier with one who was always at his side, tenacious as a shadow: the dour Templar knight Thierry Galeran, whose harsh face and unrelenting grimness were born perhaps of his great and too little secret shame. He was a eunuch. How he had come to that state, when and where and why, half a dozen people offered half a dozen tales, and no two of them alike. Richildis rather inclined toward that which had him enslaved in youth by Saracens and gelded to calm his ferocity; but he had only grown the fiercer for what they had done to him.

He had no friend, no ally, no confidant but Louis. The king cherished him, kept him close. And often, as now, engaged him in a game of chess, which he was hard put not to win.

The queen laughed as she sometimes did, as if at the mingled follies of the world. She held her cup for the servant to fill, sipped, laid it aside. The lamplight shimmered in her plaited hair.

She was nothing at all like Melisende. They were both tall, fair, more beautiful in movement than at rest—but Melisende knew the uses of stillness. Eleanor had never troubled to learn. She was restless always, mind and body. Immobility, passivity, were as death to her. She must, as a child, have been in constant mischief.

She was thinking of something now, something less delicious than some of her plots, with a frown that happened to aim itself at her husband. It could be accident, of course, and the angling of her seat and the light. Richildis did not think so.

As royal marriages went, this one was not particularly amicable, but neither was there open hostility. They tolerated each other's presence better than some, though they were not what anyone would call friends. There had been daughters, whom they had left safe in France, but no son, no heir to the throne.

Eleanor seemed not to have Melisende's objection to bearing children, but neither had she invited her husband to her bed of late; and he had not been seen seeking admission there. He was all caught up in the Crusade. He wore a pilgrim's robe always, in conspicuous humility, and beneath it a hairshirt like one of the old saints. It galled him into weeping sores, yet he would not accept salve or tending. A woman would not want to be too close to him, as averse as he was to bathing, and with the wounds, it was whispered, festering with saintly vigor.

Richildis sat next to her clean and no doubt hopelessly worldly husband, in strict propriety, not even touching him; but his presence was like a hearthfire. Now and then their glances crossed, with the flicker of a smile. To Louis they would be terrible sinners. To Eleanor . . .

If she thought of them at all, which Richildis could hardly be sure of, maybe she envied them. She had allowed them a tent of their own, which tonight was pitched beside this one, with a brazier in it, too, and comfort, and solitude. But they were here because the queen had wished it, because she hated to be alone—because, perhaps, she feared the dark and the cold rain and the quiet of sleep. In sleep she could not rule the world about her. Dreams came and went as they would, dark or light without distinction. She slept in the bright light of lamps, surrounded by ladies less fortunate than Richildis, or less fond of their husbands' presence.

At last, and after mighty effort by Thierry Galeran, Louis' king had conquered the chessboard. The courtiers about him applauded. "Oh, excellent!" Eleanor said sweetly. "May your victory presage a victory in our Crusade."

Thierry favored her with a sour glance. Some of the more pious crossed themselves in agreement. Eleanor, whose piety was negligible at best, clapped her hands and ordered wine again, though some cups were barely emptied.

Under cover of the servants' going round, Richildis touched Michael Bryennius' hand and arched a brow. He nodded infinitesimally. They had stationed themselves conveniently near the tentflap, though it denied them the benefit of the brazier. Quietly they slipped out into the brief shock of rain, and thence to the warmth and light and quiet of their own tent.

In that space they had spent much of their journey by caravan. The rugs were treasures garnered on the road, the bed a work of art, broad enough for two yet able to be folded into little more than a bundle of laths and a bit of canvas. The chests of their belongings, his armor and now hers on their stands, their weapons cleaned and laid ready at need, all were familiar, warmed by the brazier, lit by the lamp from Ch'in with its gilded dragons.

The servants had gone to their own and separate tent, and left the warmth to itself. Richildis sank into it with a sigh.

They moved in the familiar dance, undressing, laying their clothes away, each playing servant to the other as need demanded. Michael Bryennius helped Richildis

to comb and plait her hair for the night: an act as intimate as what they did under
the coverlet of woven silk and the bearskin that kept them warm in the night's
cold. She purred like a cat under his hands, aware of how he laughed at her, rich
and warm.

And yet she could say, "We should have stayed."

"Why? So that her majesty could count another pair of faces?"

"Such irreverence," Richildis said.

"Such crashing dullness. Not even a singer tonight, and no player on harp or
lute. His majesty is a monstrous poor player of chess."

"His majesty has no ear for music," Richildis reminded him. "It's mere noise to
him. The queen was sparing him the necessity of listening to it."

"What, so that she could sing her own song of the ingratitude of kings?"

"Mostly," said Richildis, "she was quiet."

"Yes," he said. "Thinking. Plotting."

"You thought so, too?"

She turned to see his face. His eyes glinted, half wicked, half amused. "Why,
madam, I am a Byzantine. We drink plots with our mothers' milk."

"What do you think she is thinking?"

His brows drew together. The mirth faded. "I would not be willing to wager,"
he said, "but if someone whom I trusted greatly were to ask . . . I would wonder
which of the men about her she had chosen to be her lover."

"I don't think so," Richildis said—too quickly, but she did not try to call back
the words. "At least . . . I think she would *think* it. But she would never do it. That
would be folly. Eleanor is a swift and reckless spirit, but a fool—no."

"She despises the man she's married to," he said. "And she is not, unlike another
queen of our acquaintance, averse to the art and craft of love."

"Melisende is gifted with great restraint," Richildis said rather stiffly.

"In that," he agreed, "she is. But Eleanor, no. Did you see how she studied to
keep all the men's eyes on her?"

"All but her husband's."

"Louis is divinely blind."

He finished plaiting her hair, bound it and kissed it, letting it be a path to her
lips. As he reached her shoulder, she stopped him with a hand on his cheek. "Do
you think she'll foment a scandal?"

"If she grows bored enough," he said, "or sees the need for a diversion, yes, I
think she well may. She's tired of him. Maybe she fancied herself tired of France,
and came on Crusade to give herself a change of scenery—but however the horizon
may change, the foreground, with Louis in it, is always the same."

"I don't believe that she's as light a spirit as that," said Richildis. "She plays it
well, but her mind is deep. Under the cleverness is a real intelligence."

"Whereas under her husband's piety is a profound lack of wit." Michael Bryennius
shook his head. "What was God thinking? To make a woman intelligent—how very
wasteful."

Richildis struck at him in mock anger. He eluded the blow easily, laughing,
darting a kiss at her palm as it flashed past.

"I think," he said from safely out of range, "that women let men do the fighting, and let them pretend to rule, because they themselves are too wise to indulge in either."

"Then the woman who wants to fight, who wants to be a king, is a fool?"

"I didn't say that," said Michael Bryennius.

"Eleanor plays at fighting," Richildis said. "Melisende exerts herself to be a king. Odd: neither wants to be a man. Simply to have what a man has."

"Precisely," said Michael Bryennius.

"You are too clever by half," she said. "What of me, then? Eleanor admires me enormously. I rule my own domain, I can shoot a bow. But I don't want to be an Amazon, or to wear a king's crown."

"You have no need of either," he said. "That's what it is, you know. Need. Fear of the dark; of oblivion. Of going to the tomb unnoticed, and being forgotten. Such people, kings or queens, no matter—they live to be noticed; to be remembered."

"And such people as we?"

He folded his arms about her. "We take the light while we have it, and let the darkness come when it must."

She shivered. "It may be very close, you know. The whole nation of the Seljuk Turks has destroyed the Germans' army. It well may destroy this one as well."

"We can pray that it does not," he said with no fear that she could discern, "and do our best to prevent it. Besides," he said, "they'll be saying in Byzantium, I'm sure, that the Germans paid for their sins on the march to Dorylaeum: for their ravaging and pillaging, and their rather perfect lack of Christian moderation. The French have been more circumspect. God may decide to reward them for it; to let them come unharmed to Jerusalem."

"And us with them," she said. "One can hope."

He drew back a little, to look into her face. "Do you want to go away? To travel apart, in a caravan maybe, or with an armed company out of Nicaea?"

She shook her head firmly. "No. No, I do not. If I had wanted that, I would have arranged it in the City."

"You still could arrange it."

"No," she said again. "I'm stubborn, you know that. I keep my word. And I gave it to this queen, to travel with her to Jerusalem."

His brows went up. "Another oath?"

"A promise," she said. "She wanted me so much, you see. Wanted what I am— what she fancies I am."

"Ah," he said: "a soft heart after all, and a weakness for strong queens."

Laughter escaped her, startling her. He was so clever with words, and not usually so unaware of it. As he frowned in puzzlement, she embraced him till he grunted, and kissed him soundly. "My lord, my dear lord, it's you she envies most, you know—or that I have you. Beauty and wit and grace enough to make a woman's heart quiver in the turn of a hand, and all devoted to me, or enough to make no matter. And so exotic, too. Beside you, my love, her milk-and-water king grows pale to insignificance."

"And yet," he said through the blush that she had contrived to win from him, "he is a king."

"And what is a king but a fool with the fortune to have been born in the proper bed? Better far the lover one finds in the road, whose beauty is unsullied, and his brow unmarred by the weight of a crown."

"Indeed," he said, "I see now. You'll be hunting down lovers as we travel, seeking beautiful boys in hedgerows and under farmers' carts."

"Boys are dull in the extreme," she said. "I prefer a man of years and experience, well seasoned in the battle that wages forever between man and woman, and," she said, sweeping him over and down and onto the bed, "apt for every mischief that a clever woman can imagine. What's a boy's bland face to that?"

"Why," he said, "to most, everything."

"But not to me." She rose above him, taking in the sight of him. No callow youth, no, nor old man either, but exactly between. Perfect; beautiful. Beloved.

Poor Eleanor, she thought as she prepared to lose herself in him. Married to a fool, and a pious one at that. No wonder she was bored; no wonder she played games of war and politics—and maybe love. If there were a man to match her, then maybe she would be content.

Or maybe not. Queens were never content; it was not in them. Not like lowly baronesses, mere ladies of the court, fine and fortunate creatures to be so blessed.

he Germans' defeat was both less ter-
rible and more absolute than the first messenger had made it. In Nicaea the French
king found the German king's envoy waiting; and that one led him in decent haste
to the place where Conrad had gathered the remnants of his army. More had survived the battle than the French had expected, and in better case. But it was still,
for all of that, a resounding rout. Only the indolence of the Turks, or perhaps their
contempt, had preserved them. They had had no attacks in this camp, nor were
the Turks abroad in the country about them. This land owed allegiance to the
Emperor of the Romans, and the Turks would not enter it. There was a pact;
treachery, some said in the armies, but the kings professed to be more glad than
outraged.

They would go on, they decided, along the shores of the sea: the French a day
or so ahead, the Germans behind with their wounded and their battle-wearied companies. It was an easier road than the inland way, and under the protection of
Byzantium. The Turks would not beset them while they traveled on it.

But that was not entirely a blessing, either. If they dallied, if they raided for
provisions, they were fallen upon by the protectors of this country, the emperor's
guardians. Nor was it a gentle rebuke; it was open attack, as if on enemies. Men
died. Pilgrims who had followed the knights and soldiers of God were broken in
spirit, those who were not killed; they turned back toward Constantinople, nor
would they go on.

" 'We are in hell,' he said to me," said a knight from Soissons who had gone to
the rescue of the Germans after they had pillaged lands stripped bare by the French
advance. "That's what he said, that poor fool of a pilgrim, with his staff and his
bag and his sore feet and not a scratch on him. 'This is not the road to heaven,
not even through suffering. This is the devil's own country, and those were his
armies who fell on us. I'm going back where God is, though I die in the trying.' I
told him God was in Jerusalem, but he wasn't listening to me. His mind was made
up."

"Maybe God isn't in Jerusalem either," said another knight, one who had stayed
with the king's army while the levies of Soissons went to aid the Germans. "Maybe
he's all the way back in France, and we were deluded into leaving it."

"Do stop that!" Eleanor said sharply, calling them to heel. They came like faithful dogs, with a suitably whipped look, cast down by the force of her frown. "God tests those whom He loves most. You know that. These pilgrims from Germany—their will was weak. They let the Devil cozen them into abandoning their vows."

"Lady," they said, bowing, contrite.

She frowned a while longer, letting them suffer; then smiled like a blaze of sudden sun. "Oh, go, be comforted. God loves you, He must. Would He have kept you alive so long if he didn't? Look at you, Thibaut, thicker with wounds than my favorite pincushion, and not a one so much as festered. There's luck for you, and God's goodwill, too."

Thibaut, the knight of Soissons, blushed like the boy he had not been for some twenty years and more. If they not been a-horseback, riding down the road by the sea, he would have been shuffling his feet. As it was, he could only express his confusion in flight: clapping spurs to his horse's sides, bolting off in pursuit of a stray sumpter-mule, with his companion hot behind.

Eleanor looked after them and shook her head. "Idiots," she said with not a scrap of the affection that she had shown to their faces. "The Devil's country, indeed! Why, this is heaven compared to some of the roads in Hungary."

Richildis rather agreed with her. Not that she herself had ever traveled in Hungary, but there was little enough to fault in this day. They rode on a clear road, wide and well kept, such as the Romans had made long ago. The sea shone blue on their right hands. The sky was a paler, clearer blue above them. The sun was bright for so late in the year, the air cool, not quite cold: invigorating. No enemies beset them, though the Byzantines were following, on guard: one could see them in the distance, outlined against a hilltop when the road dipped low toward the sea. It was a sort of paradox that even as they evaded the emperor's men by land, they looked eagerly for his escort by sea; for those were the ships that supplied them according to their bargain. It was never quite enough, they had still to forage in the land, but it was better far than nothing.

At Ephesus they paused. The Germans, who had been a day behind, caught up with the French there in the ancient city amid the ruins of the old pagans. Conrad their king, emperor as his people called him, was somewhat of a ruin himself: grey and ill and seeming older than he was. Defeat at Dorylaeum and the march thereafter had broken him, perhaps beyond mending.

He did not want to go on. None of his men did, either. They had lost heart and spirit, abandoned it somewhere along the road. Their camp when Richildis happened to pass through it was a grim and sullen place, less than indifferently clean, as if no one cared even to dig a proper set of privies. The French looked on them in scorn, mocked them in the streets of the city, called them fools and sluggards and cowardly layabouts.

Not that the French had much to brag of. They had suffered little on their march, fought no great battle, met no enemy worse than Byzantines outraged by the pillage of their country. In the way of wars and of armies, lack of privation was as ill a thing as an excess thereof. Had they had a stronger king, one less intent on worshipping at every Christian shrine in this city of the Apostles, they might have maintained a better discipline. If their queen had cared to rein them in, they would not have slipped loose as they had begun to do; but she was bored, and Eleanor in boredom was not inclined to be reasonable.

Worse, she had been quarreling with her husband. Anyone with ears could hear them of a night, his voice low, hers pitched clear and hard. She wanted them to move more swiftly, grovel less deeply to the Byzantines, take what they could and make haste to Jerusalem. He was minded to pause again, to rest troops who were, he insisted, worn down by the exigencies of travel. She laughed in his face, called him idler and idiot and weak-minded excuse for a king. He, who had never been so clever with words as she was, or indeed so clever at all, could only bluster and threaten and remind her that he was king and she, for all her pretenses, was only queen by his grace.

"And what have you?" she flared back at him. "A few scraps of land round about the Île de France, a castle here and there, and a mountain of debt to the Jews and the usurers, that requires my wealth, my lands, my dower to preserve itself from ruin. King you may be, and I but a duchess, but without me you have nothing but the boots you stand in."

"But you love your crown," he said. "You love to be called queen, to have people bowing at your feet. Without me you would have no such thing."

"I could find it," she said with ominous quiet. "Now get out. I'm tired of you."

His voice rose to a startling degree. "You can't send me away! I'm the king."

"Would you care to wager on it?" she asked, softly still, like a lioness' purr.

He left the field then. He always did. Strength of will was not a great virtue of his, nor did he stand well against his queen when she was determined to resist him. Her laughter followed him, light and cold, enough to madden most men; but he only buried himself deeper in his devotions, surrounded himself with priests, made himself more determinedly a man of God. She, as if to defy him, grew more worldly than ever, clothed herself more richly, even found a coat of gilded mail that fit her rather excellently well. In that, with a golden helmet and a scarlet plume, she rode about Ephesus like Diana of the pagans.

Under a weak king therefore, with a queen who did not see fit to trouble herself with matters that should properly concern the king, the French grew more unruly, the longer they went on.

They were four days in Ephesus—Eleanor's victory, that. When they left, they left without the Germans, and without the Germans' ailing king. Conrad was thought by many to be dying. They left him in the chanting of priests and the learned muttering of doctors, tossing in a fever that would not lift for any prayer or potion. They spared him no compassion. Jerusalem was waiting. In the grand self-ishness of the saint or the Crusade, they turned their faces toward the Holy City, and left the Germans behind to live or die as God ordained.

Still they traveled as if under a blessing: brilliant sun by day, clear stars and moon by night. They had settled into an order of march, rather free and somewhat slack of discipline but not unduly untidy. The barons took turn and turn about in the van. The queen and her ladies held the center. The king held the rear with his guards and his retinue and the knights and priests of his council.

Of them all, the ladies had the most ease. Those who tired of riding among the

Amazons could resort to the comfort of cushioned litters. At night they slept in their pavilions, warmed by braziers in the chill, or open to the air if they were inclined to be hardy.

The Germans were gone, with their long faces and their litany of defeat. There were only the French, singing in the sunlight, and their Byzantine guardhounds traveling behind and about them. They rode out of autumn and into winter, to sun that shone still but less strongly, and wind that blew cold, and clouds that gathered above a grey and foam-swept sea.

The ladies took more often to their litters then, wrapped in furs. Even the queen yielded to the lure of warmth. She held court from her litter; knights and barons wandered past, paused for a moment or an hour, rode on in a kind of easy vigilance. One never knew, after all, where the enemy might be.

At the feast of Christmas, three years to the day after the fall of Edessa, they came to a place of beauty almost miraculous in that country which was so often desolate. There a little river ran to the sea. A green valley embraced it, unwithered yet by winter's cold. In that place they made themselves a city, brightening their tents with banners, laying out their armor and weapons and the makings of siege-engines, all the panoply of war, on the sward beside the river. Their horses they put to pasture, themselves to rest. Even the least pious of them gave thanks to the Lord Christ for this place of peace. As if in answer, a cloud ran swiftly past, scattering a spray of rain—a benediction, the priests proclaimed; and no one gainsaid them.

The night was still, shot with stars. But toward the dawn a few thin banners of cloud streamed across the sky. It was a red sunrise, blood-red: such as might have been taken for omen, if any had been looking for it. But no one was. Of course there was war ahead of them. They marched to meet it. On the morrow they would take up arms and weapons again and set foot on the long road to Jerusalem.

In the hour of Lauds, while the voices of priests and monks sang sweetly through the camp, all at once, as if from blue heaven, a vast wind roared down upon them. It drowned the chanting of the office. It tore the tents from their moorings and flung them far away. It loosed such a torrent of rain as if the sea itself had risen up and crashed upon them.

It was like the wrath of God. Richildis had had some little warning: the uneasiness of the horses, and her own mare's great ill temper, that set her to fighting with the poor fool of a gelding who happened to be pastured beside her. She battered him with her heels, and every man who tried to intercede, until someone thought to fetch Richildis.

Richildis was awake and, as it happened, dressed; she had slept ill, for what reason she did not know. She bolted after the messenger, swift enough to find the battle still in progress, the gelding defeated but the mare whirling in search of a new and fresher target. Richildis, leaping in, seized her halter and hauled her down. The others got the gelding away, led him to another corner of the meadow. The mare dropped her head to graze, but uneasily, snapping at the grass, glaring about and snorting and turning her back on the bit of wind that had begun to blow.

Richildis lingered for a bit, but there seemed no likelihood of new battle. Mares being what they were, she reckoned that this one would be calm enough for a while. She said so to the horse-handlers who stood nearby. They shrugged, yawned, agreed.

One would stay to be sure of it. "You go back to your warm tent, lady," they said, "and rest a little more."

She was not minded to rest, but her tent had breakfast in it, and her still sleeping husband. She went in search of it.

The wind struck just as she reached it. It buffeted her with force enough to fling her down. She lay stunned, feeling a fool—thinking for a moment that she had tripped over her feet, or the hem of her skirt. Only slowly did her mind understand the roaring that deafened her. Wind—it was wind. And, hard on its heels, rain.

She did not try to stand against such a blast. She crawled on hands and knees toward the shadow that was—that must be—her tent. It was leaping and swaying like a dancer in a bazaar. But its pegs were holding; they were driven well and deep, and into solid ground well above the river.

Michael Bryennius had insisted on it. "I have an objection," he had said, "to sleeping in riverbeds in this country and at this season." The French had reckoned him an overcautious fool, but he had been adamant. Richildis had not seen the profit in resisting, though it set them well away from the queen's pavilion, up on the hill above the rest of the camp. It was not on the summit, but sheltered in a bit of hollow that yesterday had kept the sun's warmth somewhat after darkness fell.

Now it gave some protection against the wind—enough to keep the tent from going the way of those below. Michael Bryennius was in it, awake and dressed, scowling as he listened to the roaring without. Richildis fell into his arms.

He clasped her tightly, set lips to her ear, said as clearly as he could through the wind's howling, "Thank God. If you had stayed out in that—"

Richildis struggled. "I have to—I shouldn't—the queen—the horses—"

He held her tightly, almost to pain. "No! You'll be killed."

"But what of them?" she cried.

"God will have to defend them."

She hated him—by God, she hated that immovable calm. She could not see his face clearly, so dim was the tent; the lamp had gone out, whether from the wind of her arrival or from a want of oil. He would not let her go to light it again. He would not release her at all. His arms were like shackles.

Slowly and without her willing it, her anger quieted. Much of it was fear, and shock: that out of the night's clear quiet, such a storm could have risen. They could do nothing. Only cling to one another, cold and fireless and unfed, while wind and rain raged over them, and only a thin wall of leather between. It held, and that was a marvel; a miracle, one might have said. He had secured the flap behind her when she first came in, laced it tight. A little rain seeped in, but nothing to trouble them.

When silence fell, it was deafening. The wind had died. The rain had paused, though it began again more softly, pattering on the roof of the tent.

Richildis unlocked arms that she had not even known were wrapped about her husband. He had loosened his grip, though he held her still. She looked into his face, that was visible at last, though dimly. Perhaps it was only the faintness of light through oiled and painted leather that made him look so grey and ill.

"Let me go," she said to him.

This time he obeyed her. She staggered in getting up; her knees were weak. She stiffened them, made them carry her toward the flap. With hands that felt as heavy as mailed gauntlets, she fumbled open the lacings and eased the flap aside.

She looked out on desolation. Wasteland. Wilderness. Where had been the green meadow and the bright tent-city was a torrent of restless water bobbing with flotsam. Along the edges of it stumbled men, beasts, things that could have been either or both. The camp was swept away. Only those who had pitched their tents high, as Michael Bryennius had, were still standing on solid ground. Even they, most of them, had lost their tents to the wind; they stood under the naked and tumbled sky, dazed, dripping, spattered with mud.

Warmth brushed against her. Michael Bryennius too looked out. "God in heaven," he said.

"Yes," said Richildis. "It is God; the God of wrath."

He crossed himself backward as the Byzantines did. Without a word then, he went out into the mud and the new, thin drizzle of rain, to do what he could to aid those less fortunate than he. Richildis could do no less than follow.

he army that had come so joyfully to its Christmas camp marched out of it in grief. They had lost men, swept away in the river; beasts of burden, warhorses, siege-engines, baggage, all that had been set or pastured by the stream before it rose in flood. What had not been lost was often ruined—foodstuffs too, and barrels of ale, and wine. They marched cold and wet and miserable, nor were they granted a respite. The winter rains had come at last and with a vengeance. Every river that they met was swollen with flood, every stream overflowing its banks.

In disgust and near-despair—and how unlike their former progress, singing in the sunlight—they turned away from the sea and struck inland. But that road was no happier than the gale-wracked paths along the sea. There were Turks on it: enemies at last, infidels for a surety, and no Byzantine armies to stand between.

A week's wet miserable journey from the place of the flood, they came to a city called Antioch. It was not that great and ancient city and principate of Outremer, but a lesser city, Antioch-in-Pisidia. Maps and guides proclaimed it a Byzantine holding. Truth and hard experience filled it with Turks.

Turks ahead of them, Turks behind. At the bridge between, they closed in battle.

Here the wonted order of march proved most useful: barons in the van, king in the rear, queen and baggage and bulk of the army in the midst of them. The Amazons made no pretense of warrior strength. They clung to their litters and their wagons, and wept or prayed as arrows flew overhead. Richildis, trapped among them, could see little of what went on ahead or behind. She thought to force herself to the van, but the queen's guard had closed into a wall of steel. Michael Bryennius was farther back, with the king. She could not go to him, either. She was closed like a nut in its shell, completely walled about, advancing in fits and starts.

As they went on, the hooves of horses and oxen slipped in mud and blood, or stumbled over bodies. Some still lived: they struggled and shrieked. But the damnable guards would let no one pause. Like prisoners they pressed on, brief advances, endless halts. Sometimes they could see fighting. They could hear it always: shouts, cries, ring of metal on metal.

Richildis had taken her bow from its case and strung it, and kept her quiver of arrows close to hand. But there was nothing to shoot at, unless she turned against the knights who guarded the queen. They were admirable in their loyalty, remarkable in their fortitude—maddening, because they would not let her escape, fight, be something more than useless baggage.

At last, after endless halts and advances, they reached the bridge. It was clear of bodies but not of blood. The river below, swollen with flood, tumbled more than its wonted wrack of fallen trees, drowned sheep, bits of broken wall and shattered roof. The city ahead was shut to them, the gates barred, the walls thick with Turkish faces: black beards, long braids, the white gleam of turbans.

"Treachery," someone said near Richildis, a sound like a snarl. "That is a Byzantine city!"

"Not now," Eleanor said with impressive composure. If it frustrated her to be trapped in the army's heart and helpless to defend either it or herself, she did not show it. But then, thought Richildis, her hands were hidden, wrapped in her mantle. For all anyone knew, they were clenched into fists.

The battle of the bridge of Antioch was reckoned a victory, but its price came high. Not only had they wounded to tend, dead to bury, but as they went on, they found the country empty of people—and all provisions gone away with them. Laodicea, the city in which they had hoped to find a market or, if that failed, a rich store of goods to pillage, was empty, scoured clean. And all the land about it was barren, terrible steep mountain track and relentless slope, lashed with wind and rain.

From peaceful haven and sunlit autumn they had ascended into hell. No road was level here. It was all up, up, up, and precipitously down, then up again against the vault of the sky. Wagons could not climb those tracks. Mules slipped and staggered and fell endless furlongs to their deaths. Men must walk perforce, or risk oversetting their horses. Even the ladies struggled afoot, their litters empty or abandoned.

Nor were they granted the least bit of surcease, even from the enemy. Turks haunted the heights, even higher than they: archers taking aim at the wounded or the hapless or, worse by far, the horses. One had to fight not only land and weather but a human enemy—inhuman enough in the mind, like devils amid the torments of hell.

There at last Richildis had her wish, and got no joy of it, either: she climbed and scrambled and clambered as much as any, but with her bow close to hand; and when she could, she strung it and searched for targets. Once in a great while one presented itself. She could not spend arrows recklessly, but shoot she would and did, if she had even the hope of a clear shot. Once or twice perhaps her arrow found flesh—maybe took a life. She could not know. She could only go on, up yet another grueling slope, into the teeth of yet another merciless wind.

And she could have chosen a caravan; have traveled in comfort, with nights in caravanserais, and attacks only from the occasional pack of bandits. Instead in her folly she had elected to come home with the Crusade. Grand high heroic thought, that, but grim enough in the doing of it. She could die here. Death was a real and present thing, almost an ally; had it not flown on her arrows as they sought targets amid the rocks and scree?

She was greatly surprised, late one day, to come over yet another pass, down yet another slope, and see no mountain waiting ahead. The land was ugly enough, stony and barren, but it was astonishingly level after the mountains that had held them for so long. Far ahead was a brightness, a suggestion of shimmer that might be the sea. If truly that was so, then they had crossed this wilderness of Anatolia, and come almost to the infidels' country, the land that the Turks called Rûm.

Or perhaps not. Perhaps it was only a trick of the light as the day faded.

The queen and her train had come somehow to the van, away from their wonted place in the center. The knights about them were Poitevins, allies and vassals of the queen, who was also Duchess of Aquitaine and Poitou. She had been quarreling with the king again, and more acrimoniously as weather and terrain grew worse; she fled him, perhaps, while he dawdled in the rear, and pressed ahead.

Dawdling was his great sin; half the camp knew it, from the words she had flung at him day after day. She was too prudent to leave him, but she would ride well in front of him.

Orders had come down to the van that they would camp on the high and barren level on which they found themselves. But it was a bleak place, open to wind and arrow-flight, unappealing even after the mountain tracks. Eleanor halted there, looked about, curled her lip. She said nothing. Her servants began somewhat diffidently to make camp.

One of the commanders of the van was a vassal of hers. He was not a friend or a familiar, he was too much in love with her for that. Richildis, riding up with the last of the ladies, saw him bow to the queen and summon his men and ride off across the windy plain. A mildly alarming number of knights and soldiers followed.

Eleanor's servants looked to her. She frowned at the departing force; the more so for that the king's standard, which had been set where the camp should go, had gone with them. After a long moment she shrugged. "Follow them," she said.

"But, lady," someone ventured to protest, "the king—"

"Geoffrey says," said the queen, "that his scouts have found a better camping place farther on, but still close enough to come to before dark. It's a valley, they say, green and pleasant, with water, and shelter from this miserable wind."

"But the king is still so far behind," the bold one said. "What if the Turks see us separated, and decide to do something about it?"

"If the king is fool enough to let himself be left behind," she said with little effort to conceal her impatience, "then let him pay the price for it."

Some of those near her drew in a breath at that, but none, even Richildis, was brave enough to cross her further. Richildis berated herself for a coward even as she kept silent. Michael Bryennius was with the king. The last she saw, he had been disputing happily with a handful of prelates, one of his endless Byzantine theological niggles. He had been so evidently content that she had refrained from calling him to ride with her, had let the queen draw her away farther and farther till they were in the van and he was well behind, still toiling up the road to the pass.

Eleanor was not to be moved by any invocation of the king's name. Nor was prudence a word she cared to hear. And there was the lure of water, food, rest in a place untormented by the ceaseless, gibbering wind.

Richildis crossed herself and said a prayer to the saints who protected hapless travelers and leaden-footed kings, and let her horse follow the rest of the queen's train. The plain lay empty behind, the king's banner gone from it. As she looked back, the wind stirred the dust of their passing, swirled it into a cloud, concealed altogether the way that they had come.

Michael Bryennius had had a long and thoroughly satisfying argument with his prelates, and fine men they were, too, if given to stopping abruptly when the slope grew excessively steep. At length, as the sun began to sink, even he lost his enthusiasm for the finer points of theology, on a road that was notably worse than what had come before.

Louis, whose inclination to tarry had incited such ire in his queen, had wit enough at least to realize how late it was growing and how far they still were, by the scouts' account, from the place where he had ordered the van to make camp. He roused himself to a fair semblance of kingly vigor, ordered the column to make what speed it could, even set his own royal shoulder to a baggage-wagon that, having negotiated tracks so steep as to be all but impossible, seemed to have decided that this last and grueling slope was more than it could endure.

Its axles held, praise God, and its wheels turned with much protest but forbore to break. It lurched, creaked, groaned its way up the crest; wobbled at the summit; teetered precariously; crashed to a brief halt on a bit of merciful level. Mules and carters both paused to breathe, to nerve themselves for the even more exhausting task of getting themselves and their burden down a road as steep as the way up.

Louis could afford to pause longer while his squire brought his horse; but he waved the boy away. He had raised his eyes as they all must have done, looking toward the place where the camp should be. And as those ahead of him had done, he stared unbelieving.

There was no camp. The broad flat tableland was there as the scouts had described, wide enough to house the army, and high enough to give the enemy pause. But the king's banner did not fly there, nor did a city of tents await him, the privies dug, the horselines pitched, all the camp that he had ordered to be made.

The army ahead of him had been driven on by barons and sergeants, urged from behind by others coming over the pass and eager as they had been to take refuge in the promised camp. Others behind the king did the same, rank on rank of them, struggling, sweating, stumbling and cursing, winning their way to the end of this appalling road. All of them saw the thing that no one had expected, the camp that was not, the empty place.

And, as if at the Devil's own pleasure, the swarms of Turks that erupted from every crack and hollow in the riven earth. They had seen—they must—how the van rode far ahead, how the rear let itself fall back out of sight. They had done as Turks must wisely do. They had gathered to attack.

Already as Michael Bryennius surmounted the pass behind the king, the front line of the march was beset. He did not pause to think, still less to be afraid. He drew his sword. No time to hunt for the spears that were bound to the pack of a sumpter mule—for all he knew, the beast was a league ahead, wherever the queen and the van had gone; and Richildis with them, please God unscathed, unharried by this wasp's nest of Turks.

That was all the prayer he made time to say, all the fear he let himself give way to. Louis, layabout on the march though he might be, was a fair man in a fight. He had mounted his waiting horse, taken the lance that his squire had kept for him, suffered himself to be weighted with the vast unwieldy helm. So warded, formidable in his shell of steel, he set spur to his horse's side and thundered down from the crest.

Michael Bryennius, less heavily armored, followed in his wake, swept up in a tide of knights, squires, and yelling men-at-arms. Exhausted they might be, desperate to eat and rest, but battle warmed them like wine.

It was a grim and desperate fight with the mountain at their backs, against enemies who knew the land, who had all the advantage of its hiding-places. They could only do as Franks had done in Outremer since the first Crusade: go forward, wielding the weight of their armor and horses, overwhelming the enemy by sheer force of steelclad resistance.

Here they could not press forward far. The enemy were too many. Shrieking, flailing Turks drove them apart, scattered them, hurled men and beasts and wagons over the precipice. There was no order in it, no finesse, no fine array of battle such as kings would play upon a field.

Michael Bryennius found himself in a little gaggle of men and boys: knights and squires and a man-at-arms or two, and among them the king. Louis would never affect any splendor; he was too pious. He wore a pilgrim's robe over his mail, and had lost or discarded his helm somewhere. The nondescript bearded face in the mail-coif could have belonged to anyone. No crown adorned its brow, no mark of rank.

And that, perhaps, saved him. He was no more beset than any other man, if no less.

A flurry of Turks had driven them down the slope against a gnarled stump of tree. Someone—not Michael Bryennius—urged the king to abandon his horse and take refuge in the branches. Louis resisted, but the others were too many and too strong for him. They treed him like a hunted leopard, set backs to the trunk themselves, and battled Turks in the fading light.

Michael Bryennius paused at last, leaning against the tree. His horse was dead, had been cut from beneath him as he defended the man above him.

He would die here. He knew it as one knows that the sun has risen of a morning: as fact beyond disputing, inevitable and inescapable. Man by man, company by company, the Turks would destroy the army of the French, till no man was left standing. Then would be an end of this arm of the Crusade.

The sun, that had seemed suspended in the sky, sank with breathtaking suddenness. Michael Bryennius might not have noticed, except that one moment it was in his eyes; the next, it was gone. He was nearly face to face with a grinning, yelling Turk. He drew his sword calmly, sighted along the blade. The Turk's own blade darted out. He clove the hand that held it, and followed the great stroke round, biting deep into the body.

The man was not, God be thanked, clad in mail but in a coat of boiled leather. It slowed his sword but neither broke nor notched it. It also, and somewhat to his dismay, was not eager to let go the blade once it had sunk in flesh. The Turk was curled about it, writhing and howling. If any other happened on him, he had no weapon but the meat-knife at his belt; no bow, no spear, nothing.

But no new enemy leaped on him. It was dark already, almost too dark to see. All the shadows near him wore the shapes of Franks in armor.

With a back-tearing wrench, he won back his sword. The Turk convulsed and voided and died. The stink of his entrails was ripe, more immediate than the reek of death that had ridden all about him.

A torch flared. Michael Bryennius bit back a curse—what madman made a target of them all?

But no arrow flew through the dark. No Turk leaped yelling from a crest. As other torches kindled, stringing beads of light across the wrack of the battle, Michael Bryennius saw what they all must see, that the only Turks in that place were dead. The enemy had withdrawn, driven back by the dark.

King Louis clambered down awkwardly from his perch. There was blood on his sword: even up so high, he had found Turks to kill. He was unwounded, to the audible relief of his men; they cheered him wearily as he stood among them. He raised a hand, humble as he always was, diffident, without grace; but because he was their king, they forbore to fault him for it.

The fight was ended. There was only the grim labor of aftermath: making such camp as they could, reckoning the count of dead and wounded, and feeding themselves as they might.

The long struggle to get the baggage through the passes proved itself wise then. The tents were most of them with the van, but there were enough for a beginning; and bedding, too, and food, and wine that was more welcome than any of it, both warmth and sustenance. They made a better camp than they might have expected, though there was no hope of reaching the high level; they had to stay where they were, between the pass and the plain, and pray that the Turks had gone indeed and not pulled back to trick them into complacency.

Louis kept insisting that Michael Bryennius had saved his life. Michael Bryennius did not see what one stray Turk had to do with the king's safety or lack of it; but Louis said over and over, "He was coming for me, and you leaped, and killed him even as he struck at me. It was a splendid stroke, just splendid!"

Michael Bryennius could hardly point out that the Turk had been aiming at him. After all, Louis might have the right of it. The pilgrim's garb was disguise of sorts, but an enemy could have seen that the pilgrim was extraordinarily well guarded— might even know the French king's affectation of simplicity.

He held his tongue therefore and let himself be dragged into the tent that they had set up for the king and plied with cups of wine that he barely touched. He had a wound or two, scratches, no more, but the one on his arm had bled exuberantly— now, how had he got that? The king's own physicians fluttered and hovered. He could hardly be so ungracious as to snarl at them, but they tried his patience sorely.

The attention of kings was never a comfortable thing. Their gratitude was frankly excruciating. It won him a warm dinner, however, and a bed out of the wind, though he came to it late and weary to the bone. Even as he slept he heard the king conferring with his councillors, going on as if no weariness could touch them, droning all night long of battle and disobedience, war and treachery. They were blaming the queen. The angry, the wounded, the exhausted, needed a target; and Eleanor had been in the van. The van had disobeyed orders, had not pitched camp where it was told. Only she could have permitted such a thing, or even—some insisted—commanded it.

Michael Bryennius was already half-conscious between weariness and loss of blood, or he might have roused and injected a little sense. Certainly Louis was doing nothing of the sort. He was letting them go on, letting them curse the queen.

Hardly Christian charity, Michael Bryennius thought with his last waking wits. Hardly wise, if the king would keep this army together and eager for its Crusade. But there was no forcing wisdom on a king determined to have none of it. Michael Bryennius knew. He knew kings.

*W*hen the king and the body of the army did not appear in camp by sundown, the commanders sent scouts to find them. Eleanor was scornful. "How like him," she said. "How utterly like him."

Others were less swift to dismiss him. They were beginning to regret this choice, though it had set them in a green and peaceful place, with water, and best of all, no wind. And so close, too, to the king's chosen place, that had been so bleak and forbidding.

Yet he should have reached the plain before the sun set, and his scouts should have found them soon after and led the army to its rest. No scout had come, no messenger, no word at all.

No one slept well. The queen herself lay awake, staring at the roof of her tent. Richildis saw no regret there, no repentance, certainly no fear. But whatever she might think of her husband, she could not but pray that the army had escaped attack; that he had dawdled till nightfall and camped short of his goal. It would not be the first time, or the tenth.

Somehow this was different. Before when Louis had dragged his feet, the van had stayed with him. They had not let themselves be separated. Nor, before, had the enemy hounded them so close, or the land been so tumbled that neither half of the army could see the other. And when the Germans had been so parted from the French, there had been battle, and destruction.

It was all ill done. Richildis feared for the king and his lords and men-at-arms, for the baggage and the rest; but most of all she feared for her husband. If there had been a battle, if he was wounded or killed, she did not know what she would do. Storm heaven at the very least; raise a cry at the gates of hell.

She was a little startled that she should feel so strongly. It was a sin, probably. One should not love a man so. Such passion should be reserved for one's God.

And if she had loved God as she loved this man, she would have been a nun in Anjou, and never come across the sea at all.

The dark before dawn brought the word that they had been dreading. There had been a battle indeed; many wounded, too many dead. Men, roused hastily, went back to aid in guarding the hasty camp. When the sun rose, they would bring the king and his battered army to this place.

Of Michael Bryennius there was no word, nor had he sent any message. Richildis caught herself gnawing her knuckles. She locked her hands together under her mantle, forced composure. It did him no good if she shrieked or wailed. Not if he lived, not if he had died.

Her heart wanted to ride back with the rescue-party. Her head bade her be sensible. A woman would only discommode them; and there was little that she could do, even with her bow and her quiver of arrows. Best that she remain here, that she stand close to the queen. Already the mutterings had begun: that it was Eleanor's doing, that without her the army would not have broken in two, the van would not have gone too far ahead, the Turks would not have seized opportunity to attack. Was it not her vassal who had chosen to disobey the king's orders as to the place of the camp? Had she not acquiesced? Worse, had she not done so in open scorn of the king?

Guilt would strike wherever it could. And they were all guilty, every one of them, of abetting this folly that had proved so deadly. The anger had begun, the recriminations. And there was Eleanor in the pale cold morning, dressed defiantly in crimson and gold, refusing to weep for the poor battered army.

Her defiance waxed as the sun rose. She insisted on breaking her fast with her ladies in her painted pavilion, with the sides rolled up, for it was remarkably, almost unnaturally warm for that time of year. They remained there when they had eaten their fill, taking the soft air and listening to the luteplayer whom Eleanor had found in Ephesus. He was a eunuch, young enough to look still as if he would grow from youth into man, and he could sing as well as play. His voice was achingly sweet, lingering on a love-song that, he professed, was all the rage in Damascus.

Such a sight they must have been to the weary warriors who straggled in in the full light of morning: all at their ease, the singer singing, no cloud to mar their pleasure. They had taken no wound, suffered no pain of battle. While their husbands and lovers fought for their lives, they had slept at ease in warm and scented beds.

Richildis saw no hatred in those grey and battered faces, only a kind of resignation. Until they looked on the queen. Then they hated. Then indeed they found release for all their anger.

Eleanor could not but know it. But being Eleanor, she would never let them see. Even the eunuch felt the force of rage against his mistress. His voice faltered, his fingers slipped upon the strings of his lute. She beckoned sharply. "No! No, don't stop. Play on. Play on!"

It was bravado, but the army would see it as heedlessness. Eleanor could hardly retract it once she had said it. She sat back in her cushioned chair, warmed by the sun, and made great show of listening to the eunuch's song.

Richildis barely heard it. Eleanor's tent was so placed that most of the army had to pass by it as they came in. Richildis searched the faces, bearded and shaven, swollen with wounds or blessedly unscathed. But no lean dark Byzantine face. No rich black beard. No Michael Bryennius.

At first she expected little. As many as they had lost, there were still many more alive, and they took time to march past. But as more and more went by, and none was her husband, she sank slowly into despair. He was dead. He must be dead. If he lived, he would be here, in front of her, calming all her fears.

After despair came anger, the same anger that in the others had turned itself against the queen. How dared he not be there? Before God, how dared he be dead?

And as her anger swelled till it consumed the whole of her, a shadow appeared before her, a ghost, an apparition: the shape of a man standing in the sun. He was not maimed or badly wounded. His armor was clean. His beard was dusty, but bore the marks of careful combing. He looked much as he always had, a little paler than usual perhaps, and a great deal more tired.

He did not say anything. Her wrath must have pulsed from her, strong as heat from a fire. "You're alive," she said. She made it sound like an accusation.

He nodded. He swayed a little. Dear God: he was wounded after all, and deadly pale. She rose in terror, braced to catch him as he fell. He was a solid weight, too solid. She sank down with him.

Servants were there, squires, a knight or two. Among them they carried him off, but not, as they would have wished, toward the surgeons' tent. "Those butchers," she said. "I have more art in healing than they."

Since Michael Bryennius, even half-unconscious, agreed with her, they carried him where she bade them. Her own tent was set near the queen's, open to the air as Eleanor's own was, and with servants ready to fetch whatever she had need of. She sent them for water, cloths, herbs and simples from the queen's stores. Michael Bryennius she saw laid in the bed and relieved of his armor; then she sent his rescuers away, with careful thanks lest they believe her ungrateful. That, she was not. But he was hurt, and how badly she did not yet know. She had no time for aught else.

Someone had cleaned and bound his wounds—several of them, though the one in the arm was worst. It had been stitched, not too badly. She did what she could for that and for the rest while he lay in a stupor. He had pressed himself to come so far, she supposed; but now that he was here, he had let himself go.

She covered him at length, and said to one of the servants who seemed unable to let him out of sight, "Stay with him."

The man raised his brows but did not object. Richildis rather wished that he had. Her heart wanted to stay, but common sense told her that others of the wounded would need such care as deft hands and a packet of herbs could give. There were not so many in this camp who had spent time in converse with both Greek and infidel physicians, and learned a little in doing it.

She came back late, worn down by the numbers of the wounded, and too many who died now that they were safe among their countrymen. Pain broke down their guard; they said things that otherwise they might have kept silent. They blamed the queen. It was as much the fault of the commanders of the van, Lord Geoffrey most of all, who had given the order to move the camp. But Eleanor had had the power to forbid, and she had not. She had allowed the army to be separated. Some were even calling it treason.

They were angry; they had suffered a bitter defeat. Time would soften their condemnation, but Richildis did not think that it would vanish. There was so much that royalty could do, so far that it could go before the people lost faith in it. Yet a small thing could shift the balance inescapably. A word not said, an act undone; a camp shifted while the Turks waited in ambush.

The mood in the camp was bitter. They were not broken as the Germans had been in Ephesus, far from it, but neither were they the proud warriors who had sung their way through Asia. The sun had forsaken them. They dwelt under a grey and lowering sky, shape and image of their spirits.

Michael Bryennius was awake when she came back to the tent. She had half expected him to be up and gone, but she had caught him before he could rise. He greeted her with a lift of the brows.

"I thought you had died," she said to him.

"Obviously," he said, "you were so afraid for me that you tended me and left me."

"Others needed me more," she said.

It was not like him to be petulant. Maybe the Devil had taken up residence here, and sent his imps to vex even the wounded in their tents.

And then he asked, "Are you angry with me?" That was such a question as her Michael Bryennius would ask, in such a tone as he would use, honest curiosity, and nothing plaintive in it.

"Yes," she said. "I am angry with you. If you had died, what in the world would have been left for me?"

"It was not," he said, "as if I planned to be caught in an ambush."

"Do you blame the queen, too?"

He blinked. "As well blame the king for not moving fast enough, or Lord Geoffrey for moving too fast altogether."

"You are much too reasonable for a mortal man," she said. She sighed. "Sweet saints, I'm tired."

He held out his arms. "Come to bed, then."

She shook her head. "No. No, I have to wait on the queen. I only came to—"

"To be angry at me."

She glared. "No. To be sure that you were well. Promise me you'll sleep. I'd give you a draught, but if you give me your word . . ."

"I should be up," he said. "Seeing what I can do."

"There are others more able to do that," she said. "Lie back. Go to sleep. I'll wake you for the daymeal."

It was a measure of his weariness that he protested only a little, and not for long. She paused as he lay down, stabbed with fear. What if he was wounded worse than she had thought?

No. She had examined him thoroughly. There were only those that she had found, none severe enough to be deadly, unless it festered. And for that, she had done what she could, as best she knew how.

The queen and the king were not quarreling. They were not speaking to one another at all. Eleanor wore an air of defiance that would better have suited a scapegrace child. She had walked the camp as a queen should, given comfort to those who were not greatly inclined to welcome it. That done, she took her ease among the high lords and the king's council—if it could be called ease, to hear them fight the battle over and over. Recriminations there were none—not for that. Until they looked at her and went quiet.

She sipped wine, the last of the good vintage from Byzantium, and maintained an expression of mild interest. In a lull in the retelling of tales many times told, she said, "We will of course break camp tomorrow and go on. This time," she said, "in one army, unsundered. Can the rear undertake to accomplish this?"

"Can the van swear solemnly to allow it?" the king asked in a cold voice.

"The van would thank the rear to keep a good pace and not dawdle," she said.

"The rear would thank the van," he shot back, "to obey the orders it is given."

More than one of those caught in the fire drew in a sharp breath, but although Eleanor's eyes glittered dangerously, her lips smiled. "The vanguard will follow every royal order to the letter," she said, "by my own command."

Louis, cheated of a battle, looked shrunken and faintly lost. "Well," he said. "That's all right, then."

Eleanor's smile brightened a noticeable degree. She bowed her head regally, acknowledging not only his surrender but her own victory. Such as it was, and as little good as it could do with an army turned against her.

But Eleanor was nothing if not resolute. She would win the army back: Richildis could see how she determined on it, lifting her chin, setting her shoulders back, bracing like a soldier going into battle.

FIFTY-TWO

God or the Devil, whichever had taken charge of the French army's fate, seemed to have wearied for a while of tormenting them. The road thereafter was less ghastly difficult, winding out of the mountains and into a broad and winter-barren plain. The Turks did not follow them there. They marched unmolested, foraging where they could, eking out the provisions that the Byzantines had allowed them.

Indeed they wearied after a while of condemning the queen for her ill judgment and turned back on an older grievance: the Emperor of the Romans and his haughty and often recalcitrant servants. Michael Bryennius till now had been little noticed and seldom condemned for his race and nation, but after the battle on the mountain they seemed to remember who and what he was. They began to shun him, to walk wide of him in camp and to ride away when he approached them on the march.

He suffered it with wry humor. "Better a cold shoulder than cold steel in the belly," he said.

"That could follow," said Richildis. "Be wise now. Don't wander off. Stay close to the queen."

"What," he said, "so that the two most hated personages in the army can both be found in the same place? Wouldn't it be more sensible to divide and conquer?"

"Divide and be conquered," she said, refusing to be drawn into his antic fit. "Promise me."

"I promise," he said easily—too easily, maybe. But he was a man of his word. She had to trust him.

He did stay close, by his lights. He rode with the queen's company or not far behind it, mostly. Sometimes she saw him farther back with the king's suite. His old companions in disputation were most of them impervious to the mutterings of common soldiers. If they mistrusted him, they reckoned themselves safe enough; nor, unless he was even more devious than the run of Byzantines, could he foment treachery while he debated the mystery of the Trinity.

In Richildis' mind, the opposite too applied: no one would threaten him with stone or steel while he rode with the king's councillors. Words were only wind, even the most bitter of them—and there were many, as the march stretched down to the sea.

They came at last over mountain and plain to the city of Attalia, stone-walled sea-city full of hated Byzantines. It was a poor city, ill-provisioned; the land about it had been swept bare by marauding Turks.

As if to add insult, the emperor's governor there was a westerner, a man from Italy with a barbarian name: Landolf. He wore the garments of the east, grew his greying fair beard long and affected eastern manners, which only sharpened the Franks' resentment. Nor could he give them the provisions that they needed, though he did his poor best.

If he had been a heavenly angel with a face of light, the French would have detested him for that he was the emperor's servant. This aging ineffectual man with his imperial orders and his squalid little town and his empty storehouses was wonderfully easy to despise. And despise him they did, no more reasonable in their hunger than thwarted children.

It did, it least, divert them from Michael Bryennius. He liked this Landolf no better than they did. "Such a man," he said, "well deserves to be given a barren charge and a poor protectorate."

"Yet now we are in it," Eleanor said as they gathered after a banquet of smoked fish and too well aged cheese. The king was there, playing one of his perpetual games of chess, as if he could lose himself in fancied battles and thus escape this endless wearying war.

They had thought him oblivious, but he looked up from embroiling his queen in a fight that she could not win, to say, "I've had enough of marching. It's forty days to Antioch, they say, and most of it through mountains worse than those we just came over. This is a port; there are ships. I'll order Landolf to transport us by sea."

Eleanor regarded him with incredulous scorn. "In this season? From this godforsaken place? That weakling will never muster enough ships to carry us all."

"He'll find them," Louis said. "God will make sure of it."

Eleanor rolled her eyes. Louis did not see. He was engrossed in the game again, making it more difficult than ever for his opponent to lose.

Louis did as he had said. He summoned Landolf to him and laid down his command. Landolf gasped and sputtered and failed to say anything of use; but he agreed, in return for a price that made the king's chancellor blanch, to do as the king desired. Louis went away well pleased. Eleanor shook her head and meticulously said nothing.

Ships, as Landolf said, could not be conjured up in a night. They waited, hungry and cold and buffeted by storms off the sea. And, inevitably, a horde of Turks that swept down on them where they camped outside the walls.

No Byzantine force came to their aid. The city, seeing the assault, slammed shut its gates. They fought alone, were wounded and died alone, with the city's walls blank and heedless at their backs.

"We are not alone," Louis declared. "God is with us." But few of them had his faith. They would much have preferred a company of archers.

That battle they won, or at least failed to lose. The queen and her ladies were never touched at all; lay safe within the camp, with those who had weapons keeping them close to hand. But the army held off the enemy, drove them back from the edges and from the horselines and the baggage-wagons. A wagon or two went to the torch, but they lost little. Only blood and lives, and any trust they might have had in their Byzantine allies.

Michael Bryennius had nothing to say. He had fought among the rest, nor seen any incongruity, since these enemies were Turks; but once the Turks were driven back, the French scowled and drew away when he passed by. It was as if his aid was an ill thing, because there was only one of him and not an army's worth.

He came back to the tent that night unwounded but very tired, and with bloody hands. That was not like him. Richildis had water heated and brought in, and bathed him as she could, as he would allow. He did not resist, but neither did he help her. The spirit seemed to have gone out of him.

When he was clean, dried as much as he might be in the brazier's warmth, she took his face in her hands and made him lift it. His eyes were tired. There was no death in them, nothing broken.

She had not known she was holding her breath till it rushed out of her. She said not what she had meant to say but, "Do you want to leave? Shall we find our own way home?"

"I don't think there's any better way than this," he said.

"God help us, then," said Richildis.

The corner of his mouth twitched faintly. "Here we are in God's army, fighting God's war. How much more help can we expect?"

"A caravan would be convenient," she said, as wry as he.

"Not in this season." He sighed, yawned, shook himself. "We all pay for our sins. Mine was pride—and surety that a French army was more likely to come quickly to Jerusalem than a Greek caravan."

"We didn't know this king," said Richildis. "God forgive me, but the man is an idiot."

"Not really," he said, rather surprising her. "Pious, weak-willed, maladroit with the ladies—all of those, yes. And no great example of a king. But he's not feeble-witted."

"Does it matter if he's a master of philosophy, if he can't command his own army?"

"No," he admitted.

She let her knees give way till she sat at his feet, head on his knee, arms about his middle. The warmth of him was sweet, sweeter than the brazier. "You can blame me," she said. "I thought of this. I got us into it—I attracted the queen's curiosity."

"I agreed to it," he said. "I'm as much at fault as you."

"Then what do we do?" she asked. "If you die—how will I live?"

"As you always have," he said. "We'll come alive to Jerusalem. God will see to it."

She pulled away in sudden temper. "You're as much an idiot as the king."

"But I am," he said, "a better player at chess."

"A child could lay claim to that," said Richildis; but her temper had faded. She sighed, eased, let herself sink back against him. This time his arms went about her. Warm within them, then at last she rested.

But there are too few."

King Louis contemplated the fleet of ships that lay in the harbor of Attalia. They were a motley lot, of every size from fishing-boat to lumbering barge to a handful of horse-transports wallowing in the swell. There were not enough, not by half, to carry the whole of the army; and it was not a simple ferry-run but a sea-voyage that Louis had in mind, all the way to Antioch.

Landolf the imperial governor spread his hands at the king's words, sighed and said, "Majesty, these are all I could find. I scraped every port and harbor and village in all this coast of Caramania. These are as many as will sail in the season of storms; as many as *can* sail. There are no more."

"Surely you can find more?" Eleanor asked coldly.

The governor bowed low, lower than was strictly necessary; but he had learned to fear the queen far more than her gentle half-monk of a king. "Lady, majesty, there are none to be found."

"There would be more than enough in Constantinople," she said.

"Surely, lady," said Landolf, "but it would be days, weeks, before they could come. Do you wish to tarry here so long? We cannot feed you, lady. We are even poorer in provisions than in ships."

Since that was manifestly true, she subsided, though not without a last, terrible frown in his direction. It shriveled him admirably but conjured no more ships, nor better weather for them to sail in.

All choices now, it seemed, were ill. Louis could think of nothing better to do than fill the ships as he could. They were enough for his own household and the queen's, and for a closely-crowded small army of knights and mounted men, with their horses packed together on the transports, too tight to move.

The rest must stay behind. The Counts of Flanders and of Bourbon commanded them, grim-faced men whom Richildis vaguely remembered singing in sunlight and quaffing wine by night, so long ago that it might have been another lifetime. They were all changed now, darkened and soured by this endless and fruitless march. And now this: a choice made in necessity, the army divided yet again, and half of it compelled to make its way as it could. Landolf offered them a weak consolation: "There may be more ships," he said, "from farther away. If you will wait a little longer . . ."

There was little that they could do but agree. "We'll send ours back," Louis promised them, "as soon as we come to land. We'll meet again, God will make sure of it. Look for me in Jerusalem."

With that promise, such as it was, he embarked on the most presentable of the ships, raised his banner and turned his face toward the sea—toward the Holy City that was his dream and his destination. Others, less resolute, looked back as they crawled out of the harbor under oar and sail. No one cheered their departing. The line of those left behind stood mute along the shore. The wind tugged at cloaks and banners, faded both, tattered and worn; and lucky they were to have so much. One sound only floated across the water as the king's ship came to the harbor's mouth: the long, mournful bray of a mule.

It was dreadfully apt, and yet no one laughed. Perhaps no one dared. Louis did not admit to hearing it. He was rapt in the glory of his Crusade, blind and deaf to follies and failings. God would provide, he would say if anyone taxed him with the broken state of his army. God would always provide.

Richildis and her husband sailed with the queen. They had boarded quietly, and deliberately so. The glances shot at Michael Bryennius had been ugly; she had feared that he would be stopped, that he would not be suffered to set foot on the ship. But no one stood in his path. No one spoke to him. No stones flew. No one spat at his feet. All those things she saw in the eyes of men they passed, but in the queen's presence no one ventured to fulfill them.

It was an uneasy crossing. None of them, except perhaps the king, could forget the army they had left behind. Nor could any ever forget why it had been left; how little aid they had had from the Byzantine emperor's governor in Attalia. Michael Bryennius, lone Byzantine in their midst, speaking in no one's name but his own, reminded them inescapably of all that they had suffered. He gave them a target: a shape for their blame.

He had the books that had come with him from the City, close-wrapped in oiled leather and kept scrupulously safe. He kept to a corner of the deck when the weather was fair, rather incidentally within the compass of the queen's guards. At night and in foul weather he shared the reeking closeness of the cabin. Then Richildis was his guard and his defender.

"Are you afraid?" she asked him one night, whispering in his ear as they rocked on a long swell.

They could converse if they were discreet about it, protected by the very closeness of bodies heaped on bodies, the creak of the ship, slap of water, song of wind in the rigging. One learned in this world to be alone in multitudes, to pitch one's voice to carry no farther than the ear that was closest.

His breath tickled her cheek. "I'm not afraid," he said. "Why should I be?"

"Can't you taste the hate?"

He shrugged: a shift of shoulders against her. She settled a little more comfortably in the circle of his arms. "There's always hate."

"Someone could drop you over the side."

"And what purpose would that serve? Hate is a public thing. They'd hang me from the yards if they could. But they never will."

"Can you be sure of that?"

"Nothing in this life is certain."

"Except death."

"Not here," he said, "unless we all go down together." He kissed her temple, let the kiss wander down to her lips. There it paused a while; but it went no farther. Not with half a dozen bodies pressed up against them, and not all of them asleep, either.

"I'm safe enough," he said. "They don't want me dead. It's too convenient to despise me."

"You bear it so well," she said.

He laughed, with a catch of pain. "There's nothing to bear. It's aimed at nothing I did. I'm convenient, no more. If the emperor were here—now him they would joyfully rend asunder."

"Pray God they don't decide that you will do instead." She buried her face in the hollow of his shoulder, breathing in the warm familiar scent of him. "You may not be afraid. I am. I don't even know why. We've been in danger more times than I can count. Maybe too many? This is no worse than the Turks' attack on Attalia."

"This is worse," he said. "Pirates could take us—but it's not likely. We're out of the empire; we're sailing toward Outremer. We're going back to a war. God knows how that will end."

"Ah," she said, dismissing it. "War. I've lived with war every moment of my life."

"But not with war that could kill us—all three of us."

She went rigid. "You can't know that!"

"Crushed together on a ship, living as close as seeds in a pomegranate—I can know. I know you."

She had to stop, to breathe. It was hard. She was not even sure herself, or had not been till they took ship and there was no escaping it. Her courses were late. Her stomach, which had never been discommoded by any voyage, was desperately uneasy. Her breasts were tender, her moods inclined to shift as suddenly as wind in the sails.

"I am," she said, "upwards of forty years old. I should be too old for this. I thought—"

"Yes," he said. "You thought that it was ended; that there would be no more. But as long as a woman's blood flows with the moon, and yours shows no sign of stopping . . ."

"Except that it has." She laughed, but not for mirth. "This was not supposed to happen."

"These brave warriors would tell you that God wills it."

"Ah," she said. "God. Sometimes I wonder if He cares about us at all. If I'm meant to birth a baby on a battlefield."

"If He loves you," said Michael Bryennius, "you'll bear our child in your own country, safe in our castle at Mount Ghazal."

"And if not . . ." She silenced him before he could speak. "No, I won't say it. There's my fear. There's my silliness. Only promise me. Promise that you'll be alive to see this baby born."

"If you'll promise the same to me."

She nodded against his breast. It was enough. He tightened his grip, holding her as if with his arms alone he could drive off all fear, all dread of death and worse.

he King of the French left Attalia in the dark of the year, after a grim and embattled winter. Half his army was left behind to find what transport it could. The half that came with him had not even shoes for their feet; they were ragged, filthy, frostbitten and winter-weary.

Yet as they passed the isle of Cyprus, the winter seemed to melt away. Soft breezes blew toward them from the distant shore, fragrant with flowers. They had sailed out of winter and into spring, the brief and dazzling spring of Outremer. It seemed most apt that they should become aware of it in sight of Venus' isle, where the goddess of love had been born of the foam, long before the Lord Christ came into the world.

They came to land in the harbor of St. Symeon, not far from Antioch. Here at last after the cold welcome of Byzantium, its bare tolerance and grudging charity, they were met with high and singing joy. The Crusade had come to the Holy Land. Edessa's fall would be avenged, the infidel driven back. All that they had waited for would come to pass.

It seemed to matter little that the glory of Crusade was a battered remnant of an army crowded onto an insufficient fleet of ships. What splendor they had was sadly faded; but the sun of Syria made it bright again.

Prince Raymond himself rode down from Antioch, having seen their sails upon the sea. He had brought wonders, gifts that in Attalia they would have killed for: fresh garments, new bread and wine and yellow cheeses for them to dine on before their journey to the city. He had even brought horses to spare their poor rail-thin beasts, fine fiery horses of Arabia, and a snow-white mare for the queen who was his brother's daughter.

Uncle he might be, and sufficiently her elder, but he had kept the beauty of form and face that had served him so well a dozen years ago. He had come then to wed the Princess of Antioch—not the mother who had expected it, but the daughter who was the heir of the realm. Constance had been a child then, a maid of nine summers. She was now a woman, a tall slender golden creature with, Richildis could not help thinking, the tongue of an adder. Time had not softened it, nor had age made it sweeter. She was still a dreadful child.

But Raymond too had changed little. He was as charming as ever, with his ready smile and his open affection for the lady who was, as he professed, his favorite niece. Richildis had not known that Eleanor could simper, yet there was no other word for it. He flattered her shamelessly; she blushed like a girl. One could see then the young countess who had given herself in marriage to a king: lovely in her awk-wardness, like a highbred filly.

Louis, alack, suffered greatly beside the silken luster of the prince. He would wear nothing but the pilgrim's robe that he had worn since the Crusade began, nor bathe nor rest nor make himself presentable until he had prayed in the basilica of Antioch. He was oblivious to the banners, the carpets of flowers, the music and song that accompanied them from the harbor. Even Raymond seemed barely to impinge upon his consciousness. He was rapt in a vision of holiness.

And if he was so lost already, how would he be in Jerusalem, which was the heart of the world?

Eleanor perhaps was the wisest of them. She ignored him. She rode on the white mare beside the prince on his blood-bay stallion, laughing, joining in the song that his minstrels sang. His father, her grandfather, had written it in the spring of a year now long ago, as fair a spring then as they saw now all about them.

Never was this harsh country so beautiful as it was in this season. They rode up the river Orontes through the green valley starred with flowers, scarlet and purple and gold and white. The river rolled round the towers of Antioch, the proud and ancient city on the mountain's knees. It was all laid open to them, towers and palaces, markets and bazaars, gardens and paradises, tangled together in a profusion of centuries. Not even Constantinople was so rich in the ages, nor Rome that was half glory and half ruin. The Franks' hand was light upon it, its people much as they had been since the walls were new-built.

To Louis it was a pilgrim's joy, a queen of holy places. To Eleanor it was grandeur and delight, luxury such as she had dreamed of on that long grim march into Asia, and the pleasure of her kinsman's company only a little diminished by the presence of his wife. Eleanor bloomed in this place like a rose of Damascus, all her winter grimness scoured away. She had never been so gay or so beautiful, so very much the Flower of Aquitaine.

Richildis could have left at any time, taken her baggage—what there was of it— and her husband and gone home at last. Yet like King Louis she seemed possessed of a golden lassitude, a springtide laziness that persuaded her to tarry while the days wore away. They had suffered much, all of them, to come to this sunlit place. Suffering lay ahead of them, the war that had brought them here. Why should they not rest before they rode again to battle?

She, too. Childbirth was battle such as no man ever knew, down into the jaws of death to bring forth life. It was too early yet for that, but if she was to bear this child alive, she needed what rest she could find.

Her husband agreed wholeheartedly. He had no such urgency as simmered in her, to be again in Mount Ghazal and preparing it for the rigors of the Crusade. His affairs in Constantinople and in Jerusalem were either well in hand or out of his hands altogether. Some small business he did transact here, with allies such as he seemed to have in every city of the east. It had to do with gold, or with a caravan of spices. It gave them a house of their own, small but very pleasant, with servants and a cook and a lovely garden. One day as she sat under the rose-arbor in the dizzying scent of blooms, he brought her a gift of cinnamon and cloves and pepper, fragrant and pungent, to delight the nose and the tongue.

As she sat drinking in the mingled scents of roses and spices, her eyes sharpened upon him. He looked faintly frayed, a little more ruffled than wind and sun would account for. "Was there trouble?" she asked him.

His brows lifted. "Why do you ask that?"

"You never were a good liar," she said. "What was it? Footpads?"

She watched him consider assenting, recognize the lie, sigh and shrug and say, "French. They still haven't forgiven Byzantium for what they call its treachery."

"I call it grudging charity, myself," she said.

"More grudge than charity, they would say." He stretched, winced as if at a bruise.

"They struck you," she said, half in anger, half in anxiety.

"Not hard enough to matter," he said, "and there was a convenient passage of the prince's guard. Their captain owes me a debt or two."

"Gold?"

"Life. I found a doctor for his son, when the boy was dying of a fever."

"That's rather like you," she said after a pause.

He shrugged again. One shoulder did not rise as high as the other. She reached too quickly for him to evade her, caught him and tripped him and got his coat off, while he laughed and protested and sounded remarkably like a virgin bride. She said as much to him. He fell silent, affronted.

He was not wounded—not pierced by a blade. But whoever had beaten him had made an excellent beginning before the prince's guards stopped him. A little higher and his shoulder would have been broken. A little lower and he might not have been much inclined to beget another child.

"Hereafter," Richildis said as she tended him, "when you go out, you go guarded."

"I should hate that," he said.

"You should be dead, too," she said tartly. "Find yourself a strong young French-man to stand in your shadow, or a stray German if any's to be found: someone who will be sufficiently grateful for the wages you can pay, that he doesn't care that you're a filthy Greek."

"I am cleaner in my person than any of them has ever been," he muttered. But he stopped her before she could speak. "Yes, yes, I know. A proper hulking ox of an Angevin would do very well, if one's to be found. Or a Norman. Could I tame a wild Norman, do you think?"

"You tamed me," said Richildis.

"Ah, but you're only an Angevin." He kissed her, and seemed glad that she smiled. "I'm in no great danger, my love. There's enough hereabouts to engross any dog of a Frank, if he's not tempted to exercise his anger on a Byzantine's bones."

"If you take care," she said.

He shrugged. She held her peace. She could only harm her cause if she pressed further.

Indeed he found himself a Norman, a great blue-eyed tawny-haired ox of a youth whose utterances seemed to consist chiefly of monosyllables. He was no simpleton however—those flaxflower eyes were as shrewd as Richildis had ever seen—and he was large enough to deter even the most drunken roisterer. His name was Arnulf.

With Arnulf looming in his shadow, Michael Bryennius went where he pleased and when he pleased, and took no harm that Richildis knew of. She could rest for knowing that he was guarded; and let herself bask in the soft airs of spring.

However gentle the breezes, they could last for but a little while. Then came the furnace-blasts of summer, and the hot tide of war.

Louis in his threadbare robe with his flock of monks and priests and Templars, traveling from shrine to shrine and praying strenuously at each one, was still a king, still a lord of the Crusade. He troubled himself now and then to remember that, nor would Raymond suffer him to forget it. Louis, when pressed, reminded them all that the rest of his army had only begun to come over the sea, that he could do nothing till they were all gathered together again.

Raymond was sorely tried for patience. While the Crusade dallied and tarried and frittered itself away in traveling to Outremer, neither Edessa nor Joscelin had ceased to vex the Prince of Antioch. Now, as the army restored itself at Raymond's expense, Raymond discovered in Louis, as he put it to Eleanor in Richildis' hearing, a mewling, canting priest.

He had early taken the measure of Eleanor's feeling for her husband, and did not even pretend apology for what she could only concede was the truth. "He's shocked," Raymond said, pacing the bower that she had arrayed for herself. "*Shocked*, he professes, that we lords of the Lord's country should be so relentlessly mercenary, so mired in feuds and petty dissents. Joscelin and I should be the dearest of friends, the most blessed of Christian allies against the terrible infidel—not at odds as we so appallingly are. Who in the world taught him that Joscelin, fat Joscelin, Joscelin the toad, is a shining knight of God?"

Eleanor sighed, shrugged. "Louis has dreams. He sees visions. This is the Holy Land—how can its defenders be anything but saints?"

Raymond halted in his pacing, so abruptly that the silk of his robe swirled for yet a moment longer, a billow of gold and crimson. "God's feet! This country's crawling with saints and holy fools. But it needs men of the world to defend it— men of action; men of war. Alack for us, some of those are fools, too, and some—like Joscelin—are bloody idiots."

"He's that bad, is he?"

Raymond dropped down at Eleanor's feet. She smiled at him and smoothed a wayward curl of his hair. He smiled back, but absently. "Worse," he said. "He lost Edessa through his own fecklessness, then lost it again when he could easily have won it back. Now he's squatting in Turbessel, snarling at the infidel and leaving my borders wide open. An army from the west, suitably rested and refreshed, with such weapons and strength as it can bring to bear . . ."

"Yes," said Eleanor. "You've said." She made it sound more sweet than impatient.

"So I have," he said, unruffled. "His majesty has no desire to hear it. Jerusalem, he says. Jerusalem calls him. To what? To prayer? This Crusade began because of Joscelin—because he let Edessa fall. The sooner he is dealt with, the better."

"The better for whom?" she asked. "For the Crusade? Or for you?"

"If I am Antioch," he said, "that is nearest to Edessa, and next to fall if the infidel comes so far—yes, for me. Jerusalem is far away. I am here, and the enemy breathes down my neck."

"Jerusalem is all my husband dreams of," Eleanor said.

"Let him dream of it," said Raymond, "but let him lead his army to the aid of Antioch."

"Jerusalem has troubles of its own," Eleanor said after a pause. "It may have other uses for the Crusade."

"What other uses can there be? Edessa is fallen. We must win it back. The first step, the essential step, is to destroy the strength of the infidels. And who is strongest among them now? Who but the one who calls himself Nur al-Din. He lairs for the moment in Aleppo. If we can lure him out—if we can take him now, before he grows stronger—"

She petted him as if he had been one of his hounds. "There. There now. It matters so much to you who live in the middle of it. But we come from far away. We see differently. What's so obvious to you . . . to us it's all confusion. Crusade is more than a war over borders, or even the fall of a city."

"You parrot your husband well," he said.

"You sound like a sulky boy," she said. "Come, kinsman. Smile at me. Forget your troubles for yet a while. It's spring; it's glorious. Come ride in the meadows with me."

He let her draw him up, laugh him out of his sulks, carry him away amid the lilies of the field.

The lilies of the field neither toiled nor spun, but play they did, laughing like children. Louis in his dour devotions might well have failed to see, but others of his army were not so oblivious. They spoke aloud what everyone was whispering: that Prince Raymond and the queen were rather more familiar with one another than close kin might be expected to be.

Louis would not hear it. Quarrel though he might, and bitterly, with a queen whose whole life was the world and everything in it, and who cared little for the life of the soul; but he would hear no ill word of her. "He is her uncle," he said. "These southerners—their blood is hot. It craves a familiarity that in us cold northerners would be excessive. But in them it's mere affection."

"Such affection," his counsellors muttered: "lying in a bed of flowers, wrapped in one another's arms."

Louis would not listen. He saw what they let him see: a southern warmth to be sure, but never more than propriety would allow.

Princess Constance, rather to Richildis' amazement, was equally unwilling to give credence to the rumor. She was as besotted with her husband as Louis appeared to be with his wife. She would hear no ill of him, nor do aught but excuse him, even when he slighted her in the company of the lords of Antioch. He set the Queen of France on his right hand and relegated his princess, the rightful ruler of the princedom, farther down at table or in hall. He conducted himself as if she were nothing to him, although without her he would have held little rank and less precedence.

Richildis, married young to a man for whom she cared little, had some understanding of these noble necessities, but she had long since lost the custom of it. From the blessed sanctuary of a second marriage, a marriage made chiefly for herself, she saw in this nothing of beauty, and much that was to be pitied.

One did what one must. That was wisdom as old as Antioch, as young as the princess who sat alone and forsaken while her prince paid court to the Queen of France.

pring was brief in Outremer, and summer unrelentingly long. On the threshold of it, a messenger came up from Jerusalem under the royal banner. Queen Melisende summoned the King and Queen of France to a gathering of the High Court in Acre.

She had honored them greatly in her choice of messenger. It was no less than the Patriarch of Jerusalem himself, bringing word of more than the council. Conrad of the Germans had come to Outremer at last, healed of his sickness and bringing great gifts and goodwill from the Emperor of the Byzantines.

Louis sat bolt upright at that, startling those who were familiar with his languor in council and at the time of audience. "Conrad? Conrad is in Jerusalem? How could he be? He's far behind me."

"You tarried," Eleanor said a little too sweetly. "All the army is here at last. You could have been in Jerusalem a week and more ago."

For once he did not seize the invitation to quarrel. "I shall come there as soon as I may," he said.

"But first, majesty," said the Patriarch of Jerusalem, "if you will, see fit to attend the queen's council in Acre. Much will be decided there with regard to the Crusade."

Louis nodded, less crisply than before, but still as one who listens to what is said to him. "I shall go," he said. "If Jerusalem calls, who am I to refuse?"

"You may go," Eleanor said after the feast was over and the Patriarch had been escorted to his rest. She had retired to the solar behind the hall, to sip wine with those who were not minded yet to sleep. Louis might not have accompanied her, but she had asked and he had not seen fit to decline.

Raymond was there, too, and Princess Constance with her ladies. It was a pleasant gathering of kin, the ladies with their needlework, the men setting the board for chess but pausing for conversation, and a singer and a luteplayer and a player on the Greek pipes making sweet music beneath the sound of their voices.

Eleanor however was in no greatly pleasant mood. "You may go," she said to her husband as the singer sang of love lost and never to be found again. "I shall remain here."

Louis looked up from the chessboard with its squares of ebony and silver. He had a silver king in his hand, accoutered like a Saracen sultan. "You can't stay," he said. "The summons was sent to both of us. Queen Melisende will be wanting to meet her sister queen."

"I'll meet her in my own time," Eleanor said, "and in my own person."

"Your person is that of the Queen of France," Louis said stiffly. It was meant to be dignity, perhaps. It only sounded petulant.

Eleanor looked long at him. The force of her glance laid him bare to anyone else who felt it. He had no kingly beauty, no stately grace. He was not even clean. His hair hung lank on his narrow skull. His beard was ragged. Neither his robe nor his body had been washed in time out of mind.

He was a saintly man and an anointed king. But beside her bathed and scented elegance he seemed no more lovely than a beggar on a dungheap.

Richildis caught herself wondering what it must be like for Eleanor to suffer this man's embraces. Rank scent, vermin most certainly, and no art or delicacy—she shuddered.

Eleanor lidded her terrible eyes. "If to be Queen of France is to be your wife," she said, "then I have no desire to continue in that office."

The silence was absolute. Even Raymond seemed stunned, or he feigned it well. Louis blinked slowly. "You don't want to be queen?"

"I don't want to be your wife," she said.

"But God has joined us," he said. "We can't be divided."

She showed a delicate gleam of teeth. "Can't we? You remember Bernard, that horrible man, so full of God's righteousness that he has no room for mere charity. Didn't he condemn our marriage? Didn't he thunder at the pope to dissolve it on grounds of our too-close kinship? The pope will listen if we remind him. How can he not?"

"We are not," said Louis, "as closely related as that."

"What!" she cried in mock horror. "You gainsay the great Bernard, the mighty saint of Clairvaux?"

Louis shook his head. He had never been a match for her in temper, still less in wit, and too well he must know it. "Lady," he said as if with great patience, "the Queen of France cannot refuse to be married to its king. It isn't done."

"I'm doing it," Eleanor said. "You go, play court to the queen who keeps her grown son on a leash like a faithful dog. I'll stay here. The petition can go to Rome with the next packet of letters for his holiness. A few months, a season—it's done. The marriage is annulled. I'm free to go where I will."

"And what will you do," Louis asked her, "while you linger here? Will milord prince ask to dissolve his marriage, too?"

That was a shrewd blow, shrewder than anyone might have expected of that unworldly king. Eleanor barely blanched at it, nor turned her glance on Raymond, who sat still, watching, saying nothing. "My uncle has kindly offered me his patronage," Eleanor said.

"And his bed? Lady, has he offered you that?"

No one dared gasp. Eleanor laughed, sweet and cruel. "Oh! A sin, a palpable sin: a lustful thought. Quickly, confess it, or it stains your soul forever."

"The sin is not mine," he said, too low almost to hear.

"Oh, no!" she cried. "No, never yours. And no son to show for it, either."

"I did my duty," he said stiffly.

"Yes, once a year, on a day grudgingly approved by your priests, with prayers before and prayers during and penance after, and such a holy loathing in the doing of it that I'm amazed you managed it at all." Eleanor tossed her head, reckless as a highbred mare, and galloping on like one, too. "I am a woman, sir. A creature of flesh and blood. I am not a vile thing to be approached with shrinking and disgust, nor a pure spirit to be worshipped from afar. I am body and soul, flesh and spirit, and I am sick unto death of being married to a canting monk."

She stopped for breath, drawing it in sharply as if it were edged with pain. Such words, such vehemence, had the force of years behind them, pent up till it must escape or shatter the one who spoke them. Even those who, like Richildis, had known how little affection Eleanor had for her husband, were shocked to hear her speak so.

"Lady," Louis said, somewhat breathless himself. "Lady, you are distraught. The rigors of Crusade, the temptations of this city, the lure of eastern luxury—"

Eleanor smote her hands together with such force that he jumped. "Stop that!" she cried to him. "Just stop that! I am not distraught. I am full to the brim with your cursed piety. Go find yourself a nun, a saint, someone as cold to the things of this world as you are yourself. Set me free. Give me back the sun and the warmth and the sweet air of my own country."

"What, not the sweet air of Antioch?" Louis did not believe her, Richildis thought. He reckoned that her southern blood ran hotter even than usual; that she was gone wild with it, incited perhaps by her rake of an uncle, but that in the end he could persuade her to see reason. "Lady, I cannot set you free, as you put it. We are joined together by God and by the vows that we swore before the Church and the people of France."

"Rome can dissolve any such vow," said Eleanor. "It's as simple as a pair of accusations: that we are kin within the forbidden degree, and that I've borne you no son."

Louis' eyes glittered. "Accusations? Accusations, you say? Why don't you go even further? Why not ask me to condemn you for adultery?"

"Aha!" said Eleanor in open glee. "So you aren't as calm about this as you pretend. Of course you won't divorce me as an adulteress. You have no proof. You'll find none. And if you try . . . why, here's a prince of the Holy Land himself, lord and master of Antioch, willing to swear that I am as pure as a nun in the cloister."

"Some cloisters," muttered Louis, "are in sore need of discipline."

"Not mine," said Eleanor. "Nor shall I remain yours. I'll be free of you, my lord— if not sooner, then later. You'll never prevail against me."

He set his brows together. He looked remarkably stubborn, and hardly weedy at all. One remembered then that he was the heir of strong kings, descended from Hugh Capet himself. "I will not divorce you," he said, "nor see this marriage annulled. You will come with me to Acre, and thereafter to Jerusalem. We will present a face of amity to the High Court and the queen and the young king."

"No," said Eleanor.

Louis rose. Oh, indeed: his temper was up. He had forgotten perhaps that he was by nature and inclination a mild, saintly man. "Guards," he said.

The men who stood along the walls and kept watch on the door, the unvarying shadows of every kingly gathering, advanced at the king's word. Eleanor regarded them without fear, perhaps without comprehension. "I will not go with you," she said to the king.

"Messires," Louis said to his guards, "take her majesty into your care. See that she goes nowhere, does nothing but by my leave. In the morning we depart for Acre."

"But—" someone ventured to protest. "How can we—the whole army—we can't leave so soon!"

"We can," Louis said, "and we will. And her majesty comes with us. Madam, you may ride under your own power or you may be carried like a prisoner. You have but to choose."

Eleanor folded her arms and made herself immovable. "I am staying in Antioch."

Louis nodded to the guards. They looked a little startled, but willing enough. Quietly, firmly, and quite irresistibly, they lifted her up and carried her away to her chamber.

Raymond had sat by in silence while king and queen conducted their quarrel. But after she was gone, when the echoes of her guards' booted feet had died away, he rose. He who had been so affable, so kindly, so unstinting in his generosity, said to his royal guest, "Get out."

Louis regarded him in puzzlement. "Sir? I beg your pardon; she is your kinswoman, after all. But I am her husband."

Raymond's lips curved. It was not a smile. His teeth were bared. "Get out of my city."

"In the morning," Louis said, "we certainly shall. Until then, my lord—"

"Now," said Raymond. And when Louis did not stir, in a great bull-bellow: "Now!"

Louis scrambled up, backing away in haste and confusion. Raymond pursued him. The amiable face, the charming smile, was gone. He was crimson, suffused with rage—and Louis perhaps remembered too late that prince's reputation: affable, yes, but terrible in wrath.

Louis was feckless and given to dallying when he should move in haste, but he was not a perfect fool. He chose the wiser part. He turned tail and ran.

What war, famine, even the vows of Crusade had failed to do, Eleanor had done with her shocking display of intransigence, and Raymond in his rage had completed. Louis the gentle, Louis the monk, Louis the endless ditherer, had roused at last to a kingly resolve. He forsook his lassitude; he flung his army into motion. He swept them all out of the enveloping comforts of Antioch and set them on the road to Acre. He did it that very night, under the moon's white and startled face—impelled by fear and by the half-bared steel of Prince Raymond's guards. Raymond himself stood at their head, as if he had been the angel of Paradise with flaming sword.

Louis was driven out by steel-edged force. He was not, for all of that, too blind a coward to take care for the wife whom God and the Church had given him. He doubled and trebled the guard about her lest her uncle venture a rescue, a guard that held to its duty long after they were gone down the long road from Antioch. She could do nothing without their presence, not the slightest intimate thing.

Not even her ladies could pass that wall of guards. She had not been permitted to bid farewell to her uncle, nor allowed to pause as she was half-led, half-carried out past the swords and spears of his guards. Raymond would not go to Acre, would not answer the queen's summons. He would guard his own country against both Christian and Saracen, Joscelin and the emperor of the Byzantines and the hordes of Islam. He had cast out the French, driven forth their king. All alliances were broken, all friendships ended.

It was ill done; nor would it end, Richildis thought, with this swift and headlong retreat. They would all pay for this that they had done tonight.

The French army marched in surprisingly good order considering the lateness of the hour and the haste with which they had gathered themselves and their belongings and taken to the road. Louis was not such a precipitous fool as he might have seemed. His men had been ready to depart for some days before he roused them from their beds. If they were shocked by the summons, if they regretted the comforts that they had left behind, they were too eager for those of Acre to mourn overmuch. "And then," they said to one another in a long sigh of wonder, "Jerusalem."

Eleanor, locked in living walls by day, still needed womanly attendance at night. Louis permitted only two to wait on her: a servant of mature years and massive probity, and, rather oddly, Richildis. She might have thought that her Byzantine husband would remove her from any such consideration, but Louis did not think in such a fashion. "You are married to a schismatic," he said to her, "but your virtue is never questioned, nor is any ill word spoken of you. I pray that you may teach her by example."

If Richildis had been as reckless as Eleanor, she would have inquired, "What, to find a foreigner to wed and bed her?"

But she was too circumspect. She bowed low as was fitting, took her leave, went to wait on the queen.

Eleanor was surprisingly unruffled by her captivity. She did not rage at it, nor did she waste her substance in dreaming of escape.

No; Eleanor was not distraught. Eleanor was coldly, whitely, unrelentingly furious. So furious that she indulged in no fits of temper. She smiled, she laughed, she jested with her guards. She greeted Richildis with every evidence of honest pleasure. She demanded nothing, insisted on nothing. But her eyes were glittering, and she carried herself very erect, very still. There was a shimmer on her like the quiver of heat above a field of white sand.

Richildis waited on her in silence, assisting her with her toilet, clothing her in a warm robe against the night chill, combing out her beautiful hair. It had been washed in the morning and scented with sandalwood. It poured like silk through Richildis' fingers.

"Go on," Eleanor said abruptly. "Ask."

Richildis raised her brows in honest surprise. "Lady?"

Eleanor shot her a glance over a silk-clad shoulder. "Don't feign innocence with me. You want to know what everyone wants to know. Did I or did I not commit adultery with Raymond of Antioch?"

"No," said Richildis, though it might not have been strictly politic. "I don't want to know any such thing. Or care to, either."

"Of course you do," Eleanor snapped. "Everybody does."

"I don't," Richildis said mildly. "It's not any concern of mine."

Eleanor scowled. The expression did not become her: it made her face seem thin and severe. "Did he tell you to say that?"

"Lady," Richildis said after a pause to draw breath, to consider her words, "whether you committed incest and adultery or whether you are a pure and shining innocent, it makes no difference to me. What I would rather ask is why. Why do you want to give up the queenship of France?"

Eleanor eased visibly. So, less obviously as she hoped, did Richildis. Eleanor was craving someone to talk to, someone to ask her questions that she could answer or not, as she chose—a freedom that she might cherish in this her captivity. Richildis would not ask about Raymond; truly did not want to know. But the rest . . .

"Do you understand," Eleanor asked her, "what it is to be the Queen of France?"

"Dimly," Richildis said. "But you never seemed ill suited to it. I'd have said that you were born to be a queen."

"That well may be," said Eleanor, "but to be a queen in this age of the world, one must be mated with a king. I do not wish to be mated to the King of France."

"Not even to be queen?"

"There are other kings in the world," Eleanor said. "One of them surely will be pleasanter to the eye and nose than Louis the Monk."

"And yet," said Richildis, "when you accepted him as your husband, you accepted vows and honor and duties. You swore to uphold them till your death or his."

"I was a child," Eleanor said. "I never understood what I was promising. And he was cleaner then."

"Is it so simple for you?" Richildis asked. "Does nothing matter but your own pleasure?"

"He has often asked me the same question," Eleanor said without evident offense. "I am not a great saint and to be sure I am a terrible sinner, but a fool I am not. I have given him no son. Daughters are never enough, and he's not likely to get more of me. If I don't take my leave, his barons will urge him to put me aside, to use the pretext I gave him, that the so-saintly Bernard raised against us these long years past. France needs a prince, after all." She stretched like a cat, long and luxurious. "I want to be the one to walk away. Not to be discarded like a useless thing because it was my duty to produce an heir, and I failed in it."

"Louis would not allow that," Richildis said. "The Lord Christ said—"

"Louis is pious to the point of idiocy," Eleanor said with a spark of impatience, "but he is also a king of a line of kings. He would never propose such a thing himself. But if the barons of France urged it on him—after they had been persuaded to see the necessity of it—then he would have to give in, yes? A king must do what a king must do."

Richildis shook her head. "The minds of kings are beyond my understanding," she said.

"Are they?" Eleanor asked. "Tell me, my lady. What is it like to marry for love and not for duty or honor or power?"

"I don't think that's anything a queen can do," Richildis said.

"And may she not dream?" Eleanor demanded. "Such a dream I have, though it may never come to pass. Someone young, strong, beautiful—someone who will love me, but not dote on me; who will match me wit for wit and mind for mind; who will—yes, who will give me strong sons to mold into kings. Isn't that a pretty dream, lady? Won't it keep me warm of nights, when my so little beloved husband is late at his prayers, and I lie in my cold and lonely bed?"

Richildis felt herself blushing. Her bed was never cold and certainly never lonely. She had married as a queen could not do, to please herself.

For that matter, who knew? Eleanor was a remarkably strong-willed woman, and remarkably self-willed, too. She might even do what she dreamed of doing.

It was odd and uncomfortable. Must Louis feel so when he dealt with his wife? Or was he too saintly vague to notice, till she had thrust it in his face?

Eleanor sighed and yawned and leaned into Richildis' strokes that brushed her hair to silk and plaited it for the night. If she was aware of the quality of the silence, the chill that had crept into it, she betrayed no sign. She would not care, perhaps. A queen needed to be obeyed, to be admired, to be worshipped. She did not also require that she be loved.

Except, of course, by a prince in a dream.

he King and Queen of the French rode into Acre in grand estate, with banners flying. That the queen had come as a prisoner, that the king had constrained her lest she escape him and her queenship, was not spoken of, not in that assembly of the Crusade. It was all light, all splendor: kings and princes, lords, barons, knights and squires, priests and bishops and archbishops and the Patriarch of Jerusalem who had ridden into the city with the King of France at his side.

For a while they forgot sorrow, and forbore to count the dead and maimed and the great numbers who had never come so far at all. The conjoined armies of the West were still a great force, and the levies of Jerusalem were enough, perhaps, to give the Saracen pause.

So much splendor made Arslan dizzy. He was full in the middle of it, standing as always in Baldwin's shadow. The young king had in turn to bow to his mother's precedence, but she could hardly prevent him from taking his throne or speaking in council. Nor, to be fair to her, did she try. She was secure in her primacy, was Melisende in this eighteenth year of her queenship, the sixth of her regency.

But Arslan was not taking overmuch notice of her. Lady Richildis had come back, and Michael Bryennius with her—and a grand gathering they had had in Helena's house, all of them, even to Helena's Turks and Kutub the armsmaster of Mount Ghazal. The memory of it kept him warm for days after.

Warmer still was another thing, a new thing, new and wonderful.

Arslan was in love.

Lust he knew, as any young man knew it; and liking, and friendship such as he had with Nahar. And of course he loved his mother and his aunt, his father, his milkbrother who had grown into a king. But this was love. Love that he had heard in songs, that pursued him waking and sleeping, that made him forget to eat, that turned him from a man into a stumblefooted boy whenever he stopped to think of her—and that was nearly every moment.

He knew he should not be such a fool. She was older than he and infinitely wiser in the ways of the world. She had no use for a callow boy, still less a boy who was not yet made knight. Was she not a queen?

Even her name was beautiful. Alienor—Eleanor. He caught himself singing it when he was alone.

He was making a complete fool of himself, and he did not even care.

Of course he knew what Lady Richildis thought of her. Lady Richildis had traveled with her, waited on her, come to know her well, and did not like her at all. She was worldly, frivolous, headstrong and sometimes cruel. She cared for little that was not herself. She was not even particularly beautiful, except for her marvelous hair.

It did not matter. He saw her riding into Acre, gleaming in the fierce sun of summer, with her husband a pallid shadow at her side; and he was lost.

She did not know he existed. To her he could be only one of a hundred nameless faces in attendance on the King of Jerusalem. He did not try to gain her notice, nor do more than be near her as much as he might. That was simple enough, since Arslan attended Baldwin, and Baldwin played host to the King and Queen of France. His mother ostensibly concerned herself with the rest of the French and with the German king and his following; but Arslan could well guess the truth.

Melisende did not like Eleanor of France. Not in the least. Not even within the bounds of royal courtesy. They were too much alike, Lady Richildis said. Yet Richildis herself had been Melisende's friend from their youth, and had as little use for Eleanor as Melisende seemed to. There must be something more to it.

Maybe they were jealous of one another. Eleanor was so much younger, so much fresher in her beauty. But Melisende had the sort of face that aged like fine marble, smooth and barely lined, and was more beautiful now by all accounts than she had been as a girl. Or perhaps it was Eleanor's gaiety, her reckless delight in the lighter things of this world, whereas Melisende in these latter years had grown more markedly devout.

Arslan did not know precisely what it was. He only knew that when the queens met under a golden canopy outside the walls of Acre, the air between them grew still and cold. Instant, instinctive, and purely mutual dislike, as if God had ordained that these two ladies, so like in everything that they were, should never know the warmth of amity.

It was difficult. Arslan had been in awe of Melisende since he was a child—had been more than a little in love with her, if he would admit it. She was his king's mother, his benefactor, perhaps even his friend. And he looked on this rival of hers and could not help himself. He was lost to all good sense.

There was no one to whom he could speak of this. No one who would understand. He was not one to sing his passion in any case, nor to make a story of it to tell in the bazaar. He cherished it in himself, secret even from Baldwin his friend.

Acre was not Mount Ghazal, or even Jerusalem that had been Richildis' home for so many years. But it was Outremer, more than Antioch had been. She was home, among faces she knew, voices she remembered, land and climate that rang familiar even after so long away. This heat of summer was much like that to which she had first come from Anjou, this gathering like the one that had greeted Fulk and seen the wedding of Fulk to Melisende.

But these great lords and princes had come not to wed a princess to a man who would be king, but to raise war against the infidel. Crusade: the way of cross and sword.

They held council in the great hall of the palace of Acre, the only place that was large enough to enclose them all. She sat there among the barons in a gown that had come from Byzantium, with her armsmaster from Mount Ghazal, and with her husband.

Michael Bryennius watched the proceedings with interest and a share of amusement. Frankish councils had always fascinated him. "They speak so bluntly," he had said once. "They so seldom consider consequences—even the prelates, who should be more circumspect. They say things that one would never say in front of our emperor."

Certainly a lord of the Franks could speak freely if he chose, and to a king or a queen, too. Richildis could not imagine the constraint required of a Byzantine in royal council, the subtlety, the delicate skirting round the issue at hand.

No one was skirting anything here. They had been in council now for three days, debating what they should do with the Crusade now that it was here in Outremer. All the royalty was gathered on the dais, each under a canopy of gold, with Melisende and Baldwin in the middle: French on their left hands, Germans on the right, and prelates scattered through them like pomegranate-seeds in a sherbet. Queen Eleanor took lively part in the debate: she was in her element. King Louis said little: he would have been happier, it was clear, in the chapter-house of a monastery. Emperor Conrad, well recovered from his illness, listened more than he spoke, but seemed interested enough in the proceedings.

None of the lords from the west, it was apparent, had given any great thought to what they would do when they came to Outremer. The few who had pondered it at all had some expectation of marching to Edessa and taking it back from the infidel. They had been shocked to discover that there was more than one kind of Saracen, and that some were actually allied with the Frankish kingdom—Damascus, for example, which was in great fear of the Turk Nur al-Din; he was lord of Aleppo and would like to be lord of much more than that, and Damascus was a great prize.

Eleanor spoke for Raymond of Antioch through her husband's scowls, little dismayed by those who wished to know where Raymond was, to speak for himself. "He is in Antioch," she said in her forthright way: "in his own city, arming it against the fool and coward in Turbessel, and securing it against the infidel."

"But there's a war we cannot win, do you see?" Melisende said with every appearance of kindness, as an older queen who would enlighten a younger one. It was nicely calculated to raise Eleanor's hackles. "We've already lost it twice. Better we choose a different target. Aleppo, for example. Aleppo supports the most dangerous of the Saracens, the one whom Damascus rightly fears. He'll be king of them all in time, if he's not stopped now."

"We came," Eleanor said coldly, "to avenge the fall of Edessa."

"And so we shall," Baldwin said quickly before his mother could respond. "But Edessa itself is desert and waste. Rather we choose a place that will make us rich, that will wound the enemy deeply in the taking of it, that has great wealth in gold and trade, gardens and orchards; that, if taken, will sunder the two halves of Islam, that of Egypt and that of the east. Let us take Damascus, I say; let us take vengeance for its laughter when we marched with Altuntash against the city, and win atonement for our defeat. Then we can take back Edessa, and half the east as well."

"We cannot take Damascus," Melisende said sharply. "Damascus is our ally."

"My lady mother," Baldwin said with sweetness that he must have cultivated for a long, long while, "alliance mattered little to you when we marched to war with Altuntash. Should it matter any more now?"

"I learned a lesson then," she said. "I'll not unlearn it now. Will you, my lord king?"

He stiffened, but he smiled. "My lady mother, that was simple treachery: aiding a rebel against his rightful lord. This is Crusade. Isn't Damascus the greatest prize of all? Isn't it rich in lands and wealth, well watered, well situated, all such things as a wise king would wish to secure?"

"And," said one of the barons, "it's a war we can all safely fight. If we retake Edessa, after all, who benefits but Joscelin? And if we do as Prince Raymond asks, take Aleppo and secure Antioch, what can we gain from that? We shed blood and tears, he takes all the benefit. Whereas if we take Damascus, none of us gains more than any other. We all take the prize; we divide it fairly."

The gathering stirred at that: murmuring, nodding, quivering a little with greed.

King Louis sat up a little straighter, as if he had roused from a nap. But he spoke clearly enough, and as one who had heard sufficient of what had been said. "Aleppo we know little if at all. What is it to us but a name? But Damascus—" He sighed as if in rapture. "Damascus is a holy city, a city of the Bible, well fit to receive our Crusade. Has it not stood since Noah came down from Ararat? Did not Paul fall blinded on the road to that of all cities, and see the face of the Christ? Shall we not see that light for ourselves, as we march to wrest it from the hands of the infidel?"

His eloquence startled the council. They had not heard him in a holy transport before; had known him only as a man of few words and little wit, dull amid the glitter of his fellow princes.

While they stared, too taken aback to speak, Eleanor said with poisonous sweetness, "Such lovely words, my lord. Such entrancing sentiments. But Damascus is an ally, do you see? Aleppo is the enemy."

"All infidels are the enemy," Louis said.

"It's hardly so simple, cousin," Baldwin said in a tone meant perhaps to soothe them both, "but it is true: this war is God's own. Any who worships Allah is our rightful adversary."

"Then does it matter whom we fight?" Eleanor demanded. "Let's take Aleppo— then if we're still inclined, come back and sweep up Damascus."

"It won't be as simple as that," Melisende said, "but it's not ill thought of withal. Aleppo is the more dangerous, yes, and secures the best advantage."

"But Damascus is richer," Baldwin said, "and its taking more likely to wound the whole of Islam, not simply the *atabeg* in Aleppo."

"The *atabeg* in Aleppo is the strongest prince the Saracens have," said Melisende. "Cut off the head, the body dies. Let him live and he will come to us in Damascus, sweep over us and destroy us."

"And is this not the greatest army that Christendom has ever seen?" Emperor Conrad rose to say it, sweeping his arm over the gathering. "Here is but the head and neck of it, the gathering of its princes—and we strain this hall to bursting. Can Islam muster as many great knights and men-at-arms as we have brought together here?"

"Islam can muster more," Melisende said levelly. "Many, many more. Its well-springs are in this place, rooted in it. Ours are far away in France and Germany and the Low Countries. When one of ours dies, none rises up to take his place. When one of them falls, half a hundred spring up out of the earth. This is their country, my lord. They have advantage of numbers always, and more in reserve, never waning or failing."

"That is counsel of despair," Conrad said: and well he would know it, Richildis thought, after the march from Constantinople. "If we have so little hope, why make the effort at all?"

"Because," she said, "God wills it."

That raised a cheer, with laughter in it, but no agreement. Damascus or Aleppo, Aleppo or Damascus. The barons of the High Court inclined toward Aleppo, except the king, who these days would do whatever his mother did not wish to do. He, with the lords of the West, spoke for Damascus. Its wealth, its ancient name, its position between the two halves of Islam, and certainly the prospect of revenge for the defeat that Jerusalem had suffered in its last campaign against the city, all seemed more easily comprehensible than distant and lesser-known Aleppo.

"After Damascus," Baldwin said, "we can take Aleppo. But if we pass Damascus and march on Aleppo, who's to say that Damascus won't fall on us from behind and betray the alliance of which we are being so careful?"

That swayed a few of those who had stood against him. He pressed harder. "Orchards and vineyards," he said, "and riches from a hundred caravans. Roses, apples of Damascus; fine steel, silks, spices. All ours, all laid in our hands to wield against the infidel."

Sanity and policy showed dull as ash beside the glitter of worldly greed. One by one they fell to it, the barons of Jerusalem. Those who professed to be higher-minded were persuaded, they said, by the prospect of winning Damascus, securing it behind them, then advancing in safety to take Aleppo.

It was very reasonable, perhaps. Still Richildis did not like it. It was ill done to break alliance twice, and with the strongest of the Turks waiting for just such a chance to move on the city that he coveted. Nur al-Din could be no less tempted than the Franks by the beauties of Damascus.

Her voice was faint and thin, and few rose to bolster it. They were all gone over to Baldwin's camp. Even Melisende had fallen silent. Eleanor sat tight-lipped, too proud to protest. Whatever she said would only prove the whispers of her infidelity with the Prince of Antioch. Why else, after all, would she insist on opposing her husband's vote in the council?

It was decided. They were going to take Damascus. Arslan knew again the dizzy anticipation of war: half excitement, half terror.

The women never looked happy when their men went to war—even when it was they who did the sending. And this time it was not. Queen Melisende was much against this course of action, Queen Eleanor too, and Lady Richildis for good measure.

The queens he could elude—one was oblivious to him, the other preoccupied with her son's rebellion. Lady Richildis and Arslan's own mother, however . . .

"Do you believe this is wise?" Richildis demanded of her brother as they dined together in Helena's house. Tomorrow the council would disperse, for a while: the Westerners to Jerusalem where they would look on the Holy Sepulcher and invoke God's blessing on the Crusade; the rest to their own demesnes to gather their levies. They would all meet again at Tiberias beside the Lake of Galilee.

Richildis would go to Mount Ghazal. She would not lead her levies—that she left to Kutub, and to her brother who would lend them his more suitably Christian name and face. It would be rather splendid in Arslan's estimation, to be together again with the men from Mount Ghazal.

Clearly Richildis did not think so. "Do you want to loot Damascus, too? Are you as blind with avarice as the rest of them?"

Bertrand sighed. "What is either wisdom or avarice, when the council of a whole Crusade determines on a thing that it will do?"

"You never said a word," she said.

"And did you?"

She opened her mouth, shut it again.

He grinned, if wearily. "You can see the tide running, too. If they're going to do the worst thing, the ignorant thing, they'll do it. No voice of reason is going to stop them."

"Were we such fools," she asked him, "when we were nobles in Anjou?"

"You, never. I . . ." He took them all in with a sweep of the hand. "Remember how I came here."

"Headlong," she said. "Headstrong. Reckless and endlessly righteous. Knowing nothing of the world here, of its complexities. When did we become easterners, Bertrand?"

Maybe she did not expect an answer. He gave her one nonetheless. "Too long ago to remember," he said. "We can't go back, you know."

"Some do," she said.

"But not we."

She bent her head. She was a little pale, maybe. A little too quiet of a sudden. "I wish," she said after a while, "that I could ride to war. War is so much simpler than this."

"You can, you know," he said. "You can ride with us. Queen Eleanor is going. You can—"

"No," said Richildis.

Bertrand opened his mouth to speak. Helena silenced him with a word. "Bertrand my love, you are a knight of renown and a lord of men, but when it comes to women you're the blindest fool yet born. Can't you see she's going to have a baby?"

Bertrand's expression was beautifully shocked. Arslan supposed he could have missed it, if he was blind and deaf and never looked at his sister at all—and to be sure he said, "So that's why you've been wearing those Byzantine robes instead of decent Frankish gowns. I thought you were trying to set a fashion."

"I was trying," said Richildis, "to be circumspect. It's enough to come back after so long, without coming back to cooing and fluttering and too-frequent inquiries as to my health. I know how old I am. I know what I've been doing that's hardly advisable for a woman in my condition. I'm going to stop doing it. I'm going back to Mount Ghazal, to have my child in peace."

"Not Jerusalem?" Bertrand had recovered his wits with admirable speed. "But surely the royal physicians—"

"I'll have all the care I need in my own place, among my own people." She sounded very sure of it. She looked beautiful, too: amazing in a woman as old as she was. Arslan sighed a little. If he had not been in love with Queen Eleanor—if Lady Richildis had not been his near kin, and halfway his mother besides . . .

She was smiling at her brother the more brightly, the more darkly he frowned. "I'll be well. I promise you. Only promise me the same."

"I'm always well," Bertrand said, half growling it.

"Promise," she said.

He growled a little louder, glared, but she would not let him go as easily as that. "I promise," he said at last.

*W*ill you promise me the same?" Helena asked Bertrand as they lay together in the cool of the night, with the fan whispering over them, plied by a small imp of a servant who could do his duty even in his sleep.

Bertrand was not in the least amused. Women, he thought, were damnably persistent creatures. "I've gone to war a hundred times before, and you've never made me promise anything. Why now?"

She shrugged. Her shoulders were white in the nightlamp's glimmer. She had aged well, had Helena. She was more beautiful now than she had been as a girl: her skin finer, her hair richer, her eyes more wonderfully wide and dark. She had grown in wisdom as in beauty, and that in its turn made her all the more beautiful.

It did not make her any less baffling. "Why are you fretting for me?" he asked. "Are you afraid I've grown too old to fend for myself?"

"Of course not," she said; and she said it firmly, with no quiver of doubt.

"What is it, then? Omen? Foreseeing? Premonition?"

Again she shrugged. "I don't know. I just want to be sure."

That clearly was all she would say. He surrendered; he laid his hands in hers and said, "I promise. I'll do my best to come back unscathed, as God wills it."

She seemed content with that. She lay down and closed her eyes and to all appearances went to sleep. So too, after a while, did Bertrand.

But when he woke, when he had broken his fast and bidden Helena good day—for he would linger in the city for a day or two after the kings had left, since Beausoleil was ready and waiting for the war that he had known would come—he had conceived a thought. He saw the kings ride out, the banners and the trumpets, the bright armor glittering, the men-at-arms in their ranks, the queens each on her fine horse in her fine gown and silken veil that surely she would stop to change out of as soon as she had left the city well behind. They were full of their splendor, their strength and their holy cause. No doubt vexed them, no hesitation now that the choices were all made.

Bertrand stood in the jostle of the crowd for a long while after the armies were gone. He hardly noticed the shift and swirl of people about him, though he was aware, in a dim fashion, that he was standing like a rock in a millrace. He simply braced his feet and made himself huge and stood fast, and the crowd parted to stream past him.

When they were all gone, he went where he had decided to go. His business was brief in the circumstances; but when it was done he had a writ in his purse, copy of the one that resided with a judge of the city. Another would go in its time to the king's chancery.

It was not relief he felt. Calm, rather. At peace, one might say; but he was hardly on his deathbed, nor meant to be for long years yet. He had done something that he should have done long ago. That was all.

Richildis came home to Mount Ghazal, she thought, quietly. But as she rode toward the village with Michael Bryennius and the escort that had built itself somehow on the way from Acre, she saw banners hung from the balconies, garlands of flowers woven round them, and people running to line her path. The men and boys were shouting, the women singing: the sweet eerie song with which they welcomed one of their own returned from a long journey.

Her eyes pricked with tears. Pregnancy made her foolish, but even so, she was moved. Her people—her own people—were glad that she had come back.

The singing followed her up the way to the castle, the men and boys running, the women walking and singing. And in the castle was great welcome also, all the guards and servants, the clerks—and yes, her two maids whom she had left behind, Yasmin and Leila as swollen with child as she was. They were all gathered in the gate and the court, laughing and crying, sweeping her into a round of embraces that would have been presumptuous if these had not been who they were. Her people. The people of Mount Ghazal.

Everything was in beautiful order. Town and castle gleamed with cleanliness. The crack in the north wall was gone. The east tower was all finished, built high and beautiful. As she rode past it her banner went up from its turret: the white gazelle recumbent in a field of lilies, against the blue sky of Outremer.

Better than the women's song, better than the feast that waited, better even than the bedchamber aired and garnished and strewn with rose-petals, was the excellence of the stewardship that she had left behind her. The demesne had prospered. The accounts were minutely, meticulously kept. Whatever had gone ill, it was past, forgotten.

Of course she would examine all of it later, at her leisure. But it was a gift her people had given her, not only their welcome but their good service; and she had abandoned them, run away with barely a thought, and seldom sent word.

They had done extraordinarily well without her. She could be jealous, perhaps. Or worried—what if the world ran so well without lords or baronesses, that in the end it decided to dispense with them?

Foolishness. She had come home, and home had welcomed her with open arms. Yasmin and Leila squealed with delight to find her pregnant, leaped on her and took her by storm and carried her away to be bathed, pampered, chattered at till her head spun.

Yasmin had married a man of the town, the eldest of the nine brothers of Suraya the valiant. He had grown from a stalwart youth into a man of worth and substance, likely to be chosen *rais* when old Hamid grew weary of the office. This was their second child—the first, a son, was brought out for Richildis' inspection; and a fine strapping black-eyed child he was.

Leila, not to be outdone, had snared a Frank, a very infidel as her people would reckon it, the sergeant-at-arms of the garrison. He was a stranger to Richildis, new to Outremer this past pair of years, a big fair man remarkably like that Arnulf who still stood guard over Michael Bryennius' life and body. He was not a Norman however but an Angevin. He had been, he said, a soldier under the Count himself, but had been encouraged to go on pilgrimage after an unfortunate incident in a tavern. Richildis forbore to ask precisely what that incident entailed. A knife, another man-at-arms, a woman perhaps—it was a familiar tale, well worn with repetition.

He seemed a stolid enough creature, restful beside his vivid magpie of a wife. She chattered for both of them, would tell the whole tale of Mount Ghazal from the moment that Richildis had left it, if Richildis but gave her time.

Richildis would have time. It was early yet, but she could feel herself growing slow, sinking into the torpor of late pregnancy. She wanted to be here, home, safe; to bear her child in this place that above all was hers.

Yes, even more than La Forêt. That was so long ago now, so far away. She could remember it if she tried. Sometimes she dreamed of it: the wet green smell of its woodlands, the sun's warmth on the hills where the grapes were ripening, the hush of snow on a winter's night. Yet when she woke, she saw the world that had chosen her, the harsh dry land, the sudden greenery, the neverending rumor of war; and it was hers, her world, no more to be denied than the life that stirred beneath her girdle.

Lady Agnes wrote her still, and she wrote in return, bare words on parchment doing duty for living presence. They never mentioned Richildis' return, not any longer. It was all of other things, things that they had in common, the ruling of a demesne, the raising of foals and hound-pups and fosterlings, the training of maids and soldiers. Lady Agnes never spoke of herself, of the ailments to which a woman of her age must be subject, nor pressed for relief from her twenty years' burden. She had grown into it, Richildis thought. It had become her essence.

Just so had Richildis become a part of Mount Ghazal. In going away from it, in allowing herself to forget it, she had only heightened the joy of her return.

For Michael Bryennius it was not the same. It could not be. Yet he seemed content. He had his place here, into which he fit as smoothly as a tile in one of his people's mosaics.

Had there been no Crusade gathering to march on Damascus, Richildis would have been happy indeed. The levies had all gone, and Kutub with them, her old friend whose absence from her side had meant more to her on her journey than Mount Ghazal itself. There were fewer men in the village, and the guardroom had but half its complement. The women and the men left behind went on as they always had when the fighting men had gone off to war. Prayers were said in chapel for them and for the Crusade. Messengers who came were welcomed with wide eyes and anxious faces.

But from day to day they lived in quiet, moving slow in the summer's heat. Richildis' refuge was the bower that she had built, that opened on the garden: cool even at midday, soothed by the fall of water from the fountain. Such breezes as blew, blew through it in the sweetness of roses and jasmine. She would sit or lie there, holding court as her husband put it, with the reins of the barony in her hands, and a great sense of rightness in it all.

She could only pray that the Crusade would go as well. That they would take

Damascus, perhaps even Aleppo; that they would all come home safe and victorious under the banner of the True Cross.

Queen Eleanor in Jerusalem shone like a bird of paradise in a flock of finches. She was larger, brighter, more vivacious than any lady in the High Court; and she seemed to have determined to take the city by storm. While her husband played pilgrim, lying for long hours on his face before the Holy Sepulcher, traversing the way of the Cross on bare and bleeding knees, drowning himself in this wellspring of holiness, she found leisure for lighter pursuits.

Her pilgrimage was genuine enough, Arslan suspected. She visited all the shrines from the Tower of David to the Garden of Gethsemane, and prayed there with evident devotion; but not for hours and days as her husband did. She played, too, held court, led hunts into the hills, danced far into the night after banquets of exceptional splendor.

Baldwin was not in love with her as Arslan was, but he did find her intriguing. She seemed to share his fascination—and Arslan, whom love had not made blind, wondered how much of that was Baldwin's youth and beauty and his charming manners, and how much was his rank and his lack of a wife.

Everyone knew what she had said to King Louis in Antioch, how she asked that the marriage be dissolved. It was a fair scandal, one that she made no effort to conceal, much to the dismay of her husband's counsellors. It looked ill that the two who led the Crusade should be so at odds as to dissolve the marriage that God and the lords of France had made. It was, some said, a poor omen for the Crusade.

Arslan did not know what to think of it—no more than he knew what to say as he saw Baldwin so much in Queen Eleanor's company. "Charming boy," she called him. "My beautiful young knight." Baldwin would blush at that and remind her that he was not yet knighted, and she would cry, "What! What inequity is this? Of course you must be a knight. How can you lead a Crusade without the accolade?"

He blushed even more, and stammered, and never thought to remind her that he had been leading armies since he was a child, with or without the buffet on the shoulder that transformed a squire into a knight. Arslan, who could have spoken for him, was too wise or too cowardly to try.

Eleanor, once possessed of a cause, was unrelenting in her pursuit of it. Time was short: Louis was nearly done with his journey round the holy places. When it was over they would gather their army and march toward Tiberias, where Emperor Conrad was already, and the armies of Outremer had begun to gather.

But Eleanor would not be silenced until the King of Jerusalem was made a knight. "It can be done," she said, "after any mass in Holy Sepulcher, if a knight of worth can be found to do it. Perhaps your Constable?"

She happened to say it in front of Melisende while they all dined together in hall. Melisende, who had as little to do with Eleanor as she sensibly could, lifted a brow. "And what, pray, are you going to do?"

"Why, madam," Eleanor said in a tone that even love might have called arch, "your son is not yet a knight, and yet he will lead the Crusade. Don't you think that should be remedied?"

Melisende's brow climbed a notable fraction higher. "What remedy is needed? His majesty is young, younger than most who receive the accolade. When he comes of proper age, he will undergo it as every other young nobleman does."

"Majesty," said Eleanor, "your son is eighteen years old. Surely that's old enough?"

"We have our own customs here," Melisende said coolly. "Madam, your concern for his welfare is laudable, but I assure you, he does exactly as is fitting for a youth of his age and station."

"And is it fitting," Eleanor asked, "for a man of his years, who has led armies, to be no more than a squire?"

"My son is king," Melisende said. "Whatever he is or is not in the order of knighthood, he is, after all, above the whole army of his knights."

"But if he were one of them," Eleanor persisted, "would they not follow him all the more gladly, with all the more devotion?"

Melisende sighed with conspicuous patience. "He will do what is fitting for him to do." With that, she turned back to the conversation that had engaged her before Eleanor's clear voice rose above it: a long colloquy with King Louis regarding the foundation of convents.

Eleanor opened her mouth as if to call Melisende back, but Arslan watched her decide against it. Her face went hard then, her eyes narrow. For that little while, her beauty was gone, the silk stripped away from the steel beneath.

Melisende seemed oblivious. Maybe she was. Maybe she did not care. King Louis liked her very much: she was a worldly woman, he had been heard to observe, yet she devoted herself to holy works. He would not be dismayed to see her quell one of Eleanor's enthusiasms.

Arslan hated to see as clearly as that. Love should be blind. He should be rapt in contemplation of her beautiful face, but he could only see, just now, the two hectic spots of red on her cheeks, and the rousing of a monstrous temper.

But Eleanor did not burst out with it in front of Melisende. Prudence restrained her, perhaps. Or calculation. Baldwin was not pleased to be discussed and dismissed as if he had been a child in the nursery.

He left the hall soon after Eleanor, but not to pursue her. He went to his chamber instead, where the servants waited to ready him for bed. He sent them away with their tasks undone, all but Arslan who made himself invisible by the door.

Baldwin paced for a goodly while: door to wall, whip about; wall to bed, whip about again. On the third passage he stopped short, face to face with Arslan. "Tell me why," he said in a tight, breathless voice, "I should not summon Uncle Manasses to Holy Sepulcher at dawn and demand that he give me the accolade."

"You'll do it if you're determined," Arslan said, "no matter what I say now."

"I should do it," Baldwin said. "Did you hear what she said? As if I were a child. As if I had no voice to speak for myself."

"You didn't."

Arslan was ready: he dropped beneath the blow, halfhearted as it was. It swung harmless over his head. Baldwin snarled and spun away.

"Do you want it?" Arslan asked him. "Do you really want to insist on it?"

"What harm would it do?" Baldwin shot back.

Arslan held his tongue.

Baldwin hissed. "Damn you," he said.

Arslan crossed himself to avert the curse.

Baldwin flung himself on the bed, sprawled on his back, arm over his eyes. "Oh, God," he said. And when Arslan still said nothing: "Yes, yes. No harm, but no good, either. It's too hasty. The wrong person—the wrong queen—is insisting on it. It's not at all politic."

Arslan applauded him gravely. "All hail the King of the Franks! Lo, he groweth wise."

Baldwin lowered his arm to glare at Arslan. "Are you trying to make me lose my temper?"

"No," said Arslan, sitting cross-legged at the great bed's foot. When he was much younger he had been able to sleep lying across it. Now he had his own pallet in a niche, from which he could see and hear anyone who passed from the outer door; but he was still most comfortable sitting here, watching Baldwin decide not to have him hauled off to a life of slavery among the infidels. This time.

This and every time. Baldwin was wise enough for a young man, and he tried to be just. After a while he said, "I would dearly love to provoke my mother, but this is not the best way to do it. Knighting is more than a child's pique, or should be. I don't know that her majesty of France understands this."

Oh, it was painful to be in love, and to agree with so uncharitable a judgment.

"She doesn't know," Baldwin went on, "how things are here. None of them does. The world must be so much simpler in France—so much easier to understand. There are, after all, no infidels."

"No," said Arslan. "Only robbers and reivers and enemies of one's own race and nation."

"And Vikings?"

Arslan frowned. "I'm not sure. Maybe they're all gone—or turned into Normans."

"Same thing," Baldwin said. He sighed. "It's not a godly thing to say, but I'll be glad when the Crusade is over and the foreign kings are gone back where they came from. They are so sure of themselves, you see; and so often wrong."

"Even about Damascus?" Arslan asked, rather recklessly.

Baldwin's brows knit. "If we can take Aleppo, we can take Damascus. It's not altogether a counsel of folly."

"My father says it is. He says the real danger is the *atabeg* in Aleppo. Until we face him, we're never out of danger."

"I know he says that," Baldwin said. "He said it to me. But war is the making of choices. He said that to me, too, and far more than once. We've chosen as best we can. Once Damascus is ours, we'll be strong enough, and secure enough, to face the *atabeg*."

"One hopes so," Arslan said. "You'll not do it as a belted knight, then."

"No," said Baldwin with a flicker of wry humor. "Merely as a king."

ueen Eleanor was not pleased to be thwarted. Nor was Arslan, to be the messenger who must tell her in accents as pure as he could manage, "His majesty regrets, but he cannot honor your majesty's wishes."

Eleanor had received him in the bower that she had taken for her own, that had been a reception-hall for lesser embassies. Its grandeur suited her well. As if to honor it, she had dressed in the eastern mode, sleek as a cat in flowing silks.

She had smiled as he entered, for the servant had announced him as King Baldwin's messenger. Perhaps the smile was a little warmer for the height and youth and fairness of him—all things that she was said to favor in a man. But when he had delivered his message, the smile died. "What, is he still in leading-strings?" She tossed her head in elegant scorn. "I had thought better of him."

Arslan had never been quite so close to her before. It made him dizzy. Nonetheless he had wits to say, "Lady, he reckoned it politic."

"Politic!" She made it sound like a thing both vile and ridiculous. "What is politic about a king who clings to boyhood?"

"A squire is hardly a boy," Arslan said with dignity. "Lady, I am one, and no one calls me a child."

Ah: he had distracted her—and not to his great comfort, either. For the first time she seemed to see him, not as a pretty face and a voice echoing his king's words, but as a human creature.

He did not know that he wanted her to see him so. If she knew him, recognized him—what if he betrayed his puppy-passion? He would humiliate himself, and not even be granted the grace to die of it.

She did it. She did the terrible thing. She said, "Tell me. Do you have a name?"

He swallowed. His throat was dry. "Lady, I do. My name is Olivier, but they call me Arslan."

And why had he told her that?

Because, he answered himself. He was an idiot.

Her brows had risen. "Arslan? Is that a paynim name?"

"Turkish, lady," he said. "It means 'lion.' "

"And how did you come by a Turkish name?"

He could run away. He could bow and babble that his king had need of him and bolt. But he was was too great a fool for that. "Turks named me, lady: my mother's guards and servants, who had somewhat of the raising of me."

She looked hard at him. "You are never a Turk yourself."

He shook his head. "No, lady. I'm mostly a Frank. My mother—"

"And had your father nothing to do with it?"

"My father had not yet acknowledged me," Arslan said—and bit his tongue, but much too late.

She had understood. "Ah," she said. That was all. Not saying the word, the one that had never troubled him, but if he heard it from her he would die. From her, it would matter.

He bowed. "Lady," he said, "I should go."

"Yes," she said, but she did not dismiss him. "You are the king's squire, yes?"

"One of them, lady," Arslan said.

"You look like him," she said.

"People do say so, lady," said Arslan. And because he was mad, or because he had stopped caring: "My father was never a king, though he is a knight and baron of this kingdom. I'm kin to the king, perhaps, through Adam, but hardly closer."

"What, not through Clovis or Merovech? Or perhaps some Armenian princeling?"

"My mother is half a Saracen," Arslan said. "I suppose I'm closer kin to the Caliph in Baghdad."

She laughed with startling mirth and clapped her hands. "Oh, sir! You are delightful. Has he been hiding you, that king of yours?"

"Only with his shadow, lady," Arslan said.

She laughed again. "Clever, and beautiful, too. They breed wonderful young men here. Would he give you to me if I asked?"

"I don't think so, lady," Arslan said.

"Shall we wager on it?"

Arslan gasped for air; and prayed that she did not see. "I don't think I would like that, lady," he said.

Her brows drew together. He braced for the storm of her wrath, but it forbore to break. "Do you not like me, young lion?"

"Lady," he said as steadily as he could, "you are rather beyond likes or dislikes. I find you a marvel of the world. But I belong to my king."

"Loyal," she mused, "and beautiful, and witty and wise—it is you who are the marvel. May I borrow you for an hour an evening, to liven the dullness of the march to Damascus?"

"That is for my king to say," Arslan said.

"Then I shall ask him," Eleanor said.

Then at last she dismissed him—but not, as she said, for long.

He could hope that she would forget, though that was a dim hope; or more likely that she would be too preoccupied with duties and pleasures to remember one distraction among many. Half the young men of the High Court were trailing after her already. He would vanish among them, and gratefully too.

• • •

The King and Queen of France left Jerusalem none too soon, in not a few people's estimation. Melisende, who as always remained behind to rule the kingdom while her son led the armies to war, was unfailingly yet coldly courteous in the final feast, and again in the grand farewell as they all marched out through David's Gate. She did not linger after the high ones had passed; when Arslan looked back down the road, the glittering golden figure was gone from the gate.

It was a pity, rather, that all these kings had not taken a greater fancy to one another. Emperor Conrad and the Byzantine emperor, it was said, had found a bond of true spirits, and become friends. But there were no friendships made here.

One did not need love or even liking in order to wage war. Mutual respect and oaths sworn in common would do very well.

The French rode out singing: one of the great hymns among the king's following, and a song of the troubadours among those about the queen. Baldwin, whom courtesy had set beside King Louis in the gate and for some distance thereafter, had let his fine Arabian palfrey run ahead of Louis' more stolid mount, taking with him a fair fraction of the young and the eager. Their song was a war-song, deep-voiced and exuberant.

The stream of pilgrims, that never failed, parted to allow the army passage. They rode and marched through scattered columns of travelers from every country in Christendom. A ragged cheer followed them, prayers and blessings and demands for a blessing from one of the kings or the splendid queen come out anew in her Amazon armor.

Baldwin was in high spirits. He always was when he could escape from his mother to do what he loved best, which was to lead an army to war; but this was greater than any he had led before. It would, once they gathered in Tiberias, be the greatest army that had ever ridden under the cross of Crusade.

The True Cross rode with them, veiled now among the priests who flocked about King Louis. Everyone knew where it was, even with its jeweled splendors hidden. There was a conspiracy, as it were, to guard it and watch over it, and to protect it from any who might threaten it.

Arslan, for his part, was content to keep his place in Baldwin's shadow. He was oddly fearless. The terror that had always shaken him on the march to war seemed to have lost itself somewhere—perhaps in Queen Eleanor's eyes. He did not particularly care what became of him, if only he could ride as he rode now, with her behind, well warded among her knights and her armored ladies.

That was love, he thought. To know her for what she was, and to know war for what it was, too, and none of it mattered. She was there. That was the one thing, the only thing, the thing that made the day bright and the night blessed.

And if he was not careful he would turn into a poet, than which was nothing worse in the world.

"What are you grinning at?" Baldwin demanded of him.

He tried to bite it back, but it kept erupting in spite of him. He shrugged. "Everything," he said. "Just . . . everything."

Baldwin's sudden grin echoed his own. "Yes. Yes, isn't it?"

It did not make sense, and yet it did. They clasped hands across the stretch of singing air, set spurs to horses' sides, sprang together into an exuberant gallop.

• • •

They passed out of sight of Jerusalem, rode over Jordan and so northward to the muster at Tiberias. As they rode they met lords and knights and men-at-arms riding likewise, who joined themselves to the greater army, so that as it went on it swelled like a river in spring. The whole armed might of Outremer was moving toward the city by the Lake of Galilee.

Already as they came to Tiberias they found a vast camp spread along the shores of the lake. The Germans were there before them, and the levies from the north and west of the kingdom, Hospitallers and Templars, priests and prelates, monks in their robes and pilgrims in theirs, and whole flocks and herds of camp-followers, peddlers, sellers of every luxury or necessity that a soldier of God was likely to desire.

In their new tents that the Templars had made for them for God's charity, the French made camp in the place that had been left for them. It was some distance from the Germans, with Baldwin's camp between; and some few idlers quibbled as to which held the right and which the left hand—whether one should consider the ordering of armies as seen from the lake or as seen from the land.

Arslan was mildly glad that people had time to be foolish. It meant that they had strength to spare, to fight for and win Damascus. He, who had a duty to perform, could only walk on without offering commentary.

Baldwin, well and quickly settled in his camp, had ordered a feast for the kings and princes and the commanders of the army. It would be laid on the hill above the lake, under silken canopies set to catch the breezes that blew off the water. This was not a remarkably hot summer as summers went in this part of the world, but the folk of the West had never known its like. Those who had sense had flung themselves into the lake, disporting themselves with shouts and cries and glorious splashings.

Arslan would have given much to be among them. He had had to settle for a swift bath in the king's tent, and a new shirt and tunic—not his best; those he was saving for the feast; but presentable enough, and the tunic was silk. It was fit, he was sure, to show itself before a queen.

Eleanor was not among the tents. Passersby directed Arslan through the camp to the water's edge. There a pavilion had been set up, and a great screen of silken fabric like a living, billowing wall. Sounds of splashing and laughter beyond it made clear what Arslan had already guessed: that the queen and her ladies were taking advantage of the water's coolness.

Arslan's whole body yearned toward it. There were men in the water wherever he looked, sporting like fishes, leaping and laughing. Of the women he saw nothing: their wall concealed them perfectly. Not even a shadow showed itself through the silk.

Guards stood along the wall, figures in armor who were—he started—not men at all, but women. Of course he knew of the queen's Amazons; he had seen them often enough, and heard them too, on the march from Jerusalem. But these were not ladies of rank. Each was as tall as a man, robust and broad of shoulder, and looked as if she could wield the weapons that she wore.

Amazons indeed, and splendidly scornful of his astonishment. "I have," he said to them, "a message for the queen's majesty from the King of Jerusalem."

They did not answer him. One turned however and slipped through a gap in the wall, too quickly for him to see anything within. He swallowed a sigh.

It was some while before the guard returned. She looked slightly damp about the edges. "Her majesty will speak with you," the woman said. "Wait, and she will come."

Arslan bowed slightly. "I thank you," he said.

Perhaps he imagined her sniff of scorn. She returned to her post, and to her task of ignoring him.

There was shade at least in the pavilion, and water in a jar, cool and sweet, which no one prevented him from sipping. It might be a deadly thing to do, to taste water left so signally unattended; and if that was so, then so be it. He would die for his beloved. She would come at last and find him lying there, and maybe she would spare a moment to mourn him: so young, so fair, so nobly dead on her behalf.

He snorted. Oh, indeed; and she would return his love, too, and abandon her husband and her queenship to run away with him. A man could dream awake, and dream folly. Better he see the truth: that he was nothing to this queen among women but a pleasant face and a few moments' distraction.

When at last she emerged from behind the wall of silk, he was greatly disappointed. She had on a gown such as any lady of rank might wear in the heat of summer, light fabric of Mosul draped loose and cool. Her hair under the drift of veil was damp, to be sure, and curling wonderfully, barely restrained by a golden fillet. She was decorous in spite of it, pausing as he knelt to her, offering her hand to kiss.

She had not done that when he came to her before. Maybe she did not see him well in the shade of the pavilion after the bright glare of sunlight—perhaps she took him for someone else.

He kissed her hand as she expected him to do, and hoped that she did not mark how he trembled. Her perfume was dizzying, her skin wonderfully soft and milky fair. She freckled, he could not help but notice. She must conceal it with paint and artifice when she was not come fresh from the waters of the lake.

It was charming, as a blemish will be when it belongs to one's beloved. He let go her hand and drew back with his head still bowed.

As he drew breath to begin Baldwin's message, her voice said above his head, "Lion. Arslan."

He choked, gasped, swallowed. His face was on fire. He did not dare lift it. "Lady," he said with what voice he could manage.

He had not known that one could hear a smile. "Are you always so shy, young lion?"

"No, lady," he said.

"Ah," said Eleanor. There was a world of understanding in the sound.

If the earth had opened then and swallowed him, Arslan would have been content. "Lady," he said as best he could, "his majesty the King of Jerusalem bids you
attend him at dinner in his camp."

"And does he bid the King of France as well?"

"All the high ones, lady," Arslan said.

"Ah," said Eleanor again, this time as if in boredom. "Then I must go. One must
be politic, after all."

Arslan held his tongue.

She sighed audibly. "It's such a nuisance, this having to be politic. I'll be glad
to see the end of it."

And her marriage to the king, too, no doubt. Everyone had heard the scandal.

"Arslan!" she cried suddenly.

He looked up startled, into her laughing face. "There, see?" she said. "You can
look at me. Am I hideous? Is that why you keep your eyes so demurely lowered?
Are your boots so much more engrossing than a mere queen?"

"Lady," Arslan demanded with a flash of temper that perhaps took her aback,
"is your life so dull that you must enliven it by making sport of kings' messengers?
Your pardon, I pray you, but much as I would like to be your plaything, I have a
king to serve, and he is waiting for me."

Eleanor's laughter had died, but it gleamed still in her eyes. "Yes, do go wait on
your king. Who is not, I think, as interesting a young man as you."

"I am crashingly dull," Arslan said. "He is a king."

"Why then," said Eleanor, "so is my husband a king, and he bores me to tears.
Kings are so seldom witty. Is it the weight of the crown, do you think, that crushes
the intelligence out of them?"

"Lady, you have worn a crown; I never have."

She laughed aloud. "Oh, you are wonderful! How can I let you go, unless you
come back again? Will you come back? Shall I command your king to give you to
me for at least a little while?"

"I think," said Arslan, "that you lack sufficient employment for your mind. Lady."
He bowed low as was fitting for a squire to a queen, and left her standing there.
She was still laughing. He did not look back to see if the laughter turned to rage,
or if it went on undismayed.

rslan was not sorry that he had said what he had said, but he quaked a little after, for fear of consequences. At dinner he waited on his king, he could not avoid it, but he stayed well out of the French queen's way. She, for her part, seemed as oblivious to him as she had ever been: not even ignoring him, simply unaware of his existence. That must be an art of queens, to fail to see what one did not wish to see.

No punishment descended on him. No messenger came to Baldwin to demand satisfaction for his squire's insolence. Eleanor had had her sport. Arslan was as nothing to her again.

He was not bitter about it. She was a queen, and born a duchess; and even if she forsook all that, she would still be Eleanor. He did rather pity poor King Louis. That monkish man, no more than middling blessed with intelligence, must be sorely baffled by his splendid terror of a wife.

"Can you imagine being married to her?" Arslan asked Baldwin as he got the king ready for bed. Baldwin had been kept up late even after the King of France and the German emperor had gone wearily off to their tents, by the queen's tireless exuberance. One more cup of wine, one more dance, one more song—Eleanor was in extraordinary spirits. At length Baldwin had had to take his own leave, abandoning her to night roisterers and her own guards and hangers-on, for dawn came early, and with the dawn they would call the muster; and if all were present and accounted for, by midday they would begin the march to Damascus.

Baldwin shuddered slightly at Arslan's question. "She's splendid. Too splendid for the likes of us. She'd eat a man alive."

"She doesn't seem to have eaten Louis," Arslan said.

"What's there to eat?" Baldwin pointed out. "Dry bones and holy relics, no savor in him at all. And isn't she trying to escape that marriage?"

"Louis won't let her go."

"Won't he? I'll wager she wears him out, too, even in his shelter of priests and prayer. Just think of her with sons—she'd be like the serpent, devouring her own young."

"You don't like her at all," Arslan said in surprise. "I thought you found her enchanting."

"So did my mother," Baldwin said with a flash of teeth. "And didn't it make her livid? There's a she-wolf of her own kind and inclination, too utterly like her for words. No wonder they detest each other."

"You don't hate your mother," Arslan said.

"No," Baldwin said a little too quickly. "No, of course I don't. I don't hate the French queen either. But I don't like or trust her."

"Who does trust a queen?"

"Or a king?"

"Did I say that?"

"No," Baldwin said, "but you were thinking it." He shook his head. "Why did we begin this? Don't tell me you really are imagining being married to her."

"God's feet, no," said Arslan, and truthfully too. "I'm not a king or a king's heir; and she'll never take less."

"She won't take me," Baldwin said.

"Not even for a plaything?"

"Not even then." Baldwin's mood was light still, but in that, for a moment, he sounded like a king. "I shall find me a lady of this country, one both noble and rich, who knows the land and the people, and who understands that the infidel can be ally as well as enemy."

"I don't think anyone new from the West understands that," Arslan said. It puzzled him, it always had; but the West was far away. It could not know what they knew who lived and fought here.

"And tomorrow," Baldwin said, "we go to destroy an ally."

Arslan raised a brow. "Second thoughts?"

"Too late for that," said Baldwin. He stopped pacing and lay down at last. "Go to sleep, brother. Tomorrow we do what we have to do to get this monster of an army on the road to Damascus."

They did, indeed, what they had to do. It was the greatest army that had ever gathered in the Kingdom of Jerusalem, the greatest that had ever ridden out of the West against the House of Islam. It would have been unwieldy under but one king; under three kings and a queen and a myriad of princes and barons and knights and sergeants, it bade farewell to the blue waters, the cool airs and the green places, and marched with good speed away from the lake and into the desert.

They had mustered in the day, but such was the size of the army and the slowness of its gathering that the vanguard set foot on the road as the shadows stretched long toward evening. The rear began its march well after sunset, in the cool of evening that slid into the chill of the desert night.

It was well done. Even the hardy men of Outremer welcomed the escape from the day's heat, to travel by night and rest by day as all wise armies did in this fierce country. The men of the West lived the longer for it, and stayed the stronger.

God was with them, it seemed, and none of the infidels. That the enemy knew of their marching was inevitable; but it might be, it just might be, that no man of

Islam knew that they had settled on Damascus. They had put out through scouts and spies that they would move on Aleppo, or perhaps on Edessa.

No raiders awaited them on the road to Damascus. No armies met them. They advanced in the dark and cool, camped in the fiery heat, sought what rest they could. The ways that they took, they had learned on their last campaign against Damascus, when God's messenger, the nameless and faceless knight whom Arslan had known as the Turk Mursalah, had guided them safely home. Now they traveled in safety to the ancient city, past Bosra that had defeated them before, unmenaced, unmolested, untormented by thirst or hunger, though the heat was as terrible as it could ever be in this country in the summer.

And of a morning that was as hot already as iron in the forge, they saw before them the green shimmer and, far away, a white gleam of walls. The name of it ran down the column, borne on the dust of its passing: *Damascus. At last, Damascus.*

Arslan had kin in this place, cousins of his mother, and yet he had never seen it. He had heard of its riches till he was nigh sick of them; but no one had told him how beautiful it was, its gardens and its orchards, its streams and rivers, its walls, its towers and minarets agleam in the morning.

They camped there on the desert's edge, in the shade of trees that bore young green apples and hard knots of stranger fruits, and some even the fragrance of blossoms: oranges, lemons, citron. There was water, cold and sweet, flowing among the trees, and sweetness of grass and flowers.

Such beauty only made the stronger the will of Crusade to take this for itself. Water in this country was more precious than gold, and fruits of the earth more beautiful than jewels from the mine. Yet there were gold and gems in the city, spices and silks, things wonderful and rare.

They dreamed of them in their tents that day, while the city woke to find itself faced with an army. In the night they advanced again, seeking deeper wells and greater comfort.

Here they met at last the flicker of Saracen swords—but weak, startled, and few in number, driven back swiftly into Damascus. They could rest again unmolested, with a victory, however small, to grant them ease. It was an omen, they said to one another. A promise. Damascus would fall to them as easily as its vanguard had done.

So said the French and the Germans. But Baldwin's men, his knights and soldiers of Jerusalem, were warier. "Not all of the infidels' wars are fought on the open plain," Constable Manasses said in council. "Here in the gardens and among the trees, they'll send their raiders to cut us down one by one."

"My army will go," said Baldwin, "to hunt infidels—the serpents in the gardens."

It was a kind of fighting that Arslan had done before, but nearly always in desert places: more hunt than march, with men for quarry. He found himself in a small hunting-party, with his father for commander. It was a comfortable company, one that he had been in before: men of Beausoleil and Mount Ghazal, skilled hunters and trackers, keen to catch the spoor of an enemy.

They advanced with dizzying swiftness, as if God Himself were guiding them. And perhaps after all He was. Was this not His Crusade?

All that morning, their second morning outside Damascus, they hunted its hunters. Three times they killed: turbaned infidels armed with knives and bows. Once a Turkish arrow found target, brought down a young man-at-arms of Beausoleil who had been so unwise as to pause to pluck a blossom. He paid high for that one wild rose: an arrow in the throat, and his life reft from him as he drew in the sweetness of the scent.

As if his death had paid their passage, they found no other hunter, nor met another arrow. They drew in their net toward the place where the army had meant to camp: where, as they scoured the orchards, men less fortunate in duty had been felling trees and raising a wall against any enemy who might come.

It was a fair stronghold even as Arslan came back to it, a wall nigh completed and a gate set in it, with guards, and sentries pacing, and all the image and likeness of a castle built of stone.

Those within, he discovered, were French and men of Outremer. The Germans had gone on. Emperor Conrad, weary of the name of coward that he had borne since he returned from Ephesus to Constantinople, had taken his destrier and his knights and men-at-arms and gone to storm the city. Messengers, returning, had him at the river Barada, in a village called Rabwa under the loom of the city's walls. "Tomorrow," Conrad said through them, "we take Damascus."

Only a fool would reckon a war won before the city was taken, yet that night they kept festival in the camp. They had come farther and swifter than even the most sanguine had hoped. Damascus was taken by surprise. Aleppo, surely, could send no reinforcements so quickly, nor act to save its sister city before the banner of the Cross was raised above the citadel.

"And from within," they said, "we can hold against the world."

They were already counting out the gold that they would win, reckoning the jewels, dreaming of the women they would capture and subdue. That they themselves could die, that this lesser paradise should be their tomb, none of them paused to think. They were full of God and gold. Death would never touch them.

Queen Eleanor had been wiser than to insist that she and her ladies take part in the fighting. They had suffered themselves to be protected in the army's heart, guided through the orchards and shut up within the raw new wall. Arslan had not meant to show himself where they were, but he had an errand from Baldwin to the French king, and must pass by their tents both coming and going. As he returned to Baldwin's own tent, Eleanor appeared outside her pavilion, sitting under a tree adorned half with flowers and half with hard green fruit. She had taken off her armor and put on a silken gown; she had bathed too, it seemed, in water from one of the wells, and made herself both fresh and beautiful.

Soldiers, passing by, looked at her and sighed. She meant that, perhaps: to be a vision of beauty in the midst of war. Or maybe she only wanted to take the air and drink in the scent of orange-blossoms. That she sat in an armed camp within a barely finished wall, that a city full of infidels lay just beyond the trees, seemed to perturb her not at all. She had great courage for a woman—for any human creature. Her maids were white and silent, and one or two looked to have been weeping, but she was as lively as ever.

"Young lion!" she called as he tried to slink past.

Briefly he considered failing to hear, but her voice was penetrating. Others beyond him had heard, too: heads raised, eyes turned toward him. With as cheerful a face as he could manage, he paused and bowed. "Majesty?"

"Come here," she said.

He hesitated, but there was no simple escape. He approached her slowly, bowed again, knelt as a squire should in front of a queen.

"Tell me," she said. "Are we moving on tomorrow?"

That might not have been what she had intended to say, but it was certainly harmless. "Some of us are," he answered. "Some will stay here to hold against escapes from the city."

"But you will go on."

"I go with my king," Arslan said, "majesty."

"And I no doubt will stay here." She sighed. "Sometimes, young lion, I purely hate to be a woman."

"God willed it," Arslan said, for lack of anything better to say.

"God wills everything," said Eleanor. "What do you think would happen if I took my ladies and rode with the army? Would I be seized and clapped in chains and dragged back to this place?"

"I don't know, lady," Arslan said.

"I think I might not," said Eleanor. "Will you betray me before I can do it?"

"If you thought I would, would you have told me?"

She shrugged. "I might."

"I might, too," Arslan said, "or I might not."

"If you do, I'll never forgive you."

"If I don't, my king and your king may never forgive me."

She smiled. It was almost laughter, but not quite. "I'll gamble," she said.

He could go then, but he lingered. "You could die," he said.

"So could you."

He nodded.

She looked at him. "Aren't you afraid?"

"All the time," said Arslan.

"Odd," she said as if to herself. "Men don't usually admit to such things."

"Why, if it's true?"

"Is it your eastern blood?" she asked. "Is that why you're different?"

"Easterners say it's mostly because I'm a Frank." He paused. "My mother's like me, and she's half of each. We can't seem to talk like other people."

"Don't be like anyone else," Eleanor said. "Promise."

"That could be perilous," said Arslan.

"Are you afraid?"

She was challenging him. She was not, at that moment, any older or saner than he was. She should have been a man, he thought, to be so free of her mind and self—freer than any woman he had ever seen, even Melisende.

"How strange people must be," Arslan said, "in your country."

"Someday you will see." She sighed. "Ah, my sweet France! So beautiful, and most of all in May, when the birds are singing and the blood goes wild . . ."

Arslan squirmed with embarrassment. He could hardly say what he was thinking, that it did not need to be either May or France for the blood to rise and sing. July in Damascus, in the humid heat of afternoon, drunken with the scent of orange blossoms, was more than enough for the purpose.

"Do they have orange trees in France?" Arslan asked.

"Sometimes," she said. "And apples, and plums and pears, and lemon trees in the far south where the winters are soft and almost sweet."

"Softer than here?"

She tossed her head with a snort of disgust. "Winters are brutal here. Summers, too. Spring—that's beautiful, for the whole three days it lasts."

"Sometimes it lasts a month," Arslan said.

"Not that I noticed." She yawned, but her eyes were bright, wide awake. "Will you promise?"

"What?" he asked stupidly.

"Will you promise never to become ordinary?"

"How can anyone promise that?"

"Do it," she said.

"Are you commanding me, majesty?"

She seemed a little disconcerted—and why she should be, he could not see. "Is that all I am to you? A crown and a throne?"

"You're giving it up," he said, not at all wisely.

"I hate it," she said with sudden passion. And, a little less fiercely: "Not being queen. Being *his* queen. I'll find me another king. Someone younger, fairer. Someone whose sole pleasure in this world is not to dream of the next."

"I wish you well of your ambition, lady," Arslan said—and bowed and fled while she was still caught between temper and astonishment; before she could compel him to promise a thing that he could not agree to at all.

And was he so different? Baldwin did not seem to think so. He was not hated or scorned, though he was the king's foster-brother. He had been careful to avoid envy. His mother had taught him that, and Lady Richildis; and his father, too. It was a useful art for a bastard to know.

Yet the Queen of France, who herself was well out of the ordinary, thought him odd.

To her surely all of Outremer was strange. It was nothing like France or Aquitaine or Anjou. It was the land beyond the sea: beyond anything that the West had known.

He would see France. Someday. And Aquitaine. And Anjou. All of them. And if he was stranger than any . . . then so he was. He might after all be utterly ordinary.

SIXTY

When they left their quick-built fortress, Eleanor and her Amazons rode with them. No one had the fortitude to stop them, nor did King Louis seem inclined to try. They stayed well back at least, let themselves be warded in the center—and if the men who warded them objected to a duty that should not have been necessary, none went so far as to say so.

Arslan was in the van, close behind his father. Baldwin was somewhat behind, Louis in the rear. The French king was not, for all his monkish pretensions, a poor fighter. He was rather brave in fact, and not too ill with a sword.

The walls of Damascus loomed closer, gleaming white in the morning. Men like ants swarmed beneath: Conrad and his Germans, intent already on the attack. Turkish arrows rained down from the walls. Frankish arrows arced upward.

Arslan was perfectly, unshakably calm. Anticipation of battle could rattle his bones where he sat; but battle in front of him—that he could face with a clear eye. He had all the time in the world to make certain that his armor was on properly, his lance well sharpened, his sword loose in its scabbard. He did not wear the great helm that the knights wore, but a smaller helmet in the Norman fashion.

He was glad of that, knowing how narrow the world became in the hollow confinement of the helm, how difficult it was then to see what came at one from behind. That was the squire's task, to see what the knight could not—and it seemed that he would play squire to his father; there was no other close enough, and Baldwin was farther back and well attended.

He leaned across to help his father with the helm, lifting the great heavy thing and lowering it onto armored shoulders. The familiar face vanished in blind metal. But for the shield and surcoat with the sun's disk thereon, and the grey charger, this could have been any knight at all, any nameless fighting man in an army full of them.

The trumpets called them to order along the line of the walls. They left their horses behind with a picked company of soldiers and squires, to find again when the gates were breached. On foot in a long mailed line, with scaling ladders, with rams, with the engines that Conrad had brought up with him the day before, they stormed the walls.

And the walls fought back: arrows, spears, oil and sand heated to burning. Arslan braced his shield over his head, locked with his father's on the left hand, another man's on the right—making a roof against the fire from the sky.

A shrill cry of trumpets, a hammering of drums, a clatter of nakers, clear even above the roar of battle, brought Arslan's eyes to the gate that defied a whole company of Germans. He was not far from them, struggling to raise a ladder against a trebled horde of infidels.

The gate sprang open. He had thought the walls well manned; yet they were nigh deserted beside the army that poured out of the city upon the startled Franks. Hundreds, thousands of them, shrilling their battle cry: *Allah-il-allah! Allahu akbar!*

"God's balls," Bertrand said beside him, echoing in the helm. "There shouldn't be this many men in the whole of Damascus."

And they kept coming. Rank after rank of them, tribes and clans and nations. Turks—whole steppesful of Turks.

Those never came from Damascus, nor could have been there longer than it took to cross from the northern gate to the gates of the south. Aleppo had had the alarm, after all, and moved with preternatural swiftness. It had sent its armies, all of them perhaps, to the succor of its sister and rival.

The Franks gave up their assault on the walls, turned at bay against an enemy more numerous than they had ever dreaded to meet. What had seemed a brief siege, a quick conquest, turned swiftly into rout.

"The camp!" someone roared from behind. "They're headed for the camp!"

The baggage, the horses, the provisions—and, except for the queen and her Amazons, the women and servants. They fought with redoubled ferocity, no thought now of taking the city, only of gaining back what was theirs.

When the trumpets rang the retreat, they were already well away from the walls. They continued in good order, within a wall of shields and spears: drawing back for prudence's sake, and taking their engines with them.

Unur the emir had indeed brought in the armies of Aleppo. "They must have known," someone said that night in the council of the kings. "They had to have known."

"Not necessarily," Baldwin said. He did not seem unduly cast down, though it was difficult to contemplate a battle turned so suddenly against him. "They would have expected us to aim for Aleppo, and stood the troops to arms there. Once we were sighted here, Unur could summon the armies and expect them to come at once. Surely you aren't all taken by surprise? It had to happen."

"It wasn't supposed to happen so soon." Louis of France was not wont to speak in council, but this night, perhaps the fire of battle lingered in him still. He had fought well by all accounts, and might have broken through into the city if the enemy had not broken out before him. "We should have been in the citadel and strongly guarded before the rest of the Saracens came against us."

"War never goes as we would expect," Baldwin said with the surety of one who had led armies since he was a child. "So then. We're driven back to this camp. Raiders are running through the gardens again. We can't defend ourselves here, storm the walls, fight the new army, and keep the raiders at bay, not all at once."

"Can we not?" asked a baron from somewhere in France: a southerner perhaps with his black curls, lank now from a hard day's fighting.

"We are outnumbered," Manasses the Constable said with remarkable patience in the circumstances. All the knights of Outremer were weary of the westerners' persistent failure to understand this half of the world. "This is the greatest army that has ever marched under the True Cross, and yet we are but a tithe of a tithe of the hordes that Islam can raise against us. They are in their own country; we are far from our own. When one of us dies, none comes to take his place. When one of them falls, a hundred crowd in behind him, pouring like a river from all the lands that pay homage to Allah. We have no such fortune. We must husband our resources. We cannot spend ourselves without heed for the cost."

"Then what do we do? Run home with our tails between our legs?"

"Not yet," Baldwin said with conspicuous equanimity. "But we should consider that instead of a city lightly defended and easily taken, we face an army larger than our own, that came through a gate we could not either reach or hold."

"Should we try?" someone asked.

Baldwin spread his hands. "Should we? We're pressed to hold what we have, this southern edge of the gardens. We can't surround the city; we're too few."

"An army at every gate?" said one of the German barons.

"Then what will we have left to take this side of the city?" a baron of Jerusalem shot back. "It's as his majesty said. We can't do all that we should do. We have to choose."

"I should think the choice would be made for us," King Louis said with a touch of diffidence. "We're here, yes? We've begun the attack from this southern side. We have to continue."

"We may not be able to." That was a man near the back of the gathering, an accent more of Outremer than of France. "They expect us here, and will concentrate their forces in this place. If we go elsewhere—where they don't expect us—"

"But they expect us to keep attacking," Louis said, "unless we retreat. Should we pretend to run away, then? And draw them after us?"

No one scoffed. He was a king, after all, and a fair fighter, though he had little mind for the greater complexities of war.

Baldwin, a king likewise but more notably gifted in the art, said rather gently, "They could raise the whole country against us, fall on us and destroy us before we could come back to the borders of our own country. No, brother: we have to stay here, if we have any hope of taking the city."

"But if we withdrew," said the man in the back, "and chose a place that they would not expect—perhaps the eastern wall—"

"That would be ill done," someone else said, "if you know this city at all. It's desert there. Water is—"

"We'll carry what we can," the baron said, if baron he was; he was far back and veiled in shadow. "If we succeed, we gain much."

"If we fail, we lose it all."

"Messires," Baldwin said in a clear, quelling voice, "I think we're short of so hard a choice. If tomorrow we fail to break through the walls—then we do what we must do."

That was wise counsel, though it resolved little. They settled on it and went to what rest was granted them: little enough with infidels prowling among the trees, shattering the night with shrieks and howls and arrows out of the dark. In the deep night they fell on the horselines, cut tethers and slashed hobbles, reckless of dancing hoofs. Franks drove them off, but not before they had sent a good score of destriers lumbering into the night.

Mules, palfreys, remounts they could have spared far more easily than those great heavy beasts from the West. There were so few left, so many dead of famine and heat and sickness; yet those that remained were weapons as deadly as any sword, great battering hoofs and tearing teeth and sheer force of weight against the infidel on his swift light horse of the desert.

It was not a crippling loss, but they did feel it. The knights relegated to remounts were so much the less able to storm the walls, so much the more disheartened by the blow to their pride and their purses.

Again as before they rode out of the camp toward the city. This time no women rode with them. Queen Eleanor, out of prudence or even fear, elected to remain behind, and her ladies with her.

Arslan knew of it too late, or he would have found a way to go to her, to call her a dozen kinds of fool. The camp was beleaguered; there were raiders all about it. They could spare too few to guard it. All who could must ride and march against the city. They must take it. They could not guard the camp, too, even with the queen inside it.

Or maybe she thought that she could do some good, that she could fight to defend the camp. That would be like her. It should have sent Arslan riding headlong back, but he had gone too far. He was almost at the walls. The way behind was thick with infidels: shadows amid the gardens, shapes flitting through the trees.

The walls were black with men, the parapets so crowded that man must interfere with man, and no archer draw bow without colliding with his neighbor. More yet waited below. If the Franks hoped to raise the scaling ladders today, they would have to do it through the ranks of the enemy, against a bristle of spears.

They paused as they saw what faced them, but they were no cowards, they of the Cross. They flung themselves forward, rank on rank of them, mounted and afoot.

Arslan felt the sheer hammering force of the charge, as if he were a weapon himself, lifted in a strong hand and hurled against the enemy. He was a spear, a sword. He mowed down the hordes of the enemy.

But he could not come near the wall. None of them could. The enemy were too many. Over and over again they charged. Again and again they fell back. Each time there were fewer to renew the assault, more dead or wounded to stumble over or to drag back behind the line of battle.

There comes a time in a fight when those in the midst of it know in their bones that they have won or lost—that they should press harder or would be wiser to retreat. Arslan knew it on the sixth or perhaps the seventh charge, as he sat his heaving horse and looked about him and took count of those who were left. Baldwin was still ahorse, and Bertrand just beyond him. Louis of France—there, under the banner of lilies, battered and stained as if its bearer had fallen or been dragged in the dust. Conrad of the Germans had pressed ahead without them, a small and reckless charge amid the general confusion.

There in the lull, the high ones of Jerusalem had drawn together about their king. The word among them, contested but without excessive heat, was clear. *Retreat. We must retreat.*

Baldwin's hand swept up suddenly, beckoning his trumpeter. The man was ready and waiting. He raised his trumpet to his lips, a signal caught by other trumpeters down along the line. The clear call rang out over them, the call to withdraw.

The Germans seemed deaf to it, caught up in their knot of battle. The French surged backward nigh as eagerly as they had charged before. The army of Jerusalem went more slowly, on guard against treachery or attacks from the walls. As the space widened between them and the city, the Germans lowered their swords and began to draw back.

Arslan was one of the last to retreat. It was not that he was reluctant; but Baldwin hung back, and Arslan stayed beside him with drawn sword. Bertrand sat his grey horse on the other side, silent and faceless in his great helm. Grey Malik was wounded: there was blood on his neck and flank, bright scarlet against silver. It seemed not to distress him; he stood quietly, chewing on his bit as he was wont to do when he had perforce to stand still.

As the last of the men of Jerusalem stirred into motion, Baldwin wheeled his mount and sent it dancing after. Arslan and Bertrand followed more sedately. The Germans were coming behind, pace by pace, with pauses to loose volleys of arrows or to jeer and taunt the enemy, who shrilled contemptuously back.

Retreat it might be, but it was hard fought. The raiders in the gardens had drawn together into an army and set themselves to trap the Franks between the gardens and the walls. But there were too few, and for whatever reason the men in and about the city were not minded to aid them. The Franks broke through and forged toward the camp, harried on the flanks by remnants of the raiders.

They found the camp beset. Here at last perhaps the men from the West understood what it was to fight in this country, to be so few against so many, and more always in back of them.

They broke through to the camp, found tents struck within the palisade and wagons loaded, ready to go wherever they must. No one asked those in the camp how they had known, or what they would have done had not the army come back just then. Even as the last of them passed within, a horde of yelling Saracens fell on the camp from without. Their arrows streamed fire; they brandished torches in the hot bright daylight.

The green wood of the palisade would hardly go up in flames, but the well-worn fabric and leather of the tents, the wood of the wagons, the tent-poles, the stocks of arrows and spears and spare lances—those could burn, and would, if the enemy broke through the wall or flung fire over it.

No one had time to think. They scrambled together in marching order, the freshest and the least wounded of the fighting men in front and rear, the baggage and the women in the center, and hurled all their force into breaking through the line of the enemy. Miraculous: it gave way, broke and scattered as they thundered past.

They ran eastward, following no one knew whom; but that someone led, they could hardly doubt. Eastward the gardens shrank and faded, and the city's walls looked out on desert. Any who might have turned back found himself face to face with an army of infidels. Both raiders and forces from the city had massed behind them.

The sun's sinking found them cut off from the green country, and no wells that they could find, nor running stream: only rock and sand and thorn. They had no choice but to camp there, well back from the walls. People crowded the ramparts; jeering perhaps, though it was hard to hear.

Arslan knew what they would be saying—how could they not? Of all places to go round the walls of that great city, this would be the worst. Here was no water, no shade, no respite. Here the walls were strong and high, and no gate to weaken them. They had been herded like cattle, no wiser than sheep—straight to the worst of all places in which they could have come to rest.

It was done. There was no undoing it. No going back, no going forward in the black and arrow-ridden night. They camped where they were for lack of better place to go, and those who were wise husbanded their water, but those who were foolish had drunk it all and went thirsty to sleep; or lay awake cursing the treachery—for so it must be—of those who had led them here.

SIXTY-ONE

o one ever confessed to guiding the army of Crusade to the east wall of Damascus. No one remembered or would admit to remembering who had done it. The French and the Germans insisted that it must have been a baron or barons of Jerusalem—one or more who valued the Damascene alliance above the Cross itself. The barons of Jerusalem objected strongly to such an accusation.

Baldwin succeeded in preventing a war by the rather simple expedient of rising in the council, kicking over the table at which the highest ones sat, and saying in the shocked silence, "Yes, go on. Kill each other. Spare the infidels the trouble."

And having said that, he walked out of the council—out of his own tent and the open ground in front of it, into the firelit dark.

Arslan made haste to follow. Behind them the council erupted; but Baldwin did not pause or turn back.

Nor did he go far. They were always careful in camp to pitch tents in the same places, so that men could find their own lords and companions, and messengers knew where to go. The men of Beausoleil and those of Mount Ghazal camped to the east of the king's men, which here was on a little rise of land, just high enough to see the camp spread out below with its flicker of fires. They had no water here, but brush they had, enough to offer comfort in the cool of the desert night.

Baldwin paused in front of the largest tent, that in the flickering dimness showed merely dark. In daylight it was crimson. The guard recognized the king's face, bowed and did not try to stop him as he scratched at the flap. "My lord? Lord Bertrand?"

No answer came. He was abroad in the camp, surely; Arslan had not seen him in council, nor looked for him with any urgency. Bertrand was wise enough, and high enough, to escape gatherings that would come to nothing useful.

Baldwin raised the flap. A shaft of light dazzled Arslan's eyes. It went dark as Baldwin barred it. Before the flap could fall, Arslan had ducked beneath, close on Baldwin's heels.

Bertrand was there. He was lying on the cot, and a turbaned villain bent over him: Kutub the Turk, scowling horribly and saying in the language of his own tribe, "Thrice-idiot son of a Christian dog! How long have you been hiding it?"

"I *am* the son of a Christian dog," Bertrand said, laughing perhaps, but too faint to be certain. His breath caught as Kutub bent lower and prodded. "*Ai!* Easy, man! You're killing me."

"You hardly need the help," Kutub snarled. "When did you take that spear in your hide? Yesterday? The day before?"

"Today," Bertrand said thinly, through another gasp of pain.

"Liar," said Kutub. "Yesterday morning at latest. Iblis rot your hide, if your own idiocy doesn't."

Arslan had moved up where he could see. He made no sound, did not gasp; could not move.

How in the world the man had not only gone on as if nothing were wrong, but ridden, fought, commanded men in battle and in camp, Arslan would never know. The wound was deep, and it was ugly. Spear, most likely, or broad-bladed sword. Bloodied bandages lay beside it.

"How did you find it?" Arslan asked Kutub.

"I came in with a message," the Turk answered, "and found him flat on his back, having tried and failed to change the wrappings. Idiot."

"Indeed," said Arslan. He rounded on his father. "Why?"

Bertrand shrugged. It must have hurt, but his face did not change. "I was preoccupied. The surgeons were busy. It was nothing."

"It will kill you," Kutub said, flat and hard. "It was nothing then, no: a blade in the side, no vitals pierced, blood enough but what's that to a fullblooded man? It bled you no whiter than the surgeons would. But now . . ." He looked as if he would have spat, but thought better of it. "There's cautery, there's this potion or that, there's a poultice if I had the herbs—but it's in Allah's hands."

"God's," said Bertrand.

"Do what you can," Baldwin said from behind them all. "I'll send my own physician."

"What, a Frankish butcher?" Kutub looked appalled at the thought.

"He comes from Baghdad," Baldwin said. "A Christian, of course, but trained as the infidels are. You'd trust him, surely."

Kutub growled but held his peace.

Baldwin smiled. "I'll fetch him."

Arslan opened his mouth to object to the king's running his own errands, but who else was there? Kutub was washing out the wound with a mingling of water and wine and pungent herbs. Arslan did not want to leave his father, nor could he have done it: Bertrand had caught his hand and held it in a grip so fierce it bruised.

"Arslan," Bertrand said. "Olivier-Arslan."

Arslan knelt by the cot, bent perforce over his father. He caught there a scent that wrinkled his nose: not only the odor of unwashed body, sweat and dust and blood, but another, sweeter, darker. The scent of a wound that had festered.

Of course it had festered. The fool had wrapped it and for all purposes forgotten it, though the pain must have made him dizzy. If Arslan had done such a thing, he would have had a tongue-lashing now and a beating later, if he lived.

"Arslan," Bertrand said again. "Listen to me. If I don't come home alive—"

"You will," Arslan said.

Bertrand glared. Dear God, he was pale, as if he were dying already. "Don't you be an idiot, too. Be quiet and listen. If I die of this—and yes, I deserve exactly that—go to my man in Jerusalem, whose name your mother knows. He has writs sealed under my seal. They give you my name and countenance. They name you my heir."

Arslan did not hear, not just then. Not such words as those. "You can't die," he said.

"Every man can die," said Bertrand, "and every man does. Stop that. Listen. You are my heir, Arslan. Whatever I have, I give to you."

"No," said Arslan. He was not denying what he heard, but that he heard it at all. "You can't be—"

Bertrand let go his hand and struck him. It was a hard blow, too hard—God in heaven, much too hard for a dying man. Arslan reeled under it.

"Sometimes I think," Bertrand said, "that that was the beginning of the accolade: the father beating sense into his son. Though what sense there is in war or in weapons, God knows."

"I can't be your heir," Arslan said. It was all he could think of to say.

"Why not? You're the only son I have, that I know of. Certainly the only one in Outremer. You have the king's countenance and his favor. The queen had the raising of you. The Queen of the French is known to admire you. Worse sons have inherited their fathers' domains, and done worse with them than you will."

"But I was never—" Arslan began.

"My fault," said Bertrand. "My fault, my most grievous fault. I should have done all this long ago. I knew that I would do it; I wanted it. But I moved too slowly. I thought, you see, that I would never die."

"You won't die now," Arslan said fiercely. "Yusuf will see to it. Yusuf was physician to the Caliph himself, before he went in search of a Christian lord."

"And did the Caliph survive the learned Yusuf's ministrations?" Bertrand inquired.

Arslan hissed. "You are babbling. Is that delirium? God's feet, you're fevered. If you die—God be my witness, if you die, I'll repudiate everything you ever tried to give me."

"You can't," Bertrand said. "I wrote it down. It is yours, inescapably. Only a child of your body may inherit."

"And if I have none?"

"Your mother may dispose of it. But only if you die without issue."

Arslan's teeth clicked together. Bertrand was clever, as he should have expected. Too clever by half. And too clearly determined to let this wound kill him, as if he had no care for those who loved him.

"Why?" Arslan demanded as he had before, but more strongly now, with fiercer intensity. "Are you tired of life? How can you be? You're not even old!"

"I'm old enough," said Bertrand. "Yes, I'm tired. I'll take the cowl, I think, after this war is over."

"You can't do that, either," Arslan said. "You'd go mad inside of a month."

"Maybe," Bertrand said. "Maybe I'd be glad of the quiet."

He was not smiling, not jesting. He meant it.

Such could happen to a man when he grew older. Arslan had seen it before. Men who had fought lifelong in their own and their lieges' wars, who had been born and bred to rule over men, in time grew weary; longed to lie down, to rest, to be free of the burdens that had weighed on them for so long.

"And Mother?" Arslan demanded. "What of her? Will you give her up, too? Can you do such a thing to her?"

"We've spoken of it," Bertrand said. "She thinks that a year's retreat, or a decade's, is not of necessity an ill thing."

"Without her? Without any comfort of the body?"

"That is not," Bertrand said with perceptible patience, "as great a preoccupation for us of greater age than for you young things. The blood cools. The need—no, it never goes away, but the urgency fades. It's warmth, then, in place of the old consuming fire."

"That is perfect nonsense," Kutub said, startling them both. They had forgotten that he was there. "Here, that's the king's physician coming, unless my ears deceive me. Mind you let him do his work. You may be succumbing to some strange brain-rotting disease of the Franks, but we want you alive."

Indeed it was Baldwin's Christian Arab in his yellow turban, with his eunuch apprentice and his box of medicines and an expression of great ennui that changed not in the slightest when he saw the wound that to Arslan looked so horrible.

Baldwin himself had not come back with Yusuf. Arslan told himself that he only did his duty in going to find his king. He was not a coward, no. He was not running away from his father, from death and pain, from the things that he had heard and must perforce believe.

That his father had acknowledged him. Not in front of the barons, not to give him name and parentage before the High Court and the people of Jerusalem. No. His father had named him heir. Had granted him a kind of legitimacy—after Bertrand himself was dead.

One could, Arslan discovered, feel several different kinds of pain all at once. Grief, too. Fear. A man who let go, who no longer cared to live—in war, he could be almost certain that he would die.

And now it seemed that the army was much as Bertrand was: weakened, disheartened, torn with contention. No one slept. Few even rested. If they had been so inclined, the enemy would have prevented. All night long they suffered attacks from the city, over and over, hordes of Saracens, yelling, with torches.

And in the king's tent the council went on. They were arguing hotly—but not over standing fast or running retreat. Nothing so sensible. They were contesting the division of the spoils once Damascus was taken. Any who pointed out that Damascus was as good as lost, that they were vastly outnumbered, that they sat in a waterless camp in unprotected desert, was shouted down.

Those indeed were mostly men of Outremer. They who had been as greedy for spoil as any, woke late to clear sight and certain knowledge. They could see what the French and the Germans were unwilling or unable to see. The war was lost. They could not take Damascus from this place or with this army. The city was too strong and its defenders too numerous.

By the time the council dissolved in confusion, Arslan had long since left it. There was fighting to be done, a camp to defend. Better that than fruitless babble and more than fruitless reflection—and far better than remembering what his father had said, what Bertrand's death would make him.

Lord of Beausoleil. Heir, then, of La Forêt in Anjou that he had never seen. But Lady Richildis had spoken of it so often, in words so vivid, that he felt sometimes as if he had not only been there but had grown up there.

What bliss that cool green place would be if he could go there now. How much more pleasant than this clamorous dark, the thirst that he could not ease save with miserly sips from his waterskin, the pain of defeat and the knowledge of his father's sickness of spirit as of body. It was all more than he could bear, than he could wish to bear.

It was almost with relief that he heard, from the midst of a lull in the enemy's forays against the camp, that the kings had come at last to their senses, or been beaten into them. At dawn they would march. They would give up the siege. They would retreat from Damascus.

ord Bertrand was still alive in the dawn, laid in a wagon with others of the noble wounded. Baldwin's physician went with him, looking as bored as ever but showing no inclination to leave his side. Arslan took a little hope from that. Yusuf would not trouble with a dying man, unless that man was the king.

There was little enough hope to be had else. The Crusade that had begun so splendidly, in such high hope and grand expectation, had crumbled into a disorderly mob. The nations held together because they must, because the enemy would not refrain from harrying them. Men of the West looked with distrust, even with hatred, on men of Outremer, and muttered of betrayal.

"Oh, God's sooth," Arslan heard a man from Banias sneer at a half-dozen strutting bravos from Normandy, "and we paid the emir so well that he's kind enough to send his armies to hunt us, even now we've broken off the siege against his city."

"The paynim are always treacherous," a Norman said.

"And so are their cousins the dancing-girls of Jerusalem," said one so like him that it must have been a brother.

Arslan bumbled in before a battle could start, took no care to keep his horse from trampling ill-protected toes and shouldering bristling men apart. He offered no apology. These were commoners, plain men-at-arms. They expected little good of a nobleman.

It did distract them, as he had intended. He rode on down the line, wielding clumsiness again to herd in a troop of stragglers. They gave him no thanks, even as a company of Turkish horsemen thundered past, yelling and loosing arrows into the Frankish army.

Arslan had suffered retreats before. But none like this. None so bleak of spirit, so close to despair. They were harried without mercy, men and horses shot, cut down, left to lie, for they could not stop, could no longer carry the swelling numbers of the dead. The bleak plain throbbed with the buzzing of flies, stank with the sick-sweet smell of death.

But Bertrand was alive in spite of himself, tended by the physician from Baghdad. He lay in a drugged sleep—"Better for the pain," Yusuf said—rocking and swaying in the wagon as it crawled southward from Damascus.

Perhaps he was aware of the retreat. Perhaps he was spared it. Great numbers of the wounded had died; new wounded came to the wagons, recovered or died. He lay oblivious, unchanging as far as Arslan could see. Yusuf had cut once that he knew of, paring away dead flesh, binding the renewed wound with poultices that smelled both strong and strange.

Yusuf seemed to regard Bertrand's condition as a personal affront. He was too lofty to trouble with the lesser wounded, though he would condescend more often than not to do what could be done for the rest of those in the wagon.

Arslan found himself lending a hand, sometimes, when he had wearied of fighting, or when they had paused for the night. They were harried far out on the plain, forced into waterless and fireless camps, driven without mercy back toward Jerusalem. He seemed to hold Dame Fortune's favor: for all the fighting he did, all the arrows that flew over and past him, all the swords and spears that he met and beat aside, none touched him. He gained not even bruises, nor shed a drop of blood. God wanted him to live, it seemed, though whether he would live as heir of Beausoleil—that, he did not know.

In all that time he saw nothing of Queen Eleanor except from afar. The kings he saw often: he could hardly escape it as he performed his duties in Baldwin's tent and at his side. The French queen was keeping to herself, offering no outrageousness, wearing her armor but only for prudence's sake. Her knights and her favorites had the same whipped look as all the rest of them, the same angry incomprehension. They would never understand why they had had to run away, as they put it, from Damascus.

Even their kings seemed hard put to comprehend the need for retreat. They had agreed to it under duress, suffered it unwillingly, vexed Baldwin and the lords of Jerusalem beyond reason with their unshakable simplicity. In their world, a man was good or bad, Christian or infidel, friend or enemy. There were no shades between.

They could only win or lose a war. They did not understand how one could win a battle but lose the long fight, or how a defeat on one day might feed a victory the next. They did not think so far or comprehend so much.

Such simple people, one could think. Saracens often did, and paid in blood: for simplicity could be strong, and headlong bravery overcome the subtle maneuverings of eastern courts.

There was much bravery on that march, and much grim endurance. In camp at night, some still held out hope for the war, spoke of gathering again at Tiberias, restoring their strength, marching once more—against Aleppo as they should have done before, or against another and surer target; Edessa perhaps, or one of the smaller cities within reach of the Frankish borders.

But too many men were dead, too many hearts grown weak and cold. Such could happen in a war. The spirit could resist even the strongest defeat, rise up and overcome. Or it could sink and fail, and lose all hope of victory.

The armies of the West had stood in the muster for nigh two years. They had traveled far and fought a bitter fight to reach this place. And when they had come to it, they had found an enemy stronger than they had looked for, met a city that they could not take. Four days of humiliation, four days to discover that all their years of war mattered nothing. They were the laughingstock of Islam, the mock of the Saracens.

They were weary to the bone. They thought longingly of home: green and misty country, rain in the summer, water wherever they looked for it. They looked on the lords and fighting men of Outremer, and saw strangers, foreigners, men from beyond the sea. Men who, they were convinced, had betrayed them in the taking of Damascus.

Conrad of Germany, never the most sanguine of men, marched straight for Acre and away. He could not bring himself to linger in this country that had so shamed him. He sailed for Byzantium to the comfort of his imperial friend and kinsman, and thence again into the West.

But Louis of France was in no such haste to escape. As unfortunate as his Crusade had been, his return to France could only be worse. By now everyone knew what his queen insisted on: that their marriage be sundered, that she be set free to find another, less conspicuously godly husband. They no longer even pretended to travel together. She kept with her train to the army's center, he to the rear, while Baldwin and the knights of Jerusalem rode in the van.

She had wanted, it was said, to turn aside, to visit her kinsman in Antioch. But Louis had forbidden her. She was still his wife; he was still her liege lord. Even then she might have disobeyed, but her knights had a little sense. They persuaded her that it would do great harm to her cause in Rome if she were thought to be committing adultery with the Prince of Antioch. The pope might reckon then that setting her free would only encourage her in sin; that she should instead remain in the care and under the authority of her notably pious husband.

Eleanor had no talent for circumspection, and little for prudence, either. But she was never a fool. She could set aside her whims for a while—a very long while, perhaps—to show a proper restraint, if in the end it won her the freedom she desired.

Arslan had never fallen out of love with her. He should have. He saw her too clearly. He knew too much of her sins, her infelicities, her foibles.

It did not matter. His mother had never failed to see his father as he was: haughty, headstrong, never willing and seldom able to admit to error. She loved him nonetheless, lifelong and heart-deep. She would look at no other man, nor think of it—and men still courted her in Acre and in Jerusalem, for she remained a beautiful woman.

One could know what one loved, without falling out of love with it. Arslan had no expectation of requital, nor wanted it. It was enough that it was.

Or so he told himself on the long retreat from Damascus, as one by one the lords and knights scattered to their own places. The army dwindled day by day. Far fewer went home than had gone out. Women would weep and priests would sing the mass of the dead, over and over, through the length and breadth of Outremer.

It did not seem that they would sing that mass for Bertrand, lord of Beausoleil. He did not recover, but neither did he worsen or die. They carried him to Jerusalem—against his will, rather, for he would more happily have returned to his own castle. But Baldwin himself overruled him, speaking as king and not only as his friend and pupil. "You'll be tended where the best tending is," he said.

Bertrand, too weak to rise, could still snarl at him; but there was no opposing the will of a king. He had perforce to go where he was taken.

Arslan had never perfectly understood why westerners acted so strangely when they came to Jerusalem. It was the most holy of cities, to be sure. There were beautiful things in it: the Dome of the Rock all shining gold, the Father Mosque all silver like the moon, churches great and small, palaces, houses of princes. The Lord Christ had walked here, and David and Solomon, and the holy ones of Israel.

Yet it was, in the end, only a city. He had grown up in it, knew it as he knew his own body. He did not see why one should fall down weeping at sight of it, or drift about it in a fog of sanctimonious bliss. King Louis had been there already; but he had to visit every shrine again, walk every step of the Way of Calvary, spend whole days in prayer before the Holy Sepulcher.

The rest of them lived as they must live. Queen Eleanor, who more properly should have been Melisende's guest, was given a house in the city, and servants, and guards as she required them, and aught else that she cared to ask for. One thing only she was not given: her freedom to depart for France. Louis had forbidden it. They would return together or not at all.

She bore her misery well enough. Some would have said she was giddily happy, she with her court of adoring young men, her hunts and fêtes, her grand expeditions into the markets, where she strewed gold as if her husband's coffers were inexhaustible. She never seemed to care for the yowling of his clerks, nor to count the cost of any dainty that her whim fell on.

What Arslan saw of that, he saw from a distance, when he was not looking after his father. Bertrand had been taken to his own house, with Yusuf the physician still in attendance. There they found Helena waiting. She shed no tears, betrayed no shock at the pale shadow of a man who was brought to her in a litter. She took him in charge, saw him carried within, laid him in his own bed with his own servants to wait on him, and fought Yusuf to a standstill when he would have cast her out. Helena was a match for any man living, even a physician from Baghdad.

She in turn would have sent Arslan back to his king, but Arslan was in a mood to be stubborn. Baldwin had no particular need of him. Nor maybe did Bertrand, but Arslan wanted to be certain that he did not die after all and leave Arslan with an inheritance that he had never asked for.

Helena knew about it. There was little that Helena did not know. She spoke about it only once, a day or two after they came back. Arslan had been watching nightlong, had wandered out at dawn to discover if the cook would surrender a loaf of the bread that smelled so heavenly in the baking. Helena was there ahead of him with a new loaf and a well-aged cheese and a bowl of dates. Cook was nowhere in evidence. "Out at market," Helena said before Arslan could ask.

Arslan sat at the great scarred table with loaf and cheese and a cup of ale from the jar. They ate for a while in companionable silence. Helena was as sweetly contained as ever, no effusions of joy at her son's return, no outburst of grief over her lover's wound.

"Are you staying," she asked him after a while, "to make sure your father gets well, or to be sure he dies?"

Arslan came just short of choking on a date. "Do you need to ask me that?"

She shrugged. And was silent, which he should have let be, finished his breakfast and made his escape. But he could not help but say, "I don't want him to die."

"Why? Don't you want to be a Baron of the High Court of the Kingdom of Jerusalem?"

Arslan struck his fist on the table: a rare enough outburst that his mother blinked and looked briefly startled. "Of course I want to be a great lord of the world! But I wasn't raised to it. I've never even seen Beausoleil. He's never invited me there."

"You could have gone uninvited," Helena said.

"No," said Arslan.

She nodded slightly.

"The price is too high," Arslan said. "I don't want to pay it."

"Every noble heir pays it," said Helena.

"Not so late," Arslan said fiercely. "Not so ill. He could never call me his son in front of anyone who mattered—but he would make me his heir after he is dead. What joy is there ever in that?"

"Much," said Helena, "once the anger and the grief are past. Wealth, power, duties that can weigh heavy—but pleasure, too, and in great quantity, if so it pleases you."

"But I want that now," Arslan said. "While he's still alive. Why won't he give me that?"

"You should ask him," Helena said.

Arslan growled in his throat. He was not hungry, not any longer. He made what courtesy he could, rose and left her.

Of course he could not ask his father to acknowledge him in public, in the High Court itself, as his son and heir. He was too proud. Bertrand must do it himself or not at all.

And of course Bertrand would never do such a thing. For all the love he kept for Helena, for all the pride he seemed to take in his son, the old anger festered still. He would never forgive, not entirely, nor forget.

No more would Arslan, if this went on. He was innocent of any wrongdoing. If it was an ill thing to be born, then every living creature was as evil as the Manichees believed—and theirs was no heresy at all. The world belonged to the Devil, nor had God any part in it.

He crossed himself as the thought swelled and festered and burst. He was no heretic, whatever else he was. Only a nobleman's bastard, no more or less at fault for it than many another.

Maybe he should run away. Maybe, when the French went back at last to their own country, he should go with them. Queen Eleanor would take him into her service. He was decorative enough for that, and for whatever reason, she found him interesting. It was not as if he had nowhere to go, no place to take but that which his father grudgingly bestowed on him. He was not even indebted to Bertrand for his existence in Jerusalem. He was King Baldwin's man, friend and foster-brother and loyal companion. He needed nothing that Bertrand had to bestow.

Need was one thing. Wanting . . .

He fled the house that day, ran errands that to be sure needed doing, came back late and windblown and more tired than simple exertion might account for, and set himself to keep silent attendance on his father. Bertrand was asleep, a rarity in that he had taken no draught for it; Yusuf had denied him that comfort, bade him hunt down and capture sleep by himself, unaided. It was a restless, muttering sleep, edged visibly with pain, but he did not rouse from it as Arslan sat beside his bed.

Arslan was glad. If Bertrand had been awake, they would have quarreled. He did not want that. He kept his vigil, drowsing himself, but alert to any shift in breathing or movement from the man in the bed.

Yusuf would not say that Bertrand would recover. "He might go on like this for the rest of a reasonably long life," he had said when Arslan asked, somewhere north of Banias. "He might mortify and die tomorrow. There's no telling."

"But," Arslan had said then, "the longer he goes on, the more likely he is to recover, yes?"

"No," Yusuf said. "He should get better. If not, and soon, he never will."

That was weeks ago now. Bertrand was a little less weak, perhaps. A little clearer-headed when he was awake. But not enough. Perhaps not ever enough.

It came to Arslan as he sat there, that if this went on, he would not be able to bear it. Not for months, even years. No knight and fighting man should be so crippled, so grievously diminished.

If Bertrand was not better in a month, Arslan would go back to Baldwin. Or perhaps, if that taxed his strength too greatly, he would go to Mount Ghazal. Lady Richildis would be having her baby soon. All word from her was good, or at least not ill. She was in good health, her letters said, letters she wrote to Helena and meant for the others as well. She grew enormous rather early in her time. Maybe, she said, she was bearing a giant, another Bohemond. But the midwife was in no anxiety, and she was vigorous enough, though careful as a woman of her age should be, who hoped to bear a child alive and to emerge alive herself.

Maybe Arslan would go to Mount Ghazal to visit his aunt, to learn from Kutub the Turkish arts of war, to sit in the evenings with Michael Bryennius and hear tales from everywhere in the world, and thereby practice his Greek. He was not bound here in Jerusalem, not unless his king commanded him; and Baldwin had set him free for as long as he had need. He could go wherever he pleased.

A month, first. A month at his father's side, if he could will healing on a man who had lost the heart for it. Even Helena's presence seemed not to be enough. Maybe Arslan's would be, if Arslan refused to be Bertrand's heir if he died before he had acknowledged his son.

Arslan could endure it for a month. He would count the hours, but he would suffer through them. He was a Christian, was he not? He had learned from the cradle that suffering was a virtue. He would practice it now, for his father's sake.

Bertrand's days had blurred into the nights, a long grey fog of pain. He knew that he had traveled the length of the kingdom, that he had come to Jerusalem—and yes, beyond doubt that he was in his own house, but Helena was living in it, and Arslan. Helena he would have been startled not to see. Arslan . . .

The boy could not forgive him for what he had done. That was as clear as if Arslan had shouted it. He was making his presence a mute reproach. Taking revenge, Bertrand thought, for an injury that he in his youth must reckon unforgivable.

Bertrand in his age could hardly disagree. It was ill done, and yet what else could he do?

"Acknowledge him," Helena said crisply. He had not spoken aloud, but she always knew what he was thinking. A lesser man, or one more superstitious, might have reckoned her a witch. She was perceptive, that was all, and she knew him well.

She had no patience with what she called his nonsense: his moping and glooming, his indulgence in pain. Even Yusuf was gentler about it than she.

"You want to die," she said, "because your pride won't let you give your son his birthright while you're alive to see it. Haven't you wallowed in your revenge for long enough? Haven't you had enough of punishing him in order to punish me?"

"How is he punished?" Bertrand demanded. "He's a king's man. He's risen higher by himself than I could ever have raised him. He's the king's own foster-brother. God knows, he could even marry a queen, if he goes on as he's begun."

"Not Eleanor," Helena said in a tone so fierce that Bertrand stared at her.

"Of course not Eleanor," he said. "She's a queen already, and Louis is in no hurry to join himself with the God he professes to love so well."

"She'll divorce him," said Helena, "or he her. That's a certainty. But she won't sink her claws in my son."

"No; she'll find herself a boy who's heir to a kingdom already. My little pair of baronies are nothing that she would trouble to notice."

"Little baronies," she said, "but rich enough, and great power to be had from them, if their lord is ambitious."

"Do you think our son is?"

Helena paused before she answered. "I think that he will do whatever he judges best, for himself and his honor and his liege lord. He'll not refuse a gift given freely and openly. But," she said, "he wants a thing that you are unwilling to give. He'll give up wealth and lordship for it, if he must."

"He's a fool," Bertrand said.

"He is your son," said Helena.

Bertrand opened his mouth to speak, but no words came. He who had refused La Forêt, who had sworn never again to set foot in Anjou—he could hardly condemn the son of his own body for doing much the same, and for spite at his father, too.

Wisdom was never less than painful. Worse at the moment than his wound, which caught at his side and made him draw breath shallowly.

Helena left him to ponder his sins and his son. Whom he loved almost to despair, whom he looked on with both pride and grief. Pride for all that the boy was. Grief that he had not known of it till the boy was nearly a man. And now . . .

He closed his eyes. The dark was no more comforting than the light of day. He had never in his life swallowed his pride. He could not begin now. No, not though he died before morning.

That grace he would not be given. Yusuf was one of those few physicians who believed that a patient should know the truth. And Bertrand's truth was that he was not dying. He might live long years as he was. He might recover, though by how much, Yusuf would not foretell. Bertrand suspected that the former was more nearly true than the latter.

To live so; bedridden, weakened, slave to the heavy knot of pain that Yusuf's potions could not loosen or banish . . .

He was, by a miracle, alone. No servant lurked in a shadow. Helena had gone, he knew not where. Arslan was asleep, surely, or resting till evening, when he would keep vigil again in accusing silence.

Bertrand moved by inches. He was too weak for aught else. He was sitting upright already, bolstered in cushions; he breathed easier so. Little by little he slid his legs over the side of the bed. They felt as heavy as the beams overhead, and as lifeless.

He bade the fear be still. He was not a paralytic. He was weak, that was all, and wounded in the side, like the maimed king of the stories that the folk of Provence and Aquitaine had been wont to sing in camp of an evening. That one had suffered for his pride, too, and his myriad sins.

Bertrand's feet touched the floor. It was cool—he had forgotten how cool tiles could be on bare feet. He had to pause, to breathe as best he could, to still the spinning world. When he could almost breathe and the world was almost steady, he ventured to stand.

His knees buckled, but he clung to the bedpost. Patience, he admonished himself. He had been guarded like a prisoner, bound to his bed as to a rack. And for all the wisdom and the irascible excellence of the king's physician, Bertrand had begun to hate this confinement. Better to burst the wound and die, than to lie like a cripple.

He thanked God for the bedpost, and for his deathgrip on it. But he was on his feet. Reeling, staggering, half blind with dizziness, but he was standing. He might even, if all the saints assisted, venture a step. One feeble shuffle of the foot. Knees wobbling appallingly, breath a gasp, wound stabbing till he nearly fainted with it.

But he was erect, more or less. He was walking, or thinking of it. He—would—take up his pallet and walk. Was this not Jerusalem? Had not God wrought miracles here?

For today, for this moment, it was miracle enough that he had stood. Nor, as he fell back to the bed and lay half lifeless, had he opened the wound. Much. The pain had an almost salubrious edge. It kept him awake when he would happily have fallen into the dark.

Every day, if they would ever leave him alone, he would do this. He would get up. He would walk. He would make himself strong. He would spite Yusuf. He would gratify Arslan. He would heal, or die trying.

A month, Arslan had promised himself. A month at his father's side. And then, if nothing had altered, he would withdraw to Mount Ghazal.

He had not reckoned that Bertrand would have the same thought. Beausoleil was too far, and would demand too much of him. But Mount Ghazal that was his sister's holding, where he had always been welcome—yes, he announced, he would go there. And Arslan, if he would, would ride escort.

In the end they all went, father, mother, and son, Helena's Turks and their wives and such of their children as could not fend for themselves: a whole caravan descending on Lady Richildis at the end of her confinement. Helena did not think of it so; she pointed out with some acerbity that a woman should bear her child within the arms of her family.

And, it seemed, all of her family's servants and dependents; but Arslan did not venture to say so. He was disgruntled. He had hoped to escape alone, to find a little peace if he could. Instead all his troubles went with him.

They came to Mount Ghazal on a fine day in autumn, warm still but no longer with the fierce edge of summer. It had rained not long ago, unusual for this season; the dust was not as chokingly thick as it might have been, and the leaves of the trees, such as were left, were washed almost clean.

Mount Ghazal had grown beautiful since first its lady came to it. It was a green and pleasant place, watered by deep wells, rich and prosperous in these days. Kutub had kept its young men alive even through the terrible winnowing of Damascus, and brought them back, every one, to their wives and sisters and daughters. They were there to greet the arrivals, the women with garlands of flowers, the men with shouts and cheers for the Lord of Beausoleil and—yes—for his son, too. Bertrand, riding unhappily in a litter, managed to sit up for them, to smile and acknowledge them with a bow and a lift of the hand.

Michael Bryennius awaited them in the castle's gate. His lady was within, too great with child to stand for long in the sun, but eager as he said to see them. He was always gracious, was Michael Bryennius. He led them through a great court and a lesser one and one no greater than a cloister, brilliant with flowers, and thence to a hall that must be the new bower of which Arslan had heard: the people's gift to their lady, built while she was away.

It was lovely, splendid with tiles in the manner of the infidels, blue and gold and white. A fountain played in the court in front of it. Its doors were open to let in the sun and the warmth, its high windows likewise. It looked, with its slender pillars, as if it were made of light.

Lady Richildis reclined in the midst of it, stretched on a divan like an eastern lady. But she was hardly idle. There were women about her, stitching and weaving and writing in books. She herself had a basket of needlework, though she seemed to have put it aside some time since.

She was vast indeed with the child, but it seemed not to have drained her as babies sometimes did. Her cheeks were full, her color excellent. Her eyes seemed a little tired, but the light in them was as bright as one could ask for. She smiled and held out her hands to them all. "How wonderful," she said. "How splendid to see you!"

Lady Richildis never said such things unless she meant them. Arslan, walking somewhat ahead of his mother and of his father carried in a chair, knelt to kiss her hand as if she had been a queen. She laughed at him for it, breathlessly, drew him to her and kissed him on the forehead as she had done when he was small. As he had done then, he blushed and ducked his head and felt like an idiot. But not such an idiot as would have been glad to sink beneath the earth. No; a happy fool, ridiculously glad to be in her presence again.

He had always been a little in love with his aunt. She was beautiful even now, with her slender body all gone to shapelessness, and her hair hidden under a veil, and those shadows of weariness under her fine grey eyes. She welcomed Helena with a brief, close embrace, and her brother with no evident shock, though this thin and weakened man with his hair gone all suddenly grey could be nothing like the Bertrand she remembered. "We'll talk the days away," she promised them. "But first, rest, and wash away the dust of the road. There's sherbet for you, wine, whatever delicacies you can think of—only ask and they'll be brought to you."

"Peacocks' tongues?" Arslan asked, facetious.

"I'm sure cook can find them," Richildis said, "if you can't live without them."

Arslan bowed again, glad after all that he had come here. Here was heart's ease. Here was comfort and kin, and relief, a little, from his sorrows. All in a pair of grey eyes and a well-remembered smile.

ichildis was brought to bed some-
what before her time—not unexpected, as great with the child as she had grown.
She admitted to no fear. The midwife, who had been birthing babies in the village
since long before Richildis herself was born, professed no anxiety. She did make
haste to the castle once the summons reached her, but that was only prudent;
Richildis was her liege lady.

A woman forgot from child to child the precise length and intensity of birthing.
It was one of God's more pointed mercies. In the midst of it she had little choice
but to endure. She could not stop it. She could slow it, but what profit was there
in that? If she could make it go swifter, she would. She could certainly curse the
man who had caused her to be in this condition, though Richildis was not as far
gone as that.

He sat beside her, gripping her hands. The pain of it was a blessed thing. It kept
her mind off the pain in her belly. She could not voice what she feared: that these
were twins again, and that one or both might not be born alive. The midwife said
not, that it was only one child, but midwives had been in error before.

The hours stretched, counted in intervals of pain and painlessness. Michael
Bryennius remained with her, and Helena quiet in a corner with a book and a bit
of embroidery. The maids did turn and turn about.

The pains had begun after morning mass. They went on long after compline and
into the quiet of the night. Richildis drowsed as she could, in between battles. When
she was awake she walked, leaning on Michael Bryennius or on Helena or on the
midwife. Sometimes, late, when even Helena was asleep, it was Arslan offering his
arm, not speaking, simply being there.

She wondered then in her fog of pain and tiredness: when had he grown so tall?
He was a man, as tall as his father. The cheek she brushed with her hand to thank
him was rough with the bristle of beard, though fair hair on fair skin was difficult
to see. She could remember when he was hardly older than this child who struggled
so fiercely to be born.

He was there with her, holding her arm, when the strong pain struck, the one
she had been waiting for: the battering down of the gate. Her water was long since
broken. There was nothing left for the child but to be born.

She caught at Arslan, half-falling against him. He made to sweep her up, but she resisted with what little strength she had. "No," she gasped. "No, the stool, quickly!" Thinking as she said it that the midwife was gone, to the garderobe, to bed, who knew? And Helena was asleep, and Michael Bryennius had disappeared, and her maids were none of them to be seen. There was only this boy growing big-eyed as the truth struck him, but too brave to run away. He blanched but held his ground.

And then there was no thought in her at all except to expel this insistent burden in her belly, this core of blood-black pain. She was aware through a fog of hands gripping hers, and of bearing down, and of the hands vanishing and a young voice gasping, "It's coming! God's feet, what do I do?"

"Catch it," she tried to say. She did not know if she succeeded.

"God," he said, pure heartfelt prayer. "God in—*Oh!*"

She would have laughed if she had had breath for it. Such an expression; such astonishment. Such a small red struggling screaming thing in those big hands, and the cord glistening between.

And the midwife was there, snipping the cord, tying it, doing what must be done, all while he held the baby. It—her. A girl. A daughter. Only one after all; a robust child but no giant, and no twin, either. Richildis' womb was safely, securely emptied.

Arslan held the baby for a long time. People kept coming. The midwife, the maids, Michael Bryennius cursing the chance that had sent him out just then and failed to fetch him back before his daughter was born. He did not take the baby, no more than anyone else had. He came to stare and marvel and be amazed, but turned quickly to his wife.

She insisted and the midwife agreed that all was well. But there was a great deal of blood. More blood than on a battlefield, and more terrible, because they so loved the one who shed it.

And all the while they dealt with the blood, Arslan held the baby. She had been bathed, at least, and wrapped in a swaddling. The cradle was waiting for her. He was in no particular haste to set her in it.

He had birthed foals before. Lambs, kids, a calf or two. Puppies, kittens. But never a baby. Never before this.

She was such a little wizened thing to have cost so much. And yet, so great a marvel. So beautiful, after all. Was she not her mother's child?

He knew what it was to be in love. This was different. It was fiercer, less content just to be. He could stand apart and adore his beloved, but for this one he would be in the thick of any fight, would defend her though he died for it. For her he wanted to *do* something.

He could do little tonight but lay her in her cradle, and later, when the midwife beckoned, bring her to her mother to nurse. That was much later, after Richildis had slept, and her husband beside her as if he could atone for his failure to be with her when the child was born. Arslan had had no sleep in him. The long custom of keeping vigil over his father had served him in good stead. He sat by the cradle, quietly content. When the midwife called to him, he started. He had half dreamed that he was here all alone again, he and the newborn child.

• • •

They named her Zenobia, because, her mother said, she was born in a foreign land. It was a great deal of name for a small person, but she bore it with fortitude. She was a quiet baby, yet strong. She seldom cried, and never fussed or fretted. Mostly, those first days of her life, she lay gravely regarding the world, testing the limbs that were so new to her, nursing and sleeping in what seemed equal measure.

She had a nurse, of course. All noble babies did. Her mother's milk was scant in any event, and dried too quickly; but Yasmin, who had delivered a round brown dumpling of a baby only the day before Zenobia was born, had milk enough for multitudes. She was glad to share it with her lady's daughter.

They were all strangely careful of her, as if they remembered the two who had died. But children died; that was the way of the world, and God's will in it, for who knew what purpose. One could harden one's heart toward the child till it had grown out of childhood, or love it regardless, and mourn when it died.

Richildis could not be cold to the child of her body, more than her husband could, or any of her kin. It was not in them. Every morning they prayed for the little one, and every night before they slept, that she would live and grow strong; that she would come to womanhood.

Maybe the prayers helped her, and the love that went with them. Maybe God would be merciful this time, and not take her to Himself. No one could know, nor be sure of aught but that she lived now and seemed to thrive, nursed well and slept well and grew with the swiftness of the very young. In only a little while she was no longer a red and wizened monkey of a creature but a pink-and-white infant with wide eyes that would be dark when she was older, and dark curls, but her mother's lovely pale skin. She would be a beauty, they all thought; such a face as could break a man's heart.

They brought her to Bertrand since he could not come to her. He who had been denied his son was given the gift of a sister's daughter, not as burden or duty but as simple joy. She was not afraid of him as the servants' children were, frightened by his size and his gauntness and his pale face. She would lie in his arms, sleeping or regarding him gravely, with a hand wrapped round one of his fingers.

He was not as weak as they all thought. Not strong enough yet to walk far, nor steady enough to confess to the hours he spent in the nights, dragging himself up, shutting down the pain in his side, walking from bed to wall and back again, over and over. But to Zenobia he could speak of it, cradling her while her nurse and her kin were elsewhere. She listened; no matter if she understood. She who could not walk at all yet must wonder why he was so determined on it.

"And somehow," he said to her, "I have to find a way to ride; to get a horse saddled, to get out. I could ride, I think, better than I can walk. If I can sit a horse, I'll be a man again. I'll be strong. I'll finally—after all this time, I'll be alive."

She gurgled and sucked on her fist. She was too young to smile yet, the women said, but he could have sworn that her lips had curved at the sight of him.

When her nurse came to retrieve her, he feigned weariness so that they would all leave him alone again. To walk he needed nothing but solitude. To ride—that needed more. A groom at least, and servants to carry him down to the stableyard, and more difficult than either, to persuade the hovering flock of his kin that they should both allow it and forbear from interfering in it.

They would keep him bound to his bed until he died of pure frustration. And surely it was winter, and there were days of chill rain, raw winds, even snow; but many a morning he would wake to clear cold sunlight and remember the feel of wind in his face, and all but weep because he must breathe nothing but the warm rank air of this castle.

There was one whom he could ask, whom he could trust to understand—but that one of them all demanded the most of his pride. They were not quarrelling, if they ever had been, but neither were they at ease with one another. Arslan still had not forgiven his father, perhaps never would.

But he would understand. The longer Bertrand endured his confinement, the more difficult it became to cling to his stubbornness. And after a full week of sun, when it was almost unnaturally warm, so much so that flowers were blooming in the garden outside his window, he drew a breath and called the servant and bade him fetch Arslan.

It was a long while before Arslan came. Long enough that Bertrand knew he had been slighted, or that the boy had gone away and was in no haste to return. Yet at last he came, bringing with him a gust of wind and a scent of the open air and a strong suggestion of horses. "You were out riding," Bertrand said by way of greeting. He had not meant it to sound like an accusation, but from the tightening of Arslan's face, it was no less.

Bertrand cursed himself for a fool. Already they were at odds, and they had not been together for more than a moment.

But the sun was shining, and Bertrand was like to go mad with yearning for it. He forced himself to be humble, though it cost him high. "Your pardon, please, I beg you. I'm shut in here, and my temper is not all that it could be."

"No," Arslan said helpfully. "It's not. And here you were talking of taking the cowl. Could you live in a cloister, then, if you can't bear even this light confinement?"

Insolent. Bertrand bit his tongue and steeled himself not to answer that; not to take the bait so temptingly offered. "I need you to help me," he said—and that was as difficult a thing as he had ever said. "I don't think I can live if I have to live bedridden. If I can get out—if I can find my way into a saddle—"

"You'll fall right out of it," Arslan said. Oh, no: he was giving not one hair's breadth. Could he truly be as angry as that?

It seemed that he could be. Bertrand set his teeth and persevered. Not in words this time. In rising. In standing without falling. In walking toward him.

It was gratifying to see that hard young face wake suddenly into expression: into pure astonishment. And joy? Not likely. And yet perhaps, after all . . .

Bertrand stood in front of him. "Help me get to the stables," he said, "and onto a horse. I don't care if it's one of the plowhorses. Just get me into a saddle."

"Yusuf will pitch a fit," Arslan said.

"I don't care if he dies of it," Bertrand said fiercely. "I don't care if *I* die. I'm dying here, and in misery too."

"Of course you must go on living," Arslan said. "But I'll catch the whipping for your transgression."

"You will not," said Bertrand. "I will take all lashes that are honestly coming to me, and any that may be meant for you. Only help me to escape from this prison."

"Such a prison," Arslan said. "Lined with silk, and better victuals than a monk will ever see."

Bertrand set his lips together. "Very well," he said. "Go. I'll find another way."

"What, and get yourself killed?" Arslan shook his head. "No. I'll do it for you. It may take a day or two. Can you wait?"

"I have been waiting," Bertrand said, "for months."

"Good. Then wait a little longer." And with that, Arslan left him.

Bertrand wondered after the boy was gone, whether he could trust what after all had been no promise—and no agreement to do as Bertrand wished. But if he could not trust his own son, on whom could he ever rely?

He set himself to be patient. If in two days or three he had heard nothing, he would find another accomplice. He could be as patient as that. If he must.

rslan supposed that he was much a fool as his father was, creeping about and conspiring against the king's own and best physician. For the matter of that, neither the ladies nor Michael Bryennius would be delighted to discover what Arslan was up to. They were all convinced that Bertrand was as strong as he would ever be; that he would be bedridden the rest of his life. They did not talk about it, maybe did not admit it, but he could see it in their eyes. They had despaired of ever seeing Bertrand strong again.

Arslan had his own doubts, but he had seen his father standing and, after a fashion, walking—and not fainting or falling, either. Such determination was hardly surprising in a man who could keep an oath for thirty years and more, and hold a grudge for nigh on twenty.

If it kept Bertrand alive for another twenty years, Arslan would do it and be glad. That was his own battle, his own irresistible oath.

With everyone so preoccupied with Lady Richildis and the baby, it was not as difficult as it might have been to conspire with Muhammad in the stable. Muhammad was apt for mischief, and willing to pretend that he was taking Lord Bertrand's Malik to the west field for exercise. After all, his lordship could not ride the stallion himself, but would never be separated from him, even in illness.

Bertrand might not have been thinking of Malik; had perhaps expected a quiet mare or one of the geldings. But Arslan trusted the grey stallion, and trusted Muhammad to run the edge off beforehand.

That was simple. More difficult by far to spirit Bertrand out of the castle without rousing every servant and man-at-arms.

In the end he decided to trust again. He went to Kutub.

Kutub could very easily turn traitor. He was Lady Richildis' man, had been since Arslan was born. Yet Arslan rather thought that old loyalty might suffice, and sympathy for a warrior who must, for his life, ride again.

The Turk raised his brows at Arslan's request. Arslan held his breath. Just as he must let it out or burst, Kutub said, "Two of my lads and a diversion. Simple. But it can't stay a secret. They'll see him out there."

"Just let him get out," Arslan said. "Once he's done it and survived, they can hardly stop him after."

"You think so?" Kutub shrugged. "Well then. If we in Islam could sin as you

Christians can, I'd be running to confession for this. Isn't it a wonderful thing to be a sinless man?"

"No man is without sin," Arslan said severely. Kutub only laughed at him.

They got Bertrand out by slipping him down a rear stair and out the postern, two big sturdy young men of Mount Ghazal carrying him between them, and Arslan in the van, on watch against attack. He had chosen the time of day when everyone was either occupied or playing with the baby, midway between sunrise and noon. The servants were in the hall or in the kitchens. No one met them. No guard stood at the gate to bar their way.

Malik was waiting in the field out of sight of all but the castle's towers, out beyond the hill and toward the eastward road. He was sweating lightly but breathing easy, head up, ears alert as he watched a handful of strangers carrying his master toward him. Bertrand did not try to stop them at the field's edge, did not ask as Arslan had half expected, to walk to his horse. That was wisdom, perhaps: to save his strength for the saddle.

He did not seem surprised to see his own stallion and not some quieter beast. Perhaps he drew a breath in a sigh. Arslan, striding to hold the stirrup, could not be certain. Malik stood motionless as if he understood what he must do. Only the flick of an ear betrayed his wonted spirit.

They lifted Bertrand into the saddle. He reached as he rose, drew himself a little of the way, swung his leg over and rested for a moment. His face was white, but on it such a look of triumph that no one could utter a word.

And while they stood staring, he set heels to the stallion's sides, plucked reins out of Muhammad's hand, and sprang off at a gallop.

None of them—not one, not even Kutub—had thought to come mounted. Fools, idiots, and far too trusting.

Arslan ran a little distance, but no man could catch a galloping horse. He stopped in frustration, glanced back. The others had not moved.

The grey horse circled the field. After his first headlong leap he settled to an easy gait, light and smooth. The man on his back was grinning like a skull.

Bertrand came back to them. He was dead white, swaying in the saddle, but he was laughing. "I can," he said with the thread of breath that was left to him. "I *can* do it!"

Bertrand paid for his folly, but he reckoned it well worth the price. Malik carried him back to the castle to an uproar that he barely heard. He was carried off to bed, and collapsed there for the rest of the day and all that night, a deep and sodden sleep scarlet-edged with pain.

But he had done it. He could do it. He would again—not tomorrow perhaps, but the day after.

When he woke in the morning to the grey light and the cold hiss of rain, he laughed to see it. "I cheated you," he said to it. "I saw the sun again."

Someone moved on the edge of his vision. He started slightly, turned to upbraid the servant for creeping in without warning.

It was no servant. It was his son, and looking as if he had been there for a while, sitting in the chair by the wall. He did not seem to have slept there. He was clean, combed and dressed, and bright awake.

"Did they crucify you?" Bertrand asked him.

He shook his head. "Only a few mild lashes of words, and a great deal of expostulating to one another. They're all outraged that you deceived them for so long. Yusuf was so angry that he left."

"What, to return to Jerusalem?" Bertrand rebuked his heart for singing; but he had not loved that sour-faced creature.

"No," said Arslan. "He was talking of Baghdad. But he only went to bed. I suspect he'll tarry a while, to be sure you haven't killed yourself."

"Pest," said Bertrand mildly. "I would have been—so glad—to be rid of him."

"You'll drive him off next time you go galloping about and opening your wound."

"Did I?" Bertrand's hand went to his side. "It doesn't feel any worse that it ever did."

"Yusuf lanced it," Arslan said, "and let out a great quantity of ill humours and a shard of metal that must have been buried deep. I thought I heard him mutter that maybe now you would heal."

"Then I will," Bertrand said. He was dizzy, and not with exhaustion. "You didn't set a price on this that you did for me. Why?"

"What price could I have set?" Arslan asked.

Bertrand did not think he was as innocent as he looked and sounded. Nonetheless, if that was the game, then he would play it so. "I think you know," he said.

"Would it have done any good?"

"It might," said Bertrand.

Arslan shook his head and turned his face away. "No. Not you. Not after this long."

"Are you demanding proof?"

"No," said Arslan. "I won't humiliate myself."

"You," said Bertrand, "are the most infuriating child."

The fair brows lifted. It stabbed at Bertrand to see so world-weary an expression on so young a face. "I come by it honestly," Arslan said.

Bertrand drew a breath. It stabbed, but not as deep as it might have. Perhaps he deluded himself. Perhaps indeed he would heal. If there had been a notch in the blade that pierced him—then steel in the flesh would have weakened him indeed; and now it was gone.

Out of that hope he cobbled together a semblance of patience. "What do you require? Full Court ceremonial? A papal dispensation? Legitimacy?"

"A simple word will do," Arslan said levelly.

"There is a price for that," said Bertrand. "You must agree to be my heir."

"And if I won't," said Arslan, "I'm no worse off than I was before."

Bertrand inclined his head. This was difficult, more difficult even than he had thought. The words alone were simple enough, the wounds they dealt as deep as might be expected. But that face, that weariness, that certainty that he had seen all the blows that the world could deal—Bertrand found that most grievous to bear.

He was weak, that was all. His long wound had made him feeble. All young men grew weary of the world; it was their way.

They did not all grow as weary as this. Nor was any of them Bertrand's fault, save this one. All the things that he could have done and had not; the years he had lost, the words unsaid—they were all here, in front of him. And yet whatever he did, however he strove to make amends, he could never undo what he had done. He could not cast back time to live those years again.

"It's only the word you want," Bertrand said. "Why? Why not all of it?"

Arslan shrugged. "Lands and lordship I can get from my king. But the name of son—only one man can give me that."

"You are a strange man," Bertrand said, not meaning to say it aloud.

But it was said; and Arslan laughed at it, not particularly bitter. "People always say that to me. It's true, then, I suppose. Are you going to rebuke me for it?"

"Hardly," said Bertrand. "Many a father would give gold for such a son."

"Would you?"

"I have him," Bertrand said.

"Then," said Arslan, "what would you give up, to keep me? Can you sacrifice your pride? Can you really do what you say—can you name me yours before the High Court of Jerusalem?"

"I have never had any shame of you," Bertrand said.

"That is not what I asked," said Arslan.

"I said that I would," Bertrand said. "And I will, when I can walk into the gathering of the Court and stand in front of them again."

"Easter Court," Arslan said. "Promise me."

"If God wills," Bertrand said.

Arslan seemed content with that. Bertrand, to himself, resolved to do it sooner. Christmas Court if he could, if God was merciful. Before not only the nobility of Jerusalem but the lords and the King of France, who by all accounts would still be there. Then he could name Arslan heir to La Forêt, too, and lord-to-be of Beausoleil. Let him have it all, though he professed to want only the word.

enobia grew and thrived, and Bertrand
thrived with her, though the year greyed and faded into the chill of winter. She
was smiling, then laughing, tumbling on the floor when her nurse would let her,
while he was indeed riding before he could walk any distance at all. In the saddle
he was a man again.

The more he rode, the more swiftly he felt himself heal. Yusuf had not been so
kind as to vanish after all. He lingered, hovered, muttered, but did nothing to
prevent Bertrand from doing as he pleased. If it had been any man but Yusuf,
Bertrand would have thought that he was happy here in Mount Ghazal; that he
was in no haste to go away from it.

It was a pleasant place. People knew how to laugh here. No one went hungry.
Even the village's one leper was taken care of, given a hut of her own at some little
distance but still within sight of the castle. She had a dog to protect her, one
of the castle's hounds, and food was brought her every day, and prayers said for
her in the castle's chapel.

Beausoleil should be as well ruled as this. Bertrand could admit it in the generosity of his old age: his sister was a better lord than he, and happier in it, too. Even
in that common failure of women, that she could not lead men to war, she had
managed well in Kutub and in Bertrand himself.

Bertrand would lead men again, would ride to war, would be lord once more in
Beausoleil. What once had been as certain as the sun's rising, was now a wondrous
thing. Joyous; miraculous. Each morning when he rose, he thanked God that he
was healed. Each evening before he went to sleep, he prayed that he would wake
and find it all no dream.

He passed Martinmas in something close to his old strength. The wound in his
side was shrunk to a scar, deep and livid, that pulled when he moved too quickly,
but he had long grown accustomed to the stab of it. Yusuf gave him an ointment
to rub into it, that smelled remarkably sweet. Perhaps it helped; perhaps it merely
appeased the nose.

As Advent approached, the castle stirred to a different kind of life. Its lady was
preparing to attend Christmas Court, that this year was in Jerusalem. They would

all go, all her kin. Bertrand would ride, would come to the Holy City as befit a baron of its High Court: erect on horseback, and not prostrate in a litter.

Always when the court gathered in Jerusalem or in Acre, it became a kind of pilgrimage. The barons and their trains flowed together on the roads, friend meeting friend, enemy shunning enemy as they rode down to Jerusalem. Now and then they met companies of westerners, a German or two and many a French knight or lordling, wandering about while his king tarried in the holy places.

Bertrand had been apart so long—longer than he had imagined; and before that, ever since Damascus, he had been wrapped in a black dream of pain. This was like waking: the crowded road, men whom he had known nigh his life long and men whom he had first met in the Crusade; joy of festival, but grimness too, a war lost, a great venture failed.

None of them would renew the fight. Germany had gone home. France remained only on pilgrimage, and in avoidance of the inevitable: wars and quarrels in the West, a queen who wished no longer to be queen, coffers sore depleted and spirits broken. Happier to linger here, to pray where the Lord Christ had prayed, to wash the soul clean.

The men of Jerusalem had no such escape, and for most of them, no such despair. They were not far away from home in a strange land. This was their country. They would continue to defend it against the infidel; to protect the Holy Sepulcher, to stand watch in their chain of castles. The loss that they had suffered was one of many. After it would come victory, however they won it, however long it took them.

And Bertrand was one of them. Long ago, so long that he could barely remember it, he had been a knight of Anjou. He had looked in time to marry an heiress, to be lord of a holding while his brother Giraut was lord in La Forêt. His little sister would be wedded to a man of worth, would bear him sons and look after his affairs and be no more and no less than a noble lady should be.

How strange to remember what he had been. To look about him, to see his thin awkward sister grown tall and beautiful, married for love to a man of Byzantium, served with conspicuous devotion by Turks and Saracens, and servant herself to the Queen of Jerusalem. And he . . . no wife to his name, but a lady who in all respects had been as a wife, and a son who carried himself like a prince, and a barony on the borders of the kingdom, to which he would return when this court was ended. This was real. This was solid and strong. Anjou had shrunk to dream, a dim and misty shape on the edge of memory.

So ran the world. Bertrand wondered if his sister understood what had happened to them both—if she still imagined that she could go back to La Forêt. None of them could. Not now; not ever in this life.

Arslan in Jerusalem was like a young stallion sent away to a stranger's pasture, but now he had returned to the fields where he was raised. He ran a little wild, insofar as he ever could, which—said Baldwin—was not very. But Baldwin meant it well. He could not be a wild thing at all, not and be a proper king.

Jerusalem was full of idle French and delirious pilgrims: much as always. Nahar his friend and sometime lover had left the house in which Arslan first found her, to take her own small house in the company of three or four women both skilled and beautiful. She had ambitions, she told him. She was going to rise in the world. She was growing older; her beauty had never been remarkable, but even character did not long survive the ravages of age. Not in her occupation.

He knew better than to deny it. Nor did he doubt that she could do as she intended. She was like his mother, like Lady Richildis—like, for that matter of that, Queen Eleanor. A determined woman could shift the world, or reshape it to suit her pleasure.

Queen Eleanor had undergone, it seemed, a change of heart. She was no more enamored of her husband, but she had put aside frivolity to play the pilgrim. Sackcloth she would never wear, and a hairshirt would torment her beautiful white skin, but she put on gowns of almost monastic plainness, veiled her bright hair and lowered her eyes and showed herself all piously demure.

The pope in Rome might believe it, but Arslan found it difficult. Easier to credit that she might agree to remain bound to Louis—and that, she would not do. She kept a cool distance, was seen with him only in public and only as often as she absolutely must. Her household kept well apart from his. They had no more in common than a lord and lady of separate demesnes.

She would behave as discreetly as woman could, bridle her enthusiasms, mute her taste for strong wine and bright colors and rich things, if it would win her freedom. It said much for her strength of will that she could conduct herself so far against her nature.

She even forbore to surround herself with flocks of beautiful young men. They came, begged, were turned away. Rome must be given no cause to accuse her. She would be as pure of fleshly sin as was possible for a woman to be.

And yet she did not cut herself off completely from the world or from the beauties that dwelt in it. So Arslan discovered one day near the end of Advent, as he was coming back to the Tower of David with a company of the king's squires. They had been determining which of several taverns served the best beer, and were well gone in it, too.

Arslan was not greatly fond of beer. Ale was none too ill, but he much preferred wine. He was the most sober of them therefore, and the steadiest on his feet, as a page in French livery accosted him under the arch of the gate. The others tipped the brat on his head and left him in the water-butt, but Arslan plucked him out wet and spluttering and shivering noisily, for the wind blew cold through the great gate.

"Here," Arslan said, flinging his own cloak over the narrow shoulders. "What are you doing here? Did you get lost? Your king's praying in a church somewhere, I'm sure."

The boy shot him a look under wet curls. "I'm not the king's man," he said through chattering teeth—clearly, too, as if he had done it often before. In France maybe it was common sport for squires to dip pages in icy water-barrels. "I belong to her majesty, and her majesty wants you to come and see her."

"Does she now?" said Arslan. "And why is that?"

"She just says come," the boy said.

Arslan had to stop to discover what he felt. Joy? Annoyance? Amusement, even? He had been in Jerusalem a week and more, and never a word from the Queen of France, never a glance on the two occasions when she had dined with the King and the Queen of Jerusalem. She had forgotten him, he had thought. He did not blame her for it. She was a queen. Queens knew so many people, saw so many faces. Why should she remember his of all those she had seen?

Now it seemed she had remembered. He had duties in court, but not for a while. He was presentable enough. He nodded to the page. "Take me to her, then."

Eleanor must have been traveling about the shrines again. She was dressed in grey, with a white veil like a nun. Yet as Arslan was led in to her, she let fall the veil. One of her maids loosed her hair from its plait and began to comb it with an ivory comb. She must know how well dove-grey became her, with her white skin and her golden hair.

She did not look demure at all, though Arslan had seen her cultivating it where the world could see. Here, attended by a handful of maids and a page or two, she eased into her old manner: bold, bright, a little reckless.

"How it must gall you," Arslan said, "to rein yourself in so tightly."

"It's rather refreshing, actually," she said. "One wearies of being always outrageous—stretching one's ingenuity to find a new fashion, a new game, a new extravagance. It's almost restful to play the pious lady."

"But it is play," Arslan said. "Isn't it? No more."

She crossed herself. "I do believe in God," she said, "and in His Holy Mother, and in His Church, and all His saints. I am a middling fair Christian, though I'll never be the conspicuous saint that my husband is."

"Conspicuous," said Arslan, "yes."

She laughed. "I think you see why I summoned you. Everyone else is being frightfully dull. Even the young men—if they can't pant at my feet like a pack of eager hounds, they can't imagine what to do."

"They could pray," Arslan said, "or visit the holy places."

"That does pall," she said, "after a while." She sat back in her chair. "I didn't bring you here simply to provoke a scandal. I have a favor to ask."

Arslan held his tongue. For all his insouciance, his quick words, his seeming ease in standing before her, he was quaking within, trembling with emotions too numerous to name. One, that he was sure of, was astonishment.

"I do like it," said Eleanor, "that you never say foolish things. You're always to the point."

It was lack of imagination, Arslan forbore to say. He never thought to babble until the moment was past.

"I should like," she said, "to make a pilgrimage to Bethlehem for the holy day."

"You need me for that?" Arslan said. "Surely your royal husband—"

"I don't want to go with him," Eleanor said. "I had rather hoped in fact that your king would be of a mind to do the same. And, perhaps, his lady mother."

"It's not usually done," Arslan said.

"Can't it be done at all?"

He shrugged. "I suppose. Her majesty has done it once or twice. It's a frightful crush, even for a queen."

"I should like a frightful crush," Eleanor said.

"I'll ask," Arslan said. "I promise nothing."

"That will do," said Eleanor. She paused. "Don't you find Jerusalem rather a drab place? Even with all the holiness?"

"It's not as beautiful as Damascus," Arslan said, "or as lively as Acre. But drab? I hardly know. I grew up here. To me it's home."

She sighed and shook her head. "Oh, it's drab. Except for the golden dome, which you can only see if you stand in the right place and look up, it's all sand and dust and barrenness. Most of the churches are ugly, and Holy Sepulcher the ugliest of all. Mary Mother! You should see Rome, even as broken as it is. Or Paris, which for all its squalor is vividly alive. And Poitiers or Toulouse, Bordeaux or Carcassonne . . . oh, I miss them! I'll be heart-glad to visit them again."

"Soon," Arslan said.

She reached before he could move, and seized his hand. "You should come," she said. "You should see. Isn't your father an Angevin? He has lands, yes, that he hasn't seen in half a lifetime? Haven't you ever longed to look on them, to know what they are like?"

"Often," he said. He could not stop staring at his hand, that she held so tightly, almost tight enough to bruise. Her fingers were strong and warm, fire-warm, though the air in the room was chill. She was never cold, was Eleanor. The heat of her humours warmed her to the heart.

"Come to France when we go," Eleanor said. "I'll make you my knight. You'll have lands, your father's if you like—I'll arrange it. I can do anything in France while I'm still its queen. And when that's ended, I'll still be a great duchess. You'll not suffer in my service."

Arslan drew a careful breath. "That . . . is a generous offer."

"Do consider it," she said. "You'd be most welcome. The ladies would love you. So handsome. So exotic, with your paynim name."

"Turkish," Arslan said mildly.

"Paynim," she said. "No one in France knows or cares for the sects and factions of the infidel. Aren't they all the same?"

"No," said Arslan.

"You see?" said Eleanor. "Exotic. Different. Intriguing."

"I don't think," he said, "that I want to be a dancing bear."

"Then be a mysterious stranger," she said, undismayed. "But come to France."

All the possible objections marshalled themselves in clamoring ranks. His king, his kingdom, his kin—so many things to hold him here. So much that he had still to do.

And yet—

"I'll consider it," he said, and bowed, and let himself be dismissed.

ueen Eleanor's whim took hold of them all, once Arslan had conveyed it to Baldwin. Baldwin did not ask why Arslan was playing messenger—which was perhaps a blessing; or perhaps not. The king was in a mood to be distracted, and a royal progress to David's city, on short enough notice that the stewards and chancellors wailed in unison like a chorus of the damned, well suited his fancy.

His mother did not choose to involve herself in the expedition. "Someone should keep the holy day in Jerusalem," she said. She spoke without expression, and yet Baldwin flushed as if at a rebuke.

It did not deter him. Quite the opposite. He had been chafing at the bit since he returned from Damascus. His royal duties were plentiful, but always there was the queen regent in her chair beside him, permitting him to perform them. If she would remain in Jerusalem, he would happily travel to Bethlehem for the feast of the Nativity.

They were too much like Eleanor and Louis for Arslan's comfort. But how could a son divorce his mother?

Arslan went to Bethlehem with his king. The French queen kindly did not vex him with attention. Her knights had all turned pilgrim, some even barefoot and walking on a road worn smooth by long years of similarly minded travellers. They whose chiefest delight had been in love-songs that would make a guardsman blush, devoted themselves to the singing of hymns.

They were a pretty company, marching slowly toward David's city in fine blue weather. There were litters for the ladies, led horses for those knights and princes who wearied of walking. More than one pair of feet blistered and bled, tender as they must be from a life of good boots and level floors and no pressing need to leave the comfort of a saddle.

A Turk might call them fools, neither true ascetics—not with the fine white bread they ate in camp of an evening, or the silken pavilions with their braziers and their crowds of servants—nor honest martyrs to their faith. This was a game they played, no more.

It pleased their fancy. It freed Baldwin from his mother's choking presence, and let him command his own people without recourse to his queen regent. He would hunt out another war, Arslan thought, though the kingdom was hardly in condition for any such thing after the debacle of Damascus.

Meanwhile he would journey to Bethlehem to see the Lord Christ born again. No star guided them, but the old and deep-trodden road and the great slow-surging river of pilgrims.

Even Eleanor was moved by it, perhaps. She was unwontedly quiet. She who found Jerusalem dull must find Bethlehem a squalid little village grown bloated with humanity. Little of its holiness was left amid the sellers of relics and indulgences, the clashing clamor of prayers, the clotted masses of people. For her there was room in the inn, a house too small for all her following, so that they must crowd together or find lodging elsewhere, even camp in the fields if no house or inn would open to them.

Baldwin chose his tent and a field with a well beside it, a low hill and an olive grove within a bowshot of the city's walls. The stream of pilgrims flowed wide of it, nor did many wander there to trouble the guards or the horses. It was almost quiet, and remarkably pleasant.

For the French it was another of the wonders of Outremer: to be here in this place in this season, living the words that they had heard spoken and sung since they were children. Even Eleanor felt it: Arslan saw how her eyes went wide and lost their expression of worldly wisdom. She was as wonderstruck as any of them, and letting herself indulge in it.

Arslan wondered if he would be as greatly moved in Rome, or whether his having been born and raised in the Holy Land had rendered him impervious to the lure of a lesser sanctity. Here in Bethlehem in the clear cold midnight, hearing once more the old, old words, the story so familiar he could recite it with the priests, he was not transported as so many of the westerners seemed to be; but neither was he untouched by the mystery of it. The flicker of candles, the scent of old stone, the sweet voices chanting, all mingled into a kind of joy; a brightness of the spirit that lingered even on the dark cold return to the camp, and touched him with warmth as he woke on the dawn of Christmas morning.

They did not linger long in Bethlehem. Three days only; then they returned to Jerusalem for the rest of Christmas Court.

Amid the feasts and the fêtes and the dancing, the barons of the High Court met in hall to consider the affairs of the kingdom. Baldwin sat again beside his mother, again in tightly contained amity, yielding to her precedence as queen regent, saying nothing out of turn. Arslan reflected then what he had not noticed in Bethlehem: that there, Baldwin had been at ease. Here, there was a stillness in him, a tension buried deep yet still perceptible. Someday it would break.

But not quite yet. The escape from Jerusalem, however brief, had loosened the bowstring. It was no longer quite taut enough to snap.

Arslan, watching his king and therefore the king's mother, paid little attention to the proceedings of the Court. There were petitioners as always, lords and commons both. One of the barons wished to marry, and asked the blessing of king and queen regent. His lady-to-be had come with him, a blushing bride a good decade

older than he, but comely enough and splendidly endowed with lands and posses-
sions. Arslan hoped that he could marry as well, if he ever did—if any woman
would have him.

While he maundered as a man could do whose duty was simply to stand at the
king's back and look formidable, a new petitioner had risen from among the barons.
He was a tall man, fair brown hair gone mostly silver, face more honest than handsome, with an old scar on its cheek, and thinned still, a little, with old suffering. For a
moment Arslan saw him as a stranger, a baron whose name he knew and no more.

Then he was Lord Bertrand in his proper person, royal armsmaster, knight of the
Cross, sometime father. He did not often rise to speak in this part of the Court; his
place was more often amid the making of war and the ordering of the kingdom.
Personal petitions were rare; Arslan could not remember even one, not in all the
years that he had stood guard over Baldwin in the High Court.

Bertrand spoke well when he did choose to speak, a clear voice meant to carry.
Arslan did not listen with particular attention. It was something for Beausoleil—
some matter of title to the barony, that set the clerks to scribbling.

His own name brought him full alert, tensed as if for battle. "That squire named
Olivier," Bertrand was saying, "whom men call Arslan, who stands at the king's
right hand, whom no man has yet claimed as son or heir—I claim him. I name him
my son. He is my heir, and will inherit when I am dead."

Arslan had waited years for those words. Now they were said, without warning,
without a word of preparation, in front of the whole High Court and the French
king and queen and such of the French nobility as had troubled to attend the court.
He stood flatfooted, gaping like an idiot, with every eye upon him, and never a
word in his head.

Only anger. He remembered, rather wryly, how King Fulk had never been able
to say the right words or do the right thing in front of Melisende. Bertrand seemed
to have the same art, or lack of it, with Arslan.

He was not even looking at his son. His eyes were on the queen, who had heard
him with apparent approval. Indeed she said, "That is well done, my lord, and not
before time."

It was difficult to tell, but perhaps Bertrand flushed. "Majesty, I confess, I left it
far too long. But not, I hope, too late."

Then at last he did turn his eyes on Arslan. Arslan did not know what expression
he wore. None, he could hope. No sign of the rage that mounted till he was like
to burst with it—the more for that people were smiling, applauding, cheering him
and his fool of a father. It could not be that they liked Arslan as well as that; that
they even, in a fashion, loved him. Lord Bertrand was well known, well liked, much
admired. Of course they would approve whomever he chose for an heir, were it a
bastard fostered in the king's nursery or a howling infidel.

Some idiot had got a cheer going, and a mob of them sweeping toward him,
plucking him from behind the king, lifting him up on their shoulders. When he
fought, they only laughed and held on tighter. When he cursed them, they drowned
him out with a greater excess of delight.

They thought him modest. They called him shy. Not one of them believed that
he would more happily have buried himself under the Holy Sepulcher than be given
this grand laud and welcome.

He would not kill his father. No, he would not be so kind. He won free at last, struggled to stand on his own feet in front of the king and the queen regent. Melisende smiled down at him. Baldwin was graver: he knew enough perhaps to recognize the thunder in Arslan's eyes.

"We welcome you," said Melisende, "to the High Court—and gladly too, and with all goodwill."

He did not doubt her sincerity. She had been good to him always, fond of him in her distant way. She would be well content that this most recalcitrant of her barons, the one who would never take a wife even at her bidding, had named an heir at last.

"Majesty," Arslan said after a pause. "My lord king, my lady regent. I . . . thank you for your generosity. But I do not wish to leave the service in which I have been since I was small."

"No more will you," Baldwin said. "Though you should go to Beausoleil for a while. Its people should learn to know you. You'll be ruling them, after all, when the time comes."

"Not for long and long," Arslan said grimly.

"Indeed," said Melisende, crossing herself. "We pray so. We are very glad to see you given your due, and more than pleased to set our seal on it."

Arslan bit his tongue. He could—should—have refused it all, turned his back on his father, cast away this gift that was indeed given too late. But they smiled so, and were so happy; so content with the rightness of it.

He said nothing therefore, only bowed low to each of them and begged their leave to go. They must have thought that he needed time to master his joy: they granted what he asked, smiling still, heaping blessings on his head.

He escaped the crowds that would have held him in the court, the back-thumpings and sudden embraces and effusions of joy from people who, only this morning, would not have condescended to speak to the king's squire, the fatherless man, the one gifted with neither wealth nor lordship. He was oddly unbitter. Wry, yes, and painfully amused, even through his anger at his father.

As he had more than half expected, Bertrand found him at last. He had not made himself easy to find. High up on the Tower of David, where even the guards did not go if they could help it, with the white-and-gold banner of Jerusalem snapping above him in the hard cold wind, he leaned on the parapet, wrapped close in a fur-lined cloak, and stared out across the city to the Dome of the Rock. Its golden beauty was muted today, dulled by the greyness of the sky. There would be sleet later, and snow perhaps. The air was raw and bitter. The wind cut to the bone.

Arslan was shivering, but not enough to matter. The cold did not trouble him, nor ever had. He would live well in France, he supposed, though the French told him that it never grew as cold here as it did in their country.

Bertrand was strong enough now to brave the climb to the tower, but he leaned against the wall for a while, white and breathing hard, hand pressed to his side. Arslan offered neither help nor sympathy.

At length Bertrand's breathing quieted. He sat on the parapet near Arslan, drawing his cloak close about him. Odd that he bore the cold less well than Arslan did, he who had been born in Anjou.

"You're angry," Bertrand said.

Arslan did not answer.

"It is a pity," said Bertrand, "that I did this in my own time and in my own way. But after all it was mine to do."

"You could have warned me," Arslan said.

"I told you I'd do this. I never said when."

Arslan showed his teeth. It was not a smile. "Ah, so this is battle, too, is it? Always be prepared, you taught us. Always expect the unexpected."

"So," said Bertrand. "You're as angry at yourself as at me."

"Not quite," Arslan said.

"The Court is delighted," said Bertrand. "More honestly glad of this than I've seen it since we left Damascus. You're well liked, you know. That's a feat of sorts: to be so close to the king but to escape the gnawings of envy."

"That," said Arslan with a bitter edge, "is because I never had anything for them to be jealous of. No father, no acknowledged kin. Certainly no rank or fortune."

"You think you've lost that grace? If you had, dear fool, you'd have seen it when I told them who you are."

"I don't know how to act like a lord's heir," Arslan said. "A king's squire, a fatherless man—yes, I'm splendid at that. But this new thing . . . I'll botch it."

"I don't think so."

"You're blind."

"And you are a young idiot, and I should thrash you for insolence." But there was no anger in Bertrand's voice. That perhaps was wisdom: to be calm in the face of deliberate provocation.

"You will," said Bertrand, "go with me to Beausoleil when Christmas Court is ended."

"Are you commanding me?"

"Yes," Bertrand said.

Arslan paused simply to breathe, to will himself as calm as his father was. Those were the chains with which they had all bound him: duty, obligation, obedience of son to father. He had wanted it since he was old enough to know that other people had fathers but he had none. Now he had it, all of it, in measure that he had hardly dared to imagine. And he could not accept it as a sensible young man should. He was as contrary as a girl.

If he could have had this when he was younger . . .

But he had not. He had it now. He had more than most young men ever hoped for, and more by far than a bastard had any right to expect.

"What," he said abruptly, "if you finally agree to marry? What if you sire a legitimate son? Will I be supplanted?"

"I don't think," Bertrand said with great gentleness, "that you need to fear that."

"I did need to ask," Arslan said.

Bertrand raised a brow but forbore to speak. That was as well: they might have quarreled. He did not want that, Arslan did not think. What Arslan wanted . . .

He was tired, suddenly. Weary of all of it: anger, contention, the sheer strain of being who and what he was. And now he must change. Must become someone new, someone suitably noble, fit to inherit a barony.

The beginning of it, it seemed, was here, high up in the wind, with the sting of sleet on his cheeks. Bertrand was shivering uncontrollably, but saying no word, uttering no complaint.

Arslan sighed. With the breath went a whole great knot of resistance. "Come," he said. "Come back into the warm, Father. You'll catch your death of cold."

ichildis in her way was as angry with Bertrand as Arslan was. If she had had any warning, either, she would have arranged to be in court instead of at home with Zenobia and a touch of the rheum. It was nothing deathly, simply unattractive, what with the reddened nose and the coughing and the inclination to lie abed much later than she properly should. Therefore she had been absent when Bertrand chose at long last to acknowledge his son, and had to rely on hearsay for a full account of it.

Bertrand had done it on purpose, of course: taken them all by surprise. Richildis prayed devoutly that he would find himself a pleasant little war, and soon, to practice his generalship on; then maybe he would spare his poor embattled kin.

Christmas Court ended with suitable pomp, and Bertrand carried his son away to Beausoleil. Richildis lingered a while in Jerusalem, partly for laziness, partly for the state of the roads. A spate of storms had come in with the new year, and it was hardly fit travelling for a babe in arms. The city was never empty, but it was almost quiet, now that the high ones had gone and the Christmas pilgrims departed. The French had gone back to their pursuit of sanctity: desultory for most, whitely passionate for their king. And Queen Eleanor pretended still to be a woman of piety and discretion.

Melisende no longer spoke to her except when strict policy demanded it. They had not quarreled that Richildis knew of; had entered no open hostilities. It was the simple consequence of long custom and undiminished dislike, not aided by Baldwin's insistence on keeping frequent company with the French queen.

He did it to annoy his mother. Certainly there was nothing between them but a kind of common cause against the queen regent. They were careful to avoid scandal, to meet nowhere alone, to be seen always in the company of respectable attendants.

Melisende was not to be appeased by the semblance of propriety. She summoned her son to her of an evening, a day or two after the beginning of Lent. He came obediently, even promptly, and offered suitable obeisance; yet Richildis, who that evening was in attendance on the queen regent, sensed in him a slight, perceptibly defiant edge.

Melisende sensed it, too: her eyes narrowed and her lips thinned. She wasted no time in frivolities. "It is not appropriate," she said, "for you to dance attendance on a woman who has clearly expressed her intention of divorcing her husband and finding herself one younger, livelier, and at least as royal."

"She has also stated," Baldwin said with the stiff dignity that he always assumed these days in front of his mother, "that she has no desire to be Queen of Jerusalem."

"Of course she would say such a thing," said Melisende, "where anyone of note can hear. She cares little which realm she rules, if only its king is young and fair."

"Madam," Baldwin said, "she will not marry me, nor will I succumb to her. That I can promise you."

Melisende sat back, drew a breath. She had been braced for a war; had received no satisfaction. Yet there was still good cause for battle. "If that is the way of it, then why do you court scandal by keeping company with her?"

"Because I enjoy it," Baldwin said.

Ah: a war at last. Richildis saw how Melisende's back straightened, how she girded herself for combat. "You enjoy the harm done to your reputation? People are talking, Baldwin."

"Women have reputations," Baldwin said. "Men have pride. That is a sin, yes, but it's less easily damaged than a woman's good name."

"Then," said Melisende with the air of a lioness leaping in for the kill, "have you taken any thought for the lady?"

"Certainly," said Baldwin, unruffled. "We are never seen alone together, we are always well escorted, we do nothing to which even a bishop may take exception. I can hardly be faulted, madam, for performing the duties of host, since you so clearly find them onerous."

Ah: a hit, and palpable. Melisende sat even straighter, spoke with even more precision than heretofore. "I have done all that is proper for me to do."

"Indeed, madam? And how long has it been since you inquired after the health of our guest? Was it you who asked her to dinner two nights ago, or was it I? Have you invited her to your bower or engaged her in conversation at all since Christmas Court?"

"I have been diligent," Melisende said, "in looking after the comfort of all my guests. Of whom her majesty is only one."

"The only one indeed to be so slighted," Baldwin said. "Be honest, madam. You detest her. She's so much like you in spirit, so little like you in her actions. Where you turn to piety to wield your will, she turns to frivolity and a notable extravagance. And yet, madam, at heart you are the same. And that," he said, "is why I will never even think of marrying her. One of you is enough."

He had bowed, made reverence with correctness very close to insolence, and departed before Melisende could muster her wits to answer. When at last she rose, the door was shut and his steps had long since died away.

She did not give way to rage, or even to laughter. "That child," she said, "is sore in need of a thrashing."

"But," said Richildis, "he's not a child. Not any longer."

"You call him a man? That puppy?"

"He is nineteen years old," Richildis said. "Most would reckon him a grown man."

Melisende shook her head. She was blind, and willfully so. "He has always been young for his age. My fault, surely. I should have been more strict in the raising of him."

"Stricter then," Richildis said, "and more lenient now." But Melisende refused to hear her.

The French king lingered interminably. He stayed through Lent, through Easter, through Ascensiontide. And all the while, Baldwin continued to entertain the Queen of France, to keep her company, to guide her about the shrines, to invite her to dinner. Always in crowds of attendants, never alone. Melisende could not summon him again without raising a scandal herself.

It was not a new thing for her to be powerless, but she was long out of the habit of it. It galled her terribly. And there was not a thing she could do, nothing that would compel him to do as she willed.

No one was happier than she when at long last, near the feast of Pentecost, King Louis wavered and sighed and succumbed to the urgings of his counsellors, and consented to return to France. He had long outstayed his welcome, had visited every shrine, walked every road, prayed over every inch of this most holy of countries. He could delay it no longer. He must go home. He must be king again of his own people.

Now that they were going away, king and queen both, Melisende could bring herself to tolerate Eleanor's company again, to ride with her to Acre where the ships were waiting. Many of the High Court went with them. Richildis thought of it, but when they all rode out, she was in Mount Ghazal, watching Zenobia clamber about with delightfully alarming agility, and being addressed at length in often intelligible fragments of French, Turkish, and even Latin.

If Melisende had asked, Richildis would have gone; but no message came. Others would bid farewell to the ashes of Crusade, watch the sails vanish into the horizon, sigh with relief and return to an emptied and blessedly quiet Jerusalem.

Richildis did not go, nor any of her household. But Bertrand in Beausoleil, and Arslan who was learning to be a lord's acknowledged son, rode to Acre with a troop of horsemen. Bertrand had business there in any case, and a tryst with Helena that Arslan was not supposed to know of.

Arslan's business, as far as anyone knew, was to accompany his father and to return for a while to his king's service. But he remembered when Eleanor had summoned him in Jerusalem, and what she had said then. He was going to ask her if she had meant it.

Acre was in uproar as one might well expect. Sore depleted though the French army might be, it was still many thousands strong, well past restlessness into active boredom, and growing impatient to leave the east behind. Few had elected to stay, fewer still had found useful employment in Outremer. They were all chafing at the slowness of the departure, drinking themselves senseless in taverns along the quay, getting into brawls with anyone whom they reckoned either foreign or objectionable—which by now was nearly everybody.

Amid this tumult Arslan sought audience with the Queen of the French. He had no certain expectation of getting it, was determined not to grieve if he failed. He needed to know something, but if she would not see him, he would not force her.

And indeed his message vanished, nor received a reply. No page came to fetch him. No letter was left at his father's door. He followed Bertrand about on his various errands, arranged to be absent when Bertrand visited Helena in her own house, dined with them later at her invitation. She did not press as another mother might, to discover if he had done well at Beausoleil. She simply assumed that he had. And that, he thought, was why he not only loved but passionately admired her.

Eleanor, whom he loved but did not admire, answered him at last the day before she was to sail. He was in the city searching out a frippery, a gift for his mother. As he paused by a silk-merchant's shop, caught by the brilliance of the colors, he heard a voice that he could not mistake.

The Queen of the French was abroad in the city with a gaggle of her ladies, bidding farewell to the markets of the east. "And which do you prefer?" she was asking one of her companions, a lady who reminded Arslan of a fat white dove, all coo and flutter. "The green, do you think? Or one of these blues?"

"Oh," said Lady Mathilde, "I like this one best, like the shimmer on a peacock's feather."

Mathilde, as Eleanor knew and Arslan had to concede, was an utter idiot— except when it came to clothes. On that subject she was as sage as no philosopher would have known how to be. Eleanor wisely yielded to her judgment, and bought the peacock silk.

Arslan, suddenly and cripplingly shy, tried to slip away before the queen saw him. But he was standing just beyond the bolt of silk, between one of crimson and one of a wonderful shimmering bronze brocaded with galloping horsemen. It was that which had lured him in, and which trapped him now. "Oh!" said Eleanor. "It's just the color of your hair. Thibaut! Buy it for his lordship and send it to his house. Your father's house, yes?"

He had forgotten how quick she could be, too quick for mere male mind to follow. "Lady," he tried to say. "Majesty. You can't—"

"Never tell a queen what she cannot do," Eleanor said. "Here, you must have this silk. Make a court robe of it, such as the infidels wear. It's much too rich for a lesser man."

"What would you do," he asked her, "if I gave it to my mother? Or to . . . another woman?"

"Your sweetheart?" Perhaps he imagined the sudden fierce glitter in her eye. She was laughing, after all. "If you do that I'll never forgive you."

"Then I can't take the gift," Arslan said.

"Of course you will. You're coming to France, yes? You need something to be beautiful in."

"I am not coming to France," Arslan said. He had not known for certain that he would say it, not till it was said.

"Of course you are coming to France. You have lands there now. Your father is well and will live, they say, for years. You'll come back long before he dies."

Arslan shook his head. "Lady, I can't. Not . . . not now. It's too soon."

He feared that she would press him, but something, maybe his expression, maybe her own degree of sense, kept her silent. Instead she said, "But someday, you mean to say, it will be late enough."

He nodded.

She sighed, shrugged, smiled her sudden smile. "Well. Promise, then. Someday you'll visit me at my court in Aquitaine."

"Or wherever you are," he said, "where you are lady and queen."

"So gallant," said Eleanor. "Ladies, isn't he a wonder?"

They fluttered and cooed and made haste to agree. Arslan longed to flee, but he had not been dismissed.

And, he could admit to himself, he did not honestly want to go. Promise or no, he might never see her again. He wanted to remember her as she was now, all golden in the light from the door, surrounded by the shimmer of silks, and none of them as bright as her hair. Her face was too thin and long for beauty, and yet she was beautiful, vivid and purely alive—ill match indeed for her pious stick of a husband and his pack of priests and his eunuch familiar.

Arslan bowed low, as a man of rank should bow to a queen. "If I can," he said, "someday, I'll come to Aquitaine."

She sailed away without him. He did not go to the quay as so many others did, to see the French take ship for the west. He had seen all that he needed to see, said all that could sensibly be said. As the ships took on the last of their cargo and their royal passengers, Arslan was riding back to Beausoleil. He had made a choice, there in front of Eleanor. He would keep to it. Whatever it cost him. However long it lasted.

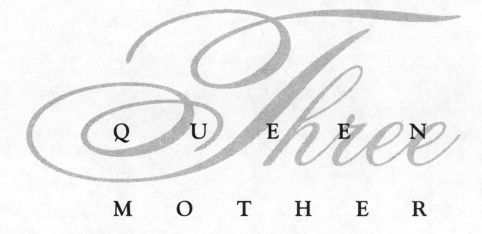

QUEEN MOTHER

(A.D. 1152-1153)

enobia had disappeared again. She was in none of her wonted hiding places in the castle of Mount Ghazal, nor had the messenger come back from the village where she might, even at her tender age, have managed to go. Zenobia was resourceful and exceedingly determined. What she wanted, she found ways to get.

Richildis closed her account-book and sighed, not entirely with exasperation. She was glad of the reprieve. "She's somewhere perfectly safe, I'm sure," she said to the tearfully terrified maid.

The servants must have been amusing themselves with the newcomer. Alia was a niece of Richildis' senior maids, Yasmin and Leila, and came from Beausoleil. She was as shy as her aunts had never been, and conspicuously in awe of her new lady. Clearly she was horrified to have failed in the charge of her lady's daughter, and on the first day of it, too.

Richildis tried to comfort her. "The imp makes a game of vanishment," Richildis said, "but she never goes far and she never does anything foolish. She's very sensible for her age."

"Sensible!" Alia wailed. "Lady, she's two summers old. What can she know? How can she—"

"Alia," Richildis said firmly enough to silence her. "Zenobia is old for her years. Stop drizzling now, please, and fetch Kutub. He of anyone will know where she went."

Alia looked as if Richildis had just sentenced her to the rack. "Ku—Kutub?" She sucked in a breath, nearly choking on it. "Lady—Lady, I—"

God's holy Mother, Richildis thought: the girl was even more afraid of Kutub than she was of Richildis. Time to have a word or six with the servants. Beginning with this young idiot's aunts.

Until then however she had a lost child and a sniveling maid and little prospect of finding the child unless she did it herself. She bound and locked the ledger and set it on its shelf, capped the inkpot, and rose, shaking out her skirts. "Come with me," she said.

With Alia quaking and sniffling in her wake, Richildis strode out of her workroom. She would ride later, she decided. Her whole body was cramped with bending over her ledgers, and her eyes were aching. She needed clean air and sun and a good horse under her. Maybe Michael Bryennius would be in similar mood, and minded to take his daughter on his saddlebow, once she was found. Zenobia would adore that.

Mount Ghazal was in its wonted order, servants at their tasks, men-at-arms at practice in the courts, horse-trainers plying their trade in and about the stables. The builders were raising the foundation of a new chapel. Richildis meant it to be high and beautiful; and a priest of her choosing would serve in it, one of the sergeants' sons who had proved himself gifted in letters. He was studying in Rome now while his chapel was being built. Richildis prayed that no prelate lured him away to a loftier benefice.

Even with a daughter who went where she pleased and never regarded her nurses, Richildis was well content with her house and her holding. She knew every corner of it and every creature in it, even to the kitchen cat that came to provide a royal escort. The insouciant curl of its tail guided her out from the keep into the first of the courts, and thence to a flurry about the gate.

There was Zenobia indeed, and riding high: perched on the saddle of a mail-clad knight. God be thanked that his horse was an equable beast, for she stood on the high pommel with her arms about the knight's neck, and never a worry in the world that either of them would let her fall.

She twisted about at her mother's approach, no more guilt in her than worry. "Mama!" she cried. "Look! Arslan-Arslan-Arslan!"

So it was, and looking splendid, too. He had been knighted in Jerusalem at Christmas Court, side by side with his foster-brother the king: receiving the accolade from his father's hand as Baldwin had received it from the Constable of the Kingdom, and good hard blows they both had been. Then Baldwin had gone back to being king and Arslan had gone to be heir of Beausoleil, for a little while; though now it seemed that he was coming back to Jerusalem.

He caught Zenobia to him and swung his leg over the pommel and slid down from the saddle, all in one fluid movement, and presented the daughter to her mother with a bow and a smile. Zenobia accepted the shift with equanimity. "I saw Arslan," she said. "I went to see him. He picked me up and I rode. When will I have a horse, Mama?"

"When you are old enough to ride it by yourself," Richildis answered composedly. She lifted a brow at Arslan.

He answered the question that she had seen no need to ask. "She was halfway down to the village," he said. "But very safe, and careful not to get underneath the horses."

Richildis heard a faint gasp behind her. Alia was more appalled than ever. Poor thing, she had never expected the likes of Zenobia.

Arslan, stronger of heart and stomach, claimed Zenobia back from her mother and set her crowing on a broad shoulder, and carried her into the keep. Richildis paused only long enough to see his escort set in order before she turned to follow.

It was odd and yet wonderful to guest her brother's son as a man and a knight, a great lord's heir and no longer a child. She could not help but remember him as he had been, steady dark eyes under the fringe of yellow hair, soft cheeks and small hands and a will that had been strong even in infancy. He had been, in fact, much like Zenobia.

Her dark curls lay against his breast, her thumb in her mouth and her eyes demurely shut, but she was perceptibly awake. Arslan held her in comfort, there in Richildis' hall, with a cup of wine at his elbow and everyone in the castle, it seemed, finding duties within sight and sound of him.

He had grown up well. The yellow hair had darkened to a fair brown shot with gold like his father's or like Richildis' own. The eyes were sea-dark, sea-grey, and as steady as ever. There was a quiet in him, a calm that he had from his mother. His voice was soft and deep, deeper than his father's. He could sing, Richildis had reason to know, but seldom did. He was not one for displays or poetry. The excesses of youthful ardor had always eluded him.

And yet, however avid ladies might be for troubadours, they seemed to find Arslan irresistible. His silence singled him out, his size and his easy grace. He was not particularly fair of face, and yet he was a beautiful creature, as a lion is. Prettier faces would fade. His would only grow stronger as he grew older. Richildis was suddenly, inordinately glad to see him here, to hear him telling tales from Jerusalem—so; he had not left it after all, but had lingered in his king's company. "Baldwin is on his way north," he said. "I've gone ahead of him, to visit my father before we all ride for Tripoli."

Richildis raised a brow. "Tripoli?" she inquired.

"You've heard all the gossip, surely," Arslan said, but without impatience.

"We've heard a great deal," Michael Bryennius said. "All the way back to the failed Crusade. Raymond of Antioch dead in a bloody struggle at Murad, and his skull set in silver and sent to the Caliph in Baghdad. Joscelin of Edessa taken captive by reivers, taken in turn by the terrible Nur al-Din, blinded and locked away in Aleppo, and no hope of rescue ever, for all anyone knows or cares of him. Baldwin and the Templars riding to the aid of Antioch, and winning it back, too, and my own emperor buying with gold the remnants of fallen Edessa. Then of course there is the Princess Constance, Raymond's grieving widow with her flock of children, refusing to wed any man that can be found for her, least of all the elderly Norman whom my emperor was so misguided as to send. Now if he had sent our cousin Andronikos the beautiful, her highness might well have been content."

"The Princess Constance," Arslan said with an air of ill-suppressed distaste, "like her mother, is a great lover of beauty in men."

"A fact of which my emperor was insufficiently apprised," said Michael Bryennius, no little blessed with beauty himself, but never minded to notice it. He sighed and shook his head. "Is she still brewing trouble, then?"

"Always," Arslan said. He had disliked Constance from their childhood: one of the few people in the world for whom he seemed to have little use and less affection. She must have been cruel to him, as she could well be: she in her lofty rank and he but a fatherless child, foster-kin to a king.

"Still," said Richildis. "If it's Constance, then why is everyone going to Tripoli?"

"It's Constance," Arslan said, "but even before that, it's Hodierna."

"Ah," said Richildis in sudden understanding.

Hodierna of Jerusalem, youngest but one of Melisende's sisters, had been wedded years since to another Raymond, Count of Tripoli. This Raymond, unlike that one of Antioch, was very much alive and notoriously devoted to his wife. So devoted that, rumor had it, he kept her as close as any eastern woman, locked in a tower surrounded by women and eunuchs. No man entire was suffered near her, nor was she permitted to show her face where any stranger could see.

And yet for all her strict confinement, she was said to have found means to escape her husband's vigilance. Raymond was a fair-haired man and Hodierna a fair-haired woman as all the daughters of the second Baldwin were, and yet her daughter—whom she had called Melisende after her queenly sister—was as dark as Richildis' own Zenobia. Raven-dark and dark-eyed. Guardsman, halfblood squire, even infidel—who knew who the child's father might have been? But it was little likely to be Hodierna's properly wedded husband.

"Indeed," said Arslan as if he had followed the track of Richildis' thought. "The Lady Hodierna has begged her eldest sister to set her free from a man whom she calls, not discreetly, her jailer. Melisende and Baldwin are riding to Tripoli to try if they can to repair the marriage. They've summoned Constance, too, and such of the court as are inclined to attend them."

"I never liked Raymond of Tripoli," Richildis mused. "His father was more than a bit of a fool. Raymond is something perhaps worse. He's said to have murdered a kinsman who might have laid claim to his domain—descendant of a legitimate heir as Raymond was sprung of bastard seed. We all know how jealous he is of his wife. Such passion is an ill thing in a ruler. It clouds his judgment."

Arslan shrugged slightly. "He's not loved in Jerusalem, but he's not actively hated, either. The king and the queen mother want to avert a scandal if they can. If Hodierna can be persuaded to reconcile with her husband . . ."

"Ah yes," Richildis said. "The world has seen enough scandal with the queen of France and her ill-made marriage."

It was not obvious, but Richildis who knew Arslan saw how he tensed at the mention of Eleanor. He had always done that, and no less now that she was nigh on two years gone, than he had done when she was there in Outremer. He spoke steadily enough, a studied steadiness. "She's still married to Louis by all accounts. She's even had another daughter."

"One does wonder how that could be," Richildis said. "The priests must have prevailed on Louis and the princes on Eleanor, till they both surrendered. One night only, I'll wager that, but it would have been enough."

"And all for naught," Arslan said, "as the lords of France would reckon it. They need a prince, not another princess."

"Eleanor would have been glad," said Richildis. "How she must have cursed her swelling womb, and prayed for a daughter, and thanked Mary Mother when the child was born. If it had been a son, she'd never have been free of her stick of a husband."

"God must want her to do as she pleases," Arslan said. "But Melisende—and Baldwin, for once agreeing with his mother—want no such division in their own family."

"It can't be done in any event," Richildis pointed out. "God was kind enough to bless Hodierna with a son. He's a squire by now, surely—old enough and to spare for that."

"He's twelve summers, I think," Arslan said. "Not a great deal younger than

Prince Amaury. They used to get on well, though they've not been together since before the Crusade."

"And how is Amaury?" Richildis inquired. "Still vexing his brother with his adoring presence?"

Arslan laughed. "Yes, still haunting poor Baldwin at the most inopportune times. It's good, Constable Manasses says, to see a younger brother so evidently fond of the elder. In Baldwin's opinion, it's a greater marvel if the elder brother can stand the sight of the younger."

"And yet Baldwin would strangle anyone who spoke an ill word of Amaury." Michael Bryennius was as amused as ever by the long battle between the brothers. "They'll be friends in the end, once Amaury stops being a nuisance and grows into an ally. Who better after all than a brother, to understand one's heart and mind?"

"A wife might do," Richildis said a little wryly, "if all else failed."

Michael Bryennius took her hand and kissed it. "And how many men are blessed to marry at their own will? Whereas a brother who shared the same womb—with him one has at least that common cause."

Richildis could not contest that, whose own brother was both great joy and great exasperation.

"Sisters too," Arslan said. "Queen Melisende and her sisters—they're wondrous amiable with each other, though they'll happily go to war with husbands, children, friends and infidels, all the world but their own four selves. Melisende does mean to convince Hodierna to suffer her husband, and Raymond to be a little less wildly jealous of any male who so much as casts a glance at her."

"And Baldwin? Does he have any hopes of accomplishing such a thing?" asked Richildis.

Arslan paused, sighed. "Baldwin will do what he can with Raymond. It's his duty as Christian and king."

"Even though he loathes the man?"

"Even so." Arslan sighed again. "I doubt even his own mother loved Count Raymond."

"It's said," said Michael Bryennius, "that Count Raymond loves himself exceeding well, and that is all in the world that matters to him."

Richildis shivered a little. She had been married in youth to a man she neither loved nor liked, but it had been tolerable, in the end. To be bound to a man whom she hated, or worse despised . . .

She had long grown out of the habit that noblewomen must cultivate, to accept one's duty to one's kin and one's lands. All that duty was embodied here in this hall, and all her desire in the man who sat beside her with his fingers twined in hers. She shaped a quick prayer of thanks and protection from harm. All joy in this world was as fragile as a breath, and could be as brief.

She took refuge in that same noble duty which she had been spared in the choosing of a husband: calling the servants to order, seeing the tables laid, regaling her guest with a feast from the fields and the orchards of Mount Ghazal.

hey all rode to Tripoli through Beausoleil: even Zenobia and her nurses, Arslan and his escort, Baldwin, Helena, the whole of that kin and kind in Outremer. Past Acre they caught the rearguard of the royal train, passed on up through it till they joined with Baldwin and Melisende and their attendants and a goodly portion of the court. It was winter still, chill and lashed with storms, but they traveled in the warmth of good company, furs and woollens and curtained litters for the ladies.

Zenobia much preferred the chill of Arslan's saddle to the musty comfort of her nurses' litter, with stones warmed in the night's fire for hands and feet. Richildis was no more willing to give up the wind in her face. It was wind off the sea, salt wind, lashed with spray. Exhilarating; deadly unless one were wise, scouring flesh from bone. Like this land that they rode through, both beautiful and perilous.

Tripoli was waiting for them, and in it the royal kin: the widowed Princess Constance and her four children, Hodierna and her son and the husband from whom she longed to be free. They exchanged greetings in the lamplit warmth of the hall, for outside it was sleeting; with dark no doubt it would turn to snow. Some of that chill lingered under the vaulted roof, between Hodierna and Raymond, and between Constance and the world.

Arslan remembered Hodierna from long ago, when she was a young princess in Jerusalem and he was a royal page. She was older now of course, no longer the lissome girl that she had been, but a rather too rich-bodied woman. Life in the harem did that to ladies in Islam, he had heard. The same appeared to be true of this lady of Tripoli. He was somewhat amazed to see her here in hall, sitting as a Frankish lady would sit, at the high table some distance from her lord. But he could hardly lock her away in the presence of her kin.

Raymond watched her always, even when he seemed to be intent on someone else: taut, wary, as the hawk watches its prey. If she stirred toward a man, he stiffened. If she laughed, his own lips tightened. He looked a little mad.

It was rather a pity, Arslan thought, that he had not been matched with Princess Constance. The infinitely jealous man would have been well wedded to the perpetually sullen woman. She carried her air of injury as if it were a chain of fine gold, polished and cherished till it gleamed.

Her children were as ill-tempered as she, though the boy, yet another Bohemond, looked as if he would have known how to laugh if his mother had not hovered so close. Later, maybe, Arslan would discover if the child needed a playmate. Zenobia was old for her years and adept already at coaxing smiles out of scowling faces.

Arslan did not mean to do it himself, but he was there and trying to be inconspicuous, and Princess Constance's eye caught him somewhere in the middle of the welcoming feast. She did not merely smile. She simpered.

And did she know, he wondered, that he was the bastard child whom she had so despised when she was younger? She must; everybody knew the heir of Beausoleil.

Indeed. He was the heir of Beausoleil. No one called him bastard to his face, or behind his back, either.

It made him faintly ill. Women had courted him before, and not always young ones. They who must marry for the good of their lands and kin were eager to find a man who was both young and presentable. That Arslan had prospects of his own only made him the more appealing. So many of the men in Outremer were younger sons, impoverished knights, even criminals sent to atone for their sins by defending the Holy Sepulcher.

Not a few of those would reckon Constance a great prize. She brought with her a principate, lands beleaguered by the infidel but wealthy still, wealth and rank and power in the kingdom. Her temper would not dismay them unduly. They could look to Raymond of Tripoli, and to the harem of the infidels. Or they might do as many another high lord did, take refuge in wars and in princely duties, and come home only to sire sons.

When the time came—nor was it greatly distant—Arslan would make a noble marriage. He had decided on it even without his father's commanding it; not that Bertrand would do such a thing. Whatever his faults, the Lord of Beausoleil would not force his son to do what he himself had never consented to.

Which indeed was why Arslan would do it. It would be a congenial lady—he had promised himself that much. If he could like her, he would be glad. If he could love her, he would be fortunate indeed. But first and foremost, she must bring profit to his family's fortunes.

Nahar would say that he was a cold young thing, and applaud him for it. She was a great madam in Acre now, had left Jerusalem for the richer pickings among the pilgrims arriving and departing. He saw her sometimes, lingered for an hour or an evening, took her to bed less often than he simply sat and talked with her. It was a satisfaction that the patrons in the upper rooms would never understand.

Nor would Princess Constance, he reflected as he sipped wine from a cup of chased silver. Queen Melisende might, if she could have lowered herself so far. She was like Lady Richildis, like his own mother if it came to that: strong-willed. Sensible.

Except . . .

He sighed faintly. There was another war, another contention in that contentious family. Baldwin was drawn taut, smiling rigidly and saying little, while his mother beside him exerted herself to be charming. She was determined to effect reconciliations all round; but she did not seem aware that she needed one in her own house. Baldwin to her was ever and unalterably a child. If he spoke, she thought nothing of lifting her voice over his. If he proposed a course of action, she ignored it. She would do as it pleased her to do, with little if any regard for the king for whom she stood regent even yet, though he was man and knight and well grown out of child-hood.

Such a beautiful family to look at, tall robust golden people; so persistently at odds with one another. Maybe they would all make peace here. Maybe the snow would turn to a fall of flowers, and the wind's howl to an angels' chorus.

The storm blew away in the night. Day dawned clear and astonishingly warm, one of the swift changes in that most changeable of countries. What snow had fallen, melted and flowed away. Flowers bloomed in sheltered gardens.

Melisende sat in one such with her sister and her niece and their respective ladies. Richildis happened to be one of them, freed of worry for Zenobia: Arslan had her in hand, peculiar occupation for a young man of his age, but Arslan had never been one to care for such things. He was a better nurse and guardian than any of the women who should more properly have performed the office. Therefore her mother could sit in the sun with the obligatory bit of embroidery, under a rose-arbor that had been coaxed to produce a scattering of blossoms. Their scent was marvelously sweet and somewhat out of season.

The royal ladies sat together in unfeigned amity. Whatever their quarrels with husbands or sons, they themselves never quarreled, had never been at odds that Richildis knew of. Princess Alys, to be sure, had had thoughts of dispossessing her daughter Constance, but Alys lived out her long exile in her dower lands, nor came forth for any persuasion. She had gone a little strange, Richildis had heard; would not leave her castle, nor walk under the sky lest it fall on her. She was as deeply cloistered as any nun, and as pious, too, by all accounts; though it was her sister Yveta who held the name and title of abbess.

Those of that kin who were in the world were here, all three, sisters and sister-daughter. Constance was never as sour-faced with her aunts as she was in court; sometimes one could even see what a beauty she was when her lips were not drawn tight and her brow unmarred by a scowl. She never forgot her grievances—God forbid—but she eased a little, once almost smiled at a sally from one of the maids.

That faint glimmer of good humor vanished soon enough. Neither of her aunts was in a mood to indulge her. "You will not marry?" Melisende demanded of her.

"I will not marry an old man, no," Constance said tartly, "nor an ugly one, nor one who smells of onions and bad teeth. What were you thinking of, asking the Byzantine emperor to find me a husband? Did you think that I would be as fortunate as some have been?"

Richildis lowered her eyes to her embroidery. It was a sore grievance to the princess that she had been sent a toad instead of a beautiful prince. She would not forgive Richildis either quickly or easily for marrying both beauty and wealth, and loving the man, too.

The queen and the countess took no notice of Richildis' discomfiture. Hodierna said, "We take the fate that is made for us."

"As you have?" Constance laughed shrilly. "And why are you here, then, aunt? Have you come to proclaim the joys of wedded bliss?"

"What is it that the infidels say?" said Hodierna, not visibly ruffled, though the blow must have stung. "For a woman there is nothing save marriage or the tomb."

"And when the marriage is mercifully over," Constance said, "there is widow-hood. Regency. Power. Tell me you haven't dreamed of it. Tell me you don't pray God to take your husband, so that you can be free."

"I can be free of him without the need to see him dead," Hodierna said. "Child, whatever our troubles with the men whom God sets over us, in this country we can't live without them. Someone has to lead the armies. Someone has to fight the infidel while we rule our domains."

"There are always knights willing to serve a woman of influence," Constance said. "Why should I marry any of them? I did my duty—fourfold, no less. I had a husband of rather remarkable beauty. God, your God, took him away from me. Why should I take anything less?"

"Because a husband is rather more useful than not," Melisende said, "even an ugly one."

"Therefore," said Constance, "you have forborne to marry again."

The elder ladies glanced at one another. They could hardly deny it: neither was in a position to convince a young and obstinate woman that she should remarry, when she had no desire to.

"My ladies," she said. "You've taught me well. From you, my dear Aunt Meli-sende, I learned that a woman can hold more than a regency; that she can rule in her own right, and keep her son tight-reined even into manhood. And in you, Aunt Hodierna, I see a woman whose husband takes excessive pleasure in keeping his wife a prisoner. You came here to be free of him. Can you honestly ask me to bind myself to a man in marriage?"

"Not all men are as that one," Hodierna said.

"Indeed; some are as Bohemond, and he is dead." Constance said it without grief after so long, but with a core of immovable resistance. "I do not wish to marry again."

Nothing that they said could shake her. She was determined; and a lady of that line, once she had set her mind on something, was no more to be shifted than the mount of Sinai.

"Muhammad could move a mountain," Melisende said. "Moses could conquer one in God's name. I can't even convince a chit of a girl to take herself another hus-band."

Constance had gone away on pretext of looking after her children. The sisters remained in the pale sunlight, tarrying till they too must go in.

"And you?" Melisende inquired after a while. "Will you be intransigent, too?"

Hodierna looked straightly at her, direct as a royal lady could be. "The man is clean off his head with jealousy."

"And has he reason to be?"

Hodierna's gaze did not waver. "If he has, then he invited it by keeping me in a harem like a woman of the infidels."

Melisende sighed faintly. "You can't even lie, can you? There's my namesake in her nursery, as incriminating a pair of eyes as I ever saw. You could have been wiser. You could have chosen a fair-haired man."

"I despise a fair-haired man," Hodierna said with sudden venom. "I *wanted* a dark one. Dark and sweet and wondrous gentle. My husband is not gentle. If he were a stallion, the mares would be glad of him."

"And couldn't you simply close your eyes and dream of dark men? Did you have to do more than dream?"

Hodierna shrugged a little sulkily. "I was bored. I was angry. All the doors were locked and guards outside of them, but I found one that I could open. What would you have done? Sat and endured, or opened the door and taken what God gave you?"

"I would never have let myself be locked in at all," Melisende said. "Nor will you again. I'll make him swear a sacred oath. No lady of our line will be treated in such fashion."

"I wish you good fortune," Hodierna said with an edge of irony.

"You in return," said Melisende, "will do your best to remain his wife. You can endure him, surely, if he lets you be?"

"If he never troubles my sight at all," Hodierna said, "I'll be as loyal a wife as I can bear to be."

"How loyal is that?"

Hodierna smiled as if she took great pleasure in the thought. "As loyal as he deserves," she said.

"My lord, think," Baldwin said with all apparent patience. "Your lady is a princess of Jerusalem, daughter of a great king, sister to a queen. Is it fitting that she be kept like a slave or like an infidel?"

Raymond of Tripoli paced his solar like a jackal in a cage. He was not an ill man to look at, middling tall, middling fair, very deep and broad of chest and famously strong. He was restless, visibly nervous, but he did not look like the madmen Arslan had seen begging in the streets of Jerusalem or Acre. He was by all accounts neither an ill ruler nor a remarkably good one. He did well enough, people said.

Except when it came to his wife. "She is beautiful," he said. "Every man desires her. And she, wanton creature—she desires them all impartially. What was I to do? I had to keep her safe."

"Women of our line," Baldwin said without expression, "are not fond of safety. Better for them the reckless edge and the free air. Trap one, trammel her, and you lose her."

Raymond ceased pacing to turn and stare at the king. Baldwin gazed back calmly. "You know," Raymond said.

Baldwin inclined his head.

"Then you also know," said Raymond with rising heat, "what a mere man must do to protect himself against them—and them against themselves. Headstrong, impetuous, high-hearted: what other women are like them? What can any man do but lock them up in strong walls and pray that they don't escape?"

"Yet," said Baldwin gently, "your lady has done so. She has summoned us who are her kin, and begged us to set her free. Forgive my frankness, my lord, but I do think that you erred. What would well cow a weaker woman has merely made her the more determined to resist you."

Raymond shook his head. "No. No, she may be your mother's sister, but you don't know her. You don't know how headstrong she is, how determined to have her way."

"Ah, but I do," Baldwin said. "Believe me, my lord. I do."

Raymond flung up his hands in a fit of sudden temper. "What do I do, then? Cut every leash and binding and let her run wild? Sit by unresisting while she fondles squires and stableboys and peasants in the fields? Let her be the mock of the kingdom?"

"If I know the women of my own blood," said Baldwin, "and I think perhaps I do, then freedom will put an end to her rebellion. Only recall how pious my mother is, how their sister is a holy abbess, and even Alys the great rebel has devoted her latter years to seclusion and to good works. Seclusion that she chose, my lord, of her own will. There's the key with them always. They and only they must choose what they will do."

"I can't," said Raymond. "I can't take that chance."

"What choice do you have? My mother is her dearest sister. I've heard her speak of the life that you've forced on your lady. I know what she will do if you persist. She has no desire to see a marriage sundered, but if you refuse to see reason as she sees it, she'll grow angry. Angry enough to take her sister's part, no matter what that would do to the bonds of holy matrimony."

"And if my lady runs direct from my embrace into the arms of a Saracen slave, what will your mother do then?"

"Your lady won't run," Baldwin said. "Mother will make her swear to do her duty while you do yours. One of you alone won't be forced to give way. She'll surrender herself to you in return for greater freedom."

"She won't do that," Raymond said, returning again to his pacing. "She's not capable of it."

"Yet if she is," Baldwin pressed him, "and will take oath on it, will you do the same?"

"If," said Raymond, "and only if."

"Then I will see it done," Baldwin said. "I . . . and my lady mother."

SEVENTY ONE

Countess Hodierna reconciled herself to Count Raymond of Tripoli in the basilica of the city before the assembled priests and nobles, the King and the Queen of Jerusalem and the Princess of Antioch with her children. They swore anew the vows that they had made when first they were wedded, set hand in hand and promised each to honor the other till death should sunder them.

Raymond spoke steadily, his eyes never leaving his lady's face. She never looked at him, but her voice too did not waver, as she promised to be faithful to this marriage that she had yearned to escape. She had broken with her own hands the locks that had barred the door to her chambers, and stood while workmen opened walls and unbarred windows. If she had gloated as she did it, who could blame her? She had been shut within those walls for ten long years. It was a wonder that she did not order them all broken down and a new palace built amid the ruins.

"And tomorrow," Queen Melisende said at the feast thereafter, "we depart for Jerusalem."

"So soon?" Count Raymond asked as if he truly regretted it. He was expansive, joyous in his victory, his marriage confirmed, his wife sworn to him beyond a doubt.

"So soon," said Hodierna. "My royal sister has duties in the Holy City, and I should like to pass the end of Lent there, and hear the Easter Mass sung before the Holy Sepulcher."

Raymond blinked. "You are going?"

"I am going," Hodierna answered him.

"You cannot."

She smiled with pure happiness. "But, my lord, I can. We swore oaths, remember? I, to be faithful, to preserve the marriage, to honor and respect you. You, to grant me freedom, to suffer me to live as a Christian lady and not an infidel slave."

"You swore also to obey me," Raymond said, "and I forbid you to go."

"You are the queen's vassal," said Hodierna. "The queen commands me."

Raymond turned to Melisende. "Majesty!"

"My lord," Melisende said with royal composure. "I have bidden my sister attend me in my own city. It is best, I think. Even Mother Church cannot reconcile a heart nurtured too long in resentment."

"But," said Raymond. "She is my—"

"You are my vassal," Melisende said gently, implacably, "as is she. Do you contest my authority to command either of you?"

Raymond opened his mouth, but—wisely or cravenly—shut it before he spoke. The color that suffused his face was wrath; yet it drained away to an ashen pallor.

No less so than Baldwin, though perhaps only Arslan saw. Arslan, nearest him, had to look past him to see what all the rest were staring at: Raymond of Tripoli defeated in his victory by the will of these royal women.

"So much weariness," Hodierna was saying. "So much strain. Among my own kin, in the city of my youth, I may find heart's ease. And when I've found it, I'll come back. That I promise you, my people of Tripoli."

"Such a pretty speech," Baldwin said bitterly. Oh, he was angry. Indeed. He kept tight rein on it till he could be alone with his mother, sought her out in her chamber long after the feast was done, when he knew that she would be lightly attended and not yet gone to sleep. Her attendance was the Lady Richildis, as Baldwin's was Arslan: comfort enough for them, if there could be any such in this meeting.

"Indeed," Melisende said to Baldwin, "and if you take issue with my sister's choice, why do you come to me? It was she who asked that I grant her this gift."

"And how did you persuade her to ask you?" Baldwin demanded. "Come, Mother. We're not in court here. Tell me the truth."

"I have told you the truth," Melisende said. "Truly—Hodierna wanted it."

"And between the two of you, you smote the count with it in front of his people. You humiliated him. There will be a price for that, Mother. A price that, no doubt, I will be the one to pay."

"And how is that?" asked Melisende. "Are we not king and queen together?"

"Are we?" Baldwin rose from the chair in which he had been sitting, and advanced till he stood over her. "Are we, Mother? Did it ever occur to you that I at least should have been warned before you did this? I promised Raymond an honorable resolution. I had to sit like an idiot while you two made a mockery of him."

"You would never have agreed to it if we had warned you beforehand," Melisende said. "Men are so tender of their pride; and young men worst of all. Child, have you no understanding of what our kinswoman suffered at the hands of that man?"

"I understand that he had been led to expect certain things, and that it was I who did the leading—because I trusted you to conduct yourselves as fairly as we. There was nothing said of her leaving him once their quarrel was settled. She is leaving him, isn't she? She doesn't intend to come back."

"Of course she intends to return," said Melisende. "She's lady and countess here, and her son will stay with his father. She'll come back for the boy at least; she's fond of him."

"As you are fond of me? So that she can rule his every move?" Baldwin's mouth twisted. "Well then. I've had messengers of my own, and the news is bad enough. Nur al-Din has his eye on this country. Take your sister back with you to Jerusalem, where you can keep her safe. I'll stay in Tripoli and soothe his lordship as I can, and help him to defend his domain against the infidel."

"That is wise," Melisende said without a tremor. "I too have had word of the Turk's intentions; more recent perhaps than yours. He has an army in motion, and it purposes to take Tripoli."

"So you allow me to stay, my lady regent?"

"I believe that you are well advised to remain," she said. She yawned delicately. "Now if you please, my child; I'm no longer as young as you. I'm tired. These bones need to sleep."

Baldwin had little choice but to bow stiffly and take his leave. He did it a little abruptly perhaps, with a shade less courtesy than might have been fitting. He did not kiss his mother on the cheek as a proper son should have done, or accept her embrace and her blessing. He simply walked away.

Raymond and Baldwin both, caught off guard by the daughters of old King Baldwin and Morphia his queen, might have found common cause; but it did not deepen their friendship. When the ladies rode out under heavy guard, Baldwin chose conspicuously to remain behind. Raymond, equally conspicuously, rode with the women. He was hoping perhaps to lure Hodierna back with him; or at least to soften her heart with his presence.

No one expected that he would succeed. Baldwin, having said a cold farewell to his mother at the gate, had gone up into the castle. A company of young knights had got up a game of dice; they called to him as he passed by, and rattled the bones alluringly. He laughed and dropped down beside them, caught the cup as it sailed past, proceeded to lose a hard-fought round.

It was astonishing, Arslan thought, how Melisende's departure had lifted Baldwin's spirits. He had been no less than difficult since they came to Tripoli. Now he was his best self again, the young king whom people loved.

Arslan had no objection to a lively round of dicing, but his mood at the moment was for something less convivial. His mother and Lady Richildis had gone back with the royal ladies, and Zenobia with them. It rather dismayed him to realize how much, already, he missed them. A man should be made of sterner stuff.

But then Bertrand had ridden with Count Raymond, though he too would come back. He was not delighted to see the ladies go, either. None of them was, except Baldwin.

Arslan wandered back down from the castle into the city. The crowds that had gathered to see the ladies depart had dispersed swiftly. There were only the usual presses of passersby in the markets and the broader streets, and knots of hangers-on here and there near tavern or fountain or castle gate.

Near the south gate of the city he heard the commotion that would be the count's return: people calling, a stallion's trumpet, a scatter of halfhearted cheers as the folk greeted their lord after his brief departure. Arslan turned his steps toward the gate through which the count and his escort would come, not thinking of anything in particular except perhaps to watch a spectacle. Lords' ridings were always good for that, even if one were a lord oneself. And, he admitted, he wanted to see if Raymond was bearing up well, and maybe to wander back behind him, with a pause in a tavern for a cup of decent wine or middling horrible ale.

He was close enough now that the gate rose tall above him. Through it he could see the road stretching away toward Jerusalem, and the riders on it. Count Raymond was somewhat ahead, as if eager to return to his city. He was a sour-faced man but a good horseman, light and erect on the back of his tall charger. One or two of his escort rode near him, but his guards rode well behind. They were at ease. He was in his own land, returning to his own city. What could he possibly have to fear?

It happened very fast. Too fast almost to see; too fast by far to stop. Raymond rode in under the gate with his two knights close behind him, his guards still some furlongs behind. There were people in the gate, travelers, guards, perhaps a pilgrim or two. Some wore turbans, white so bright it dazzled even the shadows. Infidels, Arslan thought, or began to think, dressed all in white—strange to see such a thing in this season, and so clean, too, unmuddied, unstained.

Raymond passed them, riding at the walk. His horse's hoofs clattered on the paving. He had let himself go a little, out of the sun and the sight of his people: sagging in the saddle, breathing slow perhaps, giving in to weariness.

The men in white were moving, pressing about him. The gate was not so narrow that a horseman could not ride freely past a handful of men on foot. But they crowded him. His horse threw up its head. A hand seized the bridle. Other hands caught at the rider. Steel flashed.

It was all done between one breath and the next. Raymond fell without a sound. The knives cut life and breath from him, slit his throat from ear to ear, stabbed him to the heart.

His two companions cried out and flung themselves from their horses, swords half drawn—too slow, too draggingly slow. They were dead before their blades were out. They had not even time to fight.

Arslan's throat was raw. He must have been screaming. He did not remember. He was running, other people were running, the count's guard galloping up the road to the gate. The men clad all in white—now he remembered, now he knew what those garments signified: *Hashishayun*, madmen of the infidels, murderers in the name of Allah, Assassins. They fell without a battle, died crying the name of their God. Arslan killed one of them, maybe. There was blood on his sword after, but no clear memory of how it had come there.

They had all gone as mad as the Assassins. When those were dead, the count's guards and the city's garrison went hunting. Every turbaned man, every black-veiled woman, they caught and killed. Every Muslim who dwelt in Tripoli, or who had traveled there, or who was fool enough to come in by one of the roads or from the sea, died or fled the vengeance of the Franks.

But none of it made Raymond live again. He was dead, laid in state in the castle, with his wounds washed clean and a pall laid over him. A messenger, scrambling his wits about him, had taken horse and pounded away southward to bring back the queen and the Countess Hodierna.

None of them mourned the dead with more than adequate grief. He had not been a man to inspire passion, even in those who called themselves his friends. But that a great lord of the kingdom should have been murdered in his own gate in front of his people—that, no one would forgive.

Fear walked the city. If Assassins could take down the count himself, whom could they not destroy? Lords and knights and men of property shut themselves in their houses and looked with mistrust on their servants. Strangers were locked out, and friends, and even kin. They sent their wives and children away under heavy guard, guarded themselves by night and day, lest they suffer a dagger in the heart.

"But why?"

Hodierna mourned her husband perhaps least of all. She forbore to weep for him; such a lie would demean them both. Nonetheless she was angry, and perhaps somewhat on his behalf.

"Why?" she asked again. "What had he done to draw the eye of Alamut?"

No one could answer her. Raymond had been neither saint nor great ruler, but he had had few enough dealings with the infidels, and none that anyone knew of that could have been reckoned treachery.

Melisende said as much; but before Hodierna could respond, a messenger ran in, breathing hard, with news that brought them all to their feet: "Tortosa—Nur al-Din is in Tortosa!"

Indeed. That deadliest of infidels had seen the disarray of Raymond's death, taken note of a woman raised as regent over a son too young to rule, and done what any sensible conqueror would do: moved to conquer this county of Tripoli.

When the messenger had gone away to rest and eat and restore his strength, and another had gone to Baldwin to call him to arms with all such force as he could muster, Melisende sighed and drained the dregs of her wine. "Perhaps that is why," she said. "To leave us open to the attacks of the infidel."

"Perhaps," said Hodierna, but without great conviction.

aldwin had done everything that duty and kingship demanded, to secure Tripoli against the maraudings of the infidel. He did it well as always, suffered his mother's commands and the ridings of her messengers, drove back the enemy from the castle of Tortosa and set a garrison of Templars to hold it—making certain, scrupulously, to ask leave of the Countess Regent.

"And I wonder," he said to Arslan as they rode back at last to Jerusalem, "whether she troubled to ask her son if he approved."

"Would it matter if he didn't?" Arslan asked. "He's what, eleven years old? Twelve? He's too young to argue."

"I am ten years older than that," said Baldwin, "and I'm still too young to dispense with a regent."

Ah, thought Arslan. It rankled; of course it did. But never so openly as now, as they rode under the sky, with a crowd of knights and men-at-arms within earshot.

Baldwin, always so careful of his tongue, trained to it from earliest youth, seemed to have stopped caring who heard. "She's not going to let go," he said. "You know that. Everyone knows that. She won't let me take what I should have taken long ago."

"And why didn't you?"

Baldwin laughed harshly. "You always ask the hard questions, don't you, foster-brother? How much strength have I ever had? How many friends? How many lords of either power or influence, who could stand up in court and defy her?"

Arslan looked about. Men were listening and making no pretense of doing otherwise. He could, if he wished, reckon the count of lords and barons in this army of Jerusalem. They were a surprising number. Baldwin after all had led them to battle since he was a child. Melisende never had. A woman did not do such a thing.

Constable Manasses, who always before had ridden with the king, this time was gone. He had ridden to Jerusalem before them, as escort to the queen. No small number of the Court had gone with them. But more were here.

It was a division, Arslan realized. Not conscious, perhaps, nor calculated, yet no less real for that. The lords of the kingdom had chosen their places.

Bertrand . . .

Bertrand was not here. Nor was he with Melisende. He had gone ahead of her,

called to Acre by some business of Helena's, but promising to meet Arslan again at
Easter Court.

And had he known what would happen here? He was Baldwin's teacher, his
armsmaster, but long before he had been Baldwin's man, he had sworn fealty to
Melisende. Arslan did not know that that oath had ever been dissolved.

Bertrand could have commanded Arslan to come with him to Acre. Arslan had
half expected it, been a little wounded when he said no word, simply embraced and
kissed him and said, "Easter, then, in Jerusalem."

He had known. He must have.

Baldwin was still waiting for Arslan to respond. Arslan did, slowly. "I think you
know that you have friends—and many of them."

"Enough to challenge her?"

"Count them," Arslan said, "my lord king."

Baldwin set his lips together. He did not answer, not then. Not till they had
ridden to Jerusalem.

No man of rank could enter a city gate these days without great wariness and a
strong vanguard. But Baldwin rode in as he always had, guarded but not excessively.
As always, Melisende awaited him in the Tower of David, robed and crowned and
surrounded by her ladies. Her crown had always been higher than his, her throne
set level to be sure, yet she had insisted that her comfort demanded a deeper cushion, a taller footstool.

This day as ever, she did not rise as a lady of lesser rank before the king, but
remained enthroned while he approached and bowed and kissed her proffered hand.
If she saw how his eyes burned, she took no notice of it. "Well done as always, my
son," she said, "and welcome. I trust you had a pleasant journey."

Baldwin murmured something suitably innocuous. But when she beckoned him
to the throne beside her he said, "Lady, I'm weary, and I would rest. I'll return
when the tables are laid in hall."

She frowned. But she was in a tolerant mood, or too surprised perhaps to forbid
him. He had never defied her before, not in front of the assembled court. "By all
means," she managed to say, "refresh yourself. If you should be minded to attend
the later audience—"

"I shall see you," he said, "in hall. Madam." He bowed, not particularly low, and
took his leave.

Baldwin was in a fair temper. Nothing in particular had caused it. No single slight,
no insult. Simply the sight of his mother on her throne in her glittering crown,
ruling the kingdom as she had since his father died.

"And that is long enough," he said after he had bathed and eaten a little and
retired to his chambers. Most of his attendants had seized the opportunity to rest.
Baldwin was too ferociously awake; so therefore was Arslan.

Arslan sighed and was glad at least that he could lie in comfort across the foot
of Baldwin's bed, though there was peril in that: his eyelids kept trying to fall shut.
Sometimes it was a nuisance to have a soldier's instincts, to be able to sleep wherever
he fell.

Baldwin's voice did its best to keep him awake. "I am twenty-two years old. In this kingdom a boy is a man at fifteen, a knight at one-and-twenty. And here am I, man in years, duly knighted, and still a child who cannot be trusted to rule alone."

"You have," said Arslan, trying not to yawn, "been remarkably patient."

"Some would say I've been weak. My mother would."

"So why, then? Have you been afraid?"

"No." Baldwin dropped to the bed like the child he no longer was, feet tucked up, elbows on knees, chin on fists, scowling at the world. "I kept hoping she'd do it herself. The way—the way your father did."

Arslan blinked, not entirely with sleepiness. "My father never stepped down from his barony for me. I'd fling it in his face if he tried."

"Don't be an idiot!" Baldwin snapped. "You know what I mean. You wanted him to acknowledge you. And he did. By himself. God knows he was late in doing it, but not as late as my mother has been. I don't think she's going to, brother. She has no intention of ever letting me rule."

"Have you asked?"

"Why? So that she can laugh in my face?"

Arslan groaned and sat up. "Baldwin," he said, "you're as bad as I was. You won't help yourself, and she won't do it for you. I had to make my father promise. He did it sooner than I expected, in the end, but I asked it of him first."

"Your father is a great deal more reasonable than my mother."

"You think so?" Arslan let himself fall back and his eyes fall shut. "You really think so?"

"Stop giggling," Baldwin said nastily.

"I am not," said Arslan.

"You're thinking of it."

Arslan made a small derisive sound, halfway to a snore. If Baldwin responded, he never knew it. He was sound asleep.

As Arslan had more than half expected, Baldwin did not confront his mother that day, or the next day either. But on his third day in Jerusalem, in front of the court assembled for the morning audience, he rose between petitioners and said, "Your majesty, I too would ask a boon of you."

Melisende regarded him without anxiety. It had been an easy audience, no complaints, no quarrels, nothing to ruffle her composure. She smiled, raised a brow, said, "Anything within reason, you may certainly have."

He did not smile in return, nor soften to her lightness of manner. "Madam, I believe that it is reasonable, but you may be of another mind. Tell me, madam. How old am I?"

Her eyes narrowed slightly. Her smile faded a fraction. She knew, Arslan thought, or had begun to. "Why, you must have a score of years."

"A score and two," he said, "my lady." And how ill it looked, his manner said, that his own mother could not remember how old he was.

"Ah," she said with a wave of the hand. "The time, how it flies. So: you are two-and-twenty. You had a birthday, I recall. I gave you a new set of armor and a young destrier. Was the armor an ill fit, then? Did the horse prove less well trained than I was told?"

"They are all in good order," Baldwin said. "Likewise the golden ring and the belt and the robe of Byzantine silk. Those gifts were welcome and well received. And yet, madam, did it never strike you that they marked the passing of a good number of years?"

She laughed with studied lightness. "Two-and-twenty is hardly old! Why, you're a babe in arms."

"I am not," said Baldwin. His voice was flat. "I am young, I grant you. But I am not a child. I sprouted my beard long ago."

"So I have been told," said Melisende.

She was not going to aid him, but neither, it seemed, would she hinder. That alone made Arslan suspicious; and he could see how Baldwin paused as if to gather his forces. When he spoke, it was abrupt, almost harsh. "Madam, do you not think it is past time that I claimed my right as king? I am neither weak nor feebleminded, nor require the aid of a regency."

Melisende must have been expecting this; must have prepared for it. Arslan could not believe that she had failed to anticipate the moment. And yet she said, "It can wait, surely. You've had a hard campaign. You'll want to rest, recover, enjoy your leisure. I can—"

"Madam," Baldwin said, doing a thing that he had never dared to do: interrupting the flow of her speech. "I want to be king now. I should have been king years ago."

"You are king," she said. "We were crowned side by side in the Church of the Holy Sepulcher."

"I was crowned in my minority, with you as regent over me. I ask now that I be king indeed. No regency. No power higher than my own."

"God is higher than any of us," said Melisende.

Arslan watched Baldwin refuse to give way to her mockery. For it was that, however gently she uttered it. "I will be crowned again," he said to her. "This time I will be granted the full extent of my right and privilege. I will no longer be subject to the approval of a regent."

Melisende drew a breath. The court listened avidly, as Baldwin had intended. She could not but know that he had trapped her; that she could hardly refuse him on any grounds that he or the court would accept.

She took it in good part, as a woman of long experience in the acceptance of defeat. "Very well," she said. "Is Easter soon enough? Lent is an ill time for crowning kings. On the high feast we will take crown and throne, you and I—you as king in fact as well as name, and I as before, who were born the heir of the King of Jerusalem."

"Lady," Baldwin said very quietly, "I am the heir of Jerusalem's king."

"Fulk gained his title through me," she said. "As have you."

Baldwin opened his mouth as if to protest, but chose the virtue of silence. He shut his mouth, bowed, retreated.

Richildis had not been present in court, but she was in the city, and in attendance on the queen after morning court. She had heard enough to know what had been said and not said, and to form an opinion of it.

Michael Bryennius would have told her that silence was more than wise; it was blessed. But she was seldom minded to be as discreet as that. As she helped Melisende out of her court robes and into a gown more suitable for an afternoon in the solar, she said, "You should let go."

Melisende glanced at her. "What? I've nothing in my hand."

She was being deliberately obtuse. Richildis resolved not to snap, not to be any more foolish than she had been already. "Lady, you know what I'm speaking of. From the time you took this regency, you've known that it would end when your son was old enough to rule alone. He's been old enough, as he says, for a fair number of years now."

"I am still," said Melisende, too soft almost to hear, "and always have been the heir to this kingdom. Any right that he has, he has through me."

"A king supersedes a queen," Richildis said, "even when that queen is his elder."

Dangerous, that; not deadly perhaps, but perilous enough. Richildis held Mount Ghazal by grant and by grace of the queen's goodwill. If she lost that, she well could lose her barony.

Yet she had to say what was in her to say. She could not keep silent.

Melisende did not at once cast her out. "Do you contend that a queen of years and experience, a spirit honed in the battles of courts, should yield to the fecklessness of a callow boy?"

"Certainly not," Richildis said. "Yet he is neither feckless nor callow, and he ceased to be a boy some while since. He's proved himself well in the wars. When you've allowed him, he's given wise counsel in court and in judgment. He's a son to be proud of, and he promises to be a good king—maybe even a great one."

"Of course he does," said Melisende. "He's my son. He'll be king in fact as in name, come Easter day. Is there anything more that he could ask for?"

"You'll be crowned with him," Richildis said.

"As queen beside him, not as regent above him."

Richildis shook her head. "Lady, it's not done. You know it. When a regency ends, the regent—"

"The regent," Melisende said with bitter clarity, "puts away her crown and her robes and her pretensions, creeps off quietly to some convenient cloister, and forgets that she was ever a ruler of men. Yes, I know how it is commonly done. Even I might do it, if I were not who I am. I am Baldwin's daughter of Jerusalem. My father was a king. I was his eldest child. I was born to rule this kingdom."

"And so you have," Richildis said, "since your husband died."

"And you would ask me to give it up? To walk away? To forget?"

"Not I," said Richildis. "The world—the law—"

"Damn the world! Damn the law!" Melisende looked just then as she had when she was young, years of care and queenship stripped away. "I'll die when I die. He can have it all then, like any king's heir. Isn't it enough that I'll let him rule beside me? I could blind him and lock him in a tower, or dispose of him altogether. But I'm too soft for that. Too foolishly fond."

Richildis looked at her in silence. Queens, and most great ladies for the matter of that, did not cherish their children as simpler women did. Nurses raised them, tutors had the teaching of them. They belonged to the kingdom, not to any earthly kin.

Melisende had never had any great use for her sons, even after they grew old enough to be conversable. Richildis tried to understand it. But she who loved her children with a fierce white heat, and mourned even yet those who had died, could find nothing in her to answer to Melisende's coldness.

Melisende went on, blissfully unaware of Richildis' maundering. "We'll be crowned together. He'll have what he's yearning for, and I'll keep what is mine. He can't quarrel with that."

"He might try," Richildis said, but under her breath, where Melisende could hear or not as she chose.

reparations for Baldwin's coronation pro-
ceeded apace. He suffered through the fitting of the robes. He committed to memory
the words that he would say, the things that he would do in the rite. He walked
through the steps with his mother, saw where she would stand, watched as she
pretended to take the crown upon her head. He said no word but what the ceremony
required, nor offered more than barest courtesy.

She ignored him. He was a child, her manner said. He sulked. Children did. He
would come round once he had what he wanted.

He saw that perfectly clearly. It whitened his lips and made him breathe a fraction
harder when he stood in her presence. When he was out of it, he said nothing. Not
one word.

On the night before he was to be crowned, Baldwin was permitted an hour alone
between the daymeal and his night's vigil in the Church of the Holy Sepulcher.
His mother had shared the one but would forgo the other. She would keep her own
vigil in her own chapel, and in greater comfort, too.

Arslan meant to leave the king to himself, but as he retreated from the chamber
in which Baldwin was resting, Baldwin said, "No. Stay."

Arslan hesitated. "I really shouldn't—"

"I don't want to be alone," said Baldwin.

Arslan raised his brows. "Afraid?"

Baldwin shook his head. "No. Not of that. Of . . ." He hesitated.

Arslan leaned on the door that he had not quite gone so far as to open, and
folded his arms, and settled to wait.

Baldwin saw: his eyes glinted briefly before he lost himself in his troubles again.
It was some time before he said, "I want to do a thing, and I'm not sure I dare."

"What, tell your mother she can't be queen?"

Baldwin looked startled. "How did you—that's not—" He stopped, began again.
"How do I do such a thing? She has allies everywhere. She's older, stronger, more
deeply settled in the people's hearts."

"But you," said Arslan, "are the rightful king."

"Will that matter if she calls out her forces?"

Arslan had to pause, to think about that. "I think," he said slowly, "that you
should count the number of your friends. It's much higher than you may believe."

"How? Shall I go out with a lamp like the old philosopher, and search for an honest man?"

"Don't be silly," Arslan said. "Count the ones you know. The northern barons have always been more yours than hers. Now reckon who's been seeking you out of late, who's been standing by you in court, and who's been asking to ride or hunt or play at draughts with you. I've been noticing. She has her loyal few, her women and priests, and of course Manasses and his familiars. But who else? Only a few aging barons. Everyone else is either keeping to himself or finding excuses to bear you company."

"It's not—" Baldwin stopped. "How can it be? I've done nothing."

"Nothing," said Arslan, "but grown into a man who can lead men. People saw how you conducted yourself on that botch of a Crusade. They saw your mother, too, safe in Jerusalem. They reflected even then that a woman can hold a regency, but in a warrior kingdom, among men of war, it is a man who must rule."

"She will never let go," Baldwin muttered.

"Then you must shake her loose."

"That's what I want to do," said Baldwin. "But I don't know if I can. If enough lords will follow me once I begin."

"What will you do?" Arslan asked, patiently he thought, but Baldwin shot him a look.

"What I would like," Baldwin said, "is to trick her. She'll never give way for anything I do. But if I become suddenly ill, ill enough that I can't be crowned tomorrow . . ."

"And then," said Arslan, "you gather a company of men whom you can trust, snatch the Patriarch out of his bed, and have yourself crowned before she knows what you've done."

"Why do I bother to say anything to you?" Baldwin asked, half of the air. "You always know what I'm thinking."

"You're as transparent as glass," Arslan said calmly. "It doesn't take a witch or a seer to know what you're up to."

"Then," said Baldwin, "she or her advisors—they can see it, too."

"I don't think so," Arslan said. "Remember, I shared a cradle with you. I know what you'll do, most times, before you know it yourself. None of them has any knowledge of you, not like that."

"Lord Bertrand does," Baldwin said, very low.

Arslan's heart began to pound. His hands had clenched into fists. Yet he said, "How do you know he won't choose to follow you?"

"He was my mother's knight," Baldwin said, "long before he was mine. He's never sworn himself to me, you know. Always to the queen, or to both of us together."

"Do you trust him?"

"Do you?"

They both were silent, in a sort of impasse. Arslan did not want to say that he mistrusted his father, the man whose heir he was, who had taught him much of what he knew. And yet . . .

Arslan said slowly, "If we leave him out of this he'll never forgive us. Yet if he's the queen's man in the end—he'll never forgive us for telling him."

Baldwin nodded. He frowned, troubled. "If he is mine, then I have the strength of his reputation behind me, his power and his respect in the kingdom; and he'll say no word of what I'll do until it's done. If he's my mother's, there's nothing he can do but betray me to her. Honor demands no less."

"Honor is a horned and taloned thing," Arslan said.

"I think," Baldwin said, dragging out the words, "that we must tell him. Right before I do it."

A bark of laughter escaped from Arslan. "Too late for him to run to the queen? He'll be livid!"

"I can pray he'll understand," Baldwin said.

Arslan could only nod. There was no simple way to do what Baldwin purposed to do; not with such a mother as he had. Unnatural, some would call her. Arslan reckoned her simply unwilling to accept the way of the world. None of the daughters of Baldwin of Le Bourg had any talent for submission.

Arslan wondered sometimes what their mother had been like, the legendary and long-dead Morphia of Melitene. Armenian women were not known for their strength of will, nor was Morphia ever spoken of except with reverence, as everything that a queen should be. Yet her children had grown up like a pride of lionesses.

On the eve of his coronation, Baldwin became suddenly and rather drastically indisposed. The physician who saw him was well paid to acknowledge the indisposition but not the cause of it: a dose of emetic strong enough to be thoroughly convincing.

It was also strong enough to lay him flat for a fact, all of Easter Sunday and much of the night thereafter. He had meant the coronation for the morning of Easter Monday, but though much improved, he was in no condition to seize the Church of the Holy Sepulcher and the Patriarch in it, and force that worthy prelate to set the crown on his head. He cursed roundly the impulse that had led him to take too generous a dose, but even in midcurse he fled snarling for the garderobe.

Arslan was careful not to laugh at him. He would be well on the morrow, Yusuf the physician said—not the one who had been paid to keep silent; Yusuf had been encouraged to take a holiday, and had come back too late to help or hinder the taking of the dose. It was clear what he thought of that, but physicians from Baghdad were nothing if not discreet. He fed the king a potion that, he said so nastily that even Baldwin believed him, would counter the emetic; imposed on him a diet of bread sopped in goat's milk; and departed in clearly evident disgust.

Sick as he was, Baldwin had sent out messages to those barons whom he trusted, bidding them attend him in Holy Sepulcher in the morning. His most loyal guards were ready, waiting to seize the Patriarch, and standing watch over the Patriarch's palace lest he take it into his head to depart from Jerusalem in the night. Some few watched the queen as well, but in secret lest she catch wind of it, keeping away any who might have whispered a betrayal.

Among those summoned was the Lord Bertrand of Beausoleil. Arslan had hoped in rather cowardly fashion that Bertrand would depart for his demesne at the close of Easter Court. But Bertrand lingered as many did, taking his ease in his house in Jerusalem, keeping company with the Lady Helena, visiting with his sister and her husband and their daughter. All things that he would do whenever it pleased him, but now served less well than ill. If he had been on the road home, there might have been ways to see that he heard nothing of Baldwin's intent until it was well over.

As it was, Arslan was invited to dinner in the evening. He did not want to go, nor did Baldwin command him; but the king asked, courteously, that he do it. "And when it's over," Baldwin said, "tell him."

"I should make you do it," Arslan muttered. Baldwin, still slightly green about the edges, looked ready to agree—it would have been a reprieve from confinement. Arslan escaped before either of them could do something foolish. It was foolish enough that they should be contemplating this thing, this defiance of the queen's will.

Arslan got through dinner somehow. They were all there, even Zenobia, though she went fretfully to bed before the wine went round. Arslan would have been glad to carry her off and hide in her chamber, but he had a duty to perform. Best to get it over.

The wine was good, a new cask from La Forêt. Its quality had much improved over the years. Richildis said as much, sipping slowly and with pleasure. "Lady Agnes has worked wonders with the vineyard," she said. "See how well the wine travels now. Do you think, my love, that there might be a prospect of trade in it?"

Michael Bryennius shrugged a little. "Maybe. Maybe not. It's not a large vineyard; much of what it sells, it sells in France."

"But," said Helena, "as a luxury—a cask here, a jar there, presented only to princes and prelates: the price could go as high as any of us might wish, and well repay the trouble of transporting it from Anjou."

"Such tradesmen you all are," Bertrand said, but smiling as he said it. "You aren't thinking as a nobleman should think. It's fine wine and no mistake. Given as gifts to kings and their familiars, it would make a name for itself without any taint of trade."

"Nor any taint of money, either," Helena said. "Where's the profit in that?"

"Why, a great deal," said Bertrand, "if those who received the gift grew fond of the flavor of it, and went looking for more, and bought a jar or a cask direct from La Forêt—and themselves paid to transport it."

"That," Helena said, "is perfectly splendid."

Bertrand grinned at her, cocky as a boy, and toasted them all with a fresh-filled cup.

None of them appeared to notice that Arslan was being quiet. He usually was when they gathered so, watching and listening and being vastly entertained.

Tonight he was in no mood to enjoy their badinage. The wine was fine indeed, but it sat sour in his stomach. Baldwin might expect him to take Bertrand aside and address him in confidence, but there had never been great secrets among the five of them.

This one . . .

Richildis was Melisende's lady. Of that Arslan had no doubt at all. She had had little to do with Baldwin, had shown him such goodwill as a lady might who attended his mother, but there was no more between them than that. If Arslan told her now what Baldwin meant to do in the morning, Richildis would go with it to Melisende.

Yet Baldwin had all but commanded him to pass word to Bertrand, of whose loyalty neither of them was certain. The longer he waited, the more difficult it became.

Salvation came in the shape of a fractious and very noisy Zenobia. Both women went to contend with her, Richildis out of duty, Helena because, she professed, the wine was going to her head; she felt a need to rise and move about.

Michael Bryennius accompanied the women. Perhaps he sensed something of Arslan's need. Perhaps he simply trusted in his own ability to soothe his daughter's temper.

Bertrand forbore to follow the rest. He looked gloriously comfortable, sprawled amid cushions in the eastern fashion, long legs stretched out, winecup in hand. Of the wound that he had taken in the Crusade, nothing remained save an occasional catch in his side: a pause, a slight paling about the lips, a moment to recover before he went on with what he was doing. He was no greyer, if no less; undiminished by the years, still a tall broad man with the bearing of one who had known the arts of knighthood from his youth. Baldwin would look like him, Arslan reflected, when he advanced into middle years. So would Arslan, for the matter of that. People were always remarking on how closely he resembled his father.

He had to hope that Bertrand would choose to be Baldwin's man and not Melisende's, for this night at least.

When Arslan said it, he said it baldly, without preliminary. "I have a message for you from the king. He asks you to attend him tomorrow at prime in the Church of the Holy Sepulcher."

Bertrand was still for so long that Arslan wondered if he had heard. He might be asleep open-eyed, or reflecting on things far away.

Then he said, "He's doing it, then."

Arslan did not try to pretend that he misunderstood. "Will you tell his mother?"

"Should I?"

Arslan did not answer.

Bertrand closed his eyes. After what seemed a long while he said, "I suppose it was the only way."

"None of us could think of any other," Arslan said.

Bertrand nodded. "She's not going to be happy."

"Her happiness matters little in the face of law and custom."

"Indeed," said Bertrand. "And are you prepared if there are consequences?"

"What consequences can there be?"

"War," Bertrand said.

Arslan nodded once, tightly. "We are prepared," he said.

"Good," said Bertrand.

"And will you come?"

"To the war?"

Arslan's teeth clicked together. Bertrand was not laughing. Nor for that matter was Arslan. "To the coronation," he said.

"I don't know," said Bertrand.

"He wants you there."

"His mother would be less than pleased."

Arslan nodded.

"So," said Bertrand. "He's asking me to choose."

Arslan was silent. Bertrand did not seem angry, but he had always been able to preserve a calm face even when he was outraged. Arslan had undertaken to perfect the art himself. It was useful in contending with kings and councils.

Baldwin would pay, Arslan thought, for this that he had forced on them both. Arslan only hoped that the payment would not be made in blood.

"Go," said Bertrand.

Arslan blinked. "Father?"

"Go," Bertrand said again. "Leave me here."

Arslan hesitated.

"I won't go running to the queen," Bertrand said with a hint of irritation. "What I will do . . . I need to think. Will you let me do it?"

Arslan bowed. He had to trust, as Baldwin had, that at the least, Bertrand would not turn against him. It shamed him, how hard that was. Yet he did it. There was little else, after all, that he could do.

s Arslan passed through the gate of
the Tower of David, deep in thought and barely noticing where he was, a shadow
waylaid him in the paler shadow of the gate. His hand dropped to the hilt of his
dagger; he regretted briefly that he had not worn his sword.

The shadow spoke in a voice but lately broken. "Arslan?"

He eased all at once, so swiftly that his knees buckled.

Prince Amaury regarded him in some anxiety. He stiffened his knees, steadied
his breath. The king's brother looked as if he bore news that Arslan would be
horrified to hear.

"What is it?" Arslan demanded of him. "Is the king—"

"Baldwin is still at dinner," Amaury said. "I was waiting for you."

It was hardly wise to strike a prince, but Arslan was well minded to knock him
silly. "And why," he asked with gritted teeth, "would you be doing that?"

Amaury glanced at the guards who stood stone-faced on either side. "Come," he
said.

Arslan nearly refused, but Amaury's expression gave him pause. If it was not
Baldwin, then perhaps—

"It's not Mother, either," Amaury said when they had paused in the court by the
stables. No one was there; the grooms were all at meat or abroad. The horses were
quiet, absorbed in their fodder. Someone had lit lamps in the stable, though it was
still light without.

Amaury perched on a stool of ancient vintage. It groaned but held. The rump
of a destrier loomed behind him. "Now," he said. "Tell me true. Baldwin's going to
get himself crowned in the morning, isn't he?"

Arslan forbore to be shocked. "You've been listening at doors," he said.

"Yes," Amaury said without shame, or anger either. "He thought I'd go running
to Mother. Didn't he?"

Arslan could hardly deny it.

"He should know me better than that," Amaury said. "Or does he ever notice?
Does he think I'm still seven years old and hounding him wherever he goes?"

Arslan considered him: fourteen years old, or was it fifteen? And certainly not hounding his brother. The queen had chosen her Constable to raise her younger son; Bertrand was occupied with his own late-acknowledged heir, and of all the men she would wisely choose, Manasses would have been the best of them. The Constable had kept his charge close, raised him well by all accounts, but given him little to do with his brother the king.

Amaury, it was clear, had lost none of the dogged persistence that had kept him so often and so long in Baldwin's shadow. "You don't have to say anything," he said. "Just listen. I'm not angry. I understand why he would think I'm not to be trusted. But . . . I'm strangling, too. I want to be free of her."

"And what," asked Arslan, "has she done to you? You're the second son. There's no regency for you. You're as free as anyone can be."

"May I not be free to throw in my lot with my brother?"

"Why would you do that?"

"Because," Amaury said calmly, "she might win now, but unless she poisons him or finds a way to get him killed in battle, he'll outlive her. He'll be king in time, whether she wills it or no. And I'll be at his right hand. I think I want to be his Constable, when I'm old enough to do it and not be laughed at."

Even when he was small, Amaury had always had that cold edge, that hint of calculation in everything he did. He lacked the warmth that brimmed over in his brother. Men did not love him, though they might admire his intelligence.

This could be a dangerous creature, Arslan thought. He was not frightened or even greatly troubled. Perhaps he should have been; but he had exhausted his store of anxiety in confronting his father. "So you want to throw in your lot with your brother," he said. "What do you think your mother and your guardian will say to that?"

"I am fifteen years old," Amaury said. "By law I am a man, though my lady mother may contest it. I can choose where I will go. I can swear fealty to a liege lord. I do want to do that—and I want that liege to be my brother."

"Will you swear to that?" Arslan asked.

"By my brother's life," said Amaury.

"I'll hold you to it."

Amaury inclined his head, unruffled. "I knew you would. I trust you to keep me honest, messire, and to make sure that I am honorable."

"You can't do that for yourself?"

"I can," Amaury said, "but Baldwin may not believe it. If I have you to speak for me, he'll trust me."

"Maybe not," said Arslan.

"You don't know your own power," said Amaury. "If you say a thing is so, everyone believes it. No one doubts you. You have a gift, you know, whatever you choose to call it."

"Honor," Arslan said. "Honesty. But—"

"No buts," Amaury said. "I'll see him crowned, and I'll keep silent till it's done. Then I'll swear myself to him. Will you tell him that?"

"Would you rather surprise him?"

Amaury paused as if he had not thought of that. Yet surely he had. "No," he said. "No, let him be prepared. It will matter to the people that his brother shares his rebellion."

Indeed it would. For both sons of Melisende to defy her so signally was no small thing. No easy one either, though Arslan had no doubt of what he was doing. A regent should know when to lay down her regency. If she would not do it herself, then her son and his allies would do it for her.

Bertrand sat alone until Helena and Richildis and Michael Bryennius came back from putting Zenobia to bed. Even after they had settled about him, he had no ally in the world. "Where is Arslan?" Richildis asked in all innocence.

"He went back to his duties," Bertrand said, which was true enough.

"Without bidding us goodnight?" Richildis clicked her tongue, but betrayed no suspicion. "Why, for shame. I'll take him to task for it, next time we invite him for dinner."

The others smiled; their conversation wound away where Bertrand had no mind to follow.

Soon enough they had tired of wine and chatter. Richildis went off to bed with her Byzantine. Helena lingered while the servants cleared the remains of the wine. She seldom waited so, or was so silent.

When the table was cleared, wine and servants gone, and only themselves in the lamplight, she said, "Tell me."

Bertrand had every intention of refusing. But he had never been able to resist those eyes with their dark calm stare and their conviction that he would answer. He yielded to it almost with relief. "Baldwin will have himself crowned in the morning," he said.

"Without his mother?"

Bertrand nodded.

Helena was not surprised. "She invited it, rather. Didn't she? Demanding that she be crowned next to him, if he took power to himself—proving thereby that she rules and will rule as queen regnant, and not merely as regent."

"Do you blame her for it?"

"No," said Helena. "And you?"

"I . . . don't know." Bertrand shifted, suddenly uncomfortable. "Baldwin asked me to attend him."

"He trusts you greatly, then," Helena said.

"He's a fool," said Bertrand harshly. "He demands that I choose, as if such choices were in any way simple."

"And are they not? Can you avoid them at all?"

"I would hope that I can," he said. He rubbed his face, tired beyond bearing, too tired to rest. "I could do that, you know. Retreat to Beausoleil. Refuse to take sides."

"You could," she said. "It wouldn't be like you, but you could."

"What am I to do?" he cried. "How can I choose? She was my lady from the day I came to this kingdom, when she was but a willful child and I no older than Arslan is now. And he has been my dear lord since he was born, my pupil from his youth, my king and my friend. They never loved each other beyond the bare necessity, but we who love them both—we suffer for their contention."

"Perhaps retreat is best, then," she said, "lest you tear your heart apart."

"And how can I do that, either? I was never a coward even when I ran from my

father. I've never shrunk from a battle. I've always known where I stand, and for
whom."

"In this," said Helena, "all ways are ill. Unless you prevent it. If you fetch Richildis, if the two of you go together to the queen—"

"No!" Bertrand recoiled from the violence of his own objection. With an effort
he softened his voice. "No. I promised to keep silent."

"Then perhaps," said Helena, "you've made your choice."

Bertrand opened his mouth to deny her, but no words came. He had not chosen
Baldwin. But in omitting to speak before the deed was done, he committed a sort
of treason.

He had made hard choices before: leaving La Forêt, coming to Outremer, choosing not to go back when his sister came to fetch him; first refusing and then acknowledging his son. But those had been easy beside this.

The promise he had made—yes, he could keep that, and would, whatever it cost
him. But if he must then choose between the king and the queen, he did not know
which would break first, his heart or his faith.

"He asked me to see him crowned," Bertrand said. "But—I can't."

Helena took his hand and held it to her lips, then laid it over her heart. She
did not speak. Like her son, she knew well the uses of silence.

"I can't turn against the queen," he said. "Not in secret, by sleights and trickery.
If I'm to declare for Baldwin, I'll do it in the light of day, where she can see me
and know what I've done."

That was cowardice of a sort, but Helena said nothing of it. She only said, "So
you keep your faith with both: Baldwin by keeping silent, Melisende by standing
apart while he compels the Patriarch to crown him."

"I'll get no thanks for either," Bertrand said. He paused. "Do you despise me?"

She shook her head. "I'm only half a Frank, my love. We of the east know what
it is to stand aside while the world goes mad."

"And who is mad?" he asked. "The son, for wanting what should be his? Or the
mother, for wanting what she has had since she was young?"

"Both and neither," Helena answered, calm as always. "We can pray that she
accepts the world's way, and accepts what her son has done."

"We can pray," Bertrand said. But he knew as well as she: Melisende would give
up nothing save under strong compulsion. Baldwin could not muster that, Bertrand
did not think.

Not yet.

They gathered in the Church of the Holy Sepulcher in the grey hours of the morning, two days after Easter: Baldwin the king and his company of loyal knights.
Bertrand was not among them. Arslan had not honestly expected him to be. Baldwin had asked too much of a man who loved him, but who had loved his mother
first.

The throngs of pilgrims had gone away. There was no one in the church so early,
only the acolytes preparing for mass in the chapels, and a worshipper or two near
the Sepulcher, looking as if they had slept there.

The pomp and splendor of the coronation had been taken down and put away.

There were only the furnishings of a day like any other, fine altar-cloths and banks of candles brightening the gloom. The Patriarch seemed to have descended from another and higher place, one far more royal in its dignity. His vestments shimmered as only silk will do, gold for the season, embroidered with silver and scarlet.

Baldwin had reckoned it too dangerous to slip out of the Tower of David in coronation robes, but Arslan had contrived to bring what he could. The king stood up in decent fashion, draped in a robe of the imperial purple, and over it a mantle of cloth of gold. Baldwin reckoned it a gaudy show, but he looked well in it. He stood straight, betraying no impatience as the Patriarch meandered his way through the forms of the mass. Only when it was strictly proper would he beckon the acolyte who held the silken cushion on which reposed the crown.

Fulcher of Angoulême, Patriarch of Jerusalem, was not a happy man. He was one of Melisende's favorites, chosen and approved by her. It had taken all of Baldwin's strength of will and arms and his own company of knights to persuade his eminence to leave his morning devotions and proceed to the church, there to crown Baldwin king. If Melisende should burst in now with her allies at her back and command him to halt, he would do it without a moment's hesitation.

Humphrey of Toron, who had been Baldwin's friend since the king's youth, moved in close to the Patriarch and folded his arms. He was not a tall man nor on most occasions an imposing one, but he had the gift of commanding men. Fulcher blanched slightly and speeded his pace a fraction.

However reluctant Fulcher might be, word followed inexorably upon word, until he had climbed the steps of the mass to the rite of coronation. Baldwin knelt in front of him. He glowered at the head bent so properly and so humbly, and glared at the crown on its cushion. Arslan, catching Humphrey's eye, advanced a step closer himself. He had the height that Humphrey lacked, the power to loom in silence, to threaten without uttering a word.

Between them they suborned the Patriarch. He took the crown in hands that barely trembled, lifted it high under the dome of the basilica, and lowered it onto the head that waited so patiently to receive it.

As it touched Baldwin's brow, he let go a long, and long-held, breath. All the rest was only words. Here was the truth: the weight of the crown and the right that it conveyed; the kingship that he had waited so long to take.

Arslan wondered if he felt different. He looked much as always. A little taller, perhaps; a little straighter. He wore kingship well, as he should who had been born to it. It was his proper garment. It fit him.

elisende had not been pleased to learn of her son's illness, but she had never suspected that it might have been part of a plot to defy her. When necessity forced him to put off the coronation, she suffered it. What else could she do?

She was just coming from morning mass in her chapel when the messenger arrived: a page, breathless with exertion, gasping out the words: "Majesty! The king's been crowned before the Holy Sepulcher."

Melisende stopped as if struck. "The king has what?"

"Been crowned," the child repeated, too young or too short of breath for circumspection. "He took his knights and broke into the Patriarch's palace and made the Patriarch come out and—"

"He had himself crowned by force?"

Melisende's voice was quiet, her face calm. One who did not know her might think her unperturbed. The page seemed to take comfort from her manner: he mastered his breathing and spoke more calmly, though still with headlong speed—that seemed to be native to him. "Majesty," he said, "the Patriarch couldn't argue with a dozen strong knights, even if they were unarmed in the holy place."

"No," said Melisende. "He could hardly do that."

She dismissed him with the courtesy she always showed servants and children. Already as he departed, her own messengers were running out to learn what was to be learned: who had abetted Baldwin in his defiance, and what they thought to do now. No guards had closed off her chambers, nor had any armed force appeared to confine her. Baldwin, it seemed, expected her to accept what he had done, to bow her head and fold her hands and retreat into proper womanly submission.

He was a fool. Melisende kept to her chambers, to be sure; but her allies came and went in notable numbers. Soon enough—before the week was out—Baldwin had summoned a council of the kingdom, to defend what he had done and to plead his cause.

"Let him plead," said Melisende in something like satisfaction. "Let him see how ill he has wrought."

· · ·

Baldwin did not look like a fool or a child as he stood up in front of the assembly of Jerusalem. He was a tall man and proud, holding his head high under the crown that Fulk had worn before him, and Baldwin, and Baldwin again, and Godfrey of Lorraine who led the first Crusade. He spoke clearly and levelly, speaking of the law that made a son his father's heir, and citing precedents for the handing over of regencies.

Melisende sat her throne as she had throughout her regency, crowned, clad in cloth of gold. She did not move, nor did she interrupt while he spoke. She maintained a royal dignity. She was not displaced or deposed, nor could she be without the consent of this council.

Baldwin labored to win it. "The law is clear," he said. "I am of age. I am my father's son, the heir of his body. I have proved my fitness in this council and in the field of war. Will you accept me as your rightful king?"

"It seems," said Manasses the Constable, "that you have taken matters into your own hands."

"I had no choice," Baldwin said. "The crowning that was to be—it would have continued the regency in all but name, and made her my equal in the ruling of this kingdom. Neither law nor nature would favor such a course. Yet you would have allowed it. Would you not?"

Manasses glanced at Melisende. Her face was still. "She rules well," he said, "and has ruled long."

"And now," said Baldwin, "it is time that she gave up the rule. It was never hers except in trust for me."

Then at last Melisende spoke. "I was the eldest child of a king," she said, "his heir who was born to rule after him."

"But a woman does not rule," Baldwin said, "save in a man's name."

"And why is that?" she asked. "Do you know? Does anyone?"

"God's law—" Baldwin began.

"God's law," said Melisende, "is less than precise. There is nothing that ordains that a queen and heir must give way before a child whose only right resides in the fact of his sex."

"I am no longer a child," Baldwin said.

"That is a matter of debate," she said.

"Only to you," he said, "madam." He drew a breath as if to master his temper; said with studied quiet, "Lady, it is time. You must let go."

"I will not," she said.

"Will you divide the kingdom? Will you give the infidel cause to laugh, and to hurl his armies against us?"

Her eyes narrowed. Her face was white. Then at last she let them all see her anger. "It was not I who took refuge in a lie, and had myself crowned by force. If there is to be division, there it began. Not with me."

There would be no peace between them. Not while she persisted in her obstinacy. And yet, Arslan thought, the council seemed not to see it. The older lords and barons, the knights who had fought for the Holy Sepulcher since before Baldwin was born, could not but remember how long she had ruled and how well she had done it. Arslan could hardly deny that. But the kingship was Baldwin's, and it was well past time for him to take it.

Power was a heady thing, as strong as wine. And like wine, in some it roused such a craving that they could only drink and drink, nor ever have their fill of it.

Melisende had drunk deep of ruling the kingdom. She could not give it up. And the council could not refuse her. Those who were hers, who had been hers for years out of count, could no more let her go than she could give up her queenship. They loved her. She had a gift for that; she cultivated it, as any wise ruler should do. She had only to smile at this one, exchange glances with that, invoke memories of councils long past, choices made, wars won and the kingdom preserved through her wisdom.

Against that, Baldwin could set the debacle of Crusade, his presence there at the head of the army, the suffering that he had shared. But he was young. To some, as to his mother, he was still a child.

"And what is wrong," a doddering fool of a baron asked, "with a queen ruling at home while the king rides to war? Hasn't it served us well? Can't it continue?"

"A king does not always ride to war," said a voice from close by Baldwin: Humphrey of Toron who had ridden in those wars, too, and seen both the victories and the defeat. "Indeed he should undertake to avoid war, to preserve the peace and prosperity of the kingdom. His majesty would like to be free to do that; to rule unimpeded by the interference of a regent."

"That regent is his mother," the old baron said. "Has he no respect for her? Does he forget the duty of a son?"

"She forgets the duty of a regent," Humphrey said. "Come, my lord, open your eyes and see. We have a king. It's time we let him rule."

But the old baron did not wish to see. Melisende he knew; Melisende he remembered from long ago. Baldwin was young, tried in war but not in the arts of peace. So he argued. So did a distressing number of the rest—lords of Jerusalem and Nablus; and lords of Jaffa, though Amaury the prince, who held the title Count of Jaffa, stood beside his brother and spoke for him. Melisende ignored him as she would a fractious child, spoke calmly past him, called his own vassals to stand beside her.

Amaury regarded her in anger and misery, but if she noticed, she made no mention of it. If Baldwin at two and twenty was too young to be reckoned fit to rule, Amaury at fifteen was a helpless infant.

Arslan watched the kingdom split in two. All the southern lords spoke for Melisende. Those of the north held firm for Baldwin. They were shouting before they were done, and coming close to blows.

None of them was Bertrand. Arslan had not seen or heard from him since the night before Baldwin had himself crowned. He had not gone to Beausoleil: Arslan would have known. He was in Jerusalem, then, but not at this council. Not accepting compulsion. Not making the choice that for everyone else seemed so easy.

They broke the kingdom apart. The south they gave to Melisende, the north to Baldwin, each to hold as sole and uncontested ruler. They reckoned it a fair division. Yet Melisende held Jerusalem, and therefore the Holy Sepulcher for which the Crusade had first been fought. She held Nablus; she held Jaffa in despite of its Count. Nothing that Baldwin held was of such consequence—or of such strength and wealth. She had the royal part, he the embattled fortresses, the brunt of the war against the infidel.

He laughed after, not too bitter in the circumstances. "And isn't it the same as ever?" he said to the gathering of his friends. "I do the fighting, she sits in comfort with the scepter oh so heavy in her hand." ·

"You could," someone said, "consider a reconciliation. If you addressed her face to face—"

"Should I?" Baldwin put on wide-eyed innocence, but with a twist at the bottom of it. "Should I wrangle with her in private as I have in council? What would be the profit in that?"

"A mother," the knight said. "A son—"

"A queen," said Baldwin, "who resents that she must give way before a king." He shook his head. "No. I've said all I'll say to her. I'm for the north, my lords. Who'll follow me?"

Before Arslan took the northward road with the king, he went looking for his father.

Bertrand had made no attempt to hide himself. Nor had he appeared in court. Of all the barons in Jerusalem, few had made so bold as to remain in the city yet to refuse the choice of king or queen. Melisende was said to be unhappy with him, but she had done nothing to punish him. No more had Baldwin.

Bertrand was in his own house going over accounts with the house-steward when Arslan came in search of him. He finished what he was doing, nor offered apology for keeping a guest waiting. The guest, after all, was only his son.

At length however he was done, and Guibert had gone away with his rolls and his ledgers. Bertrand ordered in wine, offered Arslan a cup. Arslan took it to be courteous; and indeed his mouth was dry.

"You leave tomorrow, then," Bertrand said after a while.

Arslan nodded.

Bertrand turned his cup in his hands. "Is he asking me to go with him?"

"No," said Arslan.

Bertrand raised his brows. "Did he ask you to come here?"

"No," Arslan said again.

"Then why?"

"Because," said Arslan. "I needed to know—will you forgive me? Because I go with him?"

"Do you believe that calls for forgiveness?"

"I am your son," Arslan said, "and your heir. If Beausoleil owes fealty to the queen, and I follow the king . . ."

"Did you ask my leave to be his messenger before he had himself crowned alone? Why ask it now?"

Arslan could not meet his father's eyes. They were too level; too burning strong. "I didn't want to leave," he said, "without your blessing. If you are willing to give it."

"And why should I not be?"

Arslan looked up. Did Bertrand flinch a little? They had the same eyes, people said. Maybe his own were as potent as his father's. "This could turn to civil war. I'm the king's man; I can't be otherwise. If you stay here, you'll be with the queen. This that I do, you could call treason."

Bertrand shook his head. He looked and sounded ineffably weary. "No," he said. "No. I know, none better, whom you must follow. I would be a fool to expect that you would do otherwise, and mad to demand it."

"Some fathers would," Arslan said.

Bertrand smiled faintly. "I was never the best of fathers, was I?"

"Better than some," said Arslan.

"You have my blessing," Bertrand said after a pause, "and with it my goodwill. We'll meet again in court at Pentecost."

That was farewell. And what else had Arslan expected? Not, certainly, to feel so strangely sad, as if they parted forever and not simply for the season between one court and the next.

They embraced as was proper, as father and son should do. If they held a little longer than usual, gripped a little tighter, neither remarked on it. Arslan had left his father before to serve the king, but never with such a wrench as this.

Nonetheless he did it, let go and walked away, nor looked back once he had passed the door.

his is untenable."

Baldwin was in a rare temper. He had come to Banias in the course of the summer's campaign, riding the borders from north to south and fending off an unwonted number of incursions from the infidel. Islam knew that the Frankish kingdom was divided, and was taking full advantage of it.

Fighting Baldwin knew, and did; and he had men enough for the purpose. But here in Banias where the cares of the kingdom had caught up with him, he found himself bound hand and foot by the want of Jerusalem.

He glared at his chancellor's account-books as if he yearned to smite them with a sword. "The chancery is in Jerusalem," he said, mocking the mincing accent of a Court dandy from that city. "The records are in Jerusalem. In Jerusalem are the treasuries. Whatever we have need of, wherever we are when we need it, its source is in Jerusalem. And Jerusalem belongs to her. I can't use it but by her leave. And to ask that . . ." He spat. "Damn her. Damn the Court that gave as much to her as she ever had, and flung me the bones."

"And left you all the defense of the kingdom, too," Arslan observed, draping himself over a chair. The solar here at Banias was beautifully appointed in the eastern style, but there were chairs to sit on rather than divans or heaps of carpets: a Frankish contribution, and rather more comfortable than not.

Baldwin snarled, perhaps at Arslan, perhaps at the ledgers that told him all the same tale. "I need Jerusalem," he said. "It's the heart's core of the kingdom. I can't rule without it."

"So take it back," Arslan said.

Baldwin erupted to his feet. Arslan thought he might strike, but his mind was on something else. "You! You think it's that simple?"

"I don't think it's simple at all," said Arslan. "But it appears to be necessary. You've done what you can to keep the north together, to keep your armies paid and in the field. It's not enough."

"No," said Baldwin, "it's not. But she won't grant me anything I ask, you know that. If I ask for Jerusalem, she'll only laugh. She knows as well as I that there's no power in this title without the city to support it."

"So insist."

"That means war," Baldwin said.

Arslan bent his head a fraction.

"Your father has been seen in court," Baldwin said, "beside her. Do you know that?"

"I know. I heard." Arslan said it with no great pain. It had been inevitable when Bertrand lingered in Jerusalem, that in the end he would go where his heart led him. Fond as he might ever have been of Baldwin, he had been the queen's man from his youth. One did not forget such a thing, or set it aside with either ease or comfort.

"Will you fight him, then? If it comes to that?"

Arslan shrugged: shifted his shoulders, that ached with sudden tension. "I will do whatever is necessary. It may not come to a battle."

"Pray God it doesn't. The infidel will be on us as fast as he can ride, and do what he can to destroy us."

"And he's doing just that now, while we're divided."

"Such a dilemma," Baldwin said a little bitterly. "I had a letter from my brother this morning. He'd rebel if he could—if I would let him. But he's too young."

Arslan said nothing. What he was thinking did not bear repeating. That this war between mother and son was neither seemly nor sensible. That one of them must give way before the kingdom fell. And that they were too truly of the same kin: headstrong, haughty, unwilling and unable to yield.

Baldwin could not defend the kingdom, either half of it, without the strength of Jerusalem. Melisende would not cede the city to him. "Ask," her messenger said, "and you shall receive whatever you need in order to drive back the infidel. But she rules in her own city. She will not give it up."

"Then I will take it," Baldwin said; and called his armies together and advanced southward from Banias toward the heart of the realm. He did not come in war unless one wished to perceive it so. He was the King of Jerusalem, was he not? Might he not return to that city with his men? They were weary with the long season's campaign. They would be happy to rest amid the holy places.

"Lies," said Melisende, and strengthened the fortifications of both Jerusalem and Nablus, arming them against their own king.

Richildis would have hidden herself in Mount Ghazal till it was over, but she had never been able to muster so much sense. Better in the heart of things, she told herself, than shut away where she could not know what would become of the kingdom: whether it bowed to king or queen, both or neither, and the infidel waiting like a vulture for its prey to finish dying.

Michael Bryennius had gone away to Constantinople to see to some affair of his family's that needed the eldest son present and speaking for himself. Richildis would go there with Zenobia before the winter's storms stirred the sea; but she had insisted that she remain at least through the summer, till matters were settled between Melisende and her son. She did not know why she was so stubborn. She had not been parted from her husband since they were wedded. She had no good reason to let him go now.

Except that she was a baroness of this kingdom, and it was divided against itself. She could not run away from that.

In the mornings she woke to a lonely bed. In the evenings after Zenobia had gone to sleep in her own chamber with her nurse to keep her company, Richildis sat alone, sometimes with a book, more often with her thoughts and her memory of her husband. It was sinful to miss him so; to yearn for the touch of his hand, the warmth of his body beside hers.

The days between the lonely hours, she spent in attendance on the queen. Melisende had taken a personal interest in the fortification of Jerusalem: unwonted for her, to walk the walls and converse with soldiers. She had always, like a proper queen, left such things to her Constable.

But this was her own city, and she would protect it even against its king.

Richildis did not know her any longer. When the news came to her of Baldwin's coronation without her knowledge or assistance, something in her had broken or turned sour. The warmth that had always been part of her, that made her seem sunlit even in grey winter, had faded and grown cold. She was sharp with everyone, short-tempered even in court, where she had been noted for her equanimity.

She should be content. She had the best part of the kingdom, the greater quantity of its wealth and the heart of its power. Yet it gnawed at her: that her son had betrayed her, that the kingdom was divided and the north turned against her.

Out of that bitterness she drew the determination to fight and not to yield. "He is my enemy," she said. "How can he be anything else? He turned against me. He defied my will. He made himself king in despite of me."

"And what did you expect?" Richildis dared to ask her. "He's young, high-hearted, seasoned in war—he wants to be king as he was born to be."

"I was born to rule before him," Melisende said.

"The world will contest you," said Richildis, "in the end."

"Not if I stand fast," said Melisende. "Men are cowards, don't you see? And so are women, most of them. A woman who is bold, who takes that is hers, who refuses to let it be taken from her—she wins the victory. Who can oppose her? No one has the strength to try."

"Baldwin might," Richildis said, but Melisende was not listening. She listened to very little these days, except her own will and the messengers who brought word of Baldwin's advance.

He neither slowed nor turned aside. He came straight on. If it was a feint, it was both strong and unflinching.

No more would Melisende flag in her determination to resist him. Her cities were strong, prepared for siege. Her people . . .

It was slow at first: a knight or two, a baron of a minor holding, a lord who by age and inclination was more easily disposed to follow a man than a woman. The priests were hers—not for nothing had she spent her widowhood in piety and in fostering of convents. But the lords and the knights saw a young king riding toward them in the panoply of war; looked to the queen and saw a woman, still beautiful but no longer young, who had never led an army, never fought with lance and sword in defense of the Holy Sepulcher. They were men; they thought as men think. They turned from her to the king who rode against her.

Baldwin had begun the march in some secret trepidation, bound by will and necessity, but as it went on with no sign of opposition, his doubts faded to vanishing. The more antic of his knights wanted to make it a grand triumphal progress, but he would not go so far. Not quite yet. They were still in the north, after all; still on lands that were by treaty his.

But with each day they marched, the southern realm drew closer. Came at last a day when they passed indubitably into lands held by Melisende and her vassals, that paid no fealty to Baldwin as king.

And no one stopped him. No army waited to bar his way. The roads were clear. Travelers on them walked wide round the king's troops, kept heads down and eyes on the road, nor offered him either aid or hindrance.

"She's pulled in her horns," said Humphrey of Toron in camp, their first evening in the queen's lands. "She'll protect the cities but she'll leave the rest to fend for themselves."

"She was always a creature of cities," Baldwin said. "Still, one would think the Constable would have something to say. I'd thought to find him with a flaming sword, guarding the gates of the south."

"We'll send scouts," Humphrey said. "If he's out there, we'll know it."

Baldwin nodded. "Do that," he said. "Do it quickly."

Manasses was, after all, on the march with an army—but slowly, as if he too had been unable to believe that Baldwin would do as he threatened. Manasses was hardly a day's march out of Jerusalem, aiming toward his own fief of Mirabel. Perhaps he meant only to pause there before he went on into the north.

"Oh, he grows old," Baldwin said when he heard that, "and he grows careless, who of all people should know what I can do when I put my mind to it."

Baldwin had become a king. He had always been one, Arslan knew that, but somehow on this too-little-impeded march, he had grown into his title. He was surer, firmer, more arrogant indeed, but as a king needs to be if he is to rule with either strength or grace. If he had doubts, he did not express them, even to Arslan.

"We march," he said, "in haste, to Mirabel. Let us be there soon after him."

"Not before?" one of his knights asked.

"No," said Baldwin. "Let him settle in comfort in his own castle, and think us far away. We'll surprise him."

Grins flashed round the circle of his council. Young men most of them, a little reckless, and no love in them for the queen or her creatures: they would be glad to make a mockery of the queen's most loyal man.

Arslan was not greatly fond of Manasses. The man had always been Melisende's, nor had time or loyalty to spare for her son and heir. Still Arslan could not fault a man for keeping faith. Arslan's father had done no less.

What Baldwin thought, Arslan did not know. He sat in the midst of them, smiling slightly, while messengers ran to prepare the army for the march. They had only paused on the road from the sea, stopped to eat and rest and take counsel while scouts brought in word from the south. There were hours yet to alter their direction, firm their purpose, advance swiftly and as secretly as possible toward Mirabel.

For Manasses' sake and for that of his spies, Baldwin sent a portion of his army toward Nablus, instructing it to turn back before it reached the city and come to Mirabel. Such might not be necessary, might not even be wise, but Baldwin commanded it in kingly certainty. This was war, and in war Baldwin had always been quicker of wit than the common run of men.

Then with the greater part of his army Baldwin made haste toward the Constable's demesne. It was a march like any other in war, swift but circumspect. As they drew nearer Mirabel, scouts were instructed to capture and hold any who might bring word to Manasses. Too few of them regretted the necessity; but necessity it was. The sooner this was ended, the better for all of them; the less likelihood of the infidel's attacking them from behind.

Mirabel was a small demesne, but strong. It warded the pass between the mountains of Samaria and the dense thickets and fens of the River Yarqon. The road that ran through it, ran from Jerusalem to the sea. Battles had been fought here, kings and rebels risen and fallen on the strength of its strongholds.

Manasses of Hierges was lord of a castle set on the eastern hill, and of a small fortress on the west that was called the Tower of the Deaf Springs. No one knew why it was called that, nor at the moment overmuch cared. Baldwin took it by surprise and with hardly a blow struck, its little garrison caught with its breeches down: half the men fuddled with their morning ale, and their sergeant actually in the garderobe. He ran out in his tunic with his braies unlaced and slipping down, to find himself face to face with the king's vanguard. He had to surrender in that condition, with the king's men offering ribald commentary.

Manasses himself had time for greater dignity, and to shut and bar his castle against the army. He stood on the walls, a still and faceless figure in his great helm, as Baldwin came up below. "Surrender!" Baldwin called up to him. "Surrender and be free.

"No," he said. Nor would he yield, as the king's army made camp about his walls.

Baldwin was grimly satisfied. By all accounts, the queen's whole army was locked up within. In her cities were only garrisons, strong to be sure, but never as strong as the force that he could bring to bear. She, or Manasses, had reckoned ill in pausing here, or in thinking to hold this place against the king.

Baldwin set his men to building siege-engines, making a great noise about it, and building them high and strong. All ways to the castle were shut, the road cut off, the queen's army enclosed upon itself.

Then when the rams were ready, the scaling-ladders, the two tall siege-towers, Baldwin flung them all against the walls of Mirabel.

Perhaps Manasses had not expected such ruthlessness. Perhaps he had thought that Baldwin would weaken; would shrink from the naked face of war. But the face that Manasses saw, for all its youth, was as implacable as any he could have seen among the infidels. Baldwin would have his kingdom. He would not stop until he had won it.

In midafternoon of the day the rams began their pounding, as the great gates began to splinter and crack, Manasses came out above them. His helm was off, his mail-coif lowered: great boldness, and purest simplicity to bring him down with an arrow in the throat. But no arrow flew. Perhaps he sighed a little with relief as he leaned on the parapet, calling to the men below, "Where is Baldwin? Bring him out! I would speak to him."

Baldwin had been resting in his tent, that too a show of bravery. He took his time coming out, dressed carefully, put on his better armor and his clean surcoat and the plain circlet that he wore on campaign instead of his crown. He was in extraordinary looks, and he could not but know it.

Manasses looked from the walls on that golden image of a king. The long grim mouth set grimmer, but a corner lifted infinitesimally, as if he had learned to laugh at his own ill fortune. "Well then," he said, "majesty. If I cede you the game, what will you give in return?"

"Your life," Baldwin said. Nothing lightened his grimness. He was angry, more angry now than he had been before he began the siege.

Manasses was perhaps touched with fear. Perhaps not; not yet. "What, majesty? Nothing else in return for a kingship?"

"Passage," Baldwin said, "to any country you choose, provided that it not be this one."

"Exile?" Manasses sounded as if the word were new to him, or too strange to understand. "Exile, sire? How have I deserved that?"

"For treason," said Baldwin, "the wonted penalty is death."

"I have but been loyal to my liege lady."

"She too commits treason," Baldwin said. "That is the bargain I offer you. Life, and exile. Or death in this place, with as many of your army who choose to resist me. They will not be so great a number, I think. See, already they draw away. They know. Queen Melisende's day is past. This now is mine."

Manasses stood for a long moment. He looked neither right nor left. Yet he must have known what those below could see: that the walls had emptied of men.

So swiftly the fortunes of war could change. The men who led the armies might persist in obstinacy, but without men to fight for them, to wield swords and spears, to bend bows in their lords' defense, there could be no war, and no hope of victory.

Manasses knew that, none better. As below him the gates ground slowly open to admit the king's men, he said harshly, "I yield. I take your bargain."

*I*diots. Cowards."

Melisende was beside herself. Manasses had surrendered, set himself on the road to Acre and thence across the sea. Nablus turned craven in the wake of it, opening wide to the king's advance. And she remained in Jerusalem, walled in the Tower of David, and when she took count of those who waited on her, the numbers were pitifully few.

Richildis was one of them. Loyalty was in no way simple, but Richildis had always been stubborn. If she paused to think, she knew that Baldwin had won, could not but win. He was young, male, king. But she had served Melisende too long. She could not change masters now.

There was no great pleasure in being one of the last to stand beside the queen. Manasses was gone and Nablus fallen. Jerusalem would yield when Baldwin came to it: that, they all knew. The world went on as it must, from aging queen to young and conspicuously strong king.

Melisende still would not see it, would not accept it. She paced her chambers like a lioness in a cage, fierce and beautiful. But there was grey in the hair beneath the silken veil, and a tautness to lips and cheeks that spoke not of youth but of desiccating age.

The Patriarch had come and gone. Amid the pious platitudes he had uttered a word or two of wisdom. "All things pass," he had said: "strength, queenship, worldly power. Only the light of heaven never changes. Will you not look to it, and set aside this vanity of earthly greatness?"

"No," Melisende had said, and dismissed him, and burst out in rage against them all.

"Where is their faith?" she cried. "Where is their plain good sense? That is a *child*. Callow, foolish, headstrong—"

"Neither as foolish nor as headstrong as you," Richildis said, too tired to be circumspect, but not too much so to tremble slightly, deep within, for the magnitude of her daring.

Melisende whirled on Richildis. "You, too? Even you would turn against me?"

"I think," said Richildis, "that you are a better and wiser woman than this, or would be if your temper would allow it. In logic surely, your right, your age, your skill in the arts of ruling, all would set you above him. But no man can forget the plain fact of your sex. No man ever will."

For a moment Richildis thought that Melisende would erupt in a passion of fury. But she was, as Richildis had judged, too wise. She stopped short, stiff-backed, white about the lips. She was thinking at last; perhaps for the first time since this war began.

She spoke slowly, as if in deliberation; though perhaps she only needed to master her temper. "There is no equity in this world."

"Did you ever think there was?"

"I think," said Melisende, "that your presumption comes close—close indeed— to lèse-majesté."

Richildis inclined her head, and not in submission.

Melisende's eyes glittered. "So. No one else dared stay, nor dared to say what you have all been thinking. You've always been braver than the rest—brave to the point of folly."

"I come by it honestly," Richildis said. "My brother is in this city, too, nor has he forsaken you."

"I do not see him," Melisende said tightly.

"Because," said Richildis, "he's at the gate, holding together such of the guards as remain. He'll fight for you if you insist, or surrender if that's your will."

"Would you surrender?"

Richildis doubted that Melisende asked it in order to seek Richildis' counsel. It was curiosity and little more. Nonetheless she answered as honestly as she could. "I would very probably resist him to the death, if I stood in your place. Though if I were wise and far less stubborn then I am . . . yes, I would surrender. I would throw myself on his mercy. He's a good lad, and ruthless though he seems—have you noticed that he's shed as little blood as he possibly may, and shown clemency to every man of yours that he has met?"

"He exiled Manasses," Melisende said coldly.

"He could have put him to death," said Richildis, "for treason against the crown."

"Then so he could do to me," Melisende said in a soft still voice.

"I think not," Richildis said. "He's a scrupulous soul. He'd never commit matricide, even for all that you've done to him."

"And what have I done? How have I sinned against him?"

"I think you do not need to ask," Richildis said quietly.

Melisende had the grace to lower her eyes. It was a great yielding of pride, for her. "The right is mine," she said. "If I had been a man, not one living thing would have uttered a word against me."

"You are not a man," Richildis said.

"Damn you," said Melisende: the strongest word she had ever said, soul-shaking for one as pious as she; but she was past caring. "Damn your clear eyes. Damn this world that for a little thing, a thing that would not matter at all were I pure spirit, condemns me to the life and lot of a woman."

Yet even she would not damn the God Who had made her so. She drew herself up, straightened her back, lifted her chin that still, though the years had traced their paths on her cheeks, was firm and strong. "I will not be broken," she said. "I will not go down in defeat."

"Have you any choice?"

Melisende shook her head, sharp and short. "I forgot," she said, "if I ever knew. I forgot . . . I fought too long with men's weapons. Now let me be a woman. Since no other way is left for me—let me wage war as my sex demands."

Richildis looked on her in great misgiving. But she smiled, a swift smile, without subterfuge that Richildis could discern; yet without great warmth, either. Just so in France did the sun shine in winter, in the lull between storm and storm.

Strange to think of France, to see it as clear as if it spread before her, and to feel nothing but a kind of poet's tenderness. So beautiful, the fields and the vineyards white with snow; so blinding bright the sun, but never as bright as the sun of Outremer.

"I must learn," said Melisende, "to fight and to rule as a woman does. You are like to be an ill teacher, my lady baroness, but since no one else has chosen to linger—teach me. Show me how a woman should properly be."

She did not need to be shown. She had learned the lesson thoroughly if not happily while her husband was alive. This was mockery, and a kind of punishment. Yet it was a gift, too. A promise. That Richildis would be rewarded for her loyalty. That, perhaps, the king would not demand that she pay too high for remaining with his mother to the end.

Richildis gathered her wits together, and such knowledge and memory as she had, and armed them all. With Melisende in such a mood as this, she would need them.

She almost pitied Baldwin. Poor thing, he would come here in the pride of his victorious kingship, in his armor and his elation, and look to be magnanimous in his triumph. And Melisende would let him have it all, but in her own way. He would win the war. She would keep as much of the prize as she could, and that would be more than he had ever thought to grant her.

For all the differences between them, the war, the contention, the love that had never been more than royal duty, as they stood face to face in the shadow of the Tower of David, Melisende and Baldwin were as like as man and woman can be. Two tall fair people with the same haughty carriage, the same fierce eyes, the same lift of the head. She had chosen widow's garb, or nun's: plain black gown over plain white linen shift, and a veil of white muslin over the tight bindings of her hair. She wore no crown, only a circlet of silver. Her face seemed hardly paler than her veil, her eyes as dark as her gown.

Baldwin beside her seemed almost gaudy. He was as he had ridden into the city, in plain battleworn mail and clean white surcoat, but bareheaded and crowned with the crown of Jerusalem. He had, on his journey, begun to grow a thick fair beard. It was short still, but it aged him nonetheless, made him seem more suitably kingly.

He had found the gates of the city open before him, the guards armed but unhostile, offering no resistance. If they had done so, perhaps they would have died. For the people had come out to welcome him, great yelling throngs brandishing palm-branches and crying his name.

The roar of the crowd had echoed in the court within the Tower, where Melisende waited with such of her ladies as remained with her, and her sisters Hodierna and Yveta, and a company of guards who might as easily have been her jailers as her defenders. It was not a long wait as such things went, nor would she be prevailed upon to ride out to meet her son. "I shall receive him here," she had said. "I give him everything that was mine. Let him come to me to take it."

Her sisters, even the holy abbess who could well have admonished her in the name of humility, kept as silent as the rest of them. Melisende would do as she would do, which was no more than she had always done.

At last he came, he and his knights and his men-at-arms and half the city of Jerusalem. He found the ladies standing in the court, no canopy over them, no protection against the sun. Some of them would be bathing hands and faces for months in asses' milk to repair the damage of that day; but none ventured to complain. It was a show of defiance, a company of women clad as starkly as nuns, facing all these men in their panoply of war.

Baldwin dismounted from his horse just within the court, walked forward without ceremony, and stood in front of his mother. He did not bow, although he inclined his head. "Lady," he said.

"Majesty," said Melisende. She did not choke on the word. No one who knew her would have expected her to.

He was at a loss, perhaps. But he who had been blooded in war while he was still a child, was never one to fall short in a battle of wills. He said, "It's ended, then."

"Yes," said Melisende.

"And do you surrender?"

Melisende drew a breath: Richildis saw how her breast rose and fell. "I surrender," she said.

"Unconditionally," Baldwin said.

"Unconditionally," said Melisende without a tremor.

There was a pause. She knew what she must do; they all did. But she did not at once move to do it. Richildis was sure for a long moment that she would not; that after all she would defy him.

Even Melisende was not so great a fool. At length, with calm that must be the walls and bars of a great rage, she sank down, bowing low and low, as a vassal bows before her king.

He looked down at her, bowed before him at last. No light of glee shone in his eyes. No grief either, to be sure; but he was keeping his gladness well in hand.

She raised her hands, palms together as if in prayer. He clasped them between his own. Her face, lifted to his, was stark white. "You are my liege lord," she said clearly, as a brave man takes cautery of a wound: because to flinch from it would but worsen the pain. "I am your vassal. I pledge to you my faith, my heart and hand, my life and limb and earthly worship against all who may stand against you. So do I swear, by this relic of the True Cross that never leaves my body."

He touched the reliquary that hung about her neck, softly and with reverence, raised her then and kissed her on both cheeks as a lord kisses his new-sworn liegeman. "I am your liege lord," he said. "You are my vassal. I pledge to you my faith and my protection, my heart and hand, life and limb and earthly worship, against all who may stand against you. So do I swear, by this relic of the True Cross and by the Holy Sepulcher."

She bowed again, sinking down to her knees. Yet it was not, for all of that, defeat. Her back was straight. Her eyes were level. She had been forced to this. But when at last she did it, she did it of her own will, because she chose to do it.

She had raised defiance to a high art, art so subtle that it clothed itself in humility. Richildis wondered if Baldwin had wits to see it. Perhaps. He was, after all, Melisende's son.

nd that was all of it?"

Helena was rarely disappointed, rarely missed anything that she did not care to miss. Yet this she clearly did regret. She had not seen Baldwin take full and free the kingship of Jerusalem.

"It was all anyone saw," Richildis said. "The rest one could imagine."

"She'll retire to Nablus," Bertrand said, "which is her dower city, and accept the life considered proper to a queen mother."

"I would wager," said Helena, "that she keeps the Church firm in her hand, and that within the year her name appears again beside her son's as Queen of Jerusalem."

"That won't happen," Arslan said. "He won't let it."

"What would you lay on it?" Helena asked him with an arch of the brow.

His own brow arched to match it. "A fine Damascus dagger."

"Done," she said. "And I lay against it a bolt of Tyrian purple."

"Done!" he said, slapping the table to seal it. But then he said, "What makes you think—"

"You know Melisende better than I. Tell me why I think she's withdrawn from the field only to come back in greater, if altered, strength."

Arslan opened his mouth, closed it. "That's how Baldwin fights battles," he said. "When he can. When he must."

"Yes," said Helena.

"She learned it from him?"

"I think," Helena said, much amused, "that a son may learn a little from his mother."

Arslan sat back. No young man could be a match for a woman of wit and subtlety. That was the lesson. He tried to take it in good part, as a well-raised young nobleman should.

"Do be comforted," Richildis said to him. "She's conceded at least to the way of the world: to rule from the shadows and to leave him the full light of the sun."

"Does any man in the world rule without a woman's interference?" Arslan demanded.

Richildis paused to think about it. "Louis of France, perhaps, now that his queen has won her freedom at last."

"Ah yes," Bertrand said dryly. "She's ruling the heart and certain other salient aspects of the Duke of Normandy."

So Arslan had heard. It was a mighty scandal, a shock to Christendom. At Easter the King and Queen of France had sundered their union before the eyes of God and man. Hardly had the feast of Pentecost come and gone before she had found, met, and married a new and far more lusty husband, a dozen years younger than she—younger by a handful of years than Arslan himself: Henry Plantagenet, Duke of Normandy, heir to the throne of England. Who happened, by chance or otherwise, to be own nephew to Baldwin of Jerusalem: son of Baldwin's brother Geoffrey, Count of Anjou, whose wedding to the heiress of England their father Fulk had left to marry Melisende of Jerusalem. This Henry was a most noble, and nobly connected, young man; a fine match for a woman with ambitions toward a crown.

Eleanor had always been swift in decision, swifter than Louis of France had ever had will to be.

"Ah," said Arslan with a shake of the head. "A eunuch rules King Louis. I wonder: does Henry know yet what he's bound himself to?"

"I rather suspect so," Helena said. "He may be a boy in years, but by all accounts he's a strong and clever man. Even the common rumor reckons that it's more than the body's lust that moved him to accept such a marriage. She comes, after all, with a duchy for a dower."

"And he will be a king," Bertrand said. "They call his line the Devil's get. A devil and a she-wolf: now there's a match to set a kingdom on its ear."

Arslan could imagine it. Could, for a startled moment, wish desperately to see it himself—to take ship and sail away.

Of course he could not do that. Baldwin as king at last, sole and uncontested, needed all the friends and servants that he had. His foster-brother could hardly go running off to gape at prodigies, or to play sweet friend to a duchess who had been and would be again a queen.

He sighed a little. He lacked the proper degree of youthful passion, he had been told more than once; and no matter that what others called passion, he called rampant foolishness.

Well, and so be it. His duty was here, in Jerusalem. He would be faithful to it as he had ever been.

Their gathering that night was a farewell feast. Richildis would accompany Melisende on the morrow to her half-exile in Nablus, but she would not linger there. With an escort of mounted archers from Mount Ghazal, with her maids and her daughter and her daughter's nurse, she would set herself on the road to Constantinople where her husband was. If she was fortunate she would find a caravan to be a part of, a company well armed against attack; for the infidel was greatly restless.

As soon as his mother was settled, Baldwin would ride to war. But Richildis would be out of it. The tides of time had shifted. She yearned for her husband; she was weary of the round of her days in Jerusalem.

The others seemed content. Arslan would rise high now that his lord was king unchallenged. Bertrand, who had remained loyal to Melisende, had received the king's amnesty as had the rest of those knights and barons who would swear fealty to Baldwin. What pain it had cost him to do that, Richildis could not be wholly certain. Not a great deal, perhaps. Melisende had set him free. He could have gone into exile as Manasses had, but he had chosen to stay, to remain lord of Beausoleil under Baldwin the king.

Arslan was in good case; Bertrand would do well. Helena was Helena, as always; neither more nor less herself for that the queen had fallen. Richildis could leave them with a clear conscience.

As she reflected on endings and partings, the servants cleared the remains of dinner and brought in the wine. One came in behind them, one of Helena's Turks. That was unwonted, and worth the lift of a brow. It was never their custom to sit at meat with Christians, nor to disturb Christians who were so engaged.

Mehmet bowed to Helena, but it was Richildis whom he approached. "Lady," he said as they all listened, as curious as she, "one has come seeking you. He says that he comes from France."

"Is he urgent?" Richildis asked.

"He says, lady, that you would wish to speak with him as soon as may be."

She glanced at the others. No one objected. "Let him come in," she said.

He was no man she knew: a pilgrim like many another, ragged and worn with travel. His accent was so familiar that it seemed strange, the accent of a man from Anjou, from near or about La Forêt.

She offered him courtesy: wine, bread, a chair at the table's foot. He took the chair, declined the bread and the wine. "Lady, I lodge in a hostel; they've fed me well."

She inclined her head. Still as he sat so close to her, there was nothing about him that she remembered. If he came indeed from La Forêt, he must have been a child when she left.

"Lady," he said, "my name is Gaultier. I was born in Miraval, but I was a clerk in La Forêt, until God and the Lady Agnes sent me on pilgrimage to Jerusalem."

"You are welcome here," Richildis said. "My house is elsewhere, but if you would lodge there—"

"Oh, no," he said. "No, lady, I'm well lodged with the good brothers of Saint Symeon. I'll not burden your hospitality."

"No burden," Richildis said, "and a pleasure, though I depart for Byzantium on the morrow. My brother, perhaps—"

Bertrand caught her glance. "Indeed," he said quickly. "You'll guest among us, sir."

Gaultier bowed to their will. "I thank you," he said, "though I'll not stay long. You are departing, lady?"

"Tomorrow," Richildis said. "I cry your pardon; but my husband is in Constantine's City. I go to join him."

Gaultier blinked, a little baffled perhaps, as pilgrims could be. The east was all so strange to them. "Lady," he said, "I bear you a message from Lady Agnes."

Richildis leaned forward. Always when she heard that name, she knew a stab of joy, and something like guilt. "Do you indeed? How does she fare? Is she well? Did the new vineyard bear fruit? Has—"

"Lady," Gaultier said, breaking in with great discourtesy, but his expression won him pardon: distress, and no little grief. "Lady," he said, "she fares ill. She bade me tell you that before I came to you she would be dead."

Dead. The word fell like a stone.

Richildis looked about. Shock, grief: but how could any of them grieve? None but Bertrand had ever known Lady Agnes, ever seen her face, ever spoken to her while she lived. Only in letters had they known her, and in messages borne by pilgrims such as this one.

She could not let herself hate them, or be angry with them because her father's widow was dying or dead.

Lady Agnes had not been young when Richildis left her—how long ago? By now she would have had threescore years and more; long enough indeed to see an end of them. Yet . . . it was too soon. She should have lived on and on, till Richildis, Bertrand, someone, came to relieve her of her charge. Until, at least, Richildis could bid her farewell.

Richildis' eyes were blurred. Her cheeks were wet. She scrubbed at them. She was weeping—she who never wept.

The others were silent, taking care not to stare at her. Gaultier had fixed his eyes on his hands, as if to look up would be to betray his faith.

"You are certain?" she said to him. "That she was dying?"

"Lady," he said to his tightly laced fingers, "a physician came from Poitiers, a turbaned Moor if you'll believe it, and he said that only God knew how she had lived so long. It was a wasting fever. She was a white shadow when I left her, hardly more than a voice; but she held you close in her memory. 'Tell her,' she said to me, 'that I lay on her no command, ask of her no duty. I only bid her remember that once she was a lady in La Forêt; and that there is no lady now, nor can be until she or her brother may name an heir.' "

"She never—" Richildis broke off. Of course she had not. Lady Agnes had had no authority but that given her by Richildis in Bertrand's name. None of them had made provision for this.

"All the while," said Richildis, "we were establishing the inheritance of Mount Ghazal and Beausoleil, we never thought—we never remembered—" Her throat closed. She forced it open. Her voice was a faint and strangled thing, but it was the best she had. "I have to go back."

"Can you?"

She stared at Bertrand. He stared back. "Can *you?*" she asked him.

He shook his head. Not even a moment's hesitation. Not an instant's doubt. "You know what I told you long ago. I gave it up. I forsook my claim to it, and its claim on me. I belong to Outremer."

"And I . . ." Richildis was cold, cold in the heart. "I have to go back. Who else is there?"

"What of Mount Ghazal?" he said. "What of your husband? Your daughter? Your journey to Byzantium?"

There was a throbbing behind her eyes, a dull ache in her skull. "Agnes is dead, Bertrand. There's no one to take the rule of La Forêt. If no one comes, if it lies lordless—"

"The count will name a new lord," Bertrand said.

She rounded on him. "Don't you care? Doesn't it matter to you? That holding has been in our family since Charlemagne was a cub. Would you see it go to a stranger? A man who might never see it, who might let it go to ruin among his greater holdings?"

"I will not," he said with all his old stiff obstinacy, "give up land and lordship here to bury myself in the wilds of Anjou."

"Do you hate it so much? Have you held the grudge so long?"

"No," said Bertrand, surprisingly without anger. "I left it behind me. I died to it if you will. It's no part of me now, nor has been for years out of count."

"So then," she said. "It's I who must go." No gladness touched her, no light of joy that she would see her home and holding again. She could only think of Zenobia asleep in the nursery above, and Michael Bryennius in the City waiting for her to come to him, and Mount Ghazal to which she had expected to return when her husband's errand was done. If she went to La Forêt, she must leave them all behind.

She could go, find someone, some kindly lord or widowed lady, to rule in her name. Yet if she did that, how would she know that she had chosen well? Wolves ran wild in the world. La Forêt was prosperous, well kept and amply defended: a fine prize for a reiver with pretensions.

She would be fortunate if she found it unscathed, even if she took ship on the morrow; if that were possible, which it incontestably was not. God knew what had become of it once the vultures began to circle, when it was known that the lady who had held it so well for so long was dead.

She raised her eyes, brought her mind back to this room in Helena's house. They were all watching her, all waiting for her to be done with her maundering. "I have to go back. I don't know—there's no one else. I have to go back."

Bertrand made no move to lighten her pain. She would hate him for that, if she stopped to think about it. He would not give way for her.

And would she give way, either?

She gathered herself to rise. "I have to go," she said, "arrange passage, send messages, tell my—husband—"

"No."

That was a voice they had not heard in a while, sounding as if it too had its share of pain, but had laid it all aside. Arslan faced them with his head up, looking oddly defiant—as if he had done anything to earn their censure.

"You'll not go," he said. "I will."

"You are the heir of Beausoleil," Bertrand said.

"And, by blood, of La Forêt." Arslan lifted his chin a fraction higher. "Think, Father. Lady. Which of us has the least to hold him here?"

"You have Beausoleil," said Bertrand. "You have Baldwin, to whom you've sworn fealty."

"Beausoleil is yours yet," Arslan said, "and will be for years to come. Baldwin has lords and knights in plenty."

"But only one foster-brother," Richildis said.

"La Forêt has nothing," said Arslan. "Why shouldn't I go? I've no wife, no child. I rule no demesne. I'm as free as man can be."

"You have not thought carefully on this," Richildis said. "Think! You were born in Outremer. What on earth would you do in France?"

"Shiver a great deal," he said. "Be lord in my ancestral holding. Find me a wife, someone both capable and congenial, and get me as many sons as she will gladly bear, and raise the eldest of them to be lord when I return to Beausoleil."

"So simple," Richildis said. "So certain."

"So inevitable," he said. He smiled at her, his sweet smile that was all his own. He could melt her with it when he was small. Now that he was a man, it made her quiver in her bones. "Lady my dear," he said, "it's you who aren't thinking. How can you leave your Michael Bryennius to run off to Anjou? He'd go running after you, you know that very well. And he'd be flatly miserable there."

Richildis tried to imagine Michael Bryennius in La Forêt. It made her head ache. "But you—" she began, though she did not know how she would end it.

Arslan ended it for her. "I should like to see France."

"And the former Queen of France?"

He flushed under the sun's dye, but he maintained the semblance of calm that led strangers to reckon him a phlegmatic man. "It would be . . . interesting to see her again."

"Indeed," said Richildis.

He fixed her with a steady storm-grey stare, till she flushed herself, and knew the sting of shame. "Lady," he said, "can you think of a better solution? I'm not needed so badly here that no one can let me go. La Forêt needs a lord. Or do you reckon me too young to hold that office?"

"I am not Melisende," she said in the face of his impudence, "and well you know it. But, Arslan, it's *cold* there."

"And it's not cold in the uplands of Syria, where I've ridden often enough, hunting infidels?" He shook his head. "Lady, you're being ridiculous. Give me your blessing and promise to keep my father in hand, and I'll go with a glad heart."

Richildis sat back, taking in the whole of him: face bronzed from birth by the fierce sun of Outremer; body honed in its wars, big and broad and strong; wits grown subtle in the courts of the east yet tempered with a wholly Frankish honesty, that rarest virtue of all, which men called integrity. He was beautiful and beloved, and if he shrank from this that he would do, he let none of them see it.

He was young. But no younger than his father had been when he came to Outremer. Now the son would return to take the lordship that his father had refused.

"You might have to fight for it," she said.

He mimed astonishment. "Fight? I? Oh, lady! And I born a noble's son in Outremer. Shall I mince and giggle and shimmer in silks, and give the lordlings of France somewhat to laugh at?"

"Not," Richildis said, "with those shoulders." She struck one of them with a fist, not lightly: in its way, it was an accolade. "You have my blessing. And my arms-master. Kutub will go with you, and such of his men as he reckons fit to brave the snows and the stares of France."

Ah, at last; she had taken him aback. "Kutub? But I can't—"

"He'll appall everyone you meet," she said, "but he'll defend you to the death. He'll give you the strength that you need to come a stranger from a far strange land, to lay claim to your father's inheritance."

"I can't take Kutub," he said. "You need him in Mount Ghazal."

"Mount Ghazal will do very well by itself," said Richildis.

"But you? Who will ride with you to Constantinople?"

"Your mother has lent me her own Turks," Richildis said, "and they are delighted at the prospect."

"I . . . can imagine." Arslan shook his head. "Lady, from all you've told me, we'll gleam like peacocks in a flock of finches."

"So you shall," she said. "And all the ladies will vie to be your consort."

He flushed at that, much darker than before, so that she laughed. That made him flush darker yet. "Oh, you are beautiful," she said, which dissolved him utterly in confusion; and that was a feat that few could boast of.

rslan had not, as Richildis had too clearly perceived, taken any thought at all before he swore his life and honor to a land that he had never seen. He had simply said what came into his head. It had seemed perfectly sensible when he said it. Had he not been dreaming of going to France? What better cause for it than to take the lordship of his father's own lands?

Better yet: La Forêt was in Anjou, and the Count of Anjou was Baldwin's own if much elder brother, son of King Fulk's youth as Baldwin had been of his middle age, and father to that Henry who had married the Duchess Eleanor. Arslan would for duty's sake attend his new liege lord at court; would see her again and know, God willing, that she was happy.

In the cold light of dawn, as he woke with a heavy head from all the wine he had drunk to seal his bargain, it all seemed much less reasonable. It seemed, in fact, quite mad. He was needed here. He was Baldwin's man. Baldwin was mounting a campaign, contemplating a new and fiercer war against the infidel. And even if Arslan were not bound to that, what of his father? What of Beausoleil? What of—

Someone rapped on the door, startling him out of his half-dream. He sat up before he thought, head and stomach reeling, and barely reached the basin before it all burst out of him.

He looked up from the basin into Bertrand's conspicuously expressionless face. "Go on," he said nastily. "Laugh. You can't pretend you don't want to."

"I can't laugh," Bertrand said. "My head aches too much." He sat at the bed's foot, carefully, as if his skull were made of glass. "That was worse wine than it seemed. Remind me not to buy its like again."

"I'll send you casks of the best from La Forêt," Arslan said.

"So you will go," said Bertrand.

"Didn't I promise Aunt Richildis I would?"

"But do you want to?"

Arslan searched his father's face. It was no more open than it ever was, but years and custom had taught him to read its subtleties. Bertrand was holding himself still by effort of will, fighting trembling that Arslan could well understand. "Who else can go?" Arslan asked him. "Aunt Richildis shouldn't; she has too much to hold her here. You won't. I—"

"Do you condemn me for refusing?"

"No," said Arslan. "You swore oaths long ago. You have to keep them."

"They were sworn in anger," Bertrand said, "and held like a grudge."

Arslan shrugged. "Does it matter? I'm going. Yes, I want to go. I'm afraid—a little. But I do want it."

"Afraid?"

"Afraid," Arslan said. "Of a strange country. Of people who don't know me, and will think me very odd, and hate me for it. Of leaving all that I know, and discovering too late that I should never have done it. But," he said before his father could speak, "I will go."

"It should be I who goes," Bertrand said, "after all."

"I think not," Arslan said. And when his father stared at him: "Your time passed long ago. You belong in Outremer now."

"As the queen belongs in Nablus? Shall I be so impotent, then?"

"Not while you're lord of Beausoleil," Arslan said dryly, "and sworn to the king."

"Yes," Bertrand said with a touch of harshness. "There are some who call it broken faith."

"There are some who sail into exile in Manasses' wake." Arslan shivered slightly. "I'll be following them, you know. But I'll be going home."

"Home," said Bertrand. The word seemed to stick in his throat. "When I dream of home, I dream of Beausoleil, or of Jerusalem."

"I don't know what I dream of," Arslan said. "I've never seen La Forêt."

"It's . . . rather beautiful. As such places go. Green," said Bertrand. "Wet. Rich with scents of earth and water. The sun is never so strong there, and the winter winds blow cold, and bear a burden of snow."

"It will be very different," Arslan said.

There was a silence, awkward as such silences had not been between them since Bertrand acknowledged Arslan as his heir. Bertrand remembered, perhaps, the chill of winter in La Forêt. Arslan wondered if he would loathe it after all; if he would come back with his tail between his legs, having failed at a task that any noble fool could perform: to be a lord in France.

He broke the silence almost gently, because he could not bear it any longer. "If you command me, I will stay."

Bertrand shook his head. "No. No, I leave you free to choose. If you decide after all to remain here—"

"I'll go," Arslan said, as much to convince himself as to withstand his father. "Do you remember how Lady Richildis used to say that she had to come here in search of you—that she couldn't not do it? I can't not go to La Forêt."

Bertrand nodded slowly. "I remember. I understand. Destiny is not mocked. It's never easily refused."

"I don't want to refuse it," Arslan said.

"Then go," said Bertrand. "Go and prosper. But promise me. When your heir is grown, when you can leave, you will come back. I don't relieve you of your duties or your obligation. You are still the heir to Beausoleil."

"I'll be sure," Arslan said with a hint of a smile, "to find a lady quickly and set to work getting sons."

"Do that," his father said, as if any mortal man could compel such a thing.

Arslan was not leaving yet, perhaps not for days. When at last they did, he would indulge in formal farewell. But this morning meeting, with both of them still dazed with wine, was a truer parting. Each had made his choices. Those, Arslan believed, were well made—both of them. He reached to embrace his father. In the same moment Bertrand reached to embrace him.

They were precisely of a size, broad alike, strong alike, holding hard enough to bruise. "I will come back," Arslan promised. "By my life I swear it."

Were those tears on his father's cheeks? They were swiftly gone, if they had ever been there at all. So too, in a moment, was Bertrand. They would meet again and often, and yet it was as if Arslan had gone away already; had taken ship and sailed to France.

Arslan had hoped to bear the news to Baldwin before Baldwin heard it from another. But such was never the way of courts. As he prepared to ask for audience, scrupulous now that his friend was truly king, a page brought a summons that brooked of no delay.

As Arslan had rather expected, he was required to attend the king at once, but the king was not required to receive him. Baldwin was inspecting the stables, approving and discarding mounts for the war that he had planned. His attendance was light but determined, and might have kept Arslan away, except that Arslan was not to be deterred by a handful of guardsmen and an officious squire or two.

Baldwin did not pause in running his hands down the legs of a destrier. "This one is shaping for trouble," he said to the master of horse. "Look, that's swelling in the hock. How old is he?"

"Rising five, majesty," said the master of horse.

"Too young," Baldwin said, "for such legs as these. Geld him and sell him. We'll not trust ourselves to him in battle against Nur al-Din."

The master of horse bowed. Baldwin moved on to the next of the horses that had been brought out for him.

Arslan had slipped in, relieved the groom of his charge, stood unsmiling as Baldwin regarded him in surprise that turned, please God, to laughter. "Brother!" Baldwin swept him into a breathless embrace. "Arslan, you scoundrel. You were supposed to dangle about my anterooms, waiting till I deigned to see you."

"Shall I go?" Arslan inquired. "Shall I do it properly?"

"No," Baldwin said with a touch of impatience. "Of course not. Here, look at this colt. How do you reckon he'll do in a battle?"

Arslan considered the young stallion standing beside him, saw evidence of youth in gangling legs and elevated rump, noted the bright eye and alert ears and slightly flaring nostrils, and said, "He'll grow up better than he seems."

"But now?"

"Now," said Arslan, "he's too young. Give him a year."

"Shall I give him to you?"

Arslan felt his heart leap once, and then go still. "I think not," he said, "majesty."

"What, is he too young to sail to France?"

"They have horses in France," Arslan said, very quietly.

"But not such horses as these." Baldwin stroked the sleek grey neck. "He's one of the Mount Ghazal breeding, out of my Bedu mare. He's not much to look at now, but when he's grown he'll be a fine horse."

"Very fine," Arslan agreed. He paused. "May I take it that you'll forgive me for doing this?"

"No," Baldwin said. "I won't forgive you. Allow you—yes. If I didn't, you'd go regardless, and let yourself be called an exile. What's that, after all, to a man who was born a bastard?"

Arslan sucked in his breath. Baldwin seemed calm, even amiable; he was smiling. But he was angry—oh, indeed. There was no mercy in him. "I . . . thank you, majesty," Arslan said: wielding his own weak weapon, to address Baldwin as king and not as his foster-brother, his companion and his friend.

He could not tell how deep it cut. Skin-deep at most, maybe. Hardly to the bone.

"Don't thank me," Baldwin said, "till you've laid eyes on France. It's a ghastly country, they tell me: wet and cold. And no one has the slightest conception of elegance. Remember what you left behind you, when you stand in the hall in your Forest Sauvage, choking on the smoke and the reek of dogs and unwashed men."

"There is a Roman bath," Arslan said, "at La Forêt. And people use it."

"In the winter?"

"It's a hot spring," Arslan said.

Baldwin blinked. Abruptly he laughed. "So they'll be clean. And you'll teach them to carpet their floors and warm their walls with tapestries, and soften their wild hearts with the trappings of civilization."

"I hope to find them a little civilized," Arslan said.

"And willing to accept a stranger who brings with him a pack of Saracens?"

"Turks," Arslan said: remembering suddenly, keenly, how Eleanor had said something very like Baldwin's words, and in the same tone half of honest inquiry and half of mockery.

"Turks," said Baldwin. "Such distinction. Will the West be capable of discerning it?"

"It will learn," Arslan said.

"Or die, I'm sure." Baldwin ran his hands down the horse's neck, over its shoulders and flanks; lifted a hind hoof and contemplated the shoe thereon, and said still bending to his inspection, "You'll depart for Acre tomorrow. The papal legate has offered his ship to you and your escort—even if those are infidels. He was not amused, but I persuaded him."

"And what will that cost me?" Arslan asked.

"Your heart's blood," Baldwin replied, "and the same promise that, I'm told, you made your father. That you'll come back."

"I never intended otherwise," Arslan said.

"Men change," said Baldwin. "Time passes. Vows are forgotten."

"Not in my family," Arslan said rather grimly.

A burst of laughter escaped the king: not by his will surely, or he would not have looked so startled. "Brother!" he said. "Oh, brother. What will I do without you?"

"Rule," Arslan said. "Fight. Be king."

"And who will make me laugh for no reason, and call me 'Majesty' only when he's annoyed with me, and stand next to me for friendship and not for what it may gain him?"

"You might," Arslan suggested delicately, "ask this of the Lord Humphrey."

"Humphrey of Toron is my dear friend and my most loyal man, and I have named him Constable of this kingdom—but he did not share a cradle with me. Damn it, Arslan," said the King of Jerusalem. "I don't want you to go."

"Are you commanding me?" Arslan asked as he had asked his father.

As Bertrand had done, Baldwin shook his head fiercely and said, "No. No, I'm not. I may be a king, but I'm not an idiot."

"You were never an idiot," Arslan said. "I'll take the gift of the horse, because you give it. I'll send you the first good colt that he sires. Who knows? I might even bring it myself."

"Don't come back just to oblige me," Baldwin said. "Marry someone pleasant as well as suitable. Someone like your aunt, maybe. Though not as sharp about the edges."

"Maybe all women in France are edged like swords," Arslan said.

"Then you're well armored against them." Baldwin straightened, resting a hand on the broad smooth rump. "I wish I were going with you," he said.

"Running away?"

"Running away." Baldwin sighed. "There's no one left who will say such things to me. What will become of me? Will I turn into a haughty image of a king?"

"Not if you say those things to yourself."

"While you say them to the Count of Anjou. Who will be father to the King of England."

"I doubt," said Arslan, "that a stranger, even a stranger who is your brother, would be as indulgent as you have always been."

"Why not? Henry's new lady was. I wager she'll be again."

"Her edge," said Arslan, "is fine steel. She'll cut me to ribbons."

"Not you," Baldwin said. "Here, take your horse. Gather your escort. Go. Before I forget to be wise, and command you to stay."

Arslan did not think Baldwin would do that. Baldwin, just as evidently, did. Arslan considered bowing as to a king; but that would be too much like mockery. He moved instead, found Baldwin there, arms open to embrace him. They embraced and kissed as brothers, till Baldwin thrust him away. "Don't linger," he said. "Nor forget me, either."

"I'm not likely to do that," Arslan said. Baldwin flung the colt's lead at him, turned his back, fixed himself conspicuously on the impatiently pawing stallion that had for the past several moments been doing its best to strike its groom with its forefoot.

Arslan almost moved to the man's aid; but his hands were full with the colt that was Baldwin's gift, and he had been dismissed. He did as Baldwin bade him: the last time that he would do that, till he came back to Outremer.

Tears were no shame to a knight of suitable nobility. But Arslan had never been one to indulge in them. He took his colt and his leave, and looked back only once. Baldwin was eye to eye with the suddenly quiet stallion, teaching the beast what men were learning swiftly, that Baldwin was his lord and king.

*I*t was all done, and well begun. Horses, baggage, men, were gathered and laden on the ship that flew the flag of the Papal Curia above the lions of St. Mark. The harbor of Acre was its frenetic self, humming with trade and with pilgrims, wide-open gate of Outremer.

Arslan had said all but one of his farewells. Baldwin was gathering his army, preparing to take a great prize: the mighty fortress and city of Ascalon, that was in the hands of the infidels of Egypt. If he won it, he would win back all the honor that he had lost in the Crusade.

Arslan would not be there to see it, whether Baldwin won or lost. He would be in France, learning to be lord of La Forêt. In the purse that he carried close to his side lay a letter from Baldwin to his brother Geoffrey of Anjou, bidding that nobleman welcome Baldwin's dear friend and foster-brother, and grant him lordship over his father's domain. That was a generous thing, and kingly, as Arslan would have expected of Baldwin.

Arslan had turned his back on regret for wars unfought and companionship forsaken. Here on the quay of Acre, there was only his mother still to face. His father had bidden a final farewell at the gates of Jerusalem, as he rode away with Baldwin to the taking of Ascalon. Richildis was gone away to Byzantium, and Zenobia with her. The mother had been calm enough, but the daughter had wept her heartbreak, clung to Arslan and screamed when her nurses pried her away. He had felt it like the drawing of a knife from a wound. When he saw her again, if he saw her again, she would be a woman grown; she would have forgotten him.

Bertrand and Richildis and Zenobia were gone. But Helena had come to Acre with her son because, she said, she had business there. Arslan knew perfectly well what that business was: to see him off. He had no power to stop her, nor was greatly minded to try.

It was rather comforting to stand beside her while the last of his baggage was carried onto the ship. His horse, his gift from Baldwin, was safe below with one of the younger Turks as a groom. The rest of Arslan's escort waited by the rail, looking fierce and foreign among the men of Italy and Germany and France. For them it was a grand adventure, better even—they professed—than riding to the king's war.

"Messire!" a sailor shouted from the rigging. "Messire, the tide's a-running. Are you going or will you stay?"

That was pure courtly courtesy from a man of the sea. Arslan bowed to it, turned
to his mother, could think of no word to say that he had not said a dozen times
over.

She relieved him of the necessity. She kissed him on both cheeks and, lightly,
on the lips. "Go with God," she said.

So simple, that; so brief to say. "Stay with God," said Arslan, and began to turn
away. But he whirled back, caught her to him, held her for a long and wordless
moment. How small she was, he thought; such a little woman after all, to have such
strength of will.

And were they not all as she was, every blessed one of them?

He was smiling as he left her, laughing through tears; running lightly up the
plank just before they drew it in without him. The tide was running indeed, and
the wind was in the sails.

"A swift tide and a fair wind for France," said one of his fellow-travelers, a man
in the garb of a Templar with a face less dour than was the wont among those
soldier-monks. "May God grant us a smooth journey."

Men nodded, crossing themselves, murmuring approval of the sentiment. Arslan
walked a little part from them to a slip of vacant space along the rail, between
Kutub and a young man from Mount Ghazal. Neither of them spoke, no more than
Arslan. They stood there silent as the ship slipped its mooring and made for harbor's
mouth. So too did Helena stand on the shore, a straight still figure in silk that
shimmered in the sun.

When he could no longer see her face, when he could barely distinguish her
among the myriad other crowding figures on the quay of Acre, Arslan turned his
back on the city and the kingdom, and his face to the blue gleam of the sea. But
he was not seeing the dance of waves with their flecks of foam. In his mind's eye
like a painting on a parchment he saw a far green country, a broad roll of river, a
black loom of forest; fields and vineyards and a castle on a hill. The castle was tiny,
the fields and orchards minuscule to eyes that had seen the splendors of Krak and
Banias, the beauties of Antioch, the gardens of Damascus. Yet they were beautiful.
They were glorious. They were, God and the voyage willing, his own.

The story of Melisende, Queen of Jerusalem, is yet another of those wonderfully dramatic historical episodes so beloved of the novelist in quest of a subject. Though not as well known as that of, say, Eleanor of Aquitaine, nonetheless it is quite as remarkable.

I have chosen to invent the characters of Richildis and her family, along with their holdings of La Forêt, Beausoleil, and Mount Ghazal. The rest of the dramatis personae, the settings and incidents, are much as I have written them. Queen Eleanor did indeed ride on Crusade in armor at the head of her troop of "Amazons"—for the whole of her story, see Amy Kelly, *Eleanor of Aquitaine and the Four Kings* (Cambridge, Mass., 1978); the book, though not entirely reliable on details of the Crusade, paints a striking picture of the lady and her age.

Queen Melisende and her sisters were quite as boldly independent as I have written them, and their men, in the historical record, are cast rather more in the heroic mold than not. There certainly was a congenital objection on the part of the women of that family to surrendering power once they had taken it; an objection that led in the cases of Alys and Melisende, to the actual display of force on the part of their disgruntled menfolk.

Alys, after she had been defeated for the second time, seems to have yielded to the inevitable. In Melisende's case however, Helena would have won her wager: within a year of her surrender to Baldwin and her retirement to Nablus, she was again appearing in royal documents as Queen of Jerusalem. Mother and son appear to have had no further conflict, nor did Baldwin challenge her control over the Church in the kingdom. She died in September 1161, leaving her power over the Church to another of her strong-willed female kin, her stepdaughter, Fulk's daughter Sibylla of Flanders.

Baldwin himself became, in the opinion of most scholars, one of the greatest of the Kings of Jerusalem. He was an excellent general and commander of armies, and a competent administrator. His first campaign as sole king, the long war and siege that ended in the taking of Ascalon on 19 August 1153, was a splendid triumph. No later war or accomplishment quite equaled it.

At the end of 1158 Baldwin married the thirteen-year-old and very lovely Princess Theodora of Byzantium, niece of the Emperor Manuel. Baldwin appears to have loved her and to have been faithful to her, but she bore him no heir of either sex.

Three years later, on 10 February 1162—only five months after the death of his mother and rival—Baldwin died of a fever. He was thirty-two years old. His queen went on to become a famous scandal, one that needs a book of its own. His brother Amaury, meanwhile, inherited both crown and kingdom. An excellent summary of their history can be found in Steven Runciman's *A History of the Crusades* (Cambridge, England, 1988), volume II: *The Kingdom of Jerusalem and the Frankish East, 1100–1187.*